# The Adventures of Rafeor

By
M. L. Chapman

# Contents

# Chapter I

The moon slowly dipped below the mountain ridge, as the sun rose into the early morning casting pink and purple rays across the sky. Starting a new day, I stared at the brightness as I rolled over and sighed. My endless chores kept me busy day in and day out, I barely finished my chores at midnight and rose with the sun in the morning. Well, let's say, I'm always tired. I rolled out of my bed and stumbled slightly as I walked towards my chest at the foot of my bed. Where I keep the meager set of clothing and personal belongings that I am allowed to own. I grabbed my slave uniform, shuffled into it, and glanced at the few personal belongings before I was taken here: a doll that I had when they came, a blanket with holes from years of use, and a fire-burnt picture of my old home. I glanced at the door and swallowed, I had to be careful, and no one knew that I owned a picture of my home. The last time someone was caught looking remorseful at a photo, they got flogged and couldn't move for days. I swallowed, it was perhaps the only item that I should not have. They do not want anyone to remember where they used to live, or where they belong, otherwise, a revolt could happen.

I sighed as I moved to shut my chest, but a loud bang echoed. I flinched slightly, already knowing who was banging. I shut the chest, stood and swallowed, slowly walked towards the door and opened it. Down the hallway, on the right, stood the hired man to make sure all of us do our jobs – his name was Michael Slyther. He was roughly six foot, a shy away from six one, broad-shouldered, wavy long black hair, and was white. I swallowed, normally he didn't enter our hut, but something pressed him to do so. I watched quietly, as Marissa's door was finally rattled open and he disappeared inside. I heard a scream and soon a bloody Marissa was dragged out by a pissed off Michael, who then looked down the hallway and spotted me standing in the doorway of my room. He sneered and barked, "What you looking at? Get to work!"

I swallowed as I slunk into the hall, and kept my eyes down as I walked past both of them. I could hear Marissa begging behind me, but I could do nothing to prevent what was to come. We all knew that it would eventually happen when the owner of us called forth a fresh bedwife. The last one he called for, three months ago, had not come back. Normally, they came back but were not the same as they once were, dull and jumped at every little shadow. The last one was named Katrina, and we had not heard of her outcome. Normally, if one of us did not comply correctly with the owner, he punished everyone that he could, to punish us all for one sole issue.

I looked up as I was beginning to get to the owners' place. Here, I had to pretend to be happy – to be thankful that he took me away from my loving home, away from my family that I scarcely remember.

I grabbed the first thing that I saw that was out of place and carried it back to its proper placement when I heard the giggling. I closed my eyes for a brief second, already dreading what was to become of me. When two of the children of the owner came out from around the corner, clearly the ones who had placed the misplaced thing in the first place. I was their target, and they knew it, and I knew it. However, I curtseyed and addressed them, **"Lady Rekina, Lady Avery, good morning."**

They sneered at me and Lady Avery snickered, "Hello dog!"

I swallowed, they knew that bothered me. The last time anyone called me a dog, I got twelve lashings and had to work through the pain, while these two watched. I bowed my head and replied, **"My ladies, excuse me as I go about to complete my tasks. Please."**

Lady Rekina smirked and moved slightly, but it would require both of them to move aside so I could continue. I waited patiently for Lady Avery to move, but she folded her arms and sneered. I lowered my eyes and walked forward, either way, I was going to be lashed for something might as well make it to be on my terms slightly. I pushed past Lady Avery, and she shrieked, "YOU DOG! YOU TOUCHED ME!"

Lady Rekina glanced at her and shook her head, she was a visiting friend of Lady Avery, not in this family. She semi-showed kindness when Lady Avery wasn't there, but it was still sheltered. She cannot admit that she felt sorry for me.

Lady Avery stared at me for a moment and then huffed, strutted off, and turned slightly to shout, "WHEN MY FATHER HEARS THIS! YOU WILL PAY!"

I looked away, hurried to put my item away, and rounded the corner. Going too fast apparently, since I collided with no other than the owner himself. 'Shit.'

We both went down and I scrambled to my feet before I offered him my hand to pull him to his feet. He huffed and puffed and leveled out before glaring at me. I looked down at the ground before curtseying, and speaking slowly, **"I apologize, my Lord!"**

He looked at me as if I had grown two heads and shook his head before growling, **"Why was my daughter yelling at you Rafeor?"**

I swallowed, and replied, **"I apologize, my Lord! I had to place something away, and I brushed past her while completing the task!"**

He stared at me and raised his hand before slapping me across the face, I did not cry out. The last time someone showed emotions to the Lord, it was their last emotion. I fell to the ground in a small heap. He kicked me four times, directly into the ribs. Still, you cannot show weakness. He sneered and spat at me as he finished his endeavor. He straightened himself back up, and fixed the wrinkles out of his pants and shirt before sneering, "**You are nothing Rafeor! I ought to sell you. This is not the first time that my daughter had a grievance with you.**"

I kept my head tucked away, so he could not see the silent tears in my eyes. I kept silent. He huffed as he walked away, pausing at the corner before speaking again, "**Get up. Follow me.**"

I dragged myself up and pressed my right arm against my ribcage, but complied with the direct order. I followed the Lord through his home, to his private suite, where he continued to walk into, I hesitated for a split second before entering. I stood in the open doorway when he spoke without turning, "**Close the doors.**"

I swallowed as I complied with his order, and shut the mahogany doors softly, hearing the door gently click close. I turned to face him, keeping my eyes downcast. He looked at me for a moment and moved against his white oak table, the same one that I had polished only last week, it gleamed in the sunlight. He sighed deeply before speaking, "**Rafeor, you have been with me for several years. You are slightly older than my daughter, and yet you two seem to be the only ones who get into trouble. You are the only one that seems to irk my daughter. Tell me, why?**"

I knew this, this was a test. A test to see if I was still worthy to be in this household. I swallowed, and replied quietly, "**I have no conquest with your daughter, my Lord, your daughter is the one who has an issue with me. I do not know why, my Lord.**"

My speech shook, and I tried desperately to clear my throat without coughing. However, a small clearing entered my voice when I was speaking. He stared at me, his eyes drifted downward, and rose slowly back up, assessing me. He sighed deeply, running his right hand through his dark brown hair unless the sun hit it right, it was light brown. His cold gray eyes hammered into mine, when he spoke, "**Undress.**"

My breath caught in my throat as I whispered, "**What?**"

He raised his eyebrows and growled, "**Undress, Rafeor. Do not make me wait.**"

I bowed my head, the only one so far who had seen me without clothing was Michael, and that was only when he flogged me. Otherwise, no one else had seen what I looked like underneath the slave uniform. I swallowed and slowly moved about to get undressed. I winced as my ribcage sent a rippling effect of pain, proving that I had at least one broken bone. But I dare not cry out. I wrangled out of my slave uniform and stood in front of him without anything. His eyes dragged across my body and he lifted his right hand and curled his pointer finger inward, waving me forward. I swallowed as I approached him.

He looked down at my ribcage, it was black and purple already, but I tried to make it seem like it was no big deal. However, since I had been here longer than Lady Avery, which made it hard to hide my emotions. He took a deep inhale of me and scoffed before speaking, "**Ugh, you smell. Draw yourself a bath Rafeor.**"

'A bath? Inside the house?' I thought. That was the first. Normally, we slaves got hosed down with freezing cold water by Michael. I turned to get my slave uniform, but the Lord spoke again, "**Rafeor, you aren't getting into that uniform again.**"

I turned around and replied, "**What?**"

The Lord swallowed before speaking, "**Last week, when the advisor for the King came, he saw you. He demanded that YOU were treated correctly, while he reported to the King.**"

I swallowed, and replied, "**Why?**"

He shrugged and replied, "**My question exactly Rafeor. What is so special about you?**"

I swallowed, I did not have the slightest idea what the King himself wanted with me. I looked at him and replied, "**Where shall I bathe, my Lord?**"

He sighed deeply and replied, "**In here.**"

I was shocked, no one was allowed to be in that bathroom except for the Lord, and not even his own daughter got that privilege. I swallowed deeply before moving towards the door, pausing before opening it, looking back at him before speaking, "**My Lord?**"

He turned his head to look at me and diverted his gaze before gesturing me inside without a word.

I walked inside, closed the door with a soft click, and turned to gaze around, only the maids of the house were allowed inside this bathroom. A slave, like myself, would not see another day if caught inside. I walked towards the bathtub and swallowed, I had never used one since I was a little girl. I gazed down into the blackness, it was black marble, with flecks of gold dotting here and there. The nozzle for the water temperature was on it, golden in color, but it was polished brass. I swallowed as I touched the nozzle for warm water. Warm water was not something I was allowed to use. I looked at the door before walking slowly towards it. Pausing at the door before gathering my nerves and calling through the door, "**My Lord?**"

I heard a sigh before the footfalls approached. I scrambled backward as he opened the door and looked at me. He raised his eyebrows before speaking, "**What is it?**"

I swallowed nervously before speaking, "**Am I allowed to use….**"

He held up his hand, shook his head, and gestured to me to follow him inside. I swallowed before following him. He turned on the hot water and after a minute, turned on the cold water function. I swallowed, this would be the first time, in my time here as a slave, that I was allowed to have warm water. He added some rose petals, and some rose oil before motioning me towards the tub. I swallowed, I did something big to get this treatment. Yes, what he did in the hallway as punishment was something I was accustomed to, but this? This was new waters. This was the unsettling part. What was so special about me? What drew the attention of the King's advisor to request me of all people?

My Lord cleared his throat and raised his eyebrows before gruffly speaking, **"Get in."**

I swallowed before climbing into the tub, I slipped once and went under the water for a moment, coming wildly back up stuttering. I breathed deeply for a moment and wiped my eyes with my wet hands. The Lord sighed deeply, and I squinted up at him. He moved backward, removing his shirt. I swallowed as I watched him strip the button-up, exposing his flat chest, four-pack, and muscles. I swallowed and dropped my gaze, he came back over and pulled out a stool before grabbing shampoo, the good item. Not the cheap shit that we as slaves got, the good stuff that smelled like lavender. I grabbed his hand and froze. His eyes flickered towards me, he raised his eyebrows before clearing his throat. I dropped my hand and expected to get slapped for touching him. But nothing happened. No pain came. I looked questioningly at him before he sighed and spoke, **"Oh Rafeor, if only I could. I would. However, what happened in the hall was not allowed. The King's advisor warned me against harming you. I let my temper slide and harmed you. Damn it."** He looked at me after a moment and continued, **"There's something about you that the King's advisor wants. I do not know what it is. And clearly, you don't either."**

I swallowed as he squirted shampoo into his hand, leaned over, and touched my greasy hair with his hands. I flinched and drew backward, away from him, at least as far as the tub allowed me to go. He closed his eyes and shouted, **"KATRINA!"**

I stared at him, shocked to hear him shout. A woman came through the door, her eyes downcast and she replied, "You called, my Lord."

He pushed back on the stool, making it screech backward, both of us winced. He stood up and turned to her and spat, **"Get her ready."**

Katrina curtseyed and replied, "Right away, my Lord."

Katrina came forward, offering the Lord a cloth to wipe his hands off, and moved towards the tub. He stood there for a moment, wiping his hands before grabbing his shirt, quickly dressing, and shoving the end of his shirt into his belt line. He left without a word.

I stared at Katrina, she was the girl that we did not know what happened to. She was the last one that he called for. What was she doing here? My face must have expressed my shock and Katrina smiled softly, and glanced at the door before whispering, "Oh Rafeor, things I have learned about you."

I raised my eyebrows and whispered, **"What about me Katrina?"**

She sighed before applying shampoo onto my scalp and massaging it into my scalp. She was quiet for a moment before speaking softly, "You are rumored to be the long-lost princess of the King. The King's advisor was here last week, and he saw you at a distance working the flowerbeds. Something that the Queen loved to do with you. He watched you for a time Rafeor, and you apparently, did a technique only the Queen used in the past. She had quit doing the flowers since you were taken in the raid apparently."

My jaw dropped, and I whispered, **"How? How do you know?"**

She smiled for a moment and glanced at the door before whispering, "Rafeor, have you noticed that there are not many white slaves around here? That there are mostly colored? You, however, are white, but just got a really really good tan due to working nonstop. And besides, Lord Verein only came into power after the raid. The times match Rafeor, I don't, however, know all the details. I was assigned to be the mistress of the advisor, but he did not seem to want me."

She paused in thought and looked down at me as she gestured for me to go underneath the water, to rinse the shampoo off. I dipped into the water and came back up spluttering. She chuckled slightly before speaking, "Oh Rafeor. I'm going to miss you."

I glanced at her questioningly, and she chuckled before glancing at the door, "The King advisor said that you were to come to him in a week, Rafeor. Surely you were informed?"

I shook my head in response. She frowned and looked again at the door before asking, "When did you receive that bruise?"

She gestured towards my chest, and I glanced down, winced, and replied, **"The Lord...."**

Katrina gasped and started to laugh slightly, keeping herself quiet for the most part. I look at her questioningly. She sighed after a moment, "Oh Lord Verein is going to get so much trouble for harming you. Same with Michael."

I froze, suddenly noticing in the past week that Michael had not harmed me once. Not once throughout the week. He kept an eye on me, yes, but he did not harm me. He did not punish me further. Now it made sense. I glanced at Katrina and finally asked the pressing question, **"What happened to you, Katrina? We received no word of you."**

She sighed and dropped her hands down before speaking, "Lord Verein decided to keep me inside the house. He had a spot opening for a maiden inside, and well, apparently, I had done a good job and he positioned me then into it. I have learned much, Rafeor, and since I was assigned the King's advisor last week, well, I was supposed to be the mole inside, and give Lord Verein details on why he came here. The only thing I told him was that the King was doing his routine endeavors of checking on his kingdom again. Now, that the years have passed, he wants the kingdom to be under his full rule once again. I did not tell him anything about you, but the King's advisor mentioned to him and Michael to not lay a hand on you again."

I stared at her and finally replied, "**You are playing a dangerous game, Katrina. What happens if the Lord finds out that you did not tell him everything?**"

She looked down at her hands before replying, "I don't care if I die, Rafeor. Knowing that you may be the lost princess means that people like Lord Verein will no longer be in power any longer. I will gladly sacrifice myself knowing that you will make them all pay for what they have done to us over the years of the King's leave."

I swallowed and felt the sudden burden of the task. What if I am the lost princess? Why didn't my family try harder to find me? Did they not want me until now? Katrina smiled grimly before grabbing the bar of soap and gently moving it along my body, especially where the broken ribs were. I winced and she had a grim smile before speaking again, "Rafeor, I have a question."

I glanced up at her and made a motion to continue, she glanced at the door before speaking, "If I am still alive through this…. Would you…. Would you remember me? I mean, I understand that you will have a huge role in this endeavor but…. Will you promise me to remember me?"

I swallowed the lump in my throat before whispering, "**I will. I promise you, Katrina.**"

She smiled softly. She had finished her duty, stood up, and went about to empty the tub when Lord Verein entered the bathroom. He looked at her and growled, "**So my assumptions were correct. You were withholding information from me. I may have been told to not harm, Rafeor, but I was given no say in your end.**"

He turned his head and shouted, "**MICHAEL!**"

Michael entered the bathroom and kind of twisted to get in before staring at Katrina and me. I had not left the tub yet and stared at them from the tub, in terror. Michael took his whip that he carried off his belt, cracked it once, and lifted his eyes at Katrina before speaking, "Katrina."

I swallowed before raising my voice, "**You will not harm her!**"

Michael paused before glancing at the Lord. He shrugged, and replied, "You do not command me, Rafeor. You are nothing. You mean nothing. You would be getting the same treatment actually if I was allowed to. But I already see that someone beat me to beating you. Wish I had the luck to."

I scrambled out of the tub, and shouted, **"YOU WILL NOT HARM, KATRINA!"**

Michael shrugged and replied, "As I said, Rafeor, you are nothing."

He cracked his whip and made both of us wince, we know the feeling of the tip of that whip. However, as soon as he raised his hand backward, he heard screams shouting sounded  from the office room hallway. He paused,  Lord Verein swallowed, looked at him, and whispered, **"They are early."**

Michael looked at Katrina and then glanced at me, before shouting at Katrina, "GET HER DRESSED. DON'T JUST STAND THERE!"

Katrina looked at me, grabbed a folded towel, gently toweled me off, and grabbed the clothing that Lord Verein placed on the chair inside. It was a silk pink shirt, with a gray skirt to go with it. She quickly helped me into the clothing, before grabbing a brush and running it softly through my hair, gently tugging on the knots, making them smooth again. She quickly braided my hair in a neat braid. I looked into the mirror, and we locked eyes for a moment, but with Michael and Lord Verein in the next room over, we could not say a word to each other.

After she was done, she slightly pushed me towards the door, and smiled before whispering, "Remember me, my Lady."

I looked at her one last time before Lord Verein grabbed my arm and dragged me towards the office doors. The doors opened on their own, and a flabbergasted butler stood there, but he was not alone. A man stood there, dressed in the royal colors of gold and cobalt blue. Short blonde hair, navy blue eyes, and an oval-shaped face, around six foot even in height. He was cute, I admitted to myself. He looked coldly at Lord Verein before snapping, "Release her."

Lord Verein swallowed and released my arm before bowing, **"My Lord, I did not know you were arriving so soon."**

The advisor stared at him and replied, "That was the point, Verein. The King himself said not to give you a time."

Lord Verein swallowed, he normally would make anyone regret not saying 'Lord' in front of his name when addressed. However, he was not going to start a fuss. I glanced at the advisor before speaking, **"My Lord, may I request that we bring every single slave girl with us?"**

He looked surprised at my request before shrugging and replying, "As you wish."

That got Lord Verein's nerves. He gripped me again, and dragged me backward, and the King's advisor shouted, "UNHAND HER!"

Lord Verein shook with anger and hissed in my ear, **"You will pay for this. You will pay."**

The click of a gun sounded in the otherwise quiet room, and Lord Verein froze. We both looked back at the King's advisor before he snarled, "I said, unhand her. Don't and I will kill you."

Lord Verein scoffed, and replied, "**You wouldn't dare.**"

The advisor swallowed and his hand shook. I knew too, that he did not have the guts to kill this man. To kill my Lord. I lowered my eyes before jerking out of Lord Verein's grasp and speaking, "**My Lord, do not trouble yourself. I'm sure Lord Verein…**"

I paused, it was the first time that I had said his name since I made the mistake of calling him by his name. I saw his eyes flash. Normally, I would be belted for that, but I did not care. And continued, "**Is okay with releasing his slaves. He has enough little girls and boys to do the work.**"

The advisor frowned and turned slightly to Lord Verein before speaking, "You don't do what I think she's referring to. Do you?"

Lord Verein swallowed and his eyes dropped down for a moment, he did not make eye contact. The advisor's eyes flashed to a different color for a brief second; he seemed to cool himself slightly before speaking, "Oh? Cat caught your tongue, Verein? Answer me."

Lord Verein looked up and locked eyes with me for a moment, snapping, "**What I do with my slaves is none of your concern. Neither is it of the King's.**"

The advisor glowered at Lord Verein before snapping, "That is against the law. That's treason."

Lord Verein smirked and replied, "**Still, you do not have what it takes to do what others would have done.**"

The advisor swallowed, we both knew that Lord Verein was correct, he would not take the life. I, however, was done with him. And the fact that he threatened me was the finishing touch to the toll. I lunged towards the advisor, grabbed his weapon, and leveled it with Lord Verein. That caught them all off guard.

I stared at Lord Verein before cocking the gun, and speaking, "**He may not have the stomach for it Lord Verein, but I do.**"

He stared at me and swallowed. I was sure he was thinking back to the day he got me. He spoke, "**You have grown, Rafeor.**"

The King's advisor sharply looked at me, and then at Lord Verein before whispering, "What?"

I sighed before speaking, "**My name. At least the name he has given me, is Rafeor. I do not remember what my parents called me before I was taken.**"

The advisor swallowed and glanced at Lord Verein before speaking, "Where did you buy her from?"

Lord Verein leaned against his desk and folded his arms, the throb in his throat indicated that he was nervous. But he did not reply. He looked at me and said, "**I will not say anything. Kill me.**"

I blinked once before shaking my head and lowered the weapon before replying, "**No.**"

He smirked and grabbed something sitting on his table and fiddled with it. "**Leave me.**"

The King's advisor was about to say something, but I placed my hand on his shoulder, shaking my head. I looked at Lord Verein and said, "**Get Katrina out now.**"

Lord Verein looked at me with rage. He looked towards the bathroom door, and shouted, "**MICHAEL! BRING ME KATRINA. NOW!**"

There was some shuffling on the other side of the door, Michael appeared dragging Katrina by her tattered maid uniform. The King's advisor took a deep inhale, showing that he recognized her and the way that suddenly acted was one of someone who had a crush on someone. He strode forward, catching Katrina before she fell in a bloody heap before Michael. Michael looked at him, raised his eyebrows, and glanced at Lord Verein. He sneered, "Sorry little one, but she was being bad."

The King's advisor stood up, his precise uniform had Katrina's blood all over it. "Bad or not, she did not deserve this treatment. Princess Rafeor, please help Katrina to the carriage."

Michael stared at him and snapped, "What is she to you? She is nothing but a slave that got too deep."

The King's advisor glowered at Michael before looking at Lord Verein, and speaking, "I will report all this to the King. He will punish you as he sees fit."

Lord Verein scoffed and Michael chuckled before running a clean cloth over his whip, cleaning off Katrina's flesh and blood from the length. He knew that he was provoking the King's advisor to do it then, but he did not care.

The King's advisor scowled and turned sharply before shouting, "GUARDS!"

A pair of royal guards stepped through the door, assessing the situation. They fingered the weapons at their belts when they saw blood, but noticed the woman below him. They glanced at the advisor before one spoke with a raspy voice, "Your orders, Sir?"

The advisor looked at Lord Verein and then at Michael before speaking, "Arrest them."

The guards blinked once and glanced at Lord Verein and Michael before glancing at each other and following his command. The one who spoke came for Michael, but he paused and whispered, "The King…"

The advisor waved him away, and replied, "I'll deal with him myself."

The guard shrugged before clapping iron cuffs onto Michael's hands, dragging him towards the doorway where the unsure butler stood. The other guard had a bit of a harder time getting Lord Verein, but after he had him pinned to the ground. The handcuffs went on and he was dragged upward and out the door.

I glanced at the advisor before speaking, "**Do you have the authority to do what you just did?**"

He looked at me and glanced down at Katrina before replying, "Honestly, my princess, no, no I do not. However, I could not take the abuse that you and everyone here have endorsed any longer. I will take the discipline the King sees fit for myself."

I replied, "**I will pardon you for this. I do have a question though, if I am indeed the lost princess, then how did I come here?**"

The advisor looked at me and swallowed. "I fear that I cannot personally answer that question, my princess."

I nodded and then went to move Katrina, when I winced. He grabbed my arm, stopping me from moving. "Why did you just wince?"

I looked down and breathed deeply before replying, "**Lord Verein…. He ah… well put it bluntly, he kicked me and hit me earlier this morning.**"

The advisor scowled and his eyes flickered another color, before going back to normal. He looked like he could not keep his temper, and for a moment, I was going to ask him what he was. Since he did not appear to be human. Human's eyes do not typically change color when they are upset or mad. However, I know, now is not the time either.

He tried to stop me from helping Katrina, but I kind of laughed at him and quietly said, "**This is not the worst injury I have dealt with when helping others with worse injuries than me at the same time. I will heal.**"

He swallowed, shook his head and whispered, "Warrior princess."

I scoffed but did not say anything to stop his words. At times, I did feel like I was a warrior, but Michael and Lord Verein were always there to squash that feeling into mush and feed it to the dogs.

We finally got Katrina to the carriage and got inside with the help of guards that were stationed there. There were three different carriages, two I recognized as Lord Verein's and one royal. I swallowed as I looked at the gold and cobalt blue carriage, before I pulled myself up into it, wincing at the pain. The guard looked at me then at the bloody mess of Katrina and then at the advisor. But he did not say a word. The look they exchanged though was a bit concerning. However, after the carriage was moving, and the horses trotted forward, pulling the carriage forward, I questioned what my new chapter was going to be. Was I the long lost princess as everyone was referring to me, or was I a nobody and would be sent back to Lord Verein after he was discharged? Those thoughts plagued my mind as the carriage gently rocked me to sleep.

# Chapter 2

I did not know how long the carriage ride was, but soon I felt them stop. I woke with a start, slightly panicked but the guard spoke gently, "Easy, lass. You are safe now."

I swallowed and licked my chapped lips before speaking, "**Did we arrive?**"

He chuckled before nodding. I scrambled to my feet, wincing at the pain, causing him to look at me with concerned brown eyes, I smiled gently and said, "**I'm fine, pretty sure just a couple of broken ribs.**"

The smile instantly wiped off his face and his eyes sparked a shade darker. But as quickly as I saw it, his eyes went to their brown color, and he glanced down before speaking, "I apologize, my Lady."

I raised my eyebrows and looked out the windows before speaking, "**Don't apologize for it. It is hopefully a thing of the past for me and the rest of the girls in the other carriage.**"

He shifted his footing before speaking, "I should mention this now, my Lady, the King did not want anyone else along with you. Do not be shocked if he dealt with them."

The way he phrased it meant that the King may kill them all, except for her. I glanced at Katrina before looking at him. I spoke, "**So you are saying the king, my possible father, is a killer?**"

The guard shrugged and replied, "Everyone has their rules, my Lady. The king said to bring no one else. I am not sure what he will do to them."

I swallowed and looked outside, now wondering who the King was.

We sat in comfort for a moment before the doors opened. To another guard, clan in royals gold and cobalt blue, he offered his hand to me as he stepped backward. I glanced at the guard inside before allowing my left hand to graze his and took it to step down, wincing. The new guard instantly looked at the other guard before snapping, "Arnold, what happened?"

The guard inside raised his hands in surrender, and replied, "Hey! It was not my doing! I just found out about it myself."

The new guard looked at me and sighed deeply. He leaned down and scooped me up into his arms, making my ribcage hurt in the process. I let out a breath of air, easing the breath out carefully. He glanced down at me and spoke, "What hurts?"

I looked down at the ground before speaking, "**My ribcage. And my back to be honest.**"

He shuffled himself slightly, and made it more comfortable, somehow to be carried still before speaking to Arnold, "Bring the other one inside the clinic. And anyone else that needs medical attention."

Arnold raised his eyebrows before speaking, "But shouldn't…"

The new guard shook his head and replied, "These women need help, I'll take the blame if he gets angry."

Arnold shrugged and muttered, "Your funeral."

The guard that was carrying me heard, he pretended to not hear him. He carried me into a white building with a red cross on it. He spoke to a nurse before they continued further into the building. I closed my eyes, the pain was starting to get to me.

****

I was laid down on a bed, a nurse shooed away the guard and came back after a few moments. She looked down at me, shook her head, and said, "You poor dear. Let me get you into something more comfortable."

She instantly stripped me out of my clothing as if it were nothing and asked a few times when she saw the bruising; she inhaled sharply when she saw the scars littered around my body. Not my neck or face, but there was enough damage underneath everything else that it counted for everything. She bowed her head, turned away, and walked out the door with tears in her eyes. The guard looked inside for a split second before closing the door, shutting me into darkness.

****

The nurse was sobbing when she got the guard to shut the door. She took a shaky breath in and wiped her tears when the aura of the King came. She bared her neck as he came forward. He looked at her and spoke, "**Why are you crying, Anna?**"

She looked at him and replied, "My Lord! She has been through much pain. So much pain!"

She continued to sob, and the King looked at the guard before speaking, "**Report.**"

The guard snapped to attention and replied, "Yes, my King! Quinn arrived with twenty-three girls, not counting the one he believes to be the lost Princess, all of them have wounds and scars from abuse. Along with Lord Verein and a man named Michael Slyther, they are in handcuffs, my Lord."

The King paused, looked at him, and then hissed, "**Bring me Quinn.**"

The guard bowed before quickly leaving, hurrying to follow his orders. The King looked at Anna and said softly, "**Anna, when did they come in?**"

Anna swallowed and replied, "Not more than five minutes before you arrived, my Lord. The one inside the room is what Sammuel brought in. The one who we hope is the lost princess and not the other one…."

The King raised his eyebrow, Anna swallowed and looked at the door. "The other one arrived dead on arrival, my Lord. The whippings were so severe that I saw bone…. She didn't make it, my Lord."

The King frowned and glanced at the door before speaking, "**Is she injured?**"

Anna swallowed and nodded after a moment, "Yes, my Lord. She is. She has a bruised ribcage, and possibly a broken bone here and there. Along with fractures, I don't know if it was the current injury that caused them or past injuries. And the scarring…"

Anna shuddered before continuing, "They only spared her neck and face from what they had done to her, my Lord. What they had done to her…. I cannot and will not wish it upon anyone. And the fact that she is still alive? She is a strong one, my Lord. Very strong."

The King nodded and placed his hand on her shoulder before speaking, "**I'll see to her Anna. Go tend to the others.**"

Anna curtseyed to him before leaving for another room.

****

The King stared at the closed door when Quinn was brought forward. Quinn looked nervous, rightfully so. I told him to bring no one else. But of course, he went against my order. I turned towards him, my eyes sparking with rage as I growled, "**Explain to me why I have one dead girl and twenty-two others. Not counting Lord Verein and Michael Slyther. Now.**"

Quinn swallowed before replying, "My Lord, I… I take the full blame for bringing them. However, I must say if Rafeor is indeed the princess, then she is in the making of a great princess."

I looked at him before speaking, "**Rafeor?**"

Quinn dipped his head and replied, "That is what Lord Verein named her when she got there. And the name that she responds to, my Lord."

I looked at the door and swallowed, Rafeor was in for a surprise when I asked to change it, considering that Rafeor was close to a dog species name. I sighed heavily before speaking, **"Quinn, you are on night watch for two months on the eastern border, alongside Davis. You are dismissed."**

Quinn swallowed and bowed before turning around and moving away from the King.

Sammuel swallowed as he watched Quinn leave. Everyone knew that the eastern border was the worst of the worst with everyone trying to cross, and Davis? Damn, he was glad that he was not Quinn.

The King looked at him and spoke, **"Sammuel, you are on guard duty on this door, and this door alone. None of the others get this treatment. Understood?"**

Sammuel bowed instantly and replied, "Yes, my Lord!" The King nodded and looked at the door again, he closed his eyes before opening the door.

****

A sliver of light came from the door after about thirty minutes of being in the dark. It was somewhat comforting that they left me to be alone, but I now wonder where Katrina was. And if she was okay. As soon as I was about to drift off to sleep, the door opened slightly. I leapt to my feet, onto the ground before leaning against the bedframe. Wincing as my ribs made a throbbing pain. I was in nothing, but I had thought of grabbing the sheet beforehand and wrapping it around myself. I cast my eyes downward before the door fully opened.

The King opened the door and flicked the lights on. His breath hitched. She was older, yes, but her hair long and black was a stark image of the Queen's, along with her height of roughly five foot six, he couldn't see her eyes, but he felt in his heart that this girl was his lost daughter. He slowly went forward, not allowing his aura to show, since Lord Verein and Michael Slyther were not a shifter like himself, they were humans.

I looked at the man before me, at least the half that I could see without looking up. I swallowed before speaking, **"Sir, I…. I am…."**

He gently shushed me, and I raised my head and met his brilliant blue eyes – the same eye color as mine, although mine was a shade darker than his. I swallowed and dropped my gaze before trying to speak again, but he beat me to it, "**Please, don't. I believe that your physical being is all I need to know who you are. You are my daughter.**"

I looked at him and my breath hitched. I went to curtsy but he stayed with me, and shook his head speaking softly, "**No, your days of curtsying are close to ending except for the royal gatherings.**"

I swallowed before speaking, "**My Lord...**"

He laughed a little before shaking his head and speaking, "**No, don't title me.**"

I opened my mouth to retort, but he chuckled a little before gesturing to the bed. I swallowed as I went to climb back in, when the sheet fell slightly, showing my giant bruise. He froze, and I could have sworn I saw his eyes flash a different color before returning to normal. He closed his eyes and breathed in deeply before speaking, "**Who did that to you?**"

I glanced at him and swallowed and replied, "**Lord Verein.**"

He scoffed slightly and shook his head before walking to the door and speaking to someone outside. He came back after a minute and asked, "**Can I see the extent of the damage he has done to you over the years? Please.**"

I swallowed but complied. I opened up the sheet and his eyes racked my body, every raised mark, every redness that never went away. Everything new and old. He gripped the edge of the bed frame before speaking, "**I'm going to make him pay for this.**"

I shrugged and replied, "**He actually went easy on me. If it wasn't for your advisor, then I wouldn't be able to wake up or move for the first two days.**"

I let out a little laugh and went silent when my eyes flickered to his. Once again, I could have sworn his eyes were a different color for a split second. But as soon as I looked at him directly he seemed to force himself to get back to normal. He was about to reply when a knock sounded, and he looked towards the door, he covered me again and after a moment said, "**Enter.**"

The door opened and two men stepped forward, the advisor and the guard that carried me inside were now inside the room. I was now thankful that the King thought of having me covered again before they saw me in this state. They both bowed deeply to the king and the advisor spoke first, "You requested me, my Lord?" The King looked at him before speaking, "**You are pardoned.**"

He had a look of shock across his face, he bowed again, and I saw a flicker of relief across his face; his facial features returned to normal, at least to me. The other guard looked shocked too but he quickly stopped and lightly smiled at me.

The King stood up after a moment, resting one hand on the bed frame before speaking, "**I want my daughter to be moved to the royal household where she can be taken care of properly. The rest of the girls that came in tow, take them into the royal household too. They will have to make do with what jobs I will assign each one of them.**"

I swallowed and spoke quietly, "**Did Katrina make it?**"

The King paused, and turned slightly before speaking, "**The girl that was with you in the royal carriage?**"

I nodded,z glanced at the advisor and then at the guard, and sighed before speaking, "**Unfortunately not. She died of her injuries before she arrived here.**"

I tightened my hold on the sheet and shook slightly, a few tears slipped out of my eyes as I cried silently – not making a sound. The guard looked crestfallen before speaking, "I apologize, my princess. There was nothing that could be done for your friend. Her injuries were severe. By the looks of the corpse, it was brutally beaten to death."

The advisor and the King blinked once, turned towards the guard, and the advisor swallowed before speaking, "Come again, Sammuel? Did you really just describe her friend's body as a corpse?"

Sammuel opened his mouth to reply until he stopped and closed it after a moment. He swallowed nervously as he glanced at the King. The King looked at him with a 'what the fuck' look before turning to me and speaking, "**Katrina, what did she do for you?**"

I swallowed before looking at the advisor and flickering my eyes to Sammuel. "**She made it possible to be here. She did not tell Lord Verein who I was. She kept a secret that she knew would come to light and would kill her. She asked me to remember her when I became the princess.**"

The King looked at me for a moment and slowly turned to the others before speaking, "**Make sure that Katrina gets a proper burial. I want to make sure that everyone knows what she did to make sure that my daughter was brought home safely.**"

The advisor bowed and replied, "Right away, my Lord."

He turned to leave, when the King spoke, "**Quinn.**"

The advisor paused, turned around to dip his head at me, but stayed inside the room as the King looked at him before continuing, "**Do not disobey my orders again, otherwise you know where you will be headed. Dismissed.**"

I glanced at the King before Quinn left, "**My…**" I trailed off for a moment, but it still made Quinn pause at the door as he looked back at me and I continued, "**I pardoned him for arresting Lord Verein and Michael Slyther. And for getting the rest of the girls out of there.**"

The King raised his eyebrows at me and chuckled before motioning Quinn away, and I could have sworn he had a bright smile across his face before he left.

Sammuel looked at the King and me and asked, "Do you need anything, my Lord?"

The King shook his head and turned towards me before speaking, "**Dismissed.**"

Sammuel bowed and turned sharply to the left before heading out the door and shutting the door. Leaving the King and myself alone once again.

****

The King looked at me before looking down at his hand and speaking, "**I'm sure you have questions….**"

I looked at him and replied, "**That I do…**"

He looked at me and responded with, "**Well….**"

I sighed deeply and winced slightly before speaking, "**If I am truly your daughter, then why did it take you twelve years to find me?**"

The King looked down at the ground before speaking, "**I fear that I do not have the answer you seek.**"

I raised my eyes towards his face for a moment and a spark of anger flew through me, and for a split second, I wished that he was not there. He glanced at me and swallowed.

"**Have you…**" He paused before trying again, "**Have you noticed that anytime you are angry or upset your eyes shift to different colors? That you do not feel like you belong with others?**"

I swallowed and whispered, "**I normally was beaten to the point beyond others. Especially when I was angry or upset. What are you? I have noticed that not only do your eyes spark a different color but so do Quinn's and the guards' eyes.**"

The King sighed deeply before speaking, "**You, my daughter, are a shifter.**"

I stared at him before whispering, "**What?**"

He sighed and looked at me before speaking again, "**Our family lines are shifters. This entire royalty is a shifter family. Quinn is a shifter, but Sammuel and a few other guards are…. Werewolves, that are hired in.**"

I stared at him and shook my head in response. Great I thought, just what I needed. Lunatics in my family. I sighed deeply, once again wincing in pain before speaking, "**Shifters. What is a shifter?**"

He looked at me and smiled grimly. "**Shifters are someone who can shift into any animal at will. You also have the ability to turn into a dragon, since you are of royal bloodline.**"

I scoffed and shook my head in dismay, he was a lunatic. He was crazy, but I thought back to all the times that I had thought of turning into a bird and flying away, always feeling that sometimes I could almost feel an effect, but just out of reach every time. I stared at him before whispering, "**Dragons are not real. They are mythical beings. If what you say is true, shift into a tom cat.**"

The King groaned and replied, "**Shifting into an animal is no easy task....**"

I raised my eyebrows at him and responded, "**Actions are more believable than make-belief.**"

He sighed before calling out, "**SAMMUEL!**"

The door opened immediately, and Sammuel entered before closing the door again. He turned and bowed to him before speaking, "You called, my Lord?"

The King looked at him and sighed deeply before speaking, "**Shift.**"

Sammuel looked at him and then glanced at me before speaking, "All due with respect sir, shifters may be able to keep their clothing on while they are in their forms, but wolves don't. We tend to shred our clothes."

The King looked at him with a look and glanced at me before speaking, "Princess Rafeor, please close your eyes. King Morphous."

I glanced at the King suddenly, Morphous, was the name that Lord Verein rarely used and it always made him glance around quickly and he always acted scared. Only Michael convinced him that Morphous was not coming back, that he was a Lord and shouldn't be scared of the fairy tales surrounding his name. I swallowed but closed my eyes, and I heard shuffling and belt clicking open before Morphous spoke, "**You can open your eyes.**"

I opened my eyes slowly, and instantly scrambled backward as I stared at a werewolf. Now it was not like the stories, of standing on two hind legs, drool coming out of its elongated snout. No, it was like a wolf. Just a very large wolf. About thrice the size of a normal one, and I have only glimpsed one while I was doing the last of my chores on a wintery night three years ago when food was scarce. I swallowed nervously before speaking, "**So you are what Lord Verein is scared of.... This is why he must have treated me differently. Why I was always watched**

**more than anyone else. If shifters are truly there, then why did it take you twelve years to seek me out? Am I not good enough for you?"**

Morphous opened his mouth, but the wolf padded his way up to the bed and dropped his heavy gray head onto the bed, next to me, whimpering softly. His big brown eyes stared up into my eyes for a moment before he sat down and glanced at Morphous, waiting. Morphous sighed deeply before speaking, **"It's not that simple. The riot…"**

I raised my hand and my eyes sparked, I was angry and I stood up, disregarding that I was nude underneath, and let the sheet fall. Sammuel growled once he saw the extent of my injuries over the years, but I heeded him no mind. For once, I was not concerned that anyone saw me nude. I felt something stir around the surrounding area, as I snapped, **"Everyone has their fucking excuses! The riot! The punishments are always targeted towards me because of the fucking riot!"**

I was about to continue but Morphous's eyes sparked a deep orange before he snapped, **"Some things are meant to be kept in the dark. Especially surrounding the damn riot!"**

I glowered at him and I felt something, and instead of suppressing my anger like I had learned to do, I embraced it.

# Chapter 3

I didn't know what happened, one moment, I was staring at Morphous's chest area since he was taller than I was, the next I had crumbled the room into ash. I swallowed, looked down at myself, and swallowed. I was staring into golden scales tipped with black. I looked up and saw the building, ablaze. I started forward, but something stopped me. I looked down and noticed that Sammuel was preventing me from going forward. I swallowed, what was I? I did this. I shook my head, slowly took a step backward, and swallowed before looking up at the night sky and imagining myself in the air. I suddenly felt myself lift, I glanced down and saw Sammuel desperately trying to keep me down but this was my fault. I killed countless people because I lost my temper. I apparently flew away. How I didn't know, but Sammuel became a small dot on the ground as I flew off.

After several minutes, which could have been an hour, I got tired. I saw a mountain, found a cave, and entered it. I was wary and tired. I went in, curled into a ball, and wished myself back to my human form. I still did not know what I had done, I didn't know who I had killed. Or what had happened. This is all new to me and I was scared. I closed my eyes and fell asleep.

****

Morphous instantly saw the difference between her normal and her anger. He had connected to the hospital staff, "**Get everyone out. This one I'm with is my daughter, but she does not understand how to control her emotions.**"

Anna was the first to respond, "Yes, my Lord."

Then the line went quiet, Sammuel looked at me before walking over to the bed like a dog, but the anger in my daughter was stronger. She stood up and walked towards me, and I could tell that she was on the verge of shifting into her dragon form, but I was willing to keep my temper in check. I did not want to kill everyone here, not until they had a chance to get out before she blew her fuse. I saw the moment that her eyes flickered to a different color then I knew that time was up, and I grabbed Sammuel in a blur of moment, and got us to safety. Just in the nick of time too. The place went up in an inferno. I glanced up and I saw a golden dragon with its scales tipped in black. The eyes were turquoise in color and she was beautiful.

Sammuel got out of my grasp, and ran towards her, disregarding the hot coals under his paws, and tried to keep her here. But I saw the moment that she looked around and came to terms with what she had done. She looked to the sky, and I half hoped that she did not know how to fly. However, she must have thought hard enough, and her dragon went up into the air and headed south, back the way she had come.

Sammuel came back after a moment and looked crestfallen for a moment before I spoke, **"You are not to blame Sammuel. All this is new to her."**

He looked at me before speaking, "Was everyone at least able to get out in time?"

I looked at him and replied, **"I did not feel any lifelines break."**

He nodded and looked towards the dot in the sky before speaking, "So, are you going after her?"

I swallowed and replied, **"I am."**

He chuckled slightly before limping away, towards the royal driveway before turning his head slightly before speaking, "Have fun with that, my Lord."

I scoffed slightly but turned to look at the mountains and swallowed. I did not know what to do. This was the first time that I saw my daughter after twelve years, and this was the outcome. I blew it horribly. I bowed my head and swallowed. I did not know how to make amends for this.

****

I looked around at the rubble before swallowing and moving closer to where Rafeor's room would have been. I wondered which of them lost their tempers first, but I also knew that King Morphous's dragon was as black as the midnight sky, and the one who had done this damage was golden with black tips. So, it was Rafeor. I swallowed as I continued further, and finally saw a limping Sammuel before I came across Morphous himself. I paused and called out, "My Lord?"

He looked at me with a look of loss, and I sighed, chuckled slightly, and spoke, "Honestly, I thought that you were the one to do that. Not her. Although I am surprised that she knew how to fly away."

He sighed deeply before speaking, **"Quinn."**

I chuckled again before raising my hands in surrender and looking at where the hospital was. I sighed before speaking after a moment, "So, why are you still here? I thought you would be gone after her as soon as you knew that no one died in that."

He looked at me and sighed. **"I don't know what to say to her."**

"Why don't you tell her the truth? You know eventually, someone is going to say how she got to that place in the first place. So, why don't you just come clean?"

He looked at me sharply and snapped, **"It's not that simple, Quinn. If she finds out that the riot was all around us as a species she's going to take drastic measures to make sure that she is not something to be afraid of. The humans have grown bolder over the century Quinn, no one is more scared of us than they are. All because of what I had done twelve years ago."**

I sighed deeply, I knew what he had done, but it still did not make a difference, someone in this kingdom was bound to tell her what happened and why she was where she was in the aftermath. Either way, this was not going to be a pretty sight. I looked at him and replied, "The humans are as much to blame as we are. They provoked you to act that way. Besides, it was twelve years ago. I doubt that the humans really remember it all too much. Considering that we have made it hardly impossible to find us. After we went into hiding."

He looked at me and ran his right hand through his hair before speaking, **"I don't know Quinn. This is something that I have tried to keep in the dark as long as possible. I wish I didn't have to tell her a single thing. However, I know that you are correct, someone eventually will tell her what happened, and I would rather not have two buildings to rebuild."**

He sighed deeply = and looked towards the mountain peaks to the south. He was about to shift when I spoke, "So, what do you want me to tell the Queen?"

He paused, looked at me, and swallowed. There was only one person that Morphous was somewhat afraid of, and that was his wife. He swallowed before speaking, **"For now, tell her the minimum facts of what happened. I doubt that it will take me long to find her."**

I nodded slightly before speaking, "Okay, but I did notice that you have not said Rafeor. You have not called out to your daughter."

He looked at me sharply before growling, **"Because that is not her name. Her name is Raphina."**

I sighed deeply and kicked a loose concrete piece before speaking, "I am going to speak my mind for a moment, my Lord…" He paused for a moment, to allow him to say something, but continued after a moment, "Raphina as you know her is gone. That little girl is now a warrior princess, and she is not going to simply take it lightly to change her name after all this time. Please understand it if she decides to keep her current name."

He scowled and shifted to his dragon form before launching himself into the air. His giant wings beat against the air to get airborne before he was up in the sky.

***

I watched until he was nothing in the sky, and sighed before I turned away and headed back to where Anna was. Anna came forward after a moment and looked at the destruction and she kind of tsked before speaking, "That damn King! That hospital was one of the newer ones too!"

I chuckled before speaking, "Oh Anna, that was not the King. That Rafeor."

Her face fell for a moment before she sighed deeply, "That poor girl. She has no idea what world she has gotten into."

I sighed as I looked at the rubble, before speaking, "Yeah…"

She looked at me before speaking, "Has the Queen been informed that Rafeor is here?"

I shook my head and replied, "No."

She gave me a weird look before speaking, "And why not? You know how she is with this secrecy that the King does. Especially after what he did."

I glanced at her and looked around for a moment before whispering, "I honestly thought that she was informed until a few minutes ago."

Anna sighed before shaking her head and speaking, "So, the Queen does not know that the eldest daughter is here?"

I swallowed before shaking my head in reply. Anna sighed deeply before turning to look at the survivors of the inferno, of the people that got out. Luckily, everyone that was there was the one that came with Rafeor, and they had managed to get every single girl out of there. She sighed before speaking, "Well, we need to get to the royal palace and the Queen will find out one way or another when the news spreads."

I swallowed and nodded before heading to assist people when Anna spoke, stopping me in my tracks, "Quinn, what is going to happen from here on out?"

I looked back at her and replied, "I don't know Anna. I don't know."

She sighed and glanced once again at the rubble before moving forward to get the rest of the girls to the royal palace to seek treatment.

****

I woke up after a moment and knew that I was not alone. I cracked open my eyes and saw that a black dragon was at the mouth of the cave. As if he was keeping watch as I was asleep. I lifted my head and growled at him. He turned his midnight black head towards me and blinked before he sighed and shifted back to a human, showing me that he was the King. I glanced down at him, great I was still a dragon. I lowered my head down and touched the coolness of the floor of the cave and my body shook slightly. I was done with everything. I wanted to wake up from this nightmare.

He sighed deeply, came forward, and placed his hand on me before speaking, "**Raphina.**"

I lifted my head slightly and growled before rumbling, "**My name is Rafeor.**"

He looked like he wanted to challenge it, but lowered his head before speaking softly, "**Rafeor, I am sorry for this to come to light so soon.**"

I scoffed and turned my head, which swung and smacked him directly in the torso. He flew, hit a wall, and crumbled to the cave floor. I inhaled sharply, I didn't mean to injure him. I closed my eyes, but he spoke softly, "**Rafeor.**"

I swung my head towards him and looked at him as he dusted himself off before speaking, "**I am sorry for everything. I am sorry that you got caught up in the riot that happened twelve years ago. Of all the damage and harm you have suffered because of me. This was mine doing. I...**"

He paused and swallowed nervously before continuing, "**I am the reason why you didn't learn how to be what you are. I am the reason that you lost the love of your family. I am the reason why...**"

A rumble deep in my throat stopped him from continuing, and I growled, "**Stop blaming yourself. Everything happens for a reason. Mine was just very unfortunate.**"

He chuckled slightly before speaking, "**Oh, but I am to blame. Humans do not know one hundred percent believe we exist. Twelve years ago, they got the glimpse of me, of what I was...**"

I looked at him and snapped my jaws slightly. He winced before raising his hands in submission. I looked away and sighed, a plume of smoke came from my nose, and a small fire came from my mouth. I looked wildly around for a moment, but he stayed where he was and smiled softly before speaking, "**So, do you know how to get back to your normal state?**"

I shook my head in response, which crashed into the sides of the mountain, making the loose stones crumble to the cave floor, rumbling the ground. I froze and glanced down before I saw him laughing slightly. "**Okay, focus on the form you want. And since you are new at this, this may take several tries.**"

I swallowed before closing my eyes, thinking of what I wanted to be, and after the second try, I was shivering. He came forward and draped his coat around me before speaking, "**Well done, Rafeor.**"

I smiled slightly as I walked towards the cave entrance and looked down. I yelped and jumped backward before peering over the edge again. We were far up the mountain, above the clouds. I looked back at him and swallowed before I whispered, "**How do we get down from here?**"

He chuckled slightly before coming alongside me and said, "**You will ride my dragon home.**"

I swallowed back my nerves before looking down the mountain and backing slightly away from the cliff edge. He chuckled again, but he shifted into a dragon after a moment and extended his left wing toward me. I swallowed as I climbed onto the webbing of his wings, and got onto one of the spikes between the shoulder blades. It was like there was a natural spot for someone to sit since it was pretty comfortable, all things considered. After a moment, he edged out, looked down the mountainside, and turned his head slightly to look at me before he pushed himself off the mountain.

For a moment, we were free-falling, and I was screaming all the way down until we passed the cloud cover and that was when he decided to snap his wings open and glide the way down and head back where the palace was.

The gentle beating of his wings lured me to sleep. And soon darkness came to me once again.

*****

I got to the front gates of the palace and slowly walked up the steps before looking at the doggy door that the King had placed inside the side. I growled slightly, but it was the only way in without scratching the door. I knew for a fact that if I scratched the door, then I would be headed down to work with Davis. I scowled as I went through the flap, it buzzed before allowing me completely inside. A security protocol was in place for the doggy door, all the werewolves and anyone who decided to be a dog had to go through a thorough examination and they knew who it was based on the foot pattern and the stance of the shifter or wolf. I sighed as I went further and finally emerged inside the royal palace. I trotted to my room and was slightly disdainful with the doggy door on the actual door too, but I had to shrug it off.

I went further into my room, before shifting back to my human form. I glanced around my room: the bed was to the right, right below the window, the dresser was on the wall closest to me to the right, and the closet was large enough to make it seem like it was a walk-in, but not exactly with a door either. My desk was on the left side, scattered with my pencils and blueprints for projects that I needed to complete.

I sighed deeply before running my hand through my hair, facing my dresser before opening the drawers and getting what I needed. The King would have to explain what happened to the seamstress because my uniform went up in flames at the hospital. It was my only one since I had been here only for a month. I wondered what my King was doing, why I was sent here to bodyguard the King of the shifters, unlike my father and forefather, who solely were guarding the king of the werewolves. I sat down on my spinning chair and sighed deeply. I knew that I was supposed to gather intel, but the only intel I had yet to discover about the shifter king was that he was lonely. That he and the Queen did not see eye to eye all the time. And that he was not someone to be scared of.

A knock sounded on the door and I glanced at the door before slipping on the pants and speaking, "Enter."

The door opened, and the Queen showed herself. I bowed deeply, now cursing myself slightly to be caught without a shirt on in her presence. Her eyes racked my body that was exposed before speaking, "**Are the rumors correct, Sammuel? That my daughter is here?**"

I swallowed slightly, I was hoping that someone else would have to explain what happened other than me. I sighed and replied, "I am confirming that she is alive. But she is not the same little girl you would think she is my Queen."

She looked at me before speaking, "**Stop addressing me as 'my Queen,' we both know that your heart is with the werewolves Sammuel. That you wish you were with your King and Queen.**"

I swallowed and bowed slightly before speaking, "Forgive me."

She scoffed slightly before speaking, "**Well, where is she then?**"

I sighed before speaking, "The last time I saw her, she was flying south."

She glanced at me, rolled her eyes, and growled, "**Flying south?**"

I smirked and grabbed my shirt, slid it on, and spoke, "Oh yeah. Morphous."

A scowl appeared on her face as soon as his name came up. So my King was correct, there was something wrong between Morphous and his Queen. What that was, was still a mystery to me. She turned to leave and paused at the door before speaking, "**Inform me immediately when she shall return.**"

I bowed to her and replied, "Yes, my Lady."

She paused at the door before turning her head slightly to the right, towards my desk and her eyes flickered to mine before leaving.

I waited a moment before walking to my desk and looking down at the blueprints, it may look like a mess, but I understood it clearly. It was a layout of the entire palace that I have since seen. There was only one place that I did not know and that was the catacombs, that were underneath me. I had no idea how to get to them, and so far my informants have been shifty as hell and not saying where the entrance was. It was all dead ends. All I remember from what my father told me to do before he forced me to become a guard at the shifter palace was that he wanted the layout. That he wanted to know all the exits, and entrances. And that was my key to go back home. I looked down at my blueprints and smirked. Once I find the catacombs, then the werewolves will overrun this shit show of a place. And take what is rightfully ours. Until then, I have to play the guard role. Until then, I have to play the 'always ready to answer' idiot as everyone else in the shifter ranks called me. One day, they will pay.

****

Anna and I finally got the injured girls up to the royal palace, and into separate rooms. The only two that did not go anywhere were Michael Slyther and Lord Verein as he was called. I wished that I could end him for what he had done to our princess, but without the authorization of the King, I could do nothing against them. They were watched every single minute while in the royal palace. We did not trust them, and they were looking around with wonder. It was more glamorous than the mansion that they had lived in.

Anna snapped her fingers in front of my face and I turned my attention to her and she rolled her eyes before speaking, "Quinn, stop daydreaming and help me with this girl. She is so thin and needs some sort of food. Wake the cook, get him to get some food going."

I stared at her before whispering, "Do you know what you just suggested Anna? Wake the cook? He's fucking nuts."

She scoffed and huffed before speaking again, "Please tell me you are not scared of Franster."

I cringed, who in the right mind named their kid Franster of all things? She rolled her eyes and walked down the hall. After a few steps, she looked back at me before waving me towards her. I swallowed back the nerves before following her. I may be the King's advisor, but it did not mean I was not scared of some of the staff that he had on hand. Franster was well, different would be an understatement. He was big, bear-like almost, and black. Yes, yes, I knew bad thoughts, but normally a black man wasn't the one that someone like Morphous would make into his cook. Especially after what happened all those years ago with the humans, and Franster, well he was a human. I glanced down at the lush cobalt blue carpet as we continued down further and soon came across Franster's door.

Anna paused before raising her hand and swallowed. I looked at her sharply before whispering, "You're scared of him, aren't you?"

She sighed deeply before glowering at me and knocking on his door. A gruff voice shouted on the other side, "GO AWAY!"

I looked at Anna and she licked her lips before speaking through the door, "Franster, we need your expertise."

A crash sounded on the other side as he must have fallen out of bed, and a curse sounded, before the door opened and he made me look like I was tiny comparatively, which was no easy task when I was at six feet already. I looked up at him and he sighed deeply, before rubbing his eyes and snapping, "What is with you shifters, always wanting to eat something."

I scowled before opening my mouth to retort, but Anna stepped backward, stepping on my left foot, making me glower at her back before she spoke, "I apologize, Franster. However, I need some sort of brothy meal. I have wounded women who needed help."

That caught Franster off guard and looked down at Anna, who was around the five-foot-five range, so by comparison, a midget to us. He sighed deeply before speaking, "How many?"

She, without missing a beat, replied, "Twenty-two."

He scowled before entering his room again, and a gruff oaf sounded from inside and soon someone else was mumbling inside. Soon, two young men came out, both of them were not more than twelve in age, and they stumbled to the door and shoved past us, heading towards the kitchen. Franster came out a minute later, grumbling but did not shove past us as the two young kids did.

He did not look like he had much sleep but continued to the kitchens, where even from here we heard the banging of pots and pans as they were moved. I looked at Anna and she smiled sheepishly before speaking, "Hey, don't look at me with that look."

I raised my eyebrows and replied, "It didn't sound like this was a one-time occurrence. He seemed to know you."

Anna looked a little smug and replied quietly, "Alright fine, no it was not a one-time occurrence. He and I know each other quite well."

I shook my head and turned to head to my chambers when Anna grabbed my arm, stopping me, I looked at her before speaking softly, "What's wrong?"

She sighed deeply, looked back where we had come from, and replied, "Some of those girls, Quinn. They are so young, yet they have the eyes of the elderly who have seen and been through a lot. They shouldn't have that dead look in their eyes. None of them should."

I lowered my gaze for a moment, looking at the flush carpet before speaking, "I know, I feel it myself. However, they will get the proper help they need now. Keep yourself happy, Anna, they will soon learn to be happy again. I'm sure it will just take time to have them understand that."

She nodded released my arm, turned towards the way we had come, and paused before speaking, "Quinn?"

I sighed slightly, but turned around and looked at her with soft eyes, before speaking, "Yeah?"

She smiled slightly before saying, "Thank you for being there for me."

A hand seemed to squeeze my chest, I licked my lip, nodded, and said, "No problem, Anna."

She smiled before she continued and rounded the corner, leaving me in front of Franster's door. I swallowed and glanced back where Anna disappeared and sighed deeply. Dating staff members was not really allowed, but Anna was catching more and more of my gazes lately. I wonder if she felt the same or not.

****

I continued down to my room and found that I was not alone in the hallway. I paused, raised my eyes from the ground, and looked around. I saw nothing, but that did not mean anything to us shifters, someone could be here and not be seen. I sighed deeply before speaking, "Who's there?"

No one shifted, but I could not shake off the feeling someone was watching me. I looked around and finally saw a picture frame crooked, and I spoke again, "Come out. I know you are there."

After a moment a beetle flew, landed, and shifted into my brother, Herald. He grinned at me before speaking, "I scared you that time, didn't I?"

I shook my head before replying, "Quit it, Herald. And no, you did not scare me. I felt I was being watched."

He rolled his eyes and leaned against the wall, fixing the frame in the process before speaking, "Oh come on! Admit it! I got you a little bit."

I stared at him before huffing and walking towards my room, which was past him. He followed me to my room. I opened my room door looking around to make sure everything was in order, which it was. I glanced at Herald before raising my eyebrows, "Wow, this is the first time you did not mess up my room."

He scowled and glowered at me before snapping, "I would have if SOMEONE did not tattle to dad about my business. What was that about anyhow?"

I scoffed and replied, "I am the King's advisor, Herald. My room is off-limits to everyone else. You are included in that."

Herald sighed and replied, "Fair point. What has been the news anyhow? Everything is out of whack, and I heard Fanster inside the kitchen tonight."

I looked out the door, that was still open before moving to close it, when Herald beat me to it. Closing the door and looking at me a little funny. I smiled and replied, "Extra precaution."

He rolled his eyes and snorted, "No one is awake to hear anything. It's bloody two in the morning Quinn."

I raised my eyebrows and replied, "All the same, you are awake. The cook is awake along with two of his helpers. Who knows who else is awake? Besides, my room has a soundproof door and walls. So, nothing in here is to be heard."

Herald looked at me with a crazed look before looking at the door and walls, as if suddenly realizing that whatever was said or done in here cannot be heard. I rolled my eyes before speaking, "The lost princess has been found, I saw her last week and I reported it to Morphous, who told me to go get her today."

To say that Herald was shocked was an understatement. He was flabbergasted, he looked around the room and finally whispered, "What the hell? Why is everyone being hush-hush on this?"

I sighed deeply and replied, "Because of what happened when she got…. Taken. No one wants to talk about it, Herald."

He eyed me suddenly and replied slowly, "There's more to it, isn't there? Something that you alone know and no one else. Am I right?"

I looked down and nodded but replied, "I was sworn to keep it hidden, Herald. And I will not disobey that order. Not without being killed for it. I promised to take it to my grave."

He swallowed and shook his head before speaking, "Damn, someone to order that to you must have been high-ranking to get you scared enough to keep that hidden. Whatever it is." I sighed and looked at him before nodding and biting my lip. He looked at me and smiled grimly, before speaking, "So, if the princess is indeed here, why hasn't everyone been informed of her yet?"

I sighed, before speaking, "There was a mishap at the hospital."

He raised his eyebrows, shook his head, and chuckled slightly before speaking, "So in other words, I will be on work duty to clean up the King's mess then? Is that your way of telling me that the King destroyed the newly built hospital again?"

I frowned slightly, Morphous has countlessly destroyed the hospital, but always made sure that he got all his people out before he did so. I sighed deeply and pinched the bridge of my nose before speaking, "Morphous wasn't the one who did it this time. It was Rafeor."

He looked at me sharply and replied questioningly, "Rafeor?"

I nodded and replied, "That is what the princess has been going as for the last twelve years, Herald. I doubt that she will go back to the name she was given back then. She is close to eighteen now."

He nodded, frowned suddenly, and said, "So, someone that has no idea what she is turned into a dragon and flew off by the sounds of it since no one was notified that she was back. Otherwise, everyone would have been alerted to be awake and surrounded her in love and welcomed her home."

I swallowed and nodded before looking out the window to the left, and sighed deeply at the darkness before rubbing my eyes, and motioning to the door, "Alright, as much as I would continue to talk to you, Herald, it's been a long tiring day and night, and I need to get some sleep before I have to continue all over again in a few hours."

Herald kind of chuckled a little at that and walked to the door, opened it, looked back, and replied, "Good night, Quinn. Get some much-needed rest."

I smiled grimly before he shut the door. I waited a minute to make sure no one else was coming to the door before I walked to it and locked it. No one else was going to come unannounced to my room tonight. They can come tomorrow morning.

*****

I landed in the strip of land that I made as the landing strip when building my palace. Someone was waiting for me there, and I saw the look on the woman before me, I sighed deeply before making sure that Rafeor was taken down safely, before shifting back to my human form. My Queen walked forward, eyeing the girl behind me before speaking, **"Why was I not informed that you had found your daughter? Why was I in the dark Morphous?"**

I sighed deeply and looked into her tear-streaked eyes and face, and looked down at the grass before speaking, **"I wanted to make sure that Quinn was correct, before telling you and finding out he was wrong. I know how much you have missed her Katherine."**

She sighed deeply and looked at the guards as they moved swiftly with the gurney bringing her daughter inside their palace.

I looked at my Queen and saw the emotions swirling in her eyes, I knew that I was the cause of some of them. She blames me for even having Raphina, that was something that would go to the grave. Raphina is not Katherine's daughter. She was the werewolf's Queen's daughter after I had an affair with her. However, since we were both of royal blood, it made Raphina the first hybrid. Between a werewolf and a shifter.

I sighed deeply and spoke, **"Katherine."**

She glanced at me before frowning. She hissed, **"You have some explaining to do. To that poor kid that you had brought into this world Morphous. Do not make me be the one to tell her that she is not my daughter."**

I smiled grimly and nodded in response. A flicker of movement came from the darkness of the alleyway, and then nothing. I walked towards it but saw no one there. I sincerely hoped that no one eavesdropped on our conversation, it would get them killed.

****

I snuck towards the landing site, where I knew that Morphous would eventually come and land, and sure enough after close to two hours before sunrise, his black dragon came into view.

The Queen came out of the common doors, but she glanced towards the alleyway I had chosen to be in. As if she knew where I was. I swallowed but stayed where I was, a movement to the shifters was what drew their attention the most.

After the guards got Rafeor down, Morphous shifted into his human form. For a moment, the King and Queen stared at each other, before the Queen, whose name I still did not know, since no one addressed her by her name, spoke, "**Why was I not informed that you had found your daughter? Why was I in the dark Morphous?**"

I stared at the two from a couple of yards away, unsure I heard that correctly, the Queen stressed 'YOUR's' out, hmmm, maybe this was the strain that was not supposed to be there. I shook my head and focussed on what Morphous was saying, "**I know how much you have missed her Katherine.**"

I frowned, I missed something that he said, but I got the name of the Queen now. I smiled slightly, when after a moment, Morphous spoke, "**Katherine.**"

I watched as Katherine looked at him before hissing, "**You have some explaining to do. To that poor kid that you had brought into this world, Morphous. Do not make me be the one to tell her that she is not my daughter.**"

That was all I needed to hear. That Rafeor was not Katherine's daughter. I slipped away and rounded the corner when I swallowed. I moved too fast, I must have caught someone's attention with my quick movement. I hope I do not get caught.

****

I stared at the ripped piece of clothing on the ground for a moment and picked it up, sniffing it. My eyes turned yellow for a split second but went back to normal after a moment. I pocketed the torn clothing before turning towards Katherine, who was watching me, "**I thought I saw someone lurking.**"

She hmphed, before heading inside, I swallowed before speaking, "**I hope in your heart, you will come to know I am sorry Katherine. It was not meant to happen.**"

She paused on the white marble steps and leaned on the bronze guardrail before growling, "**She was not something I was okay with, to begin with, Morphous. That relationship between you and her was something that should not have happened. Especially behind my back, and before he even met his mate. Werewolves are very keen on finding their Goddess-given mate Morphous, and you took that away from her first.**"

I swallowed back the lump in my throat, she was casually tossing this out, careless if anyone heard this. I glanced around, luckily, the guards were all inside. Especially because they knew that the Queen would want privacy with me. I swallowed and sighed before speaking, **"Katherine...."**

She shook her head, turned around, and headed inside without a word, leaving me there alone.

After a few minutes of standing there alone, I sighed and headed inside. I knew I had to get everything ready for when Rafeor was able to meet everyone.

# Chapter 4

I woke up on a bed, soft comfortable, not like the straw mattress I had at Lord Verein's slave quarters. I stretched, wincing slightly, the sun was halfway up in the sky and for a brief second, I feared Michael coming in and whipping me for sleeping past curfew. I closed my eyes and breathed evenly and slowly, telling myself I was okay. That I got out. I looked around the room, the walls were a dull white color, faded with the bleach of the sun's rays day in and the glow of the moon out, repeating the process. Showing that this room had not been used for many many days, or perhaps years. I looked around, saw something that was like a faraway dream, and swallowed, I eased myself out of the bed and winced. I glanced down at my chest, and saw cloth wrappings, tightly against me. I looked at the door, before smiling slightly, my father even after everything, made sure I was taken care of.

I looked at the thing that I remembered faintly again and frowned as I walked towards it on uneasy feet. I crouched, dragging the box out, and gasped. I recognized the toy on top, it was from my childhood. I looked around the room, slowly remembering things, I swallowed the lump in my throat, they kept my room as I had left it, except for a few things here and there. It was all mine. I bit my lip and looked around, I was a bit shocked, after twelve years, they kept the same room as if I never left it in the first place.

A knock sounded on the door, and I glanced down at myself, I was in shorts, but my top half was bare except for the wrappings, but it covered mostly everything. I swallowed before speaking, "**Enter.**"

The door swung open, and a woman stood there, I glanced at her and swallowed. There was not much in appearance but I could tell that she was someone of importance by how she held herself up. She eyed me for a moment before speaking, "**Hello.**"

I nodded in response, not knowing who she was. She seemed a bit taken aback for a moment before continuing, "**Do you not know who I am?**"

I paused and stood up wincing, her eyes trailed to the bandaging and seemed to want to tsk a few times before her eyes drifted to a few of the raised scars I have on my torso. She swallowed, and finally met my eyes and said, "**You poor thing.**"

I sighed deeply, for some reason, she was irritating me. I did not understand why my anger swelled, but it did. Something about her shouted danger, and the last time I ignored the feeling, it turned out to be bad for my case. I looked at her sharply for a moment before speaking, "**Am I supposed to know who you are?**"

She looked down, shook her head, and replied, "**I guess I cannot assume that you would know who I am. My name is Katherine.**"

I smiled grimly, warning bells in my mind sounded, and my eyes flickered in the mirror. I was looking over her shoulder, I wasn't surprised anymore about it after I had turned into a freaking dragon last night. I turned to face the window and she made a sound like clearing her throat, I turned my head slightly to the left, before speaking, "**My name is Rafeor.**"

She scoffed, and I turned back around and raised my eyebrows questioningly. She stared at me and sneered slightly before shaking her head and replying, "**Correction. Your name is Raphina. Not Rafeor.**"

My eyes in the mirror changed to orange and she gasped before lowering her eyes from mine for a moment before looking at me straight on again. I glowered at her and growled, "**My name is Rafeor. I am not changing it. Nor will I answer to anything else.**"

Katherine seemed shocked before she stood up straight, so she was no longer leaning against the door frame and replying sharply, "**I will call you dog then. Cause that is what your name is.**"

My eyes flickered red, I clenched my fists and hissed, "**Leave me.**"

I turned to face the window again, thinking I dismissed her. However, a moment later, a hand gripped my shoulder and she forcefully turned me about, she was a head taller than I was, well-fed, and strong, knowing who she was and what she wasn't. I winced at the force, but a sensation spread through me, and I went with what my instinct told me to do. I shifted into a wolf, I sniffed and she let out a scream.

I turned to look at her, and caught a look at myself in the mirror, I stood tall, like what the humans fear, standing on two legs hunched over. My fur was white, pure white. My eyes were turquoise. My jaw elongated. I snorted, I was what the humans feared in my wolf form apparently. Then I thought back to Sammuel. Why was I different from a werewolf? Are all the shifters like this? If so, then I understand why the humans would fear us.

Katherine caught my attention as she scrambled towards the door. My eyes squinted. My mouth pulled back as if instinctively baring my teeth at her. I slowly approached her, as if I was stalking my prey. Her breathing quickened, and I could have sworn she soiled herself. My nose twitched as I smelled the urine. I growled low in my throat, a few heavy footfalls came from the hallway, coming towards my room when Sammuel appeared, and the look of shock across his face was evident. He held up his hands and whispered, "Rafeor?"

I growled in response. He glanced down at Katherine who was in front of me, and swallowed before he glanced at me. He slowly bent down, with his hands, up reaching out with his left hand, and pulling her towards the open door before whispering, "Shhh…. Easy Rafeor. Easy. I'll get the Queen out of your hair."

I blinked once, the queen? Shit. Sammuel never stopped staring at me, he frowned before he glanced at Katherine, and whispered to her, "You didn't tell her of your title?"

Katherine shook her head in response and he grimaced, looked at me again, and swallowed. He glanced at me, in this wolf form, and eyed me thoughtfully before speaking, "Rafeor, please shift back. There has been a miscommunication surely. You don't need to act on whatever happened here."

Apparently, my wolf was one at itself. I couldn't really do anything, it straightened itself up before growling low in its throat. It was not like the dragon form last night, I could get out of it more easily, but this, this was like it had its own mind. My wolf straightened and growled, **"I do not want her near me again. She is not related to me. She is not my mother."**

To say I was shocked was an understatement. I was not at all ready for it to speak, and not sound anything like me. And by the looks across Sammuel's and Katherine's faces, I knew this was not normal. My wolf turned towards the window before snapping, **"Leave me."**

They must have bowed, and scrambled away, closing the door behind them. My wolf stared out the window, and it blinked once. After a few minutes of feeling like I was floating in my own body, I suddenly blinked again and I stared at my reflection in the glass. I was once again back to my human form. I look around… shocked.

# Chapter 5

I got the Queen out of the room that Rafeor was in, and to say I was shocked is an understatement. I did not understand why she is a fucking Lycan. So far, the only ones I knew that were Lycan, were the royals of the werewolf population. So why the fuck was the lost princess of the shifters a fucking Lycan? And the fact that the Lycan spoke in an entirely different tone than Rafeor? That was unheard of. I glanced at the Queen, the shock was still obvious on her face, and I swallowed. What was said by the Lycan, would make it impossible for someone to ignore, I was just thankful that I heard what was going on before anyone else. Even before Quinn. Before he tried to keep it quiet.

I shut the door behind us, and helped Katherine to her feet before swallowing nervously, the look in her eyes spoke unspoken words. I glanced at the closed doors before looking around us. We were alone, which was surprising. I finally got my breathing under control before speaking, "Kath…"

That was the only part that I said, and she clamped her hand across my mouth, stopping me from speaking further. My eyes flickered for a split second, but I steadied my anger and waited. After a moment she removed her hand before whispering, "**Not a word to anyone of this, Sammuel. If people find out that she is what she is, there will be major consequences. I know that you were there last night. I didn't say anything, mainly due to not realizing the extent of the issue.**"

I swallowed and whispered, "But you know who her mother is."

She turned to leave, when she stopped, looked around, and replied, "**It is unsafe to talk here, Sammuel. Follow me.**"

I looked around, the shifters tend to not eavesdrop on one another, but after what just happened, I understood her cautiousness. If word got out what Rafeor was, then that would make a huge mess. I followed the Queen to her chambers.

*****

I was shell-shocked. I was not ready to see the princess shift into the Lycan. I stared as the Queen scrambled backward and watched as Sammuel helped her to her feet after closing the door. I heard everything, and I knew the way to the Queen's chambers. I looked around slowly before following. I landed on Sammuel's back, blending into his fuzzy and black coat. My beetle form blended completely.

*****

We finally got to her chambers, after a few minutes, the Queen entered, and looked slowly around, her eyes roaming the room before she seemed satisfied no one was inside. She motioned towards the door, and I closed it. I looked at her with a bit of concern in my eyes. She swallowed before speaking, **"You must promise me, Sammuel, you cannot tell anyone inside the shifter palace. Swear it."**

I instantly noticed that she said 'shifter' and not werewolf. I glanced at her and frowned slightly. Setting my jaw slightly, I was suddenly uneasy. She chuckled a little before facing vanity, she said, **"Oh come on. Give me some credit. You had the blueprints of the layout of the palace, except for the catacombs. You had every entrance and exit marked. You are only missing that piece. I know a spy when I see one Sammuel. I do warn you though, the last one that Morphous caught sneaking around where they shouldn't be, was slaughtered."**

I swallowed and looked around for a moment, thinking of the things I could use to kill her. Nothing would stop me from completing the task for my king. She glanced in the mirror and rolled her eyes before speaking, **"Killing me is the worst that you could do to yourself, Sammuel."**

My eyes flickered to her again and I frowned before replying, "If you have known for a while now that I am a spy, then why didn't you say anything to Morphous? What is your game?"

She sighed deeply and straightened herself up before turning to face me. **"No game. To tell you the truth, I am not in love with Morphous. Never was. Tolerate is more like it. Especially after what he did."**

I cocked my head slightly and raised my eyebrows. She chuckled again and went to her dresser before grabbing a pair of undergarments, and slipping off her soiled ones. I turned slightly away from her, giving her somewhat privacy. I heard a smirk, but did not turn around before she spoke again, **"Such modest behavior, Sammuel."**

I glanced at her and replied, "I am not here for a show. I was told to keep my head down."

She chuckled slightly and said, **"And I assure you, you have kept yourself down."**

I squinted my eyes, looking through the room before my eyes flickered to her again. I leaned against the wall, crossed my arms, and spoke, "Well, you have my attention then. Why did you want to talk in your chambers though?"

She smiled gently for a moment before replying, "**Because, unlike your room and the guards' rooms, this is soundproof. No one can hear what is said inside unless they are already inside. It was made this way so that no information was eavesdropped.**"

I smiled at her, my eyes flashed golden as my wolf surfaced for a split second, that was good to know. She did not seem surprised, she instead leaned backward against the dresser before speaking, "**May I ask you a question, Sammuel?**"

I crocked my head slightly, thinking before I responded, "Depends on the question."

Katherine smiled slightly and continued, "**What rank are you in the wolves? I know you must have some rank, considering all the others do not make direct eye contact with you.**"

I smirked, loosened my arms, and pushed off the wall for a moment before replying, "I am a beta. At least, I will be once I am allowed back home."

Katherine gave me a funny look before replying, "**Why wouldn't they want you back?**"

I smiled, my eyes stayed golden as I replied, my wolf's voice underscored mine, "**Because I killed an elite warrior. In a way, it was either I served fifty years in prison, or be a spy for my king. Prison was not something I wanted to do.**"

She swallowed nervously and suddenly seemed uneasy around me for a moment before she gained her composure again. My wolf snickered at her, but drifted back into the background again, allowing me to be in control again. I shook myself slightly, "He killed the elite member. My wolf, not me. I assure you though, if you say anything, I will not think twice about committing a crime myself."

She stared at me and replied, "**You know what I think. You seem to think that you are different between Rafeor, and yourself. But there are similar things. Your wolf talked in a different tone than yours too. Why is that?**"

I glanced down and replied, "My mother was a royal wolf from a different pack. My father, though was devoted to the king, and therefore, left my mother, and well, those of royal lines can have their wolves speak differently."

I paused. Suddenly clicking something together. I glanced sharply at her and sighed deeply. "Now I am wondering, why did you connect me and Rafeor? Are you implying that she is of royal bloodline from the werewolves?"

She smiled slightly and replied, "**Morphous had an affair with the werewolf king's mate before they had met. Rafeor is her daughter, not mine. That is the riff between me and Morphous.**"

To say I was expecting that was not true. That caught me off guard entirely. I walked a little further into her room and glanced out the window before replying, "So, she is of a royal bloodline. That's what hasn't been disclosed. The werewolf king doesn't know does he?"

Katherine slowly shook her head, and replied, "**No, I doubt it. Otherwise, we would have had a war. The riot was a cover-up almost. Rafeor was six when she was 'taken', but no one really knows that. The only ones who know are; you, me, the Queen of the Wolves, Morphous, and Quinn, and he was sworn to take it to the grave. Otherwise, Morphous would kill him and his entire family line, along with whoever he informed.**"

I swallowed and replied, "So, in other words, this is the cause of the riot? To keep her identity a secret?"

Katherine slowly nodded and replied, "**Yes, and no.**"

I glanced outside again and for a moment there was only silence. I sighed deeply before speaking again, breaking the silence after a few tense moments, "Then why did Morphous send out Quinn to go 'find' her again? Why search for her?"

For a moment, she did not look like she wanted to answer, but she stood up, walked to her closet before opening the mahogany door and disappeared inside. She returned with a box. She placed the box down on her vanity, tapped her fingers on the oak wood, looked at me, and motioned me to come over to her. I walked across the walkway, looked down at the box, and looked at her. She swallowed and after a moment took the lid off. I was shocked. I took a step backward, my wolf glinted in my eyes for a moment before he faded back again. I took a shaky breath in, and my eyes flickered to her again. I whispered, "You gotta be kidding me. That's why?" She grimaced and nodded. She glanced down at the box and closed it. I swallowed and watched as she put it away again, and said, "**You have to understand Sammuel, during the riot, Morphous was in his prime time. He took things that he had no idea what or how they worked. This was one of those things. I only found it when he brought it forth as a trophy. I knew what it was, and I convinced him that it was safer in my room than his.**"

I swallowed and looked towards the window; the sun was sinking slightly. I sighed; it was a wasted day if my comrades thought about it. But so, so much information was given to me in a matter of two hours. I glanced at her again before speaking, "So besides Morphous, who knows you have that?"

She chuckled slightly and replied, "**Only you, me, and Morphous. There used to be others, but their end came quickly.**"

I nodded and replied, "Hmmm. That's putting it lightly that you killed your people."

She shrugged and replied, "**It was Morphous that put them out, not me. But you now know why. My question is, who are you going to tell this information to?**"

I shook my head slightly and didn't reply. She smiled knowingly. This was not something that you could just tell your inside dog to pass on. This was something that you had to do in person, and since I was not cleared to go back home, that made it harder. I shook my head, and she chuckled before speaking again, "**There, there. Rafeor may have been 'taken' but she was also the cover-up of this artifact. The riot was the cover-up of cover-ups. Everyone remembers the riot, but not everyone remembers the things that were taken, or stolen.**"

I sighed deeply, running my hands across my face, and frowned. I looked at her with a questioning look. "So, she was a cover-up for that. But what is her tie to it?"

She sighed deeply before replying, "**I thought you were smarter.**"

She paused before glancing at the sun, as it dipped further down the horizon. "**She is the only hybrid to be known of. You and I both know that the royals of each species respectively have not mingled in fear of a cross-bred brute. The fact that Morphous is a shifter King, means that the dragon's bloodline runs through his. And the fact the werewolf Queen has Lycan running through hers. It has been foretold that a mix-blood would appear at some point, and the horrors surrounding the creation of such have been the cause of us to be at odds with each other for centuries.**"

I kind of waved her off, and replied, "I know all the legends based on that mix. That the crossbred will be the most powerful being on the planet and will have the ability of both Lycan and shifter."

She raised her eyebrows, crossed her hands, and replied, "**And who has the most powerful being at the moment, Sammuel? The wolves? Or the shifters?**"

I opened my mouth to retort, then stopped. Suddenly it clicked on why Morphous was after his daughter again. Part of the other legend was that after she turned eighteen, both bloodlines would show. I glanced at her and swallowed, she smiled knowingly before nodding and spoke, "**Now you come to the conclusion. If Rafeor was kept here, her powers would have been discovered long before and everyone would have known what she was. But the fact that she was 'taken' in the riot, was a cover for Morphous to keep her hidden. I doubt that your Queen knows that her daughter is still alive. I believe at some point, Morphous told her that she was dead. So, she would not come looking for her.**"

I swallowed. Now I understood why Morphous killed anyone who had known and forced only a few people to keep the information secret. I shook my head and growled, "Why are you telling me all this?"

Katherine smiled and replied, "**Because, like it or not. You are caught in the crossfire of this. You know of her Lycan form, and you witnessed her dragon form last night. If Morphous thought backward, which he may already start questioning things, Sammuel, watch your back since I have a feeling, you are his next target to keep quiet.**"

I was silent for a moment and swallowed. I knew for a fact that I had too much information to stay here, but too little information to go back home. My father said don't come back until I have the layout completely.

Katherine must have known what was going through my mind since she went back into her closet, came out with a piece of parchment and handed it to me. I took it with shaky hands and opened it up and gasped. It was the blueprints of the entire palace, entrances, exits, and most importantly the catacombs.

I looked at her as I rolled it back up. She smiled knowingly. "**Better get going. Last time I checked, you were on night duty with no one on the eastern side.**"

I glanced sharply and was about to correct her, but she smiled slightly before continuing, "**I may have made it, so you are alone tonight, Sammuel. Use that time well.**"

I looked down at the map, glanced at her, and slowly backed away. All the information I now had, and everything that she told me, would get me killed instantly if Morphous found out. Or any other shifter for that matter. I needed to leave tonight. I needed to go home.

She smiled and jerked her head as I opened the door, looked back at her, and whispered, "Thank you, Katherine."

She smiled a little before snapping, "**Leave me.**"

For a moment, I was shocked at the sudden change, before I glanced out the hallway and saw two of the royal guards. I plastered on an expressionless face and bowed before closing the door with a slightly harder slam than intended.

****

The guards looked at me with a raised eyebrow and I scowled before muttering, "She called me to her."

The guards took the lie easily and I left the royal hallways and started to go to my room. I paused, glanced at the candles, and cursed slightly, I needed to get to the Eastern Wall. I switched quickly and went down another hallway. Not noticing that a beetle came off my coat after leaving the royal chambers.

# Chapter 6

I flew off Sammuel and swallowed, what I had heard, what I had learned. Fuck, I now knew why Quinn always looked a bit different after the riot. I now knew. I now knew why he was more aloof than years prior. He may be a few years older than I am, but that did not really matter all too much to the shifters. We didn't really care if there was an age gap. Now I understood though why he suddenly made it seem that he didn't want to say anything. Why he didn't want to do things after the riot, why he suddenly wanted to forget about the princess, and kind of enforced it that she was 'taken'. I now understood it all. I leaned to the wall, still as my beetle form, I closed my eyes before opening the communications to Quinn, *"Are you busy right now?"*

For a moment, he was silent before he replied, *"What did you do?"*

I swallowed and replied, *"Uhhh, why do you instantly go to the phrase that?"*

I could almost picture him scowling, as he replied, *"Because the only time YOU contact me this way is when you need help getting your ass out of trouble. So again, I ask you. What did you do?"*

With shifters, the only ones who could connect and be on the same connection were siblings and their parents, which meant bloodline. I swallowed and didn't know if Morphous would be on the same line or not, so I asked, *"Are we related to the Queen or King in any way Quinn?"*

He must have paused whatever he was doing since he got back after a few minutes, *"No, there is no connection to us. What the fuck did you do?"*

I swallowed and replied, *"Are you alone?"*

I could tell that he was debating on answering that question, but he replied after a moment, *"Give me a minute. Then I will be."*

I swallowed as I waited, I stayed where I was.

****

I knew the moment that Herald connected to our mind-link that he did something wrong. I knew it and he apparently knew it too since he did not try to argue all too much. I sighed deeply, I was helping Anna, and she instantly picked up the fact that I was not one hundred percent with her anymore. She, however, knew that Herald was possibly the one connecting since our father rarely did anymore, and my other siblings were dead after the riot. She looked at me knowingly and I sighed deeply. She rested her hand on my shoulder after a moment, she looked around and whispered, "Go, I'll be fine here alone, Quinn."

I opened my mouth to reply, but she shook her head and whispered, "There are only a few people that mind-link you, Quinn. And that is family. Go."

I sighed, turned around, and walked out of the service hall that was temporarily turned into a medical placement until the hospital was built again. Heading back to my room, I connected to Herald, *"My room. Now."*

I did not get a response, but knew he was either waiting on me or heading there.

***

I sighed deeply. I was the advisor, and I knew who was supposed to be on guard duty too, which was why I paused at the junction between corridors and called out, "AMISH! You were supposed to be on the Eastern Wall tonight."

Amish turned around and dipped his head in my direction before replying, "Uh. But the Queen said I was dismissed for the evening, sir."

I frowned and replied, "The Queen?"

Amish nodded and replied, "Yes, sir. She told me that I was dismissed from all duties tonight."

I frowned. Amish would not lie; he was always where he was supposed to be unless directed otherwise. I glanced at him before replying, "Why didn't you report to me about this? Who was the second guard that was supposed to work tonight?"

The other guard, that Amish was talking to, spoke, "It was Sammuel that was scheduled. You know that new wolf that showed about a month ago?"

I frowned, looked at him, and replied, "Sammuel was the other. Has he done the Eastern Wall alone yet?"

Amish and the other guards looked at each other, they were both senior guards, and after a moment, they shook their heads in response. I furrowed my eyebrows together, I didn't know what the Queen was up to, but I knew for a fact that the Eastern Wall was close to the werewolves, which was why it was always watched. I sighed deeply before speaking, "Amish, I apologize. However, I want you to go to the Eastern Wall. Same with you, Hector."

They gave me a confused look before Hector replied, "Why? You would be going against the Queen's order."

I looked at them both and replied, "You just said the only one manning that wall is a werewolf. Which side is their territory?"

It took them a moment before their eyes shifted colors as they caught the drift suddenly. A growl escaped Amish as he turned sharply, he went into the guard chambers, grabbed his uniform, and came back. Hector was already ready to go, but he looked pissed.

I looked at both before speaking, "If you see Sammuel, do not do anything. It does not mean that he does know that he's alone. I doubt that he knows. This is more of a precaution. I will take the blame when the Queen finds out."

They both dipped their heads to me and walked in sync towards the Eastern gate.

***

I turned to head back to my room and entered it after a moment, knowing that Herald was already inside since I didn't see any disturbances outside. I flicked the light on and turned around. Sure enough, he was sitting down at my desk, but the ashen look across his face made me pause. I had not seen him look so serious before. I walked towards him, resting my hand on his shoulder, and making him jump. I frowned, normally he would have said something and knew I was in there. Something got him worked up. I turned around to put my uniform off, but he spoke quietly, "Leave your uniform on Quinn. I have information that even the King will want to hear."

I froze, turned slowly back around, and whispered, "What?"

Herald looked up at me for a brief second before whispering, "You are going to inform the King of something for me, Quinn. Something bad."

I stared at him and replied after a moment, "What happened?"

He glanced up at me with fear in his eyes and I swallowed. Herald never had that look in his eyes before. He was always so sure of himself. I bit my lip before speaking, "Herald?"

He shook for a moment before whispering, "You know that werewolf that we got only a month ago, right? Sammuel?" I froze completely, it cannot be a coincidence that Sammuel's name came from Herald's mouth and the Queen signing off Amish tonight. I looked at him sharply before speaking, "What of him?"

Herald looked at me before whispering, "He has the blueprints of the palace including the catacombs. The Queen…"

I stopped him right there. I swallowed as I grabbed my blade before I paused before looking at him and speaking, "Herald, go to father."

He shook his head and whispered, "There is so much wrong, Quinn. I know why you have been distant since the riot."

I froze. No one was supposed to find that out. I stared at him now, fear completely draining the color from my face before I whispered, "Say nothing of it, Herald. Nothing, until I get back."

He looked at me and smiled a little before replying, "I'm leaving, Quinn. It's not safe for you or me here."

I swallowed and looked at the door before replying, "Herald, if you leave out of the blue, someone is going to notice and ask questions. You have to stay."

He lowered his eyes from mine and broke into a quiet sob, but I couldn't do anything. I glanced at the door and then at him. For once, torn between what to do. After a moment, he got his shit together before speaking, "Go."

I swallowed and left. I knew the quickest way to the Eastern Wall. I just hoped I wasn't too late.

*****

Amish and Hector got to the wall just in time, Hector hanging back in the shadows of the doorway. Amish saw Sammuel on the wall, looking down, as if judging the distance. I cleared my throat after a moment, "Sammuel?"

He froze, and his eyes flickered to mine before speaking, "I thought you were off shift tonight, Amish."

I shrugged before replying, "Eh, a day off without pay, can't really have too many of those off."

Sammuel frowned, he tucked something into his coat pocket, catching my gaze for a moment before I continued, "My question is though Sammuel, where is your uniform?"

He smiled slightly before replying, "Morphous had me shift last night before the hospital went up in flames. My uniform was lost."

I frowned, that did line up correctly. I glanced slightly at Hector, but he shook his head slightly. I looked at Sammuel for a moment, and sighed deeply before speaking, "So, care to explain why you were judging how far down it was?"

Sammuel froze and his eyes flickered to me. He then glanced around as if making sure we were alone, good thing that Hector didn't come out of the shadows. He glanced at me and removed his sword for a moment as if testing its weight. I felt a sudden calmness come over me, and I watched him before he looked at me again. "Sorry Amish. You saw too much."

He leaped forward, I drew out my blade in time and our steel connected. The blades grinding against each other. I pushed my blade up, creating sparks where they connected, before jabbing at him. He blocked the move, but it opened his right side for an attack. I slashed in an arch fast, he tried to block it, but I still caught his side. I gauged into him, he grimaced in response.

His eyes flashed a different color for a split second before his aura filled the wall, and radiated off him. I paused and took a step backward. He panted and growled, "**Enough.**"

I swallowed, only a select few could have their counterparts speak a different tone, and that was mostly the royal bloodline. I, however, kept my blade in my hand and replied, "Then summit."

His eyes flashed, and he replied darkly, "**I hope you know, I didn't want to kill you. I was merely going to injure you. But now? Nah. You're dead.**"

He charged at me, faster than a normal werewolf, proving that he had royal blood in him. I swung to the left, but he went too fast. His sword came out of nowhere and was about to slam into my chest when Hector came out of nowhere. He caught Sammuel's blade, and twirled his, casting his blade away. Mere centimeters from my chest, scratching me in the process, but not dead. I panted and glanced at Hector and dipped my head to him. He saved my life more than once through the years, and he kept proving that he would continue for more to come.

Sammuel growled and scrambled backward, his sword clanging onto the marble block, a few feet away from him. He glowered at us, before growling low in his throat. He closed his eyes for a brief second. Shifting into his wolf form. His clothes tore from his body, as he shifted.

Hector glanced at him before speaking, "Fight me, coward."

Sammuel's wolf eyes glittered in rage at the term coward. Hector took a step forward before stopping and raising his eyebrows. "Come on, coward. Fight me."

Sammuel's eyes dimmed and his eyes took more of his wolf's. He was about to attack when someone exited through the back door behind us. His head snapped up, and he drew his lips backward in a snarl.

I looked back and saw Quinn, but he was not alone, Morphous stood next to him. His eyes flashed orange, but he did not let his aura roll out since Hector and I were there. Quinn looked like he had seen better times, half of his face was red, but he looked like he was ready to defend his king. Morphous walked forward and stopped adjacent to Hector before he spoke, **"Sammuel. Give me the map, and you will live."**

He growled in response, hunkered down, and grabbed his coat in his teeth before leaping off the wall. Morphous didn't even glance down, the sudden screaming from below made me want to look down, but Morphous turned around, and sighed before speaking, **"I want all three of you to be in my office in twenty minutes."**

Hector and I glanced at each other before snapping to attention and bowed to him before turning away and going past Quinn. Leaving him and the King together.

# Chapter 7

I glanced at the King and opened my mouth to say something, but he glowered at me, his eyes still orange. I bowed my head down and swallowed in response. He glanced down at the bottom of the wall and smiled a bit before turning to me, **"Go to my office, Quinn. And bring your brother there too."**

I glanced up at him and bowed before turning around and heading that way.

*****

Guards shouted outside my door, and I frowned. No one should be doing anything. I slowly walked to my door before opening it. I glanced out before speaking, **"Thain, what's happening?"**

He glanced at me before replying, "The King has called for us, M'lady. He told us to report to the Eastern Wall."

I frowned, if any luck Sammuel was gone, but I didn't say anything and replied after a moment, **"Well, I won't keep you waiting, Thain. You may go."**

He hesitated for a moment, but he bowed quickly and ran down the hall. I closed my door and leaned against it. I bit my lip for a moment, before grabbing my knife and walking out the door.

I followed Thain's scent and swallowed as I smelled Sammuel's. It was far too fresh to be old, meaning he was still here. I looked around, I was alone. I looked at the doorway where Thain disappeared. What I was about to do was treason. However, I was the Queen, and no one was going to question my motives either. I quietly walked into the room, but as soon as I tried to sneak up on him, a voice called out, "Stop."

I paused, turned around, and scoffed. Killian was before me, and he looked like he had seen a ghost. I replied, **"I am the Queen, Killian, bow to me."**

He did not reply for a moment, but his eyes flickered behind me, and then replied, "I think I'm good, my Queen. Arrest her."

I scoffed and was about to say something, but I felt restraints being placed around my wrists. I tried to jerk my hands out, but to no avail. I stared at Killian before growling, "**Whose orders do you follow, Killian?**"

He swallowed before replying, "The King's."

I swallowed, there was no way in hell that Morphous could have known. Unless he had a mole on the inside of my room. I glanced at Killian before realizing something, he was a fucking spy for the most part, he was always where he was not supposed to be in my case. I scoffed before growling, "**Release me. I command you.**"

I rolled out my command, my aura raging around us. I saw him struggle for a moment before he replied, "No."

I glanced over my shoulder and saw Thain struggling for a moment, but he did not follow my commands either. I glanced at Killian before speaking, "**What did he offer you? Gold? Treasure?**"

He stared at me before replying, "I will not be bought. I serve the King. You should know that better than anyone, Katherine."

He turned slightly and started to head out. Thain grabbed my elbow and pulled me along, and I stumbled slightly. He seemed to want to make sure I was okay, but Killian was moving down the hallway a bit faster, and he wanted to follow him. I struggled a little bit before I snapped, "**Killian! I command you to stop and release me!**"

For a split second, I saw his footfalls falter before they got their rhythm again. He without turning, replied, "By the decree of the King, you are to be brought forth in cuffs, Katherine. Any and all threats made by you are to be remembered and accounted for. Any commands, foregone."

He said it as if it was completely fine, and I froze, Thain dragged me a few feet before I started to walk again. Morphous ordered them to do exactly what they were doing, and the last time that something along the lines of this happened to someone else of similar ranking meant that they were dead. I swallowed and whispered, "**On what grounds?**"

Killian paused, we were outside of Morphous's office doors, and he turned and replied, "Treason."

I froze and swallowed. His eyes betrayed nothing, and I lowered my eyes. He knew. He fucking found out somehow. He opened the door and held it open for Thain and me to enter the room.

*****

I made it to the King's office, along with Herald, but it was a few minutes after twenty minutes, so everyone was waiting for us to arrive. I dragged Herald through the door and bowed my head towards Morphous, who was tapping his fingers on his mahogany desk, his eyes a shade of red. I did not speak, already knowing that speaking would make it worse. Herald looked at him and was about to speak when our father came out from another room, he glanced at Morphous before speaking, "My Lord, forgive Quinn for being tardy. I had given Herald a calming medicine to get the information. I apologize."

I watched as Morphous's eyes flickered to his, and I watched as our father held against his gaze. I bowed my head, our father was Morphous's first in command of this palace. Nothing happens here without him knowing. Unless, of course, it was done in a soundproof room, then he did not know. He was Morphous's spy now since I took over his duty as the King's advisor twelve years ago.

Morphous inhaled loudly, making my running thoughts stop as I glanced at him. He looked at me and spoke, "**Anyone else know of what happened?**"

I quickly shook my head and did not reply. Herald looked at him and whispered, "My Lord, the only one that knew besides me was Sammuel, and of course, the Queen."

Morphous held up his hand, stopping him from rambling. He stood up and walked around the desk before speaking, "**Amish. Hector. Enter.**"

One of the side doors opened, and the two elder guards entered, Amish wore a small bandage on his chest, and he seemed okay for the most part. Same with Hector. They both bowed to Morphous before Hector spoke, "You called, my Lord?"

Morphous looked at us before turning his attention to them and speaking, "**Tell me the events that unfolded until now.**"

His aura raging around us, making us all flinch as they rolled. No one could refuse him. Even father looked like he wanted to submit to him, which was saying something since he was somewhat powerful in his own right.

Amish bowed his head and replied, "Two hours ago, my Lord, the Queen called for me. I came, and she told me to take the night off. I didn't ask questions, but I know now I should have. I bowed to her and left. I went back to the guard brackets and took off my uniform, and that was roughly around the same time that Hector came in from his shift. He asked me what I was doing, and I informed him that the Queen herself relieved me of my duties for the evening."

He paused and swallowed before continuing, "Hector and I were discussing where to go for dinner, and that is when Quinn shouted at me. He asked why I wasn't on duty, and I replied that the Queen gave me the night off. He asked who was supposed to be on duty alongside me. Hector responded and said Sammuel, my Lord. Quinn reinstated me back to the Eastern Wall and also told Hector to go with me. Told us to say nothing to Sammuel if we beat him there. He said he would take the Queen's wrath if she found out."

He dipped his head at Morphous and swallowed. Hector looked at Amish for a moment before speaking, "My Lord, would you wish to hear mine? It lines up with Amish."

Morphous glanced at Hector before nodding and replying, "**In your words, Hector. Please.**"

Hector bowed before replying, "About an hour to an hour and a half ago, my Lord, I got off duty. I went to the guard brackets to get out of my uniform. I met Amish there, and I asked him why he was there since I knew that he and Sammuel were due to be on the Eastern Wall tonight. He said the Queen dismissed him this evening. We were planning on going to get food at a local bar down the lane sire, and that is when Quinn came around the corner. He called out to Amish and asked him why he was not at his post. Amish responded with, the Queen dismissed him for the evening. Quinn then asked who was on the wall, and I replied that Sammuel, who is the new wolf was on shift. Quinn sent us both to the wall and told us that if we saw Sammuel not engage if we got there first. If he was up to no good. Then question it."

Hector glanced at Amish before continuing, "When we arrived there, I had Amish go onto the wall, and confront Sammuel since he was looking down at the ground. And acting like he was going to jump. I stayed in the darkness of the entrance. Sammuel tried to kill Amish, and I intervened when I felt that Amish couldn't defend himself."

He paused and seemed like he was going to end there. Amish looked at him and finally spoke again, "There's something else, my Lord, when Sammuel shifted to his wolf form, it spoke. It was not in his voice."

Morphous glanced at them sharply and replied, "**Not in his voice?**"

Hector and Amish exchanged glances and they shuffled their feet for a moment before Hector replied, "Yes sire, his voice changed. It was deeper, raspier than it was when Sammuel spoke earlier in his human form."

Morphous sighed deeply before looking at our father speaking, "**What do you make of it, Killian?**"

He frowned and replied after a moment, "Any chance that he is of royal blood? They tend to be the ones that can have two different voices when either of them speak."

Morphous looked away for a moment, frowning, drawing his eyebrows inward. Amish and Hector shifted their feet, clear signs that they were not used to being in the office. After a moment, Morphous glanced at Killian and then his eyes flickered to Amish and Hector before speaking, "**Not a word of what happened to anyone. Amish, Hector. You are dismissed.**"

They instantly bowed and replied, "Yes, m'Lord."

They exited the doors, Hector closing it behind them.

****

Morphous waited a moment before speaking, "**Killian, any chance that your son is wrong?**"

Our father looked at him and looked down at the floor before replying, "None. What I had used on him Morphous, you cannot lie to. Not without excruciating pain. And he did not show the signs of being in pain."

Morphous swallowed and sighed deeply before speaking, "**Quinn.**"

I looked at him and spoke softly, "Yes, my Lord?"

He sighed deeply before replying, "**What were you doing before all this?**"

I instantly straightened myself slightly and replied, "I was helping Anna with the girls, my Lord. When Herald contacted me through our mind-link asking if we could meet."

Our father sighed deeply, and I glanced at him and Morphous turned his head to look at him. After a moment, our father looked directly at Herald before speaking, "Why didn't you contact me instead of your brother?"

Herald looked down at the ground and mumbled something. None of us could hear him and our father growled, his eyes flashing orange. I spoke before it could get any worse, "I believe he contacted me because he knew how you would react, father. However, I was the one who told him to go to you. But I don't know if he did or not since I left my room."

Herald looked up sharply and snapped, "Because you are mean to me, father. You underestimate what I can do and you always favor Quinn over anyone else. So, how would you…"

Morphous spoke, cutting him off, "**Enough. You can discuss that on your own time.**"

Our father looked like he was going to say something, but Morphous looked at him with hard eyes and finally, our father glanced away. I swallowed before speaking, "My Lord, what is to become of them?"

That seemed to bring the King to his senses for a moment and his eyes flickered. **"That still needs to be determined."**

I bowed my head and finally, I asked, "So, my other question at this point is, where is Rafeor?"

Morphous sighed deeply before replying, **"In her room. Hopefully resting."**

I nodded, turned slightly, and looked at our father before speaking, "Father, what do you suggest we do?"

He stared at me for a moment, before a smirk came across his face, and he replied, "You should answer your own question, Quinn, you are the King's Advisor."

I frowned and was about to retort, but Morphous replied, **"For now nothing. Both Sammuel and…."**

He swallowed and looked like he did not want to continue, but he did after a moment, **"And Katherine will be in the dungeons. Away from each other. Killian, I want you to check the Queen's room. Quinn, I want you to check Sammuel's room. See what's in there."**

I bowed and was about to leave when I heard Herald ask, "And me, my Lord?"

Our father paused too, his eyes flickered to Morphous, but Morphous did not look at him. I swallowed, was I going to lose my brother, after all? However, Morphous sighed deeply and replied, **"Head your way to Anna, help her with the girls that came in last night."**

Herald bowed and quickly left, even before I got to the door.

****

I let out the breath that I was holding after I got into the hallway outside of the office. I glanced down the way Herald left and was about to walk away when our father spoke, "I thought he was going to kill him for a moment. That is what happened with the last ones that found out."

I glanced at my father before speaking, "When was that? I don't remember that."

He smiled grimly before replying, "When I was the advisor and not you. That was before your time slightly. Right when I was training you actually."

I swallowed and looked away, and he rested his hand on my shoulder before speaking, "Our job is not always the easiest son, and I know you know it too."

He released my shoulder and started to head towards the Queen's chambers before I called out, "Why are you so hard on Herald, anyhow?"

He paused and looked back at me. For a moment, I saw pain in his eyes before he blinked and pulled himself together. He cleared his throat and replied, "I'm not."

I raised my eyebrows and didn't reply. For a split second, he looked like he was going to say why, but his eyes glossed over. He turned around and spoke over his shoulder back to me, "Get going. Morphous is waiting for us."

I swallowed and glanced at the door and walked the opposite way, before I connected to him, *"You were going to say something. What?"*

He seemed to want to drop the questions, but I could also semi-tell that he didn't want to answer this question. After a moment, though he replied, *"Because Herald is not your brother by blood."*

I had a slight tumble to my footfalls, but I was about to ask what he meant, but he continued, *"We will talk later. For now, focus on your duties."*

I dropped the connection for now. I knew that he wanted to stop talking about this, but he left more questions than not.

****

I made it to a junction, where one side would go to Sammuel's room and the other would go to where Rafeor's room was. I hesitated for a moment, wondering if she was awake. I glanced down the right hallway and kind of said screw it in my mind and went down the left side, towards Rafeor's room. I knocked twice, and after some shuffling in the room, she opened her door. She looked a little shocked. I turned my head sideways and spoke softly, "You okay?"

She slowly shook her head in a no. I glanced behind her and smelled the stench of urine. I grimaced thinking it was her, but I took a deeper smell in and caught the Queen's scent, and more importantly Sammuel's. I glanced at her and spoke softly, "Do you want to talk about it, Rafeor?"

She looked at me and finally whispered, **"I... I didn't know Katherine was the Queen I swear! I'm sorry!"**

I grabbed her before she fell to her knees sobbing. I glanced down the hallway before speaking, "I need to know something really quick, Rafeor, what was Katherine doing in here?"

She sniffed and after a moment replied, "**I don't know actually. She came out of the blue and did not even address herself as the Queen. She just told me her name. She held power, but not much authority in her stance alone. Which is why I didn't think much of it. She, however...."**

She trailed off, and I frowned slightly before prompting, "She what?"

She swallowed after a moment, "**I told her to leave me after a couple of minutes, she was not being all too nice to me for some reason. I.... I have to tell you something, Quinn. I shifted into something. And the look of horror across the Queen's face was evident. And that's when Sammuel came from the right of the hall. And got Katherine out of my room.**"

I looked at her and spoke softly and slowly, "What did you shift into?"

She swallowed before shaking her head and whispering, "**If what happened during the riot, we can shift into it. I understand why the humans and other races are terrified of us.**"

I frowned; the only thing was she did not imply anything. She just said, creature. I swallowed before speaking after a moment, "What are you implying that you shifted into?"

She frowned and looked at me before speaking, "**It was what the humans think that werewolves turn into. Crouched down and long and tall. I don't understand it.**"

I frowned, what she just described loosely was Lycan, but that's not possible. At least, I didn't think so. The look across her face told me that there was more to this. I glanced at her room before speaking, "Come with me. I have a feeling you will feel better talking about what happened to your father than me."

I started to leave, but she did not move. I glanced at her before speaking, "You coming?"

She looked at me before speaking, "**What.... What if I scare him too? What if he doesn't understand what it is either?**"

I smiled softly before replying, "Of all the people in this palace, I think you two need to talk more. I understand that you only got in here last night, but he is the best person to ask questions to Rafeor. It is the best action to take. Come, I'll direct you there."

She took my hand a little shakily before letting me pull her along with me. She was shaking slightly. I glanced at her but said nothing.

****

I was pacing my office when a knock sounded on the doors, I paused and spoke, "**Enter.**"

Quinn opened the door, and he was the only one in the doorway that I could immediately see, but after a moment he looked behind the door and held out his hand to someone. After a moment, I was going to say something, but then Rafeor came to my senses. I looked at Quinn sharply before walking towards the door. Quinn looked away from my gaze before speaking, "My Lord, I apologize. I was heading to Sammuel's but…"

He trailed off for a split second before continuing, "But something told me to check on Rafeor, and good thing I did. Inside I smelled urine, but also the high stench of Sammuel and Katherine."

I frowned and looked at Rafeor, who had her head bowed and was fidgeting with her hands. I glanced at Quinn, motioned Rafeor inside, and closed the door on Quinn.

****

I stared at the door before nodding to myself and finally heading down towards Sammuel's room. I did not stop for anything this time. I got to the door, pushed it open, and let my eyes adjust to the dim lighting before stepping into the room.

# Chapter 8

I stepped into Sammuel's room and looked around. I didn't exactly expect to find anything to make me wonder what was happening, but I was glad for my quick reflexes since an arrow zinged through the darkness and would have killed me if I wasn't a shifter. I caught the shaft of the arrow, mere inches from my chest before lowering it down. I looked around, something was worth hiding in here for him. I cautiously looked around and finally found something on his desk that looked like something important. I knew better than bringing the candles inside, in case he had something light-activated. I swallowed for a moment before glancing around and shifting to my cat form.

I shifted to my calico house cat, with light blue eyes, leaped onto the table, and looked down at the drawing. At first, I didn't understand what I was looking at, then I tried to look at it as if I was a spy. For some reason, it made sense after I had that thought in my head. I saw the exits, and entrances, and the question marks on where the catacombs started. I swallowed, I had him do most of all the patrols, except for the ones in the catacombs, that was mainly restricted to the senior guards, and I was glad that I was careful. Normally, whenever we got a werewolf, we didn't have them go to the catacombs route, but if someone called out or said they could not do their shift, then usually someone had to cover. Since it couldn't be a one-man job. I was just glad that it was never Sammuel that got to do them.

I glanced around the room and noticed something else. I scanned the room for any other dangers, before leaping down onto the ground, and carefully moving that way, unsure of what else he had in position.

*****

As soon as I closed the door on Quinn, Rafeor dropped her gaze down before speaking, "**I'm sorry.**"

I raised an eyebrow and replied, "**Why are you apologizing?**"

She looked at me and replied, "**Because you are a king and King's....**"

I didn't let her finish, I walked towards her, stopped her from rambling, and gently took my right hand a raised her chin. We looked into each other's eyes before I replied, "**I will always have time for you, Rafeor.**"

She smiled weakly before moving backward, away from me. I let her. After a moment, she turned around and spoke, **"Is it normal for a shifter to have a werewolf being? Like the ones that the humans fear, and write and draw about? The ones that I would even understand why someone fears us?"**

I frowned but didn't reply. She turned around and looked at me, whispering, **"Am I a monster?"**

I instantly shook my head and went to approach her. But she held out her hands and whispered, **"No, stay away. I don't know what happened in my room, but I turned into a creature that the humans assume the werewolves all turn into."**

I stopped and frowned. **"Can you show me what you turned into?"**

She paused and replied, **"B-but… what if it hurts you?"**

I looked at her sharply, then I realized once again what I had done. **"I'm sure I can manage you if it tries to injure me."**

For a moment, she didn't look like she wanted to, but then her eyes flickered turquoise. After a moment, her bones cracked and she dropped to the ground, she let out a scream, but soon, her form panted. I swallowed. It couldn't be. She shifted into a Lycan, tall white, and fucking massive. She panted and growled. I held up my hands and didn't move, knowing movement for a Lycan, was a threat.

*****

I got to the Queen's chambers, quietly and quickly. I tried to open them with my master key but to no avail. I frowned; the master key usually worked. Although I had no reason to do what I was about to do before now, so I never had to test it. I glanced down the hallway before shifting to my fly form. It was the one insect that I tried to only do when there were no possible moves. It was also how I did most of my spying on others. None looked for flies on the walls or ceilings since they were such a common thing.

Once inside, I scanned the room for danger, before I shifted back to my human form. I stood there, and my eyes scanned the room once again before shifting to something amble and agile, a tomcat. My fur was black, pure black, and my eyes were the color of the evergreen trees in winter. Dark green, with white speckles throughout. I blinked twice, getting adjusted to the darkness and walking around the room cautiously.

****

I went into Sammuel's small closet, looking around, when I saw something shiny. I crouched down and skimmed my stomach on the hardwood to get to it. I cautiously probed it with my foreleg, before I flipped it out of the hiding spot it was in. I looked down at it and my breath caught in my throat. It was the royal seal of the werewolves. I recognized it immediately. I swallowed as I looked at everything else inside the closet with my new eyes. I saw something else, cautiously approached it, and probed it again. Before pressing myself down again in case if he had something else set up. Nothing happened. I pulled the piece of parchment out, looked down, and swallowed. Morphous had to be informed immediately of this. I grabbed the parchment, and drug dug it to the door before I glanced at the table, and leaped up there to grab the blueprints when I heard something. I froze, and looked around his room, but saw no movement. However, my back hair started to rise, my cat form knew something was there, we were not alone.

*****

I went further into the Queen's chambers and gracefully leaped onto the bed, it was suited for a Queen. I kind of chuckled to myself in my crude humor. However, I had a business to attend to, a royal business. I looked around the room, looking for threats, but saw no immediate threat. However, that did not mean there was not any. I glanced around the room, it had off-white walls, peeling slightly in the corners, and plush egg-white carpet, that was soft under paw and overall comfortable. Her vanity was over by the closet, and that was when I noticed that the closet door was slightly ajar. I leaped down, stalked towards it, and nosed my way into the room.

*****

I glanced where the sound came from and after a moment, a form came forward and dropped down as if in pain. I glanced at it for a moment and finally, an arrow showed in his right pec, and I looked at him. Yes, him. He looked at me before speaking, "My name is Daros."

I blinked once, several guards were wolves that served for years. However, after what I had found, it made me wonder if all of them were like Sammuel and had just never been down in the catacombs before. He looked at me before chuckling slightly and whispering, "Don't be afraid of me. Please, I need help."

My cat form growled in response, but he edged closer, and my form grabbed the parchment before running for the door. Alas, Daros beat me to the door and slammed it shut. Another arrow zinged through the back wall and pierced him again. He staggered backward and growled, his eyes flashing in pain before he fell.

I stared at him, he made it so I couldn't get out unless I wanted an arrow too. I growled low in my throat before connecting to Herald, "*I know you are supposed to be helping Anna, but I need you to come to Sammuel's room. And be warned. He has set traps to send arrows if the door is opened.*"

I dropped the connection and glanced at Daros before shifting carefully, away from the door, but not too far away from it in case I needed to get out.

He stared at me before whispering, "Oh, it's you."

The growl in his voice was evident that he was expecting someone else. I leaned against the wall before replying, "Why did you stop me from leaving?"

Daros stared at me and smirked. "You think that Sammuel didn't communicate with any of us wolves while he was here?"

I swallowed and slightly pulled myself upright, but he had a point, the werewolves were treated slightly like outcasts even when they had a treaty with shifters. I looked away for a moment before replying, "So, you knew what he was doing?"

He looked down and shook his head before replying, "Me and him? Hell no. Especially not after he killed my brother, who was an elite member of us wolves. I, however, am a respected ranking wolf regardless and have been told of what he has tried to ask around from the others. However, some of the members here didn't tell him squat. Especially after he murdered someone of our rank."

I stared at him and finally asked, "If you are not here to stop me, then why did you?"

He looked at me and replied, "Not all the werewolves you have here are against you in any way. We actually get treated more decently here than at home. Home is where we tend to get overlooked because we are lower-ranked wolves. Some of us, don't even have any beta blood in our blood, and yet you guys don't seem to mind as long as we do the job correctly."

I frowned before replying, "Ah. okay, but that still doesn't explain why you slammed the door before I could leave."

He sighed and looked down at the arrow shafts before replying, "Because we already know how your King is going to react. If one of us does something bad, we all tend to get treated differently. I was hoping I could convince whoever it was that came into his room that we are not all the same."

I raised my eyebrows before replying, "I don't tend to clump everyone together…."

He looked at me again and scoffed before speaking, "Everyone does, whether they try to or not. It is what we werewolves are kind of used to. However, you may not, but your king will. He already doesn't trust us down in the catacombs, so what is the difference between now and that information?"

I grimaced and replied after a moment, "He wanted to send you guys down there, but I will admit it to you, that I had a say in not having any werewolves down there."

He glanced sharply at me and sneered for a moment. I continued, "To be fair, it has only been twelve years since the riot. I don't trust people down there that are not my kin."

He sighed deeply, nodded, and replied, "I would wish to say I don't understand. But I do. You did what you needed to do to protect your home. I would do the same thing if my King allowed me to prove it. I guess I won't ever know since I will die from my injuries."

I stared at him and was about to move towards him, but he shook his head and growled, "No. Sammuel is not the typical werewolf. He killed my brother who was an elite of our kin, but he did it dirty. He tipped the blade in silver and well, you know how that would turn out. These arrows have silver components but are also something lethal to shifters. I can feel the effects even though I am not a shifter. It is keeping me from shifting to my wolf."

I swallowed and backed to the wall before replying, "I could call…"

He shook his head and replied, "No point. After the first one entered, I couldn't shift. Now the second? I'm good as dead, kid."

I scowled and was about to retort that I was not a kid, but he laughed a little before speaking, "I know you are older than you appear, but to me you are a child. I am eighty-one, and you can't be more than thirty-five, to forty-five."

He was correct, I was way younger than everyone else, and everyone seemed to want to still talk to my father over me even, but I have Morphous behind me that said otherwise. I sighed deeply before running my hand across my face and speaking, "So what now?"

Daros looked at me and smiled slightly. "You get to go to your king, while I take the next hits from the arrows."

I opened my mouth to reply when the door opened. Not only did Herald stand there, but so did Amish. An arrow zipped through the darkness of the room, and Amish caught it and broke the shaft before glancing at Daros. He frowned before looking at me and speaking, "The King requests you return to him, Quinn."

I nodded and glanced at Daros, who had a trickle of blood coming from his mouth now, and I swallowed before replying, "Get him some help, please."

Amish glanced at Daros before walking a few steps in and triggered another arrow, which Daros leaped in front of Amish and took another arrow. He grunted in pain and staggered again. Amish had a look of shock across his face, but it cooled after a moment. He slung Daros's arm through his, and he helped him out of the room.

****

Herald stared at me and was about to say something, but I just shook my head. He closed his mouth and glanced into the room, not daring to enter the room, not after what happened. I glanced at the blueprints on the desk to my left and slowly grabbed them from the table before speaking, "I know that Morphous had told you to help Anna, but I want you to guard this room. Turn into a beetle and keep your eyes open."

He glanced at me sharply and was about to say something, but I gave him a hard stare. He faltered for a moment, not wanting to refuse me.

I shifted into my calico cat again, dragged the blueprint out of the room and into the hallway, and went back in for the parchment. I grabbed it and dragged it out too. Apparently, Sammuel didn't take into consideration that we could shift into something small, and not set off his triggers. I towed the parchment into the hallway when I glanced up at Herald, who was holding the blueprints in his hands, looking at it. He seemed to understand what they were since his knuckles turned white as he gripped them. I rubbed my side against his legs and meowed a gargled one since I still had a parchment in my mouth. He loosened his hold on it and swallowed slightly. I glanced at the door and then back at him before he seemed to understand that one of us needed to close the door. He took a shaky breath before leaning against the door slightly and grabbing the knob before closing it slowly. An arrow zoomed out of the darkness, but the door blocked it, and we both heard the soft click of the door shutting.

I glanced at him before shifting back to my human form and placing my right hand on his shoulder. I whispered to him, "Watch the door. If anyone enters, let them. Mind-link me immediately though."

He nodded his head, and handed me the blueprints shakily before speaking, "What about…"

I paused and replied, "I'll report to the King what I had asked you to do. If he wants someone else there, then I will mind-link you to wait until that replacement comes."

He nodded after a moment and looked at me with fear in his eyes. I smiled slightly but turned sharply on my heel, and strode down the hallway, heading to the King's office.

****

I raised my hands slowly and spoke softly, "**I mean you no harm. Please, tell me what happened earlier. What made you surface?**"

Her Lycan growled low in her throat before she sniffed around for a moment, smelling everyone that had been in my office. She seemed to conclude that no one was inside. She looked at me before speaking, her voice raspy, "**The Queen knocked on the door, Rafeor opened it, of course, and allowed her inside. Rafeor did not know that she was the queen since she did not address herself with her title. The Queen called Rafeor a dog since that is the name we have lived with after all this time.**"

She paused, and I swallowed. I knew for a fact, that only a Lycan could make it seem that this was normal, but it was also clear to me that she never spoke before. That she was always in the background and not able to come forth. I nodded for her to continue, and it looked like she wasn't going to, but she continued after a moment, "**Rafeor told her to leave, and turned her back on her, facing the window we have in our room. The Queen grabbed her shoulder roughly and pulled her towards her. I came out, and shifted into what I am.**"

She once again paused, and seemed to gather her thoughts before speaking again, "**I came out, and the Queen let out a startled gasp, and I…. It was the first time that I was even allowed to surface, so my instincts came through. I began to stalk the Queen, baring my teeth at her. That was when I heard someone approaching, that is when Sammuel showed himself. And the look of shock across his face was a little entertaining if I am being honest.**"

My eyes flashed for a moment, so Quinn was right, there was a lot more to this story than he could explain. I growled slightly, and my eyes dimmed to an off-orange. The Lycan before me smirked before speaking, "**You are powerful in more ways than one, King Morphous, but you are not as powerful as I am. Your union should have never happened.**"

I did a second take and stared at the Lycan, and she bared her teeth slightly as if trying to smile, but it was threatening as hell. She, after a moment, closed her mouth, and spoke, "**Yes, I know of the union between you and the werewolf queen, before the werewolf king met her.**

**The moon goddess gave me the rundown of what happened. Rafeor doesn't know, so don't mention it."**

I swallowed and after a moment, to make sure she was not going to say anything else, I asked, **"So, you know about that? We'll have to talk later on that front at a later date. What should I call you?"**

She frowned and blinked at me before replying, **"I don't have a name. Since Rafeor was kept away from her kin for so long, she didn't know I existed. Nor did she until yesterday know what she was. Why did you keep her hidden all this time? That was torture in itself."**

I smiled slyly, so the goddess didn't tell her that part. Good to know, I would for the time being keep that information to myself since it didn't matter currently. I shrugged and replied, **"I cannot answer that at this current time frame. What name comes to you the most that is most fitting to you?"**

She stared at me, squinting her eyes before growling, **"At the current moment, it does not matter what to call me."**

I struggled with myself to not get angry at her response, and I could have sworn I saw something in her eyes that said she knew something more than what she told me. I swallowed, wondering what was a secret that the goddess to the wolves gave her knowledge of, I just hoped it would not mess up my plans entirely.

*****

A knock on the door sounded, and I kind of jerked, since I was not expecting anyone. I turned to see the Lycan staring at me, growling, **"Answer it."**

She moved behind the door so she would not be seen. I wondered slightly if she knew that I didn't want anyone to know of her yet, or if she was unsure of that. I, however, waited until she was behind the door, before plastering a look of indifference across my face as I opened the door.

Killian stood in the doorway, and he held a box, I recognized the box and swallowed. No one was supposed to know about that box. Although now that I thought about it, the Queen insisted it was to be kept in her room. I swallowed again and looked slightly up into Killian's eyes. He knew. Of course, he knew. I stepped aside and he walked into the room. I closed the door, closed my eyes, and turned around to face him.

Killian stood with his back to me, and put the box on the table before he spoke, "Is this what I think it is Morphous?"

He did not say what it was, thank goodness, I would have to kill him if he voiced it out. He turned around and seemed he was about to say something when his eyes flickered to my left at the door, and kind of froze a little.

I swallowed and did not speak, knowing what was behind me. He swallowed for a moment before eyeing her. He looked at me before growling, "What is a Lycan doing here, Morphous?"

I was about to reply when she replied, **"I am not a threat."**

Killian raised his eyebrows and glowered at me, "Werewolves are the only ones that can turn into Lycans. Everyone knows that. And ONLY the royals. So again, what are you doing, Morphous?"

I opened my mouth to reply, but she beat me to it, **"You know of me differently. My human form is Rafeor."**

Killian froze, his eyes flickered to mine and held them after her statement. He swallowed slightly and replied after a moment, "A union between werewolf and shifter has been forbidden by you, Morphous. And by the decree of the werewolves themselves, and that was hundreds of years before either of the current rulers' times. Who were you sneaking around with? Is this the true reason for the riot? To hide Rafeor? And to get that?"

He pointed to the box, making all of our eyes flicker to it, and I swallowed before replying, **"I don't have to answer to you, Killian. I am your King."**

He glowered, his eyes flashing red for a split second, but he managed to keep himself together. I swallowed, glanced at the Lycan, and saw her eyes squint towards me, but she didn't say a word. I turned towards one of the rooms and was about to open it when Killian replied, "You may be king, but I don't answer to a tyrant. After all this time Morphous, you had something inside our halls, that can kill anything without much trouble and kill some more? What is your end game in this, Morphous?"

I swallowed, and gripped the door handle of the other doorway, craving to be away from this conversation. I could order them both to leave, and it crossed my mind, but another knock sounded on the door. I cursed under my breath and was about to answer, but Killian handed the box to the Lycan and spoke softly to her, "Might as well hold this. Since you apparently don't want to be seen."

She took the box and looked like she was going to retort, but backed to the wall and stared at me to open the door.

****

I sighed and opened it to find Hector in the doorway. He bowed to me before he spoke, "My Lord, you told me separately if either Herald or Anna sent him elsewhere. I came to report that Herald left Anna's workstation. I had Amish follow him."

I frowned, Herald was turning out to be something I needed to terminate, but I replied, **"Thanks for the update, Hector."**

He bowed and replied, "My Lord."

****

He turned sharply on his heel and turned and walked off down the hall. I shut the door and Killian spoke after a moment, "Keeping an eye on my son are you, Morphous?"

I turned slightly before growling, **"He wasn't supposed to be where he was. He wasn't supposed to find that information out."**

Killian sighed deeply and replied, "Yet you told, Quinn."

I paused, and looked at him before replying, **"Because Quinn is my advisor, Killian."**

He shrugged after a moment before replying, "So? What does that have to do with anything? Are you going to terminate us simply because we found out?"

I swallowed, I had to play it smart too, if either Herald or Killian was found dead, questions of what they had uncovered would spread and the rumors alone would make it tedious to work with. Killian smirked as if he knew what I was thinking, and I scowled. He was my advisor before the riot, and I made sure he was treated well afterward, but I now knew that hiring in the same family was not the smartest thing I could have done. My eyes flickered to the box that now the Lycan held and glanced at Killian before speaking, **"You are too valuable to kill."**

Killian scoffed and replied, "It's more like we are too knownable. Everyone inside your palace would instantly know if something was wrong the moment they didn't see either I or Herald in the hallways. Same with Quinn, since he is your advisor."

I sighed deeply before running my right hand through my hair and speaking, **"Shut it."**

He chuckled slightly, before replying, "Might as well get Quinn back here. We need to talk about that box, Morphous. And what to do with it."

I opened my mouth to retort, but he gave me a hard stare and continued, "Don't even try to say anything, Morphous. You got yourself into this mess, but since we can't exactly do anything with it besides hide it. We can't give it back to where it came from, those people are long dead."

He gave me a pointed look before continuing, "There's only one spot that might work to hide it, but I want Quinn's opinion first."

I retorted, but another knock sounded on my door. I scowled, I was getting fed up with these knocks. It was clear to me too that Killian was getting ready to strangle someone, but he kept quiet and leaned against my desk.

****

I went to open it and found Quinn standing there. He held two pieces of parchment, and he bowed slightly before speaking, **"I was informed to report immediately."**

I glanced at Killian and saw him frown, so he didn't say anything. I stepped backward and let him in, and I could tell that it was not a surprise to him to find a Lycan. However, I had a slight assumption that Rafeor told him a rough description of herself to him. Quinn walked into the office and swallowed. I was pretty sure he could feel the energy surrounding him and us. He glanced at the box, and he stopped breathing for a moment.

I glanced at him before speaking, **"You know what it is?"**

He glanced at me before whispering, **"I would be a fool if I didn't know what it was. My question though is why do we have it?"**

I fell silent. Clearly not ready for his words. He glanced at his father and swallowed before glancing at the Lycan and speaking, **"I know what it is. More because I was the one who placed it where it was originally. Before the riot even started."**

The Lycan growled low in her throat, and her eyes flashed. I stared at Quinn, but he seemed to be fine. Killian coughed slightly, clearing his throat, and causing Quinn to look at him. Killian stared at him and spoke, "Hello. And who are you?"

He seemed to not want to answer, but replied, **"My name is Thorin. I was one of the lost souls of the place that was killed."**

He turned to stare at me before continuing, **"You are the reason why my people are no longer around. With what you wanted. Look around you great king, got what you wanted and more?"**

I swallowed, I normally would have killed anyone who spoke to me in that manner, but I also knew if I killed him, I would be killing someone of importance, and I can't really kill my advisor. I sighed deeply before replying, "**It's not what it seems.**"

Thorin laughed before replying, "**You seem to have forgotten what I had warned you when you came for it. About the destruction it would bring in the hands of a hybrid even. And what do you have in here? A hybrid.**"

I glanced at the Lycan, who had not said a word so far. Soaking in all this new information, and I could have sworn I saw her eyes flicker a different color for a split second. Great, now I would have to also answer to Rafeor when she got back control. I looked back at Thorin before replying, "**Keep it quiet.**"

I gave him a hard stare, but Thorin chuckled before replying, "**You think I am scared of you, Morphous? It is the opposite actually. I pity you. You don't seem to understand what you have done, and it angers me.**"

I snarled, my eyes flickering dark red, if one more word was said, I would shift to my dragon form and kill everyone in this room. I was about to reply when the Lycan spoke, "**Thorin.**"

He glanced at her and raised Quinn's eyebrows, but she continued, "**Leave.**"

Her aura swirled around the room, but I could tell that she was not letting it fully out either. He blinked at her, and replied, "**Of course, my Lady.**"

****

Quinn's body went forward, and if Killian hadn't caught him, he would have met the hardwood floors. Quinn panted after a moment and looked wildly around. He seemed confused about how he got there. I swallowed for a moment and glanced at the Lycan, but I could tell that she was thinking, something about how she handled Thorin pricked my side, it was almost as if she knew him, but that was impossible. Her eyes flickered to mine and she squinted her eyes but said nothing.

Quinn looked around and finally spoke, "What happened? The last thing I remembered was that I was leaving for your office."

I sighed and was about to reply when the Lycan replied, "**A druid spirit took you over.**"

For a moment, he didn't look like he believed her before he replied, "So, any chance that they can body hop?"

She looked at him and cocked her head slightly. **"Only the higher druids could do so. Why?"**

He sighed deeply before replying, "Amish told me that you, my King, called for me."

I scowled. I didn't call for him at all. Great. I shook my head and was about to walk across the room when Killian spoke, "My Lord, it still doesn't make a difference. We need to hide it."

I stopped and replied, **"For now, it stays in my room. No one is to enter without my permission."**

My voice held some alpha command, and I could tell without even turning that it had affected the ones within the room, but then the Lycan replied, **"No."**

I froze, no one has challenged my authority in a while, and I slowly turned around and stared at her. She stood there unblinking before speaking again, **"Your room is too obvious. If anything, it should go into a random room and the occupant told loosely of what it is."**

I was about to reply when Killian spoke before me, "Can't do that either. Not many people here are trustworthy enough to keep something like that a secret. The only ones that could possibly keep it in their rooms are the elder guards."

I was about to reply, but Quinn spoke, "And what then? If they see what it is father, then they will know that was the game plan in the beginning. Why did the riot even happen?"

I scowled, yes, I got the artifact during the riot, but that was not the only thing that got swept under the rug. Killian glanced at me before replying to him, "It cannot go into either Rafeor's or ours. It would be somewhere that everyone would look for."

I scowled, so my room wasn't good enough and now they were saying nowhere was good to store it. I threw my hands up and started to pace slightly, making the Lycan's eyes follow me as I paced. She replied, **"So, what's down in the catacombs?"**

Quinn glanced at her sharply, and I stopped pacing to look at her. Killian seemed lost in thought, before he replied, "Old relics, and stuff that none of the other species really know about."

He tapped his chin and raised his eyes back at me before speaking, "It is the most reasonable spot for something like it. Hide it in plain sight. Even get another two or three of these boxes, and there we go. Hidden."

He glanced at Quinn before continuing, "Thoughts?"

Quinn was silent for a moment before replying, "It depends though. How far away did Sammuel get with the layout of our home, and did he show anyone on the way there?"

I growled low in my throat, my eyes were still red, but I had learned to have my eyes red, but not lose my cool entirely. I replied after a moment, "**Don't know.**"

The Lycan was silent for a moment, listening back and forth, when I spoke again, "**But I can question anyone who was down that hallway. He had to have come from the Queen's quarters…..**"

 The Lycan cut me off, "**I can confirm that. They left my room in a rather hurry after the Queen soiled her panties because of me.**"

Her eyes glowed with laughter, and I would have laughed, but I frowned. We never actually got to finish talking about what happened. However, I doubt it now after everything that had happened, that I would find out. Great. Another mystery to add to my questions.

Quinn sighed deeply after a moment, before speaking, "So what now? What are we going to do with them?"

I opened my mouth to reply, but the Lycan replied, "**If you are referring to Lord Verein and Michael, I would want a part of that action after what I engendered all those years.**"

Her eyes sparked a different color, as the other part of herself surfaced slightly, causing Killian to glower at me as she spoke. I swallowed, I didn't know what was going to happen. He never backed away from me, but this may make him choose to. I glanced at the Lycan before I replied, "**Lord Verein and Michael were brought before the counsel this morning. The counsel didn't inform you because they didn't want you to worry about it. Isn't that correct, Killian?**"

Killian sighed deeply and replied, "That is correct. They went to the dungeons this morning. They got a five-year sentence."

She stared at us and growled, "**Five years? That's it? Why not twelve? And torture.**"

Quinn looked at her for a moment before replying, "Because the Lord Verein had his hands in with the werewolves and gave us some intel. It was enough to drop him down to that."

I grimaced, he wasn't supposed to give her that information. And by the redness in her eyes, showed that I was correct in not telling her in the first place. I was about to speak, but Killian replied after a moment, "If you want to torture them for all your suffering, M'Llady, I will help you to get down there. They may be in the dungeons, but there was no promise to live nicely."

I glanced at him out of the corner of my eye and noticed the throb in his jaw, the twitch that he lied to her face, but I wouldn't call him out. She deserved to have some fun after all she had gone through. She seemed to understand that they were promised something to get them talking, and she grinned wickedly, causing my neck hairs to rise. Damn, she was scary, I shuddered thinking of what could have happened if the werewolves knew she was still alive.

She glanced at me before speaking, "**Fine.**"

It took all my power not to laugh at her. She looked scary, but she also had a puppy aspect that wouldn't go away without much trouble. Quinn looked at her and swallowed. He was about to say something when his eyes glossed over, and he glanced at Killian once his eyes went back to normal, nodding at him slightly. I glanced at Killian and saw him side-eyeing the Lycan as if making sure she didn't understand what happened. And luckily, she was too focused on something else.

I sighed after a moment and said, "**They will be dealt with in the morning. For now, get some rest. All of you.**"

Killian and Quinn exchanged looks and glanced at the Lycan before Quinn replied, "What about the box?"

I opened my mouth to reply, when the Lycan replied, "**I'll hide it for now.**"

Killian looked like he was going to suggest something else, but she leveled him with a look for a moment before continuing, "**No one in their right mind would challenge me as I am currently.**"

He went quiet and sighed after a moment, she had a point. No one would here. Quinn, however, replied, "But you can't leave this room without someone seeing you in this form. Normal shifters can't be in that form. It's not our natural form. It's the werewolves, and only for the royals. And people seeing a Lycan leaving Morphous's office at this hour? Not the greatest point."

She sighed resignedly as if she knew deep down that he was correct. I glanced at Quinn and saw something flicker in his eyes before he glanced at the Lycan. I wanted to know what he thought of all this, but alone.

Killian sighed deeply before speaking, "If you wanted to be guarding this box, then you would have to stay inside this office. I could arrange for something to be dropped off."

I glanced at him and was about to shake my head, but he ignored me. It was as if he was waiting for her to say something. The Lycan smiled, frowned, shook her head, and finally, replied, "**As much as I want to, I know that Rafeor would eventually come back to the surface, and she wouldn't know what to do.**"

Killian seemed more interested in that statement, and I could tell that he wanted to ask her a personal question, but Quinn spoke, "Ok, but it still leaves that up to the wind, where are we going to place this tonight?"

I opened my mouth, but Killian replied, "It must be guarded. Twenty-four seven. I'll choose my most trusted shifter guards to do so. At least for the evening."

I was about to retort that was a bad thing, but he looked at me with his piercing eyes before continuing, "Unfortunately, you don't really get a say in what happens with this box for the evening. We can't trust you now, Morphous. You have to earn my trust once again. Come, Quinn."

He walked across the office, towards the door before pausing and looking at me again and speaking, "You and I need to have a one-on-one tomorrow sometime, Morphous."

I swallowed, but squinted my eyes in response too. He was ordering me to be there, and I was about to say something when Quinn spoke softly, "M'lady, if you shift back to Rafeor, I will escort you back to your room."

The Lycan blinked, smiled slightly, and looked at me before growling, "**Don't do anything stupid.**"

I growled low in my throat, and she bared her teeth in response, letting her aura roll out. I saw Quinn and Killian both flinch back. Other than that nothing else, as it was not directed at them either. I scowled and turned away, went through another door, and let it shut behind me.

# Chapter 9

I walked next to Rafeor, once she got herself to herself, she almost fell, but I caught her in my arms. She was breathing heavily before whispering, "**What happened?**"

I smiled slightly and replied, "Your Lycan surfaced. Don't be alarmed, she didn't do anything wrong. Nor did you."

Her eyes went downcast as she got her breathing under control. Finally, we were able to move out of the office. I closed the door to Morphous's office, looked up, and saw four of our most senior guards. Amish, Hector, Gillith, and Conrade, when my father said the most trusted, he meant it. These four are the eldest of our ranks, and they could even post someone in a position, for example, Gillith posted Davis where he was. I didn't know if it was punishment or not, but probably not since Davis excelled in what he did. I glanced at Conrade before opening my mouth to speak, but Gillith spoke, "Get going, Quinn. Your father debriefed us."

I swallowed, and bowed to him, showing my respect to him. He scoffed and moved towards Morphous's door, opened it, and disappeared inside alongside Hector. Amish and Conrade posted themselves outside of the door.

I swallowed, gently pulled Rafeor along with me, headed down the palace corridors, and soon disappeared around a corner. Rafeor looked at me before speaking, "**Who were they?**"

I glanced at her and replied after a moment, "Our most trusted guards."

She raised her eyebrows as if seeing if I would elaborate on that, but when I didn't, asked, "**What are their names?**"

By this point, we were outside of her room, I stopped, looked at her, and replied, "Amish, Hector, Gillith, and Conrade."

She gave me a weird look before speaking, "**Weren't they supposed to be the more senior guards? They didn't look old enough to be.**"

I chuckled and replied, "Shifters and werewolves, and pretty much any supernatural being age differently than humans do. Have you noticed that you don't look over a certain age? Have the humans ever seem aloof and treat you differently based on your age appearance alone?"

She turned towards the wall and swallowed. I hit a nerve, and I didn't even realize what I had done, until her voice changed to her Lycan's, "**We noticed, and we were targeted the most by the bullying due to it.**"

I swallowed and raised my hands in surrender, I was about to speak, but she looked at me with her turquoise eyes, something that I knew was her Lycan's eye color, and she smiled slightly before continuing, "**Don't beat yourself up on it. How could you have known? Asking questions is something that needs to happen. It just caught her and me off guard.**"

A foot scuffled on the rug, Rafeor's Lycan blinked once, and she stared back at me, looking like she was about to ask what happened. I placed my finger on my lips, and she went silent. I heard it again, and my eyes changed colors. I shifted to my cat, and stalked around the corner, leaving Rafeor where she was alone.

****

I got around the corner and saw boots. I looked up and saw a werewolf before me. He looked down and growled before moving fast. He grabbed the ruff of my neck, held me away from him, and growled in my face, "Ooh look! A pussy cat! One I'll have for dinner."

His eyes had his wolf color eyes glinting in the background, and I could have sworn his wolf would have done. So, if I didn't shift into who I was then.

He dropped me and scrambled backward. He looked very guilty all of a sudden. I scowled and rubbed the back of my neck before snapping, "What the fuck were you thinking?"

He dropped his gaze from mine, and his wolf's eye color drifted away. His hazel eyes stared at me. I scowled again and my eyes flashed yellow for a split second. He looked down at the ground and after a moment, pushed himself off the ground before bowing to me, and keeping his eyes downcast. I tried hard not to smirk, but I plastered a frown on my face, and I growled, "Answer."

He looked at me, his wolf's eyes glinted in his eyes for a moment, before fading back again, before he replied, "I apologize. I didn't know it was you."

I growled, my eyes turning yellow and staying yellow, before I snapped, "If it wasn't me, would you have eaten me?"

He opened his mouth to retort but stopped himself, looking sheepishly at me for a moment. I was about to snap again at him, but then his eyes drifted behind me for a split second, before he looked at me again. It suddenly dawned on me. This could have been a setup. I glanced away from him for a moment, but a moment too late apparently, since I had a barley bag over my head.

******

I watched as Quinn disappeared around the corner in his calico cat, it made me want to sleep with a cat suddenly, and I actually wanted to sleep with it. However, that was a question that I was pretty sure would be instantly turned down. Suddenly, my neck hair rose and my eyes flashed, but a moment later, all I saw was darkness.

*****

I paced my room, back and forth. Quinn should have been back by now. I stopped and looked at the candle, it had time stamped on the sides of it, it was a twelve-hour one, and I frowned, it was almost three in the morning. He usually returned by now. I sighed deeply, grabbed my coat, and headed out. I paused at the door though, something in me stopped me from leaving. As if by instinct, I grabbed my twin swords on the wall. They were as old as time, older than the Druid camp, and older than Morphous, but it was passed down my family line. I strapped the swords on my back and grabbed another one for my hip before leaving.

I went towards the office first, making sure that my guards were posted, and sure enough they were. I nodded to Amish and Conrade before heading toward Rafeor's room. I took a deep breath suddenly and my eyes flashed. There was a high wolf smell, and on top of that stench, there was something else. I smelled. I paused before continuing, I hoped I was wrong.

I walked around the corner, and there were scuff marks on the hardwood. I crouched down and felt the grooves, they were like someone tried to escape, and tore into the wood in the process. I smelled Rafeor in these. I blinked once, my eyes were golden, I glanced up and carefully around before following my son's scent. His scent went around the corner, and I smelled two wolves, one more than the other, proving that it was a setup. I growled low in my throat, my eyes turning slightly darker in color, but after a moment, I looked around. Everything seemed to be as if it was placed strategically but I knew these hallways, and I saw something out of place. I bent down and picked up a single grain of barley, I sniffed it. My eyes snapped to the walls and then back at it. I crushed the barley into dust before dusting it off me. I stood up and closed my eyes, I connected to Morphous, "*Morphous. We have intruders. They have taken Rafeor and Quinn.*"

His line was not live, and I tried again, "*MORPHOUS!*"

Again, nothing. I turned sharply on my heel and strode towards the office.

*****

I stared at my bed; I didn't really want to do anything. I glanced at the door and heard movement on the other end. I scowled and was about to shout at whoever it was to leave me. Then I realized it was the wrong door. It was not my door to the office. I frowned and approached it. I opened it, and there stood two werewolves. They stared at me in shock before one hurriedly tried to place a hood over me, but I growled low in my throat, causing them to stumble backward in fear.

A figure appeared behind me, but I was too busy watching these two werewolves to notice until it was too late. A hood went over my eyes, and I struggled for a good minute before blunt force hit me in the head. I went out.

****

I got to the office, and I sharply spoke, "Open the door."

Conrade glanced at me and replied, "Okay?"

His tone held a question, but he obeyed my order. I strode in and took a deep breath in. Nothing in the office was out of place, and Hector and Gillith looked at me with confused looks. I glanced at Morphous's room and went towards it. I paused and tried to listen closely, but the damn soundproofing prevented it. I took out my sword at the hip and opened the door. I smelled deeply again, and soon enough I caught the same smell. I growled and entered his room, the window clanging against the windowsill. I glanced at it, approached the window slowly, and glanced over. I saw two figures at the bottom, and they looked up after a moment; the fear in their eyes spoke volumes. They took off.

I ran out of Morphous's room and shouted, "CONRADE, GILLITH. WITH ME! HECTOR, AMISH, PROTECT THE BOX!"

Gillith glanced at me, before leaping to his feet, and our feet thundered through the hallways. I looked at Conrade before barking, "Get in contact with the guards on the Eastern Wall."

His eyes glazed over, he frowned, and replied, "Interesting. Their connection is down."

I skidded to a stop and glanced at both before replying, "SHIT!"

He blinked; pretty sure he hadn't heard me curse so violently before. I looked at Gillith before speaking, "Get in contact with the other walls. Now."

He glared at me, but followed my orders. He frowned and seemed to try again, but after a moment he glanced at me, "The chatter is gone. What do you know that you haven't told us yet, Killian?"

I glanced at him and growled, "Someone took Morphous, Rafeor, and my son, Quinn."

Their jaws dropped and after a moment, Conrade growled, "Who?"

I frowned and after a moment looked at them before replying, "Wolves."

They bared their teeth, their eyes changed color. I looked around the halls, they were weirdly empty, but I looked at them and said, "Find the other guards. Connect to them, and send out a call to the front doors. We need to get our King back."

They bowed to me, disappeared down the separate hallways, and left me alone. I panted slightly. I knew I wanted to chase after the wolves, but I also had to think clearly. I was the person in charge since the Queen was a traitor. I froze, the Queen. I looked down the hallways and swallowed. She had to have played a part in all of this. I closed my eyes, and headed to the dungeons.

# Chapter 10

The stench got to my senses first, before my eyes dimmed enough to see in the darkness. It smelled of: fear, fecal matter, urine, and blood. Currently, the dungeons held twelve prisoners. Lord Verein and Slyther's cells were side by side. So, they could hear each other's screams, but not what they were confessing to the guards. The other eight were prisoners since the riot, that Morphous kept down here. No one else knew they were alive, and he kept the circle small of those who were allowed down here.

I walked past all the cells and caught movement in one of theirs. I paused and looked at the dark black cell before I saw the eyes of the person locked within. The figure swallowed and dropped their gaze down before mumbling, "Please."

I smirked, shook my head, and turned to go further in since that was where Morphous said to place the Queen and Sammuel. The figure said, "YOUR KING IS NOTHING BUT A TYRANT! HE SHOULD DIE!"

I froze, for someone to be locked inside of his cells that was a lot of guts. I looked back at the figure and raised my eyebrows before shaking my head. He was stalling me. I turned again and headed down the corridor.

It seemed that the figure inside didn't like to be ignored, and shouted, "DID YOU HEAR ME, SCUM?"

My eyes flashed colors, but I had my back turned to it, so it didn't see the effect it had on me. I glanced down, made a note on the cell door, and continued further. Ignoring everything else it shouted. One of Morphous's rules was when you went down into the dungeons, everyone who was down there was an 'it' or a figure. He didn't want anyone to get comfortable with the prisoners. So, no names were given. Never, even the guards that were down here the most knew better than to disclose their name. Since the last time that someone got friendly, that guard was shipped out to work alongside Davis on the Eastern border.

I continued down, and the trail twisted and turned after a few meters inside, heading downward. The further you went, the less people went into it. Also, one of Morphous's doors in his office had an entrance to the interior of the prison. It was hidden, but it was the way that Sammuel and the Queen were brought down here too. So, they didn't walk through the other prisoners. So far only a handful of people knew that either of them was down here, and that close circle was sworn to never tell anyone. Not even to mention it together. That was how tight it was down here.

*****

I paused outside of Sammuel's door for a moment, debating if I wanted to talk to him. I sighed deeply before moving towards the door, unlocking it, and the door slid upwards. He glanced up and after a moment dropped his gaze before growling, "Come down here to gloat?"

I growled and he looked at me. He didn't even try to stand up, the chains around his wrists and ankles were dipped in silver, so that he didn't move. It was extremely uncomfortable for werewolves. It didn't kill them unless it pierced their skin and drew blood. However, these cuffs were made so they wouldn't. He stared down before speaking softly, "What do you want?"

I stared at him and finally growled, "What do you know of what's happening up?"

He stared at me and swallowed nervously, before replying, "Nothing."

My eyes flashed and I walked into his cell, letting the door clang behind me. He moved backward, scared. Good. I looked at him and growled, "Try again."

He swallowed, glanced at the blade in my hand, and gulped. Then his eyes flickered to the two on my back. He froze. I smiled slightly, so he knew of my blades. I raised my eyebrows and growled, "Well?"

He dropped his gaze, Adam's apple bobbed, and he stared at me before replying, "I told you. Nothing."

I placed the sword I had in my hand back into its sheath and reached for one of the twin ones. I watched him as he started to move backward, running into the corner of the wall. Panting. He knew of these blades. He knew what damage they could wield. I took it off and swished it back and forth in the air between us, and he whimpered. I looked at him for a moment before speaking, "I am pretty sure you know what my blades can do. Do you really want to test that theory though? Tell me what you know, or you will feel them."

His eyes flickered to my face and dropped and did it once again, as if he was a kid telling a lie, not wanting to make eye contact. At the same time, he knew better than looking away. I glanced at the door, swung the blade through the air, and the air whooshed, making him cower.

I glanced at him and turned my head to the side before, "Well? What is it going to be?"

He looked up at me, swallowed, and finally whispered, "Do I have your word you will not use them on me if I comply?"

I rotated the handle in my grip, and replied, "You aren't in a position to get what you want, Sammuel. I will do what I want when I want."

He swallowed, before whispering, "Please."

I sighed and leveled the blade directly at him, before replying, "Then tell me what you know, and only the truth. You know these blades, and you know what they can do."

He swallowed and replied after a moment, "Fine."

I raised my eyebrow and gestured to him to continue. He licked his lips before continuing, "I didn't come to the palace alone. I had four others with me. Last night was the night I was supposed to give them what I had learned and any information I had at that time.  However, Amish and Hector got to me first. The Queen told me that the wall was empty since it was my shift that night. I don't know how they knew that I was up to no good."

I smiled slightly, and replied, "Because my son found Amish in the halls."

His face fell, and bowed his head before whispering, "I should have known. However, my comrades were ordered not to interfere if I was taken down."

I leaned slightly against the door before I replied, "Whose orders?"

He shuffled slightly, the clinking of the chains rattled in the silence. He glanced at the blade and fell silent for a moment. Dropping his gaze down to the cell's floor before replying, "The King and my father."

I scoffed. His head whipped up and he growled, "Everyone has to listen to their alpha in command. Not even you, as a lowly shifter, can go against Morphous's ruling."

I smirked and after a moment, debated whether to tell him or not, but I shrugged after a moment and replied, "I guess it's a good thing then, that Morphous isn't my ruler. He doesn't have much against me."

The shock written across his face was laughable to me. I rarely spoke of my family line, but I looked at him and smirked after a moment. He closed his mouth and replied, "Morphous is not your ruler? Then why serve him?"

I leveled my blade at his chest, and he cowered slightly. I smirked and replied after a moment, "I am not going to disclose that information to you. Even though, I doubt that you will come to the surface again. Now tell me, where are your comrades going to take them?"

He frowned and swallowed nervously before replying, "If I am not mistaken, then straight to our dungeons on the werewolf territory."

I straightened myself up and seemed to be thinking. He seemed to be on the same length before continuing, "I hope you know, you won't get there. At least, not how you are now. Everyone will be on alert with whom they have in there."

I glanced at him and my eyes flashed purple, and he frowned. Clearly not used to seeing that color, his eyes flickered up to my face before he whispered, "What are you?"

I glanced back at him and replied, "Now, now now. If I tell you that, I'll have to kill you."

He raised his eyebrows and replied, "And? What is your point? We both know that I will never see the outside again."

I shrugged and replied, "Doesn't matter. Still won't tell you that information. Anyhow. How far away is your kingdom?"

He swallowed and replied, "It's on the border of the Eastern border, where you guys send the troubled ones as punishment to work with Davis."

I sighed deeply before pressing the blade slightly into his clothing, and he cried out as the blade tipped into his skin, not drawing blood yet, but enough pressure to puncture him slightly. He started to sob before wailing, "ALRIGHT! ALRIGHT! It's roughly forty miles from the Eastern Wall. Although, it's hard to find it."

I removed the pressure on the blade and replied, "How would it be hard? The stench of werewolves is high."

He scowled and growled, "Not as easy. It's underground."

I raised my eyebrows and replied, "Oh? Is that why we always have a difficulty in finding your territory? It's under the damn ground?"

He swallowed before replying, "Not all of it is underground. Just the entrance to the dungeon and to get inside. The upper side has a bunch of…"

He trailed off, clearly not wanting to tell me. I pressed the blade back onto his chest, the same spot. He grimaced and finally whined, "Traps! It has a lot of traps! Some like the ones I left behind in my room."

I released the pressure and replied, "How do you disable them?"

He swallowed and after a moment, didn't want to answer, but I leaned forward as if I was going to draw blood. He paled slightly and whimpered, "If I tell you that, I will never get to go home!"

I chuckled as I replied, "We both know you won't leave here. So might as well spill. How do you disable them?"

He swallowed for a moment and lowered his head. He took a shuddery breath before his eyes flickered to his wolf's eye colors. His posture changed, he took a deep breath, and looked at me with a hard stare, unwavering.

I bared my teeth at him, and growled, "Answer me."

He chuckled for a moment before replying, "**You think you scare me? You are nothing but a shifter. When I have the ability to shift into myself...**"

I didn't move and watched as his wolf tried to force himself to shift. He was rather startled that he couldn't. His eyes flew to my face, and he whined slightly. I smiled and sighed after a moment, "You can't shift with those on you. Neither can you break them. Now, answer me."

He sighed deeply and replied, "**What makes you think I would answer you?**"

I raised my eyebrows and replied, "Because I have this sword."

His eyes drifted down to the blade, he swallowed, and his eyes once again flickered to mine before he growled, "**Where did you manage to get those blades? Last time I checked, they were lost.**"

I leaned forward and growled, "Answer my question."

He scoffed and replied, "**Answer mine, first.**"

I raised my eyebrows and replied, "That's not how this works. You are chained up wolf. What is your name, so I don't have to call you a wolf?"

He sighed deeply and glanced at the iron bars of the little window, but it wasn't a window either, it was a floorboard. If we wanted to kill everyone down here, it would be pretty easy to do so. We would just close off the air vents down here, and light a fire on the only open one. He sighed deeply and looked at me before replying, "**The name given to me is Damon.**"

He looked like he was going to say something else, but after a moment he seemed to have thought better of it. He glanced at the chains and then glanced at the blade hovering above the center of his ribcage. He sighed deeply and tried to wipe his face, but the rattling and the weight of the cuffs prevented it. He lowered his arms down and released a heavy sigh before looking at me, "**I'm not getting out of here, and I know that now. What do you want to know?**"

I smirked slightly and replied, "How do I disable the traps on the top?"

His eyebrows hiked up and he chuckled slightly before replying, "**The only ones who have that power to disable them are the ones who had placed them there. It is something that the druids have taught us before your king destroyed the closest druid camp. He murdered so many people that night when he raided them.**"

I swallowed, I knew what Morphous did and did not agree with it myself either, but I couldn't openly say that either. I sighed deeply before replying, "How would I go about finding someone who did the traps?"

He raised his eyebrows and shook his head slowly, before replying, "**Most of those traps are way before either of our times. The traps themselves work even if the one who set them**

**is long dead. A few of the traps themselves are a century or more old. I doubt it that you can disable it."**

I frowned and replied after a moment, "Then tell me, where is the entrance to the dungeons and the entrance to your homeland?"

He stared at me and finally slowly shook his head and replied, **"The only way in there is by spilling werewolf blood. And it cannot be a minute old either. It has to be dripped onto the rock when the wolf is present. There is no going around that either."**

I frowned and replied, "So I need a willing werewolf to do it then?"

He looked down at his hands and replied, **"Not only that, but you also have to get one that has committed no crimes. So, you can't use me for it."**

I glanced at him, he didn't want to look at me. After a moment, he glanced up and continued, **"I committed treason, I killed an elite member. I believe Daros was his brother. However, I doubt that he is still here anymore. I was alerted when my traps went off, and so far, the arrows have only pierced a werewolf."**

I sighed deeply shook my head, and looked away. I knew I had one more place to go tonight before I could go find a willing werewolf to do our bidding. He sighed and spoke after a moment, **"Can I please get some peace and quiet? Can you leave me be for the rest of the evening?"**

I glanced at him, suddenly wondering why he switched tactics and glanced at the door slightly before looking at him. He shook his head and replied, **"I knew the moment you came in here, that you didn't want to. That you were going to the Queen's cell. I can assure you though. She knows nothing about this. If she did, I would have killed her."**

I growled lowly in my throat. He chuckled, leaned back against the wall, and closed his eyes before he sighed deeply. I frowned, turned around, and went out. He was correct, he was not my original stop. The Queen was.

I opened his door and closed it down, making sure it locked before moving down to her door.

*****

I walked down a few doors down and got to her door. I paused and placed my sword back in its sheath before touching the door. It swung upward. I heeded it no mind and walked inside.

She was dirty, head down, still in the clothing that she had come in here with. Her eyes were downcast, but after a moment she spoke, "**Did you come to gloat, Killian?**"

I stared at her and replied, "No."

She raised her head and blinked once before staring at me. I swallowed before her eyes made me want to bow to her, but no longer. I frowned, not understanding why she didn't affect me anymore. She smiled as if she knew what I was thinking before speaking, "**You aren't compelled to follow my directions or will anymore, Killian, not since I got brought down here. Especially since you were the one who brought me in.**"

I frowned, sighed deeply, and replied, "You didn't give me a choice in that affair, Katherine."

She smiled slightly, and somewhat straightened before replying, "**So what brings you down here, anyhow? I know you did not come all the way down here to say hello. There has to be another motive.**"

I sighed deeply, ran my hand across my face, and replied after gathering my thoughts, "Do you have any idea what is happening up top?"

The look of confusion answered my question. So, Damon was correct, she would know nothing, however, I had another question to ask her before I left to find a werewolf.

She shook her head and whispered, "**No. Morphous hasn't even been down here either. I actually thought you were him until I smelled you.**"

I frowned and sighed again, before replying, "The King was taken, along with Rafeor and my son."

That caught her attention, she stood up suddenly and seemed like she was going to do something, but soon she sat back down against the wall and looked at me. It was clear to me what she was about to do. I lowered my eyes for a moment and shook my head. She looked away before speaking, "**Why are we talking when you know what to do, Killian?**"

I smiled slightly before replying, "Because I thought you were involved in it."

Her heart skipped a beat, and she jerked her head towards me. She whispered, "**Excuse you?**"

I shrugged and replied, "What do you want me to do, Katherine? You gave Sammuel the blueprints and layout of the palace. What do you expect?"

She fell silent and went to look like she was about to say something but went quiet again. She bowed her head and slouched down to her seat before speaking, "**I don't know why I did. It just happened. I'm sorry.**"

I shook my head and replied, "Can't change things, Katherine, and I hope you know that too. I cannot force Morphous into accepting you back upstairs."

She was silent and glanced at me with teary eyes, but she didn't reply. I let out a puff of air I seemed to have been holding before speaking, "I do have a question though, Katherine, why did you do it?"

She looked at me, lowered her eyes, and swallowed. She didn't want to tell me. I turned towards the door, knowing I was losing time. Then she replied, **"I'm not about to disclose that to you, Killian."**

I glanced back at her and replied, "I had a feeling you wouldn't want to say anything. Goodbye for now, Katherine."

I touched the door and exited. I paused in the hallway. It was never easy to talk to the Queen, but for some reason now was different. She was more defeated, and she didn't even make a huge fuss over what had happened. I glanced back at her door before heading back the way I had come. I needed to find a willing werewolf to do our bidding. So, I could get my son, Rafeor, and my King back safely.

# Chapter 11

I woke up and instinctively went to grab my pounding head, but couldn't move my hands. My eyes were blurry and I glanced around through the slits in my eyes since they were not used to the brightness that the candles brought. I heard movement, and I tried hard to not make a sound. However, a deep voice boomed, **"I know you are awake Morphous."**

I sighed deeply, blinked open my eyes, and glowered up at the King of the werewolves. His Lycan was showing himself, his voice is normally lighter than that. I groaned before replying, **"What do you want, Nathaniel?"**

He smiled slightly and rolled back on his feet before replying, **"I want to know what you have been hiding all this time. What did you take from the Druids?"**

I frowned at him, but I made my gaze go blank, something I had learned to do so to mask my shock. He chuckled slightly and his eyes glimmered for a moment. He growled low in his throat, **"Answer me."**

I sighed deeply and sluggishly replied, **"I don't know what you are talking about, Nathaniel. Want to explain it?"**

His eyes flashed darker, and his arms started to grow a bit of the Lycan's hair, but he seemed to push it down and limit it to his Lycan's voice. Something that takes years to master, even I struggle to keep my dragon and other forms at bay when my anger spikes.

I squinted at him, he sighed deeply and seemed to have rubbed his hand across his face, before speaking, **"I know you took something when the riot happened. I know it was a cover for something. Now that my people have intel on the inside, they confirm that you took.... Wait, took is a slightly different than the term I want... hmmm.... Let me rephrase that, Morphous. What did you steal from the Druids?"**

I grimaced and replied after a moment, **"I took nothing."**

His Lycan twirled around dangerously. He grabbed my hair and yanked up my head far back, making me bare my throat to him. I growled, my eyes flashing red in response. He snarled and took a step backward before turning his head, **"Bring him in here."**

I squinted my eyes for a moment but said nothing. A moment later, another figure was dragged from a side door and I could tell it was struggling. It had a hood over its head. A chair was screeched across the concrete and slammed down a few feet from me. They struggled to place the figure down, finally smacking it straight in the face. It stopped after a moment, panting before the hood was removed abruptly and I stared directly into Quinn's eyes. Shit. He knew about what was taken and what else I had tried to hide.

We stared at each other for a solid moment, before I swallowed. I didn't know how much training Quinn had in dealing with torture since I have never tried to test that. I now wish I had.

Nathaniel smirked and finally rumbled, "**Do you want to talk now, Morphous? Or should I beat up this kid?**"

I paused, and my eyes flickered to Quinn before glancing around. I didn't recognize any of these werewolves and I could tell by Quinn's eyes that he was checking them out too. He slightly shook his head, as if we were thinking the same thing. Meaning, they had no idea who he was. I glanced at Nathaniel and growled, "**Do your worst. I won't talk.**"

He chuckled and replied, "**For a moment, I thought you were smarter than that.**"

I glanced at Quinn and saw his eyes were far away for a moment, and I swallowed, not knowing what he thought of it. Nathaniel didn't give any sort of warning and slammed a fist straight into Quinn's side. I heard a snap and knew at least one of Quinn's bones was broken. I saw him grimace, but he did not cry out. The two werewolves that were holding him down to the seat glanced at Nathaniel. Normally, a hit from their King made someone lose all their crap. Nathaniel glanced between me and Quinn before squatting down in front of Quinn and speaking, "**Who are you, kid?**"

Quinn's eyes flickered to his before replying, "A shifter."

Nathaniel frowned and was about to retort, but did not reply. He stood up and motioned to another wolf to bring in someone. He turned to face me before speaking, "**I know eventually you will break. I, however, did not think you would have an affair with someone so young though, Morphous.**"

I frowned, but Quinn suddenly began to struggle. His gaze drew away from me to him and he smiled wickedly, before chuckling. He glanced at me before continuing, "**It seems that one person here knows who I have in my custody. Go get it.**"

Two werewolves instantly left and dragged out a fragile form, who stumbled between them. Its slouched form was dragged forward. Another chair was screeched across the floor and slammed down. They forced the figure into the seat, and only one of the wolves decided to stay there. I swallowed, I hoped I was wrong. However, as soon as the hood came undone, I knew that I was correct on who it was. My daughter sat mere feet from me, and yet Nathaniel didn't know who she was. I swallowed and my eyes flickered to Quinn before glancing back at Rafeor.

Nathaniel chuckled and leaned back on his heels before rolling forward again and snapping, **"Your affair has arrived, Morphous. If you give me what I want to know, then I will not tell Katherine of your wrongdoings. Now tell me, what did you steal from the Druids?"**

I could tell that Rafeor pulled a face, and seemed that she wanted to retort, but I saw Quinn out of the corner of my eye, shake his head. She fell silent and swallowed. Her eyes flickered to Nathaniel before glancing around the room.

 The werewolf behind her was not paying much attention to her, a growl escaped her. One that only an alpha would let out. The werewolf instantly bared his neck to her, and every single lower wolf did the same, including the ones holding Quinn. Releasing him. Nathaniel whipped around and growled, **"You're one of us?"**

I swallowed, as I saw the flash of her Lycan in her eyes, and wished that it was Katherine in that seat over anyone else. She at least knew how to keep quiet. This was Rafeor's first time to be held captive. She stared at him for a moment and shook her head. Not replying. Nathaniel turned slowly to me before growling, **"Who. Is. She?"**

I looked at him before replying, **"My daughter, Nathaniel."**

He fell silent, and he glowered at everyone there and growled, **"Dismissed. All of you. Leave me."**

All the werewolves bowed and left quickly. Leaving us alone with him.

*****

His Lycan flickered his eyes around the three of us. **"I didn't know you had children, Morphous. She looks old too, so she must have been around before the riot too. Is she the reason why you had the riot anyhow? Is she the thing that you were trying to hide away so no one could find her?"**

We all kept silent, and after a moment Nathaniel looked at her before speaking, **"Who are you?"**

I glanced sharply at him, realizing that Nathaniel had somewhat forced down his Lycan. At least, to the point where he could speak without his voice booming. Rafeor looked at him before replying at last, **"My name is Rafeor."**

The look of shock across his face spoke volumes and he glanced at me. His Lycan surfaced for a split second and then disappeared. I held his gaze before he redirected his attention to

Rafeor and spoke, "**I'm sorry, but that is a dog breed. Why did Morphous name you after a dog breed?**"

She stared at him, raised her eyebrows, and smirked. She replied after a moment, "**He didn't name me Rafeor, Raphina was my former name. However, twelve years with the name Rafeor, and being whipped when you tried to tell your owner otherwise, you learn quick to not mention it again.**"

Nathaniel growled and his Lycan surfaced again; it took him a moment to regain control over him. He must have closed his eyes and rolled back on his heels before turning around and growling at me, "**Why didn't you search for her sooner, Morphous?**"

I swallowed and replied, "**I couldn't. My kingdom had suffered and I needed to make sure everything was in order. She got lost in the chaos too.**"

Nathaniel didn't appear to like my answer. His Lycan blinked once and he seemed to struggle for a moment before he shook his head and turned to Quinn and barked out, "**And what are you exactly? Rarely has anyone been close to not making a sound for my punches.**"

Quinn swallowed, and I could tell that he didn't want to answer. However, he glanced at me before replying, "I apologize, but I cannot say. Morphous doesn't know."

I froze and stared at him. He was a shifter, but I now had a feeling that something else flowed through his veins. However, his eyes never betrayed what he was. Nathaniel stared at him, frowned, and glanced at me before replying, "**You have so many secretive personnel in your arsenal, Morphous. First, a long-lost daughter who suddenly appeared after all these years, and now a shifter who won't say how he managed to not make a sound under my Lycan's punch. That is not normal, Morphous.**"

My eyes flickered to Rafeor and landed on Nathaniel's before replying, "**I'm not here to make it make sense, Nathaniel.**"

He growled for a moment before he turned to look at all of us as a whole. Shaking his head, he suddenly walked out and slammed the door behind him, leaving us alone.

******

I exited rather abruptly but I needed to. Morphous was just playing mind games with me, and my Lycan was already riled up. He was making us talk in circles, and it made me pissed off that he managed to get under our skin. I rubbed the bridge of my nose with my right hand and closed my eyes. I took a deep breath before growling, "**What do you want?**"

I opened my eyes and stared at a werewolf, the same one that was holding Rafeor. He swallowed and bowed slightly, not looking me in the eyes before replying, "My Lord, you told me to keep an eye on her when they brought her. Something is weird about her. I feel somehow connected to her, my King."

I frowned, I felt no connection to her, but that did not mean that she didn't belong here either. What happened inside that room, was something that never happened in all my years as the King. I frowned, there was only one other person who may know what happened, and that was my mate. After the riot, I knew she went out and met someone, even after everything that we have done together to fortify our kingdom, she snuck out and met someone. I don't know who she had met, but she came back looking crestfallen, her wolf sang songs of sorrow, but never told my Lycan on why.

I froze, and I walked back to the door. There was a one-way window on the door, and I looked inside and watched as Rafeor twirled her fingers into her hair, before unwrapping it again. She didn't seem to know she was being watched. I took a step backward, rage filled me. The events lined up even. I turned to face the werewolf before me, "**Bring me my mate.**"

The werewolf scrambled backward, baring his throat as he went, and scrambled out the other door. I turned my red eyes towards the room before me, if my assumptions were correct, then this was why she went out in the beginning. Until she arrived, I would let them be. I turned on my heel and walked out of the room.

******

Morphous had his head down, his hands were handcuffed behind him, attached to the chair. His face was black where they hit him to get him here. I glanced at Rafeor and noticed that she decided to stay seated. I glanced back at Morphous before speaking, "You two seem to know each other quite well."

Morphous glanced up slightly, lowered his head back down, and replied, "**Before the riot, we were close.**"

I smiled grimly, and continued, "What happened?"

He glanced up at me and blinked before glancing at the door that he went out of. "**Now isn't the time to tell you.**"

Rafeor glanced at Morphous before speaking, "**If we wait for the proper time, Morphous, then it will never pass. So, answer him.**"

Morphous groaned and glowered at her for a split second. He spoke, "**I cannot tell you now because they are watching us.**"

She smirked and replied, "**And your point? They will continue to watch us, Morphous. This is their home territory after all. We must be their entertainment.**"

I watched as Morphous eyes flashed in response, and I glanced at Rafeor before shaking my head slowly. If Morphous didn't want to talk about something, he usually was not the one to break under anything. However, I glanced at him and saw his eyes flicker to the door before sighing and speaking, "**The riot kept us apart. Our species were at war against each other.**"

He stopped talking and didn't seem to want to continue but she pressured him, "**And?**"

Morphous glanced at her and then his eyes flickered to the door before growling, "**What else do you want, Rafeor? You want to hear about how I wiped the Druids out and found the artifact they were keeping hidden away? Or the fact that I 'lost' you?**"

I growled in response, and Morphous's eyes flickered to mine. He swallowed slightly and glanced down at the concrete again. She was silent for a moment before her eyes sparked in anger. "**I guess I want a little bit of both. Why did you wipe out an entire Druid population? And why did you lose me in the damn riot?**"

I could see his jaw lock, it usually meant he shifted into his dragon right about now. I was actually surprised that he hadn't done so yet. His eyes were a dark red, and he seemed to struggle with himself for a moment. Rafeor, not knowing what to look for when he was pissed off, spoke again, "**Well?**"

He lost it. He shifted into his dragon, roaring into the underground room. The entire ceiling trembled and shuddered under the quaking. I dove towards Rafeor and protected her as Morphous's dragon blew around the fire. Scorching hot flames flew around us, but since I crashed into Rafeor and brought her down, the flames went flying over us in hot waves.

His fiery breath melted the roof, and it started to crash down upon us. His dragon spread his wings open as if trying to not kill us here. Soon, metal and trees collapsed down upon us. Soil rained down on his wings, I heard the little pitter-patter as they bounced and rolled off his great black wings, and smacked into the concrete around us.

*****

I waited in the next room over, and soon the wolf brought forth my mate. She looked at me and after a moment when neither of us spoke, I glanced at the werewolf before speaking, "**Leave us.**"

He bowed out of the room, my mate looked at me, and turned her head sideways before speaking, "**What is it? Why call me down here of all places, Nathaniel?**"

I frowned and replied, "**The night you left after the riot. Where did you go?**"

She swallowed and looked away from me before replying, "**Nowhere. Nathaniel, what is this?**"

I glanced at her and did not reply immediately. My Lycan tried hard to come forward, but he always scared her when he did. I tried again, "**My love, who did you go see after the riot? I know you went and met someone. Who?**"

The look across her face told me everything that I needed to know. She knew what I was talking about and finally, she whispered, "**You…. you watched me? I thought we trusted each other.**"

I swallowed and replied, "**I trust you. However, I also need to know. Who did you see?**"

She looked down and twirled her fingers in her clothing, a sure sign that she didn't want to say anything. She only did that when she was nervous. I lowered my eyes before speaking again, "**Was it Morphous? That you went to see?**"

She froze, and I felt an irregular heartbeat. My shoulders slumped, so I was correct. My Lycan desperately wanted to surface, forcing him back was extremely difficult now. However, I could not let him surface. Not yet. I glanced at her and asked, "**Why?**"

She took a shuddering breath before replying, "**It was before we met each other, Nathaniel. We, at the time, were lovers. Then… well… when I turned eighteen, it was snapped into me that you were mine. And I yours. I ended things with Morphous when I found your lovely scent….**"

She trailed off for a moment before whispering, "**But not until we had a child together.**"

Forcing myself not to let my Lycan out, I swallowed back a sob, but she heard it. She looked at me teary-eyed before speaking, "**It was a little girl, Nathaniel. We named her Raphina. However, I knew that most werewolf alphas would have killed anyone that was not their child, and I gave her to Morphous.**"

She took a shuddering breath, her tears streaming down her face as she continued, "**I went to see Morphous after the riot, and he told me that she was lost in the fight. My little girl died.**"

I turned swiftly, turning away from her, facing the wall as I fought my Lycan from coming out. I took a shaky breath in and out before asking, **"Did you see her body?"**

She sniffed but replied, **"No."**

I glanced at her before replying, **"Morphous lied to you then."**

She took a sharp intake and her eyes glimmered her wolf's eyes for a split second, making my Lycan quiet down for a moment. What she told us was making us want to rip both of their throats out. However, I cannot blame her. Morphous was a good-looking guy, and I was with him as friends on the day before the riot. I knew his beliefs. I knew he didn't mean any harm. I swallowed and was about to say something else, but a roar thundered throughout my prison.

By the looks of my mate, she recognized the roar. She stared at me with distrust. It was as if she suddenly made the connections as to why I had figured out her secret for the last twelve years. I glowered at her, pointed at the exit door, and growled, **"GO!"**

****

My Lycan surfaced, I watched as she winced and ran off. I waited until the werewolf came back, at least one of them. He looked shaken and looked at me with terrified eyes. I growled, **"Get everyone out of the prison. Guards and prisoners. GO!"**

He tumbled over his feet, racing to obey when another roar sounded. It thundered and shook the prison ceilings and walls. I knew his prison was old, but I wished I could have used it for another fifty years. However, Morphous's dragon had other plans for that. I grumbled to my Lycan, and we left the room entirely. Since we did not want to be baked by the scorching fire from him. We would meet again soon. For now, I needed to talk to my little brother, he needed to step up in his role as alpha of one of the packs.

*****

Morphous's dragon soon had enough of a hole where he could fly out of there. He grabbed us in his fore-talon and leaped into the air. Twirling around, he shook the residue off of himself. His giant black wings thumped against the trees, and soon he soared above the treetops. We were heading home.

# Chapter 12

I headed back up the cells' walkway, passing the ones that had been inside the cells for the past twelve years. I paused and looked back at the one who had spoken out earlier tonight. It looked at me with a deflated look and glowered at me from where it sat inside. I knew it was a werewolf and I approached the cell door before speaking, "Name?"

It stared at me and coughed a little before replying, "I know that trick."

I sighed deeply and opened its cell, making him flinch backward, and pressing himself back against the corner. Its eyes flickering to my swords, swallowing. I glanced at the blade at my hip and spoke for a moment, "Answer me."

It shook its head and I sighed deeply, before rubbing my face and growling, "Are you a werewolf?"

The figure stared at me and after a moment, it slowly nodded in response, clearly not realizing what I wanted. I squatted and looked at it before speaking, "Do you still know how to get home? The hidden entrances?"

It stared at me and swallowed, answering that himself, and finally he croaked, "Why do you want to know of my homeland?"

I stood up and replied, "Because you would know that blood has to be spilled to get into your homeland. Correct?"

Its silence was deafening, but after a moment, he slowly nodded. His eyes flickered to my swords again. "You want me to bring you before my homeland's front doors with your weapons? Is that what you want?"

I looked at him and replied, "I'll tell you something that you wouldn't normally find out. Your kin, taken the King, a woman, and my son away. They went to your homeland."

It took him a moment to conclude what he was going to do. He looked at me and sighed after a moment, "So? What do you exactly want me to do?"

I raised my eyebrows and replied, "I want you to do exactly what you said a minute before. Take me to your homeland."

He swallowed and replied, "And if I refuse?"

I shrugged and replied, "I know that the wolf has to be willing to do it. So, nothing becomes of it."

He glanced down at his cell floor and swallowed, thinking it through before he looked at me and growled, "And after? What happens afterward?"

I sighed deeply and replied, "Unfortunately, you would become an unmarked grave."

His Adam's apple bobbed for a moment, and he glanced at me sharply before whispering, "A swift end?"

I paused and glanced at him. I sighed and replied, "Yes."

He seemed to try to shake it off, but he didn't succeed, I saw the hope in his eyes. However, after a moment, he went quiet before letting out a shaky breath and speaking, "Unfortunately, you can't even use me, or anyone else in my platoon. We had been war victims and I doubt it that our blood will still work for the entrances."

He said something that caught my attention, I glanced at him and growled, "Platoon?"

He glanced up and smirked slightly before replying, "The rest of the wolves down here in the other cells. They are my men. I was their captain all those years ago. I brought them here."

I leaned against the wall with a frown across my face. I glanced back at him before speaking, "So you are a captain in the werewolf realm. How long had you been in that ranking?"

He raised his eyes at me and his eyes sparkled for a moment, but they soon lost their glow. He said, "Three years before the riot, my father stepped down. He said I was ready."

His voice broke off for a moment, and finally, he continued, "I protected him as best as I could during the riot, but to no avail. Your numbers outranked ours at the time. We were guarding our western front when your King decided to attack us."

I swallowed, what happened at the riot did not only affect the humans, but it affected the entire supernatural world. It made the humans fear everyone that was not the normal stinky being that they were. I sighed deeply, we were all to blame for escalating it that far, but it was not in the past. I couldn't be held responsible for what I had done personally in the riot.

He spoke after a moment, "My name is Wilson. Wilson Droon."

I froze, that family name was old. I glanced at him sharply before asking the question that popped into my mind, "Why did you surrender if your last name is Droon? Your ancestors were brutal and thirsty for a fight."

He chuckled darkly before growling, "The key word is ANCESTORS! My father was not like his father before him or our forefathers. We cannot be held responsible and I wished that I was as bloodthirsty as they once were. But I know myself and my wolf agreed at the time, that it was not called for. That riot was not called for. We knew that Morphous caused it to hide something, and when he attacked the Druid camp that was within our border, that is when we knew he was after them. And not more of us. We protected the Druid camp as much as we could, but Morphous was too powerful. His black dragon wiped out most of my platoon, and the rest of us surrendered. Knowing that if we didn't, we would have been killed."

I swallowed, all the information he just said was all history. And it was not through a shifter's eyesight either. It was from the opposite end of things. Something that I didn't know I needed. Morphous killed a peaceful people for what exactly? An artifact that they were safekeeping? What did he learn that was the destruction of their people?

Wilson cleared his throat after a moment and brought me back to reality. I glanced at him and saw the tiredness in his face before speaking, "I'm sorry, Wilson."

He grimaced and replied, "Were you there when the riot happened at the Druid camp?"

I fell silent, wondering back all that time. Soon though, I shook my head and replied, "No, I was elsewhere."

He smiled slightly before replying, "Lucky. My platoon was tasked to keep them safe since they helped so much in the years before our species. However, we failed."

He bowed his head in shame, and I for a moment felt horrible. I still did not agree with the riot, but I also knew against telling Morphous anything. In fear of being down here myself. Wilson, after a moment, glanced up at me and asked, "What are you going to do with this information? Are you going to kill me since I said my name to you? Or are you going to make my life a living hell and beat me to the brink of death and wait until my wolf heals me to do it again? That is what the other guards have done in the past few years."

I swallowed and shook my head and replied, "Nothing. I'll keep this a secret if you do."

He glanced sharply at me and replied, "You're different than any other shifter guards. You are polite even though you seem to want answers when you ask immediately. Who are you?"

I swallowed and after a moment replied, "My name is Killian Benik."

He stared at me, his jaw dropped before he whispered, "Benik? You are joking, right? The demon blood hybrid?"

My eyes sparked, showing purple again. He swallowed and whispered, "So, it's true then. Why are you following someone so trivial? Surely, you have been around for centuries longer than Morphous."

I sighed deeply before looking at him and growled, "I have been around for a few centuries. However, I wanted to know what happened in the shifter communities too. I became his advisor until my son was of age."

He swallowed and gulped, clearly not wanting to speak again. After a moment my eyes must have returned to their normal self. I ran my hand through my hair and was about to leave, when he called out, "Wait."

I paused and looked at him, he pushed himself out of the corner and stood up, he was rather tall but not taller than me. I glanced down at him before raising my eyebrow at him. He licked his parched lips before speaking, "If you have been around for centuries, then you should know why Morphous killed the peaceful Druids. There has to be an explanation of why."

I sighed deeply before turning towards the door and paused. I knew why. I bowed my head for a moment before speaking, "Because they had a prophecy that was passed down for centuries. That one fated day, that a werewolf queen and a shifter king would have a child together, and create the first of the hybrids in their reign. For centuries, your two species have tried hard to ignore the prophecy, until it came to light that if such a child was to be created, that it would burn the world down. Since it would have the ability to shift into anything at will, the same ability as a shifter. And also have a Lycan form that had a secondary form and mind. This child would burn the world as we all would know it. So, the forefathers of both species agreed to never allow it to happen."

The shock across his face was clearly evident. He was not ready for the prophecy, and fear was evident in his eyes. I continued after a moment, "The Druids, however, knew that one day a union would form between a werewolf queen and a shifter king, and they made an artifact. One that would harness the hybrid's ability, and therefore making whomever had the hybrid child, the most powerful species."

He swallowed and sat back down before whispering, "Do you know if such a creature exists?"

I looked at him and replied, "She does. She was exactly what Morphous made disappear in the riot. She didn't grow up with shifters to know her powers, nor did she grow up with werewolves knowing how to control her Lycan. Instead, she was sold, and only a few days ago did my son go out to find her again."

Wilson stared at me and finally shook his head before fumbling with his hands for a split second. "She? You know that one exists? If you are centuries old, then why don't you end the abomination?"

I sighed deeply before replying, "Because, there is another section of the prophecy that was passed down my family line."

He stared at me and swallowed, wanting to know what it was, but also scared to ask. I chuckled slightly before speaking, "Through my family line, it is to believe that the child will rule werewolves and shifters alike, harmoniously. The only thing is, only a Benik can manage to do that. Without a Benik, then it will do what the Druids prophesied it as."

Wilson stared and swallowed before speaking, "So… if that's true. Then why aren't you with the child?"

I leveled him with a growl, and he hunched himself down to make himself small. My eyes flickered another color before I growled out an answer, "Because your comrades decided to take her along Morphous and my son. She is that woman I mentioned earlier."

His face fell, made an O and he fell silent. He looked down and replied, "I may be a werewolf, but I will help you however I can. I want someone to lead our kingdoms properly. Not this mess, not the segregation that the forefathers had created. I know, I personally can't open the entrance, but I know where they are. I also may be able to convince someone else to open it. I had influence back in my day."

I chuckled slightly and replied, "Alright."

He swallowed before speaking again, "Killian?"

I paused, I was almost outside his door when I looked at him again. He swallowed before whispering, "I am their captain. I will not leave my men to face Morphous's wrath when he gets here. I request that you give them the same mercy you are giving me, please."

I paused, there were only eight of them. I glanced at the other cells and swallowed. I already knew that Morphous would be murderous if I had indeed done that. However, I also knew that he had kept them long enough. I sighed deeply and replied, "So be it. Come along."

Shock was written across his face, he stood up and walked towards the cell's door before tenderly placing his foot past the frame. Nothing bad happened to him.

*****

I had already moved up to the next cell, opened its door, and kept moving. The prisoners slowly eased out and looked both ways. When they saw me, they were about to shrink back inside their cells before I called back to them, "No, come along."

They all looked at me as if I was insane but Wilson spoke, "Bravo team! Group!"

Their eyes instantly held hope and suddenly they went out of their cells and stood shoulder to shoulder. They were gangly but that was due to not enough food, and no light for the past twelve years.

I glanced at them after they all ranked up, and spoke out, "I know that you have your questions. However, Wilson and I came up with…"

One of them growled, and cut me off, "How do we know this isn't a trick?"

Wilson replied, "Because he's a Benik."

The shock spread through them and they glanced at me before the one who cut me off spoke, "Forgive me, please."

I was shocked by their sudden endearment, and glanced at Wilson, I knew there had to be more to the knowledge that he knew of my family line. However, this was a case of death for them all.

I turned around and did not reply, my footfalls echoing the cell pathway. After a moment, I heard them shuffling after me. Soon, we came to the incline to the top where I paused and turned to Wilson before speaking, "Wait here."

He bowed to me slightly and shuffled backward. I squinted my eyes, he knew something. However, I knew that I wouldn't find the answers here.

****

I went out of the dungeon door and found antsy Conrade and Gillith standing in front of me. They stared at me for a moment before Gillith spoke, "Our King is gone and you were down in the dungeons because?"

I looked at him and replied, "I had to get help. There was someone down there who knew the ins and outs of the kingdom. However, they also disclosed that there was a slight issue for us."

Conrade raised his eyebrows, took a deep sniff, and growled his eyes flashing. I knew the moment that they would both smell the prisoners and I smirked that it took them this long actually. I sighed before speaking, "It has been years since they have been out. I promised them a quick death and an unmarked grave."

Gillith snarled and snapped, "Morphous had them in custody for a good reason, Killian. He will not be kind to you once he gets back here."

I raised my eyebrows at him and growled, "Would you want to be locked away for twelve years of your life, Gillith?"

He scoffed and replied, "As if that would happen to me. I am a high member of our community."

I chuckled but Conrade spoke, "Alright, say if you did. There are eight of them and only one of you."

I cocked my head and replied, "How many guards?"

Gillith and Conrade glanced at each other and Gillith replied, "No one is dead yet, but they had some sort of poison. Anna is at her wit's end trying to find what it is."

I glanced at them and growled, "How many?"

Conrade leveled me a look and replied, "Besides ourselves, and Hector and Amish, no one else, Killian. We are the only guards that were not taken down. And all the werewolves that were here, are now gone too. They pretended to guard us, Killian, and then once we were apparently weak to their standards, they decided to strike us."

I swallowed and looked down at the ground, my hands twitched. I wanted to kill someone, and Gillith saw my eyes flash red for a split second. "Can't do anything about it, Killian. We, however, need to say here. Protect the box."

I swallowed and glanced at them before nodding, "Protect the box."

Conrade backed away for a moment and growled, "Let them out of there. Let us scare them shitless."

My mouth quirked upwards slightly, and I backed away for the door to be opened.

****

Wilson stared at the two of the guards who came down, who had done some of the worst painful duties that they could detail. Everyone huddled down and I swallowed before speaking, "Hello."

The one on my right looked at me sharply and growled, "We heard that you were authorized to come out. Although do you all know what is at stake?"

A few of my comrades shook their heads and tried to make themselves look small at the same time. The one on my left replied, "You will do the duty, and then you will all be killed. Swiftly, and then be placed in an unmarked grave."

For a moment, they all didn't want to believe it. However, neither of them budged, and I swallowed before I turned to face them. "It's either that, or we go back down as a unit to face Morphous's wrath later."

They all stared at him and one swallowed, but finally, a few of their heads nodded and one muttered, "I made peace with death years ago. I'll go."

A series of 'I'll go' sounded and they all seemed to know that they would not come back. That this was their last few minutes.

****

I looked away from the eight werewolves for a moment, unsure if this was the correct path. However, now was not the time to have second thoughts. I straightened myself up and stared at the raggedy bunch of werewolves before barking, "Alright! With me."

I turned hard on my heel and Gillith called out, "Watch your back, Killian!"

I glanced back at him and smiled softly, before disappearing around a bend, with the elder werewolves in tow.

****

We watched as Killian and the prisoners walked around the bend. Conrade looked at me and spoke, "Do you think there is something more to Killian? Those werewolves bowed to him."

I sighed deeply and replied, "Possibility. They acted like he was royalty by the way they bowed to him."

We exchanged looks for a moment before Conrade spoke again, "Do you remember him telling us his last name?"

I frowned and after a moment, slowly shook my head in response, and frowned. Normally, that was the first thing that we found out. However, he managed to come in without a word on his last. Hmmm…. Interesting. I slightly scrunched up my face before walking towards the office, where the box was located. Conrade followed me shortly.

*****

I walked ahead of the werewolves, and I heard muttering behind me. I paused, turned to face them after a moment, and looked at them. They were gangly and shallow, not what they once were, however, Wilson looked at me with a look and shook his head. I sighed deeply before turning back around to continue forward, when I heard, "Just the prick he is."

I stopped dead in my tracks and turned slowly around, before speaking, "A little louder, please. What are you whining about back there?"

Wilson looked like he didn't want me to know for a split second, but he glanced at the one that had spoken first when Gillith and Conrade were terrorizing them in the doorway. I glanced at him and raised my eyebrows before speaking, "Well?"

The werewolf lifted his head slightly before growling, "You are a prick. What gain do you hold to this? And are you truly a Benik? If you are, prove it."

I closed my eyes for a moment, dealing with my demon half was something I had to keep hidden day in and day out at the shifter palace. However, we were in the Eastern woodland, and no one was well enough to see me. I opened my eyes, and they were bright purple, I allowed my demon to surface slightly, to misconfigure my face for a brief moment before falling back to my normal. The werewolves stared at me in sudden shock. I blinked once, and my eyes returned to normal before I asked, "Is that proof enough for you? Or are you going to continue to challenge me?"

My demon's voice rattled against my normal voice, making it raspier. They all swallowed, the werewolf dropped his gaze, and just shook his head in response. I turned back around when another one spoke, "Why are you serving someone younger than you?"

I paused and looked back at them before replying, "Because learning across the whole supernatural world is what I personally do."

I once again turned to walk forward, but another one growled, "Not good enough answer for my liking."

I paused, turned around again, and touched my sword on my hip before growling, "Are you not going to do what is required of you to do? Or am I going to have to put you down?"

Wilson looked at them sharply and growled slightly, his eyes shining his wolf's eyes and they all instantly looked away.

He glanced at me and nodded once, and I turned back around and continued. I wasn't going to question what just happened entirely. I knew that werewolves have different ranks, and I thought after twelve years of listening to each other's screams would have taken out the ranking they had. However, it seems I can be wrong about them as a species.

****

I paused once we were close to the border when I heard a familiar roar. I froze. The ground beneath our feet began to tremble, we were not yet off of the shifter side. I glanced at Wilson and he swallowed. I saw the stark fear in everyone else's eyes. They knew. They knew who that roar belonged to.

The ground shuddered underneath us, and soon a tree on the werewolf side tumbled down into a hole that was forming. I swallowed, I had experienced Morphous's dragon before, but not to this level. He sounded pissed off, and the werewolves all backed away. A few dropped to their knees and lowered their head in submission.

Soon I saw the dragon's head shoot out of the hole and leaped into the air. I saw two figures being carried up in his foreclaw before the dragon spun around. Shaking off the debris off his wings and body, and had it raining down upon us. I flinched as a rock slammed into my shoulder, but nothing that my demon couldn't handle healing instantly.

*****

The dragon was headed back to the shifter palace, and that was when Wilson spoke, "So, you might as well put an end to us now, Killian."

I glanced at him and swallowed. I had actually come to like Wilson, and his group, at this point. I knew I shouldn't but I did. My demon did too. He spoke in my mind, for the first time in a decade, *"Don't kill."*

I froze and replied after a moment, *"What are you suggesting I do, Falcor?"*

*"They will be our warriors, Kill. We need warriors for what to become."*

I sighed and knew he knew more than he was letting on and I sighed deeply and replied, *"And where are we going to keep them hidden, Falcor? Can't do it on either species territory."*

He scoffed in our mind before replying, *"You know where, Kill. Do not make me say."*

I rubbed my hand across my face and replied, *"That will take all day to get there."*

*"No, it won't. Me carry."*

I swallowed and glanced at the werewolves who were staring at me. I sighed before replying to him, *"And how do you suggest you do that, Falcor? They would be terrified of the form you want."*

*"I be wolf. Giant wolf. Their wolves… babies compared. They follow."*

I sighed deeply, shook my head, and he continued after a moment, *"Kill, no kill them. We need them. Best way, Kill. Best way."*

I frowned and replied, *"What do you know that I don't, Falcor?"*

*"I can't tell."*

I sighed deeply again and he continued for a moment, *"Kill, we need em'. Make it happen, Kill."*

I grumbled and he released me after a moment, knowing he didn't ask for a whole lot when he was in my mind. I looked at the expecting werewolves before I replied to Wilson, "You are coming with me. Don't be surprised though when my demon surfaces. I may be similar to a shifter, but he wants to do this. So, he will be bigger, meaner, and scarier. Do not flee. If you flee, I will have to do what I said. Understood?"

Wilson stared at me, and one spoke out, "Where are we going? Are we going back?"

I shook my head and my demon spoke out, "No, we go somewhere safe. Where army be build."

They stared at me and finally, the one who had spoken out earlier replied, "What does that entail exactly? We go to battle again?"

I, for once, allowed Falcor to have full access, and he blinked once with his purple eyes before replying, "Wolf sad. I understand. We go to a safe place. We home."

Wilson pursed his lips and looked at them all before Falcor spoke again, "Me Falcor. You?"

Wilson looked at him with shock. They all did. He blinked once and waited. Wilson glanced at the others and the shock written across their faces was evident before the one who had spoken out replied, "I am Savador Yearwood."

Wilson swallowed before speaking, "Wilson Droon."

 "Trevoric Damson."

"Xavier Dragonheart."

"Topaz Free."

"Fantar Hellion."

"Averic Broonic."

"Arcanum Ashton."

After a moment, we knew all their names, and my demon made a mental note on who spoke and when. Making their faces our known landmarks slightly, so we didn't mess up their names in the future.

They looked at each other for a moment before Falcor spoke, "Me, become wolf. Giant wolf. You stay here. Otherwise Kill, will kill you. No kill needed."

I wanted to roll my eyes, but he refused to. I still didn't understand why he spoke to others in baby language, maybe to make him more childish? I wondered if there was a more complex reason for it. However, I doubt it. When we talk, it was a mix of baby talk, but it used to be that he was as educated as I was. I didn't understand why he reverted to this.

The werewolves swallowed and took a few steps backward. Falcor squinted his eyes but Wilson spoke before he could interpret it as running away, "We are giving you room, Falcor. Room to shift."

He grinned at them, and I knew for a fact we would shred our clothes if he shifted immediately. I tried to remind him, but he shifted quickly, instantly shredding them. I sighed inwardly and knew that the seamstress would poke me with her needle again since this was not the first outfit that I had ruined in the past month.

The werewolves couldn't hide their terror, and the one named Fantar passed out in fear. Falcor glanced at him with a troubled expression across his face and looked at Wilson before speaking, "Me sorry. I didn't mean to."

Wilson gulped and replied shakily, "You are ok, Falcor. Fantar didn't know you were going to be that size."

Falcor blinked once and looked around and stopped sounding like a baby suddenly, "On my back now. We need to leave immediately. Wolves coming."

Wilson looked shocked for a moment and then squinted his eyes as if shocked that Falcor could speak normally. I would have warned them, but Falcor forbade me from warning them of the baby-ness he tended to do unless something came of it.

Wilson looked at the others and jerked his head towards Falcor. They moved gingerly towards him and climbed up onto him. He had spikes over his back, but they seemed to know what to do with the spikes. They gripped onto them, the spikes were in league with where someone would sit comfortably and be able to hold on. There was enough room for all eight werewolves on the back of Falcor, and he got up and shivered slightly – someone was stroking a spike up and down. He turned his head sharply before growling, "Stop that. Hold only."

Averic instantly stopped and cowered slightly. Falcor smiled wickedly and his eyes flashed a darker purple before he turned his head forward. He took a few easy steps forward before, turning his head again and spoke, "Hold tight. I'm going to get to our home."

They instantly leaned forward and gripped tightly and within two bounds, Falcor was booking it. He kept a mental tally of all of them being on him and ran home.

*****

Five hours later, we were where we needed to be. The werewolves slipped off of Falcor and panted, they were white and were shaking. Falcor did not stop once, not even for water. We bounded over streams that would normally make a normal wolf to swim across, and rivers that we only splashed into once, and bounded outward in another leap. Falcor knew where to go in these rivers to bound evenly, without the need to swim.

At one point, we ruled this part of the territory, now though my family line was only me, and my sons. No one else survived the war six centuries ago. Falcor spoke to me once, I thought about our family, *"Stop that. We did what what we could, Killian. We cannot turn back time."*

*"I wish we could. I want my brothers and sisters, Falcor."*

*"Even Calio?"*

I sighed, and replied, *"Even Calio."*

He hmphed after a moment and didn't reply. Calio was our eldest brother, and he always picked on us. We weren't up to his 'standards' and he told us we were weak. However, I wouldn't mind it now, I wish my family was here with us. The world has changed in the past few centuries since the dawn of the humans and the other supernatural. We had to make do with my form to be the sole form since we couldn't be out in about with Falcor's form he wanted to be as.

After a while, Falcor replied, *"I miss them too. Even Severi."*

That shocked me a bit. Severi was Calio's demon, and I sighed in our connection before replying, *"Me too."*

We went quiet for a moment before he spoke again, *"We rebuild our family. Starting with the werewolves, Killian. We start."*

*"Why?"*

*"I cannot say exactly, Killian, but we need to rebuild what we had. We need a strong army."*

*"What is so important that you can't tell me, Falcor? What do you know that I do not?"*

*"Sorry, Killian, was forbidden to tell you what would become."*

*"Who forbid you, Falcor?"*

*"Father."*

That caught me off guard, his father was in the underworld, same with Severi and our sisters and brothers' demon forms. Our human appearance died in the battle, but the demons just went under. The entrance to the demon world, however, was blocked off and only a demon spirit could enter. No forms can go down there.

As if he knew what I was thinking, *"Killian cannot leave his sons in the world alone. They still need your guidance."*

I smirked slightly before replying, *"I wouldn't abandon our sons, Falcor. They are yours too."*

*"Quinn has a demon. Herald does not, Killian. He a shifter."*

I frowned, and replied, *"But they have the same mother."*

*"Demon blood in Quinn. Eldest. Youngest is different. Herald is shifter. Like mother."*

*"Are you saying your gene skipped a gene, Falcor? I thought your gene gets passed regardless."*

*"Shifter blood has demon blood as is, Killian. Shifter was a creation species. To get rid of wolves."*

I paused, that was true. Humans when they won the war, had taken some of their children and forced them to become a different species. I remembered one case that was still active in the search. They called her Project 201, and she escaped with some of the children that she had there. However, one of her children died in an abandoned place, and she was found by a vampire species. However, demon blood ran in her blood, and the same with all her offspring. She was distinctly related to me because the demon blood they used was of my little sister's, Kylo. Kylo died in their laboratory, before being able to pass to the underworld.

*"Stop thinking about that, Killian. They tortured Kylo. They tortured her for her blood to make shifters."*

*"It still makes them family in a way, Falcor. Distant yes, but still blood-related."*

*"Not normal means though, Killian. They killed Kylo for their blood."*

*"It wasn't Astromic's idea to have that either, Falcor. They forced it to happen."*

*"I'm done talking about this, Killian. It makes my heart ache. Kylo was innocent."*

*"I agree, Falcor."*

We went quiet again, Falcor was still moving slowly. At least, his slowly. Before he spoke again to me, *"Killian?"*

*"Hmmm?"*

*"We okay?"*

*"Yeah, we okay, Falcor."*

He seemed to be happy for once in a long time. I let him be happy. I couldn't allow him to think anything else. It wasn't his fault, nor was it mine. History told strange stories. And we couldn't think about them. It was in the past. I sighed inwardly and allowed Falcor to continue in peace.

*****

After another hour, we got to the center of our lost civilization. This is where Falcor stopped dead in his tracks and sniffed the air. He placed his head down and sniffed the earth. He snorted once before speaking to me, "*Killian?*"

"*What do you smell, Falcor?*"

"*Humans.*"

I would have scowled if I could and he asked me something, and I frowned. For a moment, I didn't want to but my heart soared and my instincts came undone. This was my home. Not the humans. I replied after a moment, "*Go ahead, Falcor.*"

I just unleashed him from thinking ill of what he was about to do. He was about to bound forward, but I stopped him, "*Falcor, let the wolves off first.*"

"*Okay.*"

He twisted his head and spoke aloud, "Dismount. I have to clear some hostiles."

Wilson took a deep breath in and caught the human smell. His eyes kind of flashed his wolf's eye for a spilt second before he slid off of Falcor. The others follow him down. What they did though caught us both off guard; their wolves had shifted and stood in front of us. They glanced at us before blinking once.

Falcor smiled wickedly before tipping his head back and howling, their wolves followed. Then we went thundering through the undergrowth, and headed towards the human population that was going to meet our jaws of hell.

# Chapter 13

Morphous's black dragon landed in the land behind the palace and sniffed once. His eyes squinted as he sniffed again. He placed us down gently and sniffed once more. I inhaled and smelled something off. I glanced around, there were no guards. Nothing. It was eerily quiet. Morphous's dragon swung his head down to me, and rumbled, "**Stay here.**"

He was about to walk off, but I touched him, I thought for a moment that he wouldn't feel something so small. However, he swung his head down and met my eyes with a questioning look in them. I replied, "My Lord, allow me to see what's wrong. I can fit into places better than you can in this form."

I could tell that he didn't want to. However, he swung his head towards Rafeor and steam blew out his nose before he rumbled, "**So be it. Take this.**"

I glanced up at him and swallowed, he handed me a black scale, it was the size of half of me, and I swallowed again as I felt how light it was. I glanced up at him and he rumbled, "**Protection.**"

He turned towards Rafeor, and seemed lost in thought before rumbling, "**What to do with Rafeor?**"

I looked up at him and replied, "Curl up around her. Show her your strength in being there for her."

He turned his great black head towards me and rumbled, "**You wise for age.**"

I smiled slightly at the praise, before looking at the palace, and he rumbled, "**Scared?**"

I looked back at him and replied, "A little."

He seemed a little off guard by that answer, and glanced at the palace before replying, "**You tired?**"

I instinctively yawned at that and tried hard not to. He chuckled a little bit, before rumbling, "**Sleep first. Then go in.**"

I opened my mouth to retort, but he leveled me with a look, and I closed my mouth. He curled his black tail around me, and brought me closer to Rafeor, before curling into himself, keeping us in the center. He placed his head next to me and closed his eyes. His black wings folded inward, closing to us, sheltering us if it arose in need, and covering us in darkness.

*****

The ground shook beneath our feet, I glanced at Conrade before speaking, "Do you think he's back now?"

Conrade shook his head and replied, "Can't be them. It hasn't been more than two hours since they left."

I frowned, he was right. It hasn't been long since Killian left with those prisoners. However, I only feel that when Morphous's dragon lands. I glanced at Amish and Hector, and finally after making up my mind, "Hector, go check out the palace, see if Morphous is back home."

Hector bobbed his head up and down rapidly, left quickly, and disappeared outside. The door swung shut behind him. Conrade looked at me after a moment, "What do you think it is if it isn't them?"

I glanced at him and then at Amish before replying, "Wolves."

Both of their eyes flashed in anger, but they quickly became normal after a moment. They both looked away from me before Amish replied, "Any chance that it is Morphous?"

I shrugged and replied, "Possible. That boom usually only happens when his dragon lands."

Amish picked up the usual and frowned. He glanced at Conrade, before asking, "Usually?"

Conrade sighed deeply before glaring at me and replying, "It could also be the wolves coming back and breaking into the palace. At least, attempting to."

I smirked as I watched Amish fall silent and look at me again before speaking, "We don't stand a chance if it is wolves."

I sighed deeply and turned around to face the door. "Then I guess you better pray it is indeed Morphous's dragon landing then."

He didn't reply, I glanced back at him and saw him frowning. He glanced at the box and then at me before replying after a minute, "What are we guarding anyhow?"

Conrade shrugged and replied, "Honestly? Don't know. We aren't paid to ask questions though, Amish."

He frowned and was about to say something else, but I snapped, "Amish, remember what Killian said."

That stopped him, and he glanced at both of us senior guards, swallowed, and dipped his head toward me before replying softly, "Sorry, Gillith."

I shrugged, turned back towards the door, and didn't reply. Eventually, we would find out what that boom was. And I hoped with all my might, it was Morphous and not the wolves coming back.

****

I exited the office and headed towards the closest hallway, keeping my ears open for anything out of the normal eerie quiet that was now formed. Nothing. Good. I continued and went for several minutes, checking around the corners cautiously before continuing. Soon, I got to the palace landing strip that Morphous had, and I saw a black heap in the center of it. I swallowed as I exited the palace, and approached it cautiously. Sure enough, it was a black dragon. I sighed deeply, which stirred the dragon and I stumbled backward, scared.

The dragon leveled me a look before it seemed to recognize who I was before rumbling, "**At ease little one. Report, where is everyone?**" I swallowed and bowed to him before speaking. My voice was wobbly, "My Lord! Thank goodness you are home!"

He looked at me and seemed to want to close his tail in closer to what was in the center, but Quinn popped up and gently placed his hand on his back before calling out, "What news do you have, Hector?"

Morphous's dragon swung his head towards Quinn before rumbling, "**You should sleep.**"

I saw that Quinn was about to retort, but I replied after a moment, "We were attacked, my Lord, from within. The werewolves all attacked the shifters on shift and the ones in the guard rooms. We are unsure if any of them will pull through. The werewolves left soon afterward. The only ones that were ineffective my lord are, myself, Amish, Gillith, Conrade, and Killian. Killian left not two hours ago my lord, and he apparently took eight werewolf prisoners with him."

Morphous's dragon swung his head sharply at the end. "**What prisoners? I thought you said they were all gone?**"

He swallowed and moved slightly from foot to foot before replying, "I… I personally don't know, sire. I know that they were somewhere only Gillith and Conrade went to some nights."

Morphous's dragon snarled in response. His eyes flashed before rumbling, "**Those were MINE!**"

His nostrils flared outward, and smoke began to sweep out but Quinn spoke softly, "I'm sure if there was another way, my father would have taken someone else."

His head turned sharply to look at Quinn, and I had to hand it to Quinn, he held the dragon's gaze long enough for him to snort once before turning his head back to me. I swallowed and glanced up at the smoking nostrils of Morphous's dragon before I took a step backward in slight fear of him. His dragon breathed deeply once and let it out slowly. He finally got his temper under control before speaking, "**How many were taken alongside?**"

I swallowed and didn't want to reply, but I met Quinn's eyes for a brief second and saw him nod encouragingly. I gulped and whispered, "All of them, my Lord."

He seemed pissed off for a moment, muttering to himself, not in our common tongue so I had no idea what he said. However, I could see Quinn frown as if he understood what was said. However, after a moment Morphous's dragon looked back at me and sighed deeply before speaking again, "**Not your fault.**"

He swung his head to look elsewhere, and I could have sworn that if he didn't have anyone to watch, he would have gone hunting for them. I suddenly wondered what the deal was with these werewolves that made him want to go hunt for them once again.

****

Quinn glanced at Morphous's dragon and shook his head, apparently thinking the same, but didn't voice it. He glanced at me before speaking, bringing Morphous's dragon back to the conversation, "Hector, is the box safe?"

I nodded and was about to reply when a voice boomed out, "**BOX? WHAT BOX?**"

We all jerked our heads towards the voice and Morphous's dragon growled.

Out of the darkness, stepped out a man, but I couldn't tell why his voice made me shiver until a few werewolves that I recognized stepped out of the shadows too. They looked like they were ready to come after us. However, they also seemed to wait for this man's orders, so this must be the werewolf King. I swallowed, he was good-looking, tall roughly six foot eight, broad-shouldered, and lean. He was too far away from us to really tell what other features he had, but I shook my head to clear it after a moment. They picked the perfect time to come here when we were defenseless.

Morphous's dragon twirled around for a moment and snarled. His eyes sparked a dark red, and this guy looked at him and shouted, "**COME NOW ABACORE! SURELY YOU DON'T FEEL THE SAME WAY AS MORPHOUS! WE SAW EYE TO EYE AT ONE POINT!**"

Me and Quinn exchanged looks, Abacore? Who was Abacore? We glanced back at the guy, but it was clear to me that Quinn knew who was speaking. Morphous's dragon looked at him and rumbled, "**I have not forgotten. However, I cannot split my loyalties. What do you want, Nathaniel?**"

I glanced at the wolf and swallowed, so that was his name. I glanced back at Quinn, he had ducked down below Abacore's feet and came back up to the surface with Rafeor.

Nathaniel looked at her for a moment and replied, "**I want my stepdaughter Abacore. Give me Rafeor.**"

Abacore glanced down at Rafeor before rumbling, "**No.**"

Nathaniel smiled wickedly before speaking, "**Abacore. You are outnumbered. Give me my stepdaughter and I will leave peacefully. Otherwise….**"

The woods suddenly came alive, and wolves stalked out of the woods and their eyes gleamed in the moonlight. Nathaniel looked back at Abacore before continuing, "**Otherwise, we take her by force.**"

His voice deepened and I could tell that Rafeor was looking at him as if checking him out. However, where she was, Nathaniel couldn't really see her either. He just seemed to know that she was in Abacore's center area. I glanced at the opposing side and knew there was no way in hell that Abacore could defeat them all. I swallowed and took a step backward, which drew Nathaniel's attention towards me. He chuckled to himself before speaking, "**Abacore? You really want to see me kill your kin? I'll start with that shifter behind you. Then kill the one that is with Rafeor. While my pack attacks you.**"

Shuffling behind Nathaniel happened, but no one broke rank. They seemed to understand that failing to get to Rafeor would not work.

Abacore glanced at the three of us, unsure of what to do. However, Rafeor spoke, "**No one is taking me from, Morphous.**"

That caught everyone's attention. Rafeor stepped out of Abacore's protection and glowered at the wolves before rumbling, "**DOWN!**"

The werewolves dropped to their stomachs and whined. However, it also affected us too. I wanted to bow to her, but I fought it. I squared my shoulders and forced myself to be steady. Man, was she powerful? I could see that Nathaniel was also forcing his Lycan to be steady himself. The sweat smell came off of him in waves.

Rafeor glowered. "**I am currently happy with where I am, Nathaniel. If I need or want to learn my history with my brother kin, then I shall. Not before, and definitely not by force.**"

Nathaniel swallowed before replying, "**Don't you want to meet your mother? She is my mate.**"

Rafeor paused, looked at him, and replied, "**Not yet. I just met my father not three days ago. And I have already been brought against my will to your dungeons by your pack members. Like I said, I want to learn my father's ways BEFORE I approached you for learning your way.**"

He seemed to be perplexed by that. He replied after a moment, "**Why wait any longer Rafeor? I could make your life a living dream.**"

She growled in her throat, and her eyes changed color for a flash of a moment. She replied, "**I am not ready. I will come to you when I am.**"

Nathaniel looked at Abacore and saw his eyes were fixed on him as if challenging him to do something against her wishes. Nathaniel dropped his fists for a moment to his sides before rumbling, "**How long do you need?**"

She looked at him and replied, "**I don't know yet. I promise though that I will come to you when I am ready to.**"

Nathaniel's men kept glancing at him as if trying to make him choose violence but he seemed to think long and hard before looking at Abacore. "**If I hear that she is treated without proper care…**"

Abacore rumbled in his throat, "**You think I would allow that to happen, Nathaniel?**"

Nathaniel opened his mouth to reply but stopped himself. He glanced up at him before shaking his head and looking at Rafeor, "**My home is open to you, Rafeor. Solely to you.**"

Then he backed up and looked at his people, and seemed to discuss with his people before they turned around and left.

*****

We waited another hour as if to make sure that none of them would come back, but there was no movement again. We glanced at each other for a moment but said nothing. We shifted the conversation away from the box, but for how long? That was my question.

Quinn looked at Abacore and swallowed before speaking, "Is your name Abacore?"

Morphous's dragon swung his head down before rumbling, "**Yes.**"

I saw Quinn struggle to ask a question but I was pretty sure we had the same one, "Why Abacore? Who picked that name?"

Abacore looked at him before rumbling, "**I did.**"

Quinn and I exchanged glances and then Rafeor spoke, "**It's a pretty name.**"

I glanced at her and replied, "And yours? What is your name?"

She looked away and replied, "**I don't know. Nothing has come to my senses on what my name is.**"

I was about to say something, but Quinn shook his head, and I stopped. I glanced at Abacore before sighing deeply. He glanced down at me and rumbled after a moment, "**We are all tired. However, unprotected in elements. We go inside.**"

I nodded in response and went towards the entrance to the palace. I glanced back and saw Quinn and Rafeor following. Abacore was staring at where the werewolves had come into our territory. I cleared my throat, he swung his head towards me and sighed before he allowed Morphous to shift back.

# Chapter 14

We ran into the human encampment and the first human that met my fangs was a male. He tried to scream for help, but his head easily fit into my mouth, and I snapped his head easily. This human was on the border outside of the encampment, which meant he was a watcher. I glanced at my pack members before grinning wickedly, I pointed my snout to the right, and let out a woof, and then two disappeared that way, and another two disappeared in the opposite way. They knew what I wanted to do. Circle the encampment, and make sure no stragglers escape.

The rest of us went deeper into the human encampment. Their homes were made out of brick, something that you needed time to make, I sniffed around, and I heard a common dog bark. I woofed at it to be quiet. It went whining back home, with its tail between its legs. I chuckled to myself. I was going to have fun tonight.

****

I followed Falcor, along with Savador, Trevoric, and Fantar. We glanced around and saw that the humans had made their homes permanent and I could tell by the way the others were moving that they didn't really want to uproot these humans anymore. However, after watching Falcor rip the head off of the human that was guarding his home, was the point that made us follow him deeper.

Savador spoke to me in our connection, something that Morphous couldn't take away from us, *"What are we doing here? We just escaped prison and now we are here to kill peaceful people where they sleep?"*

I sighed in response before replying, *"Can't really argue all too much now, Savador."*

*"Yes, we can. If we all team up against Falcor, we could get away from him. We could live our own lives."*

*"Then what? Half of us will be killed, or all of us. Falcor even warned us against it. And did you notice how swiftly he took that sentry's head off?"*

*"I noticed, but I doubt that he can do it to all of us at once. We can take him down, Wilson. You just don't want to."*

*"I didn't say that."*

*"But you thought it too."*

I sighed in the connection again and broadened the connection to connect to everyone, *"Savador wants to attack Falcor. What say you?"*

A bunch of silence replies and after a moment, I thought that no one was going to reply, but after a moment Topaz replied, *"That's a death wish."*

*"No, it's not. At least, we could try it. These are peaceful people Topaz, they live harmoniously. Are we really going to slaughter an entire population of humans?"*

*"They would do us though, Savador,"* said Averic.

I could tell that Savador wanted to say something else, but Falcor paused and suddenly looked back at us. His purple eyes glowed before he spoke, "Treason behavior happening?"

Savador blanched and did not look at Falcor. Falcor looked at us all before snarling, "Well? Should I kill you all?"

I glanced at everyone who was with me before replying, "No, Falcor."

He turned his eyes to me before growling, "Then kill."

He broke open a door, forced himself inside, and screams filled the air as the occupants were slaughtered where they were. My stomach turned, but I looked at each and every one behind me and swallowed. I went towards a house, barreled through it, and let my wolf have full reins. There was no reason why I should enjoy what he did.

*****

Nearly an hour later, the sun slowly rose, and the entire human village was dead. Except for a few here and there. Falcor stood in the center, his jaw dripping with blood and the guts of his prey. I sat down farther away from him. I bowed my head, what my wolf did, what we both did… was unspeakable. However, it seemed that Falcor ravished in the gore and seemed at one with it.

After a minute, everyone else came forward, and they had similar looks on their faces, they didn't want to kill everyone. Their wolves did, but they didn't. A human ran out of a house and screamed as she looked at Falcor. She tried to run away, she was closer to Savador though, and he glanced at Falcor and Falcor stared at him. As if challenging him to challenge him. Savador glanced at me before leaping after her, and bringing her death. Her scream cut short, and then her body went limp.

Savador turned to look at me before sitting down where she was. He looked away from her corpse before Falcor spoke, "Good kill."

I glanced at Savador and begged him with my eyes to not say anything, but he turned quickly around and growled, "What is your problem with the humans? These were living peacefully."

Falcor blinked once and after a moment, he glanced around at us and concluded that we didn't know. He sighed before replying, "Centuries ago, humans took over our homeland. Killed my family, and created the shifters."

The shock written across their faces proved that they didn't know and Falcor bowed his head before speaking, "Falcor blames humans. We were a peaceful community, they came in the night, slaughtering all within their path. Similar to what we did, but in the hundreds. They swarmed us, they burned us out of our homes, and the screams of my brotherhood were loud. They killed, and killed and killed until only I was alive."

We all swallowed. We glanced at each other and seemed to come to the same conclusion, that the humans of the past were monsters. Savador whispered, "Not all humans have the same motives as they once did, Falcor."

He looked at us and snarled but rumbled after a moment, "They are the ancestors of these humans. I watched as the humans took our homeland. Made it so I couldn't be surfaced. Forced me to be in Killian's form day after day after DAY!"

He swallowed and finally concluded to say something else, "All humans are the same. They take, take, take. But never give. My family is dead because of humans."

His head hung low, and he seemed to have ended his rant. I glanced at Savador and saw his face, it was full of pity. I looked at everyone else's and saw a similar look, they didn't seem to understand it either.

I swallowed, I knew. I knew the pain that Falcor mentioned. My family, besides my father's side, was polite and were easy pushovers, but the humans saw one of them shift and gathered the town together and killed half of my family tree before my grandfather got home. That massacre was massive, not even grandfather wanted to talk about that when it happened or to teach us younger generations about it. He was sorrowful that he wasn't there to stop it.

I looked at Falcor before speaking, "Half of my family is dead too because of the humans, Falcor. It happened a few generations back."

I swallowed, since I now had my unit's attention, they didn't know about this, "My grandfather was out hunting for food. So, he was not there to protect his pack. A werewolf shifted near a population of humans that were moving closer to our territory, expanding into our territory. A human was in the woods, and it came back with enough force to kill half of my pack on my mother's side."

Tevoric looked at me sharply, he was one of the older wolves in my unit who was wise enough to stand down before Morphous's dragon. He seemed to have at least heard of that slaughter by the look he was giving me. I glanced up and saw that Falcor had moved closer to me. I turned my head to the right, to break eye contact with everyone.

Falcor spoke closer to me, "Then what happened? Did your grandfather lead a fight?"

I swallowed and knew that I had said a bit too much of my family line before shaking my head in response. Falcor sat down and wrapped his tail around himself before sitting up and squinting at me. He rumbled, "He ran?"

I glowered at him when he said that and growled, "He brought his kin that survived away from further harm, Falcor. We allowed the humans to think that they killed us all."

Falcor blinked once and looked away, and I gestured to the slaughter around us before speaking again, "Would your family be proud of this, Falcor? Would they want to know that their brother could handle this massacre?"

I should have kept my mouth shut. Falcor glowered at me for a moment before a deep rumble came out of him and he barked out, "They would have rejoiced in this! They would be proud of what I had done!"

I frowned and was about to say something but he stopped being excited as I heard Killian's voice, "But you also must understand, Falcor, that this was something that other supernatural beings do not do. You are a demon, you thrive in the chaos, they don't."

I glanced at Falcor and saw Killian's eyes for a split second before he disappeared. Falcor bowed his head slightly before looking at me and speaking, "Killian is correct. My family would have rejoiced in this slaughter since it would rejuvenate us, however, I somewhat understand. All this death lingers with someone for a long time. I still hear my sister's screams, I hear my mother screaming for me to run. More importantly, I hear Calio's voice telling me to flee. Something that I thought he would never utter. The humans killed, and killed. I barely escaped with my life."

I swallowed, I knew that Falcor was grieving but I looked around at my unit members, and saw a few hanging their heads down. They didn't want to meet my gaze, but one glanced up and blinked at me. They understood my pain.

Savador spoke after a few minutes, "Wilson, why didn't you say anything before about this?"

I glanced at him and replied, "Because my grandfather would not want me to. I know he's gone now, but he's probably rolling in his grave at this point."

Savador looked at me and smirked. I made a joke about my grandfather, one that if he was still alive would skin me alive for it.

Falcor spoke after a few minutes of silence, "We leave now. If any survivors, leave them."

He turned around and began to walk slowly towards the north as if he knew where his home was.

# Chapter 15

I left the prison cells, heading away from Morphous's dragon, and watched as the werewolves scrambled to get the prisoners out of their cells. They clamped iron cuffs onto all the able prisoners and hurried them along. I stopped walking and watched. My men knew their duties well.

Soon, I exited the prison and went to the palace, where I knew I would most likely find him. I went inside and sure enough, I saw him lounging around. I called out to him, "**Ravean?**"

He glanced up at me and kind of snarled, "**That is my wolf's name and you know it!**"

I smirked and replied, "**True.**"

He rolled his eyes and flipped up the newspaper he was reading, covering his face with it. I rolled my eyes before coming towards him and snatched his paper up. He blinked once and snapped, "**UGH! What do you want, Nathaniel?**"

I let his paper down before looking around, we were not alone in the room, so I spoke, "**Dismissed.**"

The staff instantly bowed and left quickly, however, one lingered longer than the rest, and eyed me up and down before she left. I rolled my eyes, everyone knew that I had a mate, but Ravean hadn't found his yet. He scowled, folded up his paper, and set it on the armrest of the couch before leveling me with a blank stare. I smirked before speaking, "**Any thought on what I had asked you to do, Ravean?**"

He bared his teeth, but after a moment his wolf rumbled, "**Thought yes, and I want to do it. However, Tobias doesn't.**"

I sighed deeply and replied, "**Tobias? Why don't you want to do this?**"

His wolf handed him the reins again, and he sighed deeply before glowering at me and replying, "**What do you want me to do exactly, Nathaniel? Go in and raid the other separated packs and combine them into one. Who would be the alpha, all their current alphas are not going to hand over their title willingly.**"

I sighed deeply before replying, "**We need the manpower, Tobias, it's either you do it, or I do it.**"

He glowered at me and growled, "**I vote you do it. Has it never occurred to you that YOU are the ENTIRE species KING?  They will listen to you, but they won't listen to a lowly royal wolf like myself.**"

*****

I was about to retort, when someone came into the room and plopped down into an armchair behind us. I could tell by Tobias's scowl that it was our middle brother, Logan. They didn't get along. I turned around slightly and eyed him before speaking, "**Dismissed, Logan.**"

He smirked and replied, "**Why? If Tobias is too weak to do what needs to be done, why won't you allow someone who wants to do it?**"

I glanced back at Tobias and replied, "**Tobias is the one I want to do this, Logan. Not you.**"

Logan stood up, he towered slightly before he growled, and his eyes flashed in anger. He was an inch taller but I looked at him sharply and let my wolf's eyes come to the surface, he instantly flinched back. He dropped his eyes from me after a moment, and his wolf let out a whine. He swallowed before speaking, "**Nathaniel, please, let me do something. I am older than Tobias. Why are you going to prefer him over me?**" I looked at both of them and sighed deeply. My reasons would normally not get questioned as they were now with my brothers. I loved them dearly, mind you, but they grated on my nerves. I ran my hand through my hair before replying, "**Because I know Tobias will have a leveled hand in what needs to be done, Logan. Sure, you want to do it, but your pride would get in the way of what needs to happen.**"

He went quiet, and I glanced at Tobias and knew that he knew I was correct. Logan, as much as he is older, isn't capable of doing this correctly. There would be too many casualties if he was the one in charge of this.

Logan sighed deeply and spoke, "**I guess that is a fair point. I know I need to work on my pridefulness that I have, however, I know with time you will regret choosing him, Nathaniel.**"

He turned around and walked out of the room. Leaving us alone again.

*****

I looked at Tobias and raised my eyebrows at him. He spoke, "**Is there no one else with the same qualities as I do, Nathaniel?**"

**"No one I trust as completely as I do with you,"** I replied.

He sighed deeply and rubbed his right hand across his face before replying, **"Alright. Fine, I will do as you ask."**

I smiled and was about to leave the room when he spoke up, **"Nathaniel?"**

I stopped, looked at him, and raised an eyebrow before replying, **"Huh?"**

He stood up and towered over me by two inches, but he didn't have the aura to intimidate me entirely. Sure, he had his moments, but it was a rare occasion that he let it out. He smirked and angled his head down slightly before speaking, **"Why did I hear Abacore earlier?"**

I opened my mouth to retort but he raised his eyebrows. I sighed deeply and glanced back where Logan left off before replying, **"Let's go to my office. Where we won't get overheard at."**

He frowned but didn't challenge it. We went further into the palace and soon came to my royal office. I let him in before entering myself, locking the door behind me.

*****

I left my brothers alone in the sitting room and stalked towards the bar section. As werewolves, the only booze that could affect us is homemade moonshine, I grabbed the biggest bottle that I could before ripping off the cork and downing it. The liquid burned on the way down, sizzling in my mouth. I slammed the bottle back down on the bar, shocked that it didn't break under my force. No one else was inside, it was barely six o'clock in the morning. However, my wolf warned me we weren't alone after our second swing of the moonshine. I set the bottle down, looked over to the entrance of the bar, and there stood a maid. She was cute, but not my type either. I raised my eyebrows at her before turning to my booze and growling out, **"Leave me."**

She didn't leave, she instead approached me and wrapped her hands around my midsection before reaching up, and running her fingers gently across my arms, creating goosebumps wherever they trailed. I lowered my head and breathed heavily. After a moment, I turned around and faced her before growling, **"I said leave me."**

She looked up into my eyes before replying, "But I don't want to."

I gripped her by her throat and picked her up. She clawed at my hands, trying to pry them off. I squeezed tighter and I let spittle fly from my mouth as I growled, **"It wasn't a request. Leave me."**

I tossed her across the room, and she whacked the wall, shaking the room. However, the bar had proper railings for the drinks. They rattled but they didn't fall. Probably after sweeping up glass whenever I lose my temper made them do that.

She got up weakly and collapsed after a moment before trying again. Soon, she crawled out of the room, leaving me alone. I smirked and turned back to my bottle, taking another swing.

****

A passing guard stopped and saw a trail of blood, followed it, and found a girl. She was shaking and trying to crawl up the stairs. I hurried forward and spoke, "What happened?"

She looked at me, thank goodness she was breathtaking. My wolf sang in my head, and I reached down to help her when the tingles ran up both of us. I gasped and she did too, before whispering, "Mate?"

I smiled down at her and nodded, a tear in my eye before I glanced at her completely. My wolf was in rage at the sight of her before I got him under control, and asked, "Who did this to you?"

She looked down and whispered after a moment, "Prince Logan. I wanted to make sure he was okay. He flung me across the room."

I gritted my teeth, there was a reason why Nathaniel did not allow him to do much more than drink his life away, and this was the main reason. His rage got the better of him more than once and common folk would be the ones who got the worse of his rage. I glanced back where the trail came from and frowned, normally no one was in the bar area at this time of day. However, knowing Logan, it didn't matter the time of day when he started drinking. I sighed deeply and spoke after a moment, "Can I help you stand?"

She nodded, and I picked her up slowly, she winced in response, but I couldn't do anything. The last time a guard approached Logan when he harmed someone weaker than himself was the time that Nathaniel had to get involved. And that was not a good day either. I glanced down at her before asking, "What is your name, beautiful? And why isn't your wolf helping you heal?"

She stared at me, swallowed, and looked down before replying, "If I tell you my name, are you going to reject me?"

My wolf howled in my head, and I cringed at how loud he was being before I shook my head and whispered, "No, you are mine. Why ask that immediately?"

Before she could answer, a woman stood at the top of the stairs, and called down, "There you are! You worthless lump!"

My wolf's eyes lit my face before I snarled, "She is not worthless!"

The woman blinked once and glanced down at the girl in my arms before replying, "My apologies. However, this one has no wolf spirit in her. She never got one when she turned thirteen."

I glanced down at my mate and saw her swallow hard, which meant that she had no one to help heal her, and my wolf whined softly. The pain she must be in right now. I glanced back at the woman before replying, "I don't care if she doesn't have a wolf or not. Norjor and I don't care."

The woman blinked her eyes and scoffed before replying, "What difference does it make to you?"

I glanced down again at my mate before replying, "She is my mate."

The woman swallowed and replied, "Then you know what you need to do, right?"

I glowered at her, and she simply raised her head slightly higher before speaking, "She has not a wolf to heal her. She is worthless to the werewolf kingdom. Anyone else would reject her and choose someone who would produce children without the risk…."

In a flash, I was up the stairs and snarled, "Do not complete that sentence! She is my MATE and I am the only one who will love her as she deserves."

She swallowed and lowered her eyes to me before she glanced away. She shuffled her feet for a moment before replying, "You are on the same level as I am in ranking here. Yet I want to appease you."

I smirked before replying, "My name is Finn Dragonheart, my father was Xavier Dragonheart. I am one of the only guards left here that has that last name. I wear it with honor."

She glanced sharply at me before growling, "The same Xavier that went missing twelve years ago? That one?"

My wolf pressed forward, and he underscored my voice, "Same one. And I would suggest you do your best not to fucking antagonize me."

She bared her throat and looked away from me finally. I snapped slightly before she got the message and left me be.

****

I went back down the stairs and helped my mate once again, who had heard everything. She looked down before whispering, "Why won't you reject me, Finn? I will not bring anything special to the relationship. You will be mocked…."

I placed my fingers gently on her mouth, she looked up and swallowed. I looked down at her lovingly before replying, "Rank does not bother me…. What is your name, love?"

She swallowed before replying, "Aurelius. My name is Aurelius Fiore."

I smiled and repeated her name, "Aurelius, it means the golden one. You are beautiful and I will not stand it if you don't believe so. If I need to, I will make everyone know that you are mine, and mine alone."

She giggled slightly before she winced and clutched her side, I swallowed and Norjor spoke in my mind for once in a while, he normally only spoke to me if something was upsetting him, *"Mark her so I heal her."*

*"It's too soon to do that, Norjor. I don't want to rush her. This is her life too."*

*"She in pain though. Ask her, Finn. Ask her if I can."*

I looked back down at Aurelius before speaking, "Norjor would like to mark you, so you can heal."

She looked at me before shaking her head slightly and whispering, "There is no going back if you do that. You will forever be stuck to me."

She lowered her head after a moment, a fat tear rolling out of her eye before she whispered, "I, Aurelius Fiore, reject…."

I clamped my hand across her mouth, looking disdained at her. I whispered, "Why? Why would you even think of doing that?"

She looked sorrowful before whispering, "You are a Dragonheart. Me? I am nothing, Finn."

My wolf surfaced and he glowered at her. She flinched slightly before looking at him with love in her eyes as if she knew he would never hurt her. He buried our face into her neck before murmuring below her ear, "You are not worthless. You are MINE! I want to mark you, Aurelius. I want to so badly, that I am not merely because Finn said I cannot immediately mark you. How I want to though. You are perfect for me, for us. You will help us heal. We both need to heal, love."

She pulled away from him slightly and locked eyes with him for a moment before wrapping her hands around his neck and burying her head into our neck. She was crying, Norjor cradled her to him, and she instinctively wrapped her legs around his torso when he stood up. We trudged upstairs before getting to our room.

*****

I turned around to find Tobias looking around the room as if making sure that no one was in the room. However, after a moment he turned to face me and spoke, "**Why here?**"

I sighed deeply before replying, "**Because I don't want anyone else hearing this….**"

I walked towards my desk, gripped the edge of it, and after a minute asked, "**Did you know that my mate and Morphous were a pair before she found me?**"

His heartbeat was slightly out of rhythm and I glanced at him, making sure my Lycan wouldn't surface completely, "**Did you?**"

He sighed deeply and sat down on an armchair before replying, "**I knew they were together. Caught them a few times too in the act.**"

I growled and my Lycan surfaced slightly. He raised his eyebrows at me before speaking, "**Hey! Easy there, Basil. Nathaniel is asking the questions here.**"

Basil descended out of my eyes and I swallowed before replying, "**You knew all this time and didn't tell me? Why not?**"

He raised his eyebrows at me and replied, "**Because she ended things with him when she found out YOU WERE HER MATE, Nathaniel. Although, I know that they had a child together. And that she gave the said child to Morphous. When the riot happened though, I do know also that Morphous told her that the child was lost in the chaos.**"

I froze, the wording he used in the last sentence, sounded as if he knew. I turned to face him and leveled him with a glower, questioning it, "**Why does it seem you know something about their child, Tobias?**"

He scowled and I could have sworn he wished I was different than I was, fat chance at that. He finally after a moment replied, "**The child is still alive. I know because I helped Morphous get her out of the chaos that was happening. I sold her to a human trafficking place, and that is where I last saw her.**"

I stared at him and I was shocked. He would never do that to a child, Logan though. Yeah, I would see Logan doing that, but not Tobias. I stared at him, Basil was as shocked as I was upon finding that information out.

He turned slightly and looked at the portraits of the fore-kings before speaking again, "**I know you have questions and stuff, Nathaniel. However, I did it for another reason. Remember what grandfather said about the prophecy?**"

It took me a moment before I remembered and nodded slowly. He continued, "**That the child that is born between both werewolf and shifter would one day rule either OR of our species. The child would be a great weapon since the child would have the ability to have the same factors as the shifters, and the wolf counterpart, in her case, I believe she has a Lycan.**"

I glanced sharply at him and growled, "**How do you know that she has a Lycan?**"

I tried hard this time to make sure that Basil did not surface, but he wanted to creep into my voice so badly. However, I forced him down. Tobias sighed deeply before replying, "**Cause I kept tabs on where she ended up, Nathaniel. She ended up in a human mansion. Off of either of our territories. In the south.**"

I frowned and stared at him, and asked, "**Why keep tabs on her?**"

He swallowed and replied, "**As much as I like you ruling, Nathaniel, she will eventually come for her crown. She is after all a royal too. Considering that Morphous is the king of the shifters, and your mate is the queen of the werewolves. Yes sure, she was not exactly supposed to be created. However, it happened and she is the product of love, Nathaniel. If anything, I would actually suggest you go back onto the shifter territory and force them to hand her over.**"

I frowned, and replied, "**Force? Why force?**"

He raised his eyebrows and replied after a moment, "**Nathaniel, she is a hybrid. The first hybrid between our species. What did our Druid camp say about the child, Nathaniel?**"

I frowned and it suddenly clicked. She would be the most powerful being in the entire supernatural world and whoever had the hybrid and channeled the ability, it means that the child was theirs to command. I frowned before speaking, "**How do you know that the shifters are weak right now?**"

He sighed and I knew instantly that he had done something that I would probably not understand in any given way. He was cantankerous in that aspect. When he wanted to do something, he usually did it without asking for forgiveness afterward. But it was usually all within reason, which was why he was still my top person to do what I wanted him to do.

After a moment, he spoke, "**I sent werewolves inside of the shifter palace as guards. I signed waivers for them and everything.**"

I was shocked, so that was why not all werewolves were home either. That made sense as to why they didn't all come back after the riot. I frowned and replied after a few moments, "**Did you do this right after the riot? Is that what happened to Dragonheart and Droon?**"

He sighed deeply before shaking his head in response, and replied after a moment, "**No, I unfortunately don't know where they went. However, they are highly missed by all. Especially by the children they left behind.**"

I frowned, I had forgotten that they had children, but I was glad that at least one of my siblings cared about our people. I turned to face my desk and looked at the African dark wood, so pretty in color. I didn't respond.

After a minute of silence, Tobias spoke, "**Nathaniel, I would personally go myself to get the girl, however, you know her by name at this point. I doubt that your mate was able to ignore Basil's order. And besides the fact, that you had Morphous in the dungeons.**"

I froze, slowly turned around, and was about to ask how he knew, but I stopped myself. He knew quite a bit about what happened in the palace and surrounding areas, including what my mate and I partake in some evenings. That sly dog. He smirked as if he knew what I was thinking before speaking, "**We both have things to do, Nathaniel. I will do the rallying for the separate packs, and combine them into one. You need to go get the girl. With force.**"

I scowled and stood up. I hated sometimes that he was taller than I was, but I knew he did not use that as an excuse to be a prick like Logan. I sighed deeply and he clamped his right hand on my shoulder before speaking, "**Hang in there. Also, if the girl refuses, allow her to stay where she is.**"

I stared at him and growled, "**Why would I do that?**"

He glanced at me and smirked before replying, "**Because we want her ultimately on our side. And forcing someone to be on our side is not something that we need to do. If she refuses to come willingly, then allow her to make that choice. But also tell her that she is welcome to come home any time that she wants, Nathaniel. She'll come around in a few weeks, I'm sure.**"

He started to move towards the door, but I called out, "**Where are you going, Tobias?**"

He stopped, turned around, and replied, "**Doing exactly what I need to do. You have your role in this, Nathaniel. I have mine. I know that. You know that. We all know what we need to do. I will let you do as you please, but the drugs in the shifters' guards are going to wear themselves out soon. Better hurry, brother.**"

I opened my mouth, but he unlocked the door and exited, closing the door behind him.

****

I sighed deeply before grumbling. If it was anyone besides Tobias, I wouldn't follow his directions. However, Tobias is a sneaky guy and he pretended to not want the job I had in mind, I knew it was highly because he wanted to see me beg for him to do it.

After a moment of watching the candle drip down into nothing, I grabbed my jacket, closed my eyes, and Basil boomed out on the guard communications, *"All able wolves. We are going to go after what Morphous has. His daughter."*

I closed the link, knowing that I would not be refused. I smirked internally, went out of my office, went to the room next door, opened it up, and armed myself to the teeth with weapons. Not too many to be bulky but enough that I wouldn't need Basil to come out to play either. He grumbled in response at that, but he understood at the same time why. He was unpredictable.

We got out and half of the guards were ready to go. And I glanced at everyone before taking them toward the shifter territory.

*****

We got to the border of the shifter territory, it was on the side of the landing area that I knew for a fact that Morphous made it so Abacore could land without issues. I saw a few people talking, and I heard one mention a box. Tobias didn't mention anything about a box. I glanced at everyone and commanded that they stay where they were, before I boomed out, **"BOX? WHAT BOX?"**

Their heads all turned sharply to face me, and Abacore growled at me.

I stepped out of the gathering shadows, and a few of my fellow wolves stepped forward, not to challenge my order, but to show support. I could tell that the ones before me were figuring out that I was important. I knew, at that moment, they realized that they were defenseless I suddenly understood why Tobias had told me to come now overall. They didn't have guards.

Abacore twisted to stare at me, and snarled in response, his eyes darkening to a dangerous red, and I shouted, **"COME NOW, ABACORE! SURELY YOU DON'T FEEL THE SAME WAY AS MORPHOUS! WE SAW EYE TO EYE AT ONE POINT!"**

I could also see that Morphous did not tell anyone who his dragon was, simply by how the people surrounding him reacted to the name. Interesting. I was drawn back out of what I was thinking when Abacore rumbled, **"I have not forgotten. However, I cannot split my loyalties. What do you want, Nathaniel?"**

After a moment, I saw that the one that was within Abacore's center dropped down and came back up with Rafeor. The exact person I wanted. I looked at her for a moment before replying, "**I want my stepdaughter, Abacore. Give me, Rafeor.**"

Abacore glanced down at Rafeor before rumbling, "**No.**"

I smiled wickedly before speaking, "**Abacore. You are outnumbered. Give me my stepdaughter and I will leave peacefully. Otherwise….**"

I looked back at the forest, and my kin came forward, their eyes glowing in the moonlight. I looked back at Abacore before continuing, "**Otherwise, we take her by force.**"

My voice deepened as Basil tried to surface. I noticed that Rafeor was checking me out though, at least, that was what Basil sensed, I couldn't directly see her from where she was. I noticed that the shifter behind Abacore was checking my rankings out as if concluding that there was no way that they could survive fighting all of us. The shifter took a step backward and drew my immediate attention. I chuckled to myself before speaking, "**Abacore? You really want to see me kill your kin? I'll start with that shifter behind you. Then kill the one that is with Rafeor. While my pack attacks you.**"

Some shuffled behind me but no one broke rank. They seemed to understand that failing to get to Rafeor would not work, especially when Basil was out to play.

Abacore glanced at all three, and that was when Rafeor spoke, "**No one is taking me from Morphous.**"

That caught everyone's attention. Rafeor stepped out of Abacore's protection and glowered at my pack before rumbling, "**DOWN!**"

They dropped to their stomachs and whined. However, it also affected the shifters too. The shifter in the back seemed to want to bow to her, but he somehow didn't.  I was also forcing my Lycan to be steady himself. The sweat smell came off in waves off of me. It was not easy to make Basil stop himself from shifting at the challenge.

Rafeor glowered at me before growling, "**I am currently happy with where I am, Nathaniel. If I need or want to learn my history with my brother kin, then I shall. Not before, and definitely not by force.**"

I swallowed before replying, "**Don't you want to meet your mother? She is my mate.**"

Rafeor paused, looked at me, and replied, "**Not yet. I just met my father not three days ago. And I have already been brought against my will to your dungeons by your pack members. Like I said, I want to learn my father's ways BEFORE I approach you for learning your way.**"

I seemed to be perplexed by that for a moment. I replied, **"Why wait any longer, Rafeor? I could make your life a living dream."**

She growled in her throat, and her eyes changed color for a flash of a moment. She replied, **"I am not ready. I will come to you when I am."**

I knew that Abacore was staring hard at me as if he was challenging me to do something that she physically didn't want to do. After a moment, I dropped my fists on my sides before rumbling, **"How long do you need?"**

She looked at me and replied, **"I don't know yet. I promise though that I will come to you when I am ready to."**

My men kept glancing at me as if trying to make me choose violence but I seemed to think long and hard before looking at Abacore. **"If I hear that she is treated without proper care…"**

Abacore rumbled in his throat, **"You think I would allow that to happen, Nathaniel?"**

I opened my mouth to reply but stopped myself. I glanced up at him before shaking my head and looking at Rafeor, speaking, **"My home is open to you, Rafeor. Solely to you."**

I backed away, and called through the communications, *"Back off."*

My pack members begrudgingly backed off and left with me. Leaving the shifters to sit there alone.

*****

After we got into our territory, did a wolf speak, "My Lord?"

I stopped, turned my headm and he dipped his head to me before speaking, "If I may?"

I motioned for him to continue, already knowing what everyone else was wondering too, "Why go through the efforts of what we did without getting Rafeor? Wasn't she the one you wanted?"

I sighed deeply before rumbling, **"Trust me, I ask all of you to trust me. There was a reason behind that."**

My voice held a firm 'do not challenge,' vibe, and the wolves all bowed their head in submission. We continued, and I soon was wondering why Tobias said let her be where she was. Then it dawned on me on the why. She had to come to me to be a willing weapon. I smiled wickedly to myself, all I needed to do now was wait for Morphous to screw up enough to make her come to me.

****

We got back to the palace and the wolves were released to do what they wanted. I walked in and looked around, I could smell the high stench of moonshine and knew who was already drinking at this ungodly hour. I rolled my eyes as I entered the bar. Sure enough, Logan stood at the bar and he growled, "**Leave me.**"

He said it without turning, meaning he thought I was a lowly wolf. Not surprising, since whenever he drank, he drank to forget what he was. I didn't budge, I kept Basil reigned in, so he didn't let his aura out. Logan without looking picked up the bottle he was drinking, and drained it before he threw it toward me. It crashed into the wall next to me, Basil surfaced in my eyes and he boomed out, "**ENOUGH OF THIS MADNESS!**"

He let his aura roll out, a power that made anyone within a mile feel the effects. Logan dropped down to his knee, crossed his arm, and panted under Basil's force. Basil's eyes flashed before he growled, "**No drinking before three o'clock, Logan.**"

Logan groaned against his command, but I knew his wolf would obey Basil and he lowered his eyes to the floor. No one would be able to challenge Basil. Last of all, Logan.

I turned to leave and Basil drew in his aura so that no one bowed to him as he put Logan into his place. That was when Logan spoke, "**Weak dog.**"

Basil froze, I tried to talk to him, but he cut me out, shit. I tried to alpha command him, but nothing worked. Basil turned around and growled, "**Excuse you?**"

His voice dropped to a whisper, a sure sign to anyone rational to take back what they said. However, Logan was not the rational one. He locked eyes with Basil before growling, "**Weak dog.**"

Basil growled and was about to approach him quickly, but then Tobias spoke from behind us, "**Basil.**"

Basil froze and looked back at Tobias with hard eyes, and Tobias didn't drop his gaze. He stared directly into Basil's eyes and spoke softly, "**Don't.**"

Basil glanced at Logan and bared his teeth, but turned away, knowing that what he wanted to do would look horrible on our end. Leaving Logan in the bar area alone.

***

Basil bowed his head, allowed me to surface again, and I gasped before muttering, "**Damn it.**"

Tobias rested his hand on my shoulder before speaking, "**Don't beat yourself up, Nathaniel. He gets on everyone's nerves.**"

I sighed deeply before replying, "**But I should….**"

Tobias stopped and raised his eyebrow and growled, "**You were gifted Basil for a reason, Nathaniel. If Logan had gotten a Lycan it would have been catastrophic with how he would do things. I would be overrun with the Lycan. For the most part, Nathaniel, except every now and then, does Basil override your wishes, but rarely. You two work mainly well together. Keep your head up.**"

He wandered away, and I frowned. He did not ask about Rafeor, but I had an assumption that he knew that she would reject coming by force. I sighed deeply, turned to my chambers, and went towards them. It has been a long ass night.

# Chapter 16

We followed Falcor towards the north, we were still in our wolf form, but it didn't seem to bother Falcor since he did not ask for us to shift back to ride him. Soon after a half hour, we came up upon ruins. Falcor looked around them before bowing his head as if he remembered something. We glanced around wildly and our wolves were sorrowful, I didn't understand why. Falcor spoke, "This was my home before it was raided. That ruin over to the right was the bakery. The one next to it was the butcher's shop. The ones on the left were clothing and winery. We weren't a savage people. We had differences that the humans didn't understand at the time they attacked."

He seemed lost for a moment, I looked at Savador before I glanced at Averic. I noticed that his wolf was sniffing the air again. Falcor had his back to us, but Averic growled low in his throat and that caught Falcor's attention. He turned and sniffed deeply, growled, and looked around. We were not alone here either.

I sniffed deeply, but I didn't recognize the scent. It was clear that Averic didn't either since he looked at me with a confused look. Falcor, however, took a deep breath in and blinked once. I could tell he knew the smell, but it was probably years since he last smelled it. After a moment, he allowed Killian to shift. Much to our dislike, since he shifted back at the werewolf border, and shredded his clothing. Killian, however, seemed not sorry and called out, "I KNOW YOU ARE                    HERE!                    COME                    OUT!" For a moment, nothing happened and a voice came out, "About dang time that you arrived."

A figure stepped out and the shock written across Killian's face was all that needed to be said – he thought that this person was dead. He whispered, "Calio?"

I looked at the guy before me and saw some of the resemblances between Killian and Calio. I swallowed what was going to happen now that they knew each other? I was drawn out of my thoughts as Calio replied, "The one and only Killian. You have grown soft over the last six centuries. It was a mutt that sensed my presence before you did."

I stared at him before speaking up, "And how would he have known you were alive? He said you all died."

Calio snapped his head towards me and I cowered slightly. Falcor's eyes were red. I dropped my gaze from him and trembled before him. He was about to approach me, but Falcor spoke, "Calio, they are mine to discipline."

He stopped and glowered at him before growling, "Then DISCIPLINE them Falcor? Or have YOU gone soft?"

His voice was slightly different, and I saw that Falcor swallowed nervously before replying, "I will discipline them when it arises Severi, not before. Wilson was curious, all of them were curious. Nothing more, nothing less."

Severi didn't seem to like his reply, but when he opened his mouth to say something, a voice sounded behind him, "Lord, Calio! What news?"

I could tell that he was growling low in his throat as he turned to face the slave that scrambled over the ruins and saw several others trailing after him. All human. Their eyes were dull, their timid actions showed that Severi put them down time after time, and I could tell that Falcor didn't one hundred percent agree with the collars they wore. It was a sure sign that I was glad that I was found by Killian and not by Severi. Otherwise, I think it would be the opposite way. The humans looked at us in fear before they eyed Severi with a nervous shudder. Falcor eyed them and looked at his brother before speaking, "What's with their collars, Severi?"

Severi smirked and grabbed one by the iron collar, and whipped the human back and forth, before flinging him against a building ruin. The human was screaming as he hit it, and the building crumbled slightly before dropping bits and pieces onto the human. I winced and backed up slightly before eyeing Falcor. He didn't appear to be disturbed by the actions that Severi did, but I could sense that Killian winced.

Severi smirked as he watched and replied, "They are mine to discipline, and they are mine to kill. They know that."

Falcor squinted his eyes but didn't reply. Calio looked up and down at him and raised his eyebrows before growling, "What happened to your clothing? Shred it again?"

It was clear that Calio got his demon under control again, and I saw Falcor slightly relax. Killian responded, "Unfortunately, yeah. Falcor was in too much of a hurry to allow me to take off our clothing."

Calio sneered for a moment, before his eyes flickered to us. He looked at us, as if he was doubting our capability. He sighed after a moment before looking back at Killian and growling, "I thought you would bring the eight puppies with you, Killian."

Killian stared at him for a moment, looking at us before returning his gaze to Calio. He replied, "Why does it matter to you? It is clear you have enough to take care of on your own Calio."

Calio snarled, Severi in his eyes for a split second, before he faded back again. Calio sighed deeply, looked at the humans, and replying, "If you want to call these things as beings, Killian, then you have fallen off your high horse. What have YOU been doing all these centuries exactly?"

Killian smiled slightly before replying, "Living. Learning. What mother would have wanted me to do Calio."

He stared at Killian for a moment before laughing, he bent forward and clutched his knees. He chuckled after a moment, wiping off the tears before growling, "Mother is dead, Killian. You should have lived what father would have wanted. That is how I have been living."

The humans shrunk down when he said that, and I glanced at my team before speaking, "Yet you seem perfectly okay with harming others simply because you seem to be above them. That is not how Killian has shown us to live hence far. He shows us that he can be brutal and destroy everything in his path, yet know when to end it. So far after meeting you, you have done nothing in comparison to show compassion, empathy or overall moral. You solely do everything to gain control, and do it in the wrong way."

Everyone was staring at me as if I had grown mushrooms in my ears. My eyes flickered to Calio, whose face was bright red in anger. I could tell that he wanted to kill me, but I squared my shoulders, and raised my hackles before his eyes flickered to Killian's. He snapped, "How is that not worthy of punishment, Killian?"

Killian stared at me hard and replied, "He will learn after a bit, Severi. I will not allow them to speak against myself, but he did, however, put valid points out. I don't see how that needs punishment."

Severi approached me quickly, my wolf growled low in our throat, but that did nothing compared to what my fellow pack members did. They growled and took a step forward to defend me. Severi stopped within a foot of me, before he glowered at me snarling, "Be your wretched self. You will serve alongside MY slaves all the same doing the same job! And you!"

He whirled around to face Killian, although Falcor was in his eyes, continued, "Punish them before I do! Go on! Punish them! Weakling."

Falcor growled low in his throat and growled out, "And this is EXACTLY WHY I DIDN'T LIKE YOU, SEVERI! Bossy, bossy, bossy pants! You NEVER LET ME DO AS I WANT! You are right, they are MINE to punish. Yet, they did nothing yet to require a discipline action. If anything, they stood up to you which proves that I already have some of their trust."

Severi swallowed and glanced at the humans before shaking his head and walking towards them. They cowered and hunched their shoulders inward and shook, clear signs that they were used to being beaten. I swallowed as I watched him pick up a child, no more than eight, and snapped the child's neck. The kid crumbled dead to the ground, the woman that was closest to the child let out a soft sob, but Severi didn't seem to care. He looked down at her, and kicked her five times, but none of the other humans did anything. I started forward, but Falcor spoke, "Don't."

I looked at him and hissed, "But he's killing…."

Falcor looked up, locked eyes with me, and then flickered to the rest of us before replying, "Say nothing. They are his to manage. If he wants to kill any without reason, he has that right. He knows not to harm you, and he is currently taking his rage out on his property. I know it pains you all, but you MUST let it go."

I stared at him and was about to reply, but Savador growled out, "Why are you doing nothing to prevent this?"

Falcor looked at him and replied, "Because he would do it to any of you in a heartbeat."

We glanced back at Severi, and saw that he had killed the woman, and another two while we were talking. Our stomachs turned, I looked at Falcor, and noticed that he did not look. He was looking elsewhere. It was clear that he knew that Severi would soon run out of steam, and would come back. My wolf and I wanted to mourn the ones slaughtered without cause, but we couldn't. It was similar feeling when Falcor ordered us to kill the human village earlier. However, after a while we understood why he had done it. Now though, we were questioning it. I fell back into my wolf's mind and cried softly for all those who were torn down without a chance.

*****

After five minutes, Severi was panting in the circle of dead humans. He had slaughtered and brutally beaten all of them, before killing them. It made all of us sick to our core. Savador connected to us after a moment, *"I still don't agree. We could have done something to prevent that."*

*"Like what exactly, Savador? Severi is a monster, and I now understand why Falcor had that shocked look across his face when he was the one who appeared."*

He sighed in our connection before replying, *"It still doesn't sit right with me to do nothing. Those humans have shown fear in his presence."*

*"The humans showed fear last night in ours, Savador."*

*"Ugh, I know. However, I feared for my life if Falcor saw weakness. I want to erase my memory as they stared at us in terror."*

I sighed deeply before replying, *"I agree."*

He let the connection go down on his own, and we exchanged glances after a moment, and I knew that we wanted to console each other, but were semi-terrified of what would happen. I turned my attention back to Severi.

*****

Calio growled in our mind, *"What was that to prove, Severi?"*

*"That I will kill anyone who challenges us."*

*"These ones did nothing to us, Severi. I agree with you and your motives, however, killing twenty of our slaves, that was a little harsh. We now have to get more to replace the one you killed."*

*"Have Falcor get them."*

*"Severi, you know that if he got more, they would be the same as those werewolves he has."*

*"You agree with his style of making people obey him?"*

*"Times have changed, Severi. I know that we were once peaceful, at least in our case, you and I were causing havoc. However, mother's methods result in better followers. Look how the humans around you respond to you, Severi? Does that seem like mother's way of handling things, or is it the way of father's?"*

I was met with silence and it was several minutes before he replied, *"Father's way."*

*"Exactly, Severi. Look at the eight werewolves that Falcor somehow got to be under him. Do you notice that they stood up to you? That took courage to do so. That is what mother would have suggested we did."*

*"But mother was weak, Calio. She died in that attack."*

*"But not before getting Falcor, and us out of there. She died protecting us, Severi. Father died in that attack."*

*"Then why did you say earlier that you were following father's way? You make no sense, Calio."*

I sighed before replying, *"That may be true, but the fact that the one that Falcor named Wilson, stood up to us, was a wakeup call. He was prepared to challenge us, Severi. The others seemed to back him in that thought too, since they raised their haunches at the same time."*

Severi was silent. He was thinking, and I knew he came to his conclusion, *"What do you suggest we do then, Calio? These humans fear us. Kill them all and start anew?"*

*"No."*

*"Then what do you suggest we do, Calio?"*

*"Nothing. We have shown these humans nothing but pain. They will not trust us to be otherwise."*

*"Then why change how we are if nothing changes?"*

*"Actions are louder than anything, Severi. We must stride ourselves to be better."*

*"That may be true, but how to difference?"*

I sighed and did not respond. Severi was the brutal component, and father had taken the liking in that. However, it didn't make mother happy, and father had, at some point, brought us aside and told us that mother was too weak. That she would not be able to defend herself if something happened. However, he was dead wrong. I filled Severi the memory of the night we were forced out of our homes.

*Flaming arrows, torches, and spears. Mother, dragging Falcor and myself out the back door, shoving us out. Screams filled the night of the less fortunate. The roar of father, as he protected us as long as he could, so a few of us might escape. The mighty roar of father's pain as he went down, and the attackers swarming inside. Mother, protecting us, the best she could, before looking at us before shouting at us to be safe, and flee. We were merely fourteen and Falcor eight, but we fled into the night.*

*"Stop it, Calio!"*

I ended the memory, and heard him grieve slightly. I would have lowered our head in response, but Severi had control and he would never show that sort of weakness. He took a shuddery breath in before speaking in our connection, *"Why see that memory again, Calio? That's…. That's a painful one."*

*"Sorry, Severi, but you wanted to see proof that mother was stronger than father."*

*"No more, no more pain, Calio."*

*"Okay. I won't revisit the memory, Severi."*

I waited a moment before speaking again, *"Severi, let me have control."*

*"Fine."*

****

He switched fast, I was slightly disorientated in that action and swayed slightly. I panted and looked up after a moment, and saw that we were being watched by the werewolves. Falcor, was not even looking at us, as if he knew that we would soon burn ourselves out of the rage we were in.

After a moment, I spoke up, "Let's set up camp."

Falcor looked at me for a moment before replying, "I cannot stay here, Calio. I need to head back."

The werewolves all jerked their heads towards him, as if begging him to stay, however, I replied, "Go? Go where?"

He stood up and replied, "The prophecy came true, Calio. The child lives."

I stared at him in shock. That was a legend, yet even father mentioned that our sole duty was to help the hybrid in this world – to rule the world correctly. I looked at the wolves and replied after a moment, "Do they know?"

Falcor glanced at the werewolves and then glanced at me again before replying, "They are the rest of the unit that tried to protected the Druids from Morphous's wrath. However, he took them prisoner when it was all done."

I glanced at them and it suddenly clicked, there was something else that he knew about what Morphous had, and I looked at him. Curious on what he knew. However, Falcor shifted back to his wolf form, and shuddered slightly before standing tall.

One of the werewolves, approached him and call out, "WHERE ARE YOU GOING! LEAVING US WITH HIM?"

Normally, I would do something but I watched as Falcor look down at him and replied, "I have to go. You will be safe together here."

"You protected us better than anything else. What is so important to leave us?"

"Rafeor."

"Rafeor? Who is that?"

"Child that will rule the supernatural world. Bring harmony, and bring peace. First, though I have to get back to her. You be safe, together."

He turned to leave, but another one spoke, "But you said that he would do it once you left. Take us with you."

"No."

"Why not?"

"I go back to Morphous. You are safer here, than being within his grasp."

That caught their attention, and the one who I have come to know as Wilson replied after a moment, "Averic. Fantar. Enough. He knows what he is doing, and you have to believe that he will come back."

Falcor looked at him, nodded once, before he looked at me, and connected to me for once in several centuries, *"Do not harm them brother. They are mine."*

*"Get going, Falcor."*

He leveled me with a look, before bounding away. The gathering darkness was prominent. After a few minutes, the ground no longer trembled under Falcor's footfalls.

****

I looked at the humans before barking out an order, "Get a fire started!"

The survivors scrambled to comply to my order, I glanced at the werewolves and sighed deeply. "You will do as you are told."

I turned around to leave them be, but one growled, "You are not my commander. Falcor is."

Severi wanted to put him in his place, but I replied, "He's currently not here. Gather firewood. And if you want, go hunting."

I walked away from them and left them to stare hard at my back. The humans scrambled to get out of our way. One was not as fast as the others. Normally, once that happened, we kill them, but not after our discussion. The human cowered and shook before us, but we did nothing. We continued on. The rest of the humans stared at us in shock, as one fell to their knees to help the one that wasn't fast enough, hugging him tightly. I paid no heed as I disappeared into a building that wasn't as badly ruined.

# Chapter 17

I made good time, and without anyone on my back this time, I made it back to the shared territories within six hours. Daybreak was prominent and I slowed once I got back to where I had shredded my clothing. I shifted to see if anything was worth trying to bring back to the seamstress, but nothing was salvageable. I sighed deeply before grabbing it and leaving quickly towards the shifter territory. Since I was technically on a werewolf. Soon the woods thinned out where the border was, and I shifted to a wolf form and kept Falcor in check before trudging back into the palace. Exhausted.

I entered through the dog door that Morphous and I created, so any shifter could come and go in any four-legged form they wanted. It was also used for the werewolves, and I wondered what happened to them all since Morphous was taken. However, it turns out I didn't have to wait long.

A blade came down, and held against my throat, a gruff voice barked out, "Who are you?"

I glanced up at him and blinked before placing my uniform down, the guard glanced down and saw a tattered mess before he lowered his sword before speaking, "My apologies."

I let out a woof and was about to continue forward, when he spoke again, "I would suggest you get into a new pair of uniforms. Morphous sent out word that if you came back, you were to be brought to him immediately."

I paused, I heard 'if you came back,' which meant that Morphous wasn't certain I would. Hmmm, interesting. I dipped my head to him and trotted towards my room. I may be exhausted, but Morphous would get wind that I was back before I could do anything.

I got to my room, pushed the door open with my snout, and walked into the center of the room, before shifting to my human form. I stretched and shook myself slightly. Don't get me wrong, Falcor could run fast and hard for long hours on end without stopping, but man did it make me sore after a while. I sighed deeply as I pulled open my dresser and grabbed my last clean uniform. I had to bring two uniforms to the seamstress for repair, and one was manageable to repair, but the one Falcor shredded was not salvageable. She was going to have a fit once I brought it to her, however, I cannot stop it any more than I normally could.

I slid my uniform on, and the door creaked open. I froze, my back was to the door, and I sniffed the air once. I smiled slightly before turning and looking at Herald. I said, "Hey."

He stared at me before replying, "Where did you go?"

I paused and looked at him for a moment, I still had to attach my swords to my uniform but his eyes were stuck to them. I knew that he wanted to carry them, but that did not fall to him. That fell to Quinn. I sighed deeply before replying, "I had matters to take care of, Herald."

He stared at me and shook his head before replying, "Why can't you tell me, father? What have I done? Where did you go?"

I sighed and would have replied but Falcor growled in my mind, *"Don't. He may be your son, but he has no demon. He would not understand. His loyalties are solely to the king of the shifters. Not us. Not our cause either."*

I swallowed Falcor up until now saw Herald as one of us, but I also knew that he had kept quiet too. I sighed deeply and ran my hand across my face before replying, "I am sorry, Herald. I cannot tell you."

He flinched and growled, "I was right. You want me to be like Quinn, don't you?!? You never cared about me as much as him! What do I have to do to earn your love, father?"

I winced, and Falcor spoke in my mind again, *"It will be hard, but ignore what he says, Killian."*

*"What do you know that I don't, Falcor? Why should I treat my youngest this way?"*

*"He will not understand what has to happen. The less he knows the better, Killian."*

I sighed deeply again, it was going to be a long day, and I turned around and faced the bedroom before speaking, "Herald, I am your father and you will treat me with some respect. Please, do not make me have to beat you to be submissive."

He let out a sob, and I could tell that he was shaking, but I did not turn around to console him. Falcor made it clear years ago that I was to treat him differently than Quinn. I didn't understand why, but he did it to protect us. He knew something that he wasn't sharing, and I for once wished that I had forgone his warnings and taught both of my boys the same. Alas, though, that was not something I could turn back time for. After a moment, Herald spoke, "I hate you. I hate you."

His words stung me, but I did not respond. He pulled the door and slammed it shut, closing us in darkness once again.

****

I took a deep breath in, and Falcor spoke once again, *"I'm sorry, Killian."*

*"No, you are not."*

He didn't reply. I could tell that he did not reply due to his temper flaring at that barb. We never saw eye to eye on how to raise Herald. I said at one point the same as Quinn, but Falcor said no. I couldn't really explain to Herald that my demon said no since he didn't have one. He took his mother's genes too much. Her genes overpowered mine, and only Quinn was the one who had my genes. I wondered why, and Falcor would not say why either. He kept quiet on that front.

I sighed deeply and finished getting my uniform, and weapons strapped to myself before walking to the mirror on the wall, glancing in the mirror, and fussing with my long hair. At least, trying to look presentable so Morphous knew that I took the time to do so. Afterwards, I walked out and closed the door behind me, heading to Morphous's office.

*****

I entered the palace and was shocked to see a guard stumbling around. Several. Quinn entered and glanced around, puzzled for a moment, and kept Rafeor pulled close to him. Morphous came in after a moment and he had his head down, looking at the ground before he glanced up and squinted. We all saw the same thing. Guards. Morphous looked around and called out, "**Friend or foe?**"

A guard stopped stumbling and leaned against the wall before replying in a shallow breathe, "Friend, my Lord."

Morphous glanced at me and growled, "**I thought you said...**"

I opened my mouth to say something, but another guard spoke, "My Lord, do not yell at Hector. Not an hour before, did whatever the wolves gave us lent up. We are still uneasy on our feet, but I feel my strength returning."

Morphous looked at him and frowned, before looking at Quinn and speaking, "**Any news?**"

He scoffed and replied, "I don't know much more than you do, Morphous, I was with you all day."

Morphous sighed deeply and replied, "**Oh, right.**"

Quinn looked at him with a weird look, but I asked him, "Do... do you never remember what happened when you shift into your dragon?"

Morphous glanced at me and replied, "**Only when he doesn't want me to remember. This time for whatever reason, he doesn't want me to remember.**"

Quinn frowned, and all the surrounding guards exchanged looks, but no one spoke. Rafeor glanced around before speaking, "**I am going to go to bed.**"

She stalked forward, and Morphous looked like he wanted to reject that idea, but he closed his mouth and let her leave. I looked at him and saw uncertainty in his expression, but I knew for a fact that they may have some hiccups. I sighed deeply and yawned. Morphous looked at the guards before speaking, "**How tired are you now?**"

A few of the guards looked at each other and one replied, "Strangely, not."

Morphous looked at them all before replying, "**Then I want you all to guard the entrances and exits. Windows, doors, and anywhere that an attack can come from. If a wolf comes in, kill them.**"

He started forward towards his office but stopped and swallowed. "**And if Killian shows back up, I want him to be sent to my office immediately on arrival.**"

All the guards instantly bowed, and Morphous continued down the hallway, disappearing.

****

I looked at Quinn and saw him frown, his shoulder slumped slightly before he trudged to his room. I swallowed before I called out to him, "Quinn?"

He turned slightly, before raising his eyes to me and I could see how tired he was. I swallowed before speaking, "What is so important inside the office space?"

Quinn's eyes flickered to the other guards, but they seemed to be staring off into nothing before he replied, "I cannot tell you that, Hector. Telling you that will get you killed."

I swallowed and allowed him to leave.

****

I was soon left alone with the rest of the guards, and I glanced at one. "What happened to you, Norton?"

He glanced at me and leaned against a table for support before replying, "One moment, I was with Arnold, the next I woke up with Anna hovering worriedly over me. We lost two guards to whatever the werewolves used, Hector."

I frowned and looked around before replying, "What made them turn on us?"

He growled and replied, "Their loyalties lie with their king Hector. I would not be surprised if he was the one who set them up to know how our patrols worked."

I sighed deeply and thought back to how Nathaniel appeared out of the woods, and realized that I recognized some of them who were in the ranks. I nodded slightly before turning towards the hallway to my chamber when Norton called out, "Hector, whatever you were protecting, I hope that the wolves never learn of it."

I paused and looked at him and swallowed. I knew better than to respond since I didn't know what was inside the box. I nodded once and left, and soon disappeared down the hallway, to my chamber.

*****

After I got back to my office, I released Gillith, Amish, and Conrade from their watch They had protected the box against who knew what, and I was glad for once that Killian foresaw something and did not allow me to be the sole watcher of it. I swallowed hard for a moment, wondering what I would have to do to Killian. All that Abacore told me of what he wanted me to know of was the fact that Killian let go of all the werewolves that I had tucked in my dungeons. That brought me rage, knowing that Killian went behind my back and released them. I wondered what he had done with them. However, I also knew that sending Killian to Davis was not something I could do either. Something in me had wanted to keep Killian close, and I had made it my mission to keep him and Quinn closer. However, for whatever reason, it made me not really want to deal with Herald, who should have the same reaction. However, it was different. I actually treated Herald the same as I would anyone else in my arsenal. I frowned and yawned before sitting down in my chair and leaning backward and closing my eyes. It had been a long night, and gods knew I was exhausted. There was not a reason not to sleep, since I did not know how long Killian was going to be.

****

I stopped at Morphous's office door, swallowing the nerves back, and knocked. No response, I waited a few moments, before knocking again. Nothing, I frowned and knew I heard correctly on the office door. I swallowed before grabbing the door knob and turning it to find it unlocked. After what had happened yesterday, I would have thought that he would have made sure his doors were secured. However, upon opening the door, I saw Morphous snoring away at his desk. His feet were on his desk, and he was leaning back in his chair, sawing off a bunch of snores. I smirked and looked around, I saw a long couch, a luxury that normally wasn't available. However, being that Morphous was royalty, that was not an issue.

I sighed deeply before walking forward towards the couch and laid on it. I knew better than to wake Morphous. He had been through hell and back, and I wondered what he would do once he did wake. I, however, knew that since he was asleep, I should get some sleep too. He couldn't yell at me if I was in the same room as he was. Well,  in the morning, I expected it. Not now though. I closed my eyes and soon fell into a deep slumber.

****

I woke up and yawned deeply before I removed my feet from my desk and looked around, the candles had since dripped off and were out. The office room itself was dark since there were no windows, but I knew I was not alone either. I stood up, walked towards the closet, opened it, and took out four-day candles, and lit them. I placed them around the room, and that was when I saw that I was correct, I was not alone in the room. Killian laid on my couch and I watched him for a moment. He was normally never trustful enough to sleep where he was not comfortable, but exhaustion took him. I watched as his chest rose up and down, and glanced away after a moment, he would not want me to mention how he slept.

I opened my door and saw three guards posted at my door. I frowned before asking, "**What are you three doing?**"

One flinched as if he didn't hear me and the other two exchanged looks before one replied, "My Lord, I was told by Gillith to protect this door."

I frowned and replied, "**When did he give that order?**"'

The guard opened his mouth to reply, but another replied, "After Killian entered your office, my Lord."

I smirked at their response, and I replied after a moment, "**You three are dismissed.**"

They bowed and left. I closed the door again, turned, and found Killian sitting up, and staring at me.

I crossed my arms across my chest and leaned against the door before growling, "**Explain to me why you took my prisoners, Killian. Where are they anyhow?**"

He blinked at me and yawned before replying, "They are in an unmarked grave. I killed them after I realized that you took yourself out of the clutches of the werewolves."

Abacore growled in my mind, and I frowned. He normally was docile but something about what Killian said was false. I glanced at him and replied, "**Is that the whole truth? Or are you lying to me, Killian?**"

He paused and glanced up at me. I saw a flicker of purple in his eyes for a split second, but Abacore noticed it more than I did. He spoke to me in our connection, "*Something is different about him.*"

"*I noticed. What do you think it is, Abacore?*"

"*I think he lied about what he is.*"

I looked at Killian and replied to Abacore, "*What do you think he is then, Abacore?*"

"*Me don't know.*"

I growled softly to him before ending the connection, but kept it open in case he saw something else that I didn't. I looked at Killian before speaking, "**My dragon knows you are lying to us, Killian. Want to tell us something true?**"

Killian paused and looked up before replying, "I am sorry, but I cannot tell you."

Abacore growled in my mind, "*He's hiding something.*"

"*I am now aware of it, Abacore, however, the question is what?*"

"*Me don't know, Morph.*"

I scowled after a moment and leveled Killian with a look before growling, "**I AM YOUR KING! You will answer.**"

Normally that command would make any shifter wince and cower, but Killian seemed unaffected and raised his eyebrows at me. That was the time I knew that Abacore was correct, Killian was not a shifter as he claimed. Then what was he? He could shift into anything at will like a shifter, it didn't make sense.

Killian looked down before growling, "Morphous. If you try to connect the dots on what I am. It will only confuse you further."

I glanced back at him and Abacore scored my voice as he replied, "**Tell me.**"

Killian looked up at me, leaned back into the couch, crossed his leg over his knee, and clasped his hands before replying, "I am a demon."

We stared at him and I finally got Abacore back under control before asking the obvious question that we both wanted to ask, "**What?**"

He sighed before unclasping his hands, stood up, and stretched. His muscles rippled for a moment, he shook himself slightly before replying, "I am a demon, Morphous."

Abacore snorted in our connection, and I opened the communication, *"Demons died centuries ago."*

I frowned and replied aloud, **"Demons died centuries ago..."**

His eyes flashed, and I gasped. This time he did not hide his purple eyes from me. I took a step backward, my heel hitting the door, making it rattle before he replied, "Majority did. Myself and my brother got out. I don't know if there are any others."

I swallowed before whispering, **"What about your boys?"**

For a moment, he faltered, and replied, "Quinn has one. Don't know if he is aware of it as of yet. Probably doesn't understand it if he does. Herald…. He is a shifter. There is no demon spirit in him."

His voice was raw when he replied, meaning there was something else that was hidden. I swallowed before I asked, **"If you are indeed a demon, then why stay as a servant to me? You could have forced me to your bidding."**

He smirked and replied after a moment, "You are correct, I could have. However, I do not seek that. I wanted to learn, and I did. It was educational, Morphous."

I swallowed and replied, **"What now?"**

He shrugged and replied, "Oh nothing. I continue as I am, and you…. Well, let's put it this way someone like you can understand, do not tell anyone about what I am. Otherwise, consequences have severe outcomes."

Abacore growled in response, and I couldn't agree more with that. My eyes flashed red, and he chuckled before growling, "You are somewhat weak compared to me, Morphous. Do not make me serve you a consequence so soon in finding out."

I opened my mouth to retort, and after a moment I closed it again. I looked away from him and did not reply. Abacore, however, spoke to me, *"If he is here, why? What is so important that he wants us to act normal around?"*

I frowned and looked back at him before voicing what Abacore said, **"What is stopping you from leaving again?"**

His Adam's apple bobbed up and down as he swallowed. Abacore was onto something, but he simply replied, "Nothing to concern yourself over, Morphous. I mean no harm, but I will deal harm if I need to."

Abacore rumbled in my throat at the threat, and my eyes stayed red for about thirty seconds before dimming back to their natural color again. He smirked slightly before moving towards the door and paused before looking at me. He motioned me sideways, and I complied and moved away from the door. He grabbed the door before I could say anything, opening it a crack. When I spoke again, stopping him, "**The werewolves? Did you kill them?**"

He shut the door and leveled me with a look before sighing deeply, "No, but they are hours away."

He opened the door and exited, leaving me in my office, and staring into the dark hallways. Showing that the staff had not gotten around to this section to do the candles. I swallowed and watched his dark form disappear.

# Chapter 18

For a while, I stared into the darkness of the hallway, before closing the door slowly. I was numb for a while. If what Killian claimed to be correct, then why was he here? What was his end game exactly? I looked around my office and swallowed. I would love to ask Quinn if he knew what he was, but I had a feeling even that would be considered a consequence needed action in the case of Killian. I looked at my desk and took a shuddery breath before closing my eyes, pinching the bridge of my nose, and exhaling.

Abacore spoke in our connection, *"Well, we now understand why he is different compared to everyone else."*

*"How is that a good thing Abacore?"*

*"He does things differently than anyone else. He manned the guard rotation for years before passing down to Quinn. Think about it, Morph, he did a good job. As if he had experience with it before."*

I sighed before replying, *"How can you still see silver lighting in all this chaos?"*

*"If you no look Morph, then you fail in life. Everything has a reason."*

I closed the connection slightly and thought to myself, Abacore was right in so many ways, Killian proved his worth over and over again. I had to trust him undoubtedly for a change. I approached my desk before grabbing a pen and a piece of parchment and hovered over it for a moment. I swallowed. If Killian knew what I was about to do, he would probably kill me, however, I also knew if I kept it to myself the other Kings would be on edge.

I swallowed nervously, before writing:

*To King Nathaniel and Queen Sophronia,*

*Times have changed for the worse for us as friends. I apologize for any harm and wrongdoing I personally have caused. However, under my very nose, and yours, a deeper threat looms in the shadows. You may know of my advisor for many moons, Killian, he is not what he seems. He informed me that he was a shifter, from a different family line. However, due to certain circumstances that I don't wish to conclude in this message, I found out he is more sinister than that.*

*I request a meeting on August twenty-third at seven in the evening.*

*At our old meeting place*

*Sincerely,*

*Morphous Draconis.*

I looked down at what I had written and swallowed. I glanced at the door again, before moving to address another. The werewolves and I had somewhat of mutual hatred, however, I have not personally addressed the Carpathians. They kept to themselves and I followed their way of not getting in contact, however, I had a feeling that if I didn't address them too in this manner, there may be dire consequences for me. I swallowed as I addressed another piece of parchment:

*To King Dracula,*

*I must inform you of the dire consequences that have faced me. However, writing it does not do justice to what needs to be said.*

*I request a meeting on August twenty-second at midnight.*

*At the old common grounds.*

*Sincerely,*

*Morphous Draconis.*

I glanced down at the parchment and swallowed. I shakily took out two envelopes and sprinkled resin down over the wet ink. Allowing it to dry slightly before I folded it up nicely and placed both of them into separate envelopes. I swallowed as I looked down at my seal, I grabbed the nearest candle before stamping my seal into the soft wax. I stamped both of the envelopes and addressed the envelopes to the King and Queen of the other supernatural beings.

Abacore rumbled softly in my mind, "**Who are you going to entrust to deliver these messages?**"

I swallowed and did not immediately reply to him. I looked at the door before whispering back, "*I'm open to suggestions....*"

"*Send Quinn.*"

"*What? Are you crazy?*"

"*Killian said act normal, Morph. You would normally have him do it.*"

I sighed after a moment, stood up, and swallowed as I glanced down at the envelopes before hesistantly taking them to the main door with me. I paused before entering the main hallways, if anyone asked if I was alright, I would not know what to reply. Abacore scoffed slightly in our connection before he curled himself into a ball and closed his eyes. Closing the link as he fell asleep.

Lucky dragon, I grumbled to myself. I opened the door, and now the hallways were lit and the candlelight flickered in a small breeze as it passed through the hallways. I took a deep breath in before walking out.

********

I found Quinn where he normally would be at this hour, he was with Anna, who seemed flustered about something. I walked in, assessed the situation, and kind of grumbled slightly. We were overbooked with people, injured, all because the hospital went up in flames last week at this point, and I had not made it a priority to rebuild one. However, looking around, I needed to make it a priority. There were a lot that needed medical services.

Anna went quiet after a moment, which drew my attention back to them. They were both staring at me before Anna spoke, "My Lord?"

I turned to face her and swallowed. I turned my attention to Quinn, and spoke, "**Quinn, I need these letters to be delivered.**"

Quinn opened his mouth to say something, but Anna beat him to it, "Absolutely NOT! You, Quinn, and that poor girl Rafeor are not going ANYWHERE! You were kidnapped, Morphous, and now you want to act like nothing happened? It was only two nights ago!"

I opened my mouth to retort, but she glowered at me before speaking, "Send Killian out for these letters of yours, Morphous."

I swallowed and shook my head and looked at Quinn before rumbling, "**Where's Herald?**"

Quinn frowned after a moment, and exchanged looks with Anna before replying, "Uhhh…. Probably trying to avoid building something."

I would have growled at that on a normal day, but I sighed deeply before replying, "**Get him here.**"

Quinn swallowed and his eyes fogged over, but while I was paying attention to him, one of the girls that Quinn rescued came forward and curtsied before me. I dipped my head in return, thinking none of it before she spoke, "You have shown my fellow sisters nothing but kindness living here in your humble home. How can I repay the services you have dealt?"

I glanced at her and frowned, she would be someone I could send; however, I knew that the Carpathians would suck her dry.

I looked over at Anna, who had approached and held out her hand. I swallowed, she was a medic, and I knew the rules I had in place. I handed her the envelopes, and she glanced down at the names written across them. The moment she took a sharp breath in, I knew she understood who they were. She glanced at me, glanced at Quinn, and frowned. She knew that only someone trustworthy was able to deliver these envelopes, so she locked eye contact with me and connected with me, *"Why don't you send Killian? He was your advisor before Quinn."*

*"I found something out about him, Anna."*

*"What did you find?"*

I wrestled in my mind on whether to tell her or not. However, for a medic and her patient, there was a level of security in that. I replied after a moment, *"He's not a shifter, Anna. Neither is Quinn...."*

*"What are they then?"*

*"Killian said he was a demon. That Quinn had one, but he is probably unaware of it. And Herald, for some reason, is a shifter, the demon passed him up."*

*"Huh, that suddenly makes sense in a way if you think about it, Morphous. They both act differently than normal shifters. Heal differently too."*

*"What do you mean?"*

She glanced at Quinn and saw that his eyes were still fogged over before replying, *"When Quinn was a small boy, he got angry about something, and I saw his eyes flicker a different color. Mind you, we as shifters have our eyes shift different colors as is, however, his was different. I cannot disclose more than that on it, Morphous, patient, and medical confidentiality. However, when he was a boy, he healed differently. He healed faster than a shifter and healed differently from the werewolves that we had here for a time. I don't know how to explain it exactly, Morphous. I always knew he was different."*

*"What about Killian?"*

*"Killian never sought my attention, Morphous. He could have an arrow in his arm, which he at one point did after practice was gone wrong, but he refused my services."*

*"Why didn't you tell me?"*

*"Because he said he was fine, Morphous. And I to challenge someone like him? That is not something I want to do. Killian for all the mojo and stuff he has, has an air of authority, one that I never missed. Neither did any of the lower guards."*

I swallowed and glanced at Quinn, who was blinking rapidly, frowning, and spoke to me, "My Lord?"

I looked at Anna, before speaking in our connection, *"I want to know more later, Anna."*

*"You know where to find me, M'lord."*

We ended the connection and I glanced at Quinn. "**What is it?**"

Quinn shuffled his feet slightly before replying, "He doesn't want to come. Apparently father and he had an argument last night."

My curiosity peeked, what did Killian do with Herald? I glanced at Anna and saw her frown before shaking her head slightly. She knew something else. I knew that Herald helped her out more than not, so I needed to question her slightly more than anything else. I turned my attention to Quinn again before speaking, "**Ah. ok, where can I find him?**"

Quinn struggled to reply, he dropped his eyes to the ground before replying, "He's on the Western Wall."

I nodded once and gently took the envelopes from Anna. Anna spoke, "Wait."

I paused and glanced back at her when connected to me, "*Do not say anything about Killian while you are with Herald.*"

**"Why?"**

"*Trust me on this one, Morphous. Herald and his father, do not see eye to eye. Killian is rather brutal to him compared to Quinn.*"

I frowned, that did not sound like a normal father-and-son behavior. I turned and strode out, leaving the line between me and Anna open in case she had something else to say to me.


*****


I made it to the Western Wall, and sure enough I saw the two guards on the post, and after a moment of discussion with Feilian, he pointed up at the guard's shack roof. I looked up and saw a form there. Small talk was not my forte, however, I knew as a leader I should be able to help my people as much as possible. I sighed, shifted into a bird, and flew up there.

Herald had his head down and he sniffed before growling, "Go away."

He didn't even look at who was there. I squinted my eyes, normally I would prove to anyone who had spoken that way to me in such a manner. However, I let it slide. He was hurting and something told me that this was his go-to spot since Feilian did not appear to be shocked by my questions. I swallowed and shifted before speaking, "**No.**"

That caught his attention, and he spun around; he was shocked to see me. His face dropped down to the shingles before speaking, "My Lord! I…. I thought…. I thought you were Quinn."

I sighed deeply, opened my arms, and motioned him towards me. He swallowed and crawled over after a hesitation moment. He flinched as I rested my hands against him before he sobbed quietly into my chest. I frowned before speaking, "**Do you want to talk about what happened, Herald?**"

He froze and looked at me before dropping his attention back to the shingles and whispered, "My father and I had a fight. I asked him where he went but he didn't tell me. I accused him of favoring Quinn more than me, and, well, he didn't try to argue otherwise. We went back and forth for a few minutes, and then he said something that could never be taken back. I told him I hate him."

I swallowed, besides Rafeor, I didn't really have children of my own. Katherine and I had tried but to no avail. When I die, however, I will pass everything to Rafeor. I shook my head, now was not the time to think such morbid thoughts. I was still in my prime. I swallowed again before replying, "**Do you hate him, Herald?**"

It took him a whole minute before he replied slowly, "We may share the same blood, but he will never be the father that I want. So yes, I hate him."

I felt sorry for him. I replied, "**I am sorry, Herald.**"

He looked up at me and whispered, "Why? Why are you sorry?"

I looked down at him to reply, "**Because he shouldn't have turned you away as he did, Herald. He should have loved you unconditionally.**"

He glanced down again before I noticed the rage surging within him. His eyes must have flashed before he breathed deeply. "Why did you come to find me, My Lord?"

I sighed heavily, and shifted us slightly before replying, "**Because your father and I are not seeing eye to eye right now either. I need to send our messages, and I was going to have Quinn do it since he is my advisor, however, Anna told me no. So, I need someone brave to deliver them for me.**"

He looked sharply up at me. "What did Quinn do that Anna refuses to allow him to do his duty?"

I smirked before replying, "**When we were kidnapped.**"

His mouth fell open for a moment and he glanced down before mumbling, "Oh, right."

I chuckled slightly and he looked at me before speaking, "So, what are you doing here of all the places? I would have thought that you would have one of your elite warriors deliver something so important."

I was about to reply, when Anna spoke in the connection, *"My Lord, whatever you do. Do not have him as the messenger."*

**"Why not?"**

*"It would further the rift in that family."*

**"What if I ask him if he wants to do it, Anna? If he says no, then I will ask someone else."**

For a moment she seemed to struggle with what I said. She resignedly replied, *"Fine."*

I glanced down at Herald before asking, **"Would you like to deliver the messages, Herald?"**

He frowned before replying, "Why me?"

I swallowed thinking it was his way of getting out of doing something, I was about to reply when he continued, "I would do it in a heartbeat, My Lord, but why do you choose me over everyone else?"

I smiled slightly, before replying, **"Because I only trust people to a certain extent, Herald. If you do this for me, I will make it so that you are taken care of properly."**

For a few moments, we just sat there and enjoyed the spring rays over us. He replied, "If it's despite my father, I will do it. When do I leave?"

I took out the envelopes from my pocket before handing them to him. He glanced down at them, the moment I knew that he knew where to go, his eyes turned to saucers before he looked sharply at me. I smiled slightly before replying, **"As soon as you want."**

He glanced down at the letters and gulped. He placed the envelope into his pocket, before standing up, he hesitated before offering me his right hand. I took it, and let him help me stand, the shingles let out a little sound, but they held under our weight. He looked at me for a moment before speaking, "I'll leave immediately."

He hesitated before dipping his head toward me, "My Lord."

Then he shifted to a raven, and flew off to the west, disappearing over the trees.

****

I sighed before shifting to a bird, flying down to the Western Wall again, and walking back inside. Feilian and the other guard on duty bowed to me, but I heeded them with nothing in return. I left them to do their duty without a second glance.

I entered the main palace, and moved towards my office when Killian's voice called out, "Morphous?"

I stopped walking, my back to him, and I closed my eyes steeling myself before I turned around to face him. Keeping my face blank of emotions, he looked at me and blinked. "Can I accompany you?"

A lump formed in my throat, and Anna connected right then, *"My Lord, I want a moment of your time, please. Come to my office."*

I tried to hide my smile before I replied to Killian, **"No, I am heading to Anna's office."**

Killian blinked once and replied in a hushed voice, "Morphous? Don't do anything stupid."

I glowered at him, but he turned sharply and left down another hallway. I swallowed as I made my way to Anna's office.

# Chapter 19

I flew to the west, before angling myself to the north, heading to the werewolves first. I flew for a good hour before perching in a tree, I panted slightly. Then I suddenly wondered what I was going to do. Was I just going to be able to walk straight into their territory and be like, 'Hey, here's a letter from Morphous?' that would get me killed. I frowned and looked down the tree, seeing five wolves trot past the trees, I swallowed before flying down there, shifting to my human form, and spoke, "Uhh, hello?"

The wolves whipped around and bared their teeth, raising their hackles before the leader snapped, "What are you doing here? Trespasser?"

I raised my hands before replying, "I have a message for your king."

He glanced at his comrades before growling, "Prove it."

I swallowed, before slowly reaching into my pocket, and took out the letter. I turned it towards him, so he saw who it was addressed to. That stumped them all. By the look written across their faces, they were not expecting anything. The leader wolf, frowned before speaking to someone else in the group in a hushed tone, "Batis, run ahead, and inform King Nathaniel we will have someone for him."

The dark gray wolf looked at me with distrust, before turning around and running ahead of the group. The leader wolf turned back around and growled, "Come with us."

I swallowed, before placing the letter back into my pocket, and following him further into the werewolf territory

.

*****

I walked down the hallway of the palace and got to Anna's office. I knocked twice, and I heard a muffled, "Enter."

I opened the door and saw her writing by her candlelight before setting it aside and speaking, "Morphous."

I dipped my head towards her before replying, "**Anna.**"

I looked around the room, it was very tidy, stacks of paper and books lined the walls and bookshelves, and medical papers for patients were on her desk. A couch and a chair sat to the immediate right of the door. She cleared her throat, before motioning towards the couch. I sighed and knew that I could not refuse her. I walked towards it before sitting down. She finished whatever she was working on, grabbed a pen and parchment, walked to the seat before sitting herself, crossed her left leg over her right, and looked at me expectantly. I stared at her for a few moments before speaking, "**What do you want?**"

She sighed deeply before replying, "I want you to tell me whatever is bothering you, Morphous. Why do you think Killian is what you said he was and…"

By the time that had been out of her mouth, I had mine clamped over hers. I shook my head slowly before withdrawing it slowly. "**No, Anna. Cannot do that in normal talking.**"

She glowered at me, her eyes flashing before she rumbled, "Morphous."

Her voice had a slight growl to her voice, as if when someone was angry they tend to have a different tone, that tone was one hundred percent in her tone. I swallowed for a moment before backing up, sitting back into the cushion, and opening our connections together. For a moment, she did not open the connection, but once she realized that I was not going to say anything else on this matter, she rolled her eyes and opened it. I sighed before speaking in our connections, "*Sorry, Anna, but it has to be done through connections, anything related to Killian. Everything else will be a normal conversation.*"

"*Are you scared of Killian, Morphous?*"

"*Slightly, Anna, do you know anything about a demon?*"

"*No. I was hoping you knew something.*"

"*Anna, what did you mean something is different with Quinn, Killian, and Herald?*"

For a moment she did not respond. I knew that she would have to break her patient and doctor protocol, however, this was dire business. She sighed after a moment, "*No blabbing to ANYONE OF THIS, MORPHOUS! This was strictly confidential information.*"

"*Understood.*"

"*Quinn heals differently, and like I said earlier, his eyes flashed a different color and his healing is faster than a normal shifter and wolf. However, his eyes flashed black. Pure black, no sign of what he normally looks like, Morphous. It was only a moment, but it disappeared as soon as it surfaced. He doesn't tend to come to me for bumps and scrapes as much as everyone else, and the physical exam that you had ordered everyone to do once every two years. He comes first, and he doesn't have anything wrong with him. However, one of the werewolves casually mentioned that Quinn had gotten his foot trapped in a hunter's trap not three days before the exam, and that he was surprised that he wasn't limping around. I was shocked, Morphous, when I checked him, he had no marks on him, but the guard who told me that was one of the older ones, that had always been trustworthy in the past.*"

She paused, and I replied, ***"Hmmm, what else?"***

She glanced at me and then at the door before continuing, *"It always made me wonder why Quinn could not for the life of him connect to anyone else. However, Herald… Herald could connect to Amish and anyone else he wanted without any issue. Killian, I don't believe can even connect to anyone. However, I have seen Quinn and Killian pester someone to give them a drop of their blood. The guards were very nervous about doing that, but they complied and gave blood. Only a drop, mind you Morphous, but it's enough to have a bond together."*

My jaw dropped, and I was about to say something, but Anna shook her head and continued, *"Herald is different from both Quinn and his father, he doesn't need the blood to connect to anyone, Morphous. Now that you have come to light on what the difference is between them, it makes sense all of a sudden."*

She stopped talking for a moment, and I saw her struggle. So, I asked in the connection, **"You know and understand Quinn, and we will need to touch base on Herald. However, do you know anything about Killian?"**

For a moment she stared into the abyss before talking in the connection, *"That is the mystery, Morphous. Even when he had an arrow through his arm, he didn't want to come to see me. I had to pretty much pester him to answer any of my questions, and his eyes flashed purple for a moment, a flicker before it disappeared. Not long enough to really say anything about it. Also, he seems to have the same type of healing abilities as Quinn, since, well, during his exams, he seemed to not want to allow me to draw blood from him. However, it didn't make sense to me at all. However, now with the new knowledge of what he is, it makes sense."*

***"How does it make sense, Anna?"***

*"It makes sense why he doesn't want blood to be taken, Morphous. How many times have you run across a demon or anyone who is high blood to willingly give blood?"*

I frowned, she was right about that. I didn't want to give her any of my blood, since of what happened with Astromic, who was a kid a couple of earlier centuries ago. I was actually surprised that she did not seek out my help. I was after all a king, and a shifter at that. Perhaps it was time that I found them. Anna cleared her throat and I glanced up at her, she smiled slightly before speaking in the connection, *"What are you thinking of, Morphous?"*

***"Astromic, the one that was lab created."***

*"That poor kid, I know that the human government is still after her after all these centuries."*

I frowned, I forgot about that, the human population. I stood to go, but she tsked me a few times, before snapping, "Morphous! Sit back down!"

I opened my mouth to retort but sighed deeply before sitting down again. She glowered at me before speaking, "Now, we will put a pause on what we were talking about. Tell me, what were your thoughts on what happened two nights ago?"

I opened my mouth and closed it after a moment. I sighed deeply, before rubbing my right hand across my face before yawning, **"Why bring that up, Anna?"**

"Because that is a traumatic experience, Morphous. Tell me about it. Walk me through it, please."

I sighed deeply, resignedly, since I knew that Anna would not let me go without finding out how I felt about the whole endeavor. She raised her eyebrows at me, picked up her pen, and hovered over the parchment, waiting.

*****

I was walking along with the werewolves, I was in the center of them. So, they knew I was following them, I was in my human form, and I stumbled every so often over roots and fallen matter, the wolves to the left and right of me grumbled along, growling softly. After a moment, a sizable hole in the ground tripped me, and I went down, "Uof!"

The wolves leaped to the sides and one came close to snapping at me with his teeth, but the leader wolf snapped in response towards them. He glanced at me, growling slightly, "Get up."

I pushed myself slightly, but the other wolf behind me spoke, "NO! Do not move."

I froze, and the wolf behind me cautiously approached and sniffed around the hole and spoke to the leader wolf, "Cyprus, this one is active."

I swallowed, I did not understand why they had a scared look across their expressions before I voiced out, "Active?"

They glanced at each other before Cyprus replied, "It's a time during the riot, perhaps even longer than that even. Only the werewolf that placed it here can deactivate it without killing everyone in the surrounding area."

He said it so calmly that I thought he was joking, but by the others' behaviors, I knew that this was no joke. I swallowed and glanced backward at my foot before replying, "Any chance that it's not active?"

The wolf behind me snorted before replying, "Everything has a smell. This one is active."

I swallowed before glancing at Cyprus and saying, "So, what's going to happen now?"

They all exchanged looks before Cyprus looked at the wolf behind me. "Azier, dig around it carefully. Let's see who it belonged to."

The wolf behind me snorted but complied, and soon they had the trap uncovered. Cyprus went around cautiously and looked down at the trap. He chuckled slightly before he looked at me and said, "You are in luck. The wolf that made this is still alive."

I swallowed before whispering, "Who?" A round of laughter sounded as the other two looked at the active weapon and sat down cautiously. One of the wolves replied, "Same wolf you wanted to see."

It took me a moment to come to terms, and finally, it dawned on me who. I swallowed before replying, "What are the chances that he comes out over here?"

Cyprus sighed deeply and replied, "Good question. It will be up to him if he wants to, however, he doesn't exactly know where we are either. Azier, do the call."

Azier grumbled, but sat down and howled a long howl. It was eerie, but it ended after a moment. We waited in silence before an answering call was made. Everyone in the patrol stood up and lowered their heads in submission. I swallowed and glanced towards the trees lined in front of me.

******

I sighed before leaning back onto the couch and sighed deeply. **"I don't want to bring it up, Anna. I was not that surprised."**

"Explain it to me then. What were your thoughts on that, Morphous?"

**"Anna, it was not traumatic to me. Sure, it surprised me, but it wasn't exactly traumatic."**

"Morphous."

She had a bite to her tone when she said my name. I sighed deeply and exhaled. **"I wasn't exactly traumatized by it, Anna. I knew that eventually someone was going to come and do something weird like that."**

She sighed after a moment, and put down her pen and parchment. She pinched her nose with her forefingers before speaking slowly, "Okay then. Tell me then, why did you expect it to happen, Morphous? Why did you not panic like everyone else in that situation?"

**"Anna, I had my share of experiences that are way before your time. It did not phase me in the slightest of what happened to me. It surprised me that they worked so well as a fucking**

team though, to get Quinn and Rafeor. That was…. That was a traumatic experience. Since they weren't taught how to control what is said."

She glanced at me, raised her eyebrows, and muttered to herself, "Finally, something to work with."

She glanced up at me before speaking, "Alright, I want you to explain what you felt when they brought Quinn and Rafeor out."

**"Why do you want me to do that, Anna?"**

"Morphous, please. Do it."

I sighed deeply, sat back on the couch, and began to recite what I felt, **"I was worried when they brought out Quinn first, I never trained him personally to see what his breaking point was. They placed him into a chair, and held him down. I didn't know at the time how he managed to hold against Nathaniel's punch, but now it makes sense. He didn't tell them anything, and acted as if he thought it was a hilarious predicament."**

I paused, as I watched Anna write down what I said down, I swallowed before continuing, **"As much as I like Quinn, he was not going to be the one who broke me to talk. We locked eye contact, and he seemed to understand that."**

Anna paused in her writing before speaking, "Would you allow Quinn to be killed simply because you don't want to tell information to anyone?"

I looked down at my hands before replying, **"Yes. His life is worth nothing compared to the secrets of the shifter palace, and what we have in our procession."**

She seemed shocked for a moment before she sighed deeply, put the quill down, and gave me a look. She snapped, "What do you have that someone else may want, Morphous?"

**"I cannot tell you that, Anna."**

"Why not?"

**"Because you would break under the slightest pressure."**

She swallowed, knew what I was referring to, and sighed deeply before replying, "Alright, fair. Continue with your recount, Morphous."

I grumbled for a moment, and was about to reply when a knock sounded on the door. Anna glanced at me and then at the door. She stood up, walked to the door, and opened it. In the doorway, Gillith stood waiting.

****

I stood up and stared at Gillith before Anna glanced at me and spoke, "Gillith, what can I do for you?"

He glanced at me before his eyes flickered to Anna. He sighed deeply before replying, "Herald has left the palace around fifteen hundred hours. He flew off to the west before being reported heading into the werewolf territory."

I swallowed, I had not told Anna about that yet, and I could tell by her tense behavior that she somehow knew. She replied after a moment, "Thank you, Gillith."

He dipped his head towards her, and me, before backing away and leaving.

****

Anna slowly turned around; her eyes flickered at me for a moment. "So, let me get this straight. Even after I told you not to send Herald, you still sent him?"

**"You did say that if I asked him to do it, and if he had something else to do he could have turned it down."**

"Did you say it as an order? Or as a question?"

I opened my mouth to respond but closed it after a moment, I didn't know the difference in my mind for a moment. She sighed before speaking, "Did you ask him if he was willing to take the messages? Or did you order him to, Morphous?"

**"I asked him if he wanted to, Anna. He said yes, and asked me when he could leave."**

"Did you?"

I grumbled before I replied, **"Why does it matter so much, Anna?"**

"It matters because of the rift in that family as is, Morphous! I told you that Herald and Killian are not compatible together. This will just cause a major issues when he returns."

She seemed to hesitate before whispering, "If he returns, Morphous."

I swallowed before replying, **"Anyone I send has that chance of being killed, Anna."**

She glowered at me. "That did not mean you can send someone out willy-nilly, Morphous! Herald isn't more than twenty years old."

**"He wanted to appease me, Anna. However, that is my duty. I can send anyone out as I want when it has a reason. I trust him, Anna, and I have a feeling he will not fail me."**

"He may not fail, Morphous, but it will change him."

**"Change him how?"**

"Killian and Herald do not see eye to eye as is, Morphous. This will cause a further rift in that family. One that you apparently don't know anything about. Have you never noticed that Herald is like a black sheep in that family compared to Quinn and his father? Have you never seen Herald's expressions whenever Killian is talking about Quinn and his accomplishments? Have you ever heard one nice thing that Killian has said about Herald?"

I swallowed and thought back. Now that she had brought it to light. I knew that she was right. I glanced and her shoulders slumped down before she shook her head slowly. "Leave me."

**"Anna…"**

"No, not now, Morphous. We will continue this another day. Once I get my feelings in check."

I moved towards the door and looked at her before replying, **"I…I had to send someone, Anna."**

"I know you had to, but I did not want you to send him of all people."

**"Who would have you sent?"**

"It does not matter who I would have sent, Morphous. You know your guards well. You should have sent one of the elites and not a kid."

**"Herald is not a little boy, Anna."**

"Get out, Morphous."

I grumbled but left, and soon she closed her door behind me with a soft thump. That was the closest you could get of her slamming a door close. I huffed once before walking away from her door.

******

A huge Lycan came out of the woods, along with twenty other werewolves. To say, they expected a single shifter like myself, was an understatement. Their eyes scanned the area, before the Lycan barked out, **"Spread out. Find anyone else lurking and bring them forth."**

The power radiating off of him made me flinch, but I looked up slightly and said, "Sir…"

Cyprus snarled and I instantly stopped trying to speak. But the Lycan glanced at me before growling, **"Speak."**

Cyprus glanced at him then back at me, and sat down replying, "My Lord…"

The Lycan stared at him and snarled, **"Not you. Him."**

Cyprus bowed his head at the rebuke, and I swallowed nervously before speaking, "My name is Herald. I was sent to give you a message."

The Lycan's eyes flashed for a moment and he seemed to speak to his other half before he shifted back to his human form. I stared up at the werewolf king before dropping my eyes to the ground. He was tall and scary. He flexed his upper body slightly and spoke, **"Why did you come to my territory?"**

I dropped my eyes to the ground, knowing eye contact could potentially cause an attack. "I come in peace, and I bring a message."

**"From who do you bring a message from?"**

"Morphous."

The curious look on everyone's face was evident, and the king frowned before speaking, **"Show me."**

I swallowed before replying, "I would in a heartbeat, however, it's underneath me."

He glanced at Cyprus before speaking, **"Cyprus? Explain."**

Cyprus bowed his head and replied after a moment, "My Lord, he has landed on an active one."

That caught his attention and he went to my foot. He chuckled before speaking to himself, **"Of all the ones in the area, you step on the one I personally made."**

Azier spoke up, "Does that mean you can dismantle it, My Lord?"

He glanced back at her. **"No, not this one. Everyone, clear out of the area."**

His alpha tone immediately worked and every single werewolf bowed, left, and headed further into their territory. I swallowed before I glanced at the werewolf king.

***

He looked down at the active bomb before speaking, **"What does Morphous want?"**

"He did not tell me, sir. It is in the letter I have. Although he has another one for the Carpathians too."

**"The Carpathians?"**

I nodded in response, and he frowned before speaking, "**What does he have to do with the Carpathians?**"

I shrugged slightly and he sighed deeply frowning. After a moment, he said, "**Are you a human or are you a shifter?**"

"Shifter."

"**Then what I want you to do is shift into a wolf. This sensor is made to detect wolf activity. Since you stepped on it when you are in your human form, it should trigger off.**"

"And if it doesn't?"

"**Then Morphous will have a lot of explaining to do.**"

He strode away, and I watched him for a moment before calling out, "Wait! Where are you going?"

"**Getting out of the blast radius.**"

I swallowed the lump in my throat before looking down at my foot and thinking of my wolf form and soon shifted to my charcoal silver wolf. Sure enough, it did not set it off, and I was able to step off of it.

****

After a few minutes, I howled a little bit. Not long enough to send enough werewolves to me, but enough for the werewolf king to come back.

He glanced at me before smirking, "**Ah, it worked.**"

"You weren't sure it was going to work?"

"**No.**"

I swallowed before shifting to my human form again and swallowed before taking out the letter and handing it to him. He took it gingerly in his hands as if he thought it was a trap. However, once it did nothing, he looked down and frowned. It was addressed to him and his mate, Sophronia. He glanced sharply, and said, "**Anything else?**"

I shook my head in response. He glanced at the tree line before calling, "**Patrol! Come here!**"

I swallowed the lump in my throat. If he noticed he did not say anything, five wolves trotted, Cyprus and Azier, the ones I knew by name, along with Batis, the wolf that Cyprus sent out.

The other two had no names. Cyprus bowed his head towards his king before speaking, "You called, My Lord?"

**"Escort Herald back to where you found him."**

"Yes, My Lord."

Cyprus growled and was apparently going to rough me up, at least that was probably on his mind, before his king spoke, **"Cyprus."**

"Yes, My Lord?"

**"Safely. He did nothing wrong. I do not see why I should worry about a lonely messenger."**

"He could be a spy, My Lord! Why let him off easy?"

**"Are you challenging my authority?"**

His eyes flickered his Lycan's color, and instantly all the werewolves surrounding the area went down in submission, including Cyprus. He swallowed before whimpering, "No, My Lord."

**"Good. Now take him back."**

Cyprus and the others bowed to him, turned toward me, and rolled their heads before trotting backward. I turned to follow, but their king spoke, **"Herald."**

I turned around, dipped my head down, and kept my eyes downcast. I whispered, "Yes, My Lord?"

**"Shift into your wolf form as you leave."**

I bowed and shifted to my wolf. A couple of gasps escaped everyone around me, but I thought nothing of it. I turned around and trotted toward the border patrol. Cyprus looked over at his king before leaving into the undergrowth. They knew something of my wolf form. I just didn't know what.

****

After trudging through their territory, back the way we had come, I asked after a moment, "Why do you guys seem to know my wolf colorations?"

One of the two that had not said who they were, paused in his walking, but after a moment, kept going. Cyprus sighed deeply, not stopping as he went. "I am afraid I cannot answer that question to you."

"Why not? You all seemed to hold your breath when you saw my form."

For a good solid minute, no one spoke, but Azier spoke, making Cyprus give her a look, "It is because your form is what many legends in the werewolf realm have. No one has that coloration."

I frowned and replied after a moment, "But I am not a werewolf? Why would I be foretold in your legends?"

"That is a good question. I was actually hoping you would know that answer yourself."

I frowned and looked at every single wolf before me. I said, "How would I know if I was special?"

Cyprus looked at me before growling, "Azier, enough. You said too much as is. As for you, I do not know. Your fur pattern and down to the color is in the prophecy that we had been passed down. King to king, sons to sons, daughters to daughters. It is foretold that the wolf that bore your colorations would be the most powerful. For centuries we have waited, and only to have a filthy shifter to be the one we wait for? It doesn't make sense."

I growled at the filthy shifter part, but he smirked in response and continued. After a moment, Batis spoke, "Cyprus?"

"What Batis?"

"Where are we going?"

I glanced around suddenly and knew that we did not come this way. My wolf form growled slightly before Cyprus replied, "It does not concern you, Batis."

"Nathaniel had orders."

So far everyone else in the patrol stopped, including myself. They stared at Cyprus before Batis growled, "Where are we going, Cyprus?"

Cyprus eyed us all before snarling, "Nathaniel has gone soft. He is letting someone leave our territory without a second thought. After what just happened, aren't you all curious about the why?"

They glanced at each other, but Azier replied, "Orders are orders, Cyprus. You should know since you are delta ranking."

I glanced at him and then at everyone else before speaking, "Delta?"

Batis glanced at me and rolled his eyes. "Fourth in command."

I frowned and glanced at everyone else. "Why does that matter?"

Cyprus scoffed before snarling, "It matters because it makes me more superior to these wolves."

"In what way are you more superior to them?"

"I have the rank to them. They are common wolves, trained to be here. Or also known as elites."

"Why does it matter if they are elites and not delta?"

"I doubt that you would understand, shifter, you have no ranking in the shifter compound," replied Azier.

I glanced at her before glancing back to Cyprus and speaking, "Ranking does not matter as long as the person is doing their job correctly. Are you not going to do your duty and command from your king properly, Cyprus?"

He growled in response and raised his hackles before growling, "What Nathaniel doesn't know won't hurt him."

Batis stepped slightly in front of me before replying, "We had orders to take him safely to the spot where we found him, Cyprus."

"Step away from him, Batis!"

"No."

Cyprus growled and launched himself at Batis, faster than I could react. But soon I was scrambling backward as they fought. Batis was a bit smaller than Cyprus, and Cyprus was using his size as an advantage to shove Batis down. I swallowed as the others stared in shock at what was happening before us. I swallowed for a moment before my wolf took complete reins of the situation, "**ENOUGH!**"

Everyone including Cyprus and Batis froze. They looked up slowly at me and they released each other, their tails between their legs for a moment. My wolf looked at Batis before speaking, "**You did nothing wrong, Batis.**"

He dipped his head towards me, trotting a bit away before my wolf looked at Cyprus and growled, "**It is you that is in the wrong. Explain to me what you are doing. Now.**"

Cyprus stared at me for a moment and growled, "Who are you?"

"**My name is Firefoot.**"

"Why didn't you speak before now, Firefoot?"

**"There was no reason to until now. You are in the wrong, and you know it too. You may be delta, but I outrank you."**

"What rank are you?"

**"Depending on how to look at it, I am an alpha in my own right. In your kingdom, it may differ. It doesn't matter, however."**

"It matters to me."

**"Too bad. I am not in a position to give you more information. I have my duty to complete, Cyprus. If you wish to tussle with me, so be it. However, you will be made a fool of."**

He growled low in his throat at the threat, but I blinked at him slowly and spoke, **"Well? What is your decision?"**

"Come on."

He turned around and headed back into the woods. I waited a moment before releasing Herald again. I panted, looked at the curious werewolves, and stared at them all. Batis glanced where Cyprus left before speaking, "Well, that was unexpected."

"Wha… what happened?"

He glanced at me before replying, "You have a wolf spirit in you that is higher than a normal wolf, and higher than a delta."

"What? That's not possible."

He shrugged and replied as he continued forward, "Hey don't look at me with that look. You surprised us all."

Batis had a limp and I was about to say something about it, but the others trotted to keep up with Batis. I sighed before following them.

****

After a half hour, we were exactly back at where I found them, and I swallowed. I noticed that Batis and Cyprus were side-eyeing each other, but nothing more than fighting. I swallowed and looked at the rest, they blinked at me slightly before Azier spoke, "Whatever mission you are on, is apparently important. Get going."

I looked at the rest and said, "Thank you."

The others huffed, turned away, and walked away before disappearing into the woods, leaving Batis, Cyprus, and Azier with me. I looked up at the tree I had leaped down from before shifting into a bird and flying upward. I perched on it before flying east.

******

We watched as he flew off, and Batis growled, "Well that explains something to me. Thank you, Cyprus for doing what you did."

Cyprus scowled before replying, "Now, don't give me all the credit. It was your idea to do that."

"It doesn't matter whose idea it was. It gave us a sign that times are changing," I growled.

Batis and Cyprus glanced at me. Cyprus replied, "What do you mean times are changing, Azier? Has your mother told you anything else on this?"

I shook my head and replied, "It doesn't matter what she has said or has not said. I just meant that times are changing."

Batis scoffed and nudged me with his snout before trotting away. "Come on, we better be going back home. We have to report to Nathaniel what we found out."

I sighed as I watched the raven flying off when Cyprus nudged me, bringing me back to them. I smiled before looping alongside my brothers. Myself and Batis may not have been born with the delta blood as Cyprus, but that did not mean we were not as powerful. We knew when to wait for time.

We caught up to the others rather quickly, but they seemed shocked to see us before running back to our home.

# Chapter 20

I walked away from Anna's office, with my head down, I should have known better than what I did. A clearing of the throat sounded, and I looked up and saw Killian standing there. I swallowed before raising my head slightly. He paused and ran his eyes up and down me, and speaking, "What happened inside with, Anna?"

**"None of your business, Killian."**

"I am making it my business, Morphous. What did you and Anna talk about?"

I opened my mouth to reply, but Gillith walked around the corner, and he apparently heard what Killian had asked. He said, "Now, now, now, Killian. That is confidential information between the doctor and patient."

For a moment, I had a smug look across my face, but Killian threw daggers at me with his eyes and turned his attention to Gillith, "Hello, Gillith."

"Killian."

I glanced at either of them and started to edge away before they could stop me. However, I was not that lucky, Gillith spoke addressing me, "My Lord?"

**"Yes, Gillith?"**

"There is still no sign of, Herald. Do you want us to send a party out?"

**"No, if he went out. Then he will come back once he can."**

"May I ask where my son went without having anyone inform me?" Killian's eyes flashed purple for a moment, but it was a fleeting second.

Gillith glanced at him and replied, "He left at fifteen hundred hours, and flew towards the werewolf territory. I don't know why, but it was in Feilian's report."

I swallowed slightly, so Feilian did not rattle on me on having Herald go. I wonder why he left that out of the report. I frowned slightly, but Killian scorched me with his eyes before he replied to Gillith, "Inform me immediately when he arrives back here, Gillith."

"Of course, Killian."

The air was hot among the three of us, each of us caught in a heated battle – a battle of wills, almost. Gillith probably knew there was something else going on, which was why he was stalking, however, he did not know who it was between. Killian stared at me with hard eyes, but he kept his eyes normal since Gillith was there. I glanced down the hall before speaking, **"I'll be in my office. Gillith, come with me?"**

"Of course."

**"Good evening, Killian."**

Killian's eyes bore into my back, but Gillith and I walked towards my office without a word.

*****

As soon as my office door shut, Gillith looked around the room. Found nothing, and turned sharply to me before snapping, "What is the deal with you and Killian?"

**"What do you mean?"**

"I am not stupid, Morphous. What is the issue with Killian?"

I sighed glanced at the door, and motioned him closer to me before replying, **"He's not a shifter, Gillith."**

"What is he then?"

I swallowed before glancing at the door again and replying, **"Demon."**

"Nah man, they are dead. All of them. They died back when the experiment happened centuries ago."

**"That's what I thought too, but his eyes change colors and are not the same as shifters."**

"How long have you known this, Morphous?"

**"Found out this morning."**

"Is that why Killian is following you around everywhere? So, you don't tell his little secret?"

**"Yeah."**

"Why did you tell me that?"

**"Because you wanted to know what the issue was between myself and Killian. That is why."**

"Is this something that can get someone like myself or others killed, Morphous?"

I frowned and bit my lip slightly. He groaned before growling, "It is, is it not? Damn it, Morphous."

**"What did you want me to do, Gillith?"**

"Honestly, I don't know. However, if he is what he is, then why is he here?"

**"That is the same question I asked him. He said he doesn't need to inform me of that information."**

"Like hell, Morphous! He needs to tell you something. You are the King."

He froze and suddenly realized something. He looked at the door before whispering, "But if he is what you said he is, that means he does not follow the shifter rules. That means he is an outcast and does not feel compelled to keep himself in check. Damn, Morphous, what are you going to do?"

**"I sent Herald out to deliver messages to the werewolves, and the Carpathians."**

For a moment, he stared at me in shock and replied, "The Carpathians? Are you nuts? We won't get that boy alive. Not with their feeding habits, Morphous."

I swallowed, I knew the risks before I replied, **"I know, but I couldn't send Quinn due to Anna's order, and I don't trust Killian to do it."**

"Understandable. However, why choose Herald?"

**"Honestly don't know why I did. Something just told me to do it."**

"You are going to get someone killed, Morphous, and I sure as hell hope it's not me."

I grumbled slightly, knowing he was correct. Gillith sighed deeply and said, "Anyhow, Feilian also mentioned you in his report, but the fact that the tension between you and Killian was high when I found you guys. I kept it quiet. I understand now why, but that is that. I will find the report, and destroy it."

**"No."**

"No? Are you crazy, Morphous? What if Killian reads that?"

**"You mentioned the report in the hallway with Killian, Gillith, we cannot destroy the report. He will simply ask Feilian to give him a verbal report. Either way, we are screwed."**

"Don't you mean YOU are screwed? I am not in this mess, Morphous."

**"You are now."**

He scowled and replied, "I wished I kept my mouth shut about it."

**"I bet you do, but you cannot do anything about it anymore as I can. We are stuck."**

He sighed deeply before replying, "So, what now?"

**"Now we hope that Herald gets back safely, and found before Killian finds him."**

Gillith sighed deeply before running his hand across his face, and speaking, "Why don't you just send him to Davis? Tell him that the kid did nothing wrong, and to keep an eye on him?"

**"Because when has Davis been kind to anyone? You sent him there based on the fact that he would do what needs to be done."**

"Ugh! True, that is correct. Damn, so what now?"

I opened my mouth to reply but shut it, I shook my head slowly before moving towards my couch and sitting down gingerly. **"I honestly do not know what to do. We cannot send Killian out, he will refuse. We have to act like we know nothing."**

"Who else knows of what he is, Morphous?"

**"You, Killian of course, myself, and I have a feeling someone else knows too."**

"Damn it, Morphous."

I smiled grimly before nodding my head in agreement. For a few minutes, we were in silence. Gillith looked lost for a moment and then frowned and scrunched his face slightly before speaking slowly, "If Herald is not safe here, Morphous, why don't you send him somewhere else?"

**"Where? We can't exactly send him anywhere we want."**

He glanced at me and sighed deeply before replying, "Everyone knows that you and the werewolf king were friends, Morphous. Surely, he would take the poor kid in."

**"Are you out of your mind? They will slaughter him."**

"Will they? You sent him on a solo mission to them, and a solo mission to the carpathians. Out of either of those supernatural species, which of them do you trust to make sure he is safe?"

I frowned. He had a valid point, then another thought came to my mind. I glanced up at him after a moment, and said, **"What about the experiment? The one that had the demons killed?"**

"The kid? Are you nuts, Morphous? The human government is after her."

**"Yes, true. However, it would also mean that Herald would be safe. Killian would not know where to find Herald afterward since they move so many times."**

Gillith frowned before replying, "Two of them have a reputation as is, Morphous, are you sure you want to entrust him with Herald?"

**"Have a better idea?"**

"No."

**"Any further objections?"**

He sighed and shook his head before whispering, "No."

I sighed deeply before speaking, "**I, however, do not know where she would be.**"

"Last report from Davis, he mentioned the two of them were near the town. Across the border, but that was two weeks ago."

My head shot up and my mouth dropped slightly before replying, "**What are they named?**"

He scratched the back of his head before replying, "I believe one is named Sethic, and the other is Rufenic? I don't honestly understand the IC at the end of their names."

**"Perhaps she is trying to make it sound current."**

"Perhaps, but I am pretty sure the IC is going to be dropped, eventually."

**"True."**

We sat in silence before Gillith spoke, "So, what are you going to do now?"

I glanced at him and was about to reply, when a knock sounded on the door. We both exchanged looks and I shook my head slightly. We stayed silent, but another knock sounded. I sighed as I stood up and went to the door, before turning to Gillith, "**Not a word.**"

He nodded in response.

****

 I opened the door and was surprised. Quinn stood at the door, and he was fidgeting slightly. "What do you know about, Herald?"

We at Quinn and finally, Quinn looked up and stared hard at us. "Well?"

I stepped backward, and Quinn hesitated for a split second before entering the room. I closed the door before turning to face him. Quinn swallowed and said, "No one else is in here besides us three correct? My father is not here?"

Gillith and I exchanged glances, before I replied slowly, "**No Killian is not here.**"

Quinn seemed to struggle for a moment before speaking, "I know that you have a bunch of things to do, Morphous, but I should tell you this in person. I am not alone in my mind, I have something else. Another form even, I don't know how to explain it. However, I heal differently, I…"

He rambled for a moment, before I cut him off, "**Quinn. Enough.**"

He fell silent before he took a shaky breath and whispered, "I know my father favors me over Herald, and it is solely because I have the other form that he does not. Our mother warned our father apparently that one of us children would become what she is. A shifter blood, and whatever I have would not be present in one of us. I don't think my father understood it entirely."

We all stared at him, and he swallowed before continuing, "He always told me that I was different compared to Herald and that I had more responsibilities compared to him. I was resentful towards Herald due to that. However, I do not want to experience the…."

He swallowed again, and with tears in his eyes, he whispered, "I do not want to experience the no love that Herald had endured during our youth. Herald got no love from our father, he was more outcasted. The black sheep of the family."

He fell silent, and we waited to see if he would say more, but when he kept silent. I glanced at Gillith and spoke slowly, "**Quinn, what are you confessing to?**"

"I confess that I am not a shifter. I may have shifter blood, but I am not a pure-blood shifter."

We all fell silent. He just confirmed what I had found out this morning, that the demon had passed Herald. However, finding out that it was warned about was the thing. I sighed deeply before glancing at Gillith, who had been silent throughout the entire exchange. We locked eye contact for a moment, before Gillith spoke, "What are your questions on your brother Quinn?"

"Where is he? I know you, Morphous, sent him on a mission tonight. However, what the mission is, I do not know."

I frowned before replying, "**Where do your loyalties lie, Quinn? Do they lie with the shifters or do they lie with your father?**"

He frowned before glancing between me and Gillith and answered, "With the shifters. I may have grown up with my father teaching me different things, but it did not really interest me in what he was teaching, besides teaching me to hide my other form."

Gillith and I exchanged glances, Gillith rumbled, "You have to swear on something important to you, Quinn."

He stared at him as if he had grown two heads, before glancing at me. He sighed deeply before speaking, "I swear on my mother's grave, along with my other siblings."

I froze and stared at him before whispering, "**Other siblings?**"

For a moment, he looked at me shocked before slowly nodding, "Yeah. I had a sister and two other brothers. I was the second eldest, and another one was in between myself and only one was younger than Herald. Not by much, but it would technically be Herald the second youngest."

Gillith and I exchanged glances, before Gillith asked, "What happened to your siblings?"

He swallowed before looking down at his hands and speaking, "I…I lost control of my other half. He took over and killed them all because they weren't like us. He would have killed Herald too, but our father got to me before he could."

To say, we were shocked was an understatement, we were flabbergasted. No one knew that. I glanced at Gillith and saw him swallow nervously, but Quinn spoke softly, "My father stopped me before I could kill Herald, but my mother died soon afterward. I have a feeling that my father killed her since she tried her hardest to stop me. He didn't want her family to know about what he was, and was keeping us a secret."

"How can you be a secret?"

"My father informed our mother's family that all of us perished. They even saw some of my siblings' bodies, alongside my mothers. They…. They didn't ask questions about the other two that were missing."

**"Who else knows about that history, Quinn?"**

For a moment, he seemed to struggle, his eyes flashed black for a split second before it disappeared again. Gillith and I exchanged glances, but Quinn replied, "Not many. You, Gillith, father, and possibly Anna."

"That…. That is a lot of new information. Morphous, what are you going to do with it?"

I stared into the wall closest to me before slowly shaking my head and speaking, **"I don't know. I don't know what to do."**

Quinn bit his lip before speaking, "Ummm… why don't you send Herald out to Davis?"

"Why?"

"Wouldn't that be the safest place with my father looking for him?"

**"What do you mean by that?"**

"The only reason why I knew that you sent Herald on that mission, is because my father raved to me that you were up to something, and it involved Herald. He actually casually mentioned that he would…. He would make sure that he would not see another sunrise."

Gillith stiffened and I swallowed. "**What?**"

"My father plans on killing Herald when he gets back. I want to help him leave. Please."

"We can't send him to Davis. He is too much of a hardhead. And besides that, Killian is not afraid of Davis."

"You are correct in that form, however, Davis knows stuff that can keep my brother safe."

**"What are you implying, Quinn?"**

"I read the same reports as you Gillith, but I also get another one from someone else inside his ranks. That has been in the town area that the experiment has been occupying."

Gillith and I exchanged looks, and finally, Gillith replied, "You know of the experiment?"

"I may or may not know that she is planning on moving within the next week. Her sons are hotheads which may cause them to move before earlier. However, my informer has said that they actually take in those who need to hide."

**"How trustworthy is this informer of yours?"**

"It doesn't matter that much, Morphous, as long as my brother disappears."

I sighed deeply before replying, **"We don't even know how to tell Herald."**

"Connect to him, Morphous. He is a full-blooded shifter, not what I am."

**"How are you so sure that he is a shifter and not one of you?"**

"Based on the fact that father never showed kindness to him. Based on my training to hold back my other form, and the fact that I slaughtered my other siblings. I do not know how else to prove to you that he is indeed a shifter, but Morphous should be able to connect to him since he is a king of the shifters."

We stared at each other in silence for a few seconds, he was correct. I should be able to connect to Herald, but I never tried since I always assumed that they were all the same. I sighed deeply before speaking, **"Where do you want me to send your brother?"**

"Send him to Davis. Tell him to give him to Andres."

"Andres? Isn't that the one that YOU had an issue with and requested his transfer there?"

For a moment, Quinn looked a little sheepish before replying, "I had to put someone I trusted on the wall. Don't get me wrong, Davis does not withhold any details in his reports, but it was another layer of protection. It also gave me another layer of knowledge on what was happening on that border. Which is why, I had told you to send more guards out that way a few weeks ago, Gillith."

"Oh. What did that achieve?"

"It made it so, no one had to work a full day straight without any breaks. Davis casually mentioned to Andres that they were understaffed, and I have a feeling that Davis knows that Andres is my mole inside his order."

"He wouldn't do anything to Andres."

"I'm not saying that he would, Gillith. I trust him. I understand why you sent him there of all places. He thrives in that environment. He is a loyal shifter."

Gillith seemed rather pleased by the compliments and I shook my head slowly, amused slightly. Quinn knew how to diffuse the situation and did it well. I sighed deeply and was about to speak when another knock on the door sounded. I glanced at Quinn and Gillith but they seemed perplexed.

I went to open the door, but Quinn spoke up, "Wait."

I glanced back at him with a questioning look before he continued, "My father would know something is up if I am seen with you and Gillith. I need to hide."

"Shift then Quinn, and blend in on my jacket."

Quinn glanced at his jacket and frowned slightly before glancing at mem, shrugging before shifting to a black beetle and situating himself. If I didn't see where he landed, I would have never known he was there. I sighed deeply before opening the door and found it was indeed Killian.

*****

Killian and I stared at each other before Killian glanced back into my office, seeing Gillith there and flickering his eyes to mine. He growled, "What are you discussing?"

**"It does not matter to you, Killian."**

"I am making it my business, Morphous."

**"Too bad. I am not going to tell you."**

I went to shut the door, but Killian forced himself into the office, and the door snapped shut behind him. I growled at him, Abacore glinting in my eyes before I rumbled, **"That was not an invitation to come inside, Killian. Out."**

"No, not until you tell me what you were discussing."

We stared at each other, but Killian did not budge. Gillith spoke up after a few moments, "Killian, your king does not want you inside his office at this current moment."

Killian's eyes flickered to Gillith before he replied, "What do you know, Gillith?"

"I am not going to say what I have discussed with Morphous. It has to deal with the border though. We were discussing how many guards we needed to send up there."

Killian frowned, he knew that Gillith was the one who dealt with that aspect, and glanced at me before speaking, "Meddling with Gillith's job now?"

"No."

"Then what? You just said you were discussing the border."

"True, but it was more if we can. I don't know how many people that Morphous wanted at the border since of the recent attack."

For a moment, there was tension in the air. Killian finally sighed deeply and stepped backward before speaking, "Anything else?"

"No."

"Are you lying to me, Gillith?"

"Not really."

"It is a simple yes or no Gillith. Are you lying to me?"

"I do not answer to you, Killian."

Killian stared at him before replying, "Leave us, Gillith."

"I do not follow your command, Killian. I answer to Morphous."

He seemed to struggle, he sighed deeply and closed his eyes before replying, "Gillith?"

"Hmmm?"

"Get out."

"No."

"You are driving my patience, Gillith."

"I guess we are in the same boat then Killian. I am not leaving until Morphous commands me."

Killian glanced at me again before jerking his head towards him as if trying to intimidate me to comply. However, I raised my eyebrows and crossed my arms before rumbling, "**Out Killian.**"

Killian stared at me in rage, his eyes flickered purple for a split second before he breathed out heavily and snapped, "I will wait my turn, Morphous. You and I need to have a long chat."

**"Noted. Now out."**

Killian sneered slightly, turned sharply on his heel, opened the door, and slammed it on his exit.

****

When Killian was indeed out and gone, we looked at each other. Quinn shifted back and spoke, "I know something else, too."

**"What now?"**

"I know why he won't leave."

"Why?"

"Rafeor."

**"What does my daughter have to do with any of this?"**

He glanced at me before blinking. "You have a hybrid between a shifter and a werewolf Morphous. And not JUST any werewolf. It was the Queen before she met Nathaniel."

I frowned and leaned against the door, my arms still crossed. It was Gillith who whispered, "What?"

Quinn glanced at him before glancing at me and replying, "Morphous caused the riot to cover the fact that he wanted his daughter to be presumed dead so no one else went to find her. He stole something, I won't indulge in that, but that artifact is inside the box that you were protecting."

Gillith's eyes flashed orange and he growled, "Morphous? What?"

I sighed deeply before replying, "**He's telling the truth.**"

"So, all those lives that were lost, it was all because you wanted to hide something?"

**"Yeah…"**

"I should send you to be straightened out by Davis."

I hmphed, knowing that Davis would follow every command I gave without hesitation since I was his king. He sighed and rubbed his hand across his face, and I smirked slightly. Quinn, however, looked at me as if I had grown two heads for a moment. He said, "My father told me that Rafeor will be a huge part of the battle. However, there is one factor that is the reason why he has not done anything. You know the history that has been passed down centuries ago, right? The prophecies?"

**"What about it?"**

"There was one that was passed down from my grandfather apparently. That the hybrid between the two species, yes, would be the deadliest of all beings on earth, but with our hand in the younger age of her finding out, well, let's put it this way, with only one species, she would be used to be a weapon. However, my father told me that if he helps her in training and stuff, she will unite both the werewolves and the shifters together. There will be in division between any of the supernatural species. That also includes the experiment and the Carpathians."

For a moment, none of us spoke. Gillith spoke after some time, "So, Rafeor is a weapon alone with one species. However, if she was working with your father, then she wouldn't be a weapon?"

Quinn shrugged and replied, "That is what was passed down to me by my father. I do not know what he is planning, but I also know that he will leave Rafeor where she is currently as long as Morphous does not make an idiot move."

I opened my mouth to retort, but Gillith sneered before speaking, "Too late on that aspect."

Quinn sighed before speaking, "If that is the case, then he may move her to where he took the other werewolf prisoners."

Gillith's head shot up at that statement; he rumbled, "What? Where did he take them?"

Quinn shrugged and replied, "Personally, I do not know where. However, my father did mention it was where his family grew up. Before the attack."

I frowned, I had heard of the ruins but I had never seen them. I rubbed my hand across my face and finally, Gillith spoke, "I've heard of where you speak of. However, that is a two-day travel, without stopping. Killian was only gone a day."

Quinn looked perplexed. "Then his other form must have taken over. It is the only way he got there and back within a day."

**"Do you know what he is, Quinn?"**

He hesitated before glancing at Gillith and speaking, "A demon, and one of the original ones too. His family was the one that was slaughtered all those centuries ago. I have actually heard him mutter a name once or twice, Kaylo. I think, but I am pretty sure whatever happened to her was horrific. Since I had tried to talk to him about it before, and he refused to."

**"Hmmm... I guess I need to look back at what my forefather had mentioned about that."**

"I wonder if the Carpathians know anything about it. They have lived for a long time."

"From what I have heard, the current King of their people are different from those from that era. I don't know if the King of their past is still alive, or dead. I don't know how someone rises to power in that realm. Do you, Morphous?"

I shook my head in response, and we all went in silence. I yawned suddenly, it had been a long day, and I was done with today. Quinn glanced at me. "It has been a long day for all of us. We should all go to our rooms and get some sleep."

Quinn went towards the door, but I called out, "**No, you two don't leave.**"

"Why not?"

**"Because Killian will find either of you and question you. I do not know what his style of questioning is."**

Quinn was silent and Gillith looked perplexed but Quinn replied after a moment, "As much as I dislike that you are correct, Morphous, you are correct. My father would come for Gillith in the night, find out whatever was talked about, every single secret. And then kill him, and then come for me, since Gillith would unwillingly snitch that I was involved and torture me for the intel. And I honestly don't know how that would go. Then he would either come for you, Morphous, and argue, or take Rafeor with him and disappear."

I opened my mouth and shut it. He had laid it out so clearly on how his father would do it. I glanced at Gillith and saw that he was shocked, but soon understood. He sighed resignedly before speaking, "What is stopping him from coming in here without us knowing once we go to sleep?"

"Post guards at the door of the office. Tell them no one is allowed to enter. You would have to do this, Morphous, since if Gillith did it, they would not have an issue letting Killian inside. With your direct order though, they won't refuse your order."

I sighed deeply and was about to say something, but Quinn whispered something to himself, "And it helps that you have connections to every single shifter here and not have to forcefully have a connection."

"Huh?"

Quinn glanced at him and swallowed before replying, "My father and I had to forcefully take blood from every single guard to make a connection to them. It has to be a once-a-year affair too since…. Otherwise, we wouldn't be able to. Herald can, so that is the difference in that aspect. However, my father either learned or found out that trick by accident at one time or another."

Gillith frowned and replied, "I never had to give you blood."

"No, you didn't. However, Anna has your blood, along with almost every single guard's blood."

"Oh."

"Yeah."

I sighed deeply and another yawn escaped me. Quinn glanced at me and raised his eyebrow before clearing his throat, looking at me expectantly. I grumbled before closing my eyes and thought of Feilian and Conrade, ordering them to guard my door.

I dropped their connections, looked at Gillith, and sighed deeply before motioning toward the other two doors inside my office. **"Pick a room."**

Quinn glanced at the one on the left and looked at me before speaking, "Which one is the entrance to the dungeons?"

**"That would be my chambers."**

"Ah, ok."

He went to the door on the left, opened it, entered, and closed the door with a soft click. Leaving Gillith and I to stare at each other.


*****


I sighed deeply and headed towards my chamber before anything else happened. Gillith cleared his throat, and I stopped before my door. I kept my back to him, before replying, **"Yes?"**

"Were you ever going to inform me of why Rafeor is what she was?"

**"The less people who know Gillith was my goal."**

"So, you weren't?"

**"No."**

"Good night, My Lord."

**"Good night, Gillith."**

I opened my door and entered. Closing the door before sitting down in my bed and kicking off my boots before lying further into my bed. I sighed heavily before thinking. Am I correct in what I am doing? Am I doing it for selfish reasons?

Abacore stopped my mind from rambling, **"Sleep, Morph. I keep watch."**

**"Okay, Abacore."**

I closed my eyes and fell asleep.

# Chapter 21

I left Morphous's office in a rage, how dare he? He was a simple merchant king of anything, compared to those who had ruled before him. I growled low in my throat, rounded a corner, and ran into Rafeor. Since I was going so fast around the corner, I slammed into her squarely in the center, knocking both of us over, she fell with a thud, along with myself on top of her. I scrambled to my feet and glanced down at her for a moment, before speaking, "I…"

She glanced up at me, her hair was everywhere in her face, she breathed out sharply, and her hair puffed away. She started to chuckle before speaking, "**Where were you heading at a such fast pace?**"

I opened my mouth to reply but closed it after a moment and sighed deeply as I lowered my head. I offered her my right hand, and she took it. I pulled her to her feet before, resting my left on her shoulder to steady her. She chuckled slightly before speaking, "**Don't worry about it, Killian. I am sure you did not mean to do that.**"

"I apologize, Rafeor, I did not realize that anyone was going to be awake at this hour."

She sighed before whispering, "**Yeah…. Me neither.**"

"What are you doing out and about at this hour?"

"**Couldn't sleep. I was also kind of curious where the dungeons are so, I can pay a visit to Lord Verien.**"

I could tell by the tone she had that, was filled with rage, and I kind of thought that her Lycan would be fronting, but apparently, that was not the case. I raised my eyebrow before speaking, "Do you want me to take you there, Rafeor?"

"**I'm sure I can ask someone else to get there.**"

"Not really, not many know the entrance to it."

"**Really?**"

"Really."

She sighed, before replying, "**Alright, can you take me to the dungeons?**"

I glanced at the closed candle before turning around and offering her my elbow and speaking, "Okay, come along."

For a moment, she stared at me with a shocked expression, as if she did not really think I would take her there. However, after the shock wore off, she smiled sweetly and allowed me to escort her.

****

After a few minutes of walking in silence, we got to a stone wall, I paused in front of it. Rafeor glanced around before speaking, "**Ummm, why are we staring at a wall?**"

I glanced at her slightly and smiled before reaching about a foot above her head, grabbed a brick that was sticking out slightly, and pushed it inward. The door slid open. Her jaw dropped in shock, I felt amused at her expression. I would have laughed, but I couldn't since this was not the real entrance to the dungeons, it was the hidden one. One not too many knew about it, in fact, doubtful that Morphous even knows of this one.

She stepped through the door, into the dank darkness, and looked at me. I followed her after a moment, checking down the hallways before following her. I blinked once before the door closed, enclosing us in darkness.

*****

I flew to the east, it was well after dark, and I kept faltering in my speed. However, I knew that the Carpathians were awake during the evenings. I landed in a tree and panted slightly before looking down, and noticed movement. I cracked open my beak slightly, but nothing. I stayed in the tree and kept glancing down. I did not know where the Carpathians would be, no one informed me on where to find them. I sighed deeply and my eyelids drooped. I shook my head, before gliding to the other tree, and went tree hoping.

****

It was an hour before sunrise when I stopped in a big oak tree. I panted as my head leaned forward in wariness, when a voice came above me, "Who are you?"

I jerked my head upward and saw a bat staring down at me from his perch. I swallowed before replying, "My name is Herald. You?"

195

He blinked his eyes once before replying, "What are you looking for?"

"I'm looking for the Carpathians."

"Why?"

"I have a message from my King that I need to deliver."

The bat eyed me thoughtfully before replying, "Go to the ground, and shift."

I hesitated but complied after a moment. I hopped off the branch and glided down, I stayed still before shifting to my human form. I crouched in the dead leaves and straightened myself. I glanced up at the bat and saw him blink once before he unhooked his feet and twittered down to the ground. He landed and shifted to a Carpathian. He had jet-black hair, long white nails, black clothing, and a black and red cape draped on his shoulders and back. He had a set of twin swords strapped to his back, along with countless other weapons. All of which would kill me in a heartbeat. He cleared his throat, and I glanced up, meeting his fiery orange eyes. He blinked once and they turned to a dull blue.

I swallowed and looked down again before moving a leaf around with my foot. I spoke, "What are you going to do to me?"

He regarded me for a moment before replying, "Depends. What the message is? Is it verbal?"

"No, I have a written message."

"Then give it here, and leave."

I stared at him and licked my lips nervously. "My orders were to deliver it to the King."

He stared at me for a hard minute, he lowered his hand down and his eyes sparked before growling, "No one is to see Lord Dracula. Not without bringing a gift. You have a gift for him?"

I swallowed and shook my head. He scoffed and growled, "What is in the message?"

I looked down at the envelope before replying, "I don't know. My King didn't inform me of the message."

"Why didn't he tell you?"

I shrugged, and he growled low in his throat before speaking again, "What rank in your kingdom are you? If you are a lowly servant, then I outrank you. Hand over the message, and be off."

I swallowed and touched the envelope again with my trembling hands and replied, "And if don't?"

In a blink of an eye, he was in front of me, towering over me by a foot. He glowered down at me before snapping, "Lord Dracula does not accept anyone inside his home besides his kin. You are not kin, therefore, you are an outcast. Something tasty."

He snapped his teeth down, and his eyes gleamed in hunger before it faded away. I swallowed and cowered slightly when another shout came from another tree, "NUNITO! Who are you talking to?"

The Carpathian I was talking to flinched and backed away from me. Another bat flew down and hovered for a moment before shifting to another Carpathian. He crouched down upon the dead leaves, before straightening himself. He was tall, around six foot nine, lean as a board, with weapons similar to Nunito, and very dangerous. I felt his power oozing from him.

I lowered my eyes and spoke, "My name…"

"Did I allow you to speak?"

I glanced up at the new Carpathian and swallowed. His glacier-blue eyes stared down at me, his face slightly red in anger. I shook my head and he turned his attention to Nunito.

"Nunito, you know you are not allowed to converse with ANYONE. You were to report immediately to me beforehand. You broke the one rule I gave you."

"I apologize."

Nunito mumbled, and the other Carpathian sneered before snapping, "Apologize? What do you think Lord Dracula will hear? I will make it seem that you left your post. You will be banished."

Nunito swallowed and bowed his head in shame. I stared between them before I spoke up, "Enough."

Nunito flinched, closed his eyes, and just shook his head slightly. The other one stiffened. He blinked once to Nunito before turning his gaze towards me and hissing, "Toys are meant to be seen BUT NOT HEARD! Nunito, punish your toy."

Nunito looked at me and swallowed before replying, "It's not mine."

I growled at the term 'it' and snapped, "I understand now why my King does not do matters with the Carpathians. You are a dick."

Nunito froze and snapped his head quickly in my direction, his jaw dropped slightly. The other one opened his mouth and closed it before blinking once and speaking slowly, "Your king? Who is your King?"

I straightened myself slightly before replying, "Morphous Draconis."

They both blinked once and the Carpathian glanced at Nunito before speaking, "Nunito, get back to your perch. Stay there. I will take this one."

Nunito seemed to hesitate, but soon nodded and gestured towards me to follow the new Carpathian.

*****

For a moment, there was only darkness, and after another thirty seconds, Rafeor spoke, "**So, you like the darkness, Killian?**"

I chuckled before replying, "You will see well. Let your Lycan surface slightly, and you won't have any issues."

She paused before replying, "**You want me to wake my Lycan?**"

I frowned, I didn't seem to understand that their other forms slept at different times. I sighed deeply though, turned, and grabbed a torch that I had stashed there for another visit. I picked it up and struck the wall with a small flint stone, and sparks fell into the torch, igniting it. The glow in my eyes, and Rafeor's for a moment, before I handed her the torch. She took it before speaking, "**Thank you.**"

"You're welcome."

I squeezed past her and moved further down the tunnel. The fire cast a halo of glow against the walls, and little dew on the walls showed the age of the walls. After a moment, I ran into a spiderweb, but I heeded it no mind, Rafeor, however, spoke, "**This is not the common entrance, is it?**"

I paused for a moment and glanced back at her before replying, "No, it's not."

"**Why did you take me this way then?**"

I frowned and turned back around before replying, "Because, anyone else would have turned you away from entering the dungeons. Only a select few can enter, and anyone else would need clearance from Morphous. And Morphous did not tell anyone that you were allowed."

She was quiet for a while, before speaking, "**A lot has happened in the last week.**"

I paused at a fork, eyeing the one leading downward, wondering where that one took you, but I promised Rafeor to take her to Lord Verien. I sighed and replied, "True, it has been a chaotic week."

**"I think it has happened too fast."**

I glanced back at her before speaking, "In what way?"

For a moment, we stared at each other when she looked down and replied, **"Sometimes I wish that I was back at Lord Verien's, back under the watchful eye of Michael. Where I didn't have to be anything. Where I did my tasks, without complaint, and took my beatings. Too much has happened in a week, Killian. First, finding out that I am a princess, finding out I am something that is not supposed to be. Finding out that I am a fucking Lycan, have another form…."**

She paused before continuing, **"Back then, I was able to know what each and every day was going to be like because nothing changed. The times never changed in what needed to be done. Here? I am clothed, washed, and attended to as much as I had done to everyone else I had been caring for back in his mansion. I liked the routine, as much as I hated the beatings, I knew what to expect."**

I stared at her in shock, I never knew that she had those feelings. I sighed deeply before speaking, "Why are you telling me all this?"

It took her a minute to reply, the weak wind shifting the flame to and fro. She replied, **"I want to get Lord Verien and Michael out of the dungeons. Release them and go with them."**

I stared at her, opened my mouth, and closed it after a moment. I was at a loss of words before I replied, "What about your father?"

**"Have you ever seen him come to me, Killian? Have you witnessed him ever approaching me without prompts? He may be my father, but he has not once approached me on his own. It is like I don't exist."**

I swallowed and glanced down at the left tunnel before speaking, "Let's check where this tunnel leads first before we go get them out, okay?"

She nodded in response, and I wasn't sure if she knew what I was thinking. They were not going to go to their old home. I am going to take her to my old homeland, where I had left Wilson with my brother Calio. Falcor spoke, *"No."*

*"What do you mean no, Falcor?"*

*"She is not ready to be there. She needs to go to the werewolves first."*

*"Why?"*

*"Killian, do not question it. She needs to go to the werewolves. I believe Anna, has been helping her with her shifter half, along with Quinn now and again. However, she needs to harness her Lycan before she goes there."*

*"Fine. I'll suggest it."*

*"It cannot be a mere suggestion, Killian, she MUST GO."*

*"She has a voice too Falcor. I can suggest and strongly urge her there, but I cannot force her."*

He grumbled, before he turned around and blocked our connection.

*****

The left tunnel twisted and turned, spiraling downward before ending at another doorway. I paused and looked around, nothing but cobwebs as far as my eye could see, I frowned and pressed on the door. I glanced up at it before I shoved it hard. The door creaked on ancient hinges before turning, and I looked outside. It was a hidden door – one that pointed towards the werewolf territory, no less. I turned around to Rafeor. "I know that you had said you wanted to go to their mansion and go back to what you used to do. However, that cannot happen. Why don't you go to Nathaniel's?"

I saw the anger flicker in her gaze. She growled, "**Why?**"

"Because you wanted to learn about that side earlier. Don't you want to see what your Lycan half can do, Rafeor?"

She frowned and her shoulders slumped before she whispered, "**I am curious. But I am not a high-ranking wolf, I am a…. A beast.**"

"You are not a beast. You have not been in this supernatural world for long. Keep your head up, Rafeor. It will clear up. Think about it, you will learn how to work alongside your Lycan instead of against it. Haven't you learned a bunch about the shifters and how they function?"

She bit her lip and suddenly her eyes flickered up. "**They? Don't you mean we?**"

I frowned and she eyed me curiously before speaking, "**You have another motive, don't you? What do I have to do with your plan?**"

I sighed deeply before leveling her with Falcor's eyes for a moment before he descended. She swallowed before eyeing me. I took another moment to gather my thoughts and said, "You were not supposed to find out that I am not a shifter, but since you now did, I do not blame you for connecting the dots. I am a demon, one of the last ones on the earth. It has been foretold that a hybrid, you, would one day walk the earth. However, one connection with one species would make you a weapon. You would tear down anything and anyone that stood in your path. However, in my family line, it was foretold that you would bring peace, and happiness if one of my family tree lines, was the one to point you in the correct direction."

It took her a whole minute to process what I had said, and by the time she did, she realized the connections. She glanced sharply at me. **"The riot was a cover-up, wasn't it? So that my father could safely tuck me away, no one knew where to come for me."**

She connected too many dots suddenly, and I swallowed. It was a lot to take in, but she frowned before she raised her head towards me, the wind blowing her hair. She spoke, **"I will go to Nathaniel's. My question is though, what about Lord Verien and Michael?"**

I glanced back up the way we had come before replying, "We can either bring them with us or leave them."

She blinked once before slowly shaking her head in response, **"No, there has to be another spot."**

I frowned, but replied, "Like where?"

She eyed me for a moment before replying, **"Wherever you disappeared for a day. Take them there."**

My eyes flashed in irritation. That was not going to happen anytime soon. I was about to reply and flat-out refuse when Falcor spoke in my mind, *"Killian."*

*"What?"*

*"She is doing exactly what we want her to do. Let it go, and do it."*

*"What about Morphous?"*

*"What about the coward?"*

*"He will tell more people about what we are Falcor."*

*"At this point, it would not shock them. We are different than they are, we are stronger than they are. Let them try to knock us down, Killian."*

I sighed, closed the connections, and finally looked at Rafeor who was waiting for an answer, "Alright. I'll take them there."

**"Good."**

I grumbled but knew better than to start something. Falcor would instantly say something else, and I would be at his mercy since he had not asked for control as of yet. I sighed and walked out the door. Rafeor glanced back up the tunnel before speaking, **"Aren't you forgetting them?"**

"No, I will get you safely to the werewolves, then I will take them there."

I glanced back at her before speaking again, "You did not say when. So, come on."

She glowered at me but followed after a moment. I looked up at the bright stars and saw the half-moon in the sky, I grumbled again. It was going to be a long ass night.

*****

For a moment I hesitated, but Nunito seemed to want to disappear. I sighed and trudged after the Carpathian had turned sharply on his heel and was already walking away briskly. I glanced at Nunito once more, before following him. Nunito kept his eyes away from me, but he whispered, "Run."

I glanced towards the other Carpathian but once I turned to face Nunito again, he had shifted and flown into the tree once again. I swallowed before calling out to the other one, "Where are you taking me?"

"Shut up, and come along."

"Answer me first. Where are you taking me?"

In the blink of an eye, he was in front of me, towering over me. He snarled, his eyes flashing red before he snarled, "Wherever I want to take you. Come along, and keep your fucking mouth shut."

I stared up at him and growled, "Take. me. to. your. KING!"

"No."

He smirked. Not seeming to care about what I did or said.  I stared at him and growled out, "Then where are you trying to take me?"

For a moment, he was silent. Eventually, he spoke, "No one challenges me, kid. You will come along silently. And be made into my new blood bank. Come along."

"No."

"Excuse me?"

"No. I am on a mission, and you will not stop me from doing my duty."

"Who do you think you are?"

I hesitated, I did not know who I truly was, but I knew that my father's last name normally gave people chills for some reason. I glowered at him before I replied, "Herald Benik. And I will not be what you want me to be."

He stared at me in shock before replying, "Benik? Your father is Killian or is it Calio?"

I blinked at him in confusion before replying, "Killian. Who is Calio?"

He frowned and turned slightly, and I noticed that the sun was starting to come along the horizon, I swallowed. So far, this Carpathian was a dick, but all the same, he did not deserve to die in the sun. I cleared my throat, and he looked at me sharply before glancing at the horizon, cursing under his breath. He looked at me before shouting, "EVERYONE! FLY HOME!"

I was shocked, after a moment, I heard a couple of bats fly out of the trees, and zoom past in different directions. I swallowed in shock. I did not realize that there were that many in this area.

He looked at me before turning sharply and speaking, "Can you shift?"

"Yes."

"Then shift and follow me."

I hesitated and watched as he shifted into his bat, who hovered for a moment as if waiting on me. He then headed towards the darker part of the woods. I swallowed before shifting to a raven and following.

****

It was another five minutes, and I felt the early morning rays of the sun on my feathers, warming me. I yawned once, and the bat turned his head sharply to stare at me. He then returned his attention forward. We flew in silence, and soon a dark part of the forest, a black pit, so dark that I couldn't see in front of me. I would have flown straight into a tree if he didn't flip himself upside down and grab my talons with his. He leaned his body to the left, right, and to the left again, as he directed me through the darkness. Soon after another minute, it became clear that it was not going to get lighter here. The sun could not penetrate this area, some form of magic was involved here. I swallowed in fear, wondering if I needed someone to take me outside of it once again.

Soon he let go and flapped twice before motioning me towards him. I barely was able to follow him, but did. He landed on a platform, and I landed cautiously. He shifted to his Carpathian self, and stared at me. I swallowed, before shifting to my human form.

He glanced around, before speaking in a commanding tone, "Follow."

I opened my mouth to say something, but the way he stared at me, made me second-guess myself and I closed my mouth. Something was going to happen, and I had a feeling that I needed to do what he told me to do without questioning it. I sighed deeply before following, and soon we passed several other species, wolves, and humans. However, unlike myself, they had countless bite marks on their necks, arms, and further down their torso. I swallowed nervously, their eyes were all hollow, and lifeless. I gulped in air, as I found red eyes staring out of the windows at me, watching. I hurried to catch up with the Carpathian.

After a moment, we came to a rope bridge, where we were alone, he grabbed me by the throat, and lifted me in the air, before slamming me into the tree beside us. I yelped at the pain before he hissed, "You will do as I say from here on out WITHOUT another snarky comment. Even if I have to have someone feed from you. Got that?"

I clawed at his hand, begging for air, but mumbled, "Yes, sir."

He dropped me, with disgust, when another Carpathian called out, "And here I thought you had gone soft, Akato!"

I saw the Carpathian glower at me once and turned his attention to the newcomer. A Carpathian walked forward out of the shadows before his eyes flickered to me and he took a deep breath in before his eyes snapped to him. I swallowed nervously, but the Carpathian raised his eyebrow at the new one before speaking, "Zin, what are you doing? I thought I had you do the eastern border tonight."

Zin looked at me before replying, "I had Nunito cover me."

"Nunito was with me this morning. You know the rules. Go to your post, Zin."

"Why? Nunito is the weakling in our culture, Akato, let him suffer."

"Are you questioning my authority, Zin?"

They stared at each other, unblinking, and finally, after a moment Zin looked away before whispering, "No, Akato."

"Get yourself to your post, and let Nunito go home."

Zin turned around to go do as he was ordered to, but paused before speaking, "Got a new pet there, Akato?"

"It doesn't matter to you, Zin. Go,"

Zin glowered at him before eyeing me and growling, "Give me a drink first, Akato, then I will go."

"No."

"Why not?"

I stared at Akato, shocked. He just said that he would have someone feed off of me, I swallowed but stayed silent. Akato glanced at me, before replying, "Because Lord Dracula has requested a new blood bank. You dare imp his food with your toxins, Zin?"

"I did not realize that Lord Dracula has requested a new one. He just got one last week."

"Are you challenging what Lord Dracula wants, Zin? Am I going to have to remove you from the picture here?"

"No, My Lord."

"Get to your post then, and be done with it."

Zin glanced at me with sharp eyes; he shifted to a bat and flew off to the eastern side. I glanced at Akato before whispering, "Thank you."

He jerked slightly before growling, "Sssh."

I winced but went dead quiet. He looked around before motioning forward.

****

I followed him in silence, I hung my head low as if I were submissive to him. Since that was what a Carpathian and their slaves had done, as they passed me. The human glanced at me out of the corner of his eye at one point and glanced at their master before mumbling, "Run."

I swallowed, but glanced at Akato, before shaking my head. The human stared at me with sadness and continued following his master. I swallowed and hurried to catch up to Akato.

A Carpathian couple stopped Akato, the male Carpathian glowered at me for a moment, before barking out an order, "Get back, you vile beast!"

I backed away from them and kept my tongue between my teeth. I would not speak to them. I would not acknowledge them. Akato watched me out of the corner of his eye before turning to them, speaking quietly between the three of them. After a few minutes, the couple strode past me, throwing daggers before the female one turned her head towards the darkness, snapping her fingers. I was shocked and was about to move towards them, when the creaking of the boards brought me to look towards the shadows, and saw five humans and one wolf trailing behind them. They all wore iron collars, their eyes downcast, and they looked horrible. I glanced at Akato and saw his frown, but he did not say anything.

After they passed, Akato looked at me before jerking his head. I followed him again and continued.

It was another minute later, that Akato looked around before speaking, "Good job at keeping yourself quiet. I didn't know you had it in you."

I looked up at him, and he looked around again and nodded once, so I replied, "You told me to keep my head down. I fully plan on doing that."

He smirked before replying, "Smart of you."

We continued forward, and my curiosity got to me at last. I whispered, "Can I ask you a question?"
"Hmmm?"

"Why didn't you allow Zin to drink from me?"

He paused and looked at me. "Because he is a fucker. I don't like him."

I frowned before scrunching my eyes and asking, "Can I ask a few more questions?"

He looked around and sighed deeply before motioning me to follow him. We rounded the platform, and he opened a door. It creaked open, and he gestured me inside. I paused for a moment, but realized what it would look like to any other, and quickly entered.

He entered the room and closed the door with a click before turning his attention to me again. "Alright, ask away."

I swallowed before speaking, "Why do you guys treat the other supernatural beings and humans as you guys do?"

"Not all of us are that cruel."

"How many? There are a whole lot of humans and wolves that have a collar."

For a moment, he stared at me and shook his head before speaking, "I honestly don't know, kid. It won't change anytime soon either. So, drop it. Next question."

I frowned and was about to challenge him, but a nudge in the back of my mind stopped me. I sighed deeply before asking, "What did that couple want?"

"You."

"Why?"

"Because everyone smells that you are different from everyone else. The only thing that has kept them away from you so far is because I have lied to them about Dracula."

"Why lie?"

"You would be dead otherwise, kid."

"Oh…."

I thought for a moment before looking at him and speaking, "Why did Zin call you, My Lord?"

He sighed deeply, and ran his hand across his face before replying, "Because I am Dracula's son."

I stared at him before I opened my mouth and a question formed somehow, "Then why are you at the border?"

"Because that is my duty. To be anything in our world, you have to know how to command your people. You have to earn their respect. That is how Dracula has done it, along with his forefathers."

"Oh. So, what's the plan now?"

He sighed deeply before replying, "I noticed that you were yawning on the way in. When was the last time you slept?"

"Yesterday night."

"A whole day ago?"

"Yeah."

"Sleep first, then I am going to take you to my father."

"Is it safe to?"

"No one is going to challenge me, kid. Go to sleep."

I grumbled for a moment but looked around the room before approaching the bed, and sitting gingerly down. I looked at him before speaking, "Whose home is this?"

He glanced at me, blinked once, and replied, "Sleep."

I swallowed but turned towards the wall and fell asleep.

****

I waited until he was out. I glanced at him and knew that he was by his heartbeat and breathing. I sighed, leaned against the wall, and looked out the window on the door, I was going to have to explain to my father why I hadn't drained every single drop from him, but that was what I was going to have to put up with. What I had told him was true, I was Dracula's son, but I was the last born. The youngest. Meaning, that I had no authority to bring something like this to my father, if it was Alexei then it wouldn't matter what anyone thought. I had a lot to explain when I would be bringing him towards my father.

I swallowed and watched as the clock ticked away, for a Carpathian like myself, time was irrelevant, something that mortals kept track of. However, once I glanced at this shifter, I knew that life had something else in store. I wondered if there could be ways to make other places safer than this one lone area for my kin to coexist with each other. My father kept it tightly in control, so no one stepped out of line. He put me in the guards since he knew I would do what he wanted.

I sighed again and glanced at the kid, wondering what was going to happen to him once I brought him towards my father, and possibly even my brothers.

*****

We trudged through the woods, I was actually surprised that the guards on the wall did not call out a halt or anything. But after a moment, we disappeared. I sighed deeply and Rafeor was silently walking beside me. I glanced at her before speaking, "What are you thinking, Rafeor?"

She glanced at me before replying, "**Am I doing the right thing, Killian? Leaving as I am?**"

"Don't worry about it, Rafeor. King Nathaniel will allow you inside, and with open arms."

**"What about my father though, Killian?"**

"Let his stupid being as is. You are correct, he did not give you the attention a father should. He let his people do that to you. He shouldn't have left you to figure it out."

**"But he is a King...."**

"King or not Rafeor, he should have made time for his sole heir."

That was the end of that conversation for the time being, as she mulled over the words of wisdom I gave her for the time being. Leaving us to silence, which I actually wanted over anything else. However, I understood why she wanted to talk. It was not easy to be what she was. She is the first of her kind, and I know for a fact that she will have many, many children in her future. Once she matured and found what made her swoon. I sighed deeply before speaking, "What else troubles you, Rafeor?"

**"Am I being unloyal if I do this?"**

"No, you are working with what was given to you. You cannot stop being curious and it would hamper you if you didn't do this. Morphous will understand over the long term that this is the correct time and place to do it."

**"How are you so sure of that?"**

I was silent. I let it be silent for a moment, before I replied, "Times change over time, Rafeor. We cannot change it."

**"What will you tell my father when he asks where I am?"**

"Don't you mean, if he realizes you are gone? I personally was going to wait to see how long it took for him to notice."

**"Killian!"**

"What? You said it yourself, he didn't give you the time of day to do anything with you. Let it stew, and see how long it takes."

She let out a small groan, but chuckled. **"Please Killian, tell me now that you will tell him."**

"Oh alright."

****

I stopped in my tracks, and she stopped after a moment and looked around. She didn't seem to know why we stopped but seemed to trust me. I glanced at her before calling out, "I KNOW YOU ARE HERE! COME OUT!"

A wolf stalked out of the bushes. I sniffed the air and knew it was not Nathaniel, he would be a Lycan. I kept Falcor on edge, in case I needed him to surface, but kept him out of my voice as I spoke, "Who are you?"

The wolf looked up and glanced at Rafeor before looking at me again. The wolf turned without a word, glanced over his shoulder, and padded away into the woods.

Rafeor swallowed before starting to follow. I was tempted to grab her arm, but knew that this one was a werewolf and not a common wolf. I sighed and trudged after them.

****

I woke up at three in the morning, something was telling me that I had to do a patrol myself, alone. I grumbled to myself and rolled over to face my mate, the same one who tried to reject me since she was wolf-less. Glad that she came around though, since she was perfect for me, complimented me in every form I lacked before. However, Norjor snapped in my mind, *"UP, Finn!"*

*"Why wake me up, Norjor?"*

*"Get up, or I will take over."*

*"Alright. Alright. I'm going."*

I glanced down at Aurelius before kissing her mate mark, she squirmed underneath me for a moment, her face turning into bliss before she let out a happy sigh. Norjor looked down at her and sighed before he trudged towards the door. I coughed in our link, *"Norjor. We are nude."*

*"We shift once outside, Finn."*

*"Why don't you tell me what this is about?"*

*"A gut feeling, Finn… let it go."*

I groaned in our connection, the last time that Norjor had a gut feeling about something, it turned out to be nothing, and I had to pay back whoever was doing something to the said person. I grumbled but knew better than to go back to bed. Norjor as much as we usually worked well together, was a dong when he wanted to be.

He grumbled in our connection, he heard my thoughts and I kind of chuckled at him. However, once we left our room, and headed downstairs, I wished he had grabbed something to change into. Logan was downstairs, and he looked drunk, pissed, and something else gleamed in his eyes as he glanced up at me. I swallowed before speaking to Norjor, *"Take over now, Norjor."*

*"But he scares me."*

*"Norjor. He will understand why you didn't put on clothes. Me not so much. Quick."*

Norjor grumbled but complied after a moment, blinked once, and strode down the stairs. Not even pausing next to Logan as he strode towards the door.

Logan stared at our backside, and I swallowed deeply, praying against all odds that he would let it go. However, knowing the drunken prince, that was not going to happen. And both I and Norjor knew it. However, we made it to the door before Logan called out, **"Where are you going?"**

I knew that Norjor wanted to ignore him, but sighed deeply before turning around slightly, so he had his side to turn to look, before replying, "I wanted some fresh air."

**"Does your human side agree with that?"**

"Even if he didn't, I would have taken over and done it."

He smirked and looked down at us. **"I understand it is hard for us wolves to get dressed, and undressed, but I thought you would cover yourself. You make everyone oogle you."**

"Not many are awake at this hour, the next time I come through this door, I will be in my wolf form. Not Finn's."

**"Get going. And have fun."**

We stared at him for a moment, and I frowned. Something was wrong with Logan, but I did not question it. Norjor had opened the door and slipped out into the brisk autumn air. I shivered, Norjor quickly shifted, soon, we landed on four paws, and we were off.

*"Where are we going, Norjor?"*

*"Hush."*

*"Fine."*

I let him run in silence, and we did indeed pass a border patrol, but they did not pay attention to us. Every once in a while, every single wolf went out on their own to run. It was a normal thing. We soon came close to the shifter border, when he slowed down and soon stopped entirely. He went into the nearest bushes before he laid down and placed his head on his paws. I watched through his eyes, knowing that something was going to happen around the area we were in.

****

Sure enough, I heard voices, coming towards us. A male and a female's voice. The female's voice I recognized, and realized that it was Morphous's daughter who was coming towards us. The male stopped, looked around suddenly, and called out, "I KNOW YOU ARE HERE! COME OUT!"
Norjor stalked out of the bushes, and I could tell that he was sniffing the air to see if I was a threat to them. Probably found out that I was not Nathaniel or anyone else he knew, I knew that he had something powerful since Norjor kept his distance. The male once again spoke, "Who are you?"

Norjor looked at him, then glanced at the girl before looking back at him. Norjor turned around and looked over our shoulder before trudging into the woods again.

*"You knew?"*

*"Hunch, yes."*

*"Why didn't you tell me, Norjor?"*

*"Because I knew the way you would react if I was wrong."*

I sighed and knew he was correct, I would react differently. He checked again to make sure that they were following, and sure enough, they were.

*"Do you know the male, Norjor?"*

*"Not shifter, or wolf I can tell you that. He is different."*

*"Huh?"*

*"Finn, he is not a shifter. Nor a wolf. Don't know what he is. I haven't smelt something like him before."*

*"What do you think he is?"*

*"Hush, Finn, we will find out later."*

I grumbled in our connection, looked back again, and saw them still coming after us. Soon we got to a spot where no outsiders were allowed past. Norjor turned around and stared at the male before growling, "My apologies, however, you have to stay here."

"I am not leaving, Rafeor."

"I am not going to cause her any harm. I was there when my king came to take her, but she said no. My king knew that she would one day decide to come."

He crossed his arms and growled, "She is not leaving me until I personally deliver her to Nathaniel."

Norjor opened his mouth to retort but closed it after a moment.

*"Well, Finn?"*

*"No. We cannot do it, we don't have the authority to do it."*

*"But she needs to come with us."*

*"Norjor. We cannot do it."*

*"Finn."*

*"No."*

He was about to say something else, when she spoke, **"Killian, can you sense any falsehood on this wolf?"**

Norjor fell silent, we glanced at the male and waited for him to respond. It seemed like he was struggling with someone in his mind before speaking, "No, I do not."

**"Then I will be fine with going further alone with him, Killian. Remember, your promises."**

"Of course, Rafeor."

She crossed the hidden barrier of our territory, and it vibrated once before rippling like water. I could tell that she did not know what just happened, but she must have felt it. I glanced at Killian and knew he saw something as his eyes flickered purple for a split second and faded. Weird, I thought. I haven't seen that color in a shifter before. Then I thought back to what Norjor said earlier, and my curiosity peaked, if he was not a shifter or a wolf, what was he?

However, after a moment, Killian stared at me, jerked his head towards Rafeor, and turned around and walked away. I glanced at her as we made our way to the palace.

****

I waited a good four hours before I went towards the kid. I needed to wake him, knowing that my father was going to be getting up, and he was less cranky if I did it earlier than later. He groaned before he murmured, "Five more minutes."

"No,"

I didn't know what he thought, but he jolted awake, scrambled to the edge of the bed, and panted for a moment. Fear in his eyes and the air. I waved it off and raised my eyebrow at him. It took him a minute to calm himself down again before whispering, "Sorry, forgot where I was for a moment."

I smirked in response, straightened myself up, and glanced at the door before motioning him forward. He stumbled along, shOOK himself slightly before speaking, "What if I shift into a bat or something, and you take me that way?"

"No."

"Why not? That way I don't get stared at, and you don't have to worry about the other Carpathians."

"They will still sense something is up, kid. It is better for you to be in your human form. That way they know I am not hiding something."

"But they shouldn't question you. Since you are Dracula's son."

For a moment, I was silent. He looked at me suddenly, as if taking my silence the wrong way, but I shook my head and snapped, "Remember what I told you earlier."

He nodded, and dropped his gaze, as he followed me blindly outside.

****

We past several more Carpathians, and each one of them, had at least two humans or werewolves. I could tell that the kid wanted to do something about their treatment, but he kept himself silent. Good, I thought to myself, the silent ones make it out alive. I glanced down at the forest floor, knowing that he wouldn't be able to see what I saw. I glanced at him and hoped that my father took his note seriously.

Soon, we came to the center of the darkness, and I paused, so he could admire the black marble with white running through it. I jerked my head towards the front gate and approached it. The two royal guards looked at me before one growled, "Akato, what are you doing?"

I raised my head slightly, and glowered at the guard before replying, "Heading inside."

"Were you asked to come forth?"

"No."

"Then you know what your father will do. Why risk his wrath Akato?"

I swallowed before replying, "That will be between my father and myself."

"Your death."

They backed away, and I walked forward, the kid tried to follow me. However, the guards instantly lowered their weapons blocking his entrance. I paused, and glanced at them before speaking, "He goes with me."

"You know the rules, Akato."

"I know, but he goes in."

They glanced at him before the one that had not spoken, growled out, "What is so special about him?"

"I cannot tell you."

"Tell me, or he dies," said the first one, his blade hovering over his throat.

I saw the kid swallow and his bug eyes told me that he was about to say something. I shook my head slightly before replying, "I will let my father know what you are doing here."

They lowered their weapons, and glanced at each other before the other spoke, "You are coming unannounced, Akato, and now you are even threatening his guards. You are not going to be able to get out of his throne room alive."

I swallowed before motioning towards the kid again to come forth, and they allowed him through this time. The one who has been speaking the most spoke again before we could leave, "Akato."

"Hmmm?"

"Put a collar on that toy of yours. You know how your father gets when he sees one without one in his royal household."

The kid glanced up at me sharply, but I squinted at him. He seemed to know to keep himself quiet still. I looked at the guard before replying, "I know."

"Get going, I will inform him that you will be with your toy."

I opened my mouth to reject that, but I saw his eyes glazed over already, and cursed slightly. Shit, I thought.

****

We left the guards to their stations, and I sped towards the throne room, opened the door, ushered the kid inside, and to my horror, my father already sat on his throne of bones. His hands tapped the skulls that were where the hands rested. He glanced up and held up his hand before speaking, "**Stop.**"

We froze where we were, and he growled, "**Explain.**"

I opened my mouth to speak, but the kid spoke before I could, "I was sent by my king to give you a message."

I closed my eyes, knowing the rage in my father's eyes would be prominent. "**Oh, your king?**"

I heard the sarcastic sneer in his voice, and I knew that I was in deep shit now, I wanted to cower before him. However, the kid replied, "Morphous Draconis."

The room was silent, and I opened my eyes for a moment before I saw my father freeze. He blinked before speaking, "**Everyone out. Akato, you and this one stay. Everyone else. OUT!**"

It took a moment, but the shadows in the room moved, and it was soon clear to the kid that he did not realize that the throne room would be filled with anything or anyone. I personally saw my elder brother, Alexei move from the shadow behind the throne, glowering at me as he left. Soon everyone was gone. My father pierced me with a glower, before snapping, **"You let an outsider inside my home. Why didn't you alone bring me the message, Akato?"**

"I tried to."

**"Apparently, you did not try enough. Since he is here."**

He pointed at the kid, and I scrunched down and dropped my gaze to the floor before murmuring, "He insisted."

**"You are a freaking Carpathian. He is a mere shifter."**

"My name is Herald Benik. I am not a mere shifter."

I watched as my father once again froze, and he glanced down at him. I had to give Herald credit, he did not flinch when my father stared at him. I saw him swallow nervously, but that was it. My father sat back on his throne, and with his right hand placed his forefingers on the bridge of his nose, before speaking, **"Apparently, you are not a mere shifter. Now, I know you are a Benik, I understand why my son was weak to you. You are, after all, a Carpathian killer."**

"Huh? No, I'm not."

**"Are you challenging me?!?"**

"If you want it as a challenge, then yes. However, that is not my goal. I am simply saying, I am not a Carpathian killer."

For a moment, my father and he stared at each other, finally my father growled, **"Who is your father?"**

"Killian."

My father relaxed instantly, before removing his fingers from his nose, and sighing deeply before muttering, **"What a relief."**

I frowned, knowing the difference between Killian and the other one, but it was clear that Herald did not understand the difference. I saw him open his mouth to speak, but I cleared my throat slightly, stopping him from speaking. Herald looked at me sharply and squinted his eyes at me, before reaching into his pocket and pulling out an envelope.

My father's eyes drifted to the envelope, he stood and made his way down the steps of bones. He stopped in front of him before speaking, **"Ah, the message."**

He held out his hand, and Herald instantly handed it to him and took a step backward. My father glanced at me sharply but ripped open the seal and his eyes flew to the note, and I saw him frown. He looked at Herald, before growling, **"Is that all?"**

He threw the message at his feet, and Herald gingerly picked up the note, read it, and swallowed before whispering, "I…. I didn't know."

My father turned to me and growled, "**And this is why I don't have you do shit, Akato. Why you are merely a captain of the guards.**"

I swallowed, scrunched down, and winced. Herald glanced at me and swallowed, but he spoke out, "Why does it matter that he is a captain of the guard? He is your son."

I swallowed and wanted to disappear entirely, as my father froze, turned slowly around, stared at him, and then at me with his bloodshot eyes before growling, "**We may share blood, but he… he is my last born. Nothing more. He is pathetic, weak, and a coward.**"

I flinched at each word and took a step backward, but Herald growled, "At least I know my place, I am my father's last born too, and yet he doesn't treat me like that. Not entirely."

**"Shifters and wolves treat their younger children like glass sometimes. It makes them weak. You are a weak species, and I should make you my blood bank."**

He opened his mouth to reply, but his eyes shifted before a different voice rumbled, "**No.**"

His aura rolled out, and went far and through the throne room, before being pulled back in. My father stared at him for a shocked moment, before whispering, "**And you are?**"

**"My name is Firefoot. You know the legend, Dracula, are you going to hold me hostage? Or are you going to let me go on my way? I apologize that the note is not more, but I think you and I both know that you are afraid of Calio Benik, and I believe you know EXACTLY where he is."**

The throb in my father's throat proved that. He swallowed before speaking, "**What are you going to do?**"

**"Nothing. Release me, and let me go as I was. Herald was sent on a mission, and you know that I am on my mission too. The wolves already know I exist. You now know that was my goal. Which is why I had Herald insist on meeting both leaders."**

**"It makes sense."**

**"Good. Now, that being said, my human half does not know I exist completely, so not a fucking word."**

My father dropped his gaze and I swallowed. What the hell is Firefoot? Why was my father scared of him? However, I watched as the kid suddenly scrambled backward slightly. He swallowed nervously before looking up at Dracula and whispering, "What happened?"

My father stared at him before replying slowly, "**You have a wolf spirit in you.**"

I saw Herald make a weird face before whispering, "That is exactly what the werewolves said when I blanked out."

I glanced at my father and saw him frown before he turned towards his throne again and spoke, "**Leave, and never come back.**"

Herald backed away before whispering, "Understood."

**"That includes you, too, Akato."**

I froze in shock before Herald spoke, "It's still daylight out. He will die."

**"It doesn't matter."**

"He is your family."

I shrunk down, knowing that Herald was digging a bigger grave for himself, but my father did not turn around as he growled, "**I do not like repeating myself. Get. OUT!**"

Herald looked at his back before growling, "I understand why my king does not do anything with Carpathians. You are an asshole."

My jaw dropped, and the shaking fury on my father's shoulders proved that he was treading on thin ice. Herald, however, did not seem to care, "Good bye, prick."

He turned around and walked through the throne doors, but my father kept himself facing his throne of bones.

****

I turned to leave when he spoke, "**Akato.**"

I paused and he turned his red angry eyes towards me before looking towards the door and speaking, "**Keep an eye on him.**"

"Why?"

**"Because Firefoot is correct in one way, he is right I do know where to find Calio. I want a full report on what Firefoot is doing. You will not leave that kid's side at any point, Akato."**

"The sun...."

My father sighed, before replying, "**Take this.**"

He handed me a ring, and I glanced down at it. It was the family heirloom, something that would be passed down to Alexei, not me. My eyes shot to his face before whispering, "Father, I cannot take this."

**"You will."**

"But it belongs to the firstborn."

**"Akato."**

I glanced up at him before he spoke again, **"I choose who I send on missions. It was no meaning to have you as a captain of a guard, I did it so Alexei left you alone. Also, I was forewarned that someone would come along at some point. I did not know when, but I know that I cannot argue with him."**

I swallowed, knowing the 'him' and I turned to face the throne room doors, and glanced at my father and whispered, "You don't hate me?"

His bloodshot eyes scorched mine, but he shook his head before shouting, **"OUT!"**

I smiled slightly, but I cowered and ran away. I knew that my father could not tell me anything sentimental. Alexei would hear everything. What my father said in there when it was only the two of us…. He would find out, and go after father for what he did.

****

I met up with Herald. We walked past the guards once again, but this time they did nothing to stop us. No one stopped us. Not even couples that eyed Herald, I kept going. Soon we got to the edge of the border, one more step and it would be outside of the safety of the darkness. Herald glanced at me before whispering, "I'm sorry."

I glanced at him but faced the veil and swallowed, slipped on my father's ring, and stepped out into the dimming sunlight. I winced, thinking my father lied, but nothing else happened. It was actually pretty warm. I looked up at the sun and winced as I looked into the ball of fire, that yesterday would have made me turn to dust.

Herald got out of the veil and stared at me in shock before whispering, "How are you still alive?"

I turned my father's ring in my fingers, and replied, "My father did what he did to protect me. He gave me a ring, one that allows him to walk in sunlight."

"I did not know those rings existed."

I glanced at him and swallowed slightly before replying, "It usually passes down from firstborn to firstborn. Since I was not a firstborn, I did not even dream of being out here."

"That must be a relief that it is different now. Now what are you going to do with your life?"

"I am going to accompany you."

"Why?"

"Because you seem to always be on an adventure. And I want a piece of that."

He blushed, and chuckled before speaking, "What about feeding?"

I frowned, sighed, and shrugged before replying, "I'm sure that your king has someone downstairs that I can feed from."

I saw him frown before speaking, "What about animal blood?"

I grimaced but knew that it may be feasible to do so. It was, after all, a different world out there, compared to being coped in my father's domain. I shrugged and replied, "We'll see how it goes."

He swallowed before walking forward. I walked quietly beside him. My new adventure awaited me, and I had no idea what was in store.

# Chapter 22

I disappeared into the ruin and was content to stay there the rest of the evening, however, I knew that the humans would soon come for my protection. I was their protector, even though they were my slaves. Severi snickered in my mind but said nothing. I glanced through what used to be the window of the building and watched the werewolves that Killian brought with him. They acted as a team, and everything that the humans did not have. I glanced at the human's progress and knew that if I didn't go out there to stare at them, a fight might break out. Once again, Severi snickered. I scowled and growled, *"Hush, Severi."*

*"Why should I?"*

*"Severi."*

My voice was thick with sass but he snickered in response, and I scowled again. Nothing mattered to him, he still wanted to be like his father, but we knew that his way of handling things was now in the past. That we should embrace mother's methods. I took a deep breath in, and let it out slowly before marching back out there. The humans scrambled backward, a few threw glares at the one that they were having disagreements with, but I paid no heed to them. I went towards the werewolves. One of them, cleared his throat when he saw me approaching, and Wilson glanced up at me before standing up. They had since shifted to their human forms, and they had been given clothing from my slaves, at least from those who were slain.

I looked at Wilson before speaking, "Can you work alongside the humans?"

"Why?"

"They need a firm hand, and you seem to work as a team."

"Don't you want to punish them for it?"

"Are you challenging me?"

Wilson blinked once, before glancing at the others and replying, "I would be a fool to challenge someone so violent. However, why do you want us to work alongside the humans?"

"To keep you all within the same area."

"Is that the only reason?"

I tried hard to keep Severi in check, but Wilson was making his patience run low. I murmured in our connection, *"Severi, do not lose your control. We do not need any injuries to these wolves."*

*"But he's challenging our authority."*

*"Severi, he is Killian's. Think of what we talked about. We cannot kill him solely because he is challenging us."*

*"Killian is not here to say anything against us, Calio. We need to put this one in his place."*

*"No."*

*"Calio!"*

I growled in our connection before snapping, *"Severi, you promised. Do you want me to bring back the memory? Or are you going to do the way we are trying to follow?"*

*"You wouldn't dare...."*

I forced the memory of the attack back into his mind, he winced and cried out, and after a few moments, he cried through the connection, *"STOP IT, CALIO! STOP!"*

*"Then are you going to do what we have pledged to do? Or are you going to continue to need reminders, Severi?"*

*"We do as you say."*

*"Good."*

He released me back, and Wilson stood there staring at me for a moment before he spoke, "Well?"

"Huh?"

He sighed before speaking, "Why do you want us in the same place as the humans? Is it indeed that you want to keep us in one spot to keep an eye on us?"

"Yes and no. Yes, because you seem to have a level head on your shoulders, and would be able to command the humans better than I can. You don't seem to be the one to fly off the handle with a little error. And partially to keep you together. Also, humans are easy targets for the wildlife in this area. So, in other words, you would serve as a guard."

He seemed to think it over, and he glanced at another one before speaking, "And if we do not?"

Severi wanted to growl in response, but I swallowed before speaking, "Please don't test my patience. I am trying to be good, but if you pressure me to, I will do as I see fit."

One of the other werewolves spoke up then, "I do not agree with how you treat everyone. You slaughtered twenty humans all because you were in a fit. I will not follow your rules, or wishes."

Severi desperately wanted to strangle him, but Wilson glowered at the one who spoke but another one spoke in a slight whisper, "Wilson."

Wilson glanced at him, and he continued, "I agree with Savador. I will not serve a tyrant."

Wilson seemed to struggle, and I glanced at Savador and then at the others, and glanced again at Wilson before speaking, "Is that what they want, what you personally want to follow Wilson?"

Wilson glanced at me for a moment before looking at the others, and he replied, "I apologize, Calio, however, we will not do as you say. You had ordered us to gather firewood and go hunting, which we will do. However, they feel that watching the humans is not what we should be doing."

"And just what do you think you should be doing?"

I struggled, but Severi had enough talk back from them, and he desperately wanted to put them in their place, but I hissed in our connection, "*Severi.*"

"*They challenged us, Calio!*"

"*Severi, come on.*"

Severi released control, and I rubbed my nose before speaking slowly, "I am trying to change, I hope you know that. However, you are trying my limited patience."

Savador stood up and Wilson growled at him. He stopped and looked at Wilson for a moment, and backed off. I glanced at Wilson, as he looked at everyone else before his eyes flickered to mine again. "We will do as we want."

Severi snarled in my connection, but I grimaced before speaking, "Okay."

I turned around and headed back to the humans. They had since gotten into a scuffle, and I walked towards the two who had started the fight. They cowered under my gaze, before I snapped at them, "Do. Not. Fight. Build the bloody fire, otherwise, shiver."

The humans scrambled to complete what I had ordered, and I glanced back at the werewolves, shaking my head and once again disappearing into the ruin.

****

I watched as Calio disappeared again into the ruin, before turning to my comrades. I raised my eyebrows before speaking, "Really?"

Savador glanced up at me sharply and growled, "What did you expect exactly, Wilson? He slaughtered twenty humans, or more simply because he was in a fit. If he hadn't done that or perhaps proved to us that he is trying to change, then it may be different."

"Did you not notice that he did not kill any of his subjects since that?"

"Why does that matter, Wilson?"

"It matters because…."

Another one cut him off, "Wilson."

"What do you want, Topaz?"

Topaz looked between Savador and him before replying, "Let's go on a run, hunt some deer, and communicate through our connections. I do not feel comfortable around the humans and him."

I sighed before looking at the others and replying, "Okay, let's go then."

We stripped out of the limited clothing, it was better than what Morphous had us to wear, but we all disliked on how it came to us. We had to take it from the dead humans that Severi had slaughtered. We all shifted into our wolves before running out of the ruins.

****

I ran out in front of them all, when Topaz spoke through our communications, "*Okay, now that we are a safe distance, and through our private communications, Wilson, what the heck?*"

"*What?*"

He growled slightly before replying, "*You know what! You completely ignored what we were telling you to say to him!*"

"*Annnnd? If I had indeed told him some of the vulgar stuff that you guys said, we would be dead. This is why I don't say half of what was discussed.*"

"*Wilson, you have to admit, some of the points we made were valid.*"

"*I did not say I did not agree, I am merely stating that with how Calio and his demon handled things. I did not want any of us to be slaughtered.*"

The connection went silent, as they all mulled over what I had said, finally Averic spoke, "*You are right, we should have kept half of the things we were saying alone. However, you must agree with some of it, though. He is downright bloody.*"

"*I agree with you there, Averic.*"

"*What are we going to do to stop him?*"

I sighed before growling to Fantar, "*We cannot stop him.*"

*"Oh, come on, Wilson! He needs to be stopped!"*

I was about to reply when Xavier spoke, he rarely spoke and when he did, his word tended to be the final saying, *"Fantar, we cannot stop him as much as we want to. I have a feeling that we are needed in something bigger than the current issue we face. We stay as is for now. Wilson did what he did to save us from death, and I agree with his logic. However, it does make me wonder what is in store for us."*

We all went silent. I glanced at Xavier, and saw him frown once before speaking again, *"Can anyone contact their children?"*

Silence. Nothing but silence in the communications. Morphous had somehow blocked us from connecting to them, however, now we were out of the cells. I was about to say something, but Arcanum replied, *"Why connect to them, Xavier?"*

*"Do we trust Killian?"*

Silence once again fell on the communications before I replied, *"What does he have to do with this, Xavier?"*

*"That child that he says he knows that Morphous has currently. She is the hybrid, and if that is indeed the case, there must be a war coming up. Where would you want your offspring? The ones fighting the opposite side compared to us?"*

No one spoke. He was right. We did not want our children in that mess. Finally, Fantar replied, *"We can't just connect to them out of the blue. We were gone for twelve years of their lives. And they will think ill of us."*

*"Not if they know that we couldn't connect to them."*

*"What are you getting at, Xavier?"* I growled.

*"Two of us need to go to the werewolf palace, and get any and all of our family and friends that have survived the riot and anything else that has happened between now and then."*

*"That's…. That…."*

I fell silent, it was clear by the communications that everyone else was thinking along the same line. However, Savador spoke for the first time since he spoke against me, *"And how would we do that?"*

*"Simple. Two of us leave right now, and the others go hunting."*

Silence. Nothing but silence through the communications. Finally, Trevoric spoke, *"Who do you suggest goes? It cannot be Wilson."*

*"Why can't it be me?"*

*"Because you are the only one here that will ease Calio enough so he doesn't suspect anything. Besides the fact, that you won't say half of whatever triggers his demon."*

*"He is right, you know,"* said Xavier.

I glanced at Xavier and sighed deeply. *"Okay, fine. So, who do you suggest goes, Xavier?"*

He was silent, as he mulled over who would go. Finally, he replied, *"Trevoric and myself."*

*"Whoa, now! Why not me?"*

Savador snarled. Xavier sneered in our connections, and Savador faltered in step for a moment before Xavier replied, *"Because unlike me, you decided to open your big mouth to chew out the demon, and Calio. If you disappeared, then he would suspect something happened. Myself and Trevoric have not spoken out to Calio once."*

No one spoke. He was right, they were the ones who kept silent throughout the entire duration. I sighed deeply before huffing, *"So, when do you leave?"*

*"After we take down a few deer or elk, and help drag it back to camp,"* replied Trevoric.

Xavier glanced at him sharply and replied, *"What? That's not the plan. We leave as soon as we can."*

*"Xavier, he knows we all left. If only six return, he will go hunting for us. It is best that we bring food back and then go. Besides, the blood of the kills will mask our escape."*

*"He is right on that front, Xavier, he knows we all left together."*

*"Fine."*

For a moment, we ran in silence, enjoying the night air, and finally, after a minute, Averic spoke through the connections, *"Slow down, I think I smell something coming up."*

****

We all instantly skidded to a stop and crept slowly upward, soon we came to a stop. Below us in a valley, down a slightly slanted downhill, was a herd of elk. Their large antlers on their heads shone in the moonlight. Half of them were lying down, the other half were standing, not expecting to be attacked.

I glanced to my right and motioned to Averic and Savador to start going behind them and to the opposite side. They nodded once, and crept away, keeping low to the ground. I glanced at Arcanum and Fantar and jerked my head again to the same side. They knew what I was thinking, they would be behind them all. After a moment, I looked back over, surveying the clearing before I connected to them all, *"Let me know when you guys are in positions."*

*"Copy that."* Was their reply.

Their wolves instinctually wanted to just leap into the fray, but we had taught them all to obey our commands. I glanced at Topaz and Trevoric and spoke in their connection, *"Who wants to head to the front? You or us?"*

*"I think we shall stay here, and you head that way, Wilson,"* replied Trevoric.

I nodded once, and Xavier and I moved away from them and crept slowly to the front. Xavier broke off from me, stayed still, and down in the long grass. He nodded once to me, and I grinned before heading further. We worked well as a team, even after all the years trapped and imprisoned, I would not want to be anywhere else. This was my team.

After we all got in position. I spoke in our connections, *"No youths unless they are lame. Elders a go, and if we can get two to three young bulls, that's a bonus."*

Xavier chuckled in the connection for a moment, *"Why so picky, Wilson?"*

*"Youths will do nothing to satisfy our wolves, the older ones will. We need to slaughter at least two apiece. Then eat our fill here, before we drag the other one back."*

Xavier was quiet for a moment before he replied, *"I disagree. We only take back five. No need for eight in total."*

*"Why the difference, Xavier?"*

*"Because don't forget that two of us will leave after we drag them back. Also, we do not need to waste food like that."*

*"Fair point."*

The connection was silent for a moment before Trevoric spoke, *"My wolf is getting antsy. Can we begin to attack?"*

*"Pick your target first, then once everyone picks their first one, half of us attack, and the other half waits."*

*"Copy."*

I glanced at Xavier, he was only a form to me, but I knew it was him, after years of working together. He glanced at me for a moment, before his eyes gleamed in his eyes, and he crept forward.

After half of us moved, I spoke again, *"The other half, stays in place, we will catch any that comes our way."*

*"Copy,"* said the rest who were staying place. The ones who went up first were our stronger wolves, the ones who would bring down their prey before they could make a sound. Xavier was an excellent one to do this, along with Arcanum, Trevoric, and Averic. The other wolves make too much noise, and they knew it.

I watched as Xavier's wolf parted the threads of grass aside, silently moving his feet. If anything, no one would know he was there unless you knew they were coming. I kept myself low and still.

****

I had locked onto an elder elk, he was big, his coat had a few gray hairs here and there, and he was a giant bull elk. Most likely the one that got to spread his offspring the most. I glanced out to my right and saw Trevoric stalking a young bull, and knew that, that one would probably make a fight. However, I could not say anything to any of the approaching ones. Otherwise, we will make a sound, and spook every single elk in the field.

I glanced to my left and saw Averic choosing a female, I saw his target and knew it was a brode female, meaning she was with a child. However, his wolf would know what to do. It just meant that she would be slower than the others since she was carrying. I had no idea what Arcanum was picking, but he would probably be going after a bull elk too. I shook my head slightly, my wolf wanting to growl slightly at me in annoyance, but I hushed him. If we growled, then we are no better than the others who are on the hillside watching.

Soon, I was within twenty feet from my bull before I connected, *"Everyone in place?"*

*"Yep."*

*"Then attack."*

I leaped forward, and in three bounds, grabbed the bull elk by his throat, and his blood gurgled for a moment before he went silent. He did not let out a warning. He was farther away from the others though, everyone else chose someone within the group, however, a warning call went up. The elks that were down on the grass, got up in a fright and were trying to flee. Since I had killed my bull so quietly and quickly, I lunged after another, and caught him on the rump, before being kicked. I tumbled down and winced as I landed. I growled and snarled and ran alongside the bull elk once again. I caught his throat and tugged downward, his throat opened up, and he tripped over his front legs and crashed down, his antlers carving a groove in the field. I whipped around and breathed heavily for a moment. Another bull was coming towards me, and I let my wolf lunge at him, and once again caught another bull by the throat. We swiftly brought him to an end, and I looked down before watching the life leave his eyes to become dull in color.

I watched as Wilson brought down a bull, and winced as the bull got a hoof onto his right shoulder before he went down. I smelt blood, but I could not tell from who. I glanced around, and after a minute none of the surviving elk were there, and a total of sixteen elk were down. Meaning, that we each did indeed kill more than we should have. I sighed deeply before looking at the three bodies I had and looked at everyone.

I could tell that Wilson was injured, and not just a scratch. He kept his right foreleg up, off the ground. He glanced at me and swallowed. He had only taken down one of the bulls, and none of the others. Since I had killed three of them, I jerked my head towards the furthest elk and he dipped his head in my direction. I turned my attention to the others and saw them all panting over their kills.

I walked towards the big bull I had taken down and looked down before letting my wolf surface. He tore into the flesh of the elk, and soon I heard only chewing happiness from my comrades. I kept an eye on Wilson and noticed that he did not want to eat. He kept his head low and turned away slightly. My wolf grumbled, but he stood up and walked slowly towards him.

Wilson's wolf growled in response, but mine huffed quietly, and he went quiet for a moment. I approached him and spoke through our connection, "**Why aren't you eating**?"

*"Because I need to take this one back to camp."*

**"Eat the one you caught, and drag that one back."**

My wolf pointed to the one farther away, and he looked back at Wilson. ***"But it's not all that is it? What is eating at you, Wilson?"***

*"It was an easy slaughter, Xavier. They weren't scared until they saw death."*

I frowned, he was right, they went without a fight until they noticed that they were being killed. It meant this group came from somewhere and was familiar with wolves enough to know that they normally didn't mean any harm. I frowned, as I surveyed the rest. Wilson spoke after a moment, drawing my thoughts away, *"Look at this symbol on this one's hindquarters."*

I glanced down and frowned, I did not recognize the mark, and by the look on Wilson's face neither did he.

A howl went up, my head shot up, and my comrades growled low in their throats in response.

Out of the gathering sunlight, yes sunlight, we had run and hunted most of the night away. A wolf approached, he stared down into the clearing, and I could tell by the hairs on his back and the raise of his hindquarters that this wolf would cause trouble. I glanced at Wilson before looking up at him again.

*****

Wilson winced before speaking in the connections to everyone, *"No one move."*

*"Who is that, Wilson?"*

*"No idea, but until we do, do not engage."*

*"Copy."*

Wilson glanced at me, both of us nodding in response, and turned our attention to the wolf. Wilson stood up, placed minimal pressure down, and winced before calling out, "STATE YOUR BUSINESS!"

The wolf stopped his growling, and his head whipped towards us. He snarled, "YOU KILLED MY HERD!"

Wilson glanced sharply at him, and replied, "We only took what we needed."

"What you needed? You have slaughtered sixteen of my herd!"

Wilson looked at me before replying, "I apologize, we have not eaten correctly in the past few years. Our wolves needed an entire elk to be fit."

"And the other eight?"

Wilson was about to reply, but I replied after a moment, "Gets taken back to where we are camped."

"Where are you camped at?"

I glanced at Wilson, and saw him think it over for a moment before replying, "The ruins."

"Inside Hendrix's territory? And he allowed you?"

"Who?"

He stared down at us in shock, before he sighed. "I'm coming down there to speak to you. DO NOT ATTACK ME."

"Alright."

He made his way down, and soon we saw his coat, it was silvery with black patches. He approached me and Wilson before stopping within twenty feet of us. He spoke, "Who are you?"

Wilson glanced at me before replying, "My name is Wilson Droon, and this is my company."

He glanced around at the rest and noticed that they had since inched closer. He glanced at us again before replying, "Never heard of you before. Where have you come from?"

"We came from the shifters…." I tried to reply.

He snarled in response, and jerked his head towards Xavier before snapping, "Shifters? Which?"

Savador snarled a warning, and either this wolf was too thick to notice or did not care. His ear twitched towards them, but otherwise, nothing else happened. I glanced at Wilson and he shrugged before replying, "Morphous."

The wolf instantly relaxed before muttering, "So, not those hybrid ones, right? The purebloods?"

"Correct."

"If you are shifters, why are you in wolf form of anything?"

"We aren't shifters. We are werewolves, we were imprisoned in the shifter palace. We came from King Nathaniel."

Wilson corrected. I glanced at the newcomer, and saw his eyes squint for a moment before he growled, "That king is five days had run away from us. He has no say in Ivanov territory."

"Ivanov territory?"

He looked sharply at us before his eyes flickered to the rest of our approaching company, who had been edging closer to hear what was being discussed. He sighed before replying, "You just proved that you are far away from home. Ivanov is the Lord over these hills. Hendrix is the one who controls the ruin area, all the way up to that edge of the forest over there."

He pointed his snout to the north, before continuing, "I would suggest you leave this territory and his territory. And overall, leave Ivanov's territory. He does not approve of any outsiders."

Wilson and I exchanged glances. I replied, "We aren't alone at the ruins."

"More werewolves?"

"No."

"Then what?"

"Humans along with their commander."

"Who is their commander?"

"Calio. Don't know his last."

"Calio? Who the fuck is that?"

We glanced at each other and Wilson replied, "We can take you there to meet him."

"I cannot leave my terrain. Hendrix would take that as an act of war."

"But this is Lord Ivanov's territory. Don't you have access to your lord? Explain to him what is going on."

"No one speaks to Lord Ivanov without his permission. He will kill anyone and anything that approaches him in that matter. That would be a suicide mission."

"Then how does he rule his lands?"

"He let the pack alphas decide that."

"How many alphas are in this area?"

"About eight. Hendrix has a sizeable chunk of the territory, and he keeps edging further and further into Roig's territory. So, probably going to be seven or so sooner than later."

"Huh, interesting," replied Savador, who had come close enough to listen to everything now, alongside everyone else.

The wolf glanced at him and growled slightly, but Wilson spoke, "Don't."

"What?"

"You know what, Savador?"

Savador sneered at him but went quiet. The wolf looked at Savador before speaking, "What?"

Wilson looked at Savador and motioned him to speak. Savador looked a little smug for a moment before replying, "If Ivanov was anything like our King Nathaniel, he would not tolerate the other alphas taking territory from each other, or slaughtering the others."

"The borders of your packs are secure in that way? In harmony?"

"Yeah. Everyone has their place. Most of the packs that had originally been in different parts, actually thrive under King Nathaniel's authority."

"What happens if someone forces you to be in that territory of that alpha?"

"If you are referring to it being by force? Then none, Nathaniel goes there personally and lets Basil take care of it."

"Basil?"

I sighed, drawing his attention back to me. I replied, "Basil is Nathaniel's Lycan. They work as a team. And no wolf that King Nathaniel has crossed paths with has challenged Basil. At least, not enough for him to really be challenged. Whatever fight was brought forth, is always dissolved by the time that Basil is done, and the alpha submits to him."

"So, your king is the alpha of all?"

"Yes."

"Then what are you doing out here?"

"That… that is a hard story to tell. We only came to the area not long ago. Less than a day."

He seemed perplexed for a moment. "Move your camp to my territory. Next to Hendrix, I am the second largest."

"Who are you?"

He paused and looked at the one who spoke, Averic, and replied, "My name is Roland."

He moved back towards the treeline, and Wilson called out, "I don't think we can convince the one in charge to move."

He paused before replying, "Hendrix will find your camp one way or another. He will slaughter any and all who are within his territory, who have not approached him first. And considering you have not done that, and you are outsiders. he will not tolerate it. Give your charge this message: move, or die."

He saw the conflict in our eyes before speaking, "I am sorry, but I will not abandon my pack solely because you need help. I will not sacrifice my pack for a message."

"I understand that."

He blinked at me before looking at the others and speaking, "Leave your kills here and come back. Hendrix will be having his patrol out soon on the border, and you MUST get back to your charge before they discover your camp."

We nodded once, and we turned as a team, and glanced at our kills before we took off.

****

I watched as they left in their wolf forms, and disappeared into the night. I scowled and went about my nightly routine, except for the lashing. That stopped since we both agreed to stop and follow mother's methods. I sighed and watched as the humans huddled around fires, and seemed to be better now that they were next to warmth. No more fighting happened around them. I rolled my eyes and Severi snickered. I hushed him once but kept a smile across my face nonetheless.

I went back to my ruin and instantly knew I was not alone. I glanced around and growled out, "Who are you?"

A figure came out and turned his head, his aura told me that he was a wolf and he replied, "My name is Hendrix. This is my territory, and you are invading it. Why should I not kill you?"

My eyes flashed before I replied, keeping Severi out of my voice for now, "I am Calio. This is my home, not yours."

He laughed and replied, "I think I would know if this was someone else's territory. Now, why should I not kill you?"

"Because you would not survive if you attacked me."

"Are you so cocky and think I will let you go without being killed? I OUTNUMBER YOU!"

"Numbers do not matter to me, Hendrix. Leave now, and let me be."

"No."

"Are you challenging me? Me to a duel?"

"Yes."

Severi smiled wickedly, I had let him out, and he shifted to his wolf for. I saw Hendrix swallow suddenly before he shifted to his wolf. They snarled at each other. Hendrix did not seem to know when to call it quit.

*****

We got back and soon found werewolves panting around the ruins, and we, at first, thought we would need to fight. However, after further approaching, we found out that they were all injured but alive.

Wilson moved faster, looked around, and saw Calio sitting calmly next to a wolf, a dead wolf before glancing at us and speaking, "He did not back off."

"Who is it?"

He shrugged before replying, "Someone named Hendrix."

Silence. We gasped and glanced at the dead wolf. Wilson replied slowly, "You killed him?"

"Isn't obvious?"

"He was the alpha of this area, at least this piece of territory."

"Not anymore. His pack then is mine."

"Under pack law, that is correct."

He grinned wickedly before toeing the body, and speaking, "Did you have a good hunt?"

"Yes."

"Good."

We looked at each other before backing out of his ruins. We glanced at each other and swallowed. He did all that damage, and not one human was killed. He glanced up at Wilson before speaking, "What is your question?"

"The next alpha adjacent to Hendrix's pack told us to bring you all to his territory since he knows that Hendrix would challenge, or kill anyone who was here."

"Well, he did challenge but failed to understand when to submit. I gave him plenty of times to tap out, but either his ego or his bronze mind wouldn't take defeat."

He shrugged casually and seemed rather at peace, Wilson glanced at me before speaking, "I guess I do have another question, Calio."

"What is your question?"

I glanced sharply at Wilson and saw his Adam's apple bob, before he replied, "Will you allow two of us to head back to the werewolf palace?"

I stared at him in shock, asking bluntly would get us killed. However, Calio sat back and scooted the body of Hendrix slightly. "Why?"

I glanced at the others and saw a bit of confusion in their eyes, but they knew better than to speak. Wilson replied, "Killian mentioned that you guys needed an army. What better way to do it with some of our kin? The humans don't stand a chance against werewolves and shifters."

"That may be true, but how would I know you would come back?"

Wilson opened his mouth to reply, but I spoke, "I would never leave my unit. They are my brothers."

"Even if you find your loved ones?"

"To be frank with you, Calio, we were thinking of getting our family and bringing them here. We don't want them fighting us in the war that you are preparing for."

"I guess that is a fair point. Which of you are leaving?"

I glanced at Wilson and replied, "Myself and Trevoric."

"Trevoric?"

"That is me, Calio."

Trevoric stepped forward, and Calio's eyes swept over us before he looked down at the body again and replied, "You have two weeks. Go."

I opened my mouth to say something, but Wilson cleared his throat and shook his head. I closed my mouth again, and connected, *"Two weeks is not a long time, Wilson."*

*"I know, but two weeks is better than nothing."*

*"Roland said it would take five days non-stop to get there. That would mean ten days in total to get there and back, and only four to convince everyone to leave."*

Calio looked at me and cleared his throat, bringing an end to my and Wilson's discussion. I looked at him and swallowed, but Calio smirked. "Three weeks. Go."

I opened my mouth to ask why he increased it, but Wilson grabbed my shoulder, and pulled myself and Trevoric out before hissing, "Get going."

We looked at him, and he pointed towards home, before growling, "Go!"

Trevoric and I exchanged glances before grinning and thundering away. Leaving the rest to stand there watching us leave.

*****

I watched them leave and turned to the rest before Calio called out, "Wilson."

I looked at the rest, and swallowed before entering the ruin, "Yeah?"

"Three weeks. That is it. One day later, I will start to break bones. Until they both return."

I swallowed, "Understood."

"Leave me."

"Yes, sir."

I backed out of the ruins and I could tell that the others heard every single word, and saw them all swallow nervously. They all glanced towards where Xavier and Trevoric disappeared and Averic spoke in the connections, keeping Xavier and Trevoric in the loop, *"Three weeks, you guys. Otherwise, Severi is going to break bones. And both of you need to return. No exceptions."*

*"Noted,"* replied Xavier. He tipped his head back and howled and to us. It was a little distant, but not by much. We howled along with him before falling silent.

****

I walked towards a ruin, and the rest followed me. Three weeks. Ten days in travel, and perhaps more. Less than a week to convince our family that we were separated from them to come with us.

I looked over the surrounding area before speaking, "Should we tell Roland that he doesn't need to fear Hendrix?"

"No."

I glanced at Arcanum before replying, "Why not?"

"Because he would just take advantage of the situation. You heard him. He is the second biggest in territory, and casually mentioned that Hendrix was pressuring Roig into releasing his terrain."

"What are you talking about?"

We all jumped slightly and looked towards Calio who had appeared. He smirked at our lack of hearing his approach. I swallowed before speaking, "Should we tell the next neighboring alpha?"

Calio tapped his right index finger against his chin before replying, "Nah, if he tries to come across my territory that is his business. However, I already have a lot of wolves to take care of as is."

I frowned and I could tell the others seemed perplexed slightly, but most of the ones left agreed with Arcanum, so there was that too. I sighed and replied, "Understandable. However, he did say we can come back. We did leave our kills there."

Arcanum looked like he would object, but Calio replied, "Go get it. If you need to bring humans. Take some of them."

I opened my mouth but he continued, "Your shoulder, what happened to it?"

Arcanum glanced sharply at me and must have seen the injury and glanced back at Calio for a moment. I sighed before speaking, "One of the kills got me in the shoulder before I could bring it down."

"You need to stay here."

"Thank you, but I will go with my company."

"Are you challenging my authority?"

I swallowed. "No, sir. I am merely wanting to stay with my comrades."

"You are injured. How would you be able to help?"

I opened my mouth to reply, but Arcanum spoke, "Wilson."

"Hmm?"

"Stay behind. Heal yourself."

"But…"

"No."

"Fine."

I grumbled but knew that Arcanum would get the kills back safely all the same. The others nodded in response and stood up. The five of them headed towards the exit, but Calio spoke, "Take humans alongside yourselves."

Arcanum glanced at me before his eyes landed on Calio and he spoke, "How many?"

"As many you think that would bring back all your kills."

He glanced at me before connecting, *"How many do you suggest, Wilson?"*

*"Twenty."*

Aloud, he replied, "Twenty."

Calio smirked but replied, "So be it. Get them, and go."

Arcanum looked at me and said, *"Heal quickly, Wilson."*

*"I'll try."*

*"You better."*

*"Get going. Don't test his demon's patience."*

*"Yeah, yeah."*

Then he turned and went towards the cowering humans. After Calio spoke for him, since they didn't shift back into their human forms, twenty of them came forward, and they began to leave.

****

I glanced at Calio, who had come back before speaking, "You have changed in the limited time since."

"I am trying to."

"I thank you for that."

He looked at me with a leveled look before speaking, "Come on, go into my ruin."

I opened my mouth to say that I would heal without help, but he growled, and his eyes sparked red for a moment. I dropped my gaze and limped forward. I wasn't fast enough, since Calio picked me up after a few steps, making me yelp. He chuckled slightly before speaking, "Hush now."

I went quiet and swayed back and forth with his steps before he set me down. I looked around and noticed that Hendrix was gone. But by the way, Calio was not surprised, he must have cleared him out. I swallowed as he approached and looked at the wound before tsking a few times. He sighed deeply and sat backward. "Shift into your human form. This is going to hurt, and I would rather not get a face full of fangs."

"Okay."

I shifted back and stood before him nude. I grimaced, I did not think this far through. He, however, did not seem affected by the sudden change. Then I remembered that he must not always be a raging killer all the time.

 He stopped the bleeding within a minute, got some needle and thread, and grumbled, "Don't move."

"Alright."

He went about fixing the wound and I hissed at the pain, but nothing else. If anything, what Morphous had done over the last twelve years was that he had taught us how to take pain. This was a discomfort yes, but not something I was not used to. After a few minutes, he finished and stepped backward before speaking, "You did well."

"Thanks."

He glanced around before speaking, "Go get some sleep."

I side-eyed him for a moment, but he simply walked out of the ruins and left me. Sleep overall, came over me. And I shifted again to my wolf form and went to sleep. I would not reject sleep when offered.

****

I walked out and after a few hours, the hunting and retrieving party came back. Although, three of the humans were gone. I looked at Arcanum before snarling, "Twenty went, where's the three?"

He swallowed before replying, "They fled."

I went quiet before I growled, "Did you follow them?"

"No, I stayed and watched the other humans."

"I'm going hunting then. Stay here, and keep an eye on everyone."

"Yes, sir."

I let Severi out, and he stretched out and ran. He thundered past the seventeen that came forward, and they cowered before me. However, Severi had one goal, and one goal alone. Hunt those who have escaped him.

# Chapter 23

The door to the throne room closed with a bang, and one of the side doors opened. I rubbed the bridge of my nose, sighing deeply, I knew who was going to strode into the throne room. His voice boomed out, **"Were you ever going to tell me the truth about what you just talked about, father?"**

**"No."**

**"Why did you give Akato MY RING?"**

**"Because he needed it for what he to do."**

**"Father, you should hand over the Carpathians to me. I am old enough."**

**"You know the law on that aspect, Alexei."**

I turned to face him, now that he had challenged me. His eyes flickered slightly, but he held his ground before he gritted out, **"Father, Come now, you want to be put in your place that way? Really?"**

**"You dare challenge the law my father placed down, Alexei?"**

He was silent for a moment before he replied, **"No."**

**"Are you going to challenge me?"**

Silence met me, and he finally swallowed before replying, **"No."**

**"Then you are a coward, Alexei. I would have challenged my father. You have not challenged me once, and I personally would have challenged him threefold."**

**"I am not like you, father."**

I smirked before striding to my throne and ascending the ribbed steps. Alexei stared at me before speaking, **"Father."**

**"What do you want, Alexei?"**

**"Why did you give Akato my ring?"**

**"As I said, he needed it for what he is going to do."**

**"Like what, father?"**

I was silent for a moment, and finally replied, **"How much of our conversation did you hear, Alexei?"**

He looked at me a little sheepishly before replying, "**Most of it. Except for a part. I heard the toy say that was exactly what the werewolves said. I did not hear that part of the conversation.**"

I sighed deeply and rubbed my nose before replying, "**That toy is the son of a Benik.**"

"**What? And you let it go? Why didn't you kill it?**"

"**Because there are apparently TWO Benik's around. One named Killian, who was his father, and Calio, who was his uncle. I have a feeling that the kid does not know he has an uncle though, based on his reaction.**"

"**Ah, did you tell him?**"

"**No.**"

"**Thank satan for that.**"

I scoffed before growling out, "**What else do you want, Alexei?**"

"**I want to know what is so special with the toy now. If he is indeed a Benik, does that mean he has the prophecy aspect?**"

"**Yes, that he does. It caught me rather off guard actually.**"

"**How so?**"

"**Because the kid doesn't even know he is different.**"

Alexei frowned before replying, "**What do you mean?**"

"**He doesn't know he has the spirit.**"

"**What is the spirit's name?**"

"**He called himself Firefoot.**"

Alexei went quiet and frowned. "**What now, father? Do we do what the prophecy says?**"

"**Unfortunately, I believe it to be the case.**"

"**I will get the sword masters to start preparations.**"

He turned on his heel, but I called out, "**Alexei?**"

He froze, turned around, stopped, and looked up at me. I stood up and walked back down the ribbed staircase before speaking, "**My people cannot find out immediately. The prophecy is through OUR bloodline since we are the rulers. You will tell the common folk NOTHING.**"

"**Of course, father.**"

He turned sharply on his heel and left the throne room. I watched as he left.

*****

I left my father in the center of the throne room, and my hard footfalls echoed throughout the black marble. I was heading to our sword masters' smithery, where I knew Crixius would be.

I walked down the white marble stairs, heading downward, when Zin approached me, he was my informer, my insider inside Akato's guards. I paused and my eyes flickered to him before I growled, "**What?**"

"My lord. I wanted to report to you that Akato brought someone into the veil, and…"

**"That is old news now, Zin. I told you to REPORT TO ME IMMEDIATELY!"**

Zin cowered and pressed himself against the wall before replying, "I apologize, my lord! However, Akato kept tabs on me! I had to go cover Nunito."

I scowled at him, "**Come to me BEFORE relieving anyone else, Zin.**"

He bowed to me and said, "Where are you heading, my lord?"

I paused and snapped at him, "**None of your business, Zin, get to your post.**"

"Why are you hiding information from me? I did nothing."

**"Zin, I cannot tell you. You failed me today as is, and therefore, you don't find out."**

"How many times have I failed you, my lord? Tell me!"

He raised his voice and caught a passing guard's attention. He turned and barked out, "MY LORD! How may I assist you?"

I glowered at Zin before replying, "**Escort Zin back to the brackets.**"

"Of course, my lord!"

Zin glowered at me but followed the guard back to the brackets. He spoke in my mind since I permitted him before, "*I was not done talking to you, Alexei!*"

***"But I was to you."***

"*Alexei!*"

I growled, and the guard instinctively grabbed Zin and pulled him away. Leaving me alone again.

****

I waited a moment, before heading back down the stairs, towards the smithery. A guard passed me and dipped his head to me, not speaking. It was clear the guards knew that I meant business, and rarely ever stopped me. They were beneath me, and they knew it. I was their next ruler. I finally reached the bottom of the staircase and turned sharply to the right before heading to the smithery.

I entered the blackened smithery, and I paused in the doorway. As a child, my father took me down here to show me how to operate these machines. To make my weapon, it is what the children of Dracula have to do to become members of society. I smiled slightly at the memory, but wiped it off my face as I called out, "**Crixius!**"

For a moment, nothing moved. Then after a few seconds, a voice boomed out, "**What do you want, boy?**"

"**Dracula has ordered to have the sword masters to begin work.**"

"**Why?**"

"**Are you challenging my father's wishes?**"

"**Not his, yours.**"

I bit my tongue to keep myself from lashing out at him. I replied, "**Are you going to challenge your next ruler already, Crixius?**"

"**The next ruler does not understand respect.**"

I went silent, I could not tell Crixius anything, it was not my place to inform him why. I partially wished my father was the one to start the smithery, since he had Crixius's respect as is. I, however, did not dare lower my head. Instead, I pulled myself straighter before I replied, "**I will inform my father that YOU are going against his wishes, Crixius. Let's see what he says.**"

"**What am I supposed to make, boy?**"

My lip curled up slightly, he knew my name, yet still called me boy. However, I couldn't let my anger out against him. That would prove to anyone that I was not worthy to rule yet. I swallowed before replying, "**Swords, axes, armor.**"

Silence met me, and I heard the scrape of a chair before a figure loomed in the shadows and he replied, "**What does Dracula know?**"

"**I cannot tell you, Crixius.**"

"**Yeah, you can tell me. I won't blabber to every single Carpathian. Tell me.**"

"**No.**"

"**Then how am I supposed to know how many to make?**"

I stared at him, I was about to speak when he chuckled. **"Relax, boy. Dracula has informed me that you were coming down. Also told me why."**

**"Then why did you…."**

**"To keep you on your toes. I wanted to see if you would squirm around like Marius."**

I groaned and glowered at him, **"I am not like him."**

**"Keep telling yourself that, Alexei. You may be eldest, and Marius is the third born, but you share the same blood."**

**"I am nothing like him, Crixius."**

**"I can concur with that."**

I rolled my eyes, and he chuckled again before speaking, **"You can go now, Alexei, unless you want to help wake the others."**

I shook my head vigorously; the others were downright nasty. They did not want to help me or take command of me. He chuckled in response, **"Head back upstairs, Alexei. I will take care of the grumpy crew."**

I dipped my head towards him, **"Crixius."**

**"Alexei."**

With that, I turned on my heel and went back upstairs.

*******

I made it almost to the throne room again, when the guard that had taken Zin to the brackets came forward, looking slightly spooked and also injured. I turned to him before snapping, **"What is it?"**

"My lord, he attacked me and another fellow guard."

**"What?"**

"He attacked."

**"Where is he?"**

He swallowed, pointed to the throne room, and I turned towards the guard room. Zin was an idiot. Attacking fellow comrades meant death to my father or banishment.

****

I walked towards the throne room and entered. My father sat on the throne of bones, his eyes livid as Zin cowered before him on the ground. I walked past Zin before looking at my father. My father's eyes cut to me before he hissed, "**You sly little boy.**"

Dread slightly set in, I did not inform my father of my placement of Zin in the guards of the patrols, however, it appeared that Zin had informed him of it. I glanced at Zin sharply but replied to my father, "**In what way, father?**"

"**Tell me, were you ever going to inform me of that?**"

"**Tell you what, father?**"

"**Of the treasonous actions YOU have been committing?**"

I glanced sharply at Zin and suddenly wondered what he told him. My eyes flickered to my father before replying, "**In what ways have I committed treason?**"

My father turned his head sideways and replied after a moment, "**According to this guard, you allowed him to injure his comrades.**"

I glanced down at Zin, so he did not know what I had been doing or had not chirped the wrong tune. I grinned and replied, "**I did not allow him to do that, father.**"

Zin's head snapped upward, and his eyes held shock and betrayal. I glanced at him and my eyes flashed for a moment in anger. He swallowed before looking back down. My father witnessed all of this before he snapped, "**The truth, Alexei.**"

"**I did not allow him to injure his comrades, father. I swear on my mother's grave.**"

He sat back on his throne, before speaking, "**Alright, Zin, you are banished. You have until daybreak to leave.**"

Zin's jaw dropped down before he scrambled to his feet and shouted, "My Lord! I was informed by Alexei that he would take the throne by force! That in itself is treason!"

"**Do not raise your voice at me! Get out of my sight!**"

Zin cowered before turning to face me, rage was on his face. He hissed, "You lied, Alexei! You lied and you are a snake."

I growled a low warning in my throat, but my father shouted, "**GUARDS!**"

The door slammed open, and five royal guards entered. Zin cowered before two of them since those two were his elder brothers. My father rose on his throne, standing and pointing at

Zin. **"Escort Zin back to his place of living, and then escort him to the veil. Let it be known that he is BANISHED!"**

The royal guards bowed instantly; his brothers grabbed his arms and dragged him out. Zin was in a fit of sobs at that point. The doors slammed shut after them, leaving my father and me alone.

****

My father panted in rage for a few minutes before he got himself under control again. He hissed, **"Alexei."**

**"Yes, father?"**

**"Get out. Coward."**

I bit my tongue, and turned sharply on my heel, leaving him.

# Chapter 24

I headed back to the shifter's palace and made it to the hidden door without a hitch. I glanced around and wondered why I wasn't stopped. I huffed slightly but entered the hidden entrance, and went back up the pathway. Soon I came back to the junction, where if I turned to my right, I would get to the wall again. If I kept heading straight, I would arrive in the dungeons. However, since I had promised Rafeor that I would get Lord Verein and Michael Slyther out, and brought to my camp, I could not do as I wanted – which was sleep. I sighed deeply and Falcor chuckled in my mind but did not speak. I sighed deeply before growling at him, *"What do YOU find so funny, Falcor?"*

*"The fact that you need sleep soon, and that means I will be able to take control."*

*"Falcor. You know why I cannot let you ascend completely."*

*"Oh, hush now, Killian, I would not do anything to jeopardize us. However, since Rafeor is no longer here, that means we can head back to the wolves that we have already."*

*"What do you know that I don't, Falcor?"*

*"Shush."*

*"Falcor?"*

*"SHUT IT! I hear voices…"*

I instantly let him drift backward and strained to hear the voices, and indeed I heard them after a moment. I walked forward, careful not to kick a loose rock. Soon I saw a flame, and then a guard's face. I paused and was just outside of the distance of the flame, a silhouette of the flame outreach. The guard was talking to another guard before his eyes flickered towards me and he barked out, "WHO'S THERE? SHOW YOURSELF!"

I sighed deeply, before walking into his torchlight. He blanched slightly before bowing to me, mumbling, "Forgive me, Killian, I did not know you were down here."

"It is alright, Sky. I wouldn't expect you to know of all my whereabouts."

He glanced at the other guard before shaking his head, and I caught the other one swallow nervously before turning on his heel and trying to move away from me. However, something in his movements caught my attention, it was as if he was hoping I would not call it out. Alas, for them though, I would. "What are you trying to hide from me?"

"From you? Nothing."

"Then who?"

They exchanged glances, and I crossed my arms across my chest. I rumbled, "If you want to be sneaky, the dungeons are the last place you want to be. So, what are you two trying to hide?"

"I can explain…."

"Show me."

They swallowed but complied with my order. I glanced down at the artifact, which was last time locked inside Morphous's room in a box. My eyes flickered to them and I growled, "Where did you find this?"

"In one of the catacombs."

"Why did you remove it?"

Silence. They glanced at each other, and I growled, "Answer me."

"I was going to sell it. It is nothing more than a trinket."

I frowned and looked back down at the artifact, and knew that selling it would not work. I sighed deeply since I knew what I needed to do. *"Falcor?"*

*"Hmmm?"*

*"What are the chances of Morphous feeling their bonds breaking?"*

*"None. I think."*

*"You think?"*

*"Cannot prove they won't set off something. However, their parents and family will absolutely feel the bonds breaking."*

*"I can't help that aspect…. What do you suggest we do, Falcor?"*

*"There is really only one thing we can do unfortunately for them and their families."*

*"Darn, and I really did like Sky."*

*"Why don't we bring them back with us instead of killing them outright?"*

*"Hmmm. Because they can leave at any time."*

*"Have Severi put iron collars on them, Killian? Last time I asked him, he had some sort of way of making sure of trackage."*

*"That works."*

I closed my connection with Falcor, and looked at the two guards. "You are going to be coming with me. I first just need to grab two prisoners, then we will be off."

"What? I am not uprooting my family just because you said, Killian."

"You will leave your family behind you."

"I will not LEAVE!" Growled the other guard, and he threw daggers at Sky, before snapping again, "My family is young and their mother is gone, Killian. I am the sole provider for six children. I am NOT LEAVING!"

"It's between leaving now or death."

Silence and I saw the color drain from their faces. They both swallowed before Sky replied, "De-dea-death?"

"Yeah, so which?"

"Why?"

"Because what you two dimwits had taken out of the catacombs is what Morphous had hidden. No one was supposed to find out about it. Did either of you tell anyone else of your find?"

They glanced at each other and finally, Sky looked down and replied, "I told Feilian about it."

I sighed deeply and glanced at the other guard, "And you?"

"My family. I showed it to my family."

My shoulders slumped, I had a feeling of who he was but was not certain. I sighed deeply before asking, "What is your last name?"

"Krool."

I sighed and rubbed the bridge of my nose. "Go get them. And if you are not back within an hour, I WILL kill you, and make your children watch."

He balked at me, and shrunk down slightly, before placing the artifact down and hurrying away

.

*****


I turned towards Sky before speaking, "Anyone else you failed to mention to me, Sky?"

"No, sir," he whispered. I knew he had no family, he was the youngest son of someone who had died in the riot. His siblings also perished in it. He glanced down at the artifact before asking, "What is the importance of that thing?"

I glanced at it before replying, "That would be digging yourself a bigger grave, Sky. For your safety, best not ask that question again."

He glanced at me, bowed his head, and sighed deeply, his breath was shuddery as if he was on the verge of tears. I said, "Come on, I need your help with getting some prisoners."

"Why?"

"They are going with us."

"Where are we going?"

"Elsewhere, where you cannot come back here. Or I will kill you."

"Killian?"

"Hmmm?"

"What are you going to do with us?"

I looked at him and shrugged before replying, "Not sure yet."

"Are you going to kill us once we leave the palace?"

"No."

"Then what are you planning on doing with us?"

"Sky?"

"Yes, Killian?"

"Shut your trap."

"But…"

"Do not make me repeat myself, Sky."

He fell silent and bowed his head in submission. I sighed deeply before heading towards Lord Verien's and Michael's prison cells.

****

I opened Michael's first, he had his head hung down and he took a shuddery breath in, before croaking, "What do you want?"

"You."

"Why?"

"Rafeor requested."

He went quiet, and slowly raised his head, whispering, "I swear if I had known she was royalty, I would have treated her decently!"

"It doesn't matter much now, Michael. Come."

He took a shuddery breath in before he pushed himself up, and swayed side to side before limping forward. He started to fall forward, but I caught him before righting him. He glanced up at me and croaked, "What does Rafeor want from me?"

"From you? Nothing. She has requested your check out."

"Does that mean you are going to kill me?"

"No."

"Then what does it mean?"

"You will have to wait and see."

He bowed his head and breathed in as if his ribs were broken, and croaked, "Water?"

"Unfortunately, I didn't bring any. We can get some on the way out."

"Okay."

He stumbled out of the threshold and I handed him to Sky. "Hold him steady, Sky."

Sky looked at me and swallowed, as he took Michael away from me. I walked to Lord Verien's cell and opened the door.

****

Lord Verien, was in a corner, pressed up as close to it as possible, my eyes adjusted and saw a small trickle of water before I spoke, "Lord Verien?"

His eyes flickered to me; he rasped, **"Who's asking?"**

"My name is Killian."

**"What do you want, Killian? Have you not taken enough of my dignity?"**

I chuckled darkly before replying, "Oh no, I didn't. However, Rafeor has requested your checkout date."

**"Checkout date? So, you are going to make MY DAUGHTER AN ORPHAN? How kind of her."**

Falcor flashed in my eyes for a split second, and I growled, "Careful."

He sneered and snapped, "**She is the reason why I am in here! Why my slaves have been taken, why I haven't had a decent room or bed SINCE the night before she was found by the ambassador of the shifter king! I am not going to be careful!**"

Falcor now desperately wanted to front, and scare the shit out of this puny human, however, I could not allow him to be yet. *"Not yet, Falcor."*

*"How dare he though! Let me out and I will show him something to be scared of!"*

*"Falcor, not yet."*

He grumbled, and sneered in our connection, but stayed put for now. I rubbed my forehead before speaking, "Verein, don't do anything irrational. It was time that she came to light."

**"Fuck off."**

"No."

**"Go. AWAY"**

Falcor desperately wanted out now, but Michael had limped over to the entrance of his cell before croaking, "My Lord?"

**"Michael?"**

"I'm here. Let's go."

**"You don't even know where he is taking us though!"**

"I believe it will be better than sitting in a dark cell, with no light whatsoever, and without more pain and suffering. Please, My Lord. Come with me."

**"Michael, My daughter needs me."**

Michael looked at me before speaking, "Killian?"

"What?"

"Is it possible to bring his daughter with us?"

"I would rather not."

**"Why?"**

"Because I would rather not have children along."

Sky swallowed and glanced at me sharply, but said nothing. Verein spoke softly then, "**Then leave me.**"

"But, My Lord!"

**"I am not leaving my daughter alone, Michael."**

"And how exactly are you going to protect her from here, Verein? Last time I checked, you were in prison. This is your way out. This is your ONLY CHANCE to get out, might I add."

I saw him swallow nervously before his eyes flickered to Sky and he rasped, **"Why don't you send him to get my daughter?"**

I glanced at Sky before replying, "Because he is in the same boat as you. He doesn't have a choice."

**"I don't have a choice?"**

"Not really."

**"Then why did you make it seem like it was a question then?"**

I shrugged and didn't reply. He breathed slightly and bowed his head before replying, **"Do you have children, Killian?"**

"Yes, I do. Why?"

**"If roles were reversed, would you want your children with you?"**

"No, I would think they are better at wherever they are."

**"Even if they get sold to the highest bidder?"**

I was silent for a moment and finally sighed deeply. "Where would your daughter be?"

**"Probably still at the mansion. Since that is the only place she really knows. Unless she is at Lady Rekina's."**

"Are they close?"

**"Somewhat."**

"What is your daughter's name?"

**"Avery."**

I turned and looked at Sky for a moment before growling, "Do you know where their mansion is?"

"Yes, Killian. I was one of the guards who brought them in."

I sighed deeply and snapped, "How far away is it?"

"Roughly a day run on foot."

I sighed deeply, when Falcor spoke in our connection, *"By their standards, Killian, not ours."*

*"We can't exactly run through the human-populated section of the territory, Falcor."*

*"We do it at night, Killian."*

*"Still a chance of someone seeing."*

*"We kill anyone who sees, Killian. Humans have no connections to anyone else. They don't have the same strings as werewolves, or shifters."*

*"Fine."*

Falcor faded in the back of my mind before I closed my eyes, snapping, "We will all go together then."

"Uhhh…. Killian?"

"Hmmm?"

"That would mean we need to get a carriage. And Morphous would be alerted."

"I don't need a carriage."

"Then how are you going…"

"Sky, shut it."

He fell silent and bowed his head in submission. I glanced at Verein, and snapped, "Get up."

He looked at me before forcing himself to stand, he swayed and winced. However, he hobbled over towards us before whispering, **"Thank…."**

"Shut it."

He closed his mouth instantly, and his eyes flickered to Sky's before trailing over Michael and back at me after a few moments. He lowered his eyes and breathed slightly, with a hitch in his breath before he gestured towards me to move.

*****

I moved away from the entrance of his cell before walking down the hallway. I glanced at the candle that the guards used, and noticed that Krool had less than ten minutes left to get his family down here. I squinted my eyes, and grumbled for a moment before looking at Sky and snapping, "Can you connect to him?"

He swallowed and seemed like he was about to lie to me, but I stared at him hard and he lowered his head, replying, "He went to Morphous, Killian."

"Oh? And how long did he go there?"

"He went there immediately."

"And you kept it quiet because?"

"Because he did not want me to tell you."

"I sure hope you know, I take no pleasure in what I am going to do."

He looked at me sharply and whispered, "What are you going to do?"

I let Falcor surface slightly, "I am going to go find his family, and either slaughter them where they are or take their bodies and place them around the palace. Exactly where he would find them."

"D-do-don't!"

"Are you going to challenge me?"

"No! However, I know Rosen will do ANYTHING to protect his children! Let me link him. Please."

"You have ten minutes. Then I'm going up there and do as I describe."

"O-ok- okay."

His eyes fogged over, and I could tell that it was not going as well as he had hoped. Soon, his eyes came back and he lowered his head before whispering, "He has his children hidden, Killian. He says you will not find them."

"OOH! A challenge! Finally!"

Falcor turned sharply on our heel and was about to walk upstairs, when Sky called out, "Killian?"

"Hmmm?"

"Why don't you take his children alive with us?"

I paused and Falcor replied to me in our mind, "*It will take away my fun though!*"

"*Falcor, are you really wanting to slaughter children?*"

Silence, and I knew that he was mulling it over, and finally, he replied, "*But…*"

"*Falcor, if we take the children along, we can either have them sold or take back with us. He will learn his lesson on trying to double-cross us. Either way.*"

"*I guess that is true. Fine, let's go find the buggers.*"

I smiled slightly before turning around to Sky and speaking, "Good idea, Sky. Take what he loves, and make him wish he had been with them."

Sky swallowed and watched as I disappeared, leaving him with Verein and Michael.

*****

I knew where to go, that Killian would not dare challenge. I hurried to Morphous's chambers, and banged hard on the door, waking him. Someone opened the door, and I instantly called, "My Lord!"

Then froze when I saw it was not Morphous. Quinn stood there rubbing his eyes, and I swallowed nervously before asking, "I need to speak to Morphous. Is he here?"

"Yeah, he's here. Why?"

"I… uh… ummm…"

Quinn gave me a hard look before speaking, "By your reaction, Rosen, you are afraid of something or someone. And by your stuttering, and reaction to me, it is based on my father. Am I correct?"

"Don't tell him please…"

"Come inside, Rosen."

He stepped backward, and I hesitated before stepping into the room. I swallowed nervously as the door closed behind me. I personally never been in Morphous's office, and I could tell by the pristine cleanliness that someone came daily to do maintenance. I swallowed before my eyes flickered to Gillith, who looked like he could have used another two hours of sleep before I dropped my gaze down.

Morphous came out of another door, and he paused in the doorway before speaking, "**Why are you here?**"

I glanced at Quinn and saw him yawn deeply before blinking at me with tired eyes. I glanced back at Morphous before speaking, "May I request that Quinn leave?"

**"Quinn is my advisor, Rosen, he is not going to do any harm."**

"But…."

Quinn spoke up, "Morphous, based on his reaction towards me when I answered the door, it is something with my father."

Morphous's head jerked towards him and instantly he pulled himself up straight before leveling me with a hard stare. He barked, **"What is Killian doing?"**

I swallowed, and once again glanced at Quinn, but Gillith spoke, "Whatever you have to say about Killian is not going to go back to him. Quinn has his issues with his father currently."

"Oh, ok."

I glanced at Quinn and swallowed before continuing, "He…. he's going to try to take me and my family out somewhere, where we cannot come back. Same with Sky."

**"Why?"**

I swallowed and dropped my eyes to the floor before replying weakly, "While I was on patrol down in the catacombs…."

"You took something from down there, didn't you?" Asked Quinn, completely cutting me off.

I swallowed and my eyes drifted to him for a moment before nodding my head. He glanced at Morphous and out of the corner of my eye I saw him stiffen. I cowered slightly, and finally, Morphous spoke, **"What did you take?"**

"Something in a box. I showed my family and showed Sky. Sky showed it to Feilian, but I am pretty sure that was it. Sky and I were going to sell it, and…."

**"Sell it to whom?"**

"Whoever wanted it. To us it looked unimportant, and something that could go."

His jaw dropped slightly and his hands tightened against his sides; he licked his lips and closed his eyes. I could not tell if it was out of anger, but I could tell that he was struggling with something. I lowered my eyes down again, when Quinn spoke, "Where is it currently?"

I swallowed nervously before replying, "With Sky and Killian."

**"Shit."**

I glanced at Morphous before asking, "What is it?"

**"Something I put down in the catacombs to be kept safe."**

I swallowed nervously when I saw his eyes glint orange, a sign that a shifter was irritated or angry. I looked down at the carpet before whispering, "I… I didn't know it was important."

No one spoke for a few moments, and finally, Quinn asked, "What happens if you do not go with my father?"

"Killian said he would come find me and kill me in front of my children."

Quinn frowned and sighed deeply before looking at Morphous and speaking, "Morphous, we need to hide those children somewhere. Whenever my father threatens someone, he holds himself to it. Especially with what he has too."

"What does he have?" I asked. Quinn glanced at me before replying, "Something, that you don't want to come across. However, you kind of forced it upon yourself. Morphous, his family, and himself are a target. My father won't take no for an answer, he will bid his time, and strike at the least expected time frame. I suggest that they leave."

"What?"

I squeaked. I glanced sharply at Morphous and then my eyes fixed on Gillith who had been silent throughout this ordeal. I whispered, "Gillith?"

He looked at me sharply before glancing at Quinn and speaking, "We all know the safest place for them would be with Davis. Even Killian won't go down there for them."

My jaw dropped and I opened it to speak, but Quinn shook his head and replied, "I disagree. Once my father has a target, he will go to no end to get it. I suggest they go with the laboratory shifters."

"WHAT?!? NO! They are always moving, and always on the run! That is not the life I want for my family."

Quinn stared at me and was about to reply, but Gillith spoke, "At the same time, you won't be a sitting target. Killian cannot hire, or pay someone to kill you for him. That family always moves. Never stops. Davis only knows where they are currently since they were last reported to be near a human town near him. I know not the news you want to hear, Rosen, however, this is the safest thing for your family. Without going, Quinn is correct, I have personally seen Killian go to lengths to find information. It is the safest that you can do."

I glanced at Morphous and whispered, "My Lord?"

Morphous glanced at me and sighed heavily. **They are the safest place to go. My question though, is where did you leave Killian and Sky at?"**

"The dungeons."

**"What were you doing down in them?"**

I swallowed nervously, but replied, "I was talking with Sky down there. It was the one place that we thought of that no one else would come down to. However, Killian was already down there. He was down a different tunnel. A very, very dark tunnel might I add. If Sky didn't show his torch down there, we would not have seen him."

Morphous squinted and frowned. He looked at Quinn before speaking, **"What business could your father possibly have down in the dungeons?"**

Quinn looked perplexed for a moment. "Perhaps something to do with Sammuel and Katherine?"

I swallowed, I didn't realize that they were down there. I glanced at Morphous but kept quiet for a moment before speaking, "To my knowledge, there are no cells down the way he came up from."

Quinn jerked his head towards me sharply. He frowned and looked down, with that look as if he was thinking hard. Finally, he inhaled deeply and spoke, "I know my father has told me of hidden entrances and exits of this palace. One of which is in the dungeons. A hidden entrance to it, and an exit to the western wall."

**"And you are only saying this now because?"**

"Because you never asked before Morphous, and YOU are the king of this place, didn't your father or grandfather show you the secrets of the palace before they passed?"

Morphous looked perplexed as he thought it over, and finally, he shook his head before replying, **"Honestly, no. They personally didn't explore the palace thoroughly."**

Quinn sighed deeply before looking at him with a look, he turned to me before speaking, "Leaving here is going to be the hard part. My father knows the ins and outs of this palace. He knows hidden entrances and exits. However, it is the best time to go. Out of curiosity, did he give you a time limit?"

I swallowed and whispered, "An hour."

He glanced at the time and glanced sharply at me. "So… about twenty to thirty minutes ago, right?"

"Yes."

"Gillith, find Feilian. If he is on a post, get someone to relieve him. He needs to leave too."

"Why?" He asked.

"Because Rosen said that Sky showed Feilian too, right?"

"Correct."

"Meaning he is another target for my father."

"Oh, ok. On it."

He started to move, when Morphous spoke, **"Quinn, Gillith is Killian's target too."**

I glanced at Gillith and saw him look at Quinn sharply, but Quinn didn't seem surprised, and replied calmly, "I know my father well. He will glance at Gillith, but he will not do anything about it since he is highly set on getting those who know too much. And besides, Gillith doesn't know much, Feilian is more in threat since he doesn't know how to take a hit."

I looked at Morphous and saw him frown and glance at Gillith. Gillith swallowed before speaking, "I'll go find him. Quinn, would you know his rotation?"

Quinn sighed deeply and replied, "And here I thought you would know that, Gillith. However, last time I checked the guard schedule, he's on the north wall."

"Ok."

Gillith walked past, me and paused, before resting his left hand on my shoulder and speaking, "Don't be afraid."

I swallowed nervously and was about to say something, but Gillith shook his head and opened the door, and walked out. Leaving Quinn, myself, and Morphous in his office.

****

I glanced at Morphous and swallowed nervously again. He would lose three guards in a day because of what I had done. Guards couldn't be simply replaced, they had to be trained. Taught how to do their duty, and then proved that they could manage it without supervision. I lowered my eyes and Quinn spoke, "What is done is done. We have less than twenty minutes to get your family and you out. Believe me, you do not want to wait longer."

I swallow nervously and glanced at Morphous. "But can't you protect me against him?"

Morphous sighed and replied, "**Normally, I would say yes, however, I now know that I am no match for him. The laboratory shifters are the safest you can be.**"

I swallowed and glanced at Quinn. I saw him lower his eyes slightly when I tried to make eye contact, I knew that Morphous would do anything for his people. Anyone in need, and would kill anyone to make it happen. However, this meant that Killian was a threat to us as a species since Morphous seemed scared a little bit. He would not openly say it, but I could tell by the flicker of his eyes, and based on the fact that he was sending us away, and did not turn down the idea with the project two hundred one. I swallowed and looked at both of them before speaking, "I guess, I'll go pack our bags then."

"No time. It is leave now, with the limited things on your back, and get out safely. Or be hunted."

I bit my lip and whispered, "But…"

Quinn shook his head and looked at the candle cursing slightly. He looking at me with a leveled look before speaking again, "I am sorry, Rosen, however, we absolutely need to find your children now. There is no more time we can waste. Where are they?"

"With Anna."

"Let's go then. We cannot waste more time."

He turned sharply, and headed out the door and out of the office, leaving me standing there staring at his back. I swallowed before glancing at Morphous and whispering, "My Lord?"

He looked away before speaking, **"It is the safest thing that can be done, Rosen. Go."**

I stumbled out of the office and followed Quinn.

*****

We got to Anna's room, where she had the children learning, and was in the middle of teaching them their letters when Quinn opened the door. She paused in saying, "A, A as in Apple."

She glanced at Quinn before speaking, "Quinn, can I help you with something?"

Without missing a beat, Quinn replied, "I am sorry, Anna, but I need all of Rosen Krool's children."

"Why?"

I wanted to push my way forward, but Quinn blocked my entrance, and I was slightly irritated. Quinn seemed to have frozen, and I glanced over at Anna and saw her eyes too were glazed over. I scowled, and after a minute, Anna and Quinn shared a pointed look but she sighed deeply before calling out, "Neo, Victor, Conway, Rae, Ayer, and Dimitri. Please, hurry and pack your school bags, and go with Quinn."

My children scrambled to put their ink pens and parchment away, and I swallowed. They shouldn't have to run away, away from what they know. Their lives were going to be uprooted and I was the whole reason. Quinn glanced at me and pulled the door closed as the children were moving to get out of there. He gave me a pointed look before speaking, "What is done is done. However, you should not have a look of fear across your face. And do not tell me I do not know what I am talking about. Your children will know something is wrong within the second they see you, Rosen. Be strong for them."

I gulped in the air quickly and breathed in a quiet whine. Quinn glowered at me and I looked down and steeled myself. Soon, the door opened and my son, Dimitri came out, alongside the others. I swallowed and plastered a smile on my face. He looked at me and then at Quinn before speaking, "Dad?"

I swallowed nervously, and Quinn lightly elbowed me in the side. He cleared his throat before speaking, "Lean your bags against the wall there. You will leave right now with your father."

"What? Where are we going?" Asked Conway, and I looked down and Quinn said, "I cannot answer that immediately. Hurry now."

They glanced at me but complied with Quinn's order, and followed us after we headed away from their classroom.

Dmitri fell in step with me and linked, *"Father?"*

*"I'm sorry, Dimitri. I am so sorry."*

*"Why?"*

*"Because we have to leave immediately. We cannot come back here. Ever."*

*"What did you do?"*

*"Remember that trinket I found?"*

*"Yeah…. Wait, that is the reason why we have to leave? Because of that thing?"*

*"Yes."*

*"Just give it back father! Then we don't have to leave!"*

*"I'm sorry, son, but we cannot stay here."*

He stopped walking; Quinn paused and looked at him before speaking, "Come on."

"No."

"I'm sorry, but you need to."

"I am not leaving my friends, and uprooting my life here. I like it here."

Quinn glanced sharply at me, but replied to Dimitri, "You are a little too young to understand what is happening. Your father will have the answers you seek."

"I am not leaving."

"Oh? Who said anything about leaving?"

Quinn and I froze, I glanced over Quinn's shoulder and saw Killian leaning against the wall. I swallowed before speaking, "Ki-kil-Killian."

His eyes flashed purple for a moment before he cleared his throat, "Thank you, son, for finding them all. I'll take them from here."

Quinn swallowed and glanced at me before speaking, "Father."

Killian glanced at him and looked relaxed, but I saw him grip his sword on his hip. His eyes bore into Quinn's and flickered to me every few seconds. Shit. I took a step backward, and that was when Dimitri glanced at me and swallowed. He seemed to suddenly realize why I hadn't said a word towards Killian, except for a shaky one.

Conway looked at Killian and linked us all, *"Slowly back away. No sudden movements. I know of a way out. Thankfully, we all have learned how to shift already."*

*"Which way?"*

*"Father, don't question it. Slowly back away."*

I didn't want to but followed my children backward. Slowly. Quinn seemed to know that something was discussed through a link, and he looked at me for a fleeting second, blinked once, and turned his attention back to his father. He knew what he had to do for us.

*****

Killian watched us for a moment but Quinn asked a question, "Father, I have a question."

"Oh, and what is your question?"

"Why weren't you in our room earlier today, or last night for that matter?"

"I…. uh… I had things I had to do."

"All night?"

"Yeah…"

"Like what?"

"Ummm…. Why are you asking that question, Quinn?"

"Because I am merely curious. Why are you trying to hide it from me?"

"I am not trying to hide it from you. I am just not sure where your loyalties lie currently."

"Why, they lie with you, father, and probably will forever."

"Quinn, you know that you cannot lie to me."

"It's no lie, father. I love you."

"That is a strong lie there, son. Never knew you were a sentimental one."

"Good time to change that though. We never say it enough towards each other."

"Good point."

"Father, Anna is having trouble with the children in the classroom. Would you mind stepping in there, and observing the room for a few minutes?"

"Uh… unfortunately I have things to do."

"But Anna really needs help, father."

"Why don't you do it?"

"Because I do not scare the young ones enough. They will be scared of you though."

"They shouldn't fear me though."

"That's a good joke, father, you know you love to scare their fathers, and their fathers pass down what they did today to their families. You scare anyone who crosses into your path."

Killian's reply was one I could not hear since we ran around a corner and followed Conway through different hallways. Speed walking so we are not thundering down the hallways. Soon. Conway opened a window and looked at all of us before speaking, "Now we shift, and fly."

"What? No!" I hissed.

Conway looked at me and replied, "Father, we need to leave. Quinn can only stall his father for so long. And since I did notice that Killian was always holding his sword, and staring you down. It usually means that whoever is on his target list is to be killed."

"How did…."

"It doesn't matter how I know that information. Shift. And we fly out of here."

I grumbled but shifted to a crow, and my children shifted to the same bird. They glanced at each other, before hopping on the window sill and leaping out the window and falling before opening their wings and gliding towards the treeline.

****

It took me a couple of minutes of being in the classroom to realize that I did not have my targets in sight. However, Anna did, in fact, have issues with a few boys in the classroom, which was instantly shut down when I opened the door and entered. They huddled downward and all swallowed nervously.

Anna glanced at Quinn and seemed to almost ask why, but he shook his head. I did not know what was happening but soon sat in the back of the classroom listening to Anna, "A, a as in Apple. B, b as in Bumblebee. C, c as in Cat. D, d as in Dog. E, e as in Elephant. F, f as in Fish…."

I stood up after she got to O, she paused, looked at me, and spoke, "Killian? Where are you going?"

"I apologize, Anna, but I need to attend other duties today."

"But, I thought you would stay for the rest of the hour."

I glanced at the candle and frowned before realizing that she was also stalling me. My eyes snapped to her before I opened my mouth to speak, when one of the children spoke out, "Please? Pretty please? Stay for the rest of the school day?"

I looked at the child and groaned inwardly. This kid had his puppy eyes out, and he pooched out his lip. I sighed deeply and sat back down, adjusting my swords, and leaned slightly forward. Anna smiled sweetly at me, as she continued the session.

*"What are we doing, Killian? We HAD OUR TARGET IN OUR SIGHTS!"*

*"Hush."*

*"KILLIAN! YOU ARE LETTING THEM ESCAPE!"*

*"Shush, Falcor."*

*"I. WILL. DEVOUR. THEM!"*

I grimaced at his volume, and leaned backward, rubbing my forehead slightly and grumbling, *"Falcor, we both know that they cannot get that far from us. Why scream?"*

He was about to reply when Anna cleared her throat, and my eyes shot up, and saw the entire class giggling. I swallowed before speaking, "I apologize, Anna, what did you ask?"

"Would you like to tell the class a little bit about what you do for the palace?"

I frowned and Falcor began to laugh in our mind. I growled slightly at him, and he fell quiet, but I still heard his snickering. I sighed deeply before speaking, "I enforce the rules, and make sure that the guards are where they are supposed to be. Make sure the maids know which rooms to dust, and overall clean. Distribute the chores so everyone has their tasks to complete."

I fell silent and saw twenty pairs of eyes watching me before a little girl raised her hand. I nodded to her. She bit her lip slightly and asked, "But aren't those Quinn's duties?"

"Myself and Quinn share the responsibilities of running the palace. It is a two-person job."

Another child raised his hand, and he asked the typical question, "Why did you choose to do that type of work? Is it easy?"

"When you are first learning how to do your duty, it can be a little hard. You will make mistakes, but if you don't, you don't learn anything new. I like the challenge of the job, and every day is something different. And once you know your job well, it is easy, and becomes a rhythm."

That seemed to make them all quiet. I glanced at the candle and saw that it was, in fact, an hour passed since I came in here. I stood up, and heard a bunch of awe's before I turned my full attention to Anna, "Anna, I apologize. However, I must now really need to leave."

"Of course, Killian. What do we say, class?"

"THANK YOU, KILLIAN!"

I smiled, as I exited the classroom. Falcor bright in my eyes before he growled, "*Let me out, Killian.*"

"*No.*"

"*Why not?*"

"*Because you will go on a killing spree simply because.*"

"*If you had not been in that classroom I would have already gotten to get Lord Verein's daughter! Now we have to hunt for the runaways!*"

"*I was thinking…*"

"*Thinking? What the fuck were you thinking?*"

"*We let them run…. And then go hunting once we drop off everyone back with Calio.*"

"*Give them three days to disappear? Are you mad?*"

"*It will give us something to do while we wait for Rafeor.*"

"*Hmmm. Fair point. How far do you think they will go?*"

"*Only one way to know for sure, Falcor. We let them run.*"

"*Fine, on one condition.*"

"*Depending on your condition, Falcor.*"

"*I am in control when we go hunting for them.*"

"*No killing anyone that is not our target though.*"

"*Fine. However, that only lies with those who are surrounding them. Not the ones harboring them.*"

"*I guess that is fair.*"

"*Damn right, it is fair, Killian.*"

I grumbled but did not reply. He was in a mood and I understood. We were caught in endless questions by our son and somehow got roped into going into Anna's classroom. I sighed and walked towards the hidden dungeon entrance since that was the way we were leaving.

# Chapter 25

I walked alongside the wolf, leaving Killian where he stood. Since the wolf said he could not go further into their territory. The wolf had not spoken since we left, and I was itching to ask a question. Finally, I sighed and stopped walking. It took him a moment to stop and look at me with a questioning look. I smiled slightly before asking, **"Where are we going?"**

"We are heading to Nathaniel."

**"We've walked quite a bit already, I thought by now we would have reached it."**

"Normally, yes, we would. However, you are in human form and I have to take you a different route than normal."

**"Do you want me to shift to a wolf?"**

"Uh…. I don't know if that would be any better. Since no one knows who you are."

**"Doesn't Nathaniel know I am coming at this point? What was that shimmer when crossing into the territory?"**

He opened his mouth but closed it after a moment, he was confused too. He sighed deeply and replied, "In honesty, he did not send me to get you. I just had a hunch that someone was approaching. Even my human half was not very happy when we went out."

**"Oh. So, there is a chance that I could be attacked?"**

"Chance, yes. However, once they realize who you are, that will change. But not before they have done some sort of damage."

**"Oh."**

I fell silent, and my Lycan spoke to me in my mind, *"Let me shift please, Rafeor."*

*"Okay."*

I looked at him and spoke again, **"Do-don-don't be surprised by my form, please."**

He cocked his head to the side with a questioning look in his eyes before he replied, "Why would I be surprised?" I smiled weakly and allowed my Lycan forward. After a few moments, she stood in all her glory, and I saw him shrink down before her.

He swallowed before whispering, "H-ho-how is that possible?"

**"I am the first of my kind, I am a shifter, and a werewolf hybrid."**

"Hy-hyb-hybrid? You are a cross?"

**"Yes, I have what my father is, who is a shifter. Can shift into anything at will. Along with what I believe is my mother's, as a werewolf."**

"You aren't supposed to be. Our species have been careful not to mix! For this exact reason!"

**"Are you going to attack me now that you know what I am?"**

He swallowed and after a moment, looked away. "I already know you would make a fool of me if I tried."

**"Damn right, I would."**

He fell silent and looked towards the woods ahead of us; he seemed to be talking to someone before the bushes rustled.

****

After a few moments, five wolves stepped forward, each growling. I glanced at the wolf before speaking, **"What is this?"**

He looked at me, before replying, "Your end. You will die before you go further into our homeland. Freak."

I winced in response, and my Lycan growled a warning. The other wolves kind of froze but growled and raised their hackles ready to fight. It was going to be six to one, and I swallowed nervously before speaking to my Lycan, *"No killing them. But wound them."*

*"Wound them? They are the ones challenging us, and called us a freak!"*

*"I know, but we cannot do much else. This is my wish though. Please."*

*"If they try to go for anything vital to our life, that is off."*

*"Okay. I give you full control."*

My Lycan smiled in response, as I drifted back into the back of our mind, so I do not see what she has in store for them.

*****

Basil was restless, and I grumbled as he tossed and turned, and making Sophronia get out of the double-king bed, and move away from us. I scowled at Basil but kept quiet. Whenever he was this restless, he knew something was happening, but didn't know what. After about five minutes, he jolted up and would have roared in rage, but I snapped at him in the connection, *"DOWN!"*

*"NATHANIEL!"*

He roared, making my mind rattle against our skull, and making me wince. Something was up. He rarely if ever did this. *"What is wrong Basil?"*

*"We need to get to the border. NOW!"*

I grumbled, but slid off the bed, and stood up. My muscles moving, but Basil growled, **"Let me out."**

**"Why?"**

**"Do you not trust me?"**

I fell silent, and sighed before replying, **"Do not kill anyone."**

**"Only if they are not doing anything harmful."**

**"Fine."**

I allowed Basil full access and he still roared. I grumbled at him in the connection, but could not do anything about it. Sophronia glanced at me and spoke, **"What is going on, Basil?"**

Basil looked at her and growled, **"Shift."**

Her wolf instantly shifted and looked at him in surprise. Basil howled once more, answering the calls. Basil crouched down, and hovered over Sophronia's wolf before rumbling, **"Evenor, do you feel anyone close to you?"**

She blinked before whispering, **"I feel something, Basil. It feels like a part of me is waiting."**

Basil looked at the door before standing to his full height and charged at the door. It splintered before him and I mumbled, *"Damn it, Basil."*

*"We fix later."*

*"If you had opened it, it would not need to be replaced."*

*"Hmpth."* Was all I got out of him in return. I sighed as I watched through his eyes. He went out of the chambers and instead of walking like he normally did on two feet, he went on all fours. Proving that something was wrong. Normally, he would never get down on all fours, and the wolves that he had awoken with his roars, let's just say they went pale when they saw that.

He bounded forward and made the entire hallway frames tremble on the wall. I winced as several fell off, glass shattering, but he paid no heed.

Soon we were down the stairs, well under a technicality, Basil ignored the stairs and leaped off the landing in one bound, and landed on the ground floor twenty feet below. To say, we did not scare anyone was a lie, we made a few wolves scatter, and Basil seemed to have loved it since he grinned wickedly at them. He ran out on all fours, and the front doors splintered as he forced his way out of them. I scowled in our connection but knew what he would say, so I stayed quiet. The wolves followed and were pelting after Basil, since he already made it to the treeline, and disappeared.

*****

I knew how to fight, but I stayed in place, waiting for the attackers to make the first move. The six approached cautiously, and two veered to the left, and the same with the right. I swung my head side to side, to keep all of them within my gaze, but it was six to one, and the odds of me making out alive were actually less since I was just taught how to fight with the shifters. I could tell that Rafeor was starting to wish that she did not leave Morphous's but I felt like Killian was correct, that it was time to head over to the werewolves to learn their ways. So far, they had only taught us that they did not agree with what happened and that they would go to great lengths to kill what they believed to be a sinful thing. In that case, it was me. I brought back my lips in a snarl, when off in the distance, I heard a roar.

The wolves stopped their approach, and leaned down slightly, as if unsure. But the wolf that had brought me into their kingdom continued to approach. His lips were drawn back in a snarl, but then another roar sounded, and this time he stopped and looked backward as if he was unsure of what to do now.

The others glanced at the one who called them forward before one spoke, "Why did you bring us here, Norjor? Now we have to deal with Basil. Whatever got him worked up. I bet is something to deal with this."

"Because this is a freak of nature! This thing is a hybrid. Between the shifter and wolf!"

The others glanced at me then, and one sighed deeply before replying, "Norjor, is any of this because of your father? Xavier was a legendary warrior, and an unknown outcome, however, it does not make sense for his son to make this accusation towards someone unknown."

"So, you agree to let this thing live? Because this thing is a daughter of Morphous and mother of a werewolf! Remember the prophecy?"

"Prophecies have more than one outcome though. You cannot say that your future is going to be laid out in stone. What prophecy has do you think that this one will?"

I stared at them, these seemed to understand what prophecy he was referring to, but at the same time challenged it. Norjor looked conflicted towards his comrades, and he snapped after a moment, "What would your mother say about ignoring the prophecy?"

"What she doesn't know won't harm her, Norjor. Come along patrol. We need to report back to Nathaniel anyhow with our patrol."

Trees beyond them snapped, the ground trembled, and the werewolves glanced at each other before one sighed and spoke, "Speak of the devil. Norjor, you better have a good reason for this. I am pretty sure that this one is what Nathaniel informed us, guards, to keep an eye out for on our patrols. Which is why they have been more frequent."

Norjor swallowed and glanced at me again, but sat down and hung his head.

*****

The ground stopped trembling, and a few trees back I saw glowing eyes approaching. A twig snapped and the wolves went downward slightly with their tails between their legs. Then out stepped another Lycan. We locked eye contact, and he breathed deeply and his eyes flickered to the patrol, and his eyes fixed on Norjor. He growled low in his throat before rumbling, "**Azier, you and your patrol were the only ones that I had out. Did Norjor join you?**"

"No, My Lord, Norjor came on his own."

The Lycan swung his attention to Norjor before rumbling, "**Explain.**"

Norjor opened his mouth and then closed it again before hanging his head and tucking his tail in further. The Lycan growled low in his throat, his eyes flashing, and his talons growing slightly longer.

I swallowed before I spoke, "**Norjor met Rafeor and Killian at the border. About an hour ago now. He was taking Rafeor further when Rafeor allowed me access. Since we did not want to be attacked.**"

The Lycan froze and slowly turned its head towards me. His eyes sparked for a second before he rumbled, "**Did I ask you?**"

**"No."**

**"Then why did you speak?"**

**"Because I do not sit still."**

His eyes flashed again and he rumbled, **"You said Rafeor but where is she?"**

**"I am alongside Rafeor."**

He looked at me and blinked once. He stopped growling and looked at Norjor. **"Norjor? Report. Now."**

He looked like he wanted to disappear suddenly, but he bowed his head and replied, "I-I-I...."

It took him another moment to speak, "My Lord, I had one of those hunches, and went to the border. I apologize, My Lord."

**"It does not make a difference to me who comes outside during the evenings, Norjor. However, I am displeased with you. Cyprus, report."**

Norjor jerked his head upward and swallowed. The Lycan noticed that but ignored it. It was evident to him that he wanted more than one voice in this.

"My Lord, we were on the eastern border patrol this morning. We were checking all the typical areas for normal patrol when we heard Norjor call out in a howl. Since he was not supposed to be out, we came towards him and caught another scent. We, I, apologize now, My Lord, but we approached the other Lycan, and were not friendly to say the least. When we heard your roar, we backed off, but Norjor decided to continue, but after another moment, you roared again, and he stopped his approach."

The Lycan swerved his head towards Norjor before growling, **"Is that true?"**

"Yes, My Lord."

**"Patrol stay here. ASH!"**

A gray wolf approached, his soot-like ash in color, but his eyes were blackish brown, depending on how the shadows played with them. He bowed to the Lycan before rumbling, "Yes, My Lord?"

**"Take Norjor to the dungeons."**

"Of course, My Lord."

"Du-dun-dungeons? Why?"

**"Because you were not supposed to be out here in the first place. Last time I checked, you were door-posted."**

"I apologize, My Lord! But you can't seriously mean the dungeons! My father was Xavier Dragonheart!"

**"Then your father will be ashamed of his son's performance. Ash, take him."**

"Come along, Norjor."

"NO!"

He leaped over Ash and tried to run towards the border, closer to me, but I lunged down and grabbed his scruff on the neck. He yelped in shock, twisted himself, and latched onto my arm. I snarled as his teeth sunk into my flesh. I released him before he could do more damage. However, he dropped to the ground and tore away.

****

Ash started forward, but the Lycan spoke, **"Leave him."**

"My Lord?"

**"If he comes back, take him to the dungeons."**

"And if he doesn't?"

**"Then it is his loss."**

Everyone stared at where he disappeared, and finally, Ash whispered, "He'll come back. He just found his mate."

The Lycan looked at him sharply but said nothing. His gaze fell to my arm and scowled before he spoke, **"Come along. Patrol, if you have other sites to go to, continue. Otherwise, come."**

"We have a few more spots to look at first, My Lord."

**"As you were then."**

"Thank you, My Lord."

The five wolves left, and started heading back into the underbrush before disappearing. I took a step forward, but Rafeor blinked once, and we swayed before she shifted back. Ash got to us faster than the Lycan and eased us down to the ground slower than when we were falling.

The Lycan sighed before approaching, when off in the distance I heard a female voice, "**Who is that? She smells. . ."**

That was all we heard before we went unconscious.

*****

I woke up in a room. It was plain for the most part, the walls were off-white, a bed that was pretty comfortable, and a dainty wall adjacent to the door. I winced as I tried to move my arm, and a voice spoke to my right, "**Careful.**"

I jerked and snapped my head towards Nathaniel who sat in the armchair next to the bed. I couldn't tell if it was originally there, or if he had it moved inside the room. There was another chair there too, but no one was in it. He sighed deeply and brought my attention back to him before whispering, "**Wh-wha-what happened?**"

He sighed deeply and ran his right hand through his hair before replying, "**You came across the border, and apparently someone thought you were a threat to the kingdom and they tried unsuccessfully to do further harm to you.**"

I glanced down at my arm before whispering, "**Oh, the last thing I really remember was when I was replying to the wolf that brought me here. He was such a nice wolf before I shifted. Then he called out and a patrol showed up. After that, I don't remember anything.**"

Nathaniel looked down at his hands that he had since clasped between his knees. "**Why didn't you simply send a note or something to me? I would have met you at the border.**"

"**It wasn't one hundred percent planned. It was on a whim thing. Killian suggested it.**"

"**What does Killian have to do with any of this?**"

I shrugged before replying, "**Honestly? I don't know what his deal is. He insisted that I go to the werewolf kingdom, but did not entirely seem too pleased when the wolf said that he couldn't go further. It was strange, we crossed into the territory, but there was a veil...**"

"**It alerts me whenever someone non-werewolf passes through it.**"

"**So, you knew that I was in your territory then?**"

"**Not exactly. Basil, however, did.**"

"**Basil?**"

"**My Lycan form. His name is Basil. He does want to know how you have a Lycan though. That is his mystery.**"

**"I was born with her."**

**"What is her name?"**

**"I don't know. She hasn't told me if she does have one or not."**

**"Normally they don't tell you what it is. I had to find out a different way to learn what Basil's name is. It was tricky but so rewarding to know."**

We sat in silence before he looked at me and continued, **"So far, there have only been three Lycans throughout this area. Mine, and one other that I met in passing at one point. Then you. There has to be a reason why you have a Lycan. Would she be willing to speak to me?"**

I looked away, as I replied, **"I don't know."**

He stood up slightly, startling me before I hunched down into the bed further, and gulped. He was freaking tall. He smirked slightly before moving towards the door, opening it, and calling out a name. Soon, a guard came forward, they talked for a moment, and the guard disappeared. After a few moments, a girl slipped inside. She glanced at Nathaniel before dipping her head in submission, her eyes red with tears and her face blotched. My Lycan stirred in anger, but the girl smiled at me before speaking, "Hello, my name is Aurelius. Aurelius Fiore."

My Lycan relaxed suddenly and I smiled slightly. **"My name is Rafeor."**

She cocked her head to the side slightly, before looking at Nathaniel and speaking, "My king."

She made little shooing motions, and he chuckled before looking at me and leaving.

****

The door shut gently behind him, and Aurelius slouched slightly and sniffed once before I asked, **"What's wrong?"**

"Oh, it's nothing."

**"It's something if you are crying. What's wrong?"**

She swallowed and tears began to run down her cheek. She sobbed a little before she whispered, "My mate marked, mated, and told me sweet nothings. But he apparently did not feel like staying. I am worthless! I have no wolf, so no one fucking cares about me! They pity me, but they don't really care."

She fell silent and bowed her head, and swallowed her saliva before continuing, "It doesn't matter. I should have seen it coming. He was a freaking Dragonheart, and I…. I fell for his lies."

**"I doubt that he would want to leave. Who was he?"**

She looked at me in shock before replying, "Y-yo-you do-don-don't know?"

I shook my head, she frowned, and glanced at the door before replying, "His name was Finn, and his wolf was Norjor."

**"What happened to them?"**

"He was the one who got you into the territory. According to Azier, and she….. She's one of the few who treat me well. I trust her."

**"Oh. I didn't personally know."**

"It is quite alright, I guess. Is there anything you need, my lady?"

**"I am no lady, please, call me Rafeor."**

"It is not proper for the low life like myself, to call someone by their name. Unless given permission. At least, that is how everyone here goes about it."

**"Well… good thing is, I just did permit you, and even without my permission, I would want someone to call me by my name. What do they have you call them?"**

"Normally, my lord, my liege, my…."

She tapped her index finger against her chin, thinking before continuing, "My overlord."

**"If I had anything to say about that treatment, it would stop. Everyone should be treated equally."**

She smiled slightly in return. "Alas, your world is not the norm here. I have been called several things, and a few offensive especially when I keep away from those who want to mate with me. I guess I should have let them."

**"No, I disagree with that. You have a mate, and it sounds like he really likes you. When he cools off, I'm sure he will come back to you."**

She frowned and looked away before mumbling, "He should reject me and take a chosen mate."

I moved off the bed and approached her before I replied, **"No, don't let your thoughts talk you against someone who will always hold you dear."**

She glanced at me before replying, "You are rather wise. How old are you?"

**"Eighteen."**

"How are you only eighteen and so wise?"

I grimaced and replied after a moment, "**You have to grow up fast, at least where I came from.**"

"And where did you come from?"

I opened my mouth to reply when the door opened and a woman peeked her head inside and snapped, "You worthless lump! get her bandages replaced, then come out here! You have much to do and absolutely no time to chit-chat!"

I stared directly at the woman before I snapped, my Lycan probably on the surface. Or at least in my eyes, "**Excuse you.**"

Her eyes snapped to mine before she swallowed slightly and replied, "Forgive me, my lady. However, she has the entire upstairs to do, on top of changing your bandages out."

**"And you are doing what exactly?"**

"Why? I am her mistress. She has to do what I tell her to do. Otherwise, she knows where she will be located."

Aurelius shrunk down at the threat and swallowed before moving towards my arm. I moved it out of her reach before I snapped at the woman, "**I do not know who you are. However, you are rude and cruel. No one should work under you since you are an asshole.**"

Aurelius froze and glanced at the woman. The woman looked at her with a glower, before she replied in a clipped tone, "And you are nothing. Nathaniel should toss you out in a heartbeat. You are nothing but trouble."

**"What was that?"**

The woman stiffened and her eyes grew huge before she removed her head from the gap and started to close the door.

I strode across the room, when Aurelius whispered, "Rafeor!"

**"What?"**

"You… you don't have anything covering."

I glanced down and swallowed before looking at her sheepishly, grabbing a throw blanket before opening the door.

****

The woman bowed low to Nathaniel and glanced at me with a shocked expression across her face before it disappeared. Nathaniel glanced at me, and smirked before asking, **"What is going on?"**

**"She is being an asshole to Aurelius, all because…."**

I stopped talking and frowned before continuing, **"Because she does not have a wolf."**

Nathaniel glanced sharply at me before turning his attention to the woman before snapping, **"Is that true?"**

She swallowed and did not reply. Her eyes cut to Aurelius and I saw her rage in her eyes, and I stepped into her direct line of sight for a moment, blocking it. Her expression was worthy of one that would scare everyone, but Nathaniel growled, and his eyes sparked before he rumbled out, **"Answer me."**

She extended her neck in submission, and she whimpered, "It is true, My Lord. Everyone does."

Nathaniel blinked once before he rumbled, **"Not anymore. She is to be treated fairly."**

"Of course, My Lord."

**"Aurelius, why did you not say anything?"**

"Because I…. I was threatened many times to keep it quiet, My Lord."

**"By whom?"**

Aurelius glanced around me and saw the woman shaking her head side to side, but it was not missed by Nathaniel. He growled in response, and she cowered slightly before him. His eyes flickered to me before speaking, **"Rafeor, please get some clothes on. Aurelius, can you please assist her?"**

"Of course, My Lord!"

She pulled gently on my shoulders, and I stepped backward, glowering at the woman, before I closed the door with a small click.

****

Aurelius stared at me before speaking, "Why did you do that?"

**"Because no one should go through that. Least of all you."**

"No one is going to stop it."

**"Not even with an alpha command?"**

She opened her mouth to say something but stopped and frowned after a moment. A small smile came across her face and she shook her head before replying, "Any who have done so, had ended up either in the dungeons or dead. It highly depends on how Basil is in the mood or not."

**"Is Nathaniel a good leader?"**

Her eyes flickered to the door before she replied, "Yes, he is some of the best of what he does. He doesn't tend to go off on people. Unlike his brother, Logan."

**"Logan?"**

"Nathaniel has two brothers, Logan is the second born, and he is a piece of work. And Tobias is gone on leave for the time being. Last I heard of his whereabouts is that he is heading towards the outlands."

**"Why?"**

She shrugged before replying, "Don't honestly know. Probably on important business for Nathaniel."

**"What about Logan? Why didn't he send him?"**

"Because Logan is a piece of work. Nathaniel keeps him at home most of the time so he doesn't do anything wrong."

**"Like what?"**

She glanced at the door before whispering, "Like killing people for the fun of it. Nathaniel found out that he was in a drug ring, and they weren't only doing drugs, they were also slaughtering humans."

That made my eyes flash in rage, and this time my shifter half did it. My Lycan didn't. Aurelius frowned before asking, "If you do not mind my asking, Rafeor, but what are you exactly?"

I swallowed before replying, "**I am a hybrid.**"

"Between what?"

**"Shifter and werewolf."**

"Oh…. that makes more sense now on what Azier told me about then."

**"You… you aren't scared?"**

"Why should I be? You are nice, and are the first person to show me kindness today, besides Azier."

I glanced at her and she smiled slightly. Her face was still red from crying, but she seemed at peace now compared to coming inside the room. I sighed deeply before moving towards the wardrobe before opening it.

****

Seeing all the fancy dresses and clothing, I glanced at Aurelius before asking, "**Anything simple?**"

She walked over and chuckled before shaking her head and replying, "Apparently, Sophronia did not want you in simple clothing. She had the seamstress stock this room with dresses while you were out."

"**How am I supposed to fight in these?**"

"Fight?"

"**Train how to be a werewolf. Or tame my Lycan form as Killian mentioned it as.**"

"Why? I don't believe you are supposed to fight in these. These are what Sophronia has however informed the seamstress to make for you. I don't believe that she wants you to do anything like that."

"**But I need to learn how to control…**"

The door opened and Nathaniel entered. He kept his back to the wardrobe before speaking to the wall, "**Everyone now knows to call you by your name Aurelius, and treat you like anyone else. It is not your fault that you were not given a wolf, and therefore, I have alpha-commanded everyone.**"

"Thank you, My Lord."

"**One other thing, Aurelius. If you keep anything from me like this again, dire consequences are in store. I do not want any member of my staff or community to be treated unjustly. The fact, that yours went for so long without my knowledge is unforgivable, and I wished that you had said something beforehand.**"

"I apologize, My Lord."

He turned slightly, and he either completely ignored my nudeness, or was so used to it, that he did not seem phased by it. He spoke, "**Aurelius, do you know where the female elite chamber is?"**

"Yes, My Lord?"

**"Take measurements of Rafeor, and go get her a change of clothing. There is no way in hell she is going to fight in those clothing."**

"Of course, My Lord."

I watched as she quickly grabbed a measuring tape, before checking my length, and heading towards the door. She hesitated a moment, before she bowed to Nathaniel, and left promptly. Leaving me alone with Nathaniel.

*****

I looked at Nathaniel before speaking, "**You seem like a just leader."**

He smirked and walked towards the bedframe post, rubbing it slightly with his hand and replying, "**I am when Basil is not in a mood. However, once you were within our sights this morning, he seemed to calm down a bit afterwards."**

"Any chance that it was the veil that happened?"

**"That is a possibility. He sensed it triggered."**

**"Ah."**

I looked down at the ground, it was not carpet, not built into the ground at least, but there was a sheepskin rug. I asked, "**What are we going to learn today?"**

**"That highly depends on if your Lycan is willing to come out and play. If not, then not much more than what Morphous had trained you with."**

**"I wish Morphous trained me. Instead, Quinn and Anna trained me. Along with the guards. But otherwise? Not much training. The only thing that I was fully trained on was how to shift and know how to change back into my form."**

**"I wish I could say I was surprised, but honestly, I'm not one hundred percent surprised. Does he even know you are here?"**

I swallowed, looked away from him, and shook my head slowly. "**No, he does not know that I am here."**

He sighed deeply before replying, "**Do you want me to send a message to him?"**

"Killian should have already reported it to him."

"Killian?"

"He was the one who assisted me to the veil before Norjor told him that he couldn't come forward anymore into your territory."

"Ah. What role does he play in the life of Morphous though?"

"I think at one point he was the advisor for him for a few years, but I don't one hundred percent know. Killian does not really talk, and the only people I have really interacted with while I stayed with Morphous are: Quinn, the current advisor, Anna, the nurse or school teacher, and a handful of guards who agree to help me practice. Otherwise, no one else."

"Any normal defense? Did you learn to hit anything on your own?"

I opened my mouth to reply when the door opened and Aurelius came back in with a set of clothing. She bowed to Nathaniel, before approaching me. I blinked and saw the happiness radiating off of her but she glanced at Nathaniel before her eyes flickered downward again. I glanced at her and was about to ask her something, but Nathaniel sighed deeply "**Rafeor?**"

"Huh? Oh! My bad, not really. They kind of showed me how to shift into other creatures, it was mainly that. Some have favored animals to shift into and others had different ones."

I shrugged and he scowled slightly before looking at Aurelius and asking, "**Have you Aurelius, been taught how to defend yourself?**"

She paused and glanced at me for a moment. She replied, "No, My Lord."

"**After you are done with Rafeor, I would like you to get some gear. To join us in the training room.**"

"But I have a bunch of chores…."

"**Your chores have been waived, Aurelius. At least, until Finn gets his wolf under control again.**"

"**How do you know it is his wolf? And not himself?**"

"**Based on how he spoke. Whenever Basil speaks, no one refuses him. However, his voice also booms out and is usually filled with alpha power. I know Finn personally would have never left his mate behind, no matter if she was wolf-less or not.**"

Aurelius swallowed before asking a question that I did not know was possible, "Would that mean that when he does come back, you will put down Norjor?"

"**I am not going to enclose that information to you at this time, Aurelius. I hope that Finn will willingly go into a dungeon cell, so Basil and Norjor talk. Just a talk mind you, but if Basil thinks that he is a threat, he may do what he thinks is correct.**"

"So, there is a chance that we both become wolf-less?"

Nathaniel looked at her and had a grim look across his face. He did not reply, but it was an answer in itself. She lowered her eyes before whispering, "Why did Norjor do what he did?"

**"Because he thinks that my Lycan and myself is an abomination and I should be killed. I was not supposed to be here."**

Aurelius looked sharply at me, and I could tell that Nathaniel knew what I was talking about and his facial appearance confirmed that. He sighed deeply before he returned his attention to Aurelius, "**Alright, go get your gear, please.**"

"Okay, My Lord."

She curtsied before him, left out the door, and probably headed back to wherever she came from with the uniform.

*****

I glanced at Nathaniel before speaking, "**You know something about her, don't you?**"

He swallowed, and his eyes flickered to me before replying, "**She doesn't know what I am about to tell you.**"

"**Okay?**"

"**She is my niece. My brother Logan had her. At least, she was in somewhere where she wasn't supposed to be. I don't know if Logan simply got her to keep an eye on her or not, but either way, she is a good kid.**"

"**How long has she been here?**"

"**I brought her here when she turned six. And that was twelve or so years ago. So, I believe she is eighteen or just barely turned it. It would make sense though that she is at least eighteen since you have to be eighteen to find your mate.**"

"**Do you think I have a mate to your standards?**"

"**There is a possibility, but I honestly do not know.**"

"**Where is the training room?**"

He smirked and turned towards the door before replying, "**Come along. It is time that you get in some practice. Either with me personally or one of my warriors.**"

"**Will they treat me horribly?**"

**"They would not dare to,"** he rumbled.

I noticed his eyes flashed another color as he replied, and felt something else, but it was barely there for me. However, a few guards on the other side of the open door bared their necks to him. I locked eye contact with him for a moment before speaking, **"Hello, Basil."**

He blinked once and turned his attention away, but I could tell by the grin across his face that he was pleased.

****

After about half of an hour, we made it to a high-ceiling room, with floor-to-ceiling windows, and dark red drapes coming down. A few candles were stationed every few feet, but they were unlit, and the natural light filtered inside the room. Large square mats were lined in the center of the room, and two wolves were fighting in one.

 I paused to watch them before my eyes flickered away. The one observing their training called out, "TIME!"

They stepped away from each other, breathing deeply. Their shirts were off, and it was clear that they had been training for a very long time, since their bodies were honed in, and had lean muscles. One walked to one side of the side I was watching him from, and he paused as he grabbed a cup of water and locked eye contact with me. "What are you staring at?"

I swallowed sheepishly before heading towards where Nathaniel was waiting. I could practically see Nathaniel glower at the warrior, but he said nothing as I approached him.

He cleared his throat, and Basil rumbled, **"Under no circumstances should ANYONE HERE treat Rafeor any differently."**

"UNDERSTOOD, ALPHA!"

They all chorused, and I glanced back at the one who had spoken to me. He raised an eyebrow at me. I smiled sweetly before looking at Nathaniel, well should I say Basil since his eyes glint in Nathaniel's eyes. I touched his arm briefly, and a collective gasp rose, but Basil looked down and blinked before he faded away.

Nathaniel smirked before calling out, **"Marius, come over here, please."**

The warrior that called time, came forward, and a few of the werewolves backed away from him and lowered their heads in response. He was tall, around six foot, with broad shoulder and lean, and had wavy dark brown hair. His shirt rippled with his movements, and he was barefoot. Compared to everyone else, he was the sole one who was without foot coverage. He approached, and I could see that his eyes were a light blue with a hint of green. He bowed to Nathaniel before speaking, "My liege."

Nathaniel nodded his head at him for a brief second before he turned his attention to me and spoke, **"Can you please pair Rafeor with someone who knows how to train someone new?"**

"Has she had any training beforehand?"

He looked at me as he replied to Nathaniel, and I swallowed before replying, **"I-I don't believe I got anything to go on."**

"I guess I'll have to pair you with another naviance. And monitor it myself. Nathaniel, a word alone?"

**"Stay here, Rafeor."**

**"Alright."**

They walked out of the training room, since this place was full of warriors' training, and clearly did not want anyone eavesdropping on their conversation.

*****

The warrior who spoke to me earlier glanced at the others before walking up to me. He spoke after a moment, "So, what is so special about you that YOU get Nathaniel's personal attention?"

**"I mean it could be the fact that I am not a full-blooded wolf."**

"Oh? And what exactly are you?"

"SAIS!"

He flinched and backed away from me, before he whispered, "We are not done, bitch."

I growled low in my throat in response, and my Lycan flickered in my eyes for a brief second.

****

Marius strode over, and every step spoke to power, proving that he was ranked. He growled again, "Sais. Back off."

"I apologize, Marius."

Sais dropped his gaze from meeting Marius, but his eyes flickered to me before his wolf lit his eyes for a brief second. Marius growled a warning, Sais backed away, and turned and headed back to the mat.

Marius looked at me before speaking, "Alright, basics."

He clapped his hands, and I flinched for a split second, but he noticed it instantly. He kind of paused before frowning. He was about to say something when Sais called out, "What are you doing here?"

Marius turned around, and I could see Aurelius cower before Sais, and that was enough for my Lycan, since she boomed out, "**EVERYONE. DOWN!**"

Marius and the entire hall dropped down to their knees, and a few trembled as if they were trying to fight her power. Marius looked up at me, and my Lycan's color of eyes radiated from my gaze. He lowered his eyes once again to the ground. Aurelius was pressing herself against the floor, and I hissed at my Lycan in our connection, "*Release them.*"

"*Why should I?*"

"*Only one was in the wrong! Fix this!*"

She huffed in the connection, but pulled back her aura before she spoke again, "**Sais, stay down.**"

It was as if a hidden force was lifted, and everyone was able to move once more, except for Sais. He struggled against her aura, but he looked up and locked eye contact for a split second before lowering his eyes again.

Marius swallowed before whispering, "Ah, so the rumors are true then. Everyone, besides Sais, you are dismissed."

The entire room was soon echoing with movement, and the warriors left besides Sais, and Aurelius – who looked confused and was about to leave but I locked eye contact with her and shook my head. She swallowed as she watched the warriors leave the training room. Soon, we were the only ones in the room. Marius glanced at me before speaking, "Please release Sais from your command."

My Lycan blinked once before growling out, "**Fine.**"

She stayed in control, on the verge of surfacing, but she released him.

****

He fell forward before Marius walked over to him, grabbed him by the throat, and lifted him into the air. I stared in shock at such treatment. Sais's eyes bulged out of his head for a moment, and he clawed at Marius's hand for a moment, but Marius's wolf showed in his eyes. After a moment, Sais stopped fighting and hung in his grip. His breathing was raspy, but other than that, it did not appear that he was lost of breath completely. Marius rumbled out, "You know the same thing that everyone else knows, Sais. That Aurelius is not a product to be messed with. Should I call back, Nathaniel?"

**"Call me back for what, Marius?"**

Marius glanced at Nathaniel, who stood in the doorway, and it appeared to me that he did not know what just happened before Marius returned his attention to Sais, who upon seeing Nathaniel began to struggle again. Nathaniel squinted his eyes for a moment. **"What did he do this time?"**

Marius looked at me, and Nathaniel's eyes flickered to mine. He growled, **"What idiot thing did you do to bring her Lycan forward?"**

"It is my fault," whispered Aurelius.

Nathaniel glanced at her before returning his glare to Sais. **"Marius, please put him down."**

"Of course, my liege."

He placed Sais down, and he gasped for breath before he swallowed hard and spoke, "I-it w-wo-won-won't happen again."

**"What did you do?"**

"I-I-I…"

**"He yelled at Aurelius, in a threatening manner."**

Sais's head whipped to face me, and his eyes flickered for a moment in rage, but Nathaniel rumbled, **"Is that true?"**

"Unfortunately, it is, my liege. Aurelius came in not too long ago, and Sais yelled at her."

**"Even after Basil had that order in the pack link? You defied his order?"**

Sais swallowed nervously before whispering, "I-i-it w-wo-won-won't ha-hap-happen again!"

**"It won't happen again since you are dead."**

Basil had finally surfaced completely, and he stalked forward, but my Lycan called out, **"Stop."**

Basil paused and turned to her and his eyes flashed in rage; he bellowed, "**I AM THE KING HERE!**"

"**I. AM. SHADOW. You will obey me.**"

Basil blanched at the amount of power that she suddenly released from herself, it went up the walls to the ceiling, and then withdrew and vanished again. Everyone was gasping for air when she reeled it back in.

Basil swallowed before he locked eye contact with her again, his eyes dimmed to Nathaniel's eyes. He just released Nathaniel. Nathaniel blinked a few times before panting, "**Well, we now know what her name is.**"

"What the hell?"

"What do you want to do with Sais?"

Nathaniel glanced at him and then at me. "**Well, Shadow, what do you want to do?**"

"**Not in the mood to do anything with him. However, he should know his place now. If you step out of line again though, Sais, I will be your worst nightmare.**"

Sais swallowed nervously, and he lowered his head in submission. Nathaniel glanced at him before shaking his head and rumbling, "**Sais.**"

"Yes, My Lord?"

"**You are on cleaning duty for two months.**"

Sais lowered his head in shame before replying, "Yes, My Lord."

He walked out of the training room, and he stopped by Aurelius before he hissed something to her, and departed. Shadow noticed that Aurelius shrunk down and she growled low in her throat in response. Sais looked over his shoulder at me, he swallowed and hurried out, and leaving Marius, Nathaniel, and Aurelius to stare at me.

****

I swallowed and after a moment, Shadow released me, and I stumbled around for a moment and panted in shock. I raised my head and whispered, "**I…**"

Marius started to chuckle before clasping Nathaniel on the shoulder and speaking, "Wow! And here I thought Basil was bad. Before you came down again, Nathaniel, she had the entire training room on their knees. Including myself, which is no easy feat."

Nathaniel looked at me and smirked. "**It sure surprised me that Basil released control back to me when she yelled at him. Normally, whoever orders him around is in pieces.**"

I swallowed in shock before I whispered, "**What's going to happen now though?**"

"Nothing, you just showed everyone that you are not someone to mess with. Nathaniel may have ordered no one to mess with you, but for the majority of these fellows in this hall, they tend to find loopholes in that order. Now though? They will not mess around with you, and I have a feeling will leave Aurelius alone."

"**What about Sais?**"

"He hates being on cleaning duty. That is his punishment. Although, he did challenge Basil's direct order from this morning, and I am surprised that I don't have to clean him off the floor."

He said it so simply that it must not be the first time that Basil lost his temper and killed someone in this training room. Nathaniel sighed before speaking, "**So, since everyone was dismissed, who are you going to pair them with?**"

"I will personally train both of them, Nathaniel."

"**Works for me.**"

He turned to leave, but Aurelius spoke, "My Lord?"

"**Hmm?**"

"Can I please sit this out today?"

"**I still want you to watch though.**"

"Okay."

He nodded to Marius before leaving out the doorway, leaving Marius alone with Aurelius and myself.

Marius smirked before rubbing his hands together, "Alright. Where to start?"

# Chapter 26

I glanced at Aurelius before smiling back at him and replied, **"Where do you suggest we start?"**

He opened his mouth to reply but paused and tapped his finger to his chin. "I guess basics. Do you know how to prevent yourself from being pushed over?"

I shook my head in response, and he glanced at Aurelius and saw her swallow nervously. He smirked before speaking, "Alright ladies, before we start practicing anything. Let's tell each other our names, where we came from, and…. One thing that is unique to you alone. I'll go first. Hello, my name is Marius, and my wolf is named, Onyx. I am a gamma, third in command. I train the warriors and help train the elite warriors with the beta. I was born here, and raised by my elder brothers, who have since moved on to their positions at other packs. I have not found my mate yet. And…. I love putting people in their places."

He looked at me expectantly, and I swallowed before replying, **"My name is Rafeor, I have a Lycan named Shadow apparently. I was a slave for the majority of my life until Morphous sent his advisor to get me out…."**

I looked down at the ground before speaking, **"I am what is called a hybrid. My father is Morphous, and my mother is a werewolf. And before anyone asks, I do not know who my mother is."**

Aurelius did not look shocked, but Marius certainly did. His jaw dropped before he coughed a little, to clear his throat. "Well, by golly. That is a lot of information. Is that why you flinched when I clapped my hands earlier?"

I nodded in response, and he sighed deeply and glanced at Aurelius before speaking, "Before we go too deep into that information, Rafeor. What about you, my lady?"

Aurelius blushed when he addressed her with that. "I beg your pardon, Marius, but I am not anyone to be called my lady. I am a low wolf in ranking."

"It does not matter. You are a lady, and therefore I shall address you as one."

She once again blushed bright red. She dropped her eyes to the ground and replied, "My name is Aurelius Fiore, and I don't have a wolf. I am wolf-less. I was the person that people call worthless, a weakling, a…."

Marius growled low in his throat, Onyx showing in his expression. He replied, "Aurelius, you are NOT WORTHLESS."

"You only say that because Nathaniel holds you at a high level. Everyone else either pitied me or treated me like trash. It is alright, Marius."

"Abuse is never alright. If I had found out, I would have put an absolute end to it."

"Thank you."

Onyx stayed in his eyes for another moment, before he flickered out, Marius sighed deeply and spoke, "Anything else you want to add, Aurelius?"

"I just found my mate the other night, and…. His wolf decided that he needed to head to the border, and found Rafeor at the border."

"Congratulations on finding your mate! What's his name?"

"Finn Dragonheart and his wolf is named Norjor."

Marius frowned, he looked at me for a brief second before replying, "Finn is honorable, and will come back to you, Aurelius. I have personally trained him and had trained with his father. They are both great warriors, and I know Finn is not happy with his wolf."

**"What are the chances of him being killed when he comes back?"**

"None, Nathaniel has already informed the patrols to leave him alone when he comes back. Although, they were informed that he needed to go to a cell when he comes back."

**"Ah. so…. What now?"**

"Now? Well, I want to know what happened exactly at the place you came from. That way, I don't do anything to trigger you."

I swallowed nervously and replied, **"How would you know what would trigger me?"**

"Simply by asking what you went through. What did they do to you?"

I looked down and swallowed. **"Are you sure you want to know?"**

"In order to help train you in a way that you won't freeze, I need to understand why you would. Please."

"It is okay, Rafeor, we are not here to judge you."

I looked at Aurelius before swallowing my nerves; Shadow linked me, *"Do you want me to tell them?"*

*"No, I'll try it first."*

*"I am here if you need me."*

*"Thank you, Shadow."*

She hummed in response, she kept the connection open and I swallowed before speaking, **"I am the reason why the riot happened twelve years ago. Morphous did it to hide me from the world. I was… six, or seven when I was sold into the trafficking."**

I swallowed and sat down on the ground. Marius and Aurelius sat down too, crisscrossed with their hands on their knees, and back straight. I looked down at the hardwood floor before continuing, **"I was sold into a mansion, the Lord there took me and maybe twelve other girls of various ages. I was the second youngest, and I don't really remember all too much except for pain, and being taught that I cannot leave. One of the girls who came with me had a bright idea of trying to escape after hours, and she managed to leave. However, she was found shortly afterward, and everyone was beaten to a bloody pulp. Including myself. We were whipped until we were bloody raw, and…."**

Tears began to stream down my face and my voice cracked. So far, no one has asked me how I had grown up. They assumed that I had talked to someone about it. Marius stood up, walked away for a moment, and returned with a glass of water and a towel. He gently laid it beside me before touching my shoulder and whispering, "You are never going back there. Before you finish telling the story, please let me get, Nathaniel."

**"Why?"**

"Because he needs to know this too. What you went through is something that would have never happened if you stayed inside the werewolves."

**"Okay."**

Marius looked at Aurelius before walking out the door.

****

Aurelius glanced at me, scooted herself over to me, and laid her hand on my knee, whispering, "You are strong, Rafeor. So very strong."

**"How do you say that?"**

"You survived what others would have succumbed to long before you. You are a warrior."

**"I wouldn't say that."**

**"But she is correct either way."**

I looked up and saw Nathaniel striding across the room, followed by Marius. Who smiled slightly, and I swallowed before asking, **"B-bu-but do-don't y-yo-you…."**

**"I may be King, Rafeor, but I always have time to stop and listen to history and what someone went through. Unlike Morphous, I actually listen to my people."**

I looked down at my hands and saw that they were trembling. I took a shaky breath before whispering, "**Ah.**"

**"Would you feel more comfortable somewhere else?"**

**"I-I…. I don't know."**

"Hey, it's okay either way, Rafeor. If you want to stay here, we will all stay here. If you want to move, we will move. If you want either myself or Marius out of here, we will leave."

I glanced at Aurelius and saw her smile. I weakly smiled back at her before turning my attention to Nathaniel and replying, "**Here is okay.**"

"Do you want either myself or Aurelius to leave?"

**"No."**

"Let us know when and if you ever do. We do not want to pressure you, Rafeor."

**"Thank you."**

"You're welcome."

He winked at me and I blushed slightly and my Lycan chuckled in our connection. I sighed before speaking, "**Should I restart?**"

**"No, Marius informed me of what was said beforehand. Continue where you finished."**

**"Oh, okay."**

They all sat down and I looked down at the grain in the wood, gathering my courage and speaking again, "**Even after we were whipped until we couldn't move, or didn't want to move. We were still tasked to do our chores, which for me was to attend the main house. I had to wear clothing and scrub the floors. I had to redo the floors more than once, because my blood was dripping off of me, and…."**

Nathaniel growled in response, and I stopped and glanced up at him. Basil lit his eyes before I whispered, "**Are you okay?**"

**"No, if I had known you existed…. You would have a very different childhood."**

**"Oh."**

"Unfortunately, we cannot turn back the time to change how we would have done things. Nathaniel, are you going to be able to contain Basil?"

**"I guess it highly depends on how upsetting Rafeor's story is."**

Marius nodded in response and turned his attention to me, before speaking, "Please continue, Rafeor."

I swallowed before glancing at Aurelius and continuing, "**Anyway, my blood had hardened over time. I had learned to keep my pain at bay, lock it away. For years, I believed that I was a human since they were all humans. So, when I came of age and got my Lycan, she…. She caused trouble at one point, and they beat me to the brink of death. The other girls, for some reason, were not treated horribly after that, and I was the sole one who was targeted the most for the beatings. I took them in stride, especially when we got a few new girls, their backs were bare of scars and…."**

**"Can I please see your scars?"**

**"Why would you want to?"**

**"Because…"**

He trailed off. Not responding after that. Marius replied, "Because I want to see what you endured throughout your life. Please."

I swallowed but reached down, and grabbed the hem of my shirt, which was long sleeves compared to everyone else, since I wanted to cover my arms from the abuse. I turned around and lifted the back of the shirt upward – I heard a snarl and fabric ripping.

****

A hand rested on my shoulder, at least a hairy one. I looked up and saw Basil standing there, he panted and his eyes flashed once before he rumbled, **"If I had known… if my mate told me what happened….. I would have fought tooth and nail to get you here."**

"Your mate?"

**"Evenor is beside herself. The reason why Sophronia stocked her room is because…. Because Morphous had told her that their daughter had perished in the riot."**

"Sophronia is her mother? But… how is that…. Possible?"

**"Before I found her to be mine, she and Morphous were a thing. He was my best friend growing up, and since he had a child with my mate, I…. I had reacted how anyone else would have."**

"Now that all makes sense. I was curious how Rafeor got into dealings with Morphous in the beginning. She mentioned that her mother was a werewolf, but I did not know who. It also makes sense why Evenor has not had a child since."

**"In what way?"**

"She was grieving, Basil. She was grieving her firstborn. However, I have a feeling that she would be ready to have another child with you, Basil. Since her firstborn is here, and as well as she can be in her circumstances."

**"Hmmm…. I guess I need to find that out….. I am sorry, Rafeor. I did not mean to startle you when I shifted."**

**"It is alright, Basil."**

He smiled slightly before he turned around and looked at Marius, **"Any chance that Onyx wants to tussle?"**

"Do you think that is the greatest idea with Aurelius and Rafeor in the room?"

**"They can move as we fight."**

Marius looked like he was going to reject, but I spoke up after a moment, **"Ummmm…."**

Marius glanced at me, before speaking, "Yes?"

**"Shadow wants to tussle with someone."**

Basil looked at me and replied, **"Are you okay with her taking over?"**

**"Yes."**

"Before she ascends, go to that door, and change out of the gear. We do not need more than one angry seamstress after us for two pairs of clothing."

**"Okay."**

I started to walk away, when Aurelius spoke, "Rafeor?"

**"Yeah?"**

"I am sorry, but I need to go."

**"Where?"**

I glanced back and saw her twist her fingers slightly before she worked up the courage to reply, "I…. I need to…"

"Aurelius?"

"Yes, Marius?"

"Is any of this because you do not have a wolf?"

She looked down before she replied, "Perhaps. I would just get in the way."

**"No, you wouldn't."**

"I got no one in here besides myself, Rafeor. You…. you have Shadow, and Marius has Onyx, and King Nathaniel has Basil. Everyone in this room has a wolf spirit, and…. I have nothing."

**"Why does that matter to you so much?"**

"Because at one point I remember that I did! I remember having someone else, and then she got taken away from me!"

**"WHAT?"**

Shock radiated through the room. A clear sign that he was not informed that she had someone. Marius's jaw dropped and I swallowed before speaking, **"What do you mean by that, Aurelius?"**

"I barely remember, all I remember is that I was of age, and then something had killed my wolf. Then I had become wolf-less."

"Now…. who in their right mind would take a wolf away from someone?"

Basil stiffened, and I looked at him before looking at Aurelius. Surely, what Nathaniel had informed me of earlier did not happen. That his brother had anything to deal with this. Clearly, Basil was on the same wavelength though and his eyes blazed before he muttered, **"I'm going to kill him."**

"Kill whom, Basil?"

**"None of your concern."**

Basil strode to the door, but Shadow called out, **"Stop."**

He stopped, panted, and slowly turned around before growling, **"Shadow."**

**"It would not change anything if you do."**

**"It would give me satisfaction that he had met his end."**

**"But you would have to kill a pack member to do it. It is not worth it."**

He seemed to struggle for a moment, but Shadow stayed in my eyes, and voice before continuing, **"You have a lot of explaining to do, Basil. And you promised me a tussle."**

Basil swallowed and looked at Aurelius before glancing at Marius, sighing deeply and replying, **"I guess I do."**

He walked back into the room, and Marius glanced at Shadow. "What do you know that we do not?"

She looked at him before replying, "**That is not my information to give out. If Basil or Nathaniel wants to say something, they have that authority.**"

"I guess that is fair."

Marius glanced at Basil. "Do you want us to leave, Basil?"

**"No."**

He rumbled. He glanced at Aurelius. "**I will have to explain later, Aurelius.**"

"If you kept it a secret for this long, don't worry about it. I am sure that if it was important to me, that you would have told me beforehand."

**"I guess that is true."**

She smiled slightly, and looked at me before speaking, "D-do you want me to stay, Rafeor?"

**"I would like that, yes."**

"Okay, then I'll stay here."

**"Thank you."**

"You're welcome."

****

I headed towards the door and kept it ajar since my Lycan did not know how to open doors. She knew how to destroy them, but I did not want to destroy the door. After a moment, after I had taken off my clothing, I reached into our connection, "*You ready for this, Shadow?*"

*"I was always ready, Rafeor."*

*"I give you permission."*

*"Thank you, Rafeor."*

I fell onto all fours and screamed in pain as she once again took control and rearranged my bones. I could hear Aurelius had started to walk towards the room, but Marius had grabbed her to stop her approach. Then I heard nothing. Saw nothing.

****

I opened the door and walked out, I had to duck to enter the training room and stood to my full height of seven foot one. I towered over Aurelius, and Marius by about two feet, or in Marius's case a foot. He looked up at me in shock.

Basil was facing the wilderness out the window before rumbling, "**How many times have you shifted before now, Shadow?**"

"**Not enough. It is extremely painful to Rafeor. I have to reshape everything to accommodate my form.**"

He nodded and turned to face me, and he had to even glance up slightly, not by much, but it was enough for him to scowl before grumbling. I smiled wickedly. "**I cannot help it that I am taller than you, Basil.**"

"**That you cannot.**"

"By the goddess…. You are beautiful."

I glanced back at Marius, who had his hand around Aurelius's forearm. I blinked in response and replied, "**Thanks.**"

"You're welcome, Shadow."

My heart fluttered slightly, but I did not realize why, until Onyx whispered, "Mate."

"What?"

"Shadow is my mate."

"**Are you sure, Onyx?**"

"She smells like fresh air on the mountain. I smelt it when she entered the room. I… just did not want to say anything."

"What? Why wait?"

"Because I…. I feared that she would not want me."

"**Why wouldn't I want you?**"

"Because you are not a werewolf directly. You, Shadow, are a Lycan, but your human half…. She does not understand the significance of finding a mate. The different customs. Marius had told me that I should accept that you would never look at me that way."

"Oh! I never thought of that."

Basil frowned and looked at me before speaking, "**What does he smell like to you, Shadow?**"

"**He smells like lilacs. Irresistible lilacs.**"

"What should we do? Does Rafeor have the same connection? Or… is it different with her?"

**"That is a good question. Shadow, do you want to ask Rafeor that question?"**

I shrugged and connected to Rafeor, who every time I take control, cannot possibly know what is happening, *"Rafeor?"*

*"Yes, Shadow?"*

*"Do you have any feelings towards Marius?"*

She was quiet for a long minute, before she replied, *"I feel something, like I am drawn to him. He smells of the lilacs at the mansion to me. Why? What does that mean?"*

*"I think it means, he is our mate."*

*"Are you sure?"*

*"I am positive."*

*"Do you want him, Shadow?"*

I paused and thought about it, did I want someone to become a daily in my life? Then I thought of all the hurt that we had experienced and knew that love was something that no one could exactly squash. I swallowed before replying, *"I want him."*

*"Do you trust him?"*

*"Do you?"*

*"I asked you first!"*

*"Yes…. I trust him."*

*"Then I do not see an issue here, Shadow. If their customs are indeed true, then we were given a great gift."*

*"I agree."*

I dropped the connection but kept it open slightly. Only just so Rafeor could hear.

Basil looked at me before speaking, **"Well? Does she have the same connections?"**

**"She feels drawn to Marius. She doesn't understand how it all works. And to be frank, neither do I."**

"I will always cherish you Shadow."

Replied Onyx, and he continued after a moment, "I will never let you go. I will never reject you. I will always hold you dear to me."

**"Even when Rafeor has a nightmare? When she wakes up screaming?"**

Everyone's eyes flashed in anger, and Aurelius whispered, "Mates are not like boyfriends or what the humans have. Mates will always be beside you. No matter the circumstances. That is, as long as they live."

"Truer words were never spoken."

Aurelius blushed darkly before ducking her head. Basil chuckled slightly before asking, **"So… do you still want to tussle with me?"**

**"I would not turn that down, Basil."**

"As long as you do not do any harm to her."

**"That is if he can."**

**"Is that a challenge?"**

**"If you want to call it a challenge. Sure."**

Basil grinned wickedly, and he would have launched himself directly at Shadow, but Onyx spoke, "Get on a mat you two."

**"Fine."**

We walked to the mat, before squaring each other off.

****

Onyx released control of Marius and he cleared his throat slightly, drawing our attention slightly before he spoke, "I want a clean fight here you two. No talons, do not draw blood on either opponent. Block and defense only."

**"You are taking the fun away!"**

"I am not, and you are a Lycan, Basil who knows how to be yourself. Shadow is new to this. You will do it the common way until I get a good reading on how Shadow does."

**"You are only saying that because she is your mate!"**

"I am not, and you know how I train others. You did not have an issue of that before now."

**"I guess that is true."**

We squared off, and finally, Basil swung a hit and landed square on my shoulder. I snarled as I heard a snap. Marius snarled, but he stayed in place. Basil smirked but soon lost it when I came at him and swung hard and smacked him down onto the mat as if he was not trying to prevent himself from falling. He fell with a BOOM!

He grumbled as he rolled to his feet, and repositioned himself before he went to jab at me, but I blocked him again, and again. And finally, he got angry, that he wasn't really making any hits, and his pent-up anger came flooding out of him, and he went his full speed. If I was a common wolf, he would have killed me. However, since we were both Lycan's I loved the challenge. Marius was correct, he did know that he would beat the shit out of me because I did not know how to defend myself entirely since I was new. I heard Marius snarl at one point since he hit hard in my solar plexus. Sending me flying in the air, and slamming into the wall.

Marius growled low in his throat, but I got back up and wiped my nose, which stained my white fur with red before I looked up at Basil and growled, **"Is that all, old man?"**

Basil growled low in his throat and bounded off the training mat, ignoring Marius as he shouted, "STAY ON THE MAT!"

Basil attacked me on the normal ground, and the wall splintered behind me, but I gripped his forearm and tore. Drawing blood, he snarled in response before he backed away from me. I grinned wickedly, and we squared off again.

It was another hour or two before Basil called out, **"Alright. Enough."**

We were both panting and staring at each other's wounds. I had gashed him several times, and it was clear that he did not keep himself intact with his anger since he had gashed me several times. Marius strode towards us, before speaking, "About time."

**"Oh? How so?"**

"Have you seen the state of the training hall?"

We glanced around suddenly and he sheepishly replied, **"Oh, well… I guess I made more work for the staff to do."**

"And you did not listen to me, Basil. I said NO TO DRAWING BLOOD!"

**"I was checking to see how fun she was, Marius."**

"It does not matter. You ignored my order."

**"I am your king, Marius. Your word doesn't matter one hundred percent to me."**

He tightened his fists at his side before he closed his eyes and shook his head. "Why do I even bother?"

**"Because that is your duty?"**

Marius sneered back at him. However, I swayed on my feet, that was the first time that I was allowed to fight, and have a worthy opponent. And well, I sent Rafeor to the surface, and she shifted back and fell. She thudded to the ground and was out.

# Chapter 27

I woke in a different room, and this time I sighed deeply before looking around. I knew I was safer than when I first arrived. There were two armchairs, and Marius was in one of them. He looked up and smiled slightly at me. "You're awake."

**"Wh-what happened?"**

"I am assuming Shadow did not get any fighting practice until then?"

I shook my head and replied, **"Morphous told me to keep her a secret from the shifters even. She was not allowed out."**

His eyes flashed for a moment as Onyx surfaced for a brief second before Marius sighed, and rubbed the bridge of his nose before speaking, "Well… I can assure you that Basil and Shadow will have another chance to do it again. Once… both of you learn your limits."

I looked down at the bedding and frowned. **"Whose bed is this?"**

"It's mine."

I glanced sharply at him before replying, **"Ummm… why?"**

"Because…. It is what Onyx wanted?"

**"Oh."**

I fidgeted for a moment. **"What do I smell like to you?"**

It took him a moment to respond and he replied with a gush of wind, "You smell like the fresh air on a mountain. I love that smell, the fresh crisp air, that always carries the freshness of the air. No stench, just fresh clean air. What do I smell like to you?"

**"Don't laugh, but you smell like lilacs to me. Like the flowers I had to plant every year when I was at the mansion. They always brought me peace."**

"Do you understand some of what happens with a mate?"

**"No, I don't. Do you?"**

"I do."

He paused and licked his lips before speaking, "It is typical for the mated couple, to mark and mate each other in the first day of meeting. However, since…. You are different. I don't think that is the best thing to do with you."

**"What does that entitle?"**

He smiled slightly before a light blush bloomed over his face as he replied, "It implies that when we make out…. Wait…. How much were you taught in the bodily functions?"

**"Ummm…. I wasn't. I know I got what an older girl called a period when Shadow appeared. But no one was taught how to do anything. We were only taught how to…. Survive."**

His eyes flickered for a moment, before he replied, "I guess that is something that needs to be addressed before we do anything in that matter. I am willing to wait as long as you need to feel comfortable, Rafeor. Even if I need to wait several years, you are the only girl that I will want."

**"Aww! You are making me cry!"**

He chuckled slightly when a knock on the door sounded, and he sighed deeply before looking at me and speaking, "I guess we will continue this later, my love. Aurelius is pretty nervous that you fell again, and…. Basil felt bad when it happened again."

**"Oh…. what did you think of it?"**

"Honestly? I was pissed. If I wasn't in control of Onyx he would have attacked Basil for harming his mate. However, Basil would have slaughtered us where we stood. So, there's that."

Another knock on the door sounded, and he sighed as he got up, and stretched before moving towards the door. In the door way, stood Nathaniel.

He looked at me and spoke, "**Oh my gosh, you are finally awake.**"

"No thanks to Basil drawing out too much of Shadow."

Nathaniel opened his mouth to retort, but Aurelius pushed past them both, and walked to the bed before speaking, "You nearly gave me a heart attack! Don't do that again!"

**"I wasn't planning on it, Aurelius. How long was I out?"**

"Twelve hours."

**"What?"**

I squeaked. I looked around at everyone, and Nathaniel looked at the ground, still looking rather guilty before he replied, "**Yeah, we had to have a nurse check you. She said you had a bad concussion and needed stitches for some of the scratches that Basil inflicted.**"

I swallowed and bit my lip. No wonder why Marius looked like he had been up all night. He most likely was. I bowed my head slightly, whispering, "**What now?**"

**"Now you heal, and get to know your mate."**

I glanced at Marius who had a lazy grin across his face and I smiled slightly in return. **"I would like that a lot."**

**"Come on, Aurelius, let's leave these two new mates to figure it out."**

Aurelius smiled at me as she waved goodbye, and left after a moment. Following Nathaniel out of the room, and closing the door behind her. Leaving me and Marius alone.

****

I followed Nathaniel out of the room, before I asked, "My lord?"

He stopped walking and looked back at me before replying, **"Yes, Aurelius?"**

"Would it be alright if…. If…"

I lowered my head down before continuing, "If we had a meeting together?"

**"About what?"**

"About me…. And possibility of what you would do when Finn arrives? If he comes back that is."

**"Come to my office with me. I do have some paperwork that I need to fill out, but I will give you my undivided attention."**

"Thank you, my lord."

I curtsied before him, and followed him to his office, which was the one room I was accustomed to since it was the main room I cleaned the most when he was not occupying it. Nothing has changed, the African blackwood desk and matching chairs, the collection of books in the book shelves off to the left, with a cozy armchair next to the window. The cherry wood floors, freshly cleaned and scrubbed every day to keep the shine.

Nathaniel walked around his desk before sitting down, and motioned towards the two chairs before the desk. I swallowed and gingerly sat down, never once was I allowed to sit anywhere in this room besides cleaning the floors. I looked up at Nathaniel as he pulled out a quill, and ink before pulling a parchment out of a stack of papers before reading it.

The parchment was the only thing that made noise after a few minutes, he wrote down something on it and moved to the next one. He frowned when he read something, but other than that, no muttering – nothing to tell what he was thinking. It was clear he knew what was most of the work, since he did not say a peep about any of it. Finally, he got to the end of the pile, I saw an envelope, he paused before he sighed, and broke the seal.

He glanced down at what was written and his eyes sparked a little with Basil, but he put it down before he shook his head, and looked at the calendar across the desk, and flipped it to August, and went to the twenty-third and marked it as meeting. Then he tossed the note onto the other pile and then turned his attention completely to me.

*****

I swallowed before I spoke, "My lord?"

**"What are you curious about, Aurelius?"**

"You seemed to have known more about my life. I saw the look that Basil and Rafeor exchanged. When I mentioned that I had a wolf before she was killed."

**"That is because I do know more than I let on. Especially on that aspect. However, I doubt that now is when you want to know about that?"**

"Please, my lord? What are you keeping from me?"

He sighed and lowered his eyes to the desk before speaking, **"I believe you are my niece, Aurelius. Logan, was in a bunch of bullshit before I managed to get him to stay within Basil's line of sight. On one of the busts, I think it was the second to last bust, I went in there, and…. He had you in his arms. It was many years ago, and I don't know much else. It concerns me though, you were not of age to get your wolf until later in life. What happened to her?"**

My jaw dropped as I thought of what he just said before I whispered, "Y–yo-you're my…. Uncle? Why didn't you say anything?"

**"Because Logan told me that I was not to treat you like one. He said to keep you here, and I believe he kept you here to keep an eye on you."**

"Why?"

**"Excellent question that I am pretty sure I will find out relatively quickly. Especially learning that you had a wolf, and became wolf-less while you were here."**

"I wasn't here when I lost her. I got her very early."

**"How early?"**

"I think when the riot happened is when I lost her."

**"You think?"**

"I think."

**"Why aren't you for sure of what happened?"**

"Because I tend to not want to think about it."

**"I guess that is a fair point. Aurelius, what was your wolf's name?"**

"Her name was Alice. She was my complete self. She was extremely joyful…. I haven't heard her in so many years."

Basil glinted in his eyes, before he swallowed and his eyes faded back to his normal eyes before he cleared his throat, **"I'm sorry, Aurelius. If I had known…."**

"Don't worry about it, my lord, it happened many years ago."

**"But I should have known. I should have been informed!"**

His rage surged forward as Basil surfaced. I swallowed, but I knew that Basil would not harm me. I looked down at my hands before twisting my fingers slightly together before speaking, "My lord?"

**"What is it?"**

"What are you going to do with Finn when he arrives?"

**"Basil needs to talk to him. Figure out what his plan was with Rafeor."**

"Are you going to kill Norjor because of it?"

**"I hope not, but if Basil deems him a threat…. I'm sorry, it could be a possibility."**

I lowered my head and scrunched in my shoulders before I whispered, "Give him another chance. Before he has to live wolf-less. It is… it is not something I want anyone I love to carry the burden of."

The creak of the chair made my head rise. Nathaniel came around, crouched down before him, and gently took my hands into his before replying, **"I know I cannot promise anything, Aurelius, but I have a feeling that Norjor will be fine. He may… get a disciplined talk, but I don't think he will need to be put down."**

My breath hitched, and I shrunk down before I whispered, "Just like Alice."

His eyes flickered before he stood up, and rumbled, **"No, not like Alice. Alice seemed to have come to her end too early. Tell me. Who took your wolf?"**

I extended my neck in submission as I replied, "I-I-I don't know who he was. He had a vile, and it smelt high of wolfsbane! I got Alice when I turned five! It was one year before you found me."

He stared at me and he trembled before he whispered, **"You were….a pup?"**

"Yes, my lord…"

**"Logan has some explaining to do."**

He started to walk across the office and almost got to the door when I asked, "Where are you going?"

**"To ask my brother what his fucking problem is."**

"Don't make it worse."

**"Huh? Make what worse?"**

"His anger towards you, Basil. He hates you already, and I have a feeling he would target me if you brought it up. Please…. Don't."

He sighed deeply and I saw the moment that Nathaniel got control back, and his shoulders slumped down before he whispered, **"What am I going to do?"**

"Nothing."

**"I cannot do nothing about this, Aurelius. He knows something about this."**

"That may be true, but I also know that your relationship between you two is strained as is. Also, he scares me, and I don't really want a drunk angry werewolf to come to my chambers."

**"He will not go to your chambers."**

"He has done it before. More than once. Especially when… when I had brought attention to myself."

**"And how did you bring attention to yourself?"**

I looked down and twisted my fingers together before I mumbled, "I… uh, may have caused several guards to chase me through the halls because I dropped a wasp nest on them."

**"Why did you do that?"**

"Because they were being unnecessarily cruel to me that day. I saw a live wasp nest in an alcove above the guard post. I got stung a few times, but it was, honestly, rewarding to know they got the blunt of the angry insects."

He frowned and looked at the door, tapped his fingers twice on it, before he walked back to his desk. He didn't sit down, he leaned against it before thinking. He frowned a little before speaking, **"What did Logan do that night?"**

I swallowed hard before whispering, "He… uh… I would rather not answer."

**"What. Did. He. Do?"**

I bared my neck when Basil rumbled, and replied weakly, "He tied me to the bed post, and…. And whipped me a few times. Then…. Then… he…"

I closed my eyes and shook slightly before continuing, "Then he let in the guards that I dropped the nest onto into my chambers."

I did not continue, I still had nightmares from that evening, and I did not want to relive what happened. He leaned forward, Basil glinted in his eyes and I saw hair growing on his arms, and saw him tremble. I shrunk down before whispering, with a small sob, "Please… don't make me say more. Please."

He stood up and closed his eyes, and after a moment the hair disappeared and Nathaniel spoke gently, "**Aurelius, if anyone crosses a line again like that. I give you permission to end them.**"

"E-en-end them?"

He opened his eyes and emotions swirled in his eyes before he replied, "**I want you to learn with Marius, and I will step into some of the training too. You will learn how to defend yourself. And if any idiot comes at you for doing anything in that matter again. Kill them. End them. Do whatever you need to do, to get away from them. And if you cannot, link me.**"

"But I… I am no one."

"**That all changes, Aurelius. I am not going to sit idly back anymore. You will be treated differently since I am your uncle. Logan can come to me if he wants to argue.**"

"B-bu-but h-he-he'll st-sti-still c-co-come af-aft-after me…"

"**No, he won't. Where is your chamber, Aurelius?**"

I cowered slightly before Basil, and he once again drifted back away from Nathaniel and he closed his eyes before pinching his nose and looking at me. I swallowed and said, "In the maids chambers."

"**Not anymore. I'll have you moved.**"

"What? But… my daily…"

"**Are gone. You will no longer be expected to do those duties.**"

"What will I be doing then?"

"**Whatever you want to do with your day.**"

I swallowed nervously before replying, "What about… everyone else? They will know something is different, considering that I am being moved. On top of being ordered to not…. Not treat me horribly anymore."

"I don't care, Aurelius. If you want something to do, you can help Rafeor while she is here."

"While she's here?"

He sighed deeply before replying, "**I have a feeling that she will once again leave.**"

"B-bu-but she has Marius as a mate. Surely, she won't leave him."

"**What do you know about the prophecy, Aurelius?**"

"Prophecy? What?"

He glanced at the books before walking over to them and looking at them. He finally reached up and pulled an old bound book, with a few pages sticking past their bondage, and gently flipped through them. Finally, he came across where he seemed to want, before he walked back to his desk, gently placing the book down, and tapped it. I glanced down and swallowed, the text was old but was written well. He asked, "**Do you know how to read?**"

I glanced up at him and lowered my eyes. I replied, "Not really. I had learned a little, but… not enough to do anything."

"**Then I will have to teach you. For now, though, I will read it to you.**"

He gently took the book back, and sat down in his chair before clearing his throat and reading aloud, "**My children, I must forewarn you of the dangers of cross-contamination with other supernatural beings. I must emphasize that YOU SHOULD NEVER mate with another species. Even if they are your given mate. The druids spoke of a hybrid long before my time even, and I must emphasize that if such a monster should be made, it should be destroyed.**"

He paused before looking up at me and speaking, "**I should have mentioned that it was my grandfather who wrote this. My apologies.**"

My jaw dropped, so that was why it was my children at the beginning. I swallowed and my eyes must have bulged slightly and he had a grim smile on as he continued, "**Do whatever needs to be done to destroy the beast. However, the one that I was personally warned of by the Druids, is the one that will be a cross between us as a species and the shifters. Therefore, I have made rules and regulations that we, as a species, should not interact with them. Except for leaders, on this topic, we need to monitor all of our borders and make sure the ones below us follow the rules. So, a beast does not become present.**"

He stopped again and looked down at the script before continuing, "**The prophecy that was given to me was that one day, someone in the royal family on both sides would come together to make a child. This child will be the end of all we know. All that we have held dear to our kin. This child will be the destruction of the world.**"

He placed the book onto the desk and clasped his hands together before speaking again, "**Now my history…. At least a little so it makes sense to you.**"

He paused and swallowed slightly before standing up and speaking, "**Before I start, do you want something to drink, Aurelius?**"

"Ummm… do you want me to go get a drink, my lord?"

"**No, we can have someone else.**"

"Ummm…. A water please."

****

He hmm-ed before opening the door, and talked to a guard outside his door, and I saw the guard flicker his gaze into the room before moving to do as he was told. Nathaniel came back in after a moment and sat down. After a few minutes, a knock sounded on the door. "**Enter.**"

A guard pushed the door open and carried a tray with two cups. He placed the drinks down on the desk before bowing and backing away. His eyes fell on me before they flickered to Nathaniel's, and he exited.

I reached forward to grab my drink, but Nathaniel stopped me. He grabbed my hand and shook his head for a moment; he sprinkled something into it and stirred it. After a moment, the water turned a weird color and Basil flashed in his eyes. He bellowed, "**GUARD!**"

The door opened, and a few guards held their weapons at a ready. They kind of paused before they slumped slightly and noticed there was no immediate threat. They looked expectantly at him as he stood up; he growled, "**Who poured this cup of water?**"

The guard who had brought it forth cowered slightly and stammered, "Lo-log-Logan."

"**My brother, Logan?**"

"Yes, my lord!"

"**Bring him to me.**"

"Yes, my lord!"

The guards ran out and I heard their thundering feet. I whispered, "Why did you stop me from drinking it, my lord?"

He turned his attention to me, and growled, "**We are family, Aurelius, so therefore, call me by my name, and same with Nathaniel. However, it is because the water is tainted with poison.**"

"Why would anyone poison water?"

"**Why do you think?**"

"To keep someone quiet."

"**Precisely.**"

I swallowed, hunched down and soon an angry roar sounded down further the hall. A few grunts of pain before Basil growled, "**Go to the library area, Aurelius. Pull the red-bounded book towards you.**"

I tenderly walked over there, found the red bounded book, and pulled it towards me, a set of stairs came into my view. I swallowed and looked over my shoulder before whispering, "Where does this lead?"

"**Just enter it, and pull the bar back with you. No one else knows that this exists. And listen in on this conversation. Do not say anything though. Understood?**"

"Yes, Basil."

I entered, pulled the bar back, and sat down on the steps. I was shocked that it eased back into the proper place before disappearing. Also, was very surprised that I could still see out into the room. I wondered how many times he had used this area to get away from people. I shook my head and waited.

****

It was quite a few minutes, and it felt like forever until I heard Logan's voice in the doorway, "**What do you possibly want with me?**"

"**Why did you poison the water?**"

Silence. I watched as they were at the desk and were looking at the water. Logan replied, "**I didn't poison it.**"

"**Don't lie to me, Logan. Why did you poison the water? Is this your way to get back at me for what Basil did?**"

"**I am not a beast like Basil, Nathaniel. I said I did not poison the drink. Now let me go back to what I was doing.**"

"**No. I have a few questions to ask you before you leave.**"

"**Like what exactly?**"

"**Did you put Norjor up to attacking Rafeor at the border?**"

Silence, and finally Logan replied, "**No, I did not put him up to it.**"

"**Are you lying?**"

"**No.**"

"**Swear it then.**"

"**I swear that I did not….**"

He coughed and spluttered as he dropped down and heaved whatever he ate onto the cherry wood floor. Nathaniel growled, "**You are lying. Fine, I will let Basil have full control. Goodbye, brother.**"

Logan glanced sharply up at him before swallowing hard. Basil had his back to the bookshelf but Logan had clear view of it. He cowered before Basil as he rolled out his aura.

"**Tell me why you poisoned the water, Logan.**"

"**I promise you, I personally did not poison the water.**"

"**You know who did though?**"

"**I know who did.**"

"**Who?**"

He looked down at the ground before replying, "**I prefer not to say, Basil.**"

"**I don't care what you want or don't want to do, Logan. Tell me.**"

"**It was Sais…. But it was not you that he was targeting.**"

"**Who was he targeting then?**"

"**The same person I am wondering where she is. Do you know where the brat of a maid is?**"

"**Who?**"

"**Aurelius. You know who.**"

Basil rocked onto his heels slightly and rolled back after a moment. "**It does not matter if I know where she is or not. Now, answer my question. Why did you task Norjor to attack Rafeor?**"

Logan glowered at him and growled, "**Where is she, Basil? Is she somewhere in this room?**"

"**It is none of your concern where she is, Logan. Answer me.**"

"**Fine, I tasked Norjor to attack the beast. Like it was foretold to be done to it. It is an abomination to our species, and you know the history of what it could do.**"

"**Something can change between now and then. We can write our own history.**"

"**So, you are simply going to ignore what grandfather had said, and the same with the druids? Are you mad?**"

"**No, not mad.**"

He scoffed before replying, "**I guess that is a fair thing to say. No one would want someone who was mad when they have a leadership role. Now, where is she?**"

"**I am not going to tell you that, Logan.**"

"**Tell me.**"

"**No.**"

"**Why not?**"

"**Because you will kill her if I tell you where she is.**"

"**I guess that is a fair assumption.**"

They both fell quiet for a few moments, before Basil asked, "**What do you have against her anyhow, Logan? Why such hatred towards her?**"

"**What do you know of her, Basil?**"

"**Only a little information. Why did you have someone kill her wolf?**"

Logan looked shocked and his eyes flew around the room before he gripped the chair near him and snapped, "**Where is that snake? She was not supposed to tell anyone that.**"

"**Answer me.**"

Logan bared his neck to Basil and sighed deeply before replying, "**She got her wolf too early, Basil, and that wolf was causing issues. I had to put an end to it before it got out of hand.**"

"**Before what got out of hand?**"

"**Before the others found out what she was.**"

"**Meaning what exactly?**"

"What do you want me to say exactly, Basil? Do you want me to say I'm sorry to her or you? No, I am not going to apologize for something I carefully thought of. Besides, her wolf was getting into mischief and was going to blow everything I was doing away. I had to stop it from happening."

"What were you doing that needed someone to be put down like that?"

"I was doing undercover business in a different pack, Basil. You, however, never asked why I was somewhere and just assumed the worst."

"Remind me, what did Nathaniel find you at before?"

Logan fell silent and finally, he hedged, "I learned my lesson after that time. I was trying to do something else."

"Like what?"

"Why should I tell you everything? That was before the damn riot happened, Basil."

"Because a young woman is wolf-less because of your actions."

"I guess that is a fair point."

He paused and turned his attention towards him again. "I was at the other pack because I smelled my mate."

"What? Where is your mate?"

He looked down before replying, "She died during childbirth, Basil. I got two children, and…. Aurelius is not one of them either."

"Who is she then?"

"She was the alpha's daughter."

"Remind me again who the alpha was?"

"His name was Glen, but he did not make it out of the fight you caused. Most of the pack fell before they surrendered to you, Basil. You left a little girl without her family."

"What pack was that again?"

For a moment, Logan did not seem to want to reply. He finally did, "It was the Willow's moon pack. They bordered your territory to the north."

"The same pack that kept attacking us?"

"I guess that Glenn had it coming on his own. However, you did leave Aurelius to not have her family."

"Why did you decide to keep her then?"

"Because she…. She was the closest thing that I would be able to keep. Aurelius is not my blood-related child, Basil, but she was my mate's child."

"Who was your mate?"

"Her name was Amanda Fiore. Which is why Aurelius has the last name, Fiore."

Silence. I swallowed as I tried to keep myself quiet. That was the most information anyone has said about where I came from.

Logan glanced around the room before he sighed deeply and continued, "**What do you want from me, Basil? What else do you want to pick me for?**"

"**Do you know what happened to Norjor? He ran off.**"

"**I…. well… may have to tell him to kill the beast, or flee.**"

"**Why do that?**"

"**Because he failed.**"

"**I am glad he failed, Logan.**"

"**Tell me, why are you glad he failed that mission I had him do? We all know that Norjor would have left on his own anyhow. He did actually go himself, I just sent him a message through the link to do it.**"

"**Why?**"

"**I already told you why, Basil. It is because she is a threat to our species. Did you disregard everything that grandfather wrote? I see that you had brought out his book, and have the prophecy pages turned. Doing some casual reading again on it are you?**"

"**A bit.**"

"**If we had killed that beast before she entered the veil that would have been better, Basil. That way she would not get known.**"

"**Do you want to kill my mate's child?**"

"**Your mate? I thought that Sophronia could not have children.**"

"**That is what I thought too… until I talked to Evenor, and found out that she simply refused to.**"

"**Damn. So, what are you going to do now?**"

"**See if I can have a child with her, of course, Logan.**"

"**Darn, and here I thought when you passed on, I would be able to get to be king.**"

Basil growled low in his throat before he replied, "**Over my dead body.**"

"I guess that is fair. I have done many questionable things over the years."

"Questionable? If you weren't my brother I would have killed you for half of the things you have done so far, Logan."

"As if you could."

"Do not test that theory, Logan."

"I'm not."

"Good."

They fell silent and Logan leaned against the desk, tapping his fingers on the desk. He seemed content to keep it silent, and finally, Basil faded from Nathaniel's eyes. Nathaniel sighed deeply and spoke, "**So, Sais poisoned the water, and Aurelius is not your blooded child, but she is Amanda's child. Does that mean…**"

"It means that my mate did not wait for me. When I met her, she already had Aurelius and was towing around a child with her. Glenn kept a sharp eye on me, but he allowed me into his pack since the mate bond."

"Were…. Were you happy?"

"Honestly, no. I was not happy. I had resentment towards Glenn, and when I caught him planning a raid on the royal pack, I was going to tell you. That was when Aurelius caught me, and…. One thing led to another and her wolf surfaced. That is when I had to put her down. Although, I regret it. Her wolf only came to be because of traumatic behaviors."

"What do you mean?"

"She may have been a daughter of Glenn, Nathaniel, but he did not treat her like a daughter. No, he treated her like shit. And since I was new to the pack, I could not really do anything about how he treated her. She got her wolf early because of the abuse she was getting. Amanda couldn't do anything about it either, and since I was there, Glenn did not touch her."

"She…. she was beaten?"

"The only good thing that happened when you came after me, Nathaniel, was that you put down Glenn and erased his existence from this world. However, my mate died a month or so earlier, so, I was not all too well."

"What happened to your two children?"

Logan looked down and after a moment replied in a hushed whisper, "**They died when Morphous attacked the druid camp. I had them being trained there.**"

"I'm sorry."

"It is what it is."

"What are you going to do now, Logan?"

"Hopefully, drink until I pass out."

"That's not a good thing to do, Logan. You should…"

"ENOUGH! I am done with what YOU expect me to do, NATHANIEL! I am going to drink my sorrows away, and just be fucking glad that I am not hunting down Aurelius."

"What would you do if you did find her?"

Logan fell silent and replied after a few seconds, "Honestly? Don't know. She is the last thing of my mate I have, but she is also a bitter love-hate thing."

"Would you kill her?"

He was silent and glanced at Nathaniel before replying, "I don't know."

"Are you lying?"

"No, I am not lying."

"Swear it, then."

He seemed perplexed for a moment; he gulped a little and replied, "I swear I will not kill her."

"Would you order someone else to?"

"I don't want to answer that, Nathaniel."

"Answer me."

Basil rumbled out again, and Logan hung his head before he replied, "Possibly."

"I forbid you to."

"Yes, Basil. Can I depart and get ahead on my drinking?"

"Go."

Logan turned sharply on his heel and paused at the door before looking back at Basil and speaking, "Do not tell anyone of what was discussed. Especially not Aurelius."

"Go drink your sorrows away."

Logan clenched his fists together but departed after a moment, and shut the door. Leaving Basil to stare at the door.

****

It was another minute before Basil released Nathaniel, and Nathaniel opened the hidden doorway, and stared at me. Different emotions swirled in his eyes, and I whispered, "I guess I am not your niece."

**"Apparently not. But you are…. Still a distant family member."**

"How?"

**"You were brought into the family when Logan found his mate."**

"Does anything of what he described make sense though?"

**"As much as I wished that it was wrong, Aurelius, yes, it makes sense. It makes so much sense that I am surprised that he did not say something beforehand."**

"So, what now?"

**"Now we move you out of the maid's room."**

"But I am not your…."

**"It doesn't matter, Aurelius."**

"Ok, my lord."

**"Aurelius?"**

"Yes?"

**"Please call me by my name."**

"But we have no blood in common."

**"It does not matter."**

"It matters to me."

**"Too bad."**

"Fine."

It was another few seconds before I asked, "Where are you going to put me, Nathaniel?"

**"Beside my chambers."**

"But that is where the royals are."

**"You are a distant family member, Aurelius. You are my step niece."**

"That may be true, but that still does not make sense for me to be moved there. If that is the true reason. What about Rafeor?"

**"What about her?"**

"Does that mean she's your family?"

He was silent for a moment, he replied after a heavy sigh, "**I guess that does make her my step-daughter.**"

"So, shouldn't she get moved besides your chambers?"

**"Under technical terms, yes. However, Sophronia has not yet talked to her."**

"Is she scared to?"

**"I think so."**

We glanced at each other and I looked down before twisting my fingers together and speaking, "I guess, that is fair. She was believed to be dead."

**"Truth."**

I smiled slightly, and walked towards the door, pausing and looking at Nathaniel before speaking again, "So after I get moved, what do you want me to do?"

**"Whatever you want, I don't really want you to clean. You had done enough as is. And just so you know, Basil has decided to let Norjor be as he is."**

"What are the chances that he comes back?"

He leaned against his desk, and looked down at the parchments; he frowned and did not immediately reply. It was a few seconds that he replied, "**I will have to send a search team for him.**"

"What will you tell them?"

**"I will tell them to bring him back alive."**

"Who would you send?"

**"That is my decision I will have to make, Aurelius."**

"Okay."

He smiled slightly, and looked back down at the parchment, and sighed deeply before speaking, "**It has been a long day already, Aurelius. For now, you can go to the spare chambers next to mine, and stay there for the evening. We will move your belongings over tomorrow.**"

"Thank you, Nathaniel."

He looked at me and smiled a little, but it did not reach his eyes. He nodded towards the door and replied, "**Have Cyprus escort you back to that room.**"

"I thought he would be on patrol?"

**"He helped bring Logan over here."**

"Oh. okay."

**"Good night, Aurelius."**

"Good night my…. I mean, Nathaniel."

He chuckled slightly as he turned to face the fading light of the sun. I exited his office, and moved away, and Cyprus fell in step beside me.

****

After a few minutes, we made it to the new chambers and I paused before hesitating to open the doors. Cyprus looked at me and spoke, "It won't hurt you."

I scowled at him before replying, "I know that."

"Then why hesitate?"

"Because yesterday, I was a maid."

"I guess that is fair. Go inside, and sleep well, Aurelius. I will remain outside your door tonight."

"You don't have to, Cyprus."

"Have to, and want to are two different things. I want to. It is not an obligation. Besides, Azier wanted me to protect you since everything has happened."

"Ah, that makes sense. Thank you, Cyprus."

"You're welcome."

I opened the door, stepped into the room, and looked around. My jaw dropped and I lowered my eyes as I began to shut the door, when Cyprus pushed the door open. His eyes scanned the room and he grumbled before he pulled me out of the room, and slammed the door closed. I stare at him in shock before muttering, "Never mind here. I'll take you somewhere else."

"Why?"

"Better not ask questions you don't want to know."

"O-oh-okay."

He glanced around the hall before pulling me along and disappearing down a side door and heading outside. I was confused for a moment before I spot Azier waiting, and then the entire patrol. They worked well as a team, and there was no evidence that they would treat me differently because I was wolf-less. Azier smiled at me, but did not speak. They simply turned around and disappeared into the woods, and I followed cautiously.

Soon, we made it to a shack in the woods, and Cyprus spoke, "Alright, go to sleep."

"Why did you take me here?"

"Because Sais wants you dead."

"What? Why?"

"It doesn't matter right now, Aurelius. Go to sleep."

"Does Nathaniel know where we are?"

"It is better that we keep the circle of people close on your whereabouts are at the moment, Aurelius. At least, until Finn comes back."

"Oh… okay. Good night."

I entered the shack and found a bed, and a few other things, but it was very minimal in other things. It was supposed to be an outpost and it was taken down years ago, so it was very dusty, but they left the building out there for extra sleeping area. I sat down on the bed, lay on the bed after a moment and closed my eyes. I was tired, and exhausted and it did not take long before sleep took me.

# Chapter 28

I pressed the brick, opening the hidden entrance to the dungeons, and entered. Not bothering to check my surroundings, since, well, I was not planning on returning anytime soon. I went deeper into the darkness, and soon I smelled Sky and the stench of the other two, oh god, do they need a bath. However, no time to get them to one. I rounded the corner, and headed into the prison, and came face to face with Sky.

He was shocked to see me before he swallowed before speaking, "Oh, it's you. I… I thought it was someone else."

"And who were you hoping for?"

"No one."

He dropped his eyes to the ground as he whispered it. I saw his Adam's apple bob, and knew he was lying, but did not entirely care either way. I glanced at Michael and Verein before snapping, "Time to go."

"D-do-don't you have someone else to get?"

I paused and counted a few seconds before I replied, "He managed to escape me for the time being. He will be hunted down when I drop you with my brother."

**"Does that include my daughter?"**

"Yes, so come along."

They shuffled a little bit, before leaning against Sky, and I could see Sky was somewhat struggling to keep them standing since they were both clinging to him. I, however, did not remotely care at this point. I turned sharply on my heel and barked, "Follow me."

****

We went further into the dark tunnel, without a torch, and I heard that Sky was having trouble with both Michael and Verein, but I did not care. Soon, I got to the exit and pushed onto the brick and the door swung open. Sky gasped in shock, normally, I would have smirked, but I was in no mood. The sun was sinking at this point, and I scowled as we walked out, I glanced at Sky before speaking, "Shift into a stallion."

"Why?"

"You will be carrying these two."

"Why don't we get a carriage?"

"Because, as you said, Morphous would need to be alerted. And I would rather he didn't."

Sky looked up the wall and swallowed, he seemed like he was going to test the theory, and I snapped, "I would not suggest you do anything stupid."

He looked at me and his shoulders slumped before he bowed his head towards me. I turned my attention to the humans and spoke, "Either of you ridden bareback?"

Michael looked at me and was leaning heavily on the rock wall before replying, "I have, but I am unsure whether Lord Verein has or not."

He glanced at Verein, and I glanced at him and saw him struggling, but he did not seem to be entirely there either. He was beaten more than once for their crimes, and since they did not have any spiritual beings with them, that meant they heal as they are, as fucking weak humans. Falcor scoffed at me and I growled a warning in our connection, and he fell silent, for a few moments. I looked at Lord Verein before speaking, "Well?"

Verein looked at me before rasping, "**Have done it, but in no condition to do so....**"

He wheezed and coughed a little before coughing up blood. I swallowed and knew that Morphous had interrogated them severely before he had lessened their terms of crimes. I sighed deeply, pinching the bridge of my nose and speaking, "How long have you been coughing up blood?"

**"I think when they were beating me up good and proper, that they hit a lung."**

"Hmmmm…. And you still beat the girls you had to that point too, didn't you?"

"He did not really harm them all too much. That was my task to keep them in line."

"Oh? And…. if they indeed were doing the same behaviors as what you two are experiencing? What did you do to them?"

Silence, and I saw his Adam's apple bob; he replied, "Put them in an unmarked grave."

Falcor flashed in my eyes for a brief second, but I tried my best to keep him low in appearance since anyone could look down the wall and shout at us to halt. I sighed deeply before motioning towards Sky, and he lowered his head and came towards me.

I looked at him before growling, "Go to the carriage point, and get one."

"Who is going to pull it?"

"At this point, you."

"Alone?"

"Yes."

"B-bu-but they are equipped for two shifters or two horses to pull…."

"Get going, Sky."

"Yes, Killian."

He turned and headed towards the carriage area, before disappearing. I looked at the two humans before speaking, "Follow him."

"Okay."

They moved along the wall and pressed themselves into it. To keep their footings, and balance. I looked at the shapes of the guards and knew that they were most likely doing a guard change soon and that Feilian would be there. I already knew his schedule and would expect to see him on this wall too. I waited and waited. Nothing. Falcor pressed on our connection, *"Did Morphous take away our prey?"*

*"It looks like it."*

*"And why did you not listen to me earlier?"*

*"Hush, Falcor. We will find Rosen and his children."*

He hummed in the connection, but did not reply. I sighed as I watched the wall, but Feilian did not appear. I scowled but muttered, "Figures. Let's go, Falcor."

****

We moved along the wall, quietly so as not to alarm the guards above. Soon we made it to where the carriages were stored, and I instantly noticed that Sky had disappeared. Falcor flickered in my eyes for a moment before I asked Michael, "Where is he?"

"I-I-I…"

He fell silent before trying again, "We rounded the corner, and he was gone. I'm sorry…."

Falcor surfaced, and I couldn't force him back this time. I had let his prey go far too many times, and he growled, "He is good as DEAD! Let me out, Killian! Let me out!"

*"Falcor! No!"*

"You had your chance. Too many preys have escaped me! I will slaughter all!"

"A-al-all?"

Falcor looked at Michael, blinked once, and sighed deeply before muttering, "Ugh, I forgot I had two. Soon to be four. Kil, we come back later?"

"*Later.*"

"Fine, fine. Come along, I take it that you know how to attach a horse to a carriage?"

"Y-ye-yes."

"Good. Hook me up then."

Falcor shifted to a demon stallion, and his mane was the color of blood, and his coat black, his chest had rivets in it like gills. He took a deep breath in and let it out slowly. The two humans shrunk down when he fully was shifted and swallowed, their Adam's apple bobbing in fear. He turned his eyes to them before nickering.

 Michael swallowed hard, before resting his hand on his muzzle and leading him towards a carriage. It was a dark brown one, and Michael backed Falcor into the placement before swallowing nervously. Falcor towered over him by several feet, and he was mean. Falcor snapped once, showing that his teeth were razor sharp, not rounded. Michael slouched a bit down before, he went about finding the set-up equipment.


*****


I led the humans towards the carts before I looked around. I was kind of surprised that Killian let me go alone without him considering that he had Rosen leave without an escort. How stupid could he possibly be? I thought. After a few moments, seeing that Killian was not coming any time soon, meant that I could fucking leave, and hide. I looked at the humans before whispering, "See ya!"

One of them, looked like he was going to argue, but I was too far away for him to do anything. I disappeared into the palace and ran straight into Quinn. Quinn looked like he was out of breath and stared at me in shock before speaking, "Sky?"

I swallowed hard before growling, "Are you going to turn me back into your father?"

"No."

"Are you lying?"

"I would not lie to you. According to Rosen, you were also involved, and YOU were the one who showed Feilian that thing."

"Oh…. I thought…."

"He may be my father, Sky, but we are not similar in that action."

"Where can I hide from him?"

He sighed before replying, "My father most likely will come back to the palace, Sky, and the only safe place is with the experiment."

"Are you nuts? Them?"

"That is where Krool is heading with his family. They are the only ones that move frequently, and…. Most likely will keep you safe at the same time."

"What about staying here?"

"You know that is not possible."

"I still have to leave my home?"

"It's either leave or go with my father. Wherever he is taking you."

I swallowed and did not want to do either, but also knew that Quinn would not lie directly, he was Morphous's advisor and that was what kept me in. I swallowed hard before whispering, "What about Morphous? Is there anything he can do?"

"He personally sent Krool that way, Sky. I am sorry, but they are the only ones that will keep you safe."

"Where are they?"

"Davis mentioned that they were in the same area as him. So, head that way."

"Wait, why can't I just be with Davis?"

"Because when have you ever seen him actually be fair to anyone?"

"I guess you have a fair point. So, I am to leave everything I know? Simply because I found that thing?"

"If you had left it where it was placed, and did not tell anyone about it, you would be exactly where you belong. However, with this issue, and the fact that now my father is going to be leaving and such, this is the only situation. You and I cannot do anything else unfortunately, it is set. If you stay, my father will slaughter you for deserting him, and if you go he will have to hunt you down to find you."

"There has to be another way!"

"OR you could see where your new path lies, Sky. You could find out where he is taking you. You would not be able to come back, BUT you would never have to feel like you have to always look over your shoulder either."

"B-bu-but…"

"I'm sorry, Sky, but those are your options. Leave with my father, and won't have to look over your shoulder for the rest of your life. OR flee, and hope and pray that the experiment and her family can protect you."

"Have you ever met the experiment?"

"Personally? No. They are always too far away to go find them."

"But aren't you curious how different they are?"

"Sky, it is time for you to make your decision. Are you fleeing and finding out that answer yourself? OR are you going to go back out there and leave with my father?"

I stared at him and swallowed nervously before whispering, "W-wh-what do you suggest I do Quinn?"

He licked his lips and sighed deeply before replying, "I cannot make your decision, Sky, I cannot. That is your decision."

"Oh, come on! Where is your father taking us?"

"Us?"

"He's taking the humans that were in the cells with him. And heading towards the mansion where Rafeor was to get the Lord's child."

"Ummm…. Not sure where he is going, but I know that…. I can't tell you that part unless you are going with him. However…."

"I know he is a demon."

"You know?"

"He told me and Rosen down in the dungeons."

"I am pretty sure he is taking you wherever he went the other days ago."

"Where's that?"

"I have never been there. I have no idea."

"So, my choices are, either leave with your father on an unknown path or flee to the experiment and always look over my shoulder?"

"Unfortunately, those are your only two options. Morphous cannot protect you, as much as he wants to. He is no match for my father, and quite frankly, neither am I. No one here would be able to protect you, Sky. It would kill hundreds of us, to protect one being."

"Oh…."

I swallowed hard before turning back around and started to head back out, when Quinn called out, "Wait."

I stopped and turned my head in his direction before he continued, "Grab food before you leave."

"Why?"

"That way if you do indeed go the route I think you are choosing, then you can just say you were getting provisions for the trip."

"Oh. That is rather smart."

****

I turned back around and jogged through the palace, and soon came to the kitchen. I swallowed before entering the door. The cook was stirring a large vat before he snapped, "What do you want?"

"F-fo-food for five."

"How many days?"

"Ummm…."

Quinn entered behind me and glanced at me for a moment replying, "Food for five, and enough for five days. Including water, and…."

"Get out."

I stared at the cook and had my jaw drop before he turned to someone behind him, "Nicolas, get what they want."

"Yes, sir."

The cook turned around and growled, "OUT!"

I stared at him and backed out of the door. Quinn started to follow before he looked at the cook, and spoke, "Thank you, Franster."

"Get out of my kitchen."

Quinn chuckled slightly but complied with his request. A few minutes passed, and I swallowed. Surely, Killian would be gone by now, and I would have to debate on heading towards the mansion myself or leave and always look over my shoulder. Soon though, a boy came out and looked exhausted for a moment before mumbling, "Here you go."

"Thank you."

"No problem, sir."

He disappeared back into the kitchen, and soon more yelling happened on the other side of the door, but I dared not enter the room again. I looked at Quinn before holding out my hand. He hesitated for a brief second before shaking it. I smiled grimly and whispered, "Thank you, Quinn, for all you have done."

"You're welcome. Now go."

I turned on my heel and headed back out to the carriage area.

*****

He tried his hardest to get Falcor hitched to the carriage, but Falcor, well, never been hooked to a carriage and his demon self was not exactly a walk in the park. He was a vicious beast, and Michael had learned the hard way, you fucking stay away from his razor-sharp teeth. He had a bleeding shoulder, and I grimaced and snarled through the connection to him, *"Easy there, Falcor!"*

*"It is his damn fault!"*

*"How is it HIS fault?"*

*"He is not moving fast enough."*

*"Falcor, he is a human."*

*"He will learn to be faster this way, Killian."*

*"Remember that Rafeor wants them safe."*

*"Oh, shut up!"*

*"Falcor?"*

*"What?"*

*"Watch it."*

*"Make me."*

*"Do not tempt me to make you do something."*

*"As if you could."*

*"Falcor?"*

*"Enough."*

He closed the connections, and I lost to him. I tried hard to press myself out into the connection, but alas, he was more powerful than I was currently. He had sleep, I didn't. I sighed in our connection before snapping to myself, *"Well, great…"*

The side door opened and I felt Falcor tense and seemed ready to fight. Michael swallowed hard before he backed away from Falcor, but soon I saw Sky come out. I was surprised to see him and I could tell that Falcor was too.

*****

He walked out of the palace and swallowed as he saw something he had never seen before. It was coal black, with blood red mane, and what looked like gills on the chest. Blood was splattered on the ground and he glanced at Michael and saw him bleeding; he looked quickly back at the beast before him. He swallowed as he walked forward and carefully placed the food and water canteens down, holding his hands out in surrender and spoke, "I apologize."

"Were you going to run?"

"I would be lying if I said no. I apologize though, I ran into someone and they suggested I come along and bring food for the trip."

"I should make you go without eating."

"I am sorry."

*"Falcor?"*

*"What, Killian?"*

*"He came back and brought food. What more do you want?"*

*"My other prey!"*

*"We will go hunting for them at a later date. For now, look at the silver lining. He understood his chances of living are slimmer when he runs. When he comes, he will work, but he will not need to look over his shoulder. He will be relatively safer that way. Also, we did not bring food."*

*"So that's it? You are not going to punish him?"*

*"Look at it this way, we will not need to go hunting."*

*"I guess that is true."*

He mulled it over before speaking aloud, "You are safe for now. However, I must warn you. Try to do that vanishing action again and I will kill you."

"Understood."

His voice wobbled as he answered weakly, but that was it. I knew that he was going to learn very hard and that Falcor would hold him to it too. He approached slowly and spoke again, "Should I be the one pulling?"

"You should have been, but…."

He trailed off for a moment before looking at him sharply and snapping, "But I am semi-ready to go now."

He nodded, saw something, and frowned before he grabbed a chest halter, and I instantly knew what he was thinking. I was going to tell him to forget it, but Falcor did not allow me to speak. I held my breath as he looked at it and then looked at Falcor. Falcor took a breath in, and his gills moved slightly before he let the air back out. As if showing him that it would not work. He swallowed before speaking, "I need to put this piece on."

"That is exactly how I got this bite! Do not."

He looked over his shoulder at Michael before turning his attention back to Falcor and speaking, "This piece will help me steer you. May I please place it on?"

"I will bite you if you try."

He swallowed hard before he straightened himself slightly. "Then how am I going to direct you?"

"Simple. You do not."

"That is not how this is going to work. It needs to go on."

"If you value your movement currently, I highly suggest YOU leave it off."

Sky frowned and sighed deeply, lowered the chest harness down, and seemed perplexed for a moment. He replied, "If you are so keen on having this thing off, then switch with me."

"Why?"

"Because I know where we are going. You don't. If I didn't place this on you, you would not know which way to turn. And we would have issues as is, since no one has seen a horse like yourself before."

"I am not a HORSE! I am a demon!"

"In the form you are in currently? You are a horse to our eyes. No one has seen a beast like yourself. This will help keep people from ogling yourself."

"Michael. Take this stuff off me."

"Yes, sir."

He approached cautiously and took off the other equipment and soon Falcor shook his head, closed his eyes, and allowed me to shift back. I went back to what they were used to and I could see that Sky was nervous but was not immediately going to do anything.

I blinked at him before speaking, "Under any circumstances. Do not attempt to do that again. Understood?"

"Yes, Killian."

"Good. Now, shift."

He shifted immediately into a chestnut stallion. He stood at seventeen and a half hands and shook his mane before nickering. Michael approached him, and directed him carefully, as if afraid that he would get bit again, however, I knew that one of the things that the shifters have done over the decades is getting used to different ways of being trained. They have tamed their wild half over everything, and that was something that I still had to work with Falcor, who had snorted in our connection but did not make a comment. Soon, after only a few minutes, Michael had Sky set up and ready to go. He threw his head around and nickered softly again.

*****

Another stallion trotted out of nowhere, and I turned around, confused for a moment before another shifter approached. He looked at the humans for a moment before speaking, "Going somewhere?"

"It does not concern you."

"I am in charge of the carriages. You are taking one of the oldest and most unstable carriages. They are going to be dismantled."

"It will serve its current function."

"And what function would that be?"

"I am not in the position to tell you."

"I am in charge of these carriages, given access by Morphous himself. I was not informed that someone needed a carriage to leave. I request that you dismantle your stallion and…."

"Do you noy know who I am?"

"Sir, you are Killian…."

"Exactly. Killian. Why does it matter that I have not consulted with Morphous?"

"Because he needs to authorize the department."

"You just said you were going to dismantle this carriage, meaning you no longer need the use of it anymore. Therefore, he would not need it anymore."

"Regardless. Orders are orders, Killian. You should know better than anyone else here."

I forced Falcor to stay back, before I replied, "I am leaving here."

"No."

"Are you challenging my authority?"

"Morphous had specifically informed me that absolutely no one was to leave without his express permission, Killian. Regardless of rank. I am sorry, but my hands are tied."

"Are you seriously going to make me do something I don't really want to do?"

His Adam's apple bobbed but he raised his head a little higher before he replied, "By the King of the shifters, you are not going to take that carriage anywhere."

I swallowed, I knew that Morphous had done that so the youths did not go on rambunctious adventures without someone in the know. However,, this meant that I either had to kill him or take him with me. Falcor pressed on the connection and I opened it, *"I get to kill him?"*

*"I don't want to kill him."*

*"Why not?"*

*"Because he is following the directions that even I know."*

*"Try again, and insist that you leave then. If he does not comply….."*

*"Shush, Falcor, I will try to make it so I do not have to kill him."*

He grumbled but did not reply. I glanced at the shifter before speaking, "Let me go in peace. I am trying hard to keep the death toll down. Do not make me add another."

He swallowed hard before he looked at the stallion beside him; he replied, "I am sorry, Killian, however, I cannot let you leave."

"So be it."

I swallowed as Falcor pushed the connection, and quickly the shifter before me was severely injured, he would die if Anna did not get to him immediately. Even then it would probably too late for him. The disturbing aspect was that Falcor did not touch our weapons, he used his speed and talons to do the damage to the shifter.

The stallion reared and let out a shrill voice, and I winced as Falcor released me. I glanced at the stallion and saw that the eyes were staring far off in the distance, a sign that the stallion was scared, or calling for something. A mighty roar sounded, and Falcor snarled in response, we both knew who had roared. Time to leave, promptly.

******

I felt the pain rattle through the bond of the shifters. The disadvantage of being the king of our species, you felt each other's pain, and especially life-threatening damage. I knew whose I was feeling, and instantly knew who it was too. Quinn reported to me immediately after Sky left him by the kitchen, and came to report Killian. Now, I wished that I had him down in a dungeon, where he would not be able to get out. I snarled low and Abacore pressed on our connection, and I let him surface. He roared. He did not say a word, but he did make the entire palace tremble by the volume of his roar. He glinted in my eyes as I watched my reflection in my window, and knew he was on the verge of shifting. I, however, kept him in close, and connected to Anna, "*Get to the carriage portions of the palace.*"

"*Of course, my lord!*"

I dropped the connections and Abacore pressed on the connections again. A little harder, and I frowned before grumbling to him in the connections, "*We can't have you shift inside here, Abacore.*"

"*LET ME OUT MORPHOUS! He attacked one of our own!*"

"*I know he did! But we cannot destroy our home!*"

"*If you do not want me to shift right here right now, then get the heck out of here! I'll give you four minutes to get out of here. Two hundred forty, two hundred thirty-nine, two hundred thirty-eight....*"

I closed the connection and hurried from my room. Since one thing that Abacore would do when he got down to that last second, was indeed shift. And I couldn't afford to have to rebuild my home. Plus, all the lives would get disrupted once again. I was still having crews at the site for the hospital. At least, rebuilding it since Rafeor shifted to her golden dragon with the black tips. I froze, I had not talked to Rafeor in a long time. Not once a week, I tuned into Abacore's time limit, *"One hundred fifty-five. One hundred fifty-four...."*

I bit my lip before rushing out to her room. I knocked on her door, well, more of banged on her door. No response. I knocked again. No answer. I swallowed hard before I turned the handle and peered around the door and saw that she was out. However, what got Abacore to stop the countdown was the fact that he did not smell her scent fresh, *"By smell alone, Morph, she is not here. And HAS NOT BEEN HERE FOR TWO DAYS!"*

I grimaced as he bellowed in our mind, and frowned. I thought I was doing an alright job being a father, but apparently, I wasn't. Abacore huffed in our connection but did not say anything. I swallowed and looked down at the ground and tightened my hands into fists, before Abacore whispered, *"Ninety-nine. Ninety-eight. Ninety-seven. The time is still going, Morph. Ninety-five. Ninety-four..."*

*"Then go ahead and shift."*

*"I thought you wanted to wait outside?"*

*"Abacore, it doesn't matter currently. Shift."*

*"Gladly."*

He let out another ferocious roar, as he shifted into his black dragon. The hallway around him exploded, and the roof above us tore open like a melon. His head snapped out and he roared again. He had to fight his way out of the ruined section of the palace, but he eventually got out. He was in control. He was a beast. He was going to rain hell on Killian.

# Chapter 29

*Hunting*

I glanced at the humans before leaping into the driver seat, and snapping, "Hurry and get inside!"

They scrambled to the carriage door, flung it open and I snapped the whip across Sky's back; he leaped forward and fought to get moving. Shit. shit. Shit. I thought. I forgot to take into consideration how much the humans would weigh. However, once he surged forward, we were off. We crashed into the gate in front of him, which would normally prevent anyone from leaving, but the stable hand must have left it open.

Soon we hit the main road and were going as fast as Sky could go. A little slower than Falcor wanted. He kept grumbling but kept quiet otherwise. He was slightly angry with me and my judgment on leaving the shifter just barely dead, but he seemed to understand why now. If Morphous willingly released Abacore, then all hell was going to break loose. I'd seen both sides, if Morphous was in control, then it was easier to handle the dragon. However, if Abacore was in full control, he would totally give Falcor a run for his money. He was dangerous, he was powerful, and he was always full of rage. Which was why Morphous would rarely let him completely ascend. However, that last roar was what Abacore sounded like. That death note. Hardly anyone escaped alive when that sounded.

Falcor brought me back into the focus, *"Let me out."*

*"Why?"*

*"Because otherwise, we will be toast. We will come back for the human's child at a later date, Killian. We need to flee towards Severi."*

*"That will still take too long."*

*"KILLIAN!"*

I winced at his volume as our minds jostled, and he forced control. I winced again as he shifted to his dragon, something he had not done in centuries, not since we had trained to be what we were. It was hard to shift, but soon he unwound his four wings, and acted as if he was going to roar, but then must have thought better of it, with all things considered.

He grabbed Sky's chestnut stallion around his girth and grabbed the carriage with his other talon fore-claw. He beat his four wings together and rose into the air. I could tell that Sky and the humans were terrified, but I could do nothing. My wariness finally overcame me and I whispered in our connection, *"Be safe, Falcor."*

*"Go to sleep now. I got this."*

A yawn overcame me and that was his answer. He was now in full control. Once I was out, I was out for a solid three hours at a time typically, however, this was different since it was a day and a half that I had not slept. I hoped that Falcor was not going to do anything to get us killed.

*****

I flapped my wings and got high above the cloud cover before angling myself towards my homeland. I had to work overtime to get airborne with all this added weight. The carriage was heavy, the stallion was heavy, and the humans were okay, but they were adding weight to the carriage. I flew for a good ten minutes before I set down the stallion and the carriage before huffing out, "Shift and get into the carriage."

Sky instantly shifted and his bugged eyes would be hilarious but I knew I did not have time. I snapped my jaws at him, and he shimmied out of the harness before entering the carriage, where I had strategically placed them all so I could do a better lift-off. I gripped each side of the carriage and launched myself into the air again, flapping my wings hard against the air to get airborne. I heard an off-distance roar and knew my time was up. I flew off, heading towards Severi.

*****

I roared in the sky again and knew that everyone within the palace was cowering. I did not release my fire, I knew better than that. I leaped into the sky and saw something out of the corner of my right eye, a mighty beast, blood red with white spikes. We locked eyes for a moment before it flew above the cloud cover – not alone might I add. It was carrying something big. I snarled, my eyes sparkled in rage once again, and I roared into the sky.

*****

I flew hard and as fast as I could. Knowing full well that Severi was the only one who would be able to fend off this shifter king. He was always the one who was proving that we could shift into our dragon, much to our mother's dislike since she said countless times that there was no point in being bloodthirsty monsters. However, father approved and that was Severi's role model and he ignored mother's words. However, I have a feeling that went down the rabbit hole once he saw me and the werewolves' behaviors together.

I flew for a solid two hours, flying away from the shifter and werewolf kingdoms, away from normal civilizations. Away, and away. Still, though, I heard the roar of the dragon. Severi was the only one who could do something about this now. I just hoped that I get back in time before it caught up to us

.

****

I flew off after the beast, knowing for sure it was who I thought it was, and knowing that he was going somewhere. At some point, someone tried to tell me to come back, but I tuned everyone out and pushed myself after him, after my prey. He was as good as dead.

I caught sight of him landing again, and I immediately pushed myself a bit faster, since he had landed. However, after a minute, he got back into the air, and I roared in rage. I could practically see that he faltered for a moment. He was dead. I would make sure he never saw another day.

****

I glanced back at the black dot, that was maybe two leagues away, he was gaining distance. He always kept me in his sight, and I swallowed hard. I could not land where I would normally, and I swung the carriage one way and then the other, contemplating killing them to get away. However, I was the one who would see them fall to their doom and knew that Killian would instantly not trust me enough to be in control again. I swallowed and closed my eyes, there was a weak connection between us brothers, but I connected to Severi, *"BROTHER! HELP ME!"*

*"What did you do that needs my help? Also, how far away are you? I could not contact you when you were that far away…."*

*"I'm not far, Severi, I have a few more of my subjects to add. However, I did something to piss off the shifter king."*

*"Let me guess, he is after you. How far away is he from you?"*

*"About two leagues away."*

*"How far away are you from the homelands?"*

*"Flying wise, no more than two hours."*

*"So, you want me to leave my subjects solely because you screwed up?"*

*"If he catches me, Severi, he will kill me."*

*"What did you do to make him so pissed off at you?"*

*"I prefer not to say, Severi."*

*"It's not what you want to do. BUT IT IS THE ONLY WAY YOU WILL GET ME FROM WHAT I CURRENTLY AM DOING. So, again, what did you do to get the shifter king in a hissy fit?"*

I swallowed back my pride for a moment and knew that Severi would not come without the knowledge of what I had done. I also had a feeling that he went to check on Rafeor and found her gone. That might have been the tipping point in this case. I sighed deeply before replying, *"I nearly killed one of the shifters, if medical didn't reach him in time he would be dead. Also, I believe it is because I have the artifact, and he wants it back. Along with the possibility that he just found out I took his human prisoners and took them, along with a prisoner that Killian refused to kill for the artifact…. And…."*

*"You are rambling, Falcor. You are trying my limited patience. Only two sentences. Go."*

*"I took a few prisoners and forced one family to flee, and took something that will enhance the hybrid's ability. Also, informed the hybrid that she will need to leave and go to the werewolves for the training."*

Severi was silent for a solid minute, and I was getting antsy with his silence. Soon though he replied, *"So it was one hundred percent your fault for having a…. What form is he in?"*

*"Dragon."*

*"A dragon? I thought he couldn't be a dragon."*

*"Severi, please. Can we discuss this later? When you know, my life isn't threatened."*

*"Fine, but you owe me an explanation when I assist you. How far away are you now?"*

*"Roughly around an hour fly, and I can barely see the ruins."*

*"Keep coming, brother then. I will come out to meet you."*

*"Thank you, Severi."*

He did not reply. I knew I had a lot to explain when he came. I looked again behind me and saw that Abacore was coming faster as if I had slowed down. I glanced around and realized that

I had indeed slowed myself down. I swallowed and flapped my wings hard and strained myself to get going. He had gained a league and I could tell by his echoing roar, that he saw me.

He never really lost sight of me either, dragons have a nasty habit of seeing for several leagues away, without an issue. In his case, since he was the shifter king, it may be the case that he could always see me, and where I possibly even might land. So, he might see the freaking ruins, and some of the inhabitants.

******

I saw an old compound, it was old and broken and falling apart. It was probably a good hour fly further but I could see it. It made me mad. No, correction, it made me furious. If he thought that he would get to those ruins without encountering my razor-sharp teeth and talons, he was surely done for. I roared again and I saw him falter before it seemed that he strained to push himself harder, and faster. And by the way, he flew, he was getting tired and I grinned wickedly. He would soon either drop what he was carrying or land somewhere where I would smolder him and roast him alive. Either or works. I personally wanted a fight and I hoped that he would give me one.

Morphous tried to talk to me in the connection, but I ignored him until he bellowed, *"STOP!"*

I faltered for a moment and growled at him in the connections. Finally, listening to him, *"Where are you even going, Abacore?"*

*"After my prey, Morphous! He is getting away!"*

*"Have you ever thought of where he is leading us?"*

*"It doesn't matter, Morph, he will be a goner!"*

*"He is a freaking demon, Abacore! We do not know what is in store! He is the only one we know of. Have you even LOOKED at his DRAGON form? It freaking has FOUR wings. Not two like yourself!"*

*"I've noticed, Morph, but he is slow!"*

*"Can you SEE that he is carrying a freaking carriage? Those things are heavy as hell. And IF he is carrying anyone inside, that adds to its weight. Go home, Abacore."*

*"No."*

*"ABACORE! YOU WILL DO AS I SAY!"*

*"Not this time, Morph."*

*"Abacore, if he gets the upper claw…."*

*"Then you can tell me I was wrong."*

*"We have a kingdom to rule!"*

*"You have grown soft over the last century, Morphous. I'm tired of your laziness. We do this."*

*"Abacore…."*

I blocked his connection, cutting him off, so I could not hear anything else. I felt his anger through the bond, but could not hear the words he was cursing.

I tuned into my prey, gathered the energy I had saved over the past few centuries, and bolted after him. A sonic boom sounded under my wings, and it rolled throughout the terrain, the trees surrounding underneath bent down and probably killed countless creatures with one wing snap. He was mine!

****

I looked behind me, I felt the air around me tremble, and heard the creaking of the trees behind me. I was shocked. Morphous had leveled an entire forest to flat, killing anything that was inside it. I swallowed and looked down at the carriage, there was only one fucking way I was going to survive, and that is letting these go to their deaths.

I screamed internally and woke up Killian who, had slept only three hours, and looked around through my eyes. He saw everything I was thinking, along with the options we now have. He sighed in our connections before mumbling, *"Go low, and drop the carriage."*

*"What?"*

*"Go low! Drop the carriage when you are roughly a hundred feet in the air. It may be an old model, but it will hold up somewhat. That is the ONLY way we will get survivors. They will have injuries, but otherwise, alive."*

*"But, Morphous!"*

*"Falcor, that is Abacore. You WOKE him up. Do not be surprised for him to come harder, and faster than ever before. We have not experienced him to go his hardest. He is angry. He is pissed. Get going. AND WHATEVER YOU DO, DO NOT GO TO THE RUINS!"*

*"Why not?"*

*"Because that is WHERE we had left everyone. We cannot have them in a dragon fight."*

*"Oh, right."*

I suddenly flew to the right, and I could hear Abacore's angry roar that he was not prepared for that swerve. I went lower and lower. Soon, I was roughly fifty feet in the air, and I closed my eyes for a brief second before releasing the carriage. I could not wait around to watch, I gained altitude and flew further away, hoping that Abacore would leave them alone.

****

I watched as he dropped the carriage, and I desperately wanted to roast whatever it was. However, I remembered what had happened yesterday night. When Rosen Krool arrived at my office, that he and Sky had taken the artifact out of the catacombs and were going to sell it – thinking nothing of why it was down there in the beginning. I swallowed and had an inkling of where Sky was, and as much as I wanted to roast the carriage, I honored Sky's father too well. I was not about to kill his sole surviving child, even in my rage. I would never forgive myself for that action. I sighed deeply as I flew over the carriage, if it was still there on the way back, I would bring Sky back to the palace afterward.

Morphous broke through the connections after several attempts, *"STOP!"*

*"MORPHOUS! You HAVE to stop screaming at me!"*

*"Then freaking THINK!"*

*"Morphous, we have been over this!"*

*"Where are we?"*

*"Uhhh…. Past the borders."*

*"EXACTLY THE POINT! We are WAY past our homeland! And WAY past HELP!"*

*"I don't need help."*

*"Abacore…."*

I growled at him in the connections, and he stopped for a moment before he sounded frustrated before he growled, *"What would YOU do once you do indeed manage to catch up with your prey Abacore?"*

*"Kill it."*

*"Really? You would kill your old advisor and friend?"*

*"He played us, Morph, I do not think of him as a friend."*

*"Fair, but have you THOUGHT this through? What are you going to explain to Quinn or Herald?"*

*"Huh?"*

*"What are you going to do with his offspring?"*

*"Throw them into the dungeons."*

*"Has Quinn ever shown any similarities to Killian? Has Herald?"*

*"No…"*

*"Then do not kill them, or throw them in the dungeons. They have their own lives to do, and I personally have not had any issues with Herald. Quinn did at the start question my authority, but otherwise, he is the best of the advisors. They are meant to challenge everything we do. Abacore, leave."*

*"No."*

*"Abacore! LEAVE!"*

*"NO!"*

I locked the connection down a little harder. I could tell that he was trying hard to break through it, but to my credit, it held fast. Morphous would not hamper my plan to catch, and slaughter my prey. He was a goner.

*****

I flew away, and sure enough, Abacore left the carriage alone, which made me wonder if he knew what was inside. I panted, and soon flew over another forest area, but flew back after I spotted a herd of elk, not wanting to kill the innocent creatures. A familiar howl sounded to my left and I jerked my head sideways and saw Severi crouching down in the woods, he had three humans dead before him. I swallowed as I stared at their mangled bodies, and landed next to him after a moment. Well, near him knowing full well what would happen if I thought of coming closer to him, especially, when he is angry about something.

He turned his bloody face towards me and snapped, "Where is your dragon buddy?"

"He's coming."

"Now, before he shows up entirely, what did you do?"

"I… uh…. I might have killed a shifter…. Wait, I already told you what I had done. Why ask again?"

"Because I want to know it again. You caught me in the middle of my hunt."

"Hunt?"

"Yeah, these three idiots thought that they could flee since I sent them on a trip to bring back some food the other day. I had just found them."

"Oh, I thought you were done killing your subjects?"

"I am. Unless they think that they can get away with running. That is my line that no one shall cross again."

"I guess, that is fair."

"Damn right, it is. Now, tell me more about this dragon. What did you do to bring the shifter king ALL THE WAY OUT HERE?"

I opened my mouth to speak when an echoing roar sounded not too far away. I knew that he could see us and that he would land soon. I looked at Severi before replying, "Why don't you ask him since he is here?"

He rolled his eyes before howling long and low. The ground trembled, and after a minute I glanced at Severi in shock, since when did he get a freaking army of wolves under his command? However, the boom of something larger sounded and I swallowed hard before shifting back, allowing Killian to have command.

****

I sighed deeply and rubbed my eyes before I scowled, moved towards the corpses, and grabbed a pair of their trousers. No way in hell would I grab one of their shirts, but the pants, sure. I glanced at Severi before shaking my head in annoyance and speaking, "Help me move him back to his kingdom. I don't really need to kill Abacore."

"Abacore?"

"That is the name of the shifter king's dragon. We cannot kill him, but we can wound him."

"What do you know about him that I don't, Killian?"

"He is the hybrid's father. We cannot kill him since we want her to come back with us willingly. Therefore, we merely redirect him back home."

"What did Falcor do that pissed him off so much?"

"Relatively speaking, Severi, it was not entirely Falcor's fault. I have dealt my blows to get him this pissed off. Now, the last time I checked, which was not that long ago when I woke back up, it was Abacore in full command. Not Morphous. So, both myself and Falcor manage to wake up the beast."

"So, what do you plan on doing now?"

"The hard part, Severi. Talk to the beast. At the same time trying not to get killed."

"Ah."

"Yeah. Do you want to either watch or join me?"

He glanced down at his kills and looked back up at me. "Now what would I gain if I joined you?"

"The fact that I am believed to be the last of my kind. You would be a surprise."

"Oh? How many species think that we have disappeared? Sure, let's get this over with and see his surprised expression."

I smiled slightly, turned around, and walked through the tall grass that was growing, knew that eventually, this needed to be trimmed since this would be our homeland once again. And it will be maintained as it once was – as I remembered it to be

.

****

Finally, after ten minutes of walking around roots and rocks and overall overgrowth, I made it around the bend where a pack of wolves had surrounded Abacore, who looked like he wanted to rip them to shreds. I called out, "ABACORE!"

That caught his attention, his head snapped up, and he growled a low rumble in his throat. His eyes blazed in rage. I held up my hand before I continued, "You are a LONG way from home. Please, go back."

**"You slaughtered my people. You killed the carriage handler!"**

I swallowed and replied, "I did not kill him, Abacore, I apologize on my demon's behalf. Please, go back home."

**"You will have to MAKE me leave, Killian! I am out for blood. And it is not these measly wolves either. I. Want. YOURS!"**

I swallowed and replied after a moment, "Abacore, can I please talk to Morphous?"

**"No."**

"Why not?"

**"Because he is a pushover! And you will corrupt what I want!"**

****

I swallowed again and was about to reply when Calio rounded around the bend. "Stand down."

The wolves instantly backed away and looked at him expectantly. A sure sign that I missed something big since they normally only did this if their alpha was challenged and killed. Calio approached a little closer and looked up at Abacore, his eyes trailing him before speaking again, "You are a long way from home, Shifter King. I apologize if my brother brought you here without…."

**"What do you mean by brother?"**

The wolves cowered, and Calio's eyes flashed red for a moment, a sure sign that Severi was wanting out. I was actually surprised that Calio was handed back the reins. Severi always wanted the fight, however, I could see the locking of Calio's jaw before he replied in a clipped tone, "Please, do not cut me off again. You and I are similar, shifter king, you want to make your subjects before you tremble at your feet. However, there is a limit on how well I can manage my other half. I suggest that you shift down to your human form, and we will talk like civil people."

**"Is that an order? I don't take kindly to being ordered around, toothpick."**

Steam rolled out of his nostrils, his eyes sparked in rage, and I swallowed hard. If Calio wasn't careful, then he would lose the entire pack of wolves and even the surrounding areas.

Calio raised his eyebrows and replied, "You are on my territory currently shifter king. I can order you to be attacked. However, being the diplomate that I am, please… shift so we can discuss what my idiot brother had done."

I glowered at the back of his head at that terminology before hissing, "Calico!"

He glanced slightly back at me before returning his attention to Abacore and speaking again, "Well? What shall it be?"

Abacore blinked once before growling, **"I should roast you all alive."**

"Yet you won't because you are out of your terrain. This is our homeland and you are invading it. You are alone, and I…"

He paused and gestured towards the pack, before continuing, "Have an army at my command. Shift, and we will discuss this. You do not need to release your other half, if you do not wish to. However, a dragon is not the greatest thing to be in the presence of. Wouldn't you agree?"

Silence. I personally could tell that he was struggling to see a trap behind Calico's words, but he finally relented, rumbling, "**You not attack?**"

"It highly depends on what happens. However, I will not be the one who initiates the attack. I understand that you are at your weakest point once in the human stage, as well as we all are, however, do not think twice about double-crossing me, dragon."

He huffed before shifting to his human form, and I could tell by the wolves that they were startled at how powerful he was and shifted into something so small afterward. I could tell that none of the wolves around us knew who he was, and I had to make a note of that later. For now, I was to observe what Calio would do now.

Calio turned his head slightly towards me, growling, "Come along, brother."

"Of course, Calio."

He growled softly, and his eyes sparked once but other than that Severi did not surface further. I followed him down the slope and the wolves surrounding the hillside parted before us, they growled low in their throats at me, but Calio paid them no heed. I let Falcor surface slightly and they cowered before me. I would have smiled if it wasn't a dire situation. Soon, we came to about four yards away before stopping. I could tell that Calio was judging him, and could practically tell that it was the same with Abacore. However, after a moment, Calio spoke, "So what did my idiot brother do this time to get a shifter king to come out past his borders?"

Abacore blinked once before rumbling, "**You keep mentioning that he is your brother. Why?**"

"I asked you a question first. Please answer, and I will tell you."

**"That is not how I roll. You tell me first, and I will answer."**

I could tell that Severi was having an argument with Calio and that he was not really winning on keeping him under wraps, and soon, I was right. Severi's eyes snapped into play and glowed red for a moment before Calio forced him back. But not before Abacore could see the red in his eyes. I saw him swallow hard; he growled, "**You are another demon? I did not think that any of them survived the attack all those centuries ago.**"

Calio closed his eyes and pinched the bridge of his nose before grumbling, "To answer your question, yes, I am a demon, and I am older than Killian. You are starting to make me lose the fight with my demon for not teaching you a lesson about ignoring our question. However, since you are a King of sorts, you are to be treated with respect. Now that I have answered your question, what did he do?"

**"He killed the carriage handler, who had followed the rules that BOTH Killian and myself agreed on. However, it appeared that he thought he was exempt from that rule. Also, I believe he is the sole culprit for having my daughter to be gone! And…."**

Calio held his hand up and turned to face me before speaking, "Killian, is anything of what he is saying correct?"

Abacore snarled in rage, but Calio glowered at him. Severi glinted in his eyes, and he went silent. I swallowed before replying, "I apologize, brother, however, he is correct. We made the rule so that no one ran off in the middle of the night, and couldn't be found. And, I knew that it would not be the easiest thing to get out of the palace, due to that exact rule. And…."

"You are rambling, Killian. I see that never changed."

"I apologize, Calio."

I swallowed and looked at Abacore before speaking again, "I am sorry, Abacore, that this happened. I did not mean to kill him. I swear. I…. I regret doing it, or having a backseat to having him die."

**"You think sorry is the only thing that you can do? I want to kill you for what you have done!"**

"Abacore, is it?"

**"What do you want?"**

"I want you to think about something. Is one death the only reason why you are hunting my brother or is there another reason?"

Abacore glowered at him and his eyes sparked in rage, but he grounded out, **"You are downgrading the death of my family member. I don't think you understand the love and loyalty I had with the carriage handler. However, he, I believe, is the last one who had seen Rafeor, AND on top of that, made me lose an entire family AND…"**

"One thing at a time, please. Killian, explain something to me. Why did you kill the carriage handler?"

"It was not intentional. I tried to talk him out of it and let us go. However, he had his foot down, and I… I couldn't control my demon. He took over, and…"

"You couldn't control Falcor?"

I swallowed and my eyes flickered to Abacore before falling back onto Calio's again. He raised his eyebrows and growled, "Oh, didn't tell him that did you not?"

"No."

**"Tell me what?"**

Calio turned his attention to him before replying, "His demon's name. Do you know who he is?"

**"No."**

"Do you want to meet him?"

"Calio what are you doing?"

Abacore looked between and rumbled, **"Yes, I want to meet him."**

Calio looked back at me, growling out, "Killian, let him surface."

"I do not know what you are going to do with him. But fine."

*****

I zoned out, Falcor surfaced and he tried hard to not show his fear, but it radiated off of him for a moment. He calmed himself back down and hunched down for a fleeting second. Calio cleared his throat and looked expectantly at him before speaking, "Falcor, explain something to me, will you?"

"Y-ye-yes, Ca-Calio?"

"Why did you kill the carriage handler?"

I cowered before my brother and whispered, "I let my anger get the best of me…"

Severi flashed in his eyes and growled, "Louder, so Abacore can hear you."

My eyes flickered to his before raising my voice, "I let my anger get the best of me, Abacore. I am so so so sorry. I will not do it again."

**"You are banished from the shifter palace."**

I glanced sharply at Calio and was about to say something but Calio frowned and looked at Abacore before speaking, "You judge him roughly. If I am not wrong, then you are the one who should overall be banished from your kingdom and should be hunted down. Sonchis, do you know of anything about what this shifter king has done?"

A wolf, about hip height to me, looked at Calio with a look before replying, "I am not sure, my lord."

"Give your best guess, Sonchis."

He looked at Abacore before replying, "Based on your tone of voice, my lord. He had done something horrible and wrong. I am going to assume that he tried to cross into someone else's territory to gain land?"

"I would say close, but it is not quite that either. Falcor, what DID this shifter king do?"

I swallowed and did not know where Calio was going with this, but replied, "He killed the Druids off the face of the earth. Got several people killed, well, a couple of thousands. Also…"

"Enough."

I fell silent and looked at the wolves and saw their eyes flickering in rage before Calio asked Sonchis again, "So, Sonchis, what would you do?"

"Kill him."

"Oh? But you don't know him completely."

"Doesn't matter. Druids were a peaceful people, I always wondered where they all vanished to. They were being protected by the werewolf king further inland."

"You know about the werewolf king?"

"I have spoken with Wilson recently."

"Ah, that explains it."

Calio turned his attention to Abacore and spoke, "As you can see, Abacore, everyone here does not want you in our homeland. Alright, what I want you to do, is leave."

**"Not without him."**

"I am afraid that is not possible, Abacore. He is my younger brother, and therefore a sibling bond is in place. I will not allow him to be slaughtered."

**"Are you challenging me?"**

"Completely challenging you if you decide to attack us. You will have to get through me to get to my brother."

"Correction, my lord, he would have to get through me to get to him."

Sonchis positioned himself in front of Calio and the pack raised their haunches ready for attack before Abacore looked around. **"Why protect him?"**

"Why attack him when he has not slaughtered thousands?"

I bit my lip and knew that the wolves thought I did not kill anyone, but Calio glowered at me, and I kept quiet for now. Abacore glowered around, and growled, **"Fine, I will leave. What is your name?"**

He directed it to Calio but Calio smirked darkly, replying, "As if I would tell you that."

**"ANSWER ME!"**

Severi surfaced and he bellowed out, "YOU WILL LEARN YOUR PLACE!"

Abacore hunched down and lowered his eyes in submission. Severi panted in rage before biting out, "Leave my territory. And not in a fucking dragon form, Abacore. You can be in wolf form, but otherwise, NOTHING ELSE."

**"And what would you do if I don't?"**

"I will hunt you down personally. If you think Falcor is someone to be scared of, then I am much worse. Leave my territory and do not come back. Not without an army behind you since YOU ARE NOT ALLOWED ON MY TERRITORY AGAIN. GO!"

Abacore winced, backed off, and kept his head down before he turned to leave. He looked at Calio and spoke, **"I will kill Quinn and Herald when I get home."**

I stared at him and opened my mouth to speak, when Severi replied, "If you kill his offspring to get to us, that way. You should know that your daughter is fair game."

His eyes flickered to his eyes for a moment, and held it for a solid thirty seconds before he looked away, and swallowed. He was letting his anger surface, and finally, he disappeared from Morphous's eyes.

****

Morphous swayed back and forth before he fell and winced as he slowly looked around. He cursed and slowly rose before holding out his hands. Severi glowered, "Get off my territory."

**"I will. I apologize to you…. What is your name? Please, I do not mean any offense."**

"My name is Severi, and my human half is named Calio. I suggest you leave."

He looked at me before speaking, "**Killian, what Abacore said…. I will not let him touch Quinn or Herald. I simply request…**"

"You are overstaying your welcome. Leave."

Morphous glanced at Sonchis before snapping, "**Enough wolf. I am speaking, and you will obey.**"

"Like hell. My alpha is Calio. You would have to challenge him to become alpha."

At some point during their banter, Severi released Calio and Calio commanded, "Enough."

Sonchis fell silent and glowered at Morphous before turning his attention to Calio. Calio looked at Morphous. "What is your request?"

"**I request that I get my daughter back. I know you had someone inside the carriage and did not believe you would have taken Rafeor with you.**"

"I did not take her with me."

"**Where is she then? She has not been in her room…**"

"She is currently with the werewolves. With King Nathaniel."

"**Why not discuss that with me BEFOREHAND?**"

His eyes flashed for a moment, but Calio spoke, "Uh, uh, uh. Do not even start."

Morphous glanced at Calio and bowed slightly to him before looking at me and speaking, "**I just wished that you had consulted me in that information, Killian. You were my advisor before your son.**"

Falcor disappeared into my mind, and I was finally able to speak without speaking through him, "I apologize, Morphous."

He nodded and looked at Calio, asking, "**Out of curiosity, what is your last name?**"

Calio looked at me, raised his eyebrows in question, and I looked away before he turned his attention back to him, "Our last name is Benik."

His face went white and he glanced at both of us in shock before replying, "**So the rumors are true then. That the family line of the Benik's are surviving.**"

"Yes, now, my limited patience has ended, Shifter King. Please, leave my territory. I suggest wolf form since you will need to travel several leagues to leave."

"**Of course, Calio. Thank you for not killing me.**"

He shifted to his giant black wolf and the werewolves surrounding took a glance at Sonchis who had not budged, and stayed in place. But I could tell that they were wary of the size of him.

Morphous looked at Calio before dipping his head and looking towards the horizon and running.

It was a moment later that the wolves began to trot after him, making sure that he left the territory without taking anything along with him – leaving Sonchis, myself, and Calio standing there in silence.

Calio looked at Sonchis before growling, "Go to the ruins, Sonchis."

For a moment, he looked like he was going to refuse, but one glower later, he was high-tailing it back to the ruins.

****

Calio waited another minute before turning his attention to me, growling, "That… was… hmmm.…"

"I apologize, brother."

"It was thrilling though. Come along, brother, we can talk on the way back to my kills."

"Okay."

It was a few minutes before Calio spoke, "So what are you going to do now? You were banished from the shifter realm."

"I promised Falcor I would go hunting for those who escaped him. Along with going to get a girl from some mansion past the shifter realm."

"When do you leave for that?"

"After I bring the three that I had in a carriage back here. They are on the edge of the ruins, probably around three or four leagues away from there. Falcor had to drop them there."

"Ah, well, after I dig unmarked graves for these.…"

He went silent and I glanced up and saw why the humans were gone. He looked around before he growled, "What the hell?"

I went forward carefully, crouched down, and found multiple wolf prints before I looked over my shoulder at him and spoke, "Are you the only wolf pack in this area?"

"No."

"Well, it appears that whoever joins this part of the territory, got to them."

He came over, crouched down, and snarled. Severi was bright in his eyes as he snarled, "It appears I need to teach every bloody wolf here that I AM THE LAST ONE TO TAKE SOMETHING FROM!"

I swallowed, stood up, looked where the prints went, and started to follow. However, after a moment, Calio called out, finally able to control Severi, "Killian."

"Hmm?"

"We will leave this for the time being. We need to find the carriage that you brought."

"But…"

"Shush, Killian."

"Okay."

We turned around, unaware of the wolf that was watching. His eyes the color of burnt amber, and his coat a mix of black and gray, his height would rival anyone of alpha rank. He looked down at the killed humans, sniffed them once before he turned around, and walked back to the center of the wilderness. He would wait. He would find out who was in his territory.

# Chapter 30

I woke up in the shack, it was past the time that I normally get up, and for a split-second, fear set into me. I would normally get harshly scolded, and have extra chores added to my already large amount. I swallowed as I looked around the shack again though, and soon memories of what happened yesterday came into my mind and I cracked a small smile. I stood up and walked to the door, hesitating slightly before opening the door. The birds were chirping around, hopping from tree branch to tree branch, and the trees swayed gently in the breeze. I took a deep breath in and watched as the sun began to rise, a twig snapped and I jerked my head towards the sound. Azier approached me. She was in her wolf form, but I knew who it was. She glanced sideways and nosed her way into the shack, and I closed the door, already knowing what she was about to do. She shifted to her human form, and I swallowed hard if only I had my wolf, I could not think about that though. After a moment, Azier stood before me, dressed, since this is where they store clothing, and she smirked in response. I smiled slightly at her as I approached her for a hug. She embraced me and squeezed slightly before rocking us slightly side to side, giggling as she did it. She smiled before releasing me and stepped backward as my arms dropped to my side. She looked me up and down before speaking, "Wow, you woke up earlier than Cyprus would have thought. I am surprised though that Nathaniel had sent Cyprus to escort you."

"Why are you surprised?"

"Because we are typically always the ones to do the night patrols. Not watching someone."

"Oh, are you…."

"Aurelius, it doesn't matter. I would hang out with you anyhow. It was just a little surprise, that's all."

"So, who did the night patrol then last night?"

"I think Ash, and his team."

"Ash?"

"I don't really know if you know who Ash is, although I wouldn't doubt it that you had run across him more than once. Just didn't know his name."

"Oh, what about Sais?"

Her eyes flashed in response but she quickly tried to cover it again, before she could do anything. I swallowed, her wolf was pretty but she was dangerous. Any wolves were, and to be frank, living with werewolves was a little frightening when you didn't have one. I bowed my head after a moment, and Azier placed her right hand against my shoulder before speaking, "We took you here because we cannot trust him."

"Will he be banished?"

"No."

She let her hand fall away, as she turned slightly to face the wall before continuing, "You know the saying, keep your friends close, but your enemies closer?"

"Yeah, vaguely."

"Yeah, that is what Nathaniel is thinking of doing. Until Norjor and Finn come back, then we will keep our distance. Sais along with the majority of the pack does not know where you are located and do not get comfortable, it is only a matter of time before we have to move to another site."

"Why move?"

"Because this site may become compromised."

"Oh…. do…. Do you know why you are even protecting me?"

"I do not question Basil's link, neither does any sane wolf. He appointed us to protect you at any costs until Finn comes back, Aurelius. We cannot be bought, we cannot be tortured for information. We cannot be swayed from our duties."

"Basil had you do this?"

"Aurelius, why ask? You are worth being around. Stop fretting about what Basil does and start looking towards the future. I hear that Finn is highly sought after."

I blushed and she chuckled slightly before grinning at me. I bowed my head and walked towards the bed before speaking softly, "I found out information yesterday, Azier. Something that now makes sense."

She frowned and glanced at the door. "Link with me, Aurelius."

I glanced up at her and swallowed as I linked with her, *"I learned why I don't have a wolf."*

*"What? You had one?"*

*"I had one when I was very young. She came too early, and she was killed."*

*"Who killed her?"*

*"According to Logan, himself, but there is something else….."*

*"Logan? The king's brother, Logan?"*

*"Azier, there is something else. But yes, him."*

She stared at me and her wolf glinted in her eyes but she replied, *"What else?"*

*"Logan is my stepfather."*

*"Wait…. But he…. He killed your wolf…. What?"*

*"Yeah. And I only know that he is my stepfather because I…. I guess I can't really out the king with his privacy areas. However, I found out that Logan is my stepfather, AND that he had two children…."*

*"Wait…. Are you… are you supposed to tell anyone this, Aurelius?"*

*"I wasn't supposed to hear any of this, Azier."*

*"Then don't tell me everything."*

*"But…"*

*"I am sorry, Aurelius, but I cannot be the one to be told everything. However, it now makes sense on WHERE Basil was going to place you."*

*"Oh, ok."*

She came over to the bed and rested her hands on my shoulders before speaking aloud, "Hey, keep your head up though. It means that you are not someone to pick on."

"But no one knows, Azier."

She frowned and glanced at the door before replying, "It doesn't matter. However, I believe it is time that you go to the training room now. We don't want to keep Marius waiting."

I swallowed hard before whispering, "But what about Sais?"

"Don't think about him. We won't leave you today."

"But wouldn't that make it hard on you? You and your team members?"

"Aurelius, we were tasked with keeping you safe. That is our current duty. None of my team would do anything else. They want to serve."

"How are you so sure?"

"Come on."

She opened the door and I saw the rest of her team members: Cyprus, Batis, Brego, and Ghost. They were all in their wolf forms, but I knew their colorations at this point. I swallowed and knew that Cyprus, Batis, and Azier were siblings, but Brego and Ghost were their most trusted friends. I looked away before speaking, "Hi."

They blinked at me and Azier gently bumped into me before whispering, "Let's go."

"Alright."

Brego and Ghost turned around and trotted away, leading the way out, Cyprus and Batis looked at Azier for a moment before walking away. I swallowed as I walked, suddenly realizing that they had left the way they did to keep me as safe as possible. Keeping the most prized being in the center, since I noticed that Batis went off to the left, and Cyprus went off to the right, disappearing into the woods. I knew they were all within eyesight of me. Azier bumped into me and linked her elbow through mine before slightly pulling me towards the mansion. I let her lead me towards it.

*****

I paced back and forth before slamming my fists against the desk. Where could that brat of a man be? I thought she did not have friends. She did not have anyone. I stared hard at the indents that my fists had made in the wood, I smirked slightly before straightening myself slightly and shaking my hands off, glancing down at the redness of my hands. I glanced around my room and knew that it may look like a disaster to someone who didn't know what to look for, but everything was where it should be. A knock sounded on the door, and I sighed deeply as I walked towards it. Pausing as I caught the scent on the other side. What did he want? I thought as I opened the door.

In the hallway, stood Enix, and he looked pissed. I rolled my eyes and stepped backward before gesturing to him to come inside. I closed the door after him before speaking, "What do you want, brother?"

"I want you to explain something to me, Sais. There is a rumor that you poisoned a drink this afternoon, one that I should mention could have been Nathaniel's."

"Ah, that little itsy bitsy detail."

"Why?"

"Because he was not my target. There was someone else I was targeting, Enix, and that someone was in the office with Nathaniel."

"Regardless of whom you were targeting, Sais, what the hell were you thinking? What if you had poisoned the king? What then?"

"Then it would have fallen to Logan...."

"Are you nuts? No one would follow Logan. He is not smart enough to lead the entire werewolf population. On top of what he used to do… he doesn't have the respect that Nathaniel or Tobiashas ."

"Ugh, shut it."

Enix growled at me before snarling, "You know that Nathaniel is going to possibly banish or kill you depending on how Basil is in the mood or not. There would be nothing I can do to stop him from doing it either."

"Ugh. Shut up."

"Is this some sort of joke to you, Sais? What would our father say to this behavior of yours anyhow? He would be ashamed that his youngest son tried to kill someone."

I did not reply, and looked at a pile of scraps before replying, "Are you done lecturing me, Enix?"

He stared at me before shaking his head and growling, "What is wrong with you, Sais? You used to be a better man, a better brother, a better warrior. Now though? I am surprised that the new Lycan did not banish or kill you."

My head snapped up before I replied, "She's a Lycan? How is that possible? I thought only Nathaniel had a Lycan."

"As if I would tell you that piece of information after what you have done as is. Has it occurred to you, that being on cleaning duty is something that you should be doing right now, instead of moping around in your disgusting room?"

"It is not disgusting, Enix, I know where everything is."

"Sure, you do. However, I would suggest that you do what Basil ordered you to do."

I scoffed and turned slightly, growling after a moment, "Enix?"

"What?"

"Get out."

"Nah, I'm good."

"I wasn't asking. Get out."

"Sais."

"Out."

He came over to me,  stopped within striking distance, and rumbled, "No, I am here to babysit you since you cannot be trusted."

"On whose authority?"

"Nathaniel's."

I scowled before growling, "Get out of my face then."

"No. I do have another question."

"What is your question?"

"If you did not target Nathaniel, then who did you target?"

"The bitch, Aurelius."

"Why?"

"Because she refused me. She is nothing but a freaking tool and is milking everything that she can before she is…."

"Did you not hear that she has a mate?"

"I heard, I was surprised that Finn did not reject the bitch."

"Why are you so cruel all of a sudden towards Aurelius, Sais? There has to be more than the reasoning you gave."

I paused and did not reply. There was something else, but I was forbidden to tell anyone, otherwise, I would die. I sighed deeply before replying, "I am tired of this conversation, Enix. if you are going to follow me around, so be it. However, fucking keep your fucking distance."

I grabbed the door before he replied, "Sais."

"Hmm?"

"I should warn you. You are on thin ice with Nathaniel. If it wasn't for me, you would be in the dungeons currently. I argued to keep you where you currently are. Do not make me regret that decision."

I paused before turning the door knob and exiting the room, followed closely by Enix.

*******

We entered the training room, and I looked around before coming to terms that I was no longer in the need to keep the room tidy. Another omega was wiping the floors down, and the patrol walked straight through the area where she was waxing. I could see the look across her face, the crestfallen look before she got more wax out and tried to wash their muddy prints off again. I froze and stared at the backs of Cyprus and Batis, speaking, "How rude can you four be?"

They froze and turned their attention back to me. Cyprus looked at Azier, returning his attention to me again and speaking, "What?"

"Did you not pay attention to what she is doing?"

They glanced at the omega, who might I add wanted to disappear suddenly, and cowered before Cyprus. Cyprus looked at me again before raising his eyebrow, "Huh?"

I shook my head before replying, "Unbelievable. You have just walked across a freshly waxed portion of the floor without a single glance at the ground before you. Have you always treated the omegas as trash as you are currently as they work?"

"I…"

Cyprus trailed off and frowned as he looked down at the floor before noticing that it was shining against the ground. He looked at me again before speaking, "I will keep a look out from now on, Aurelius."

I rolled my eyes, and was about to drop down to the ground before a voice I knew and caused dread in my stomach, spoke from behind me, "Oooh, what is this? The five that are ALWAYS tasked to do the night patrols to be….With her?"

I felt Azier tense beside me before she looked over her shoulder at Sais and replied, "Sais."

"Azier."

For a moment, there was a tension in the air among the eight of us, the omega caught in the center of it, and was cowering before us. I glanced down at her and wanted to help her to her feet, but she just withdrew further back until her back slightly hit the wall.

I glanced at Sais and sighed before speaking, "What do you want, Sais?"

His head jerked to mine; his eyes flashed before he rumbled, "Did I give you…."

"Sais."

Azier glanced further back and blocked my vision on who spoke, but I knew the voice, it was Enix, who was I think five or six years older than Sais who was seventeen currently. Enix was a better man than Sais and was someone who always made sure that nothing was coming off. He was highly respectable and would make a great delta if he ever claimed it. However, I knew that this family line did not seek out ranks, but I could tell that Sais may one day challenge it. I swallowed, a day that I hoped would never come to be.

Enix approached and his footfalls echoed before he rumbled, "Sais, you know better."

"Shut it, Enix."

"No."

Sais looked at his brother with a hard look, but I could tell that the one to win that fight would be Enix, he was built and stood at six foot three, and Sais was only six foot, so a few inches taller than him. His hair was wavy black, and his eyes were normally relaxed. However, these were the most intense eyes I had seen him wear, his wolf slightly surfacing which was rare to see. Sais looked like he was about to challenge his brother when Cyprus spoke, "Sais."

Sais looked at Cyprus before grunting in response, and Cyprus continued, "Behave yourself. Or should I mention that Basil wanted to kill you? You had crossed enough lines, and the last one was last night. If Enix did not do what he is currently doing, you would be in an unmarked grave."

I saw Sais swallow hard; he growled, "He doesn't scare me."

"But he should…"

I whispered as I thought I said it in my mind. However, he went rigid as he threw daggers at me, snapping, "You should have drank that poison! Then you would not be here! If only you had done so!"

"That is treasonous action that you speak of, Sais. Have you forgotten who you are standing before?"

He went silent as he observed who stood before him, he glanced sharply at me and spoke, "I can take you all cowards!"

"Sais."

Enix tried again to intervene, but Sais lost his cool and tried to do something, but since the floor was freshly waxed, the obvious thing happened – he slipped and skidded past me and Azier, and hit the other wall. He growled out, his wolf flickering in his eyes as he scrambled to his feet.

Azier stepped slightly in front of me before speaking, "Enough."

He glowered at her. "No!"

******

He took a step forward when a voice called out, "What is going on out here?"

I glanced up and saw Marius walking downstairs, barefoot as always when he was heading to the training room. He stopped and assessed the ones in the hallway. What he thought was a mystery, but he looked at the omega before speaking, "Alice, can you please leave?"

"Of course!"

She scrambled away, and I swallowed as I watched her run away, something about the name Alice made me long to talk to that name. I bowed my head, but Azier elbowed me slightly, I snapped my head up and swallowed as I saw Sais staring at me with rage in his eyes. However, he did not try to do anything. That would result in his death, and he knew it if he moved.

Marius looked further before calling out, "Enix, what is going on here?"

"I apologize, Marius, I did not realize that Aurelius would be down this hallway."

Marius glanced at me, replying, "Did anything happen?"

"No, Marius, nothing happened," I half whispered.

He looked at me and smiled slightly before turning his attention to Sais and speaking, "Sais."

"Yes, Marius?"

"Do not make me do something that I will have to live with for the rest of my days."

I could tell that Sais wanted to challenge that but soon looked away as Marius glowered at him when he noticed Onyx surfaced slightly in his eyes. I swallowed hard but kept my head up, I was not going to compromise myself to Sais – not again.

Sais pulled himself up and stood on shaky legs, rumbling, "I will find you later, bitch."

"SAIS!"

He froze as Marius barked out his name, he turned around and looked at him before replying, "What?"

"Apologize to Aurelius."

"No."

"Apologize."

Sais straightened himself and growled out, "No."

Onyx glinted in his eyes and was about to reply when a voice called from above Marius, **"You are testing my patience, Sais. Did I not say that you would regret doing anything else to Aurelius?"**

Power oozed from the stairs, and even Marius winced as the power passed him, but it was not directed at him. It appeared that Shadow had learned to channel the power towards a certain person, and I saw Sais go white before he stuttered, "I-I- I.."

**"Enough. Marius, move out of the way, please."**

Marius moved to the right and Rafeor appeared, but her eyes were turquoise which I had noticed was the eyes of her Lycan. Sais lowered himself slightly before mumbling, "Please…."

**"You challenged my authority. You challenged…"**

Marius placed his hand on their arm, and she fell silent slightly before closing her eyes and rumbling, **"Get out of my sight, Sais."**

He scrambled out of the hallway, but not before glowering at me as he passed me. Azier's eyes flashed, but she did not do anything. However, I noticed that she had a hand grabbing her blade on her hip, watching him, not trusting him. The hallway was tense until Sais had disappeared.

Enix looked at me before speaking, "I apologize for his behavior, Aurelius."

"Enix."

"Yes, Marius?"

"If he steps out of line again, then he will be killed."

Enix swallowed before whispering, "Understood."

Enix turned around and started to follow where Sais went.

****

I looked at Marius and Rafeor before smiling at Rafeor. She was in control again, but she frowned as she watched as Enix left, knowing that Sais would be dead if Shadow took control of her. She sighed and looked at Marius before smiling at him, and speaking, **"Are we still doing the training?"**

Marius glanced at me and said, "Aurelius? Are you still up to train?"

"Yes, Marius."

"Good."

He paused as he looked at the five before speaking, "Cyprus, Azier, Batis, Brego, and Ghost. What are your plans?"

"We were tasked to do whatever Aurelius was to do until Finn came back."

"Ah, so you are joining us?"

"Yes, sir."

"Good. Then we must not delay further then. Come along."

They moved across the floor and I swallowed as I tried hard to not think about what Alice would have to do to get it to gleam again when she came back to do her work.

****

Cyprus linked me, and I opened the line before speaking, *"**What is it, Cyprus?**"*

*"Forgive me, my lord, however, you told me to report to you."*

*"**Go ahead.**"*

*"We had a small issue with Sais, luckily Marius and Rafeor arrived before he could do anything. However…."*

*"**Sais is good as fucking DEAD!**"*

*"M-m-my…."*

*"**Give a moment, Cyprus.**"*

*"Yes, my lord."*

I dropped his connection as I sighed deeply. I had not left my office when Aurelius left, I knew that Cyprus would not take her to the room. We had agreed that it was not safe inside for her while Finn was out, so I had given him and the team the task of keeping her safe, and keeping me updated with anything major.

I sighed in my connection with Basil before speaking, *"**Basil?**"*

*"**We should have killed that bastard when we had the chance to!**"*

*"**We shouldn't kill him.**"*

*"**Why the fuck not?**"*

*"**Have you forgotten who his father is?**"*

Basil was quiet for a moment and finally, he hedged out, *"**Not forgotten on who he was, Nathaniel. Cannot forget him.**"*

*"He may have crossed many lines as is Basil, but we should think of something else besides death for him. In honor of what his father had done."*

*"What do you suggest we do with him? Enix is good, but Sais? Sais is corrupted."*

*"I know, but we cannot kill Kaylon's son. We can probably banish him, or imprison him, but we should not kill."*

*"I miss Kaylon."*

*"I know, I do too."*

We fell into silence, before Basil asked, *"**What now, Nathaniel?**"*

*"**Now, we find out what Cyprus has to report. See if Sais should be banished or imprisoned.**"*

*"**Okay.**"*

I waited another moment before reaching back out to Cyprus, and he instantly opened the link again, speaking, *"My lord?"*

*"**Go ahead with your report, Cyprus.**"*

*"Of course."*

The things he recounted for me, made me want to strangle Sais, but Kaylon was in the front of our mind now and after a few minutes, Cyprus stopped talking. I waited another heartbeat before asking, *"**Anything else?**"*

*"No, my lord."*

*"**Alright, keep me posted.**"*

*"My lord?"*

*"**Yes, Cyprus?**"*

*"May I ask you a question?"*

*"**Go ahead.**"*

*"What is so important about Aurelius?"*

I paused before sighing deeply, and Basil linked me for a split second, *"**It is better if they knew.**"*

*"**Alright.**"*

I turned my attention to Cyprus's link before replying, *"**I would rather tell you that in person, Cyprus. Come to my office.**"*

*"Do you want me to leave Aurelius?"*

*"Are you in the training room?"*

*"Yes."*

*"Then she is safe, bring along the rest of your patrol. You all need to know this."*

*"And leave Aurelius?"*

*"Rafeor and Marius are there, correct?"*

*"Yes, my lord."*

*"Then she will be safe. I will personally inform Marius."*

*"Thank you, my lord. See you in a couple of minutes."*

He let the link close, and I instantly linked Marius, *"Marius?"*

*"Yes, my liege?"*

*"I'm filling in the patrol on the importance of Aurelius. She will be with you and Rafeor."*

*"Anything else, my lord?"*

*"No."*

*"Okay."*

He dropped the connection and I waited.

*****

It was indeed a couple of minutes before Cyprus knocked on my door. I opened the door and Cyprus bowed his head to me before Azier followed him inside. Soon, the patrol was inside and I closed my door before speaking, "**I am sure you have your questions. However, I need to clear something up now. Do not tell anyone else this information. No one else is to know.**"

"Yes, my lord!"

They all clambered at once. I sighed deeply before walking around my desk and resting along its edges before speaking, "**Aurelius is my step-niece. She was Logan's mate's daughter, whom I recently found out was killed in childbirth a month or so ago before the fight with the Willow moon pack. Which is why her last name is Fiore.**"

I paused as they absorbed to information and Azier frowned before asking, "If she is family, then why was she positioned into the maid work?"

**"Because Logan did not want her to be known that they are related somehow. Apparently, Logan had other children, but when Morphous attacked the druids, they perished alongside them."**

Bergo jerked his head in response to that, and looked at Ghost before speaking, "Are we sure that his children are dead? Or did someone take the children?"

I frowned, I hadn't thought of that and I looked at him with a questioning look across my face and he swallowed before speaking again, "In our legends, there is a wolf that is more powerful than all. With markings and patterns, that when Herald showed up…. And his markings…."

He trailed off and went quiet after a moment. I frowned, but if that was the case, then what about the other child? I thought. Did Morphous indeed save both of the children and did not slaughter everyone? I suddenly wondered. However, Cyprus spoke drawing me out of my thoughts, "I was curious on that aspect too. Now that it makes sense. Could Herald be one of the lost children that Prince Logan had lost? How many children did Logan have with his mate?"

**"Two."**

"Unknown about the second one, but could it be possible that Herald is Logan's son? Since our legends are based on royal blood having a higher-ranked wolf. But does that mean the other part of the prophecy is correct too? That the war is coming?"

Silence surrounded us and I was about to reply when Bergo replied, "Well, if we think about that aspect, Rafeor is here. And she is a hybrid. However, I think there is more than one prophecy regarding Rafeor. However, we need to touch base on that later. My lord?"

**"Yes, Brego?"**

"Anything else on Aurelius we should know about?"

I thought a moment before slowly shaking my head in response, **"Not that I can come up with."**

"Okay. Do you want us to head back to the training room to be with Aurelius?"

**"Not yet, we now have some digging to do."**

"My lord?"

**"Yes, Cyprus?"**

"If Aurelius is indeed royalty, at least partially, does that mean that she gets royal guards following her?"

I paused before shaking my head and replying, **"No, if I do so then Logan will throw a fit."**

"He doesn't want anyone to know what Aurelius is?"

**"Aurelius is the last of what he has of his mate. He will not cast her away, even though that she is not his by blood."**

"Oh."

I glanced at Azier and noticed that she looked like she knew something, and I had a hunch that Aurelius had told her something. I sighed before asking, "**Azier, you are offly silent.**"

She looked up at me and bit her lip slightly, replying, "There is one other thing that you did not discuss, my lord."

**"What is that?"**

She hesitated before linking me, "*The fact on why she doesn't have a wolf.*"

**"She told you?"**

"*Tried to…*"

I looked at the others who seemed a little distrustful of what Azier and I spoke about. I sighed deeply before speaking aloud, "**I guess there is one other thing about Aurelius that you guys should know.**"

"And that is?"

**"She used to have a wolf."**

Silence. Their eyes were a mix between their wolves and their natural eyes, as they processed that information. Finally, after a few moments, Brego spoke, "What happened to her wolf?"

**"Logan told me that he had to put the wolf down. She caught him doing something, and one thing led to another, and he had to kill her wolf."**

"What could possibly happen for that to occur? He made a young woman suffer abuse…."

Brego trailed off and looked away, shaking his head before Azier asked, "So, Logan is her stepfather, and yet he was the one who killed her wolf. And…."

She trailed off as if could not wrap her head around it. Ghost looked at me after a moment, his eyes were very light blue, so light blue that they looked white, but he rumbled after a moment, "It doesn't matter. We have a friend that needs our help. This new information is needed, yes. But it is not something we should use to be pitiful towards Aurelius. She must know this information, correct?"

**"Yes."**

He looked at Cyprus before speaking, "We will not treat her differently then. We know her history, but that is something that she may have warmed up to us to tell us in person. We will support her throughout the heartaches that she will have. At least, until Finn comes back. Which reminds me, why didn't you have us track Norjor?"

**"Because I needed someone to keep Aurelius safe. Especially after Sais tried to poison her."**

Their eyes flashed in anger at that, and Cyprus asked the question, "May I ask you a question, my lord?"

**"Of course."**

"If Sais indeed poisoned a thing of water, then why is he allowed to move as he is?"

**"It is in honor of his father, to be frank."**

"Who was his father?"

**"Kaylon."**

A collection of gasps went up. I smirked slightly and knew that they all remembered Kaylon. After a few minutes, they fell silent, and finally, Brego asked, "So in honor of Kaylon, his son is safe from what you normally would do to a wolf that had done what he had done?"

I swallowed and bowed my head slightly, staring at the floor before replying, "**Indeed.**"

****

Azier glanced around the room and sighed deeply before speaking, "What is done is done. However, one question remains."

**"And what is that?"**

"If the legends are correct, that a war is coming, then are we prepared for it?"

Her question was severely left-field, I thought she would ask a question about Aurelius, but that was a valid question. I opened my mouth to reply but stopped after a moment and sighed deeply before replying, "**No, we are not. I was not planning on doing anything on that front.**"

"If the legends are true, then Rafeor is the greatest weapon to be. However, if Herald is indeed a lost child of Logan, then it would make me wonder what is in store. I thought that they would not be roughly the same age."

I sighed deeply as I was about to reply when Ghost spoke, "Cyprus, one day at a time. We will make everything work. I have a feeling that is why you sent Tobias out toward the outlander's territory. To collect their ruthlessness?"

I frowned and replied, after a moment, **"How did you know that?"**

"Are you forgetting that Tobias had children already Nathaniel? Or should I say, Uncle?"

I fell silent and shook my head in response, I forgot that Tobias had children, and Ghost was one of them. He smirked in response before turning his attention to his comrades and speaking, "Alright for now, we should head back to the training center. So, we can catch a few sparring lessons ourselves. Cyprus, are you up for the challenge to go up against me?"

Cyprus grinned widely, and replied, "Of course, Ghost."

He smiled slightly before turning his attention to me and asking, "With your leave, my lord?"

**"Oh, go ahead."**

"Thank you, my lord."

Ghost opened the door and they all exited except for Azier. Who looked at Batis before shutting the door behind them.

*****

She turned towards me before speaking, "We need to talk."

**"About?"**

"We need to do it elsewhere, Nathaniel. Don't you have somewhere hidden?"

I paused and looked at her before gesturing towards the bookcase, pulling the red bounded book towards me, and opening the hidden passage. If she was surprised. she did not show it, and entered the room, and up the stairs. I looked behind me, before shutting the entrance.

*****

I followed Marius and the others into the training room when Cyprus and Marius exchanged glances as they headed out of the room. Azier squeezed my arm and smiled slightly before speaking, "You will be safe with Marius and Rafeor for a while. We will come back in a bit."

"Where are you going?"

"We have to report to Nathaniel."

"Oh. Okay."

She squeezed me again and walked after her patrol. I swallowed as I watched them disappear down the hallway leading away from me, and glanced at Marius who was watching me. He smiled when we made eye contact and it eased my mind slightly as he did. I knew I would be safe with Marius.

Rafeor walked close to me and bumped into me with her shoulder, before smiling at me. She did not say anything, but she got me to smile back, which I assumed was her goal. She grinned at me before she skipped away. Yes, skipped away. I saw Marius's eyes flash with Onyx before he looked at me, he appeared to be happy, and I noticed though they did not have a mated mark on them. I swallowed and touched my mate mark, wishing that Finn was there with me.

Marius spoke, "Alright, Rafeor, come back here. Aurelius, come forward please."

I walked across the room and sat down next to Marius, who had sat down, and after a moment, Rafeor came and sat down. She looked expectantly at Marius. I glanced at him and frowned but did not say anything. He sighed before speaking, "Before we train today, we need to stretch first. Keep one leg stretched out in front, or to the side and lean forward. You should feel a little burn or your muscles pulling. But do not go to the point where it hurts. Try to touch your toes with your fingers."

I did as he said, and as much as I tried, I could not reach my toes. I kept trying, but it was indeed a burning sensation and I knew better than to push myself further. Soon after, we switched to the other leg, and then Marius spoke, "Good job, ladies. Now, lift one arm into the air, over your head, and with the other hand grab your wrist. You should feel some pull again."

I did this one and winced as I heard my shoulder pop in response, and I could tell that Marius heard it too. He frowned before he looked at Rafeor, and noticed that she had tried to pull her shirt back down since it had ridden up. I could see Onyx in his eyes again, but I could not tell if he was aroused or if he was in anger. However, he dimmed away, and soon Marius was in control again. He glanced at me before speaking, "Switch."

We switched arms and soon after a few moments, he stood up and spoke, "Okay, now that you are properly somewhat warmed up. I want you to run the perimeter of the hall. Four times."

"Four?"

I asked in disbelief. He smirked in response and replied, "Yes, four, and normally anyone who questions my warm-ups, I would add another two. Don't question me again, Aurelius."

I went white and shrunk down slightly in response. He smiled slightly before turning to Rafeor and speaking, "No shifting. Human form only."

I swallowed and knew that it was solely because of me that he said that. But I could tell that Rafeor did not think that. That I was the only one to think that, and she replied, "**As if I was going to.**"

He chuckled in response and raised his eyebrows at us. "Well? What are you waiting for? Get going."

****

I should mention now that, normally, the only running I would do is when someone forgot to do a room when we had someone important show up. That was the point that I would do the running. What he asked for us to do, damn was I going to feel it tomorrow, or worse yet afterward.

Rafeor and I jogged the first lap around, but even she had issues, she grimaced once before muttering, "**He acted as if this was easy….**"

I would have laughed if it wasn't for the stitch in my side already. I was sweating profusely. Around the second lap, was when the patrol came back, except for Azier. However, they did not seem perplexed by that. I heard Marius speak to them for a moment before they waited for us to pass them before joining.

I glanced at Bergo before breezing, "Hello again."

"Hello, Aurelius. Alright, after you are done, you and I are going to square off."

"What? You have to be kidding. I'm already regretting having to do this."

He chuckled, before running ahead. He did it so quietly that both Rafeor and I exchanged glances, as the four of them rounded the corner silently, as if they were not there. Our footfalls were loud and smacking the floors. Theirs? Hell, they were silent.

They rounded the next corner, and the next one.  Soon, they overcame us even and made a whole lap by the time we reached the fourth lap. By then, my legs were jelly and I stumbled, and finally, my body had enough, and I would have fallen flat on my face if it wasn't for Ghost to catch me.

375

He eased me down before looking down at me. He raised his eyebrows before Brego made it to me, coming to a stop. He looked down at me, and I panted before wheezing, "I…. I… c-ca-can't d-do t-th-this…."

Ghost and Brego exchanged glances as Ghost looked down at me with a smirk. "Oh Aurelius, you cannot be tired already. We have only done a small warm-up."

"You have been doing this way longer than I have though! This is the most running I have done."

I saw the laughter in their eyes, and I groaned back at them and whispered, "Go away…"

Cyprus came around the corner, slowed down, leaned down, and passed me a cup of water. I took it and panted before wiping my brow and looking at him. He smiled down upon me before speaking, "We should have known that you are too soft for the challenges."

"Am not!"

"Are too!"

"Am not!"

"Are too!"

He stuck out his tongue at me. And for whatever reason, that made me get up and lunge at him. As if he knew I would do that, he took off running. I ran after him. I followed him for a whole lap before stopping, breathing hard. Sweat dripping into my eyes and everything. I felt gross. Cyprus chuckled before coming to a stop a few feet from me and looking at me again, "And here I thought you were slow. I actually had to push myself a little."

I scowled at him and would have said something, but Marius spoke, "Enough."

I looked over at him and saw Rafeor standing beside him, breathing hard a little, but not by a lot. She was more fit than I was. I lowered my head in shame as if they knew what I was thinking. Ghost and Brego came towards me, bumping gently into my shoulders. Ghost spoke, "You did good for the first time. Normally, no one gets past the first lap around."

"Huh?"

"Most people don't finish their first lap before they quit. You did good at keeping your pace, and keeping your spirits up," replied Brego, who looked at Ghost, having their private conversation and smirking at me again. I rolled my eyes as I looked at Marius, who stood patiently waiting for them to finish teasing me.

Once he had our attention, he went to clap his hands before stopping himself midway, speaking, "Alright, Brego, you are paired with Aurelius. Do not harm her. She heals the same as a human, unfortunately."

I looked down and swallowed hard, but Ghost grabbed my chin gently, lifted it upwards, and spoke softly, "It does not matter, Aurelius. If you have a wolf or not. You are you."

The way he said it, I could almost tell that he knew that I had lost my wolf, not being born without one. I lost her. I could see the flicker in his eyes that he knew. I tried to bow my head against his, but he shook his head before whispering, "It matters not, Aurelius."

I didn't reply and looked away as he released me gently. I glanced at Marius and saw him frown slightly, but did not intervene. Whatever was going on was something that he did not entirely know either. However, I did not want to say anything. Especially now. You never know who was watching the training hall.

*****

Brego led me toward a mat in the center of the training hall. He stepped up the three steps up, and I followed him. I swallowed as I saw small divots here and there, knowing that someone had smashed someone down hard enough to leave marks. He snapped his fingers a few times and I drew my eyes up to him before smiling slightly. He frowned but did not make an effort to really do anything else. He glanced at Marius who had come over, and Rafeor and Batis came up onto the platform. I could tell that Batis was uncertain about what he was to do with her. Marius approached both the pairs before speaking, "Block and defense. No shifting. No drawing blood. Defensive and offensive. Since Rafeor and Aurelius are new to this, Batis, Brego, and I expect that they will have bruises, but nothing more than that. Got it?"

"Yes, sir."

"Yes, sir."

They both replied and glanced at each other smirking. I rolled my eyes and panted before asking, "Can't we wait a few minutes?"

Marius looked at me, and then glanced at Rafeor before smirking, "No."

"Ugh!"

I groaned, and Marius smirked, but walked away from us without replying. He sat down with his legs in a relaxed position and spoke, "Alright. Rafeor, you are on the defensive side. Aurelius, you are offensive."

I glanced at Rafeor and saw her grumbled, but she asked the question I was curious on too, **"What is the difference between those exactly?"**

Marius opened his mouth to reply, but a voice boomed out, **"What is going on here?"**

****

Marius winced and glanced up at the balcony that was above the training room. An area that I was previously never allowed to enter. Only older maids were allowed up there to clean it. I glanced up at Logan, and I knew by the tension in the air, that no one seemed to want to answer him. Even from here, he smelled of booze. I glanced at Brego, but he shook his head slightly. He glanced at Marius and waited for him to say something.

Marius sighed deeply before speaking, "Can I help you with something, my lord?"

**"It highly depends on what SHE is doing with you."**

I had since turned my back to him, but could tell that he was pointing at me. I swallowed hard, and tried hard not to shake. By the way that Brego shifted his footing, he knew something. I glanced slightly at Rafeor and saw her clenching her fists, and her eyes flicker different colors as if she was going to have her Lycan surface.

Marius glanced at me and replied, "Your brother ordered that she was to be taught how to defend herself."

I could sense that Logan was staring daggers down at my back; he growled, **"And what is HE to her?"**

I could tell that everyone in the room shifted their feet, as if they knew who he was to me even, and I finally turned my head to look up at him before replying, "He is my king."

He looked down at me with a scowl, surely expecting something else. However, no one moved, or said anything else. I could sense that Ghost and Cyprus had moved slowly forward from the other training mat, as if they would be a match for him. I couldn't tell if Logan noticed or not, since he was drunk.

Soon, they were beside our mat. Cyprus called up, "Care to join us Logan in our training?"

**"No."**

"Why not?"

**"Because I already know who you four are. You are Nathaniel's CHOSEN ONES! The batch of wolves that are even slightly above the precious elites. The ones that are…"**

**"What was that brother?"**

I didn't know when Nathaniel entered the training room, but Azier followed him after a moment, and were both looking up at Logan. Logan sneered at him before snapping, **"We all know that you favor these five wolves! Admit it!"**

**"I do not have to admit anything, Logan. They are, after all, close to becoming part of the royal guards. Training to be them actually."**

I glanced at Brego and noticed he looked at Cyprus before smirking slightly, before returning his attention to Logan on the balcony.

I could tell that he was shocked. To say, I wasn't would be a lie too, it made sense now on why they were the most trusted guards, and patrol. They were the ones who were filling in times that no one else wanted, and they did so ever so diligently. I glanced at Ghost and Cyprus, and knew that they both were the ones who should already be in the royal guards – since that was the highest ranking you could be, and they both were higher than omegas. I glanced at Brego and Batis, they did not have delta or gamma blood, but they were both powerful wolves. I glanced at Azier, and did not know what was so special about her, but knew that she was someone to not mess around with. This was, after all, her team, not Cyprus's or Ghost's. She was the one that got them together. She was the starter of these five.

My attention drifted back to the conversation, which was currently between Logan and Cyprus, "Oh come now, Logan! You haven't had any training in a few years, surely you are itching to fight off some steam."

**"You just want to make a fool of myself!"**

"Am not!"

**"Are too!"**

"Not!"

**"Shut your mouth, Cyprus! You know that you would make a pancake of me in a heartbeat."**

"Your words not mine, Logan."

Logan snarled and his eyes glimmered. Nathaniel glanced at Cyprus before speaking, **"Cyprus?"**

"Yes, my lord?"

**"Do not push Logan into fighting you. You will wish you weren't in the crossfire."**

**"Oh? Even my elder brother is scared of me! See, Cyprus? He is keeping you safe."**

"I would like to challenge that though, Logan. When I do become a royal guard, how would I learn more better than training with you? At least once a week. To see if I can successfully beat you. Either way, it is a good training session. That way I learn, and you get to practice, instead of the route you are down."

**"What is that supposed to mean?"**

"I want you to be my training comrade, Logan. I want a fight. I want a challenge. Don't get me wrong, Ghost is pretty good, but I know his moves as is. Since we have worked together for years and years. Why not have you be my training partner for a few hours?"

Logan was silent and stared down upon us all. Nathaniel held out his left hand, and started to count backwards. When he hit one, Logan replied, **"Fine."**

He gripped the railing, leaped off the balcony, rolled to his feet, and popped back up. He fell with a thud, but that was to be expected since he was even taller than his elder brother. He fell roughly twenty or so feet to hard wood floors. He strode over and gave me a hard look before facing Nathaniel and speaking, **"Don't you have some paperwork to do?"**

**"Perhaps, perhaps not. However, watching training is also important."**

Logan scowled at him but said nothing else. Since I think he knew that Nathaniel usuall at least twice to four times a week did check on the training. Which made it more enjoyable to the pack, since their king was checking in on them. It boosted everyone's moods up when he showed.

****

It was about a half hour before Logan panted and backed away from Cyprus, who was panting and looked scary. He looked like he would kill someone with that look. We had all taken a break, when they squared off. More of to see them fight, since none of the normal guards have seen the five fight, it even drew some passing guards' attentions. And it quickly spread that the five were in the training hall. Soon, around forty wolves were watching the match.

Logan had won, of course, but Cyprus had given him a good run for his money at the same time. It was a ferocious match, and one that Cyprus would continue to feel. Logan may be drunk, but he was not drunk enough to not beat Cyprus's butt.

Cyprus panted and looked around the room, and his eyes landed on me before he grinned wickedly. Ghost approached them, got onto the mat and looked at Logan before speaking, "Do you still have steam, Logan?"

**"Why? You want a butt whipping too?"**

"Like Cyprus mentioned earlier, it would be a good training experience. But if you want to call it a butt whipping, then sure. That is if you can give me a butt whipping."

He was taunting him, and a collective "Oooh" was heard from the ones watching. They looked at each other. Soon, after a few minutes, Logan seemed perplexed. Ghost was much more hardcore compared to Cyprus, who had his butt whipped by him. However, Ghost was somehow related to them. I forgot personally on whom his father was, but I knew it was between Tobias and someone else in the royal pack.

*****

I glanced at Marius, and saw his frown. His eyes roamed the room every few seconds, and I knew that he was uneasy about something, but I wasn't sure what though. Rafeor and I made eye contact, and she made her way towards me. She grabbed my arm, and walked a few feet away from the crowd before whispering, "**Have you seen how they have fought so far? It is so beautiful!**"

I rolled my eyes and was about to say something, when a hand came over my mouth, and at the same time across Rafeor's. She stomped on their feet, and whoever it was grunted in pain before we were hit across the face with something. The world went dark.

# Chapter 31

An unknown amount of time passed when I came to my senses. I groaned and looked around the room, it was dark, the only light was in between an industrial-style fan, whenever the blades moved just right at least. I looked across from me and saw Rafeor slumped in a chair, she looked to be asleep, but I could be wrong too. I didn't know if she knew how to pretend hardcore, or not. I swallowed as I looked around the black room, and finally, after what seemed like forever, a door banged open and I saw Rafeor jolt slightly, showing that she was awake, but was keeping herself still. I wished I had done the same, since the guy strolling over held some intimidating weapons. Well, should I say torture devices?

He placed the tools onto a metal table before turning around and looking at me, smirking. "What a pretty lass you are."

Based on his voice and everything, he was a human. I swallowed before speaking, "What are you going to do to me?"

"Isn't it obvious? You are going to be mine to play with. Mine to torture, mine to find out what you are."

"Huh?"

He rolled his eyes before replying, "I come from a long line of supernatural hunters. You were in a group full of others, according to my source, but you don't have the same fighting spirit as they do. That one."

He pointed at Rafeor before continuing, "Apparently made a huge fuss, and tried to escape. However, my source was sure to knock her out. Luckily for me, she is still out. I heard that she has a nasty temper."

I swallowed before whispering, "Why?"

"Why? Why what?"

"Why are you doing this?"

"Because I am a supernatural hunter. This is what my family does."

"So, what is going to happen to me then? To both of us?"

He picked up a boning knife before he replied, "I'm going to make your beast inside you surface, then I am going to kill it. Once the beast within is dead, then I will re-train you to do my wishes and become another round of supernatural hunters. Starting with that mark on your neck."

I squirmed in my seat before growling out, "Don't touch me! You have no idea who you are dealing with do you?"

"You are correct in that. I have no idea who I am dealing with. However, it is not going to matter either way. You will both meet your end. One way or another."

I swallowed before replying, "Why us?"

"I think it was because you got separated from the main group. That is what my source said."

"Do you know who your source is?"

"He didn't give me a name, but he did have a tattoo like yours on his neck."

I swallowed, anyone mated to a werewolf had the mark on their neck. However, can be on different sides, but mainly on the right side. I swallowed and whispered, "You know what that tattoo is though, right?"

"No, and you shouldn't be worrying so much about who brought you here. You should be more worried about what I plan on doing with you. I should be causing you fear, and when she wakes up, along with her. Fear. Nothing but fear."

I glanced at Rafeor and replied, "You should release her, and keep me. You have no idea what you have unleashed."

"No one is going to come for either of you. No one will find you, and you should already come to terms with that. Now, hush up."

I swallowed but opened my mouth to say something but closed it when he glowered at me. I swallowed hard. "No."

"You are challenging me?"

"Yes."

"You, foolish girl."

He strode towards my chair, and grabbed my chin roughly, before jerking it upward. As much as I tried to, I could not force the fear out of the mate bond. I knew if Finn still loved me, he would feel the fear – the rawness of it. He leaned down before snapping, "You both stink. Perhaps, I should strip both of you to nothing, and hose you down."

I swallowed and replied, "You would not dare to."

He shoved me, and since I was tied to the chair, I fell over with a bang. It echoed on the concrete, and I sent Finn everything I was seeing – hoping against all odds that he would come for me. But it was only a dream. Since the night Rafeor had come was three days ago, and there was no sign of him coming back. I swallowed and side-eyed this human before speaking, "Do not touch me."

"I do not care what you want, bitch."

I scooted the seat a little bit, and tried to kick him, but only shifted the chair around at the same time. I was scraping my arm up on my left side, but to hell with it. I would heal with time for that. I didn't care that I healed the same as a human, I glowered up at him before speaking, "Who else are you torturing?"

He paused before tapping his finger on his chin, eyeing me thoughtfully, and replying, "Not many others. The rest are not as pretty as you, though. Once that mark comes off your neck, and hopefully after everything else, you will be alive afterward."

"What would you do if I told you I cannot do anything that you think?"

He frowned and replied, "Are you implying that my source got someone who isn't supernatural?"

"Yes, it is the same with her too. She is not to be messed with, not because she has something, but because of whom she is family to."

"What about you?"

"I am nothing more than an extra. I am almost human."

"Almost human?"

I swallowed as I replied, "Almost human, because I do not have anything remotely concerning your lineage. You should let her go, and I will be whatever you want of me to be."

"I want you to beg for me to kill you in the end."

"Ki-kil-kill me? But you said…."

"You talk so much. If you had closed your yapper, then I may have kept you for my original purpose. However, that ship has long since sailed. You are dead."

"Wait. Wait. Y-yo-you can't kill me."

"No one else knows you are here, princess. You are as good as dead. Same with her."

He turned around, and with a shocker to him, she was gone. However, I had watched her look up at me when he forced me to the ground, but his attention was solely on me. I urged her to leave. It took some convincing, but it was something that she needed to do. She had swallowed, but Shadow was in control and had left with a promise of coming back for me. I knew that she would since so far Shadow and Rafeor were honorable and had been nothing but nice to me so far. I swallowed as he turned his attention back to me, growling, "You knew?"

"Knew what?"

"Do not fool around with me! You knew that she escaped!"

"Yeah, I guess. I did know that she left."

"She will not get far. Heck, she probably isn't even past the main hallway."

He chuckled to himself as he turned around, headed back to the doorway, and paused before calling out, "Whatever you do, do not try to move. Rosco, watch."

I craned my neck to see a dog, a massive brute of a dog, mind you. His eyes flickered to mine before he growled low in his throat. His master exited the chamber and went whistling down the hallway, looking for Rafeor.

*****

I swallowed and spoke softly, "Rosco! Come here, Rosco!"

He growled low in his throat but did not move from his spot. He had a clear view of the room around us, and I knew that if Rafeor was still in the room, it meant that Rosco would know. If that was the case, how did she escape? I wondered. Rosco looked like he would murder anyone who would come towards him to leave, but I am not sure what he would do with Shadow in response. She was something that even I was a little afraid of.

**"Aurelius, Up here."**

I jolted slightly and turned my head to the side, and saw Rafeor up in the rafters. I suddenly wondered what she was doing up there. She was supposed to be heading out. I swallowed and was about to reply when Rafeor whispered, **"We have a problem, Aurelius."**

"What is the problem?"

**"We are on a boat."**

"What?"

**"We are on a boat."**

Silence, I looked up at her and whispered, "How are you so sure we are on a boat? Boats are made of wood. This is not wood."

**"I overheard some of the crew mention that it was the first of its type. That's what they call a barge. It's metal, Aurelius."**

"But metal is hard to make and hard to come by. Who has that type of money to make something like this?"

She glanced at the door, before replying, **"A lord across the canal we were adjacent to. He is hefty with…"**

*****

The door banged open and five humans came inside, one of which was the same one that left a few minutes prior. Their eyes swept the room, and finally, one pointed and said, "There!"

The human looked up at Rafeor before growling, "Come down here."

**"I'm good up here though."**

"It is not what you want. Come down here."

**"Nah, I'm good."**

He approached me fast, and I could not move since I had not broken free of the holds yet. He grabbed my chair roughly before jerking it to its upright position and holding a knife to my throat. He stared up at her before snapping, "Come down, or I slit her throat."

"Are you insane, Malcolm? The lord has requested that BOTH arrive in good shape!"

The one holding me went quiet, and frowned before turning his attention to the one who had spoken, "Dammit, Earl!"

"What? You know what the lord has ordered!"

"Earl! Shut your trap!"

"Or what Malcolm? You will tie me up and make me squeal? You already know what the lord would do if you did so."

Malcolm grumbled but he released me, and glowered at Rafeor. "Get down here!"

**"No."**

"Down!"

**"I'm rather good up here, Malcolm. You should know that whoever your lord is, he is going to be in a tight squeeze."**

The other four looked up at her and Earl replied, "Oh? And why do you think that, girl?"

**"Because you have no idea of the hornet's nest you just kicked over."**

They all frowned and glanced at Malcolm. Earl hissed, "Who are they? They were supposed to be lowly servants."

Malcolm swallowed and replied, "My informer…."

"Informer? You nuts? Malcolm! They were SUPPOSED to be nobody! The lord is not going to be happy when he comes to terms that he will have to pay them off to keep them."

**"Keep us? Doubtful that you will be able to keep us. Especially when they learn of whom has us."'**

Earl looked up at Rafeor and swallowed before asking the question that hung in the air, "Who exactly are you two? And why do you assume that your lords cannot be simply paid off for the two of you?"

I glanced up at Rafeor and she smiled before replying, **"My name is Rafeor, and this is my friend, Aurelius Fiore."**

They glanced at each other, but Malcolm started to laugh before speaking, "Fiore is nothing special. They have nothing across this side of the channel. Rafeor, you are nothing but a peasant, and you need to come down here."

**"Nah, I'm rather comfortable up here. Have any of you questioned HOW I got up here?"**

They looked at each other and glanced at Malcolm. I could see that his Adam's apple bobbed, and Earl replied, "Malcolm…. Did you do what I think YOU did?"

"Ummm…."

"You did, didn't you? You took a supernatural away again. Malcolm, this might be the last time you breathe easy. Or should be your last. Rafeor, please come down here. We will allow you to go. Along with Aurelius."

The other three looked at him sharply before one whispered, "That is not what the lord wants either! He wants girls, and these two will fetch a fortune on the other side."

Earl looked like he wanted to sucker punch this guy, and for once Malcolm looked like he was going to laugh in response. Although Rafeor raised her eyebrows and replied, **"Nah, I'm good up here."**

"Please come down?"

Earl tried again. Rafeor shook her head in response, and Earl looked at Malcolm before speaking, "You will have a lot of explaining to do to the lord when we port in two hours."

**"Two hours?"**

Earl looked up at Rafeor before nodding and speaking, "We are almost across the channel. We will arrive within two hours."

"H-ho-how long has it been?"

Earl looked at me and replied, "Five hours."

I looked up at Rafeor and knew what she was thinking, that was a long time to be at sea for, and that was plenty long enough for someone to notice that we were missing. I wondered what was happening at home. I swallowed and I looked at Earl before speaking, "Can't you take us back?"

He looked at me and shook his head before replying, "Nope. You are now stuck."

"But I thought that the lord would want someone who is not important."

"Unfortunately, for you two, we have several people across the channel who would love to have someone untouched. Both of you girls look young enough to go to a whoring house."

A collective chuckle surrounded that statement and a shudder when he said it made my skin crawl. I could tell that Rafeor knew what he had said, and she looked down at them before speaking, **"That is not to be your best interest. You should release us when you have the chance. Do not wait until Morphous hears about this. Nor when Nathaniel comes after. Neither of whom you should want to cross paths with."**

"Who?"

Earl asked, and this time he stared directly at Malcolm as he asked it. Malcolm swallowed hard before answering, "Supernatural...."

"You got to be kidding me. Did you seriously take two of their ranking people?"

"It doesn't matter, neither of them knows it was me!"

"It doesn't matter if they know it was you or someone else, Malcolm! The lord is going to have a handful to keep these."

"I thought you were going to sell them to a whoring house to get rid of them."

"I was originally going to, Malcolm! But knowing that they are going to be hunted down is something else entirely. They might as well go to the lord. Say nothing, of where they came from. Hopefully, these two men do not come after them hard."

**"Do not bet on that. Heck, I would not even question if they are already on their hunting party."**

Earl looked up at her and replied, "And you, come down here! You know that it is not safe up there."

**"Neither is it safe down there with you five."**

He was silent for a moment before shaking his head, looking at Malcolm, and speaking, "You should wash these two. They do smell."

Malcolm grunted in response when Rafeor called down, **"I would actually suggest to leave us be. Smell and all."**

"And why is that?"

**"Because of whom we were taken from will come. It does not matter to him on where, or whom he kills."**

"You both stink, though."

**"Would it matter if you were dead?"**

"No…."

**"Then leave it alone. If the lord wishes that we would be washed, then have him do it. Not you. It will be safer for you in that way too."**

No one spoke and looked at each other, and finally, after a few moments, Earl looked at Malcolm before hissing, "You are in charge of them. But as the lord wants…. No INJURIES!" He turned to leave and paused before looking back up at Rafeor, followed quickly by the other three foot soldiers. Leaving Malcolm to stare at the door as it banged shut.

*****

He glanced up at Rafeor before speaking, "You think your lords will come for you? You are dead wrong."

Rafeor did not respond and she glanced down at me, speaking, **"Aurelius, you okay?"**

"As good as I can be tied to this chair, Rafeor."

**"You want to untie her?"**

"No. If you want that, you would have to do it."

He walked back to his desk of tools and grumbled as he put them back into the duffle bag that he had, and kept his back to us. I saw the moment that Rafeor was about to come down, but I shook my head in response. She froze but seemed perplexed for a moment. She did not know why I would say no.

Malcolm turned around after a few moments and looked up at Rafeor with a scowl across his face, muttering, "Damn it."

He walked towards me with measured steps and stuck me with a needle in the neck. I winced as he did it, and soon I saw darkness creeping into my vision. And then nothing.

*****

I looked around the training hall sharply, something was amiss, and not just my senses. I could tell that Brego sensed something too, but none of the five were around Aurelius and Rafeor had left my side. I looked around for my mate, and could not see her through the crowd. I pushed forward and looked around. "Rafeor?"

I called out but no response. I looked through the masses, and called again, "RAFEOR?"

No response, I got a few wolves looking at me suddenly, as if they had just heard who I was calling for. They looked around and I heard one speak, "I don't see her, Marius."

I pushed through the crowd, calling, "RAFEOR! This is not funny! Where are you?"

No response. The ground trembled as Ghost tossed Logan to the mat again, but I couldn't care less currently. My mate was missing. I was starting to get frantic, and Nathaniel rumbled out, "**Anyone see Rafeor around?**"

"NO, MY LORD!"

A chorus of no's came from the surrounding wolves. I locked eye contact with Nathaniel and he frowned. He had talked to Rafeor about leaving alone, but soon Azier called out, "Wait, where is Aurelius?"

Nathaniel looked around the room, since he towered over the majority of the wolves, he could see that she was not there either. Basil glinted in his eyes before he rumbled, "**SPREAD OUT. FIND AURELIUS AND RAFEOR. NOW!**"

The surrounding wolves dispersed immediately, a few shredding their clothing as they allowed their wolves to take over, finally, they sniffed to an area not five feet from the back of the crowd before growls echoed.

Nathaniel came forward and Basil glinted in his eyes as he inhaled deeply. His eyes stayed Basil's as he caught the same scent I smelled. Sais. Basil panted for a moment before he rumbled, "**FIND THEM.**"

Wolves tore out of the training hall, and a few slipped on the freshly waxed floor, but they kept going. They ran outside and down to the dock. They skidded to a stop when they whined and sniffed the dock.

Basil came forward and sniffed the air, it was a matter of less than thirty minutes, that they were here. He looked to the horizon, towards the other side of the channel, and growled, "**GET. THE. SHIP. READY.**"

A chorus of 'Yes, my lord,' surrounded him, he turned sharply on his heel, and headed back to the palace where he bounded up the stairs.

****

I swallowed as I watched as they left, I should have never let them out of my sight. I was done for if Nathaniel decided it to be done for. Well, I guess under technicality when Basil thought that. I swallowed hard and looked around the room. The only ones who stayed were myself, the five, and Logan – who looked like he was trying to hide something. He swallowed hard and shuffled his feet.

Ghost stared at him before growling, "I sure as hell hope you do not have anything to deal with this, Uncle."

Logan looked at him and growled, "**Do not assume the worse of me all the freaking time, Ghost.**"

"Then do not make it easy. You are shuffling your feet as if you are scared. Tell me, did you have something to do with this?"

Logan did not reply and swallowed again. "**You know the prophecy yourself, Ghost! That she was not supposed to be.**"

"And what of Aurelius? Was she just collateral damage? You know for a fact that Nathaniel has taken a liking to her now."

Logan paused before growling, "**What do you know of Aurelius?**"

"He only told me that I have a cousin, Uncle. Not one, but two."

"**Two?**"

"Yes two, well, he more of told me that Aurelius is one by your lost mate, and the other one is yours."

"**Impossible. My children have perished.**"

"Really? Have you met Herald? He has a wolf spirit as well as being a bloody shifter, or is he really a shifter, I wonder. Is he something you had hidden to keep away?"

**"NO! MY CHILDREN HAD PERISHED WHEN MORPHOUS ATTACKED THE DRUID CAMP!"**

"Are you for sure on that, Logan? Did you see their bodies?"

Silence, and he finally, whispered, **"N-no-not b-bo-both…"**

He trailed off as he thought and his shoulders slumped down before he looked at Ghost, growling, **"What are you getting at?"**

"I'm more of making you think of what Nathaniel is feeling. Rafeor may not be his blood child, but his mate is her mother….."

He trailed off and looked at Azier. "Azier, any chance that you can get a message to Morphous?"

"Why?"

"Because he is the father of Rafeor, and if my calculations are correct, they are by boat. And roughly an hour ahead of us. A dragon can catch them a whole lot faster than we can."

Azier glanced at Cyprus before replying, "We should go as a team as always, Ghost."

"Alright. Uncle, I am disappointed in you. Your actions are exactly why Nathaniel keeps you close."

He turned hard on his heel, as he left the mat, leaving Logan standing there staring at his back.

****

Basil tore into our chamber and ripped the wardrobe open before getting out gear to fight with. Sophronia came into the room and leaned against the door before speaking, **"What's wrong, Basil?"**

**"Rafeor and Aurelius have been taken."**

**"By whom?"**

**"Someone who will die."**

**"I'm coming with you."**

**"No."**

"Basil, that is my daughter you are going to go after. I am coming with."

"No, you stay home."

"Basil."

"No."

She went silent before she growled, "**I am your mate, Basil. You will allow me to come along.**"

Basil looked at her hard before growling, "**I love Rafeor and I will not let anything come to her. Sophronia, you WILL stay home.**"

She stared at me with rage in her eyes. "**You cannot make me stay here when we are talking about my daughter, Basil. I am going.**"

"No."

"Tell me why you say not then!"

"I need you home."

"As if I would sit idly by as you go into battle for my daughter!"

"Our daughter."

"Basil, she is not yours by blood..."

"She is still my family. She bears your blood, and Shadow is my sister kin."

"Shadow?"

"Her Lycan name."

"She has a Lycan?"

"You are not going with me, Sophronia, but yes, she has a Lycan."

"Who took her?"

"Sais."

"Not possible, Basil."

"Why say that?"

"Because I have been with Sais the entire time that you were down in the office and training room. Yes, they ran across each other in a hallway, but I met Sais when he left the others in the other hallway leading into the training hall. I would not lie to you, Basil. I can even show you the memory."

"Show me."

She cast the memories of the past two hours into my vision, and sure enough the time frame lined up. She left Sais in her office, as she came into our chambers since Basil had roared more than once already. After a moment, Basil asked, **"Then who the hell took them then?"**

**"I don't know, but it is hell is not Sais."**

Basil went silent before looking at her and rested his palm across her face in a loving way, rumbling, **"I do not want you to go."**

**"Basil."**

He was losing the needed strength to say no to his mate, but Nathaniel connected to me suddenly, *"Tell her that she needs to stay behind to man the palace. We are taking the five, along with our beta and gamma. She is the only one we trust to man the palace while we are gone."*

Basil swallowed and looked at her before speaking, **"I don't want you to go because you are the only one I can trust to run the palace while we are gone. I am taking everyone who is immediately in rank. Beta, gamma, and the five along with me, Sophronia. I do not trust the delta enough to do it."**

It was a few moments of being stared at, not in the nose area where many stared at, but in the eyes, before she sighed, looped her arms through mine, and squeezed my torso in a hug, **"Bring them home safely, Basil. But you should also get Morphous."**

**"Why?"**

**"Because he is her father, and once he finds out that she was taken from you, he will turn into Abacore, and help get her back. You know Abacore would help rescue his daughter too."**

Silence and she looked up at me with watery eyes. She whispered, **"I am sorry, Basil."**

**"Hush, Sophronia, I would not want anything differently anymore. Times have changed, and I now know that even Morphous had tricked more than one person into believing that Rafeor is gone. How wrong he was to rob you of your daughter. I would have loved her with all my heart."**

**"Would or are going to?"**

**"Going to."**

**"You will be a good stepdad to her, Basil. Now. GO!"**

I grinned down at my mate before I gripped her tightly and whispered in her ear, **"I will bring her and Aurelius back safely, my dear."**

She giggled in response as she gently pushed me away, before turning around and walking away.

*****

Goddess, I loved my mate. I looked at the wardrobe when Ghost connected to me, *"My lord, you get ready, we will go get Morphous."*

**"Thank you, Ghost."**

*"You're welcome, my lord."*

He dropped the connection and after a moment, Cyprus connected, *"We found something else out, Basil."*

**"What?"**

*"Sais was not in the training room. They masked themselves in his scent since they knew that he was the one on thin ice. But that is not the only thing."*

**"What are you beating around the bush for, Cyprus?"**

He hesitated for a moment before replying, *"Logan did it. He orchestrated the entire thing. He did the challenge, knowing that would draw attention from other guards, and it did."*

**"And you are sure of this?"**

*"He confessed to Ghost before we left."*

I breathed deeply and thought, what would I do with him? Cyprus connected, *"My lord?"*

**"I. Will. Kill. Him."**

I stared at the wardrobe and was close to becoming what everyone feared, but Nathaniel pressed on the connection before speaking, **"As much as I want to slit his throat too, we would be taking Aurelius's father away from her. We cannot take him away. We also cannot kill our brother as much as we want, Basil."**

**"He BETRAYED US!"**

**"He is going to learn his lesson later, Basil. For now, we need to head and get ready to go. Rafeor and Aurelius are waiting on us. They are counting on us to come to rescue them. Logan knows he is on thin ice, and this may be the time that he is taken to the bridge."**

I frowned, knowing what Nathaniel meant by that, and scowled as I walked away and ducked under the door before moving towards the armory. Already knowing that the five needed time to get Morphous going.

******

I woke up in a dark chamber. I don't know where I was, but I knew it was not on the ship anymore. A creaky door opened further, past my door. I swallowed back the bile in my throat, as the door to my chamber opened, revealing not only Malcolm but another older human. He looked at me with a hard look before turning his attention to Malcolm and speaking, **"This is the slave that you brought me? I sent you and your team to get MORE than two."**

"I apologize, my lord, these were the only two that we could get at the time."

The lord glowered at him and looked at me again. He entered the room and looked down at me before speaking, **"Do you speak?"**

I swallowed as I whispered, "Who are you?"

Malcolm took a deep breath in, as the lord smirked before turning to him, **"Ah, so it does. You were told to bring me illiterate slaves. Not ones that have learned!"**

Malcolm leaned backward before whispering, "I apologize, my lord. It will not happen again."

**"I know it won't because you are done."**

"My lord?"

**"Guards! Take Malcolm to the chamber, and clean up the mess afterwards."**

Two guards stepped forward, grabbed Malcolm roughly, and dragged him backward, the fear in his eyes evident that he knew where they were taking him. I looked at the lord before speaking, "NO!"

The guards paused, and Malcolm glanced at me in shock. The lord looked at me sharply before growling, **"Excuse me?"**

"No, to whatever you are going to do to him."

**"And I have to listen to you because?"**

"I am Aurelius Fiore, you will release him."

**"Who?"**

"N-n-no one! She is no one!"

Malcolm scrambled to say, even though they had all heard what I had said. The lord looked at him sharply before turning his brown eyes back at me and snapping, **"Where did you come from? Whose house?"**

"From Nathaniel. Across the channel. I know he is big elsewhere."

**"Nathaniel?"**

He turned slowly to face Malcolm before whispering, "**The same Nathaniel that has peace treaties with us? That NATHANIEL?**"

Malcolm shrunk down and whispered, "I-I-I…. I don't know if it is the same, my lord!"

The lord turned back around before speaking to me, "**What is the name of his wife?**"

"Sophronia."

Malcolm swallowed hard. The guards shrunk down too. It may be a long way away from here to the other side of the channel but they surely knew who I spoke of. The lord turned to face Malcolm before hissing, "**I will not kill you because she said no, but get him out of my sights.**"

The other guards dragged him away, and Malcolm looked over at them before swallowing. He knew he was good as dead as he got off the boat whenever that was.

****

The lord turned around after a few moments as if he had gathered his strength before asking the question that I knew was going to come, "**What about the other woman that came with you?**"

"Rafeor?"

**"I think so."**

"She is his daughter. I am his niece."

**"Shit."**

He exited the chamber, paused at the entrance but slammed the door closed at the same time, locking me inside.

*****

It was quite a while before the door was opened again, this time Earl stood in the doorway before he spoke softly, "Please, follow me."

I got up off the bed and walked towards him. He turned and walked down the concrete walls. We started to go upward before I saw any lights. I saw plenty of other women, and all

397

were not doing well. They all were hollows of what they should be. I swallowed as I looked at them before hurrying to catch up to Earl.

He walked to a chamber, knocked once, and opened the door before gesturing me inside. I walked inside, and as soon as I crossed the threshold, he closed the door and a lock clicked behind. I looked at Rafeor as she stared at me. I could tell that she did not get drugged here, but she was in pain, and holding her side slightly.

I walked gingerly towards her and hugged her. We stood there for a while before she whispered, **"We are in trouble, Aurelius."**

"Why?"

**"Because this lord is not a friend of the shifters or any supernatural beings."**

"How is that possible? He told me that he had a treaty with Nathaniel, and when I told him of Sophronia, he took me up here from wherever he had me. He and the rest of the people acted scared."

**"Shit."**

"What?"

**"Well, when Nathaniel does come, he will meet out with a fucking army. This lord is very wealthy on this side of the channel, Aurelius."**

"You have to believe that Nathaniel will come rescue us."

**"He doesn't even know where we are though! We were taken right under his nose!"**

"That may be true, Rafeor, but keep your head up! We will be saved. I know it."

**"The only question is how many lives will Nathaniel risk to get us out."**

I opened my mouth to respond but closed it. What was our lives worth compared to the pack? A worthless wolf-less pack member, and Rafeor? I swallowed as I tried hard not to think about it.

# Chapter 32

We crossed the veil and paused, this was not the furthest away we have been from our kingdom, but it was the first that it was in a dire situation. I connected to everyone in my group, *"So, what exactly is the plan? We can't walk right into their palace, and say we need Morphous."*

*"And why are you starting to question how we are going to do it?"*

*"Have you forgotten the last time that there were werewolves inside this palace? What happened? They will not trust anything we say."*

*"Oh, right."*

*"It doesn't matter, Azier. As soon as Morphous hears our cause, he will come with us. I am sure of it."*

*"Before or after he takes us to his dungeons?"*

*"It will not come to that, Azier. Hush now. We are coming upon their border."*

We let the connection be left open, but no one spoke. We all knew that we needed to be ready for anything.

****

A shout went up and soon three shifters held spears and pointed them at us before one spoke, "STATE YOUR BUSINESS!"

I glanced at Cyprus and he sighed before stepping forward and speaking, "We come in peace. We need to speak to Morphous."

The guards glanced at each other before the same one replied, "Currently he is out."

"When is he due to be back?"

"The king of the shifters was not expecting anyone from the werewolves."

"I apologize, but we need to speak to him."

"He is not in right now."

"Where can we find him then?"

Silence and a few shuffled their feet. Finally, another one replied, "He left without intel on his whereabouts wolf. Now go back home. You are not wanted here."

"I apologize that I am not wanted. However, we need to speak to Morphous."

"Not possible. Go home."

"No."

"Do not make me sound the alarms. Go back to your territory."

"No."

I glanced at Cyprus and saw the vein in his face throb a little, and knew that he was not in the greatest of moods, but he would not stop being courteous to the shifters. Especially since they are doing their job rather well.

*"Why are we keeping quiet on the reason behind we came, brother?"*

He glanced at me before replying, *"Because we do not know if they even know Rafeor."*

*"She did come from here first brother. Come on, surely at least one of them knows her."*

He huffed in the connection, but I knew that he agreed. Ghost, however, spoke, "What is your name?"

"My name?"

"Yes, your name."

"Why?"

"So, when we finally meet Morphous, that way we can inform him that his guards prevented the important message from being heard."

"What important message?"

"Why do you think we have come from our homeland to come to yours?"

"To make us think you are going to attack again."

"Five wolves? Against the entire shifters? Does that make sense to you?"

The guard swallowed hard before replying, "No...."

"So, take us to Morphous."

****

The guard went to speak when a voice spoke from behind them, "He is currently not here. He went after my father."

The guards parted and a shifter approached, and they looked at him expectantly. The guy looked at the others before speaking, "You three are dismissed. Go back to the wall."

"Yes, Quinn."

"Thank you, Quinn."

"Of course, my lord."

They have various responses, and Quinn looked at us before flickering his attention to Cyprus and speaking, "I am Morphous's advisor. What can I do for you?"

I glanced at Cyprus and Ghost glanced at me before shrugging his shoulders. We had stayed in our human forms, knowing the territory well enough that we didn't need to shift. And would make it easier to speak to the shifters too. Cyprus sighed deeply before replying, "We need to inform your king of something dire."

"Dire?"

I looked at Cyprus and was about to speak but Ghost spoke, drawing Quinn's attention to him, "Rafeor was taken."

"Taken? Where?"

"We are unsure of what the captors were planning, but they went across the channel."

"That's eight hours sail to reach the other side."

"Correct."

Quinn looked like he wanted to go, but he sighed before speaking, "I would take you to Morphous immediately, but he is not here."

"Where is he?"

Quinn opened his mouth and closed it again before shrugging. "To be bluntly honest, not entirely sure. I do know he went beyond the shifter territory. Since no one can link him or Abacore."

"Do you know when he will come back?"

"I would average perhaps another day."

"A day? By then Rafeor would be dead."

"Hey, I unfortunately can't really send anyone after her. That is Morphous's call."

"I thought that she was his daughter," growled Brego.

Quinn's eyes flickered to him before replying, "It is not my fault that Morphous is out."

"If Morphous is not here, then who is his second in command? Surely not you? Isn't he married?"

"Katherine is not available."

"And why not?"

He swallowed before looking at the wall and whispering, "She committed treason. She is in the dungeons."

Silence. We were not expecting that information. I glanced at Brego and then at Cyprus. Nathaniel was not going to be happy when he would find out that Morphous was gone.

****

I turned towards the woods, back to our territory when a roar sounded. It sounded far away, but it echoed.

Quinn glanced towards where it sounded and sighed a breath of relief before speaking, "Speak of the devil. He's coming home."

I looked at Cyprus before Ghost spoke, "Is he quick to anger?"

Quinn looked at us before replying, "It highly depends on if Abacore is in control or not. If Morphous is in control of his dragon, then not really."

"But if Abacore is in control?"

His Adam's Apple bobbed before he swallowed nervously, giving us the information we needed. We just had to hope he was in control of the dragon.

*****

I landed on the patch of land that I had made possible to be Abacore's landing place. When I knew I wasn't alone. I turned my head towards the East and saw Quinn approaching. I flared my nostrils and smelled wolves. Abacore flared in my eyes and I shifted to our human form before snapping, **"What are the werewolves doing on our territory?"**

Quinn stopped within a few feet from me and swallowed before speaking, "They bear dire news, Morphous."

**"What dire news?"**

He opened his mouth, but a young werewolf came forward, bowing to me, and speaking, "May I address you?"

**"You may."**

"My name is Cyprus. I bring news from Nathaniel."

**"What news?"**

"Rafeor was taken across the channel. He requests your aid."

**"My aid?"**

"Yes, sir."

**"Why?"**

"Because we know that Rafeor is your daughter. And you should be heading to rescue her."

My eyes flickered to another werewolf, he approached and bowed to me before speaking, "My name is Brego, and I am with my comrades. We were to bring you to the ship."

**"The ship?"**

"They are ahead of us, my lord, they have your daughter along with someone else that needs rescuing."

**"Who else?"**

"Her name is Aurelius, she is a friend of Rafeor's."

**"Collateral damage by the sounds of it."**

"You won't go after your daughter?" replied Cyprus, drawing my attention to him, and I swallowed before replying, **"She left me without telling me."**

"She is eighteen. Legally she can go as she pleases."

Abacore flared in my eyes and he flinched back and took a step backward. I scoffed and turned towards the palace, about to leave them when a female's voice spoke, "You say you love your daughter. However, you are a fucking coward. If you think you can just walk away! How dare you! Rafeor will want both of her parents. Not one. Two!"

I froze, turned slowly around, and squinted my eyes at the woman before growling, **"You are in no position to yell at me!"**

"THEN FUCKING ACT LIKE A FATHER! She was taken right under our noses and sent across the channel. You know it well enough that it takes eight hours to reach the other side. They left not more than two hours ago!"

**"Why should I help her? She left me!"**

"BECAUSE YOU WEREN'T TRAINING HER! You had others train your daughter in how to be who she is on your side. She has the ability of shifter and werewolf. She is the first of her kind and she is scared. Wouldn't you want someone to come to rescue you if roles were reversed? Would you want someone who you had only met three days before to rescue you? Or someone that you have spent two months with? How…."

"AZIER! ENOUGH!"

She winced and cowered slightly, and looked at another werewolf.  He stood tall, and his eyes blazed in wolf light before he turned his attention to me and spoke, "My apologies. She does tend to go off the charts when she is passionate about someone. Come along, patrol. We need to report to Nathaniel."

The patrol turned around to leave, and I turned towards the palace, but Quinn spoke, "Morphous?"

**"What?"**

"This isn't like you. You wanted to know your daughter. Are you really going to let what happened cloud your judgment? She is your blood."

I paused and looked at him, and then my eyes flickered to the werewolves, who had paused, but had their backs turned to me. I swallowed and growled, "**Blood or not. She has chosen her course.**"

I started heading back to the palace, but soldiers came out of the door all armed to the teeth. I stared at them before growling, "**What are you doing?**"

"We are heading to rescue Rafeor, my lord. She is the hybrid and you know the legends. She will be a force for all of us. We need to rescue her."

I swallowed and did not speak and turned to face Quinn again. "**Get ready to go.**"

"Yes, my lord."

Quinn glanced back at the werewolves and left promptly afterward. He was going to get ready to go.

***

I turned my attention to the werewolves before speaking, "**Stay here.**"

The werewolves glanced at me and simply nodded in response. I turned sharply, entered the palace, and headed towards the armory.

****

I picked up two swords, the finest I had in my armory, and turned them in my hand before sliding them into their sheaths and strapping them to my back. I grabbed another sword, this one went against my hip on my left side, since I was a right-handed dominate. A few of my comrades were hurrying on getting their equipment and placing it on themselves. We all wore loose-fitting clothes, so we could move in them and fight in them. My eyes blazed since Basil did not relinquish his control as of yet, but everything was going smoothly, until Batis contacted me, "*There was a problem with Morphous.*"

**"What is the problem with him?"**

I was surprised that even though Basil was in my eyes, I saw his reflection, but he allowed me to speak as normal, I shook myself off as I caught the tail end of what he was saying, "*Didn't want.*"

**"Wait what?"**

"*Morphous more or less said he did not want to go. He said she left him, and…. Well… he was prepared to leave her to whatever happened to her.*"

Basil growled in the connection, and he fell silent. I tried to reign him back in but to no avail. **"*HE IS HER FUCKING FATHER! HOW DARE….*"**

"*MY LORD!*"

Ghost's voice echoed and forced Basil down as he shouted back. Basil growled low in his throat, but Ghost growled equally threatening before he snapped, "*Batis, you left off the most important part. The fact that HIS people were the ones that pushed him to follow. Morphous is going, along with the majority of the shifter population.*"

Silence, I was not expecting that news. I knew that the shifters would not come unless they knew something else about Rafeor. I swallowed as Basil desperately wanted to tear out and go without anyone, but I kept a firm hand on him before speaking to Ghost, **"*Thank you, Ghost for the update.*"**

"*You're welcome, my lord.*"

They let the connection drop. And I glanced around and saw the werewolves with their eyes flickering, they must have heard Basil even though they were not included in the link. I sighed before speaking, addressing the room, **"We go after my family."**

A collective 'hooah's' sounded, and the clanging of metal as they left the hall. I smiled, my pack. My people. They were ready to get something that was stolen from us. No matter the costs. They were going to bring her back home.

****

I entered my armory and grabbed a few swords, and twirled one in my hand, but did not do anything with it. I was thinking, why should I let Quinn and Herald be? They were the ones that were the offspring of the man who betrayed us. Why wouldn't they be different? They were the enemies. They would one day come back and haunt us. Morphous stopped my train of thought immediately, *"No, Abacore."*

I huffed at him in the connection and rumbled, *"She left us. Morph. She should learn that we will not drop everything to come rescue her…."*

*"Are you even hearing yourself, Abacore? You would let Rafeor go back to that old life? Because I can assure you that is what will happen if we do not go after her."*

He grumbled, but did not say anything, and when he was about to reply. Anna came into the armory before speaking, "Morphous?"

**"Hmm?"**

"Even if she decides to be with the werewolves, you know that she will still be your daughter, right? Quinn informed me of what you had said. And to be frank, that werewolf girl who spoke out of terms with you is highly correct. You are her father and she would want you to help in getting her back."

I turned around and Abacore growled, **"You agree with the wolf? Are you mad?"**

Anna's eyes flashed before she snarled, "ABACORE! HOW DARE YOU! I understood why you and Morphous were doing other duties to keep the palace running smoothly, and safely. However, YOU even stated when she first arrived that YOU would train her! Yet YOU only trained her to shift back into her dragon and how to somewhat control herself. You left a novice with no training, no love, no support. Even though YOU PROMISED IT! I do not blame Rafeor for leaving when she did, Abacore. By the sounds of it, she is learning her place and learning how to be what she is. And considering that she has only been with them for three days, the fact that the werewolf challenged you speaks wonders already of how she is fairing in their territory."

Abacore fell silent and looked away before releasing me back, his eyes flickered out of my eyes. I swayed back and forth for a moment and grabbed the bench to stabilize myself before murmuring, "**I am sorry, Anna.**"

"Sorry gets nowhere, Morphous. You know I spoke the truth. We, as the staff trained your daughter in the ways of being a shifter. You more of assisted in keeping it available to the people. Otherwise, you did nothing."

"**Anna!**"

I turned to look at her in shock, and she glowered at me before snapping, "Now stop shuffling your feet, Morphous. Get going, and save your daughter."

She turned sharply on her heel and paused at the door before calling backward, "Do not keep them waiting. They will leave without you. And then you have many grounds to cover."

She let the door slam shut behind her as she left and soon I was left alone in the armory.

*****

I headed towards the dock and turned around. Only a quarter of the pack would remain, along with my mate, I looked up in the window, where I knew she would most likely be waiting. Sure enough, she was watching down upon us as we left. This brought back memories of the days of the old too, when we would sail during the summer months, and very early winter, bringing back loot from across the waters. We had to stop that about thirty years ago and made peace treaties instead. We got goods still, but without the bloodshed, without the fight.

I walked across the planks of the dock, and I heard the cawing of birds. I looked up and saw crows and a few ravens flew down. They landed on the posts surrounding the dock and one shifted before the others. He stood perched on the dock post, as if it was easy to stand on it, before calling out, "WE ARE HERE TO GET RAFEOR!"

I looked at the tensed werewolves, a few of them flinched backward as they looked at the shifter. He was older, and he was armed to the teeth. I looked at one of the few werewolves that flinch before linking him, "*Who is he?*"

The werewolf looked at me for a split second before replying, "*His name is Gillith. He is one of the top shifter guards. He is one of the few that would have sent someone to the Eastern Border.*"

I looked back at the shifter and saw the experience in the way he held himself, and sighed before speaking aloud, **"Welcome, shifters."**

They stared at me, unblinking. The werewolves were restless. The druids had done a fair job at keeping the veil on the ground, but would not be possible to prevent anyone from flying over. Although, not many could fly, and Morphous and I had a mutual understanding that we would never have our troops come into another's territory without consent. Hmmm, I wondered what was keeping Morphous at bay.

****

Soon the flapping of giant wings sounded, the shifters glanced upwards and a few hopped off their perches, into the air, hovering. The werewolves surrounding them shrunk inwards on themselves, they have only seen memories of the dragon, but not many had the experience to see him.

Abacore came flying down and landed on the back lawn, probably much to Sophronia's disdain since he landed in her flower beds. I scowled slightly as Morphous shifted to his human form, he crouched down before standing up. He looked at the gathered forces before turning his attention to me and growling, **"Why wasn't anyone watching her?"**

**"It was not my intention for her to be taken, Morphous."**

Tension began to rise, and Ghost stepped forward before something else could be said by Morphous, "Enough. What is done is done. What matters is that we will go get her. Both of them."

The wolves around him let out whoops and hooahs and he turned around to stare at the shifters before addressing them, "Does it matter to any of you on sharing the task of getting them both back home? Or is the task too daunting for shifters?"

A collective growl happened, and I could see the shifters' eyes flash in anger. Whatever Ghost was doing, it was working. At least, if his goal was to make the shifters angry then it was working flawlessly.

Gillith stepped off the dock post and walked towards Ghost, stopping within feet of him before speaking, "You and I seem to think alike. What is your name?"

"My name is Ghost. Yours?"

"Gillith."

"Welcome."

"Thank you."

Gillith turned around and called out, "COMRADES! DEPART!"

The birds glanced at Morphous before leaping into the air and shifting mid-air into albatrosses. They soared above the wind and glided away.

Gillith turned his attention to the werewolves before eyeing the ships we were about to board. He glanced at Morphous and spoke, "Morphous?"

**"What?"**

"We need your dragon form."

**"Why?"**

"To pull the boats."

He glanced at the four boats in front and he shook his head before snapping, "**I am not pulling them across the channel, Gillith.**"

Gillith looked like he was going to challenge him, but he stopped himself and sighed deeply. He turned to look towards someone who had not taken off. I looked over and recognized him as Morphous's advisor. He swallowed and walked into the hilly area of the yard, and shifted. He screamed as his form took control. His eyes were black as coal, and he panted as his dragon surfaced.  His wings were black as night, his body black with red-tipped scales. He had four wings, and he was massive.

I glanced at Morphous and saw his jaw part, as if in shock. Gillith, however, did not look surprised, almost as if he had known. I looked at Morphous and suddenly wondered if he had any idea that his advisor was something so dangerously powerful. Whatever he was.

Gillith walked slowly towards the dragon, who rumbled in his approach. His eyes flashed colors before it rumbled, "Step no further."

Gillith paused before calling out, "Easy. We need your help."

"Why should I help you?"

"For Rafeor. You should assist us."

His coal-black eyes were hard to see, but he rumbled, "What needs to be done?"

"The boats need to be towed behind you."

"How many?"

"Four."

"Fine."

He leaped into the air, and faltered for a split second, before gliding towards the dock. He landed close by before rumbling, "ROPES. CHAINS. ROPES AND CHAINS. BRING FORTH."

The surrounding werewolves looked at me in fear, before I snapped, **"Get what he has said out."**

A few of the werewolves scrambled onto the boats and brought out ropes, but the chains were something that they did not have. A few took off towards the palace, where a werewolf standing in the doorway was handing them chains. A lot of them too. Soon, they came back with them.

I turned to face the dragon before speaking, "**What is your name?**"

He looked at me before hissing, "It matters not."

I swallowed and felt Basil stir at not being answered, however, this was not the time to get worked up over something. I looked over at my pack members and knew that they did not want to approach the dragon. He was frightening, and since he was closer to me, I could see the gauges in his scales and knew that someone, at one point, had tried to do several harmful things to this dragon. His teeth were razor-sharp, almost like a sharpened pike, it was pointed to the point. He growled a warning. His eyes were black as coal, no iris, it was a black hole almost.

I looked towards Gillith who was already tying rope and chain together. He looked up at me and smirked before speaking as he continued to work, "It took a long while to get him to come out."

**"Do you know his name?"**

"Yes, and no. I am not going to tell you. That was AFTER he nearly killed me several times before I stumbled upon it."

I growled, Basil glinted in my eye, and the dragon behind me chuckled before he rumbled, "My name must be EARNED. Not a given. My shifter half is named Quinn. You may address us as that. I will respond."

"Shifter half?"

He turned his coal-black eyes to him before rumbling, "Quinn's father is Killian Benik, and he is a demon. I am a demon. Our mother, however, was a shifter."

"So, you are a hybrid? What is the difference between you and Rafeor?"

"Rafeor is a mix between royalty wolf and shifter. I am a demon and shifter. We are much different."

"Are you safe to be around?"

"Depends."

"Depends on…"

"ENOUGH!"

Ghost looked hard at the werewolf that had drawn Quinn's demon's attention and he turned his attention to it before speaking, "My name is Ghost. We are currently sitting back and waiting on YOU to assist us across the channel."

His dragon blinked once with its massive black eyes before rumbling, "As if I would let them."

Ghost blinked in confusion for a split second, and knew that he was not in the place to question it. He shook his head and the dragon huffed out a laugh before turning his attention to Gillith and hissing, "Isss itsss readysss?"

Gillith swallowed before holding up to him. He took one step forward before turning his head towards us and rumbling, "Get in your boatsss. We leave asss sssooon asss I getss my attachmentsss on."

"Why are you hissing?"

Ghost asked what everyone else was wondering, and the dragon blinked and what I assumed was an eye roll, growling, "Just get on the stupid boats. When I am secured, will I need you to tie it to the head of your ships?"

Ghost smirked, turned to his comrades, and glanced at me before nodding his head, I turned my attention to everyone surrounding me, waiting on my orders. I allowed Basil to surface in my voice, "**BOARD OUR SHIPS!**"

A collective 'hooah's' sounded in response, and they boarded the ships without delay, waiting for the dragon. I turned my attention to Morphous before calling out to him, "**Morphous, would you like to be on my ship with me?**"

He looked at me and swallowed, but he shifted into an albatross, flew into the wind, and soon disappeared out of sight.

*****

It was another moment before Gillith walked slowly towards me with a long chain, he had four others in his hands before he held out another to Ghost, Marius, and my beta, Rispin. All captains of the other ships. They took the chains and headed to the front of the ships, before looping it onto the arch of the dragon's head of the ships. There was a lot of slack between Quinn's dragon's connecting them, and Ghost looked at it and looked at the dragon that sat there idly. He spoke, "Is it taunt enough?"

"Would you rather go flying?"

"No."

"Then don't question it. Believe me, when he gets airborne, it will not be slacked."

Ghost nodded and went to the head of the ship, gripped onto the loose end of the chain, and leaned backward. A few werewolves attached him to the mass of the boat, same with the others since that is the instructions that Gillith had told them to do while the dragon was speaking.

Soon, I was attached and looked at Gillith before speaking, "**Are you joining us?**"

"Not with you. I am going to be riding him."

He pointed at the dragon and the dragon's eyes flickered for a moment, but his grin was evident. He was going to have fun being ridden, and I saw Gillith swallow before he leaned towards me slightly and whispered, "Heads up as a warning. He is still green to being held in. It is probably in your best interest to have your pack strap in if possible."

I swallowed and looked back at them, knowing that they heard what he said, since we are werewolves. We hear things that we were not really supposed to know all the time either. I swallowed before speaking, "**Okay, lead on.**"

He stood up and approached the dragon slowly, who bared its teeth at him. But nothing else. He mounted the dragon and gripped the thorn tips before jerking his hands forward sharply, the roar of the dragon echoed and made all of the wolves flinch in response, except for the five, myself and my beta and gamma. They were ready. We were coming to get Aurelius and Rafeor.

Ready or not? Here we come.

# Chapter 33

The door rattled open and we both flinched as the door opened. The Lord came in, and much as I wished that Rafeor was wrong, I noticed that he was now carrying weapons. He looked at us as we clung to each other before speaking, **"Why are you two so jumpy?"**

**"Because you are going back on what you had told Aurelius downstairs."**

He looked at Aurelius, chuckling before replying, **"I guess that is a fair point. You will soon be owned to me and me alone. You two will be my housewives, and be what I want."**

**"Over my dead body will I do that!"**

**"Do not tempt me, bitch! You were going to be that if you were illiterate. If only Malcolm had followed my directions!"**

**"Did you know that Malcolm had wanted us because we were believed to be supernatural?"**

**"Supernatural? Nothing is that as they say. People across the water are all saying that, but it is nothing more than lies."**

"Are you so sure about that? Then why are you carrying so many weapons?"

**"Because I know Nathaniel may or may not come after you two. It highly depends on whether you lied or not to me when you said who you are. My guess is, that you lied and nothing is to become of it."**

**"Then why risk carrying weapons?"**

**"Risking weapons? I am not risking. I own this entire frontier and everyone knows it. No one is going to challenge it."**

That was met with silence, and finally, I looked at him before speaking, "If that were to be the case, then why are you carrying weapons? You weren't when you were downstairs, at least not as many as you currently have on hand. Are you more scared to let someone see?"

His eyes flickered between us before he snapped, **"I do not answer to slaves. Either way, you will get to work."**

**"No."**

**"Are you seriously going to challenge what I want in my own home right now?"**

**"Yes."**

**"Get on your hands and knees, bitch."**

**"No."**

**"You dare challenge my authority?"**

**"Yes."**

He went silent, blew out an angry breath and shouted behind him, **"GUARDS!"**

I glanced at Rafeor and she looked at me out of the corner of her eyes, and leaned down before speaking, **"Do not do a thing for them. We are not their slaves."**

"Rafeor, you just said that you know that Nathaniel would not come through."

I hissed at her, but apparently too loud since the lord startled me by saying, **"See? A lie. You will do as I say and without complaint."**

Rafeor looked at him and replied, **"No."**

The lord scowled before growling, **"You are getting under my skin girl. You will do as I say."**

**"No."**

**"Yes."**

**"Not going to happen. No."**

The lord tightened his fists before looking at the guards and speaking, **"Remove their clothes, and tie that one to the bedpost, and that one to the bedpost on that bed."**

"Yes, my lord!"

They chorused.

****

They marched forward, and Rafeor put up a good fight, and, I, well, let's just say that being in sweaty clothing and being taken away from my home, made me more obedient. I actually helped them get my clothes off, but they still roughly removed them, dragged me to the bed, and hauled me onto the bed before restraining my wrists.

It took six guards to get Rafeor to be bound to the bedpost, and it was not without any broken bones, at least one of the guards had a broken nose, or a finger, a hand or something else entirely. They panted as they stared at her, and their eyes flickered to mine. I swallowed and knew that no one was supposed to see my body besides Finn, but I doubted that I would see my mate again. I swallowed hard and winced as one of them approached me, with a hungry look on his face. I squirmed against the bondage and winced as I pulled myself a little too roughly against the ropes, tightening them against myself.

He looked at the lord before asking something I wished I never knew, "My lord?"

**"Do as you wish to either of them, boys. Keep them alive, but do as you please."**

He closed the door, shutting the six guards inside, with both of us bound to the bed. I looked at Rafeor and saw her eyes flickering with different colors. I swallowed and wondered why she didn't shift yet. Was she waiting on something? I did not get to know my question, as the guard came into my span of attention all over again.

*****

He crawled up on the bed, and ran his hand up my side, chuckling darkly, "You will be better than any whore I had dominated."

I shuddered before whispering, "Please don't."

"Oh? Am I too good for you?"

I swallowed before whispering, "I have a mate back home! Please leave me alone!"

He chuckled before looking at the other five before speaking, "Mate! She claims she has a mate! Oh, my goddess, little girl. You are mine to torture, mine to dominate."

"Not alone, Dax."

He looked up and smirked before replying, "Of course not, Calvin. Want to make her squirm with me?"

Calvin smirked once before walking towards the other side of the bed, ran his hand on my legs, and paused on my hip bone, before moving it towards my jewel that Finn said was his alone. I swallowed as I squirmed against him and screamed, "LEAVE ME ALONE! HELP! SOMEONE HELP!"

The guards winced at the volume before one grabbed something out of his pocket, and held it out to Dax. "Make sure that her dirty little mouth is busy, Dax. We don't need the entire mansion to hear her screams."

Dax grunted in response, moved again on the bed, and Calvin yanked my head up as Dax secured the cloth around my mouth, gagging me. I tried to call out, but it was muffled again. I swallowed and squirmed around but to no avail.

For whatever reason, Rafeor could do nothing. I looked at her and suddenly wondered why she wouldn't help me until I heard one of the guards speak, "Damn, she has a pinprick of something on her neck. Sam, run down to the dungeons and ask Malcolm what he gave this one. She is so docile, but has a nasty mouth to her."

I glanced at Rafeor and suddenly remembered something, wolfsbane can cause your wolf to go to sleep for a certain amount of time until it coursed through your body. It usually took close to twenty-four hours for it to make its course out of your body. It suddenly made sense why she was being so docile besides her mouth. If Malcolm had indeed drugged Shadow, then we were in a world of being only human. A world in which men assumed that we were nothing but theirs to own and play with. And that frightened me more than anything else.

*****

I walked away from the room and headed into my office when a knock sounded on the door. I glanced up at the candle and snapped, "**Enter.**"

The door swung open to a petite woman, roughly seventeen in age I would say. However, the laws surrounding them, made it so they cannot be touched. Otherwise, dire consequences ensued. I looked at her with a raised eyebrow before speaking, "**What do you want?**"

"I want to know who you have in your spare room. Who are they?"

**"They are not your concern."**

"I am making it my concern, father."

I jerked my head up from what had captured my attention and swallowed. I knew I had daughters, but they were rarely seen but not heard. I squinted my eyes before snapping, "**Who taught you how to read? Or speak?**"

"Mother."

**"Which one is your mother again?"**

"Ugh! You don't even know? I guess mother was right, you would not know who I am. Along with ALL your other daughters. You only value your sons."

**"Sons know their place, women need to learn theirs."**

"So, I will, once I become eighteen, correct? Will I receive the same ungodly treatment as those two in the spare chambers? Is that my fate in your eyes?"

I frowned and moved away from my desk and approached her, now that I could see her up closer, I knew who her mother was. It was the redhead whom I had a one-night stand with eighteen years ago, she was a beauty then. Perhaps even now, but that was many, many seasons ago. I turned away from her before snapping, "**Get out.**"

"Why should I father?"

**"Or I will make sure that when the candles strike midnight, you will not be alone once you turn of age. Get out."**

"I hate you father."

**"OUT!"**

She backed out of the door and closed it with a click. I faced the window and smiled as I watched the hired and my personal troops be stationed in spots, ready to go against Nathaniel if he decided to show himself. I smirked, sat down in my chair, and closed my eyes. I was currently safe, and I knew it.

*****

It was nightfall when the torches went up. Since we were raided many, many seasons ago, I glanced out the window and saw the channel. Saw nothing out of the norm, walked out of my office, and headed to my chambers. I was tired, I hadn't finished anything that I had to do in the paperwork. Sign off on payments, and make sure the maids were doing their proper tasks. I knew that it was going to be fun tomorrow evening, since I planned on having the one that defied me today in my chambers, probably tied to my bed. Since they squirmed around more when they were.

A shout went up outside, I turned my head towards the window that I was passing and saw an albatross land on the shore. I frowned, it had been a few seasons since I had seen these large birds come back to this side of the channel, they usually were on the opposite side. I felt a cold sweat, across the channel I saw Nathaniel. Shit, surely this bird couldn't be a warning bell.

I backed away from the window and heard something else, it sounded like thunder, but it was a clear night sky tonight, I swallowed. Surely, it couldn't be that, I had heard a dragon flying before, once, when I was a boy.  But that was many, many seasons ago. Surely, there were no dragons.

In the flickering torch light, I saw more and more albatrosses arrive. They looked like they were normal birds, but I thought frantically and remembered something that my father had said once, that there was more than one ruler across the channel, and none of them were exactly friendly. Especially when someone took something special from their homes. I swallowed and glanced down the hall, and knew that my chambers were the last place I should be. I thought quickly and realized that the one person who may know who the girls were, was downstairs in a dungeon cell. Alive, but still in a cell. I swallowed as I tried hard not to run, but I failed miserably and kind of ran towards the entrance of the dungeons. Hoping against all odds, that I was remembering something wrong. Surely, Nathaniel would not get someone else involved in this affair.

*****

I was one of the first to land on their beach, and looked across their torches area, and I saw unsure humans staring at us on their beach. At least, further up. They were watching the harbor, and I blinked at them. A few more of us arrived and landed on the sandy side since further up was rocky. These humans were going to be slaughtered if they did not know when to run. I heard the beating of Quinn's demon, and I smiled slightly before turning to look at the thirty of us who had landed. I nodded once, and we shifted.

Shouts of surprise sounded from the humans and I called out, "THROW YOUR WEAPONS DOWN!"

A few startled forward, but a shout went up, "STAND YOUR GROUND!"

I glanced at the few who were with me and shrugged before removing a blade, and walking forward. When I heard Gillith shout, "OUT. OUT OF THE WAY! OUT OF THE WAY!"

I scrambled through the sand, before shifting to a wolf, and landed hard on my paws, pushing myself hard away. It was right in time too, since Quinn's dragon appeared and the screams of the humans were deafening. They were not ready for that. I looked at them before shifting once. I was at a safe distance before calling out again, "THROW YOUR WEAPONS DOWN!"

The humans scrambled backward, but none of them dropped their weapons. I glanced backward, but since I knew where the others were in the darkness, I knew the humans could not see Quinn's dragon all too well as he was black as the night. I shrugged and waited for the others to come forward.

****

I was glad for the slack in the chain when Quinn's dragon got airborne. I now understood why Gillith had it that way. I swallowed though, if Gillith had not informed the king to not tie ourselves down, besides myself and the other captains, then we would have lost several of our pack members. We were somewhat halfway out of the water and tilted upward. Gillith had a handful directing the dragon the way that we needed him to go. He kept on wanting to go whatever way he wanted to go, and it was proving a slight difficulty to manage. However, my task was simple, well not really. I was one of those who were tasked with holding a chain.

I glanced at the other ships, two had different lengths of chain, so as not to crash the ships into each other as we bounced through the rough seas at night. My father told me stories when he was just old enough, that their father took them Viking, and the best time to come in was at night when nothing was alert. Seas were choppy at night, but was easier than heading in during the day when their targets could see them coming.

I noticed that Rispin was having a slight issue, his chain kept moving out of his hands, and I glanced at the other ships, and saw that they were having slightly the same issues. I glanced at Brego who was in my ship and connected to the others, *"Help tighten your chains down team. Otherwise, you will have to row in."*

*"And how are we supposed to do that when the dragon is moving like this Ghost?"*

*"For crying out loud, Batis, it is not THAT hard. Just tell the wolves around you before you do, and they have more line."*

*"Oh,"* he replied.

I glanced at Azier and saw her moving towards the head of her ship. She had allowed her wolf to surface, but only enough for traction. She hauled herself to the mass, went underneath Rispin's arm, and skillfully tackled the chain, making it so it was more taunt, but enough to make it easier for them to manage, but not hard enough for the dragon to have an issue. Once she was done, she shimmied back down, and that was when we hit a harsh wave. She jolted towards the side of the boat, but three of the front-row wolves leaped up from their seats and grabbed her in the nick of time. They hauled her to her feet and made room on their bench for her to sit.

I swallowed, we almost lost Cyprus and Batis's sister. I glanced at the other two ships and noticed that Cyprus had watched it happen too. His eyes flickered to mine for a moment before heading towards Nathaniel, since he boarded his ship. He quickly got the chain to be tighter and moved slowly backward, and Nathaniel gripped his shoulder slightly and stopped him from moving.

I glanced at them for a moment longer, but then looked over at the other ship, and saw Batis trying desperately to get the chain situated, but it whipped through Marius's fingers and flew wildly in the air. Their ship stopped as soon as that chain disappeared. I shouted, "NO!"

Which caught Gillith's attention, but when he tried to get the dragon to do what he wanted, it refused and roared, rattling the chains.

An albatross came into view after a few minutes, and I called out, "HELP!"

The bird looked down at us and blinked once before it seemed to count how many ships were there. It looked like it was going to ignore us, but finally sighed, turned around, and flew back. Soon, a giant splash happened, and I would have looked backward, but I knew I couldn't. My task was to take care of the chain.

Soon, the missing boat got ahead of us, as a huge black dragon was flying, and carrying the boat across the water, not in the water either – Out of the water. I saw the shock and fear as Batis looked over the rim of the ship, looking down upon our heads, before it overtook our dragon, and headed to the distant land that I could see barely on the horizon.

*****

The ships moved forward onto the sand behind us, and a few of the werewolves leaped out and tried hard not to lose their food, but failed. However, none of the humans witnessed it since Nathaniel leaped out of the ship and boomed out with his Lycan, "**WHERE. ARE. THEY?**"

The humans shrunk down, Nathaniel walked forward, and paused beside me, his eyes sparking in anger, he bellowed, "**GET. MY. FAMILY. BACK. TO. ME!**"

A brave or stupid human shouted back, "GO AWAY! YOU BEAST!"

Nathaniel looked at the one who shouted, he rumbled, "**How dare you.**"

Even I knew when he was no longer playing, and I had never fought alongside the werewolf king either. I swallowed and looked at the humans before calling out, "We are ONLY after Rafeor and Aurelius! Hand them over to us, and then we will leave."

Nathaniel's head jerked towards me slightly, since no one had said Aurelius's name to any of us shifters. He looked back at his pack, but his eyes landed on Ghost and Cyprus, he rolled his eyes, knowing that the five may have told some of the shifters something when they went for Morphous.

We were at a stand-off. They had the upper ground, but that was not going to stop angry werewolves and shifters. We came for two people, and we were not going to leave without them.

Regardless of the bloodshed that was about to happen. If they wanted a war, they had it on their doorstep. Ready or not, blood was going to paint the grass and rocks.

# Chapter 34

We stared at each other, and finally, one brave human stepped further than the rest, making the rest look at him in shock. He swallowed and I could barely see him, but our eyesight was better than his, and he could see by the numbers that we were not playing around. He kept coming forward and stopped within striking distance, and I could see that he was just a young boy. I glanced sideways at Nathaniel, but he did not do anything. He tightened his grip on his weapon but did not approach. I sighed and started forward, and stood within a few feet from him before speaking, "Hand over the two young ladies, and we will leave. There is no need for the massacre that will occur if we are refused."

The human swallowed before replying, "How do I know it is not a trick? You all look armed to the teeth. Along with the ability to be whatever critter you want."

I frowned, his voice, was not one of those that belonged here. I glanced at Nathaniel before speaking, "Are you… are you a slave?"

His throat bobbed before muttering, "I was taken from my homeland earlier this year, sir. How could you tell?"

"Someone else has the same voice, broken sounding."

"Oh."

He glanced behind him at the mass of humans, who did not budge from their spots before returning his attention to me, "What is your name?"

"Mine is Conrade. Yours?"

"William, but they don't call me that. It's all get over here boy, and…."

'GET AWAY FROM THEM BOY!"

A voice boomed out, and I looked beyond William before seeing a white male, coming forward he looked pissed. Coiled around his belt, however, I spied a coiled whip. I growled and turned my attention to Nathaniel. "Nathaniel?"

William shrunk down when Nathaniel looked hard at us before I motioned him towards us. For a split second, I thought he would refuse, but he approached, and quickly five werewolves came forward and approached too. I recognized one as Batis but the others were a mystery to me. I swallowed and looked up at Nathaniel and spoke, "Not everyone here is by choice, sir, some are forced."

"How are you for sure on that?"

"B-be-bec-because…."

Nathaniel looked at the human, and Basil flashed in his eyes, but William swallowed hard before continuing, "Because some of us did not get the chance to refuse. We were brought against our will to leave our homeland."

**"And would these people you speak of, lay down their arms and surrender?"**

William swallowed hard, his Adam's apple bobbing in fear. He replied, "Most of them would if it was not for their owners. Who is watching us like a hawk, making sure we don't bail."

"I SAID. GET AWAY FROM THEM BOY!"

A whip cracked behind William, and he shrunk down and fear lit his eyes. However, I had looked past him and saw about a quarter of them flinch in response to it. I knew the moment that Nathaniel saw that aspect and his eyes flashed for a split second before he rumbled, **"If you value your life, human, then you will lay down your whip, and surrender."**

Basil rumbled in his voice, making William shrink down and cower. I looked at him before speaking, "Would you surrender to us?"

He looked at me with fear in his eyes, whispering, "No use of a…. Of a whip?"

**"None,"** replied Nathaniel, who had tuned in to what we were speaking of, and he swallowed before removing his sword and tossing it to the ground. The collective gasps behind him were from the other quarter. William turned around before calling out, "THEY WILL NOT WHIP US! They will keep us safe. COME WITH ME!"

For a moment, it looked like they were too scared to move. Their overlords chuckled before one called out, "Freer of slaves? These are not what you want in your army."

**"They won't be in our army though, they will be free men and women."**

Silence, even some of the werewolves behind us moved slightly with what Nathaniel said. I looked towards the humans before speaking, "Anyone who throws their weapons down, will NOT be killed. Those who dare to carry their weapons will meet their end."

For a moment, I thought that they would listen, and throw down their arms, but they glanced at their overlords and must have come to grim terms with what was to become of them if they did so.

William stared at them all, before shaking his head and moving towards us, backing up before calling out, "REVAN! HORST! Come on!"

Two of the humans looked at the man who had approached, coming after William in fear, but they slowly approached. Another overlord, however, snapped his whip before bellowing, "ANY SLAVE THAT STEPS ANOTHER FOOT FORWARD WILL RECEIVE THE END OF MY· WHIP!"

Nathaniel growled low in his throat, and hair started to pin prick all over him, as he tried to keep his Lycan under control, however, it was a losing battle. I could tell that the five werewolves that came forward could see it as a warning bell. They took a slow step backward and drew William with them, slowly mind you. I swallowed, I was in front of him, if he indeed lost the battle with his Lycan from surfacing, then I was good as dead, however, Nathaniel looked at me. **"Shift. Into. Wolf."**

I glanced back at the five and swallowed before turning to the humans and calling out, "IF ANYONE WOULD LIKE TO LAY THEIR WEAPONS DOWN DURING THE FIGHT. THROW THEM AWAY FROM YOU, AND GET ON YOUR KNEES, AND KEEP YOUR HEAD DOWN."

I looked behind me and saw Nathaniel's eyes flickering between his and Basil's. But at this point, it was mainly Basil's eyes that showed his hair coming in. I linked the rest of the guards, *"WOLVES ONLY! DO NOT FIGHT ANY OTHER WAY! I have a feeling that Basil will not know the difference between you and the humans."*

A chorus of groans happened, but we would do it the werewolf's way. I glanced at William before speaking, "Head towards the ships. Keep your head down, and under any circumstances try to run away."

He nodded his head vigorously, headed towards the ships, and was followed by snarls from the werewolves and shifters behind us. I turned my attention forward and shifted to my wolf, which was gray in color with black spots. My paws barely touched the ground before the human before me, the one that was after William, cracked his whip at me, and caught me in the shoulder, drawing a line of blood. I snarled, bounded forward, and attacked.

****

The battle was not fair, we were built and trained to fight, and these humans were hired by whoever owned the mansion behind them. They were easy kills. And once their overlords indeed were too busy to pay attention to their slaves, they threw down their weapons, and sank to their knees in submission. None of the werewolves or shifters attacked them afterward. It was as if they knew the terms of surrender, and I swallowed. I didn't think I would have that authority, but I could see Basil rip through a human as if he were nothing. Blood poured out of the wounds he had inflicted first, and I swallowed as I was glad I was not the one he was attacking.

Soon, all the humans that had dared try to fight were slaughtered. Only a handful of the overlords had tossed down their swords but did not go down before us. And they were all shouting, **"NO! WE THREW DOWN OUR ARMS! THAT WAS THE…."**

A strangle gurgling sounded, and one by one, they dropped down to the ground. Severely wounded, but on the verge of death. A form hovered over them, growling, "You were told to drop to your knees and have your head down. That was the surrender image."

I looked over and saw Quinn, he was deadly now and had welcomed his other half, which was not more than three or four days ago. He looked at me and grinned wickedly, he was the only one who was not in his wolf form, but he did not have any harm from Basil which surprised me.

A werewolf came forward, and shifted after a moment, before panting, "You shifters fight well."

"Thanks. You as well."

The werewolf smirked before turning his attention to Quinn and speaking, "What are you entirely?"

"I am a shifter and demon."

"Another hybrid? Wow, dangerous. I wonder what your offspring will be if you choose to have them. Times are changing. Soon, there will not be full-bloods anymore."

He trotted off before I could reply, and seemed to catch Quinn off guard entirely. His jaw was parted in shock, and I watched as the wolf disappeared into the werewolf population. One blink, and he was gone.

I looked at Quinn before speaking, "I thought you would have been a wolf."

"Nah, wolves are messy with their kills."

He gestured around, and I didn't even have to look knowing he was right. There would be spilled guts everywhere, on top of the gore that was evident. The sun started coming up, illuminating the slaughter and the blood coating everything, including the used-to-be white marble building. I glanced at Quinn before whispering, "I somehow wished that they would follow our directions. There is too much bloodshed."

"This happens in every war though. Too many die, and not enough to replenish the counts. This is what war looks like. Take a good look at it, Conrade, since another one is coming."

"How do you know another one is coming, though?"

He looked at me and did not reply. Instead, he walked towards a group of the surrenders before speaking, "Stand up. Keep your heads down, hands ALWAYS where we can see them."

The humans did not refuse him and did as he said. I swallowed and wondered what he knew. What could possibly make him believe another war was coming?

*****

I had made it to the dungeons in record time and panted as I pulled myself together. I had spared no one in going out to the front, so no one was seeing the fear in my eyes. I composed myself before heading to Malcolm's cell and opened it. He looked up in shock at me before bowing his head and whispering, "Did you come to kill me, my lord?"

**"Tell me something, Malcolm. Did you solely get those two because they are supernaturals?"**

His Adams apple bobbed in fear and he gulped. "W-wh-what of it?"

**"I want to know who your source was. Was it the same source when you managed to capture that young male one?"**

"They were different. The young male, was in his wolf form when I managed to capture him. I uh…. I think whoever gave me the two girls worked for whoever it was though, since he mentioned his name."

**"What was the supplier's name, Malcolm?"**

"Logan was the one for the wolf. I believe he was doing something to distract the others when we got the girls, but unsure of the other source that handed the girls over. However, they both had the mark on the neck, same as Aurelius."

I frowned before replying, "**Any chance that they are not what I think they are?"**

He swallowed before clasping his hands, and moving slightly so he was as comfortable as possible in the current situation he was in. He replied, "Doubtful, my lord, they bore the same mark and around the same area too. I think they are what my father would have said as werewolves. I know that another species is across their territory, but…. I have not personally seen the other type of supernatural."

**"Werewolves? You sure?"**

"Look, I know I screwed up big time, Kiesin. However, I know what to look for. Yes, they are werewolves. I should have taken the source with me, to try to force his wolf to surface and…."

I held up my hand to stop him before he could continue. I hissed, "**So you knew they were werewolves?**"

"I knew one was for certain a wolf, Aurelius, has the mark. Rafeor? Is it? Doesn't have the mark, but I was informed that she was given something to tame or dull out whatever she has."

I stared at him before whispering, "**Do you by chance know WHAT was given to her?**"

"I believe, if she is a werewolf, then it would be wolfsbane. It would make her wolf dormant, kind of blocking it. I personally have not administered it before since that takes the fun away from the hunt. However, it does make sense."

I rubbed my hand across my face when he spoke again, "What is going on out there, Kiesin?"

I paused, heard the growls and screams already. I swallowed before replying, "**I believe Nathaniel is here. Along with someone else. Do you know what else is across the channel? What other supernatural there is?**"

"I don't know. I already told you I don't know about the other species. I know that they must be big enough for Nathaniel to not attack. So… eh?"

I frowned before speaking, "**Any chance that your father mentioned something to you? And you simply ignored it? Something that you didn't believe to be true?**"

He frowned before replying, "Alright, he did mention one other species. I think he called them changers. But unsure of their proper term. He said that they can change into anything at will. Mentioned that the government on that side, is hunting a wayward experiment that escaped. Said that the one who escaped is very dangerous, and I should try to stay away since I don't have anything to keep them in."

**"Do you believe that they would be powerful enough to make Nathaniel think twice about invading them?"**

"I think the experiment has not settled down, Kiesin."

**"Any chance that someone else has the same qualities as the experiment?"**

"Hardly unlikely, but possible. Why? What is happening? What are you keeping away from me this time, Kiesin?"

**"I saw a freaking dragon."**

"A dragon? A fire-breathing dragon, dragon? I think they are all extinct, Kiesin."

**"I know what I saw, Malcolm. I saw a freaking dragon. So, is there a possibility that there ARE pure-blooded changers?"**

"Of course, that is the possibility, Kiesin."

**"Well, great. I think Nathaniel got the pure-blooded changers involved then."**

"Why would they even bother? It is not like we have something that they would want. Unless…."

He frowned and swallowed hard before looking at me again, "Unless the reason why we got Rafeor is because she is something that is not supposed to happen. My source mentioned that she was the one that we should ALWAYS inject the serum every three days."

**"And you are just mentioning this now because?"**

"To be fair, I am down in the dungeons, Kiesin. Can't really tell you shit."

I scowled before turning towards the door and speaking, **"Come on, Malcolm."**

"Why?"

**"Because you were my top guard before this."**

"I would rather stay down here."

**"Why?"**

"You hear those death screams, Kiesin? Those are human screams. The growls are wolf. So, no, I am not going up there."

I scoffed at him before snapping, **"Coward."**

His Adam's apple bobbed, but he did not reply to the barb. I left his cell door open, in case he thought better of staying down here in the end.

******

I got upstairs at the worst time. A set of wolves were passing the entrance down into the dungeons when I opened the hatch. They swerved their heads at the creaking of the hinges and stared at me. I swallowed before exiting and falling to my knees. I knew better than to try to grab my weapon, there were just a few too many to try to defend myself.

A wolf came forward before shifting to his human form, I was not expecting to be staring up at a man fully clothed though. I have heard that once a werewolf shifted, then it would rip the clothes right off. He stared at me before speaking, "You have nerve coming back up from your dungeons. Who are you?"

**"I am...."**

I swallowed, and finally, lied, **"My name is Malcolm. Please, show me mercy."**

He cocked his head sideways before replying, "That would require Morphous and Nathaniel to decide your fate. Take him."

The wolves approached and swarmed me, jostled me to my feet, and kept me in the center of the group. I swallowed hard, Nathaniel knew who I was, and he would instantly kill me. I gulped in air and looked around the marble walls, thinking that this was the last time I was going to see them. I never appreciated the beauty of them before now.

I was led to the hall where the majority of my staff could come for their days off, and at meal times. That was where Nathaniel was residing, I did not recognize the man beside him, talking. They stopped talking together and turned around. Nathaniel's eyes flashed before he rumbled, **"You. How dare you."**

The wolves snarled and backed away from me, the one who had shifted into his human form raised his eyebrow before speaking, "You know him?"

**"That is Lord Kiesin. The coward."**

Snarls filled the room, and I cowered slightly before whispering, **"Please. Have mercy."**

**"Why should I give you mercy, when YOU have captured my family members?"**

**"I didn't know they were yours!"**

**"Anyone across the channel is either my people OR Morphous's. You took our family members."**

**"Both of yours? I thought you did not have someone else reeking power in your kingdom, Nathaniel."**

A closer snarl happened, and the man shoved me down onto my knees before snapping, "That is King Nathaniel to you. Same with King Morphous."

I swallowed as I winced in pain at the force, the man before me did not look like he could hold his own, but he did. He was dangerous. He wasn't radiating power, but it was oozing from him. The guy beside Nathaniel spoke, **"Enough, Feilian."**

"Yes, my liege."

He took a step backward but did not stop glowering at me. He kept his hand on his sword on his hip, and I tried hard not to see that there was not a drop of blood on the weapon. I looked up at him before whispering, "**H-ho-how d-di-did y-yo-you k-ki-kil-kill m-my....**"

"**We were in our wolves form. We have no use for weapons, except for our claws and teeth.**"

I swallowed hard and bile came up when I realized that he meant that my men were gone, and possibly were not recognizable since they were slaughtered horribly. I bowed my head before whispering, "**Please have mercy on me.**"

"**Why should I?**"

"**Because I send you goods from my side. Who else will do that?**"

"**With what happened here, Kiesin, I doubt that that is what you are thinking. I can go back to the ways of the old.**"

"**You would go back to killing innocents because you want to slaughter?**"

"**Correction. I would go back to what we used to do, simply to give you a lesson.**"

His eyes flickered in the candlelight for a split second, and he seemed to struggle for a moment, before his eyes returned to normal. The man beside him looked at me and spoke, "**Nathaniel, we should put his head on a pike. Make a message to his kind.**"

"**Nah, we should leave him.**"

"**Why?**"

"**Why are you questioning my motives, Morphous?**"

"**Because you were the one who was out for his blood this morning.**"

"**True.**"

I swallowed hard before standing up and speaking, "**I will give you whatever you want in return. I swear I will...**"

"**You don't get a choice in this matter, coward.**"

"**You know my NAME! Use it, you dog!**"

The entire room froze, and Morphous looked amused for a moment. He glanced at Nathaniel before shaking his head. Nathaniel was growing hair out of his arms, and his voice took a rumble, "**What. Did. You. Call me?**"

I swallowed, and backed away, at least tried to. The wolves in the hall growled a warning. Nathaniel walked down the steps, headed straight to me, and bellowed, "**ANSWER ME!**"

I hung lower and finally dropped to my knees before looking at the ground and murmuring, **"I apologize. It will not happen again!"**

Nathaniel grabbed me by the throat and raised me high in the air, snarling, **"You are correct. It will not happen again. You know why?"**

I gasped and clawed at his hand, which only tightened on my throat. I croaked out, **"W-wh-why?"**

**"Because you are not going to survive another minute."**

My eyes bulged, and he tightened his hand further, cutting off my air entirely, and I internally screamed, as my face turned bright red. Soon, turning white due to the loss of blood. The whole hall was watching in satisfaction and finally, I saw blackness creeping into my eyes. I gasped hard, and soon the darkness won, and I saw nothing.

*****

Basil dropped Kiesin after a moment, I knew he felt the weak heartbeat in his hand, however, he wouldn't kill the coward. He had something else on his mind for him. He looked at the crowd before speaking, **"Find them."**

The hall erupted into movement, as the wolves scrambled out of the hall and into the rest of the mansion. Basil waited, and soon turned around and raised his eyebrow to Morphous who stared at him.

Basil scoffed before releasing control back to me. I sighed and led my hand through my hair before speaking, **"Why did you refuse to come, Morphous?"**

**"Because she went without my permission."**

**"Is that the only reason why you did not want to come, Morphous?"**

He swallowed for a moment and replied, **"Along with the fact I didn't want to be alone with you. I have wronged you, and made…"**

**"Morphous?"**

**"Hmmm?"**

**"I have come to terms with forgiving you, at least with Rafeor. Not the other things that drove us apart. Those I will never forgive you for, Morphous."**

He met my eyes for a moment. **"I am sorry that it came to that, Nathaniel. I had enjoyed our old friendship before everything happened."**

"**Remember, it was you who had caused the tear in the friendship. Not I, and definitely not Sophronia.**"

He swallowed hard before whispering, "**I know.**"

Nathaniel turned around to look at the remaining werewolves and the shifters who did not leave before speaking out, "**Get out.**"

The shifters hesitated for a moment, but Morphous nodded at them. They left quickly and disappeared.

*****

He turned around before speaking, "**Since we are now together. Why did you send Herald out to me to deliver a message?**"

I swallowed for a moment before eyeing the room, knowing that someone could overhear what we had to discuss, however, it seemed empty. I looked at him and replied, "**Well, it seems rather stupid now that you have seen Quinn.**"

"**Why is that?**"

"**Because Quinn has what his father has…. A demon. When I wrote those letters, it was before any other form of event. I do have to say something else, Killian, as of now, is banished from the shifter territory. As he probably should be from yours too, Nathaniel. He cannot be trusted.**"

"**What did he do to get you to this point?**"

"**He killed an innocent, you know the law I have fairly well. He even helped me with some of the rulings too. However, the thing that led to that though is that he has lied for years about what he is. Quinn only surfaced stuff because of what has happened.**"

"**What are you not telling me?**"

I swallowed as I looked around the room and spoke, "**You have heard the rumors? That the Benik's are back?**"

"**Interestingly, you had mentioned that, Herald claimed to be one.**"

"**His father is a Benik. At least, he claimed to be one.**"

"**So, the line of the demons is still a thing? I thought they all died out centuries ago.**"

"**I think they survived, and while Abacore was chasing him, Killian led us to the outlanders' territory….**"

I paused, looked around, and swallowed hard before continuing, "**There are wolves over there, Nathaniel, and they are powerful. However, that is not the most terrifying news. It's the fact that Killian went to his brother. He has a sibling left. I think his name was Calio, and his demon if I remember correctly is Severi. I would suggest we stay away since they seemed quite at home in the outlanders' terrain.**"

I saw Nathaniel's Adam's apple bob, before he replied, "**Are you sure it was the outlanders' territory that you flew after him to?**"

"**Positive. It was probably a five-day horseback ride there, but with Abacore, it was only a matter of a few hours.**"

"**Shit.**"

"**What?**"

Nathaniel turned away from me and looked elsewhere. I walked into his line of sight and growled, with Abacore glinting in my eyes. I rumbled, "**What do you know that I don't?**"

He sighed before replying, "**I sent Tobias over to the outlanders' territory.**"

"**What business do you have with the outlanders?**"

"**It is none of your immediate concern, Morphous. It is werewolf business.**"

I opened my mouth to retort when yells were heard, I growled, "**I want to touch base on this again, Nathaniel.**"

"**If we can find the time to do so.**"

I scowled and knew that it was the way it had to be. I turned my attention to the doors.

*****

Six human guards were shoved through the entrance. They were in various stages of being undressed, and a few had weapons, coiled whips, beaters, and small knives. I growled as I smelled something familiar on all of them. Rafeor. I strode towards them, and they cowered as they stared up at me before I growled, "**Why do I smell Rafeor on all of you?**"

One swallowed hard, before spying their lord on the ground, a bruise already forming around his neck from where Basil had wrapped his hand around his throat. He looked up at me and whispered, "Just kill us and get it over with."

"What game are you playing, Dax?" Hissed his comrade who was beside him. I glowered at them, and Abacore pushed for control. When Nathaniel came over, he froze before Basil

433

glinted in his eyes and power oozed out of him in waves. Making the werewolves bare their necks in submission, and making the shifters adjust their stances. He might not be their king, but he rolled out enough power that they knew and felt it. Nathaniel lost control of Basil. He lost the mental will to keep him in.

*****

**"WHY DO. I. SMELL. AURELIUS. AND. RAFEOR. ON ALL SIX OF YOU?"**

The humans cowered further to the floor, and Basil shredded the clothes that he had brought. He growled at the six humans and approached fast. He was in his Lycan form, down to the hair and strength. He towered over me by several inches. He looked down at the humans, he pulled his teeth back in a snarl, saliva dripping out of his gaping maw. They looked at him in stark terror. One had released his bowel and the urine smell along with the feces was prominent in the air. Basil leered over the humans before snapping, "**ANSWER.**"

Dax swallowed before whispering, "W-w-we."

Basil's eyes flashed and he snapped his jaws once, the snapping of his teeth rattled against each other, making them hunch down further. Dax looked at the one who was beside him and whispered whispering, "Fal?"

Fal swallowed hard before whispering, "We robbed them of what girls want to keep."

I barely heard what he said, and I saw that several werewolves in the back, along with my kin were frowning. Basil looked down upon Fal before growling, "**Louder.**"

Fal leaned down, but even though his voice trembled, he spoke, "We robbed them of what girls want to keep."

**"And what do girls want to keep?"**

"Their dignity, and their…. Their…."

He swallowed hard, not wanting to continue. Basil's eyes flickered to mine, seeing that Abacore was not in them, he growled, "**Abacore? You coming out?**"

I swallowed, I had put him down tight, but I sighed and knew that it was only a matter of time before I could not contain him anymore. I closed my eyes and his eyes flickered in and stayed. He blocked my access and made it impossible without being imprisoned to be brought backward.

*****

I took a deep breath in and scowled when the once fresher air was tinted with the smell of fecal matter. I glowered down at the humans before snapping, "**Where are Rafeor and Aurelius? And what exactly did you take from them?**"

Fal swallowed and leaned backward, I knew Basil was holding back his aura, but I didn't even bother drawing backward. I let it all out. I even saw Basil shift his stance for a split second, and I smirked. It was something he hated, the fact that I was more powerful than he was.

I looked down at Fal with a raised eyebrow, looking at the hall before thinking aloud, "**This is a pretty house, although it will be nothing but rubble when I am done with it. So, tell me. Where are Rafeor and Aurelius? And WHAT DID YOU SIX TAKE FROM THEM?**"

Dax swallowed before whispering, "We took their dignities and their…. their…. "

He swallowed a lump in his throat and whispered more quietly so, even I had to strain to hear, "And their virginity."

I stared at the six and my eyes sparked red, before I snarled, "**You what?**"

Dax looked at Fal and swallowed hard again before he met my red eyes for a fleeting second. He looked away before whispering, "We took their virginities. They are no longer innocent."

Howls of outrage sounded and sounds of shredding fabric echoed throughout the entire hall. The humans were as good as dead. I looked down at them before growling, "**You have committed treason.**"

"Not according to our lord. He allowed us to do it. He said as long as we left them alive, we were good."

I turned towards the Lord's body, snarled, and moved faster before Basil could do anything, I shifted into my dragon and stuck a talon directly into his chest, making him wake up due to the pain. He gasped and clawed at my black talon with his hands, and I snarled at him. He froze and shook as his life source was ebbing away. I looked at Basil before snarling, "**FIND THEM BASIL. We both know that YOU have their scent and know what to look for. Find them.**"

The werewolves growled low in their throats, but Basil looked at his kin before snapping, "**ENOUGH! He is correct. I have their scents, and I will find them wherever they are.**"

He was about to stride through the hall, but one of the humans spoke, "We placed them in the dungeons along with the wolf that we had captured days before them."

"**What wolf did you take from my kingdom?**"

"He was in wolf form up until a few hours ago. I think when we brought Aurelius down there, they knew each other since they were sobbing together."

I frowned, looked at Basil, and knew the moment that he knew who they had. He turned slowly towards the humans before bellowing, "**HOW DID YOU GET FINN?**"

I swallowed, looked at the humans, and looked down at the lord, as I watched his life draining out further. I knew that once I removed my talon, he would die. However, I wanted him to hear everything, and witness what was to become of his guards who had done the deed.

Basil looked at me and growled, "**Do not remove your talon yet, Abacore. I want Kiesin alive.**"

I cocked my head sideways but did not reply. The only way to save him was to give him shifter blood, and I did not want to give this lousy thing a drop of my blood. However, I looked over at Quinn who had come into the hall alone. He looked at the guards before speaking, "Hands on your head, and keep them there. You move, and you lose your hand."

The humans instantly complied with his order, not taking any chances on who was giving the order. Quinn looked at Basil and did not seem to be daunted with his aura. He said, "I will go with you, Basil."

Basil looked like he was going to refuse, but Quinn's eyes flashed black for a split second and he shook his head slightly before turning away again. Quinn paused and looked at Feilian before speaking, "Feilian, did you mention that you had found the lord coming out from a hidden door?"

"Yes, sir."

"Please lead me and Basil to this door, and come back here."

"Of course."

Feilian looked at me, before bowing and leaving with Quinn trailing him. Basil looked at me with a hard look, before following them.

# Chapter 35

We got down into the dungeons without an issue, all the guards seemed to have been sent out to the massacre outside, besides the six who were doing unsavory things to our people. I looked at Basil and saw that he was not crawling exactly, but he wasn't exactly walking either. I sighed, stopped walking for a moment, and shifted to my wolf form, drawing Basil's attention to me immediately. His lip curled upward, but he did not speak.

I went further and soon came to a cell that was opened. A man sat inside, and he reeked but it was not the smell of urine, oh no, he reeked of Rafeor and Aurelius, and one other smell. Basil knew the smell. He snarled, "**NAME. NOW.**"

The human swallowed hard before raising his head and replying, "Malcolm, sir. My name is Malcolm."

He hung his head down and whispered, "I'm sorry. I did not realize that they were important to you, Nathaniel, and who I assume to be the other leader."

He looked at me expectantly, and I huffed before shifting back, making his eyes pop slightly. He swallowed hard, his Adam's apple bobbing before he dropped his eyes to our feet. I spoke, "Tell me something, Malcolm, what did you gain in taking two innocent lives away from their homes?"

"Nothing but misery."

"Good. Basil, we should take this one back with us to the other side."

**"Why?"**

"Because he would do well for target practice. We have to get ready for war."

"War? What war?"

I looked at Malcolm before chuckling, "A war that probably won't reach through this side of the channel."

I turned sharply on my heel, left the cell, and left a confused Basil and Malcolm behind me.

****

It took only a few moments for Basil to catch up to me before rumbling, "**What are you talking about?**"

"You don't know?"

"**No.**"

"Oh, well, my father had found something on his leave, and he, well, told me to prepare for a war. The prophecy is going to happen, Basil. Are you ready for it?"

"**You know about the prophecy?**"

"I know your and Morphous's prophecy, which is bogus. That Rafeor is going to drive everyone apart. If she is used correctly, then she will bring peace, and unite the shifters and werewolves together."

"**Is this the reason why you wanted to come down here with me alone?**"

"To be truthful, yes. Yes, it was because of that. However, the issue is. The only way that Rafeor would be able to unite the packs AND shifters, she would need a Benik involved."

"**So, you?**"

"Truthfully, I always thought it would be my father who would do it, however, since Morphous banished him, he can't come back. So, it may as well be me."

Basil swallowed for a moment before replying, "**What about Herald?**"

I paused and looked at him for a solid thirty seconds before sighing deeply and speaking, "He's not my brother. We grew up thinking we were, but before my father was banished, and without Herald knowing. We talked. It turns out my father got him from a Druid before Morphous killed everyone. The Druid said that his destiny is already set in stone."

"**Druid camp?**"

"Yes, Druid camp, Basil. Meaning, if my research is correct, that would put him in the same age as well as your brother Logan's child."

"**Impossible.**"

I shrugged walked further, shifted into a wolf, and allowed my animal spirit to take me to the correct cell this time, leaving Basil to think in silence.

*****

I sniffed the cell and smelled Rafeor and another scent. I looked at Basil before motioning to the door. He grabbed the metal, and ripped it backward, his forearm flexing, but otherwise was the only form of struggle. The screeching of metal sounded, and as soon as it was off, Rafeor and Aurelius cowered. Along with a male, I growled at him, but he raised his hands towards me, and Basil whispered, "**Finn?**"

"I am sorry, my lord. I have failed. I tried to come back. I swear I did."

He lowered his head and swallowed before whispering, "I understand if I need to stay here with what Norjor did."

"**No.**"

He raised his head in shock before Basil rumbled, "**Did Logan set Norjor up for that attack?**"

"He did. He also had a hand in getting me here."

"**In what way did he have a hand in that?**"

"He told Norjor where to run if he…. If he failed what he was told to do."

I glanced at Rafeor and saw her eyes squint for a moment before she looked over at me. She had never seen me in my wolf form, all the other guards at the shifter palace had shifted, not me though. I sighed as I shifted back into my human form, and she ran and hugged me before whispering, "**Quinn!**"

I smiled slightly before wrapping my hands around her more firmly and glanced at Basil before speaking, "Shush, you are all right now, Rafeor."

She let out a small sob and buried her face into my neck. I looked at Basil again, but this time, I was looking into Nathaniel's eyes. He was still in the Lycan form, but he spoke softly, "**Rafeor, do you have feelings for this…. This man?**"

Rafeor went backward before replying, "**Not in the way that you are thinking, Nathaniel. He was the one who got me out of the mansion that Verien and Michael were in charge. It is a close bond, but nothing personal.**"

I swallowed hard. I wanted to have my personal feelings locked down good and tight, but Nathaniel looked at me with a pointed look, and I looked away. He knew what I wanted to hide. I wanted to have Rafeor look at me with love in her eyes, I wanted her to be mine, however, I have heard the rumors in the werewolf population, that she was mated to someone named Marius, and I have run across him once so far. He was a well-built wolf, and he had a rank. He would make Rafeor feel safer, and quite frankly, it was not my destiny to be with her. I knew that as is.

I looked away from Nathaniel's pointed look but did not release Rafeor entirely. She glanced at me and pushed gently at my arms. I sighed before I released her. Finn looked at me and sighed deeply as he looked up at Aurelius and murmured, "I promised you, Aurelius, that I would always come back. However…. I…. I…."

He bowed his head, and she rested her hand on him before speaking, "It was not your fault that Logan did this to you, Finn. Nathaniel, what are you going to do with Logan?"

**"That is an excellent question, what are you going to do with the person that made it possible for us to be here in the bloody first place? He was the one behind getting us here!"**

I glanced at Rafeor and whispered, "I thought you would have spoken with your Lycan, especially when you are angry and scared like this. Why isn't she surfacing?"

I saw her swallow hard before touching her neck, and I moved closer to her and saw the pinprick along with cuts and lashes. My eyes blare black for a solid ten seconds, drawing attention towards me. Nathaniel held up his hands before speaking, "**Not here. Not now.**"

I forced my demon backward before closing my eyes and muttering, "Sorry."

**"Quinn? What was that?"**

"It was my demon. I have the same thing that my father has, Rafeor."

**"Oh, well. That makes sense if you think about it."**

I huffed in response, and turned slightly, towards the door before speaking, "If you want to know what it is like, it is never quiet in my mind. It is always a constant talking. Nothing ends."

I touched my forehead and walked out of the cell. Knowing that if I stayed longer inside, then he would come out, and currently, I could not allow him out. He would slaughter everyone here, except Rafeor.

*****

I watched as Quinn left, and I turned to Nathaniel with a confused look. He smiled with a grim look before turning his attention to Finn. I looked out the ripped door before looking back at what was happening with Finn.

When we had been shoved into this cell, we were thinking we were going to be alone, but it was with great sorrow that Aurelius had found her mate here of all places. It now made sense why he didn't come back. Because of how far away he was, if we hadn't been brought here, he would have never been found. And would have forever been thought that he would rather live without his mate. I swallowed and closed my arms across my chest, and winced. The lashes that the guards have done, on top of the brutal entry…. That was….

A hand gripped my chin and I flinched backward, and the hand fell away, before Quinn's voice came into my hearing, "Rafeor! Shush, you are okay. You are not going to have that experience again."

I took a shuddery breath, looked around, and saw Nathaniel looking down at me in shock. I lowered my head in shame, but Quinn shook his head before whispering, "Don't. What you experienced is not normal, Rafeor. That behavior that they had inflicted is not going to happen to you again. I won't let it happen again. Look at me, Rafeor."

I looked up and whimpered, he crouched down beside me before whispering, "Shush, you are okay, Rafeor. You are okay. You are safe."

He stood up and offered me his hand. I swallowed hard before taking it. He pulled me up to my feet. **"How are you so calm in this, Quinn?"**

"Because this is what some of the older warriors go through. Anna had called it post-traumatic response. Or something along those lines. They get flashbacks to what happened to them. They get sent back to wherever they are. What were you thinking before?"

I frowned and replied slowly, **"I was thinking about what happened. I was thinking about the pain I am so used to…."**

Quinn's eyes flashed once, but he forced whatever he had down for a moment before looking over my shoulder at Nathaniel and speaking, "Get her mate down here, Nathaniel."

Nathaniel looked at him sharply but looked at me with what looked like pity. His eyes fogged over for a split moment before replying, **"He will be down in a few."**

Quinn nodded and backed away from me before speaking, "I am sorry, Rafeor, however, I need to keep my distance for the time being. King Nathaniel, if I may leave you?"

Nathaniel looked at him in shock for a moment, before he shrugged and replied, **"As you were."**

Quinn bowed to him and looked at me with a sad look, but he left the cell and did not come back.

*****

I looked at Nathaniel with a pointed look. **"What was that about?"**

Nathaniel looked at me and sighed deeply before replying, "**I believe he is having issues with his other half, currently. I think he would have done something if he didn't leave.**"

"**Is it because of me that he is having trouble with his other half? Is that why he is going to keep his distance from me?**"

"**I wish I could comfort you in that he will come around, but I do not know the terms or fight he is dealing with internally. He said something about the prophecy, but other than that I have no idea.**"

"**Prophecy?**"'

"**Yeah. Wait, you don't know the prophecy?**"

"**It depends on which one you are referring to.**"

"Which one do you know?"

"**The one that I would destroy all that is here. And more.**"

I swallowed hard before facing Finn, saw him struggle to his feet, and leaned against the wall before he replied, "Would that one come true? I sure as hell hope it does not come true."

He glanced at Nathaniel, but Nathaniel shrugged and replied, "**Honestly, prophecies are hard to read sometimes. Nothing is set in stone, except for a few loose here and there pieces. However, the meeting of this was set in stone, but probably not the outcome.**"

"In what way? Would the outcome be different?"

"**The fact, that Morphous came along with us. Along with the majority of the shifters. We worked alongside each other to get here.**"

"I thought that we were not allowed to co-exist with the shifters."

"**That is what my father and forefather had ordered. However, I was, at one point, friends with Morphous when we were both young rulers.**"

"What happened?"

"**Prefer not to relive it. It was the breakage of the camel's back though, and will not be friends again, but mutual aid will happen. As long as the prophecy does not come to play.**"

"What part of the prophecy do you not want to come to play?"

Nathaniel looked at me for a split second and sighed deeply, lowering his eyes and replying, "**When Rafeor brings an army to our doorstep to slaughter all and any in her path.**"

"**What?**"

I squeaked. I did not want to know that side of the prophecy, but I knew that it was horrid either way that I had heard. It was horrid. I swallowed and was about to say something when I smelled the lilacs coming down further from the cell. I looked at Nathaniel and spoke, "**I-i-i...**"

Nathaniel shrugged and replied, "**It is not set in stone, Rafeor. Things can change.**"

I swallowed hard as Marius embraced me and whispered in my ear, "I am so sorry, baby."

I clung to my mate, looked at Nathaniel, and out of the corner of my eye, I saw Finn fighting with Norjor surfacing. His hands were white, and he was sweating. Nathaniel looked at him before speaking, "**Back off, Norjor.**"

Finn's eyes flew to Nathaniel's, and Basil's eyes lit in them for a brief second, and instantly Norjor disappeared. I swallowed hard and knew what the reason was behind it. He did not believe I could rewrite what the prophecy was. I swallowed hard before looking elsewhere. I was the freak.

****

It was another five minutes of standing down in the dungeons before Nathaniel sighed deeply drawing everyone's attention, "**Let's get out of here, and go home.**"

I swallowed hard but followed Marius out of the cell, and headed towards the entrance. I stopped as I spied Malcolm. I swallowed again and looked at Marius who had stopped and looked back at me, with love in his eyes. I looked back at Nathaniel who had stopped when I did. He had a confused look on his face, he spoke, "**What is it, Rafeor?**"

"**I want to bring him with us.**"

"**The same man that brought you here? The same one that probably knows why Shadow isn't able to speak or shift?**"

I looked at Malcolm before replying, "**He may have brought us here, but we have done more than that together. I want to know some things that he alone can answer.**"

"Like what?"

I looked at Marius as he spoke, and I frowned before twirling my hands together and speaking, "**Like why? Why did he send for us, and no one else?**"

Nathaniel looked at Malcolm, and Malcolm swallowed hard, but it was Aurelius who spoke, "And because he would look pretty well as a servant."

Malcolm's face fell when he heard that. If he thought he would get away scot-free, he was wrong. He swallowed hard before looking at Nathaniel with a pleading look in his eye. Nathaniel sighed deeply before replying, "**Alright, fine, Marius, take him.**"

Marius looked like he did not want to lay a hand on him, but followed his king's order, and grabbed Malcolm roughly, before dragging him to the front. I frowned at the action but did not question my mate in front of everyone here.

****

We got out of the hatch and entered the room that it was in when something caught my attention. I walked towards it and touched it, and Malcolm looked over his shoulder. "I would suggest you don't touch that thing. Lord Kiesin does not want anyone to touch that artifact."

**"What is it?"**

"The lord called it the…. The stabilizer. It was some relic that his grandfather got from across the channel."

Marius released him, since there were now guards, and came towards me, and looked down and saw something. His head jerked back to Nathaniel before whispering, "It can't be."

Nathaniel walked forward now and looked down and Basil spoke, "**His grandfather got this?**"

"Y-ye-yes…."

Nathaniel took it into his hand, and made me loose feeling it, before turning his attention to him and speaking, "**His grandfather is dead, correct?**"

"Yes, he died a few years ago now."

Nathaniel finally won and looked down at the artifact, and my curiosity bubbled, what was it? I was about to voice my question when Finn looked at it and swallowed hard before looking at Nathaniel in shock and whispering, "By the gods, I thought that artifact was gone."

Nathaniel looked at him and then at everyone else that was in the room, the only two that he could not force to obey him were myself and Malcolm. Everyone else was a werewolf. Basil surfaced again before growling, "**Not. one. Word of this.**"

"Yes, my lord!"

The guards chorused and that was the end of it. The wolves would hold that order since Basil was the one who ordered it so, but the humans would be the odd ones. However, disobeying his order was not sought after either. He was fucking scary and would make them disappear if they spoke out of terms. I knew that he would try hard not to kill his pack members, but I also knew that time would only tell what would happen.

Nathaniel looked at me and Malcolm before handing it over to Marius, who had pockets and pocketed the artifact in one fluid motion, disappearing in his pocket. I would have missed the pointed look both Nathaniel and Marius had given if I had looked anywhere else. Marius swallowed but did not say another word.

I swallowed, it was something, but they appeared not to say anything. I looked at Marius for a split second, but he avoided my direct gaze, confirming that it was something that I should not have found, or know about. I glanced at Nathaniel and saw him look anywhere but at me. I sighed and went towards the doorway when I paused before speaking, "**Whatever that artifact is, keep it safe.**"

Marius snorted and Nathaniel looked at me in shock, but I left before they could stop me. These halls were filled with soldiers of ours. Both shifter and wolf, therefore, I would be safe from any harm.

# Chapter 36

I went into a room, that had caught my attention, I pushed the door open, and entered. It was plain inside, but it was one of the richer rooms, with red silk curtains, white marble walls, and a canopy bed. I ran my hand against the bedding, and swallowed hard, as I sat down on it. A lot has happened, and one that I did not want to repeat. I looked down at the floor and saw a finger sticking out. I swallowed and got down onto my hands and knees, and peered underneath the bed. A terrified child along with two others stared at me. I blinked at them before whispering, **"Shush, come here. You are safe."**

They seemed to want to sink further back into the bed, but the older child looked like he was battling odds with himself, and finally pushed himself out, slowly. He stood up and stood roughly at my waist height. He looked up at me before whispering, "Are you here to kill us?"

**"No, what is your name?"**

"Johnathan."

**"What about the other two Johnathan? What are their names?"**

He looked at the bed and swallowed hard before replying, "My youngest sister is named Annie, she is five. She doesn't speak. And my brother is not right in his head. He is what father called a retard. However, his name is Espi."

I swallowed hard before asking, **"Why did your father call him a retard?"**

Johnathan swallowed, before speaking, "It's okay. She's friendly."

It was a few moments before two other children scrambled out, and one was stark white. He had pink eyes, stark white hair, and he was very frail in appearance. Johnathan looked at me before whispering, "He is different. Father would have, you know, when he was born. However, mother forbade it."

I stared at the two children, and for the first time in twenty-four hours, Shadow surfaced. She whispered in my connection, *"Mine."*

*"Shadow? You okay?"*

*"Tired, Rafeor, very tired."*

*"What do you mean by yours though before you go?"*

*"Mine to protect, mine to have. They go with us, Rafeor."*

*"What about their family, Shadow?"*

*"I think that their parents are either gone or fled. No one else is here with them, Rafeor."*

I turned my attention to Johnathan before asking, "**Where are your parents?**"

He swallowed hard, glanced at his siblings, twirled his fingers together, and dropped his voice down, I could tell that he was keeping quiet since I knew that his siblings understood at least half of the things he had said. "Father was out in the front when…. When we were raided. Mother…. Mother died a few seasons ago."

I frowned and winced as my back ached, drawing my attention to my pain. I had forgotten how it felt, but I knew that I would be able to survive with them. I sighed before motioning towards the door and headed towards it. Johnathan whispered, "Where are you going?"

I paused at the door before replying, "**Come along with me. You will be safe.**"

"I may be safe, but Espi won't. They will…. You know…."

He glanced at Espi and his pink eyes stared at me. He spoke very brokenly, making Johnathan wince, "I-i-it o-k-ok-okay John-John-Johnath-Johnathan. I-i k-kn-know."

My heart gripped and Shadow whispered to my connection, *"He is mine, Rafeor."*

*"How will we get him to be safe? They are correct….."*

*"Trust, mate."*

I swallowed hard but did not say anything. I did trust Marius, but I also didn't know if I was strong enough to do it. Shadow whispered in my mind, *"We are not alone in this, Rafeor."*

I swallowed hard but did not immediately reply. I knew what I was going to do, I drew on Shadow's aura, and I pulled on my dragon, whose name I had recently discovered to be Remmu. With the joined aura, my eyes blazed a mix of Shadow's eyes, which are turquoise and sea green with Remmu's. I opened the door, and motioned for the children to follow me. They hesitated, but they finally complied.

The halls were filled with shifters and werewolves, and they turned their heads sharply when I walked past them with the children in tow. I heard one wolf whisper, "That is an abomination."

I turned sharply on my heel, and with him Shadow peaked and growled, "**Excuse you?**"

He cowered for a moment, and his wolf submitted to Shadow instantly. Shadow looked around the hall, at the werewolves before growling out, "**They are mine. Anyone who calls them anything horrid, you answer to me.**"

Her eyes peaked slightly, and she rolled her aura out, and the werewolves hunkered in on themselves before she reined it back in. Shadow released me a moment later, and I stood panting slightly, but could not do anything else. Everyone saw my wounds, since, well, I did not put a garment on, it would hurt too much. The fabric would cling to my wounds, and they would get infected. I saw a few eyes trail after me, but Marius exited whatever room he had been in, rolled out his aura, and everyone who was looking looked away instantly.

****

Marius came towards me cautiously and looked at the three children. His throat bobbed slightly before he turned his attention to me again. Shadow flickered in my eyes for a brief second, but she faded, and I swayed slightly before whispering, "**Shadow...**"

"Shush, little mate."

I tried to keep myself awake, but for whatever reason, I dropped. But as I did, I heard Shadow whisper, "**Protect them, Marius. Mine...**"

Then nothing.

******

I had caught my mate and heard what Shadow barely whispered as she dropped before she passed out. I looked at the three children, who looked terrified. I stood up after a few minutes before speaking, "Hello, children. Would you mind telling me your names and ages please?"

The older boy whispered, "My name is Johnathan. I am twelve years old. This is my brother, Espi, he is ten. My sister, Annie, is five."

I blinked and looked down at my mate and heard Onyx whisper, "*So young, Marius.*"

"*I know.*"

"*What are you going to do about them, Marius? You and I cannot take care of them.*"

"*We can do what we can do for them, Onyx. Besides, Shadow seemed to want them. Are you going to refuse your mate what she wants?*"

"*No, and neither should you.*"

I chuckled slightly in response, making them look even more scared. I sighed slightly before speaking, "My name is Marius, and my wolf is named Onyx. I am a werewolf."

Johnathan swallowed hard. "Are you going to kill us?"

Onyx surfaced in my eyes and voice for a split second, before I reined him back in, "No. You are safe now."

I swallowed hard before speaking, "I will try to make you more comfortable, but my King and the shifter King are planning on departing soon."

"What is going to happen to us then? And all the other children that are left here?"

"Other children?"

Johnathan swallowed before replying, "Y-yes, sir. There are other children that Lord Kiesin took in to do the hard-to-get places. We may have been born inside the mansion, but there are others that he had bought."

"He bought children?"

"It is a common practice on this side of the channel, sir."

I looked at the gathering werewolves, their eyes showed wolf light, as they fought to keep their wolves in control. I looked at Johnathan before speaking, "Do you know where we would be able to find them?"

"If they were not sold, they would be in the…."

He trailed off, scratching his head, but Espi spoke, it was broken but he still tried, "Th-they wo-wou-would b-be in t-th-the c-cellars. A-al-along w-wi-with t-th-the b-ba-barn."

I heard a few werewolves scoff at the boys' speech pattern, but I could tell by the look across Johnathan that he had been trying really hard. Johnathan shrugged after a moment, "Espi would know where they are located since he was allowed to be with them. Since I am how I am, I was not allowed to be with the other children. They were viewed as beneath me, according to father."

"Who was your father?"

"A b-ba-bad m-ma-man," replied Espi, and Jonathan lowered his eyes to the ground before he whispered, "Father wouldn't let Espi do anything. If he gets a cut, then he bleeds and bleeds without stopping, becoming more pale than he already is."

Annie let out a whine when he said something, or when she finally caught on to what they were talking about.  Her voice went up higher, a female wolf came forward squatted down, and held out her hands. Annie went straight into them, crying.

Johnathan looked at her with wide eyes for a moment, and I looked down at Azier's mother, who I thought had stayed behind. She grabbed the young crying child, and her eyes flashed once before she spoke in our connections, "*She is something special. All three of these children are. These ones come back.*"

"*What do you see that we cannot see, Taryn?*" Asked another wolf that was nearby. I looked at the wolf that had asked and knew that he was one of those who would never challenge what she would say. I looked at everyone around and only saw three wolves have a grimace across their faces, but otherwise, everyone else seemed to welcome the children.

"*I see them becoming something that our pack needs. Something that would help us.*"

It was very vague, but everyone in attendance seemed to be fine since that was her typical response. They looked at the children, before one of the ones who would challenge her, spoke, "How are you so certain they are good for the pack, Taryn?"

Something about him, saying it aloud made the rest of the pack take a deep breath in. As if they could not believe he would challenge her. Taryn looked up from comforting the small human child, replying, "Are you challenging what I say already, Hecktor?"

"So, what if I am Taryn? You spout out all these outrageous things and thoughts and we are expected to take it in good graces for the most part."

I stepped forward slightly, and was about to speak, when Johnathan spoke, "STOP!"

Hecktor looked at him in shock, before his wolf surfaced in his voice for a moment, "A little boy like yourself should be seen but not heard! You are nothing but a peasant, and you will rot here."

A large amount of aura swirled through the entire party that had been here, and Taryn smiled slightly before she looked behind me. I knew who was behind me, simply by the paleness on the wolves' faces, but they did not submit, which meant it was another royal blood.

****

Ghost appeared with the others in his group. He strode towards us, before gently placing his hand on my shoulder, and I stepped out of the way. Ghost stared at Hecktor and spoke, "Hecktor, are you challenging what Taryn is saying once again?"

Hecktor's Adam's apple bobbed as he swallowed nervously. With Ghost. he kept himself uptight, and tight as a bowstring, you would not know you made him upset unless he spoke out. Hecktor looked down at the ground before whispering, "Don't you have somewhere else to be, Ghost?"

"Normally. I would be elsewhere, however, my duty is also stopping someone from being stupid. You are in that category, Hecktor."

"How dare you! I am not stupid!"

"Then act like it, Hecktor. You are challenging Taryn, who was trained by the Druids in their ways and has passed down her skills to her daughter. Do you really expect me to stand idly by as you challenge the only one who can prevent something from happening, and not step in, Hecktor? Are you really going to question Taryn again after all this?"

Hecktor looked like he was going to say something, but his friend, placed his hand on his shoulder, drawing his attention to him. He shook his head slowly. Hecktor looked at Ghost with a look of hate for a moment before he pushed past the other wolves in the area, heading away down further from us.

Ghost watched them leave, before turning his attention to the three children and speaking, "Welcome to the pack, children. Best to stay away from Hecktor for the time being, until Nathaniel says something."

Johnathan stared up at him before whispering, "Who are you?"

"My name is Ghost."

"Did you pick that name or did your parents give you it?"

"Ghost is the name of my wolf. However, no one has called me by my actual name."

"Why?"

"Because everyone seems perfectly comfortable calling me Ghost. I am not opposed to the name either. Neither is my wolf, who likes hearing his name every time someone calls us."

"Doesn't it get hard to be only called by your wolf's name? Wouldn't…."

Ghost smiled and Johnathan leaned backwards and swallowed. However, Ghost stopped and looked at me before speaking, "Marius, King Nathaniel is wanting to head out. He informed me to find you."

Johnathan lowered his head, but Ghost looked at him, continuing, "I apologize. What is your name, child?"

"Johnathan."

"I apologize, Johnathan, however, I had to report to Marius about the status that our King has said. I was not trying to ignore your question. Now, to answer it, no it is not hard to be called one name. I actually prefer it compared to having more than one name to respond to. Ghost relish being called every time someone talks to us. It is what we are, we have no set boundaries and no one cares that I continue to be Ghost. It is a personal choice."

"Oh, over here, if you try to change your name, you get flogged."

Every single werewolf that was in hearing, well, they did not handle that fully and clothing turned into ribbons as countless wolves surfaced.

Ghost blinked once before clearing his throat, and looked at the wolves before rolling out more of his aura, making a few steps sideways slightly. He looked at the children before speaking, "Taryn, would you mind if you assist with these current children?"

"No, I do not have issues with that, Ghost."

"Thank you, Taryn."

He looked at the pack members before speaking, "Head outside, and find a few members that are in their human forms, to assist in finding the other children if there are any left here. I want them alive."

A few huffs sounded from the wolves, but they would not dare attack a child. They huffed since the children did not understand. They trotted off in different directions. Soon, the hallway was empty except for the five, Taryn, the children, myself, and the limp body of Rafeor.

Taryn looked at Rafeor and brushed her hair aside before she sat slightly and frowned. She looked up at me before speaking, "Marius, we need to clean her wounds and get her some bandages before we depart."

I opened my mouth to say something, but Ghost spoke, "I will take care of that Taryn, Marius at the moment needs to assist Nathaniel."

"Ah, alright. Go find out what Nathaniel wants Marius, but you should be nearby in case you need to mark her. If her injuries are too severe for her to naturally heal from."

I growled low in my throat at the thought of that, and Taryn sighed deeply as she stood up with Annie in her arms. Cradling the child before leaning slightly, to adjust the weight. She looked at me with a soft smile before speaking, "Go and assist Nathaniel, Marius, I got them from here."

"Thank you, Taryn."

"You're welcome, Marius."

I looked down at my mate and swallowed hard, but turned away from her and the children and went to find Nathaniel.

****

I found Nathaniel near the throne room and saw that he was having an argument with Abacore. The tension in the air was prominent as I approached. I caught Abacore's attention and he turned his head towards me, growling a warning. However, Nathaniel growled out, "**Abacore, no.**"

The dragon growled low in his throat, and that was when I saw why they were arguing in the first place. Lord Kiesin was alive, but barely with one of Abacore's talons in him. Blood oozed from his wound that I assumed swept further down into him, and possibly out the other side. I glanced at Nathaniel before speaking, "My lord, Abacore. You had called me?"

It took a moment for Nathaniel to look away from Abacore, but finally, he looked at me before sighing hard and replying, "**How many prisoners do we have in total, Marius? How many extra bodies do we need to cart over the channel?**"

"Ummm… a lot more than what is already being watched by the shifters."

**"What do you mean? You found more?"**

"We have a bunch of children, Nathaniel. Apparently, Lord Kiesin bought children and sold them if they did not do their duties."

Abacore growled but did not lift his talon. Nathaniel looked at me sharply before turning his attention to Kiesin and growling, "**Is that true, Kiesin? Do you really sell and buy children?**"

He spluttered, and went red slightly, whispering, "**Kill me, Nathaniel.**"

Nathaniel glanced at me before speaking, "**Where are the children, Marius?**"

"Currently, they are being located. Rafeor had found a trio of children, and they informed us of the hidden children and roughly where they would be hiding."

**"Once they are found, take them to the ships."**

"Of course, my lord."

He had a grim smile for a moment, but he turned his attention to Abacore before speaking, "**Abacore, please.**"

**"No."**

Nathaniel looked like he was going to sigh, but I asked, "What is going on between you two?"

Nathaniel looked at me before sighing deeply and replying, "**I want to bring Kiesin across the water, alive. But Abacore is against that.**"

I looked down at Kiesin before speaking, "If Abacore takes out his talon, he is as good as dead though."

"**There is a way that he can survive. Abacore knows it well, and what the humans had done six or so centuries ago with the experiment project they had, they found out shifters have healing blood. It only takes a drop of blood and it cures all issues. It can bring back people from death too, Marius.**"

My jaw dropped and Abacore rumbled a warning, but I looked at Nathaniel, speaking, "If you want him alive, then why don't you ask another shifter to do it? If Abacore is not going to help. I am sure someone else will."

Abacore growled low in his throat, and he squinted his eyes in response. Nathaniel looked at me with a look, like really, and he looked at Abacore. "**That could work, but it works better with Abacore's.**"

"But it is possible to use someone else's?"

"**Yes, it could work with someone else's.**"

I turned my attention to Abacore before a thought hit me, and I glanced at Nathaniel. "Hey, Nathaniel?"

"**Hmmm?**"

"What are you planning on doing with him when you get the blood, and get him across the channel?"

"**I plan on torturing him until I cannot tell who he was. And let him slowly heal, only to repeat.**"

I glanced at Abacore as he looked at Nathaniel with sudden interest. I asked, "Would it be possible to have Abacore assist in the torturing?"

Nathaniel froze for a moment and glanced sharply at me and then looked at Abacore, who looked very interested. He blinked at Nathaniel and he and Basil seemed to have a lengthy conversation before they came to the same conclusion, or agreement in their case. Nathaniel looked at Abacore before speaking, "**That could be worked out. What do you say, Abacore? Do you want to help me make his life a living horror?**"

Abacore seemed to think about it, but I saw the glint in his eye. He finally relented, "**Fine, sounds good to me.**"

I swallowed hard, as he looked at me expectantly and suddenly. Nathaniel looked at me, too. I looked at both of them in confusion before speaking, "Why are both of you looking at me with a similar look?"

**"Because we need his blood. And you are usually spot on in getting blood quietly."**

"Ummm, surely not from Abacore? He would roast me alive if I got his blood."

**"I would not roast you alive. I am allowing you to get my blood. If it was forceful then I would roast you alive."**

"Uh…. I guess thanks. Why can't you do it, Nathaniel?"

**"Because I do not trust him enough to take my blood anymore. We may offer mutual aid to each other, but other than that, nothing more. You are the one who suggested the idea, therefore, you are the one to extract my blood."**

"And how do you expect me to extract your blood, Abacore? Your scales would prevent that from happening."

**"You would simply go in between the scales to get to my hide. Then with your sword or blade, whatever you want to call it. You are going to stab into me, and extract my blood."**

"Wouldn't that hurt you more than anything?"

**"Stop stalling and do it."**

I swallowed hard, but I approached him grabbed my hip sword, and slid it out of the sheath before coming towards him. He loomed over me, looked at me with a look, and finally repositioned himself slightly, With his other clawed arm, he rotated it, before showing me an already lifted scale. I looked at him in confusion before approaching slowly, finding it was a regular spot where someone else had extracted blood. I looked sharply behind me, at Nathaniel, and swallowed hard, before I slashed into him.

Abacore growled in discomfort, but his blood oozed from the wound. I looked around and was slightly confused about how to direct it to Kiesin. Nathaniel spoke then, "**Cup your hand into the blood, Marius, and get a small amount. Then carry it slowly to Kiesin. Then force the blood into him.**"

"Ummm… okay."

I cringed as I held my hand against the black scales of Abacore, and caught some of the blood that was spilling with my hand. It was warm, and it was the color of crimson. I tried hard not to gag but I was very pale when I walked towards Kiesin.

He tried to struggle, but he was in no condition to move and I forced the blood into his mouth, and much to his horror some of it made it down his throat. He gurgled and coughed, and after a moment, Abacore removed his talon. I stared in wonder as the fatal wound closed up, and sealed completely.

Kiesin scrambled backward and stared down at his lost blood before he looked at us with this… feral look in his eyes. He whispered, "**H-ho-how is that possible?**"

**"Shifter blood is something that can cure any and all illness. It is what the humans across the channel had found out by accident when they created the experiment. And when she escaped, they believed she was the sole one who could have that power. So, they have unfortunately been hunting a kid for centuries."**

**"Shifter blood can heal anything?"**

Nathaniel raised his eyebrow slightly before replying, "**Haven't been able to test its powers fully.**"

**"There is an abomination of a child living in my mansion. That should be given something since he is a… freak."**

"You better not be talking about Espi."

**"You know him?"**

"My mate found him and his siblings in a room."

**"Normally, a child born like that would have been slaughtered at birth. However, their mother forbade the father from harming the damn thing."**

**"You would kill a child?"**

**"I would kill something of that sort. Yes, I would kill something that is not normal."**

I glanced at Nathaniel's eyes and saw Basil trying to force a shift, but Nathaniel wasn't allowing it. I glanced slightly at Abacore but saw that he had released control to Morphous, and Morphous was standing nearby, and looking at his forearm. I saw a scratch and swallowed hard knowing I was the one who caused it. He looked at me and smiled slightly, before rolling down his sleeve and shrugging it off. I looked at Nathaniel before speaking, "Where would you want me to place him?"

**"Do we have extra chains?"**

"Depends on if Quinn's dragon has issues again. Otherwise, we may have enough, but it would be unsafe for our pack members."

**"Quinn's dragon won't take you back this time. I will, we have too many innocent lives this time."**

"And pack lives don't count as innocent because?"

He paused and looked at me sharply before replying, "**Because you all can swim. You have wolves that will heal you if you are sick, injured, or otherwise incapable of being you. Humans, however, do not have such things. Therefore, you were rather safe.**"

"What about the boat that snapped off last time?"

Morphous sighed and glanced at Nathaniel. "**You werewolves used to sail across the channel every single year for months. That was what? Forty years ago now that you had stopped?**"

"**Roughly that long, yes.**"

Morphous looked at me before speaking, "**So, therefore, your parents had fought across the channel.**"

"**Only thing is, though, Morphous, you attacked someone who was in werewolf territory.**"

"**And how did you manage to get on that topic when we were talking about fighting across the channel, Nathaniel?**"

Their energies swirled around, and I felt Basil stir in the energy in the air. I swallowed and saw Morphous squint his eyes in challenge, and Basil's eyes flashed once. I spoke softly, "Stop."

They froze and their eyes flickered to me before I looked at them with a look.


****


All the while they were bickering and had Marius busy trying to stop a fight from brewing, I slipped out of the room. Not through the main entrance, no, that would make me walk right into others of their kin. I slipped into the hidden routes, only the people of the court knew this route. I disappeared into them and hurried along.

I needed to inform the King on this side of the channel, that their prayers were answered. That there was a cure for whatever their son had. I just needed to make sure I got out here alive.


****


I opened my mouth, to continue to speak, when Morphous's eyes flickered to where Kiesin was. I turned around, and he was gone. I froze and looked around the room, there was nothing, no sign of having the door open or anything. I looked back at Nathaniel before he looked at Morphous before speaking, "**We will need to touch base on this later, Morphous.**"

"**What happened twelve or so years ago, Nathaniel, happened for the good of the people. Sure, it killed the Druids, but they were…**"

"SHUT. THE. HELL. UP!"

I bellowed at them both. Onyx was in control of my voice. Basil snarled in response, but Onyx snarled back at him before he turned his attention to Morphous, asking a question, "If it was good for the people, then why did you kill the warriors protecting the Druids? Did you not understand that they had a family to go back to?"

"**I did not kill them.**"

Silence. Finally, what seemed a whole minute, Nathaniel spoke, "**What do you mean you did not kill them? Are you saying you took prisoners, Morphous? And kept them down in your dungeons? Are they still down there?**"

"**They were down there until Killian took them out.**"

"**What does Killian need with my missing pack members?**"

He went to reply when Onyx cleared his throat, stopping them. Nathaniel closed his eyes and pinched his nose before turning slowly around and speaking, "**Marius, you are trying Basil's patience. Do not think that you can do anything…**"

"Yet we are standing here and discussing interesting things of the past, while Kiesin is escaping somewhere. Your call on what to do, my lord."

Nathaniel sighed deeply. "**As I said earlier, Morphous, we need to talk later. Once we get back home. We need to talk about some of this that has come to light. However, now is not the time for that. Onyx, release control BACK to Marius now.**"

Nathaniel rolled out his aura, and Onyx relented immediately since he could not challenge Basil's direct order, nor Nathaniel's.

*****

I gasped and looked up at Nathaniel before whispering, "I apologize, my lord…."

The doors banged open and Ghost approached. He surveyed the room, and seemed to have concluded that whatever was spoken of outside was correct before speaking, "We need to leave now."

**"But we don't have, Kiesin."**

"Taryn says that if we continue to stay here, the people he is getting in contact with will come with enough force to come and kill the majority of us. We need to depart now."

**"Who has that type of power?"**

"We have located a staff member, and she informed us that there is a King on this side of the channel. Lord Kiesin has to pay this King a hefty toll every year for the amount of protection. The men we had fought earlier, were merchants and what little Kiesin had left. The King over here has everyone else. Once word gets out that we have raided across the channel, then we will be attacked."

Nathaniel's eyes bore Basil's eyes, but he spoke, **"What is the name of their so-called King?"**

"I am unsure, my lord, the maid did not want to say his name. However, she did mention what is semi-common knowledge on this side of the channel. That the King's sole heir had some sort of accident, and his injuries are causing some sort of issue."

We all froze, we had to heal Kiesin and tell him something that not many knew. Morphous bowed his head before muttering, **"And that is exactly why we are hush-hush on what shifters are capable of doing."**

I swallowed and Ghost glanced at Morphous before speaking again, "I would love to know what had happened, however, the boats are loaded with the ones going back with us. We have come across two more war boats, and we have to take them since the survivors have taken two of our boats."

**"Are the other two boats watertight?"**

"Unsure on that, my lord, we won't know until we get into the water further. It highly depends on how the sea treats us too."

Nathaniel sighed deeply before starting forward, when Morphous spoke, **"How many pack members came across the channel with you, Nathaniel?"**

**"Roughly three-quarters of the pack. Why?"**

**"Because there is another way to get across without boats. Except for the four that you had brought."**

"And you are just bringing this up now because?"

**"I do not answer to the likes of you."**

I looked at Morphous more closely and knew he was fighting with Abacore, but there was nothing that I could say. I went to say something, but Ghost cleared his throat. I looked at him with a look but he spoke softly, "While we are here chit-chatting like nothing is coming, the faster that Kiesin is getting closer to his target. We need to leave. Now."

Abacore looked like he was about to challenge Ghost, but Ghost looked over at him before speaking, "Abacore, do us a favor, do whatever Morphous was going to think of doing. If we can do that, it would save us time, and get ready for the evasion that we know will come."

Abacore huffed once and glowered at me before he strode away and out of the doors. He called out to the shifters, his voice far away, so we did not really hear what was said.

I looked at Ghost before speaking, "You knew that Kiesin would leave?"

"Correction. Taryn knew that he would. However, we could not alter the train of events. This one has to go as it currently is."

**"Why?"**

"That is something I cannot tell you, Nathaniel, as much as I wish I could. We cannot change what is to become of the current shifters we know."

With that, he turned around and left. However, I thought hard about what he did say. And suddenly it dawned on me on the wording he had done. I glanced at Nathaniel and knew he came to the same conclusion, something big was bound to happen to the shifters, and not the experiment entirely either. Ghost was referring to Morphous and his clan. We glanced at each other and swallowed hard, we knew that whatever Ghost and Taryn knew, it was drastically important that the current train of events were to occur. For what reason, was the question.

# Chapter 37

We glanced at each other before we left the now quiet halls of the mansion. The sun was setting in the west, casting pink and orange clouds. We heard weird sounds as we got closer to the ships and saw that all of them were further out of the bay, we would have to swim to reach them. The werewolves crowding around were all talking in hush tones, as they watched the shifters. We got closer and soon found out what had their attention and were equally shocked. The shifters were shifting into these great big beasts of sea beasts, and a few roared into the darkening skies. They were scaly and had long teeth with long snouts.

Quinn approached us, he did not look at all surprised before tossing a grape into his mouth. I looked at him before speaking, "What the hell are you eating?"

"A grape, do you want some?"

He offered me a small cluster, which I did indeed take, and popped a grape into my mouth. Working around the seeds, and spitting them onto the ground. They were juicy, fresh and ripe. Their skin is not rubbery or anything. I glanced at the creatures before speaking, "What are they?"

"They are what is called a plesiosaurus."

"A… what?"

"Let's say they are going to make several people think twice about following us when they see them."

"How are they going to help us get across the channel?"

He popped another grape into his mouth before replying, "They are water-mainly creatures. They can be on land, but they do prefer to be in the water. Therefore, they will be faster than my dragon and Abacore."

"Why didn't we do this when we came across the channel?"

"Because up until now Morphous didn't allow us to. Along with the fact that it takes a lot of energy to become one of these sea beasts. We could have gotten across the channel, yes, but then you would be the ones taking the brunt of everything. The ones that are shifting into these creatures are the ones that did not really do much. Or are too impatient for sitting around doing nothing."

"How are you acting that this is nothing?"

"Because if you think about what we, as the shifters are, then this is a walk in the park."

"I thought you weren't a shifter."

"I'm half."

"Half with what?"

"Demon."

"Oh."

"Yeah."

"Have you ever killed someone because your other half took control before you could stop it?"

"I would rather not answer that question, wolf. Anyhow, time to go."

I was about to say something when Nathaniel cleared his throat, stopping me, and looked over at the children who had come out of the mansion. Several of them bore signs of starvation, along with recent beatings. I closed my eyes and counted to ten before sighing deeply. These children went through so much and all because of the damn lord that owned this establishment. He should have been on this carriage back to the other side of the channel.

Nathaniel cleared his throat again, I looked at him in shock and moved sheepishly toward him. Leaving Quinn to be what he was going to do, which was nothing.

*****

Nathaniel looked at me, speaking, "**Do not get attached to all of these children, Marius. Most of them have to be sent elsewhere.**"

"Except for the three that Shadow declares as hers. Those three are ours."

"**Do you have any idea how hard it is to raise a child, Marius? Let alone three?**"

"I don't know, but I do know that I will do anything to make sure my mate is happy. And if it includes raising children so be it."

He smirked slightly but did not reply, as his eyes softened when they landed on Rafeor and Aurelius, who were with a small group that was supposed to be watching Aurelius. I looked at him before asking, "So if Aurelius is indeed your niece, as rumors go. Why hasn't she been treated as it?"

"**Because Logan.**"

"Aurelius is Logan's child?"

**"Technically, step. His mate had a child before they had found each other."**

"Is that why he had done some questionable things? Because she is not his blood-related?"

**"He is grieving."**

"Grieving and giving a fuck…"

****

Ghost approached us, and spoke before I could finish my conversation with Nathaniel, "My lord, Marius. We have a slight issue."

**"What is the issue?"**

"Some of the children refuse to get onto the boats."

"Why?"

"Because we are the ones who had killed their fathers, brothers, and in some cases lovers. They blame us for their deaths."

"We should leave them then."

**"No, no child gets left behind."**

"What are your orders then, my king?"

**"If needed, tie them with rope and put them into the boats."**

I looked sharply at him before speaking, "If you want those children to trust you on the other side, Nathaniel, you cannot do that. They would be terrified of you."

**"Like I had said, Marius, we cannot keep them all."**

"What do you mean by that, Nathaniel?"

**"I mean it, we can't keep them all as much as it pains me. There are simply too many mouths to feed."**

"Then why bother taking them across the channel when their lives are going to be shit either way? They would be sold over this side, and be traded and stuff on that side. That is NOT how you acted like a while ago, Nathaniel."

**"What do you want me to do exactly here, Ghost? We cannot take all of them, and not have a proper home for them. I already know that the shifters cannot take more in, and we can't really do it either."**

"So, you are going to give up what the little hope that the majority of them have? Is that what you are going to do with them, Nathaniel?"

**"What do you want me to do exactly here, Ghost?"**

"I want you to do the right thing, Nathaniel. How often do you get the chance to right the wrongs from someone else? These kids are innocent in whatever is happening. It is not their fault that their fathers and brothers decided to fight against something that they cannot possibly win against. That is not their motive. That is not in their control."

**"It may have been out of their control, yes, but they are still the offspring of them. We cannot simply take care of all of them."**

"What would Sophronia say if she was here, Nathaniel?"

Nathaniel groaned before muttering, **"Fine! Fine. They go."**

Ghost tried hard not to smirk. I looked behind him and saw Taryn watching and saw her smile I looked at Ghost and suddenly realized that they had known that Nathaniel would try to get rid of more than half of the children. Whatever they knew was something that was regarding these children. I swallowed hard before speaking, "You knew he was going to refuse at first until you brought up Sophronia."

Nathaniel removed his hand from his face to watch Ghost give me a lazy smile before he turned hard on his heel, and disappeared into the crowd.

****

Nathaniel grumbled slightly, knowing that I was right. Ghost brought up his mate solely because they knew he was going to reject the children. I looked sheepishly at Nathaniel before speaking, "So, with the shifters being as they are, how are we all going to get into the boats?"

Nathaniel opened his mouth to answer when Morphous approached. Nathaniel looked at him before raising his eyebrow, and Morphous smirked slightly before speaking, **"That is a simple solution. Quinn and I will still be dragons, and some of your pack members will be riding in the ships, yes. But some will also be riding us."**

"Riding? What do you mean by riding?"

**"You would get to be high up in the air and be flown over the channel."**

"Is it safe to do that?"

**"It depends."**

"Depends on what exactly?"

**"If you can hold onto the dragon."**

"And if someone were to let go of a dragon?"

**"Best not think about the outcome, Marius. If you think about it too much that is not going to go well."**

I glanced at Nathaniel and saw him staring at Morphous before Morphous shook his head. **"No, you are not going to be riding on Abacore, Nathaniel. He does not trust you."**

**"And whose fault is that entirely, Morphous?"**

Morphous looked away from him and walked off, and Nathaniel sighed deeply as he watched him leave.

I looked at Nathaniel before speaking, "Are you ever going to tell me at least on what happened between you and him?"

**"Probably not, Marius. It is in the past."**

"If it is indeed in the past, then why are you bringing it up more than once on this rescue mission?"

Nathaniel turned his head towards me sharply, but did not reply, and finally walked away, towards the ships.

*****

Quinn moseyed himself to me, still popping a grape into his mouth and speaking, "Well, that was moderately entertaining."

"What was?"

"You and Nathaniel."

"You heard what we were talking about?"

"Should I apologize if I say yes?"

"What if we were talking important pack business?"

"Nathaniel knows better than to do that around shifters as is. He knows that our hearing is acute."

"What are your thoughts on our conversation then?"

"My thoughts? Hmmm…. That is an excellent question to be had there, Marius."

He popped another grape into his mouth, and I stared at him before asking, "How are you so calm in all of this?"

"Because I know that being anything but calm is not going to help anyone. I am Morphous's advisor. Therefore, I need a calm head in all of this."

He shrugged as if it was a common practice. Popping another grape into his mouth. I watched as his face twisted up in disgust before he spat the grape out, scowling slightly at the remains before taking another one off the stem and popping it into his mouth. I sighed deeply and looked at the children loading the ships, and sure enough, about half of the pack could not ride the ships.

I heard many of the werewolves start to freak out about having to swim across, when Quinn spoke, "Thankfully, for us, there are three of us who can shift into dragons."

"Three?"

"Morphous, myself and Rafeor."

"My mate can become a dragon?"

He looked at me with a sad look for a split second and Onyx huffed in my mind in laughter before it dawned on me what the look was. I stared hard at Quinn before asking, "Do you have feelings for my mate, Quinn?"

"I would be lying if I said no, Marius. I have seen you two together, from a distance so far and you treat her as a princess. I wouldn't be able to treat her that well. However, I am going to warn you, Marius, she suffers from post-trauma, and will have nightmares, flashbacks, and may not recognize you as her mate while this is all happening. I am not telling you this to drive you apart, but you need to know this. Our medic back home said that she may experience some of the trauma from being where she grew up too."

Onyx tried to force himself into my voice, but I kept him locked down. I swallowed slightly but did not look away from Quinn as I replied, "We will work with it together. You and Rafeor seem to be close."

"I was the one who got her out of the mansion."

My jaw dropped and Quinn continued, "She may not feel the same love that I have for her, Marius, but I can assure you this. If you do her harm, you will die at my hand."

His eyes flickered black when he gave me a warning, his demon surfacing and darkening his voice. I swallowed hard before he turned sharply. I called out, "Please! What is your name?"

Quinn paused and looked back, his eyes his normal blue now before he sighed deeply and replied, "Do not tell anyone else who his name is. You have to promise it."

"I swear on the moon that I will not tell another living soul."

Onyx underscored my voice as we both made the vow, and he would not back away from doing it for his mate. Quinn blinked once before his demon surfaced again and he replied, "Thakur."

A chill ran up my spine, something told me that his name meant something, and he grinned wickedly before speaking again, "If you are brave enough, Marius, then ride me."

"But if Rafeor is going to be her dragon, I should be riding my mate."

"That is up to you, Marius. But hold out your hand."

I squinted my eyes at him in sudden suspicion before I held it out to him. He walked back to me before biting Quinn's finger and drawing blood. He looked at me expectantly, saying, "Cut your finger, Marius."

"Why?"

"Because our destinies are intertwined. This way, we can speak to each other."

I hesitate before I spot Ghost in the background nodding at me encouragingly. I swallowed, he and Taryn along with the rest in his patrol were the best of the best. If they said to do something, it was better to ask questions later than anything else. I sighed as I cut my palm. I winced at the pain but knew the moment that Onyx would heal the cut.

Thakur pressed his split-finger onto my cut, and I gasped at the sudden surge of power. Finally, I felt another link snap into place. I stepped backward before allowing Onyx to heal the wound and open it up. Thakur looked at me with a smile before speaking in my mind, *"Now we can connect to each other. The difference between a normal shifter and myself is that distance is not an issue. Demons can connect quite confidently. The one key is to not be days away from each other. Since our territories are next door to each other, it is not a matter of an issue."*

*"But doesn't it drain either of us?"*

*"To be honest, unsure. Since I have not spoken to anyone besides Falcor, and Quinn."*

*"Falcor?"*

*"Killian's demon. Or should I say, my father."*

*"What about the brother? Does he have a demon?"*

*"No. he does not have a demon, and neither is he a shifter."*

*"What is he then?"*

*"He is a…. I am sorry, I cannot tell you that information yet. Time will tell on what and who he is."*

*"Isn't he Logan's son?"*

*"You are correct in that aspect. So, you do know something about him."*

*"The only thing that I do not know is how Killian got him."*

*"Killian visited the Druid camp three months before the attack. The Druids gave him Herald, and Logan's other child."*

*"Wait, if that is the case, then where is the sibling?"*

*"Unfortunately, for us, she had died. I went on a rampage when I first surfaced or became of age. Killing the majority of all of Quinn's siblings. Except for Herald, and that is only because Killian got back in time."*

*"She's dead?"*

*"Unfortunately, yes."*

*"Oh…."*

A shout broke our connection, and I looked behind me and heard thundering footfalls. Thakur looked beyond us, and sighed deeply before speaking, "Well, it is time to go."

I looked at him sharply before speaking, "You knew that the humans would get this far? And you have been stalling?"

"Under technical terms, no we were not stalling. We had children to load, and get them going. So far, the only ones here, are the ones that could not go on the ships."

"So, what are they waiting on then?"

He smiled slightly before walking away from me a few feet before shifting into his dragon form and roaring into the night sky, connecting to me, *"To be honest, me."*

I looked at Nathaniel and saw him watching the treeline, and knew that he was getting agitated.

****

A soldier came out of the woods screaming a war cry, and a couple of others ran afterward. I looked at the rest of the werewolves, there were a lot of shifters on the ground, but they looked like they were not going to move. I was about to shout at them to run, before a shifter moseyed towards me and spoke, "Mount up. The werewolves go first."

"What about you?"

"We will be fine."

He helped me onto Thakur, and I sat on his neck, near his head. And about thirty others got to get up onto him. Thakur turned his head sideways, to assess the oncoming humans, before he rumbled in our connection, "*Tell them to hang on.*"

"HANG ONTO HIS HORNS!"

"YES, MARIUS!" They chorused.

They leaned forward, before grabbing the horns in front of them. Thakur spread his wings out and flapped them four times before bunching himself slightly and leaping into the air. None of the pack members fell off, they were death gripping his horns, and finally, he leveled out and flapped towards the other side.

I turned to watch as the other pack members boarded the other two dragons, and watched as they launched themselves into the air. I now knew which one was Abacore's dragon, and now it kind of evened out who the other one was since Quinn mentioned that only three could shift into the dragon forms.

The shifters met the first line of humans, and it was only the last of the werewolves getting onto the dragons, that they held the line. I stared at their fighting techniques and swallowed. They knew how to fight, and move with precision and nothing was sloppy in their movements. They were all trained fighters. I could tell in the pack link that I was not the only one watching them fight. They might only be holding the line for us to escape, but that was still showing that they knew how to fight.

A line of horses appeared next, but since the pack was now up in the air, the shifters one by one shifted into a small bird and flew upward, before angling towards the sea. Once they were too far away from the shore to get shot down by an arrow, they shifted in mid-beat and changed into more albatrosses. They barely had to flap their giant wings as they glided underneath us and over the ships.

# Chapter 38

We thundered across the fields and tree line, however, our target was getting onto dragons of all things. I urged my stallion forward, trying extremely hard to reach them before they all took off. However, the soldiers up front had no defense against fighting them. Anyone that attacked, was killed quickly. Soon after the giant dragons got airborne, the fighters stopped, changed into birds, and flew away. We had tried to shoot a few down, but they were too quick.

Finally, they got farther away, and our arrows could not reach them, and then we watched as they changed into something else mid-air, and that was when a horn blew from our side. We slowed our horses down and turned them towards the black majestic stallion that our king rode. He was roughly six foot two, with raven black hair, and wearing his royal colors of black and crimson red.  He stared as the dragons and the four Viking ships were moving across the sea. He bunched up his reins before yelling, "**NO!**"

The horses threw their heads up in fear, and they moved around. However, the only ones who rode on top of them were the more senior warriors, who knew how to handle riding a horse. I urged my stallion closer to him, so we could speak in private since I was his advisor.  I glanced at my king before speaking, "**My lord? Your orders?**"

He looked over at me before speaking, "**Get the ships out. We are going after them.**"

"**Of course, my lord.**"

I angled my stallion sideways before shouting, "**GET THE SHIPS OUT AND READY TO SAIL!**"

The soldiers that were not dead, moved to obey my orders, and I looked over at my king before speaking, "**So Lord Kiesin was correct.**"

"**It appears so.**"

"**Should I send someone home to get him out of the cell he's in?**"

"**No, I will need all hands to get the specimens.**"

"**Are you sure you want all of them, my lord?**"

"**Are you questioning my authority now, Blackwell?**"

My stallion stomped his foot on the turf, and I shifted my seating before replying, "**No, my lord.**"

"**Good.**"

We looked out of the harbor and watched the small specs of the dragons and ships disappear before I spoke again, "**Are you going to be bringing Esfire with you, my lord?**"

"**I was thinking that.**"

"**How will you get him across the channel?**"

"**The same way that we always do when we bring our wares over. The barge.**"

"**Lord Kiesin's?**"

"**He doesn't own anything over here anymore except for his life now, Blackwell.**"

"**Of course, my lord.**"

We watched as the men moved the barge into the harbor before loading a few of the stallions that were already dismounted by the slightly higher-ranked officials. I sat on my stallion, rubbing his sweaty neck before speaking again, "**Are you sure you do not want to bring Lucius with us, my lord?**"

"**He would be a sitting duck if we brought my son along with us. He can't go.**"

"**Are you sure that by forcefully taking them across the channel is the only way, my lord? They did kill around twenty men already to flee.**"

"**It sounds like you are scared of what is to become of this, Blackwell. Are you too scared to join your king?**"

"**Of course not, my lord!**"

"**Then stop questioning my movements.**"

I knew better than to respond. He was in no mood to speak. Lucius was barely alive, and his wounds had not been fixed. We would go across the harbor to get the one species that could heal him, and save his life. Along with everyone else's that we could.

*****

It was about an hour later when the barge was ready to go. We urged our stallions forward, and since the barge was made to hold stallions and riders together, we rode ours right into the belly of the ship. Our stallions jerked their heads backward but they did not refuse either of us. They trusted us enough that they would follow us willingly into the fires of hell if needed. We boarded the barge, and after another close to an hour, we set sail. The moon was the only light we could use across the channel. Daybreak would be our attack time if the winds were correct.

# Chapter 39

I flew underneath Abacore when I felt like something was wrong. I looked backward at the fading shore when I spotted something that was not there before. I linked Morphous since I knew that Abacore was busy, *"My lord?"*

**"What is it, Feilian?"**

*"I think that the humans are following us."*

**"Impossible."**

*"Can we send others back to check?"*

**"Has anyone else noticed this? Or have you kept it to yourself so far, Feilian?"**

*"I am pretty sure I am the only one that has noticed so far, my lord."*

**"Then say nothing."**

*"But if they are indeed following us, then we should put a stop to it."*

**"Feilian, you are a shifter. Think about it, what do we have that humans do not have?"**

*"Uhhh… the ability to shift into anything at will, and oh, yeah, I guess we should not investigate that."*

**"So, you now understand why we are flying away instead of flying to meet them correct?"**

*"Yes, my lord."*

**"Good. Now, do not tell anyone else."**

*"Of course, my king."*

I let the connection drop as I looked at the others and saw a few glanced backward and found the same thing that I mentioned to Morphous. I swallowed hard, knowing why we were being followed, but that was only because I stumbled onto it by accident when I was talking to Morphous. He did not tell me the reason, but I worked it out myself – which was more entertaining than anything. I swallowed as a few looked back and realized that the humans were on their way behind us. I glanced up at Abacore before connecting to him again, *"My lord?"*

**"What is it, Feilian?"**

*"The others are piecing together what is happening. I think you should say something in the connection before they leave."*

He sighed before closing our connection and mind-linking everyone, *"**Absolutely no one is to go backward. If the humans are indeed coming after us, then we need to get home.**"*

*"But it would be safer if we turned back and took care of them before they reached the other side of the channel. That is where the majority of the females are."*

*"**Are you questioning my authority, Quinn?**"*

*"Not entirely, Morphous. I am simply saying if we wait until we cross the channel, then we will have to fight them on our turf. Why not send a squad to take care of them before they reach our side?"*

*"**Because unlike yourself, none of my people are demon-ed.**"*

*"I cannot help that fact, Morphous. However, I can solidly say, that we will be okay if we send about twenty shifters back. At least to attack whatever ship they are using than anything else."*

*"**Absolutely not! No one is to go back there. End of.**"*

The entire shifter population was quiet throughout the entire link, and I felt their unease about bringing the enemy across the waters, finally, Gillith spoke, *"My lord, if I may?"*

*"**Go ahead, Gillith.**"*

*"If they are indeed after us, then we should turn some of us back to deal with them. Not all of us need to fly immediately home."*

*"**No.**"*

*"Why not?"*

*"**Gillith, and everyone. Think of WHAT happened with the last time we healed someone with our blood. What happened?**"*

Silence. Gillith replied weakly, *"One of us was captured about six or so centuries ago, and used for the experiment. At least in blood type…."*

Once again, silence. No one spoke. That was not something that we wanted to repeat, and finally, no one wanted to go backward. However, Gillith spoke, *"If that is the case still, Morphous, then we are still leading them to our homeland. Do you want to lead them directly to where we call home?"*

*"**They would have to go through the werewolves first to reach us. And you fought against the humans alongside the werewolves yesterday, Gillith. How would you rank their fighting?**"*

*"As much as I want to say they are good fighters, Morphous, we train harder than they do. Sure, as a species they fought well against the humans, but they struggled to be alone. That is their weakness. Along with the fact that the werewolves are not the enemies, we are mutual aid, Morphous, and therefore, we should not bring a war on their front porch."*

*"What do you exactly want me to do then, Gillith? If we turn back around, they are after us."*

*"Don't you have a connection with Nathaniel, Morphous? Connect to him that way."*

I heard the beating of Abacore's heartbeat as he thought on that, and finally, after a moment Morphous dropped the connection and Abacore turned his head slightly towards Rafeor's dragon, and stared at Nathaniel.

*****

I felt a weird connection, at least a long-forgotten connection stirred in my mind, and I glanced sharply at Abacore before letting it open. Morphous sighed in the connection before speaking, *"We have a slight issue that has been brought up to our attention, Nathaniel, Basil. One that you should be aware of."*

*"And what would that be, Morphous?"*

*"The fact that the humans are now following us."*

I stood up expertly on top of Rafeor's neck looked back at the fading harbor and saw the boat coming. I looked at Morphous sharply before speaking, *"How long did you know that they were coming after us, Morphous?"*

*"Not long, I didn't notice it. Another of my clan saw it coming. He informed me of the issue."*

*"I know you well enough, Morphous. How long ago did this clan member of yours tell you of this?"*

*"Fine, about twenty or so minutes ago. It was not that long ago that they noticed the boat being brought out of their dock."*

*"Alright, then what is your course of plan exactly, Morphous?"*

*"My plan would require them to beach on our land. Or more like your land as we flee into our territory."*

*"You would leave us without aid in this?"*

*"You were the one that pressured Abacore to give Kiesin blood. Therefore, this is somewhat your fault that the humans found out that we have healing blood."*

*"Alright, that is a fair point, however, we are not as well trained as you are apparently. My pack members commented on how well you held the line back there."*

*"We do train rather hard, Nathaniel. We kind of have to."*

*"I do wish you did not have to do that so hard, Morphous."*

*"We cannot escape what we are entirely, Nathaniel. Now, what is your idea if you have one?"*

I looked back towards the ship that was coming after us and glanced down at the sea beasts that had long necks and were swimming swiftly through the sea. I glanced back at Morphous before speaking, *"Any chance that more of your clan can shift into those?"*

I turned my head down, and scared the wolf on top of me, while he was cursing. I saw the sea beasts before I replied, *"That is probably the last thing I want to do."*

*"Why?"*

*"Because they are shifters and they would go after us. They are after the shifters. You… you are not like us at all, Nathaniel."*

*"I guess that is true. So, what is your idea?"*

*"My idea is to wait until we get across the harbor and let you handle them when they get over here."*

*"Morphous, that is the coward's way of doing things. That is not how you should handle this."*

*"I am trying to do what is best for my people, Nathaniel. If it is to flee, so be it. I am sorry, but that is how it should be."*

*"No, what about Quinn's dragon? He is technically not a shifter."*

Abacore frowned and I glanced over at Quinn's dragon before speaking, *"There are only werewolves on him, Morphous. Therefore, they would assist him."*

*"But he is something else. And would you dare see how many Rafeor's mates can handle before he was taken down?"*

*"Marius may be not expendable, and neither is none of my pack members on his back, but they are the only ones who would be able to go. Considering that Rafeor cannot do it, since she is the first hybrid between us, and you cannot go since you are pure blood. And none of your clan should go either. Therefore, he IS the only solution, Morphous. As much as it pains me, he should be the one to be used in this case."*

I could tell that what I had said, made Morphous think. He was thinking hard about it before replying, *"I am going to include him in our connection, Nathaniel."*

*"Fine."*

The connection dropped for a few moments before Morphous opened it back up with Quinn involved now.

I could hear Quinn's sigh before he spoke, *"My lord, Nathaniel. What can I assist with?"*

**"You are the only one who is not a pure-blood shifter. Therefore, you should be the one to turn around and attack the ship that is coming."**

*"What about the werewolves on my back though? None of them would survive it if my dragon decided to shift mid-flight to something else."*

**"Stay in your dragon form then. Then drop them off on the deck before flying off again and attacking it from the air."**

*"So, you are willing to get your pack members in danger?"*

**"We have children back home, Quinn. This is the only way that we can stop a fight from happening on our shores."**

*"What about, Marius?"*

**"What about him?"**

*"He should not be the one going on this fight. Marius should trade spots with the wolf on Abacore's head."*

**"Rispin is my beta, therefore, he is my second in command."**

*"Look, Marius may be the gamma in your pack, your third in command after Rispin. However, I already know that Rafeor would turn back around to help her mate if Remmu or Shadow catches on to what is happening. You are simply stopping what she would do."*

**"Remmu?"**

*"You didn't know? Well crap, my apologies. However, yes, Remmu is Rafeor's dragon's name. She is rather scary when she speaks. So, be careful. However, you must not say her name. She would not trust you if you call her by her name."*

**"Stay on task, Quinn."**

*"Sorry, my lord. But yes, we need to switch Marius with someone. Otherwise, Rafeor will turn around to help her mate. Have you noticed that Remmu has only flown fast enough as my dragon? She is watching her mate."*

I was silent and knew that Morphous was thinking before I replied, **"What about someone else besides Rispin?"**

*"Who do you suggest entirely?"*

I was about to respond when Ghost spoke in our connection, shocking everyone, *"I am going to apologize now. However, no one is going to prevent this ship from crossing the channel."*

*"Why not?"*

*"Because of the fate that is already set in stone. I have seen what would happen if something were to happen to this ship. Neither outcome would be suitable. No, no one is to attack it now."*

**"But once we land, then you will be attacked."**

*"That may be true, but you Morphous, and the entire shifter population would need to vacate and leave for home."*

**"You would condemn your pack members to fight a battle for us?"**

*"Morphous, if something happened to the shifters now, we would be lost. The entire world is balanced, and currently, this needs to happen. Make sure that every single shifter gets home, besides you Quinn."*

*"Why besides me?"*

*"Because if you went, then we would be in a bad situation. You need to stay, and let your demon surface completely."*

*"That would result in more than human deaths if I let him out like that though."*

*"No, it won't."*

*"How are you so sure?"*

**"If Ghost is saying that you will be able to wrangle your demon back into yourself, then believe it. He has not been wrong yet on something like this."**

*"And you are an expert on demons now, Nathaniel because you have dealt with them?"*

**"Enough. Ghost, are you sure you know what you are doing? We would assist you if needed."**

*"As you said earlier, Morphous, they are after shifter blood. Therefore, you all should go home. However, you should know this…. If you know where Astromic is, then you need to find them. They are not safe."*

**"How would I find them?"**

*"Listen to your clan members. Especially the ones watching certain borders."*

*"And how do you know about Astromic?"*

*"She is the key to something. Same with the entire shifter population that she has under her command. They are part demons, even if it was forced, but they are the ones you need to find, and protect. Otherwise, everything we know it as will crumble."*

We would have continued to speak back and forth, but Rafeor's dragon roared and it stopped all communications as we tuned back into what was happening in front of us.

*****

There was more than one ship coming after us, but instead of being behind, they were coming from the sides. They weren't thankfully coming from the front, but it would be easy for the ones in the air to escape, but the sea beasts were the ones in danger. Quinn's dragon stopped flying forward and hovered where he was. He looked towards me before rumbling in the connection that Morphous still had open, *"I know we should try to flee. However, the plesiosaurus's. Has no way to disappear. Normally they would dive deep and disappear and resurface when they are in a safe distance. However, they cannot since they are carrying cargo."*

**"The people are not cargo."**

*"Sorry, wrong wording. However, the plesiosaurus still cannot dive to get away. Therefore, they are being prevented from doing what they naturally want to do. Morphous, some of the shifters need to shift into other plesiosaurus, or some other sea beasts, to deflect them away."*

**"Feilian, Gillith, Conrade, and Hector. Shift and deflect the ones approaching on the sides, but do not engage with the one from the back."**

*"Understood."*

They stopped flying, dropped down to the sea, disappeared for a moment before huge necks surfaced, and they dove down below sea level.

There were a lot of things happening at once, a few of the werewolves were moving in their placement below, on the ships and it looked like I was taking a bit of encouragement from Nathaniel to let it go, but the werewolves were itching for something. Finally, Ghost connected, *"The plesiosaurus are not going to be the only ones that need to fight these from the sides. These are not human. At least not completely."*

**"What do you know that we don't, Ghost?"**

*"Taryn says they are not human. At least, the crew that is rowing towards us is human, but the ones that would attack are something else."*

**"What are they?"**

*"Something that the shifters should not engage entirely."*

**"That is a very vague response. What are they?"**

For a moment, Ghost was silent, and I glanced down at the ship and saw him talking with Taryn before he replied, *"I can only tell you their name. They are what is called a Sazornora. They…. I cannot say what will happen. I am sorry."*

**"What are you not saying?"**

*"I am sorry. But I cannot tell you what they will do."*

He dropped the connection with being on the same mind-link with them, and only connected to me, *"Nathaniel. Drop the connection with the shifters. Now."*

**"Why?"**

*"Just do it."*

I felt Morphous's question in the mind-link before I spoke in the shared connection, ***"I am sorry. But I am going to need to concentrate on what is happening now. As should you. Let's drop the connection."***

***"Nathan…"***

******

I dropped the connection before Morphous could finish my name, and Ghost sighed deeply before speaking, *"Nathaniel, I am going to tell you what they are and what they will be doing."*

**"Why can't the shifters know this?"**

*"Because it would alter the course of the future. We cannot inform them. I am sorry, but the drastic events that are about to happen must happen. Otherwise, the life we know as is will change for the worse. It is a hard truth."*

**"So, you are basically saying that if the shifters find out what they are now besides what they are called it would change everything in the long term?"**

*"Correct."*

**"Why are we allowed to find out what they are then?"**

*"Because eventually, you will need to sign a peace treaty with the leader of their species. Without the treaty Nathaniel, they will wipe the werewolves out of the entire world."*

**"What does Taryn say about this, Ghost?"**

*"She says that you need to listen to what I have to say, Nathaniel. I may not be her son, but I am her daughter's closest friend and she therefore confines me in that way. Therefore, I know what Azier, Batis, and Cyprus have to manage, and not tell a single soul either. Same with Brego, he knows things that would cripple the time frame, but he had sworn an oath to not say a word about anything. Damn it. I am rambling. However, she says that you need to listen."*

**"I am listening to you, Ghost. It has to be something drastic with the way you are acting currently."**

*"As much as I want to help the shifters, Nathaniel, we cannot assist them. Not without condemning our own future. We have to let the ones that Morphous sent down to attack their ships go."*

**"What do you mean? They are going to die?"**

*"Nathaniel. I am sorry, but all of the four shifters that Morphous is sending out will die. The Sazornoras are here to slay the shifters. They do not take their blood since they would simply counteract it."*

**"But those four are Morphous's high-ranking officials."**

*"I understand that they are those to Morphous. However, we cannot prevent this from happening, Nathaniel. As much as I liked Feilian and Gillith, and the other two. We cannot prevent it from happening. They will be killed, and they will sink to the bottom of the channel. However, they will give us enough time to escape, and the Sazornoras will leave us be for another couple of years."*

**"How are you thinking that is a silver lining?"**

*"I am sorry, Nathaniel. You cannot tell the shifters of what is to become of their comrades if you did. Then it would alter everything."*

**"What are they?"**

*"They are what is called a Sazornora, Basil. They are the supernatural hunters. The human government assigned them the case of hunting down the shifters and the experiment. That is the reason why I stressed to Morphous about finding her and her clan members. Because she and her offspring know how to blend into the crowd and move around."*

**"We have dealt with supernatural hunters in the past, Ghost. They are no different than those ones."**

Ghost was about to reply when Taryn spoke, *"My lord?"*

**"Go ahead, Taryn."**

*"As much as it pains me to say this, we cannot alter what is to become of the ones that Morphous has sent. Nor can we warn them of what they are besides the name that they call themselves. They are no ordinary supernatural hunters. They may be hired by the human government, but they are by no means human. None of them are human. They are four to five times stronger, faster, and dangerous than we can fight. Same with anyone who crosses them. I had a vision, Nathaniel and it showed it from more than one angle. One of the angles would be if you informed the shifters of the Sazornoras and what they would do to their comrades currently, and that would be a horrid reality. Another one was how it would go as it should, and the werewolves would be safe from them, along with several other supernatural beings. The only ones that are not safe from them are the shifters."*

**"But not all the shifters are the experimental shifters though, Taryn. These ones are the purebloods. Therefore, they should not be killing these shifters."**

*"Oh, I am sorry, Nathaniel. I truly am. However, it does not matter to Zhukov who he kills and who lives, as long as they are shifters. If we were to interfere with this, Nathaniel, he would hunt and kill every single werewolf on the earth, just because you denied him whom he originally was hunting for. As much as it pains me, Nathaniel, you have to let this go."*

**"Those that are going, Taryn. You knew they would die didn't you from the start. Is that why you acted differently around them of all the shifters?"**

*"Yes and no. Yes, because I knew they were going to die on this trip sometime. However, no because I was not treating them that way because of it. I was treating them that way because I could sense that they were solid good soldiers, and would be a horrid one to lose. However, we cannot say anything else."*

**"So, in other words, the Sazornoras are after shifters only and will leave the others alone? Is that correct?"**

*"As of current if we do nothing, yes. However, if one of the werewolves tries to rescue the shifters that have gone to attack the ships then we have an issue. However, I don't think that anyone would take the plunge into the frigid temperature waters willingly."*

**"Taryn, so you are pretty much-condemning shifters to die, and you know that."**

*"Nathaniel, you cannot stop what is going to happen. If you do, then the Sazornoras will attack any and all supernatural that they find."*

I was torn and looked over at the boats that were coming when Ghost spoke in the connection, *"Don't do it."*

**"I am going to do what I think is right, Ghost. So, be it."**

*"You are going to condemn the entire supernatural world to horror if you do this!"*

**"So, be it."**

I blocked the connection between Ghost and Taryn and knew that they were trying hard to reach me, but I didn't allow it to be open either. I swallowed hard and looked at Morphous before connecting to him, **"Morphous. Get your people back onto the ships. Do not engage those ships."**

**"What do you know that we don't?"**

*"Nathaniel, don't!"*

Morphous glanced down at the ship and Ghost and Taryn stared up at us in paleness. However, I swallowed and looked over at Morphous, but Quinn's dragon spoke in our connection, *"MORPHOUS!"*

**"What?"**

*"I am sorry but YOU cannot find out what Nathaniel found out. And Nathaniel?"*

*"What?"*

*"You are a coward."*

**"Apologize now, Quinn! That is out of line."**

*"No, Nathaniel knows the issues if he indeed tells you what is about to happen. He has seers, Morphous, and his seers are telling him not to tell you a single thing of what is to become. Therefore, you should not listen to what he was about to say."*

**"You know what he was about to say?"**

*"I vaguely know what is going to happen, and know that there are certain consequences if they are attacked other than by the ones that are currently approaching."*

**"I order you to inform me of what is happening, Quinn."**

*"Unfortunately, I cannot tell you, Abacore, as much as I want to. It will alter too much of the future if either of us tells it. Therefore, you need to let it go."*

**"TELL ME!"**

*"No."*

**"Nathaniel?"**

**"I am sorry, Abacore. I guess I cannot tell you what is to happen."**

**"And you wondered why we stopped being friends."**

I felt a jolt of hurt through the connection and winced and finally closed the connection with them and hung my head in shame. Ghost nudged the connection before I allowed it open, *"Thank goodness, that Quinn's dragon spoke about this."*

**"They are about to die Ghost and you are simply going to do nothing!"**

Ghost let the connection drop, and I did not speak.

****

I looked at the ships approaching and saw two of the sea beasts disappear while one was distracting the occupants on the ship before the other one came flying up from the depths of the sea, and flipped the ship over completely. I watched as the boat turned over, and glanced at the other one on the other side and saw that it was over too. I thought that maybe Ghost and Taryn were wrong, that it was just two human ships but soon I was proven wrong. Some of the occupants of the ship got onto the haul of their ships and fired arrows at the sea beasts. I felt

Rafeor stop flying as her dragon felt the difference as the shifters were killed. I looked over at the other side and saw that the other two were dead too. Their bodies sank into the water, but they were indeed letting them go down without taking their blood. However, they did indeed buy us enough time to get to the other side.

I knew that the entire shifter clan felt their deaths of them. They looked like they would have flown over to aid, but Morphous must have forced them to stay in rank and they flew onward. I looked down at Ghost and Taryn and saw them hang their heads in sadness. They all knew that they had to be the ones sacrificed to make sure that we got to safety. I swallowed hard before looking backward. With my eyesight, I saw ten standing on the haul of their ship staring at us as we flew onward. Same with the other ship that was over. There were ten on the other, so a total of twenty. That was how many of the threats would be a cause for the shifters. Twenty. I swallowed before looking towards the shores that were coming up.

****

It was another hour before our ships were released from the shifters that had towed them across, and we helped the prisoners and children off the ships. I glanced up at Morphous, who had once again landed in Sophronia's flower beds, and watched him glower at me in anger. The shifters walked past me and headed towards Morphous before mounting his dragon. Two stood on his taloned arm, before he took off into the air. I watched as they flew off, leaving Quinn there alone.

Quinn looked at me and smiled slightly before speaking, "It had to be done, Nathaniel."

**"Will he ever forgive me or you for not telling him what was going to happen?"**

"If roles were reversed, Nathaniel, would you?"

**"No."**

"Then you know your answer."

**"What is going to happen to you if you go back to the shifter territory?"**

"Thakur will make sure that Morphous does not do anything drastic."

**"Thakur?"**

"That is his name, Nathaniel."

I looked at him closely and saw how worn down he seemed. I replied, "**You knew coming across the harbor would result in more than war deaths. Didn't you?**"

"Thakur knew what was to become. We need to get ready for another battle, however this one…. This one is not like the others, Nathaniel. For this one, which you will face later down the road, you need to think for the goodness of your species alone. Not the coming battle with Rafeor, no…. Another one is coming. One that you need to think of the werewolves and no one else."

**"What do you mean?"**

"He means that something else is coming, Nathaniel. Something that goes hand in hand with the supernatural hunters."

I turned to face Ghost and the rest of the patrol as they approached – crunching the rocks as they came forward. They still had their weapons strapped to themselves, and I looked towards the sea before speaking, **"How long do we still have before they come across?"**

"I would say another hour or so. They are carrying close to an entire army."

**"We should have kept the shifters over here."**

"No, they are after the shifters. Quinn's demon is the sole one that would help."

I looked at Quinn and saw him frown and kick a rock before speaking, "I cannot promise that the werewolves will be safe if I let him completely out though."

"It is okay if a few of us go down," Ghost replied

I glanced sharply at him before rumbling, **"Nuh ah. It is not okay for a few to die, Ghost."**

"Sacrifices must happen, Nathaniel. It is part of life. If we do not have Quinn's demon, the humans will slaughter a quarter of the pack. If Quinn's demon does indeed fight, then we would only lose a couple of wolves. It is for the pack that we need the demon."

I was silent and glanced at Quinn before sighing deeply and throwing up my hands before starting to walk away.

Quinn's demon spoke, "Wait."

**"What?"**

"There is a way for me to not attack the werewolves."

"And what way are you speaking of?"

"One that many would hate, but may be the only way to make sure that in my crazed state, I do not kill everyone."

"We are listening."

"Give me a drop of your blood. Each."

Ghost stared at him and looked at Azier and Taryn walked closer before she looked at me before speaking, "As much as we want that, we cannot."

**"Why not?"**

"Because there is a catch. Isn't there?"

"There is."

**"What is it?"**

"You would willingly be giving me blood, and be made into my army."

**"My pack swore an oath to fight for me and me alone."**

"That may be true, but my package of the blood would reverse that."

I swallowed hard and knew that losing the pack would not be the route I should go. Losing a few werewolves though, also, was not the course of action I wanted either. I looked at Taryn before speaking, **"I am leaving it up to your discretion, Taryn."**

I turned around and left, and knew that Taryn would know the correct course of action to take.

****

Taryn looked at me and finally, she shook her head. "It sucks yes, but we will not allow you to take our blood, Thakur."

I blinked at her once before smirking and shrugging in response. I picked up a stone before twirling it in my hands and speaking, "That is your call, Taryn. However, you do know the next course of the future and all the different angles."

My eyes flickered up to her face, and I saw her swallow hard, but she did not reply. She knew what I was referring to. Ghost growled low in his throat, but did not say a word. Knowing that something was going to happen, and one that they should not alter in that course. I shrugged and dropped the stone again before walking towards a fallen oak tree – awaiting the attack.

# Chapter 40

I should have known that they would stoop so low. They knew that Feilian, Hector, Gillith and Conrade would die. They KNEW! I should have seen that someone else would die and I could do nothing to prevent it. I should have. I landed hard onto the grass that I had made for Abacore, and felt in the shifter mind-link of what everyone was feeling. We all had been connected to them. We are one connection, and we all were feeling their deaths. I bowed my head and Abacore threw his head back and roared into the sky. The remaining shifters, had exited the palace, with tear streaked faces, since we all feel a life drop if one of us dies.

Anna approached slowly and looked at me. I was still in Abacore's dragon form, and she whispered, "Morphous? Please shift back."

Abacore turned his head towards her, her eyes were glistening in tears, but Abacore did not want to shift back. He wanted to fly to the werewolf palace again, and rain fire on the whole lot. However, Amish came over before looking up at me, whispering, "A-ab-Abacore. Please, there…. There is nothing you can do."

Abacore looked down at Amish and finally released control and allowed me to shift back. I dropped to my knees and lowered my hands to the grass. My body shook as sorrow filled me. I lost my advisors besides Quinn, I lost my best friends.

Amish approached slowly and placed his hand on my shoulder, lowering himself down to my level before speaking softly, "They may be gone, Morphous, but surely we can return in a couple of days to get their….. Their…."

A sob escaped him, and Anna slowly approached and rested her hand on his shoulder. The rest of the clan circled around us, the ones that had joined us in the rescue had their heads bowed. They were all shaking since they had lost their friends, family and their captains. We all had our heads bowed down when I finally got myself together slightly before turning to look at some of them that had went, "**We need a few teams….**"

"Morphous, not now. There is nowhere any of you should go."

"I am sorry, Anna, but Morphous is right. There has to be a few teams to go already. We have to find the experiment and her children."

"Why?"

Amish looked at me before looking at everyone else, saying, "I got friendly with a werewolf named Batis, and he informed me that we need to find the experiment and her family. Because we are being hunted."

**"Hunted? Hunted by what?"**

Amish looked at me with a look. "Isn't it obvious on what is hunting us now, Morphous? He told me that when we were on the way across the channel. I didn't believe him at first, but now with what happened? Can you honestly say we aren't?"

"If that is the case, Amish, how trustworthy is this werewolf you speak of?"

Another shifter approached, forgot his name entirely, since Quinn and Gillith had rotated the guards, but he whispered, "He is trustworthy, Anna, he was in the five."

"The five?"

"There are five werewolves, I guess technically six, but there are five werewolves that are pretty young. However, the sixth werewolf is a seer. And I am not entirely sure which are the seer's children, but a couple of the five are her children. Batis is in the group."

Silence, I looked at Amish and spoke, "**You knew that a few of us would die, Amish?**"

"I knew that someone would die, since we were attacking across the channel. Accidents happen Morphous. I…. I… wasn't informed of when. So, when none of our numbers dropped across the channel I thought that Batis made a mistake. That he was only bringing a darkness around us. I…. I didn't know that it would be my best friends that would die!"

He wailed the last sentence, and everyone lowered their eyes in anguish. Conrade, Gillith, and Hector had always done things with Amish. He was the only one that I did not send out. I bowed my head. A sob broke out from someone, but otherwise, everyone else was rather quiet with their mourning.

*****

Anna looked over her people, the ones who had arrived back and looked down at Morphous and knew that if he knew going in, that one or any of his people would perish in this attack. Then he would have not attended. I bowed my head, Gillith, and myself had been up to no good. There was a rule of no one dating the medical team, in case of favoritism, but Gillith was my lover. I, however, was going to have to feel that pain and mourn him at a later time alone, since I could not out him like that. I could never bring myself to bring anger upon him. I swallowed hard before looking at the shifters that had gone on the mission. There was a few that had their eyes glazed over, and they were hallow of what they once were. I had seen everyone's up and downs, and this is the most pain that I have seen in any of them.

I swallowed hard before speaking, "No one leaves without me talking with all of you first."

"Anna…."

"No, Amish. This is the way it needs to happen. I have not checked any of you for wounds yet…"

**"Anna, I apologize but we do need to have them go now."**

"Why?"

**"Because I gave a human blood to keep him alive."**

"You…. you healed someone that was not….. Abacore, you knew what would happen if that got out."

**"It is not entirely my idea, Anna. It was Nathaniel's idea."**

"And you listened to Nathaniel because?"

I growled low in my throat, but Anna's eyes flashed green. I finally lowered my eyes in submission. I knew better than to challenge Anna, I had made it so any medical had more rank than even their leaders. I lowered my head but Amish spoke, "Regardless of how they had found out. Anna, we do need to go."

"No."

"Anna…."

"I said no. Are you challenging a medic?"

Amish swallowed before replying, "I am."

Silence. Everyone knew that if you challenged a medical personal you would, well, it would not be pretty. Anna stared at him and I swallowed before looking at the rest of the clan before speaking, **"We will need roughly twelve people to go in total. Anna will see them first, before they are cleared to go."**

Anna looked at me with a hard look, glanced at Amish, but she looked at the clan and said, "Whoever goes needs to come forward first. Come along."

For a moment no one moved. Finally, twelve shifters moved forward, their heads bowed but they had something written across their faces.

*****

The rest of us stayed outside and finally, after close to two hours, Anna and the twelve that followed her inside came out, and she nodded. They approached Amish before resting their hands on his shoulder and shifting and flying off in different directions. They didn't ask where they needed to go, they went without questions. It was almost as if Anna knew where to find the experiment and her children.

I looked at Amish and knew that he knew that Anna was going to punish him for speaking out of term and challenging her. She walked down and looked at everyone, and knew that the majority of us were kind of holding our breaths in, waiting to see what she would do. She finally looked at Amish. "Amish."

"Yes, Anna?"

"You are dismissed from all your duties for the next three months."

"But…"

"Four months."

Amish went silent. Knowing that if he tried to say anything else, he would lose more. He swallowed hard and looked at me for a moment before whispering, "What would you like me to do during that time, Anna?"

"You will heal."

Amish bowed his head in submission and I knew that normally if someone loses a loved one, they work hard to forget who they were. Anna was pretty much punishing him to a life full of anguish since he wouldn't have anything to fill his time with.

I looked at Anna and knew that she would not change what she had decreed, and the rest of the clan looked shocked. A few of them probably thought that was a vacation. But now that a few had pieced together what they would have done if roles were reversed. They soon understood that this was the punishment. They looked sideways at Anna now and knew better than to challenge a medic.

*****

I sighed deeply before speaking, "**Do you know where the experiment is with her…**"

"Shut it, Morphous."

Abacore flashed in my eyes for a moment, but I closed my mouth. I tried to bring Abacore's energy in, but he finally shifted and roared into the sky. Anna did not look surprised, but the next words out of her mouth would have chilled someone to the core. "Abacore, stay here. Or I will drug you."

Abacore whipped his head towards her and bared his teeth. A big no-no. Anna's eyes flashed green before she looked at the rest of the shifters, and she ordered, "Get the chains."

No one in their right mind would challenge her now, and they rushed to get what Anna ordered. Abacore bared his teeth, steam streaming from his nostrils, and his eyes darkened to a red, but Anna did not budge. Amish scrambled slowly away, so Abacore did not take him as a threat and headed inside to disappear.

Anna looked at me hard for a moment and growled out, "Abacore, shift back into Morphous's form."

**"No."**

Anna shook her head in anger and turned slightly as the chains were brought forth. Abacore eyed them and growled low in his throat before he rumbled, **"You will not chain me down."**

"Then shift back."

Abacore bared his teeth at her, and Anna shrugged before grabbing one of the long chains. I had given her a document saying that she could chain up Abacore if he did not comply with her orders. I know that he would have roasted me alive if he had seen that document, but I had made sure I had him blocked for it. As in how he was blocking me out since I would have forced him to release control due to what was about to happen.

Anna approached and looked at Abacore before speaking, "Shift back now."

**"No."**

"Abacore, I am giving you a chance to do it right. Shift back and take your punishment. Or we do it the hard way. Your choice."

He bared his teeth at her, and smoke began to fill the clearing in the sunlight that was now streaming in the clearing. It was rising and twirling in the breeze that was coming in. Anna glowered at Abacore. "You created and agreed with Morphous on the rule of do not challenge the medical team. Yet here you are challenging me! SHIFT. NOW!"

**"NO."**

Anna glowered and her eyes turned orange and she hissed, "You are doing this to yourself, Abacore. This is not Morphous, I know that he would have shifted back on his own accord. I know that you are in full control. You, however, have witnessed what I had done to Amish, and you and I both know that he is going to suffer from that as in consequence. Shift now, Abacore. Or so help me."

**"Do your worst."**

Anna's eyes sparked once before she focused on herself and pulled at the tie that I had created for her. One that would pull from the clan if in need. I felt the pull and I was positive that Abacore could feel it too since he took a step backward. He bared his teeth at Anna again before roaring into the sky and leaping into the sky. He angled himself to head away, but Anna shouted in the mind-link and out loud, *"DOWN, ABACORE!"*

As much as Abacore wanted to keep flying elsewhere, he would not be able to. He was kind of stuck on where he would be. He flapped his wings twice before he plummeted to the earth. He crashed into the earth and sent earth flying every way. He skidded to a halt right before running into a giant sycamore tree. He tried to push himself up but Anna's power radiated out and he crumbled to the ground but did not release control.

Anna threw chains over him, and indeed drugged him when she finally had him chained down. Finally, after a bit of fighting off the drug as much as he wanted to, he released control and I could take back over. I shifted back into my being, and I staggered since the drugs were intense.

*****

I looked at Anna and was about to say something when Herald came out of the woods speaking, "What the heck happened here?"

I lifted my head to stare at him in shock before Anna noticed someone behind him. She took a step backward before Herald glanced back at his company. He spoke, "This is Akato, son of Dracula."

**"I thought the Carpathians could not walk in the sunlight."**

"My name is Akato. I am the youngest of Dracula's sons."

**"Why are you here?"**

"I have orders from my father, that I intend on doing."

**"Like what?"**

"Like making sure the son of this Benik is safe. Considering that he has a prophecy surrounding him."

"Wait what? What prophecy are you talking about, Akato?"

Apparently, Akato kept some things to himself, and he glanced at Herald before looking at us. "We need to speak in private. However, it is not only the shifters, it includes everyone that is the supernatural world."

"Why are you just mentioning this now, Akato?"

"Hush, Herald."

Herald stared at him before muttering under his breath. Anna looked at me with a hard look before she followed him.

****

I looked at Akato and said, **"We will have to speak at a different time frame, Akato. At the moment, now is not the time."**

I turned to leave towards the palace when Akato replied, "Time is never a great thing shifter king. Whatever happened when your dragon form with your medical team? That was brutal punishment. I can see how you rule by just how your medical team responds to others challenging them. This is a fine establishment."

I looked at him with a look and he scoffed, "However, time is not up for everything you should know that...."

**"Shut your trap! A lot has happened between when Herald left and when you decided to show yourselves. We will touch base on this at an alternated time frame."**

"Are you preparing yourself for war shifter king?"

I froze and looked at him with a hard look, but did not respond and trekked back to where the palace was and disappeared into the palace. Not looking back to see if he followed or not.

# Chapter 41

I sat down on the fallen oak when Azier approached me. I knew it was a female wolf since they tend to walk carefully compared to their counterparts. She gingerly sat down and watched the waves lap against the shore before speaking, "You know something that will happen. How is that possible?" I looked at her and sighed before leaning over, grabbing another stone, and twirling it in my hands before I chucked it into the channel. After a moment, I said, "Trust me, you do not want to know what will happen Azier. It needs to happen. Taryn knows what will happen."

"Taryn is my mother, and yet she has said nothing besides the fact that some of us are going to die since you will attack us by accident."

I swallowed hard and looked away, and Azier shifted backward slightly, whispering, "You are going to attack us by accident, right?"

"I cannot confirm anything with you, Azier. What will happen is going to happen."

"Please answer me this though, if you can, is any of my brothers or my immediate team mates going to go?"

I looked at her and saw the sadness in her eyes as she thought that. I sighed deeply, picked up another rock, and threw it into the channel before speaking, "Not in your small patrol group."

She sighed a relieved breath and stood up to walk away when she froze. She turned slowly around and locked eyes with me for a split second, she bowed her head before turning around and running. She finally understood who I was referring to. I swallowed and saw her embrace her mother. Taryn looked over her shoulder at me. I shook my head, but she seemed to know what would happen. Soon the rest of the patrol approached her, and hugged her. I was unsure of what was said but knew that they would never forget what happened today.

I turned my attention back to the channel and saw the boat coming. I sighed before standing up, Quinn was in the back of my mind, *"Try hard and not to kill Taryn, Thakur. Please."*

*"You know I cannot alter what is to happen. She knows and she seems to welcome it too, Quinn."*

*"You are going to drive them against you. You know Ghost will try to protect her."*

*"I know."*

*"How are you going to get her away from him?"*

*"Quinn?"*

*"What?"*

*"Drop it."*

*"But…."*

*"Quinn, believe me when I say this. I take no pleasure in what is to happen. But it is a must."*

*"Azier is not ready to take her mother's position yet, Thakur."*

*"She will need to learn to grow up fast to become what she needs to be, Quinn. Allow me full access."*

*"I give you full access, Thakur."*

*****

I felt the bond drift slightly out of place, and my eyes blazed black. I took a deep breath in, relishing in the fear emitting from the werewolves as they watched the ship approach. Relishing in the strong heartbeats in the area, and relishing in what was to become of a certain few. I might not like what I was shown in my vision, but I knew that Taryn understood and knew more than I did if it did not happen.

I glanced over at the small huddle and got a side-eyed look from Ghost before his head jerked slightly as he looked at Taryn. He swallowed, approached her slightly closer, and showed me that he would indeed be the problem one to get around.

I sighed and looked at the incoming ship and waited for the time. I knew that the attack would happen soon and knew that about six had to die – and one of them would be in that cluster over there.

*****

We watched as four sea beasts dropped from the sky, and attacked the two ships coming from the sides. Our king stood on the deck of the barge, watching in shock. I looked at him before speaking, **"Your orders, sire?"**

**"Head a course."**

**"What about the survivors of the attack?"**

He turned his head towards me, but his eyes flickered to the attack, and we watched in shock as the four sea beasts died. Whoever had killed them let their corpses fall below the channel waters and disappear into the depths. We stared in shock, as the rest of the changers and the rest of the whatever they were fled past the ones that were killed as if they did not care that their own were slaughtered.

My king turned slightly before speaking, "**STOP THE SHIP!**"

I swallowed as the ship came to a stop before it stilled in the channel. We were right outside of the two ships that were taken out. The twenty people looked up at the barge before a rope ladder was thrown down to either side. They would still have to swim to reach it, but it would get them up faster than anything else.

After a few minutes, they boarded the ship, and the older one strode over to our king before speaking, "**Thank you for stopping.**"

"**What is your business on this side of the channel?**"

"**So, you know of me.**"

"**What is your business on this side of the channel? I know I did not authorize your clan to be on this side of the channel.**"

"**I apologize. However, there was no need to be told where we could sail our ships. You know what we are after. You dare declare war?**"

"**The human government on that side of the channel has issued your services. Not this side of the channel.**"

"**That may be true that they did the money dip, however, if I recall correctly. You are after the same thing that we are.**"

"**You know what I am after?**"

"**You and I are after what is called shifters. Their blood can heal anything, and bring people back from the brink of death. The human government had created an experiment to wipe out the werewolf and Carpathian creatures to make more room for themselves.**"

"**So, you do know my end game. However, what are you planning on doing with the shifters as you call them?**"

"**Slaughter the whole lot.**"

"**Why slaughter them if they can heal anything? They would be useful in the long term.**"

"**Because that is what the job is. We are told to kill the shifters, and leave no survivors.**"

"**Any way that can be changed?**"

"None. I already know that the human government on the other side has deeper pockets than you do. Since they are a united front. Therefore, they all pitch in for our spending."

"What about leaving two of them for us? That way we can get what is needed for what we need to do."

"What your king's son has is not something that normally you would survive from. Everyone else knows that he is good as fucking dead. Admit it, you yourself, have questioned it. Why all this madness for ONE LIFE?"

"My son has more class than you."

"Are you seriously going to challenge me to this? I am not in the mood, they just tipped my ships over. Unless you are going to let me have your barge."

"This is my crew and my ship. You are in my waters."

"Careful. It almost sounded as if you were challenging what I can do."

I watched from the corner of my eye and saw my king blanch slightly before he replied, "Please leave my ship and get back to yours."

"We would get back to ours, but first, SILAS!"

"Yes, father?"

"Pick one to kill."

I was about to say something, but my king stepped forward, speaking, "Don't! We need every able body to be ready to fight for what you call shifters!"

"I can tell you one thing now, you would cross into waters that are not in your waters. Therefore, into our business. So why should I allow you to escape with your lives when you are heading into the waters that we are aiming for? Oh! Also, shifters run scared when they know that they are being hunted. Even if you managed to get across the channel, you would not find the shifters. Probably a big pack of werewolves, but not the shifters."

"How are you so sure that the shifters would not meet in the harbor like anyone else?"

"Because the shifters we are tracking are typically cowards."

"Were these the ones that attacked your ship, the ones that you consider cowards? Or are they different from the ones that were created?"

"They are different."

"Then let us go after the ones that had been different, and you carry on your course of hunting the ones that you were tasked to kill."

"**You make it seem like there is a difference between laboratory shifters and the purebloods.**"

"**There is, isn't there? A difference between them?**"

He stared hard at me before turning to his son, who held a crew member by his throat before speaking, "**SILAS?**"

"Yes, father?"

"**Release him.**"

He grumbled but dropped the crew member to the deck. I watched in horror as the crew member coughed up blood and wheezed. I stared at him before I asked, "**What are you?**"

My king glanced at me sideways, swallowed, and gave the man before us a look. He smiled wickedly before replying, "**We are called Sazornoras. We are supernatural hunters.**"

"**If you are supernatural hunters then why are you singly targeting the shifters?**"

"**Money.**"

"**What are you going to do with the rewards? I thought you would be bounty hunters and need to bring back your specimens for review before you earn your rewards.**"

"**Blackwell.**"

"**Yes, my lord?**"

"**Shut. Your. Trap.**"

I closed my mouth and saw the Sazornora smirk in response before he turned his attention to Silas, speaking, "**Silas, work on flipping the ships back up. If any of our cargo survived, make sure it is ready to go.**"

"Yes, father."

He leaped into the frigid temperature waters, swam towards the ships, and grabbed a piece of rope before looping it along the side of the front, turning the ship right away.

The man turned his attention back to us before I could finish watching what was happening. However, one thing that I did know was, that these were no ordinary ships, they were hard to turn for anyone normal. I swallowed hard and wanted desperately to step backward in fear, but I knew that this creature would only take it as a win. He grinned wickedly at me before turning his attention to my king, "**So, with everything. I will allow you across the channel, but do not be surprised if you are met with werewolves only.**"

He turned to go back when my king spoke, "**If we were to cross paths again, what is your name?**"

He paused and looked at us. His eyes turned hard in appearance, and I swallowed hard and took a step backward in response. He smirked slightly before replying, "**My name is Cassius Zhukov, and these are my children. It is best that you stay out of this side of the channel after you attempt to get what you are after. Head back home, and not further inland. We are in the treaty waters currently, but do not wait until you are within my side of the channel before you attempt to be an idiot.**"

Shock from the crew stretched, no one called our king that before, and survived. A crew member, surprisingly enough, the same one that was caught, charged at Cassius. Cassius, without flinching, took the blade right into his side and single-handedly took out the crew member. He removed the sword from his side, drawing his blood from the fresh wound – shocking the rest of the crew and myself when he did not drop down dead.

Cassius looked down at the dead crew member before looking at us and speaking, "**You attacked me? You do realize what you have declared?**"

"**I declared nothing, Cassius, my member did not understand what was to become of the issue. I apologize on his corpse's behalf.**"

I stared hard at him in shock. I saw his Adam's apple bob in fear, but his voice was steady. Cassius twirled the blade slightly before he threw the blade straight at me, I could do nothing as it speared directly into my chest and out the back. I screamed out in pain, but he smirked. "**More insurance that you need to find the shifters. You will fail since they only know how to flee. However, if you want your advisor to survive, along with your son, you need to find a willing shifter. CHILDREN!**"

"**Yes, father?**"

"**Time to depart.**"

I was in intense pain but could do nothing before they disembarked. They got into their wooden boats before they rowed away. They were strong, and since their cargo did not survive, they were rowing alone. Cassius looked at our king before calling out, "**DO NOT GO FURTHER INLAND! YOU WILL ONLY MAKE IT HARDER FOR YOURSELVES!**"

We watched as they rowed away, and soon disappeared.

*****

I panted in pain, grimaced in pain, and called out, "**SAIL OUT!**"

My king looked at me, as my blood pooled out of the wound, if we removed the blade, I would die instantly. He knew it, I knew it. Everyone on this ship knew it. He blinked hard but turned around and looked across the channel. My only chance was the shifters. My only chance for life.

******

I watched as the ship came closer. I stood up, stretched, and glanced around. The werewolves were shifting into their wolves, and some stayed in their human forms. I noticed that Taryn refused to shift, and her eyes caught mine a few times, I dipped her head in acknowledgment. Knowing that she would have shifted if I had known her wolf form.

I closed my eyes for a moment, relishing in the tense air before the battle that was to come. I opened my eyes and smiled wickedly. I touched Quinn's blades gingerly since I was debating on using them or not.

A werewolf came towards me, and he slowly walked over. I glanced at him with curious eyes for a moment before he spoke, "I will fight alongside you."

"You could get hurt if you do."

"Maybe, maybe not. War is always dirty and harsh. I would be surprised if no one was injured."

I sniffed slightly, caught his delta blood, and raised my eyebrow before speaking, "You are delta blood. Are you fourth in command?"

"No, my father is though."

"Ah."

I turned my attention back to the ship and saw it dock, about a few hundred feet from us. I looked over my shoulder and saw the pack look towards the palace, that was when I realized that Nathaniel was not out there. The pack was restless. They were waiting on their alpha.

I looked back at the ship and walked forward, the wolf hesitated before speaking, "We need to wait for Nathaniel."

"Wolves, wait. I am not a wolf though."

He swallowed hard and glanced at a wolf, a big black one. I saw him shake his head toward the one that was speaking with me. I blinked and looked at him before speaking, "Stay with your pack. And stay out of my immediate way."

He stared at me and backed away before turning around and walking back to the black wolf. The wolf looked at me with green eyes, before blinking once. I turned my attention back to the ship.

******

It seemed like no one wanted to come off the ship, and finally, I walked forward. I looked at the hull of the ship before calling out, "HELLO?"

A few timid humans looked at me, and their eyes rose. I saw impressive numbers of the werewolves behind and swallowed hard. They disappeared back inside and soon a mid-age man approached. He was flanked by four guards, he called out, "**HOLD YOUR ARMY!**"

I smirked but did not respond. He came about fifty paces before they stopped before speaking, "**Please, any chance any of you are shifters?**"

"I am sorry, but they have already gone home."

"**Any chance that one can come back?**"

"None. Now if you do not want bloodshed, go back home."

His hand tightened on a sword on his hip before he swallowed hard and spoke, "**Are you in charge of this side of the channel?**"

I opened my mouth to say something, when Nathaniel's voice boomed out behind me, "**No, he is not. I am.**"

I looked behind me and stepped sideways, I may want a fight. However, something else happened that was not foretold. It was apparent that Taryn felt that something was different too. I looked at her with a look, but she shrugged and I turned my attention back to Nathaniel.

******

Nathaniel looked at the human king before he raised his eyebrows in confusion, none of the guards he had brought were carrying any weapons. None, absolutely nothing to defend themselves against us.

Nathaniel glanced at me for a split second and then looked back at the small cluster, and Taryn shrugged once and that was that. He turned his attention back to their king before speaking, "**You come onto my shores, and yet you do not carry a single weapon. At least, your guards don't. Why?**"

"**Because we had crossed paths with someone who claims to own these shores. However, he has not claimed them by the looks of it.**"

"**Who are you referring to that owns these shores?**"

"**Ummm…. His name was Cassius Zhukov.**"

Nathaniel glanced at me with puzzlement, and I shrugged. Taryn walked forward when I noticed that his eyes glazed over. The patrol followed her. Ghost kept glaring at me every so often, and kept his hand on his blade at all times. I didn't blame him either. I would be killing her if the things I had seen were to go in the order they should. I could tell by the way that Taryn acted though that she knew this was one of the possibilities. However, I could also tell by her movements that she really wanted it to happen the way that we both knew. I swallowed, what could be the worse outcome if she was scared? I couldn't tell you it. Even if I wanted.

I turned my attention to Taryn approaching Nathaniel before bowing and speaking, "Did you say Zhukov?"

"**Yes. You know him?**"

Taryn looked at Nathaniel with a sharp look before glancing back at me, and speaking, "He is the leader of the Sazornoras."

"**That is what he called themselves, yes. So, is there any chance that a shifter did not go too far inland?**"

"**Unfortunately, they all went home. There is no way to get in contact with them again.**"

"**Please, surely one stayed behind. I am desperate.**"

"Why are you desperate?"

He looked at me with a look before looking at Nathaniel swallowed and looked down. "**My son is on the brink of death. Since Kiesin had survived what he did with shifter blood, then I could also save my son. Along with my advisor.**"

"What happened with your advisor?"

He looked at Taryn and swallowed. His eyes flickered to Nathaniel and I could just tell by his movements that he was used to women being in the room, but seen not heard. Nathaniel looked at him with a look before he looked back at Taryn and spoke to her directly, although more in a disgruntled way, "**He was….**"

A man came out of the ship and was walking, in the sunlight. It gleamed off the blade, I cocked my head sideways and knew that I was probably scaring these guys shitless. But I looked at Ghost and motioned him closer to me, he eyed Taryn, and came over.

I looked at him before speaking, "It seems that the train of events is changing, Ghost. I am going to release Quinn. However, I am unsure how steady he is afterward. I just want you to be over here in case you need to support him before he regains his footing."

"You and Taryn knew something that would drastically change how things are currently."

"Yes, we did. However, it appears Taryn knew that this was one of the possibilities too. Although, the fact that she wanted the other way, is a little frightening."

He looked at me with a look and glanced at Taryn but seemed to know better than to ask questions.

*******

He nodded once and I felt the connection between myself and Quinn snap back into place. I closed my eyes and drifted backward before Quinn indeed needed assistance to keep his balance.

This, of course, had one of the guards' attention, and he was watching me as I switched with Quinn. His blue eyes blinked and he nodded to Ghost to release him when the guard spoke, "Are you a shifter?"

That drew their king's attention towards me, and I sighed deeply before speaking, "Not fully."

"What does that mean?"

"It means that what you want to be done is not possible with me. My other half would prevent it from happening the way you want it."

"But you would be able to get the shifters over here though. If you can change who you are, and your voice. Surely you can…."

**"Enough."**

The guard fell silent and looked down before whispering, "I apologize, my lord."

Their king glanced at him with a hard look, but it was only the back of his head. Since he did not turn around to face his king. I looked at him before speaking, "I am sorry, but the shifters would not willingly give you their blood. No matter who it is for."

"**And you are so sure because?**"

"Because I am King Morphous Draconis's advisor. Without his consent, none of the shifters would give you a single drop of their blood without a fight."

"**Surely, he can make an exception.**"

"**Unfortunately, for you, I know Morphous personally. Once he has it in his mind that someone will exploit what their blood can do, then he will make it so no one can go against his order. I am sorry, but your mission has ended.**"

Their king bit his lips slightly before speaking, "**What about your species?**"

Nathaniel smirked slightly. "**The only way to be healed by our blood would be if you consume enough of it before we bite you. You would forever be tied to me, and my clan.**"

He stared at Nathaniel for a solid moment. His eyes flickered to me before whispering, "**What about you? What would happen if you gave blood?**"

I opened my mouth to respond when a small blue bird flew over to me. I glanced at the bird and knew who it was, without her shifting. I sighed deeply before turning slightly and whispering to her in mind-link, "*Anna, what are you doing here?*"

"*Doing what Herald wants.*"

"*My brother is back?*"

"*Yes.*"

I swallowed hard before replying, "*Did Morphous allow you, Anna?*"

"*He cannot go against a medic.*"

I smirked a little before turning slightly and speaking aloud, "I guess you do have someone willing to give their blood to your cause. However, they do not go back across the channel. Do you have your son?"

Their king's Adam's apple bobbed before he replied, "**No, the voyage over here would have been too strenuous on him. He would have not made it.**"

I saw out of the corner of my eye that Anna had hopped down and shifted a few feet from us before she approached, making the guards go to their hips, only to come short.

*****

Nathaniel glanced at Anna before bowing slightly and speaking, **"Hello, what is your name?"**

"My name is Anna."

**"Did Morphous give you the okay to be over here?"**

"He cannot challenge me."

Nathaniel blinked twice and frowned. However, Taryn looked at Anna with a smirk before she spoke, "Something that the shifters have in place I believe? Correct?"

Anna looked at her and smiled slightly before replying, "Morphous cannot challenge a medic. He gave me unlimited authority."

Nathaniel's jaw dropped and I could tell that he would ask her more questions, however, I cleared my throat and glanced back to the king before speaking, "He would need to come over the channel."

**"He would have not made it! You would be condemning my son to death!"**

I opened my mouth to reply, when Anna rested her hand on my shoulder, stilling me before speaking, "Quinn, get a bag or a jar. Nathaniel, any chance of there being a needle somewhere? One that one of your medical team is not using?"

Nathaniel glanced at Taryn before speaking, **"Taryn, please go with Quinn in finding what she needs."**

"Of course, my lord."

Ghost looked perplexed for a moment, and he attempted to follow for a moment, but Nathaniel called out, **"Ghost, you stay here."**

Ghost stared at me with a look, but I shrugged and followed Taryn towards the palace. Through all the werewolves that were getting antsy with waiting. They were ready for battle but did not know it was not coming. However, Taryn did not say a word to anyone as we went to the palace.

*******

As soon as we crossed the threshold into the palace, Taryn spun around and slapped me. I was shocked before rubbing where her hand landed and asking, "What the hell?"

"You said something to Azier, didn't you? Or more of enforced that SOMEONE she loved would perish, didn't you?"

I stared at her and replied, "I am unsure what Thakur had discussed since I had given him full control. It was weird being in my mind, and not seeing anything."

She glowered at me before shaking her head and muttering, "Fuck off."

I stared at her with a look before asking, "You know something that you were hoping is not the case. Why are you so scared?"

She paused and looked back at me before replying, "The reason why I am scared is because of what is coming our way now."

"It would have happened either way. We tossed the Sazornoras into the water. In front of that metal ship, Taryn. It was not entirely our fault."

She sighed deeply and looked down at the hardwood floors before looking around and speaking, "There was a reason why I did not want to say anything, Quinn. It is because I knew the different outcomes. The one we are now on would result in every. Single. Shifter, dying. Or being hunted for their entire lives, Quinn. It also…."

She paused and looked around carefully before dropping her voice to a hard-to-hear tone, "It also means that the werewolves will be without a kingdom that Nathaniel has built. This is no longer going to be here, Quinn. The outcome that I died was the one that the shifters yes, would still be hunted but would not have to flee every single night. However, that has been altered."

A voice spoke from behind Taryn and she jumped and looked behind her. I spied Marius, who I had faintly remembered coming inside with Rafeor beforehand. "You would have been killed to save the whole future, Taryn?"

"Marius, How much of that did you overhear?"

"Enough to know that some events are going to happen that we do not really want to happen."

He worded it so that if someone else was eavesdropping, they would not really know what he was referring to. Taryn gave him a knowing look, sighed deeply, and hung her head in submission. She looked up at me, with a red handprint across my face before she spoke again, "I am sorry that I had slapped you, Quinn. I know whatever your other half says is not what you entirely want either. With or without your knowledge."

I swallowed and looked at Marius, who was watching me like a hawk. I was inside their home, after all, and I knew that the werewolves were tense after the betrayal that had happened. Especially since we cannot trust them enough to be honest. I glowered at him before speaking the obvious, "It was not the shifters that caused the further rip with the werewolves. You attacked us from the inside."

He shuffled his feet and said, "Not all of us agreed to do that, Quinn. Most of us were kept in the dark of what we were to do."

Thakur flashed in my eyes, but I forced him back. Taryn sighed deeply before speaking, "Stop it you two. That is now in the past."

****

I looked at her and was about to say something, when Ghost strode into the palace, speaking, "So I see that you have not gotten what your medic has asked for Quinn."

I turned around to face him, and to say he was surprised with the handprint across my face, was an understatement. He glanced between Taryn and Marius before his eyes flickered to me, raising his eyebrows in question.

I rolled my eyes and went towards the bar. I smelled the alcohol from the doorway and was surprised that they even had any since, well, it was well known that the werewolves cannot really get drunk unless they consume quarts of it.

Ghost paused before following me and speaking, "What is in here that you possibly want?"

I went behind the counter, looking around, and finally found tubing for their system. It appeared to be a really good system since I had never seen the like of it before. I frowned, but took some of it, before cutting a section of it off. Ghost seemed to be white as a ghost, no pun intended when I did it. I looked up after a moment, "What?"

"That…. That was Logan's."

"He'll understand the reason behind it."

"Except he won't. He will take his anger out on the first person he sees."

*****

I shrugged and moved to grab a jar when a blast of alpha power radiated around the room as a voice whispered dangerously, "**Who destroyed my system tubing?**"

I looked up from the counter, and held a jar of some sort of alcohol before replying, "That would be me."

His eyes flickered to Marius who looked like he would use his weapon on his hip, and he slowly moved Taryn behind him. It was done slowly, but I could tell that they all were tense and ready to defend Taryn. The newcomer looked back over at me before growling, his eyes flashing with his wolf's eyes for a moment, he said, **"And who might YOU be? This is werewolf territory, you have no business being inside our home."**

He was edging around the counter, there were two exits, but I knew by the look written across Marius's face, that he would be able to get to the other side within seconds if provoked. Ghost stared at the newcomer before speaking, "Logan, he is a…."

**"Last time I checked, Asaro, I was not talking to you."**

Ghost flinched back and looked away. My eyes flickered to Ghost and knew that Asaro was his real name, not his wolf's name. I turned my attention to Logan before speaking, "My name is Quinn. I am here for an empty jar, a needle, and…. Stumbled on your tubing system and knew that it was something that could be used for what it is for. I apologize for wrecking your system."

He blinked at me, his wolf surfacing more, more alpha power radiating off of him before he snarled, **"The same Quinn as the shifter's advisor? That QUINN? WHO. THE. FUCK. GAVE. YOU. AUTHORITY. TO. BE. IN. THE. WERE. WOLF. HOME? WHO!"**

I swallowed hard before replying, "Nathaniel gave me the go-ahead. Myself and Taryn were tasked to get what was requested. I apologize."

He turned around slightly, so he could see Taryn hiding behind Marius with fear in her eyes. He took a deep breath in and seemed to relish in the fear that she was giving off. He growled, **"Taryn. Come here. Now."**

Ghost stepped in front of Taryn as she shook her head in response. His hand rested on his blade before he spoke, "Logan…. Don't."

**"I said, Taryn. NOT you, Asaro! This is the second time that you stepped out of line with me."**

Logan strode forward and raised his hand to backhand Ghost before Thakur released his aura. It pushed hard against Logan's and then he reeled it back into ourselves, when Logan froze and slowly turned himself around to stare at me. Thakur stayed in my eyes, black as coal, before he spoke quietly, "You will not harm them, Logan Vigolf."

Marius, Ghost and Taryn gasped. No one addressed any of the royals by their last name, not unless they wanted a fight. Logan stared at me hard before growling, **"And who might you be so bold on saying my last name?"**

"My name is Thakur Benik."

Silence. Taryn locked eye contact with me for a split second and her eyes showed something indescribable and she looked quickly away. Logan stared hard at me and swallowed before looking away and drawing his aura back into himself. He bowed his head before speaking, **"So, it's true then. There are some demons left on this earth."**

"Correct. Along with my father, I believe I also have another family member somewhere close. Best not to do anything out of the norm though, Logan. Same with you all."

"Does King Nathaniel know that you are that?"

"He knows enough. He doesn't need to know my last name yet."

**"Why not?"**

"Because it is not up to anyone to decide on that fate besides myself. You will not warn others about who or what I am without dire consequences. Taryn, you seem to understand why we cannot say or speak of certain events. What do you see that others do not know? Especially around my namesake."

Everyone's eyes turned to see that Taryn swallowed hard before shaking her head slowly and whispering, "I cannot say what I know yet. There are too many moving parts in play currently."

Thakur released me as soon as she said that. I swayed slightly, gripping the counter before breathing hard and whispering, "There may be moving parts, but we cannot be blind to what is to come. However, Thakur and you may know of more than one outcome. However, on the course, we are currently on, Taryn, how.... How is it looking?"

She swallowed as she looked at my eyes. There was nothing in them from Thakur and she looked at everyone else before whispering, "I am sorry for what you have to go through, Quinn, however, I only see you as the oddball to what is going to happen. Nothing is set in stone as of yet, but.... What I have seen you will never get a day's rest."

I swallowed and looked down at the tubing and jar of alcohol before opening the jar. I sniffed it, screwing up my face at the smell. I took out five glasses and poured everyone a shot, and a majority of it into Logan's glass.

Taryn stared at me before speaking, "What are you doing?"

"Drinking. We have been through a fucking lot already. Might as well take a shot for the nerves."

"That is not a healthy coping mechanism."

I shrugged and replied, "May not be, but I know for a fact, I would not be able to drink back home."

"Why not?"

I looked at Marius before replying, "Morphous has outlawed alcohol back home. Unless it is for medical supplies."

We would have gone back and forth, but Anna connected to me, "*Quinn, I need my supplies now.*"

"*My apologies, Anna.*"

I sighed deeply before pouring the rest of the jar into their cups, moving with the now empty jar, and tubing before looking at Taryn before asking, "Where is the needle?"

She looked at me with a confused look, before it dawned on her why we came inside. She looked at Logan for a moment, before backing out, "Right this way."

*****

We left them there, when Taryn whispered, "I am sorry that I cannot assist you more with what I see. However, I…"

I stopped walking and it only took her a few steps further to realize that I had stopped. She turned to look at me before I spoke, "Taryn, I understand that some things that you see are to come to pass, and arrive. Whether we want it to or not. Therefore, I know that you cannot say certain things. I understand. Believe me. I do understand that most of the things you know, you wish you didn't even know."

She swallowed, acknowledging that I was correct. That she did not want to know what she had seen, in most cases. I sighed before gesturing for her to continue. She hesitated for a moment, but she soon took me to her medical team area.

*****

We walked into their operation, and a werewolf looked up. He was older, around sixty which for a werewolf was not that old. He looked at the jar, and tubing, and raised his eyebrows before speaking, "What can I do for you?"

I noticed that his voice held authority, and Taryn glanced at me for a moment. "Iverson, do you have a clean needle?"

He crossed his arms, as he leaned back against the wooden table behind him, looking at the equipment I held, and eyed Taryn with a look. "It highly depends on what it will be used for. There is only one logical thing for tubing, which by the way, Logan will have a fit over. I believe where you got that tubing from. Along, with the empty jar that by the smell of it, once contained moonshine. The only logical thing that I think you need those and a needle for would be extracting blood from someone, and being able to transport it somewhere. Am I on the correct path?"

I stared at him before speaking, "Uh… yeah. You are actually spot on."

He turned his hazel brown eyes towards me before speaking, "Whose blood is going to be taken where?"

"A medic from Morphous's palace. She is going to be giving someone blood. She requested a jar and a needle."

"Did she request the tubing, or was that your idea?"

"Mine."

He nodded slightly before looking at Taryn and speaking, "Taryn, you are excused. I will go out and do what is needed."

"But…."

"Taryn, we may have different customs to the shifters, however, I still have the authority to order some people. Please do not make me have to restrain you."

"Why would you restrain her? She has a job to do…."

He looked at me before speaking, "Do all shifters have to follow what their medical has said?"

"Yes."

"Then why are you questioning my judgment?"

I swallowed hard before replying, "Because your King will expect Taryn, not yourself."

"He may expect her, however, she is on leave for the time being. She knows why."

He gave her a hard stare, and she swallowed hard before looking away. However, not before she grazed her stomach with her left hand, where it lingered for a moment before it fell to the side. I swallowed, surely, she cannot be with child.

Iverson looked at me before clearing his throat. My eyes flickered to his hazel ones before speaking, "I'll get the needle, and then we will need to leave."

"Of course."

He looked at Taryn before moving to do what he had said he was going to do before speaking with his back facing us, "Taryn, get going. I will have my assistant go check on you in a few minutes. They will link me if you are not where you need to be."

Taryn looked at me and whispered, "I am sorry, I guess I cannot escort you back, Quinn. Have a good day."

"Are you with child, Taryn?"

Both of them froze, and she looked sharply at Iverson. He turned around, with a needle in his hand, before he spoke, "And how did you find that out?"

"Based on her movements. On your actions. There would only be one real logical reason why you both act like that."

He glanced at Taryn and smirked slightly. "Have you told anyone else about this, Quinn?"

"No, and I don't understand why she would want me to kill her if fate had different scenarios."

Taryn closed her eyes and flinched backward a step. Iverson looked at her with a hard stare before looking at me with an equally hard stare. He pinched the bridge of his nose, while he seemed to struggle with his wolf for a moment, "Taryn… what is he talking about?"

"I saw something I wished I never witnessed, Iverson. I am sorry. But they cannot grow to their adulthood. They can't. At least, not be with me."

He looked at her with a hard look, before looking at me with a hard stare. His wolf surfaced as he rumbled, "Do not speak of this to anyone else, Quinn. You can consult your medic, since the patient and doctor are on strict no outside business UNLESS to pass information from doctor to doctor."

I swallowed and knew what he would do if I told someone else, but a voice spoke out from behind me, since I was still in the doorway, "Wait, you are pregnant, Taryn?"

She flinched when she heard the voice, and turned slightly to face Ghost, before looking at Iverson. He sighed before looking at me with a hard look. "Asaro, Ghost."

Ghost looked instantly at Iverson before blinking once. Iverson spoke, "I command you that you do not say a word to a living soul under the moon. Swear it."

Asaro seemed to want to refuse, but Ghost rumbled, "I swear by the moon."

Asaro looked at me with a look but knew that he could not go against the pact. He swallowed hard before looking at Taryn, turning on his heel, and leaving promptly.

*****

I looked at Taryn and swallowed. There had to be a reason why she did not want her not even here yet children not known. However, Iverson came over and cleared his throat, and glanced at Taryn before speaking, "You better get moving, Taryn. The time is ticking down."

Taryn swallowed hard and exited through another door, not replying or saying anything to me. I looked at Iverson before speaking, "I thought that Taryn's mate disappeared...."

Iverson's wolf surfaced, and he twirled around and slammed me into a wall. I grimaced in pain, but let myself take the blunt force of it, and stared into his wolf's green eyes. He rumbled, "Not. One. Word."

I swallowed hard but nodded in understanding. He released me and took me through the front door and towards the harbor again.

******

We got to the harbor when the sun was sinking, and Nathaniel glanced at me with a hard stare before speaking, "**What took you so long, Quinn?**"

I went to open my mouth to reply, but Iverson replied, "That would have been my fault, Nathaniel."

Nathaniel glanced at him and dipped his head a little before speaking, "**I apologize, Iverson, I did not know you would be delivering the supplies that Anna had requested.**"

"No worries."

He glanced at me with a hard stare, but looked at Nathaniel before speaking, "Where is she?"

"I am here."

Anna came out of the crowd had her sleeves rolled up and looked at Iverson. They locked eyes for a moment before Iverson looked away, but not without me hearing, "Mate."

I glanced sharply at him but swallowed. I knew that Anna would not be able to do anything about it. I was unsure of werewolf policies with the medical team. However, I looked at Anna and knew that she had felt something. She, after a moment, cleared her throat and looked expectantly at me.

I swallowed before speaking, "My apologies, Anna. I did not mean to delay you."

"It is okay, Quinn. I am sure you had your reasons."

I swallowed and glanced between Iverson and Anna, and knew that Iverson was trying hard not to say anything louder, or act differently. I could also see that Nathaniel saw something and squinted his eyes in response.

Anna cleared her throat, and I handed her the items. She glanced at Iverson before speaking, "Are you their medic?"

"Yes."

"Then you know what I want done correct?"

"Correct, ma'am."

He was keeping it business, but I could see the longing in his eyes, as she pushed her sleeve higher up before stepping closer to him. I saw his wolf flickered in his eyes as if he desperately wanted to live with her, but he looked away for a moment before Nathaniel approached so that the humans could not hear a word.

*****

I glanced at Anna and saw her look down before speaking, "I understand what is happening. However, I cannot accept it. I would be taken out of practice if I allowed my personal feelings…."

Iverson swallowed hard, his eyes filled with unshed tears, but Nathaniel spoke softly, **"Please don't do what you think is right, Anna. please. Our customs are different to the shifters."**

"They may be different, King Nathaniel, but I am a shifter, and he is a werewolf. We cannot mix."

"The moon goddess is never wrong, Anna."

She looked sharply at me, before she lowered her eyes, and whispered, "So you believe that this could work, Quinn?"

"I do. This is no way to punish you, Anna, this is a way to rejoice in love. Something that the shifters cannot really understand. This is a union. A blessed union."

She looked at Iverson before swallowing hard and looking at Nathaniel again, before closing her eyes and lifting her arm again. "Before we do anything drastic, we need to do what I came here to do first. Please."

Iverson swallowed hard, but he inserted the needle into the tubing and placed the end inside the jar. Then he found a vein and inserted it into her arm. If he was relishing in the mate sparks, he did not show any signs.

After about half of the jar was filled, he went about to stop, but Anna spoke softly, "Don't."

He looked at her with a look but continued doing what she wanted. Soon, the jar was almost filled to the brim before she swayed back and forth. I walked forward, and placed a hand on her shoulder, earning a growl for Iverson. I glanced at him with a look, and he looked away for a moment, swallowing in response.

*****

After a moment, it was right at the brim before he took out the needle from her arm, and pressed onto the puncture area before handing the jar to my outstretched hands. I screwed the lid on tight, before looking at Anna. I was slightly concerned, but after a moment she sighed deeply, looking at the man with the sword stuck inside him. He looked to be in great pain before she spoke, "With shifter blood, you have to ingest it. You have to take it by mouth. One gulp."

The man screwed up his face in horror but glanced at his king and fellow comrades before he hesitated forward. I offered him the jar, and he opened it before raising it slowly to his lips. He took a giant gulp of it in, and Anna nodded once to me, before I gripped the sword handle, and ripped it out of him. A shout from his comrades, but when he did not drop down dead they froze. They watched as his body returned to normal.

He panted as he looked down at the bloody sword and looked at me with a shocked look before speaking, "**How?**"

"Shifter blood heals all. Take the jar back home with you. Keep it in a cool dark place. It should be good for at least twenty people. Do not come back over the channel for more," Anna replied. She gave the king a hard stare before she fell into Iverson's arms. Her strength gave out.

Nathaniel turned to look at their king before speaking, "**I request that you get back home. And do not come back.**"

He swallowed hard before he took the jar from his advisor and whispering, "**Thank you.**"

He turned back around, and his men followed him up the gang plank and disappeared inside their ship. Then it somehow backed up, and soon disappeared.

********

Nathaniel looked at Iverson, then looked at me with a look before speaking, "**Take her inside, Iverson. Quinn, a word.**"

I nodded and Iverson picked up Anna and walked back towards the palace.

I looked at Nathaniel as he turned to look at the pack before calling out, "**EVERYONE IS DISMISSED!**"

The pack instantly left. Some going into the woods and some into the palace. I swallowed as I looked at Nathaniel, looking at me before speaking, "**Go home, Quinn.**"

"I thought…"

**"Leave."**

I bowed and shifted to a bird before taking off. Not understanding why he would want a word, only to tell me to leave immediately afterwards.

# Chapter 42

I stared at the sword, it was handed back to one of the others since it was not theirs, and when I refer to them as theirs, I mean across the channel. Much to my distaste I had to clean off my blood off the steel. I looked at the others, they were watching me as if expecting me to drop dead. However, when I didn't, it made them slightly fearful. What happened, was a shocker to everyone, and it showed how much it truly did. No one expected me to survive.

I walk towards my king before speaking, "**What are you going to do with the blood, my lord?**"

He looked at me and then glanced at the rest of the men, who were waiting on his response before whispering, "**I think we need to discuss that in private with the council. It is not just me that needs their voice in this debate anymore. This changes everything.**"

"How does it change everything?" Asked one of the other guards. Our king glanced at him before speaking, "**It means we have a source that can heal any injuries.**"

"That may be true, my lord, but…."

He trailed off for a moment, before looking at me for a split second before finishing, "But what is your current plan? You sound as if you are going to attack them for the shifters. And possibly on catching them for their blood…."

"**That is exactly how it is going to be. I just need the other council members to approve it.**"

Silence. They glanced at each other before I voiced what I thought, "**But the one that gave you the blood said don't come back. They gave us their blood, and you and I both know that they were ready to fight. The entire pack was ready to tear into us.**"

"**Are you challenging my authority, Blackwell?**"

"**I am challenging you on your word, my lord. You said you wouldn't come back. Therefore, you are going back on it.**"

He looked like he wanted to backhand me, but didn't in front of the others. Since they wore similar facial expressions to me, which was like judgment. They agreed with me in that aspect. He gave them his word that we would not go back, but yet alone, he was saying he wanted to prepare for capture -which was against what we had agreed to do.

He turned around, holding the jar of blood, I still did not like the copper taste in my mouth, but knew that without it, I would be dead. I looked at him before speaking out of terms, "**If you are going to go against what we have agreed to do, Drake, then count me out.**"

He froze, and turned slowly around to face me, speaking, "**Excuse me?**"

I swallowed hard, knowing fairly well what might happen, but I didn't care. "**If you go back on your promise to them, then count me out. I will not help you in this capture mission of yours.**"

"**Arrest him.**"

No one moved. He looked at everyone before his eyes flickered back to mine before he glowered at everyone else. Before barking out, "**ARREST. HIM. NOW!**"

No one moved. They shuffled their feet, but none of them moved to arrest me. I looked at him with a slightly raised head. "**I have supported you throughout your campaign, Drake, but if you do this, you will not get my support.**"

He stared at me before fuming, "**And this is why you do not have someone who talks back to you as a fucking advisor! You are supposed to support every single decision I make, Blackwell. And the only thing that you have done is nothing but ridicule me!**"

"**If you had given me a chance, Drake, then yeah, I would have been the one you viewed. However, I will not stand idly by while you go back on your word. This is what I am challenging you on, not your way of running the kingdom that you have earned through wars. And have gained peace throughout the land now, but that is the king I followed. Not this...**"

I waved my hands around in the general area before continuing, "**Ever since Lucius got in a tussle with someone, you seem to forget that you were once that low.**"

"**HOW DARE YOU! ARREST. HIM!**"

He looked pointedly at the guards behind me, but they did not look at him. He turned to face the others on deck, but none of them moved. They all had heard what was said since this was not a private conversation. Everyone had heard of what was said on the other side of the channel, and they all swallowed.

I looked down at the ground before speaking, "**Drake, you and I are friends, and I view you as a friend still. However, if you attack the shifters who gave you enough blood to heal at least twenty of us, along with your son, then I don't see it being worthwhile for me to stick around. I went in with you through blood and gore, Drake, and now you are acting like a madman.**"

He stared at me before he bent over and set the jar of blood onto the deck, slamming his fist into my mouth. I stumbled backward, and I instinctively held my hands up, as blood poured out of my mouth. He split open my lips and knocked a tooth out. I spat it out onto the deck before looking at him. He was fuming, but I held my head high before speaking again, "**You just lost my support. I am no longer your advisor, Drake.**"

I turned around and saw everyone on the ship staring at me, and I swallowed. If this was done in the solitudes of the captain's quarters on this ship, they wouldn't have known. However, it had been changed. I glanced at Drake, who looked like he was ready to murder someone, and someone near the edge shouted, "THERE'S A SHIP COMING AFTER US!"

I ran to the side, leaned sideways, and looked out. Sure enough, there was another ship. Not as fast as the one we were on, but it was pretty quick for it being how it was made. I glanced back at Drake before looking at it again and speaking aloud, "**Continue forward.**"

"**No, stop the ship.**"

I looked at him with a look, but he had pulled himself upright. He glared daggers in my direction. The men looked at me but the ship soon came to a stop, and the ship caught up. The rope ladder was thrown down and whoever it was started to climb the ladder.

****

They landed hard on the deck, before straightening themselves out and flanking each other. There was a total of five and they looked at me, before turning their attention to Drake and speaking, "We had received word that the shifters had given you something. We request that you hand it over, in the name of Logan Vigolf."

"**Who?**"

They glanced at me before their eyes flickered to Drake before speaking, "Logan Vigolf. He is King Nathaniel's brother. He requests that you hand over whatever was given to you by the shifter."

"**And if we don't?**"

They blinked once before one fingered the blade on their hip before speaking, "We have the authority to get whatever was given by force. Do not make us follow through with what the order was."

They arranged themselves slightly, not enough to trigger a fight but enough to signal to us that they would indeed fight for it. I swallowed and glanced at Drake, and knew that his son's life hung in the balance for it. I looked at them before speaking, "**Would you be able to come across the channel first? We give it to one other person before we hand it over?**"

"This is not your winnings. Hand it over now, or we will attack you. Your choice."

**"I am sorry, but your King has authorized it to come back with us in its amount given. Would you dare challenge his authority?"**

They looked at me in shock, they shuffled their feet slightly, clearly not expecting me to pay attention to how the pack was ruled. Not one wolf approached us unless they were given expressed permission by Nathaniel. At least, that was what I had witnessed. They were ready to tear into our throats, but they seemed to wait until their commander gave the word. Since he did not give the authority, they did not attack.

Their eyes flickered to Drake before the same one started to speak, "Is this how you are going to do this? You are going to challenge someone who can take you out within three minutes?"

I looked at Drake and saw him inch backward towards the jar. **"What my advisor said stays. You would be challenging your alpha's order."**

I tried hard not to look at Drake, but I did side-glance at him. I was shocked that he backed me up after everything that had happened before they had boarded. My attention was brought back to them before I could even move, the lead one had slashed me across the stomach with his blade, opening me up. I scrambled to catch my insides before falling to the deck in shock.

*****

The lead one looked down upon my dying self, before speaking, "We are in no ways finding joy in slaughtering your crew. However, you are forcing our hand. Who shall I slash next? Hmmm?                                                    Who?"
Drake stared at me with horror before cawing sounded, and we all glanced upward. A black raven landed and after a moment shifted, revealing Quinn. He stood up and looked at the wolves before us before he spoke, "Now now now…. As soon as I got up into the air, back at the beach, did I see why Nathaniel sent me off abruptly? You five are not supposed to be here."

 "Neither are you. You were supposed to go back home."

Quinn raised his eyebrows before replying, "I go where I please. You, however, are going against what Nathaniel has ordered. Therefore, you are going against Basil's direct order. Should I inform him?"

They went quiet, and only one shuffled his footing but they all looked like they had seen a ghost. The lead one swallowed hard. "And how would you inform him exactly? You are no wolf."

"I may not be a wolf, but my brother is. Therefore, his connections to the pack link are there. Along with my ability to connect to Rafeor."

"Rafeor is nothing but a...."

"If you value your life, do not continue that sentence."

That caught them all off guard. Quinn glanced up slightly and saw a large shadow hovering in the air before Marius dropped down to the deck. He glanced at Quinn before the blackness disappeared.

Quinn looked a little smug at what happened, but he cleared his expression when he looked at the lead one before speaking, "You are without a right in this form. Stand down, and head back home."

The lead one swallowed hard before another spoke, "We were ordered…"

"Ordered? Nathaniel has not ordered anyone to follow this ship back home. Therefore, any order that came from elsewhere is not authorized."

They swallowed and the lead wolf replied softly, "We outnumber you, Marius, you are being weak. Let's take him."

He took a step forward, before I spoke with a shaky wheeze, "**Stop.**"

The wolf looked down and raised his eyebrow before snapping, "Might as well finish you off."

He raised his sword into a strike position, but Marius rumbled out, "If you kill him, Hecktor, then you will be banished. Along with anyone here."

They all froze. The lead wolf stayed his posture before he looked up at Marius and swallowed hard. "You have no authority to do that, Marius."

Marius swallowed slightly but did not move an inch, before replying, "King Nathaniel has given me permission for anything that happens at the moment, Hecktor. Therefore, you are out of bounds."

The waves moved the ship slightly, rocking it slightly before Hecktor looked down at me with a wild look in his eyes. He finally lowered his blade from my throat and took a step backward. He panted slightly before he raised his eyes to Marius and spoke, "How did you get here, Marius?"

Marius glanced at Quinn before replying, "It appears there is more than one way that Quinn can travel."

Hecktor looked at Quinn for a moment before he looked at Marius, looking down at me before closing his eyes, and slashing downward – only he was met with another sword. They were mere inches from my throat and I swallowed hard.

******

I saw Drake standing over me, sweat on his brow before he flung Hecktor's blade out of his hand, and looked like he would kill me. He glowered at Hecktor before speaking, "**Do not harm my advisor.**"

Hecktor stared at him and breathed heavily for a moment before he snapped, "Then you might as well kill him yourself. There is no way he will be able to survive his injuries."

Drake swallowed, but his eyes found Quinn's apparently. Quinn had picked up the jar and took it over to me. We were within striking distance of Hecktor and his goons, but they did not strike him. As if they knew that striking against him was an act of war. I took a swallow of the blood and grimaced at the taste, but knew better than to spit it out. I swallowed it, much to the horror of Hecktor and his goons.

The shock written across their faces, as my wounds had stitched themselves up made it much more enjoyable to witness though.

Quinn glanced at me before looking at Hecktor before speaking, "You attacked someone that is not even in your jurisdiction. Why?"

Hecktor swallowed before replying, "Our orders….."

"Who ordered you to do this, Hecktor?"

Hecktor looked at Marius before replying, "Logan."

"Logan has no authority over Nathaniel. You went beyond Nathaniel's rule. Basil had insisted that if one of the wolves had gone against his direct rule, they would be banished. Therefore, you are. Along with the small group that you had convinced to join you."

"What?"

One of the five squeaked out. He threw daggers at Hecktor before speaking, "Marius, please…."

521

"If you had not listened to Logan and his ruling you would not have to leave. You, however, decided against what Nathaniel has decreed and therefore you lot are banished. Along with whoever is inside the boat you stole."

"But I am loyal to the crown!" Replied another wolf.

Marius looked at him with a hard stare before replying, "You were going against King Nathaniel when you had boarded this ship, Sais. You alone stood on thin ice already. You saying that outwardly is somewhat comical."

"I was not referring to Nathaniel as my king."

Marius growled low in his throat, and Quinn straightened himself up, before speaking, "If I am not mistaken, you are speaking treason. In the shifter palace, that would result in death."

"Well, good thing that I am not a bloody shifter then. Hand over what Logan wants, and we will leave."

"You are banished from going back home, Sais, along with you, Hecktor. And…."

"Can I have a trial, Marius?" Replied one of the werewolves in the five. Hecktor and Sais shifted their footing but did not snap at their comrade, they were blocking who it was. But by the look written across Marius's face, he did not expect them to be there.

The figure stepped out and looked at him with hopeful eyes. Marius's shoulders slumped forward before he whispered, "According to Nathaniel and Basil, anyone who went against his direct order, has to be banished on sight. Therefore, you are banished."

Their face fell and he looked down at the deck before whispering, "But…."

"I am sorry, but I am not going against Nathaniel."

"I understand." They whispered. They had their head hung low and Sais looked at me before speaking, "I guess I should have killed you when I had the chance."

"You should leave, Sais, otherwise my demon will come into play. And believe me, you do not want to experience what he wants to do to traitors."

"I am no traitor."

"Going against your king is treasonous and being called a traitor is taking it lightly. Therefore, traitor."

Sais gripped his sword handle tightly, but he did not withdraw his blade, seeing as how Drake stood ready, and striking against Quinn would bring a war. However, he glanced at Hecktor as if looking for his next move.

Hecktor stepped backward, and Sais took a step backward, same with the rest of the ones that boarded. The one that seemed to want a trial, seemed to understand that if he stayed, he would not be able to survive. Hecktor glanced at Marius before speaking, "Until we meet again, Marius."

"Hopefully that is a never thing, Hecktor. I would have to follow through with what King Nathaniel would want any of his people to do with banished people."

Hecktor swallowed hard and glanced at me before smirking and backing to the ladder before descending backward. Followed by the rest of them.

******

I glanced up at Quinn before reaching my hand out. He gripped my hand and helped me to my feet before he turned to Drake and spoke, "I am going to stress this a little bit for you. Do not come after the shifters for their blood. There is a reason why we only gave you that amount, be glad with what was given to you already."

Drake swallowed hard before whispering, "**But the shifters can heal any injuries. We can be saved as a whole!**"

"You seem to be forgetting who gave you the blood. Anna warned me that this might happen. We were all warned that if we gave blood willingly or forcefully, then this may occur. However, the selfishness of the human species in general always makes me wonder if you are indeed the correct species to rule most of the world."

Drake swallowed and looked down at the deck before speaking softly, "**Our numbers are growing, Quinn. Soon there will not be enough space for the werewolves and the shifters.**"

"What is that supposed to mean exactly? Are you that stupid to threaten us?"

Drake glanced at Marius and swallowed before looking at Quinn and speaking, "**This side of the channel has authorized the hunters. I will be doing the same, although I will be ordering them to bring me a supply of shifter blood.**"

"I should kill you where you stand."

Drake's eyes flew to Quinn's fury-laden eyes but he did not touch his sword at his hip. Drake swallowed and brought his sword outward slightly, before I spoke, "**If you kill him, you ensure that it will indeed lead to a manhunt. Don't do it even if it tempts you. You will get nowhere.**"

Quinn looked at him with a hard look, but he glowered at Drake before speaking, "Your advisor has some good qualities in him. You ought to keep him around. Otherwise, I will hunt you down and slaughter you."

I swallowed and glanced at Drake, but knew that he would not look at me for the life of me. I knew that his stuck-up self would prevent us from being friends ever again, but knowing he had gone up against a werewolf for my sake, made me wonder why he risked his life. However, I knew better than to voice it out loud. Especially in front of an audience.

Quinn looked directly at Drake as if he knew that he would have sent me somewhere. He swallowed and lowered his sword. Quinn nodded once, before turning to Marius and speaking, "Time to depart."

Marius glanced at Drake before speaking, "Do not come back. Nathaniel let you go with your lives. Do not make him regret it."

He approached Quinn, and as one, they shifted together into a bird and took to the skies - disappearing after a few minutes.

*****

I looked at Drake before looking away, knowing that I should get as far away as I could from him. However, after a moment he spoke quietly, "**I am sorry, Blackwell.**"

I looked at him and swallowed hard before speaking equally as quietly, "**So what now?**"

He looked up before speaking louder, "**We go home, and we leave the shifters alone.**"

The rest of the crew seemed to let go of a gush of air as if they were all holding their breaths. Which I assume they were. He turned around, before speaking, "**Blackwell?**"

"**Yeah?**"

"**I know that I have no room to request this, but will you continue to be my advisor?**"

"**Yes, my lord.**"

He looked over his shoulder at me and smiled with a weak smile, before he turned towards the crew members. "**Get us home.**"

The crew instantly leaped to their tasks, and soon the ship moved and soon we were on set sail homeward. I glanced back at the shores that we were leaving. Without the shifters, I would be dead, and without Quinn and the others, I would be dead. Overall, the shifters would have my full support. I was unsure of what would happen from now on, except for the one fact, that if I needed something, I would make the voyage across the channel for the aid of the werewolves and the shifters, at least personally.

# Chapter 43

We returned to the beach, where I looked at Nathaniel who was waiting. I landed and shifted, and Marius stumbled away gasping. He panted and stared at me momentarily before whispering, "How are you fine after flying and shifting still?"

I smirked before replying, "I am a shifter and a demon Marius. I am used to shifting into more than one thing."

He looked like he would say something, but Nathaniel cleared his throat and Marius straightened himself up before dipping his head at him. Nathaniel's eyes flickered from him to me before speaking, **"Was I wrong in sending you that way?"**

"Unfortunately, you were correct, my king. Logan had sent a ship after them and…."

**"Logan?"**

"Yes, My Lord."

He sighed deeply before looking at me and speaking, **"Quinn, you can go home for real this time. It has officially become a werewolf business."**

I bowed to King Nathaniel before speaking, "I thank you for being so generous King Nathaniel. I will leave now."

"Quinn?"

I paused and looked back at Marius before looking at Nathaniel. Marius swallowed before speaking, "Thank you for taking me with you."

I smiled back at him before turning around Nathaniel spoke just in time before I shifted, **"Quinn, one other thing."**

"Yes, King Nathaniel?"

**"Do not tell anyone at the shifter palace where Iverson's mate is."**

"Anna will eventually go back on her own accord."

**"Perhaps, perhaps not."**

I shrugged and replied, "Only time will tell what happens from now on, King Nathaniel. Anything else you need to tell me before I take off?"

**"No. You are dismissed."**

I dipped my head in his direction before shifting again and taking off.

****

I watched as Quinn flew off and let out a breathy breath. I looked at Nathaniel before speaking, "Out of curiosity, how did you know someone was going to betray you? Along with sending Quinn out there? How did you know you could trust him?"

Nathaniel looked at and said, "**My office. Then I can answer your questions.**"

I dipped my head towards him, we turned around and headed towards the palace, where we found an irritated Logan pacing back and forth.

*******

Nathaniel paused in the doorway and for a split second, seemed to contemplate something, but soon seemed to come to terms with it. There were many wolves and several guards around. Nathaniel, without missing a beat, spoke, Basil underscoring his voice, "**Gray, escort Logan to the dungeon.**"

Silence. Logan froze mid-step and his eyes flickered upward. He whispered, "**On what grounds?**"

"**Treason.**"

If it was silent when Nathaniel spoke, it went dead quiet. Logan swallowed hard before speaking quietly, "**I did nothing wrong.**"

Nathaniel side-eyed me and moved his head slightly. I swallowed slightly, if I spoke out then I would have a target on my back. However, Nathaniel was the rightful king and no one would follow Logan without being downright nuts too. I pulled myself to my full height before speaking, "Not according to the wolves that have recently been banished. They had your name on their lips."

If you weren't watching carefully, you would have missed the panic in Logan's eyes, it was there only for a second, but long enough for Nathaniel and most of the wolves in the area to growl a warning. They noticed. Nathaniel seemed to struggle with Basil for a moment since his eyes flashed Basil's eyes every few seconds, but then it faded away.

Logan took a step backward, and Gray took a step forward before speaking, "Come quietly, Logan."

Logan glanced at Gray and then looked back at Nathaniel, snapping, **"If you want me to be in the dungeons. You, Nathaniel, will have to place me there. Otherwise, I will kill anyone else who dares to try."**

"More treasonous talk. You are digging yourself a bigger hole that you cannot possibly crawl out of Logan. Go quietly, or we will restrain you."

Onyx was heavy in my voice, and Logan glanced at me sharply before growling, **"It seems as if your gamma is too scared to take me on, Nathaniel."**

Onyx snarled a warning, but Nathaniel rested his hand on my shoulder, and I felt Basil stir in the air around me. I swallowed and knew Nathaniel was not having an easy time controlling his Lycan. He was about to speak when Shadow spoke, **"He is not a scaredy cat like yourself."**

Logan's eyes flashed something, and he turned towards the stairs before snarling, **"I am no cat!"**

Shadow raised her eyebrows, she may be in Rafeor's body form, but she seemed like she was goading him into a fight. Nathaniel glanced at her and shook his head slightly, but either Shadow saw or simply ignored it, was a mystery. She stared at Logan before speaking again, **"Cause, after all, you were the one who ordered my capture and sent me across the channel to begin with."**

Logan stepped backward, and if I wasn't watching, I would have missed his flinch. However, since I was watching him, more than my mate, I knew that she could defend herself rather well since she gave Basil a run for his money when she threw him around more than once. Crap, I missed what was said. I glanced around the room, read it like a book, and knew that Logan was only drawing himself into a hole where he would never see the light again. I looked over at Nathaniel and swallowed hard since I only saw Basil glinting in his eyes now.

Logan looked around the room, and spoke again, **"Nathaniel, you are too scared to take me to the dungeons? That is the only way I would go down there."**

**"Are you sure you want to be alone with me?"**

Rumbled Basil, and Logan bared his neck in submission since Basil rolled out enough royal aura to make everyone, except myself, Logan, and Shadow drop to their knees. Even though it was not directed at anyone else but Logan. Although, I have to admit, even I wanted to back away and drop down to his aura. However, I forced myself to stay standing, even though it took a lot of strength to do so.

Shadow looked at Basil before speaking, **"Basil?"**

His eyes flickered to her, and he growled low in his throat, warning, but Shadow bared her teeth slightly in warning, and speaking, "**Let Nathaniel have control.**"

"**Why should I?**"

"**Because you are not thinking properly, Basil.**"

"**I am too thinking correctly!**"

"**Are you though? You are making every single wolf around you bow for no reason besides making Logan bare his neck.**"

Basil drew in his aura, and the rest of the ones in the room quickly got back to their feet and seemed ready to do what needed to be done. Their eyes flickered to Logan.

Logan stared at the wolves before him, turning around slowly and speaking directly to Basil, "**You have gone soft, Basil. You are whipped. You should have handed the reins of control of this kingdom to me. Who would be the best in this pack, would be a leader.**"

Basil would have replied, but Sophronia came out of nowhere. She blasted him with her aura and was pulling from the pack at the same time. Logan dropped to his knees and looked at her with shock written across his face. She glowered at him with her wolf-lit eyes and rumbled, "**How DARE you, LOGAN! Crawl to the dungeons. Now.**"

Logan seemed to want to struggle against her order but soon found out that she was too powerful for him to fight. He bowed his head and slowly crawled toward the dungeons. For whatever reason, he did not shift into his wolf, but I felt his wolf refused to allow him to shift.

Sophronia looked at Basil before speaking, "**I will take care of this grievance, Basil, release control to Nathaniel. Then take Marius, and Shadow into the office. Everyone else, besides Gray, you are dismissed. Gray, assist me with the doors please.**"

"Of course, my lady."

Everyone else left quickly, none wanted to step on Sophronia's toes and moved away instantly.

******

Basil flickered out of Nathaniel's eyes, and he locked eyes with his mate, twirled her into his arms, and kissed the living daylights out of her before he let her go. She staggered slightly before he chuckled, and she lightly smacked him on the chest. She turned sharply to face me before said, "**Do not leave anything out in this meeting you are going to have, Marius. I want to know the details. Nathaniel, honey, keep the link between us open please.**"

He bowed slightly towards Sophronia, his eyes twinkling in love, but he did not reply. She rolled her eyes at his antics and followed Logan after a moment, disappearing.

******

I looked at Nathaniel after a moment before speaking, "What the hell was that about?"

Nathaniel looked at me cheekily before replying, "**Let's get to the office first.**"

I nodded once, and looked at my mate, before extending my arm towards her. She took it and we went towards the office.

*****

We entered the office without further ado, and Nathaniel shut the door with a click. I opened my mouth to speak, but he held up his hand, stopping me in a heartbeat. I saw his eyes fly around the room, but he squinted slightly, a book was placed on his desk, and he approached it and sniffed. Basil growled slightly before Nathaniel turned towards the bookcase and motioned us to follow him. I frowned, until he pulled a red bounded book towards himself, and a secret entrance opened up and he motioned for us to enter. I hesitated for a split second, but Shadow entered without hesitation. After we were inside, I saw stairs heading downward, and also spiraling upward. Nathaniel pulled the case backward and soon we were closed within it.

Nathaniel turned slightly, put his fingers to his lips, and we nodded in response. Knowing full well that we should not speak behind the case. I glanced towards the room and was shocked that I could see inside the room, it seemed nothing was out of the norm, but I understood that there were some things that Nathaniel wanted to keep hidden. We went upward, and it spiraled upward for a few twirls around before we came to another office room. Although, this one, was not in the normal case of entrances. It stared into a wall.

Nathaniel entered the office without much more ado, sat down in the office, a puff of dust danced around, and he waved it from his face before looking at me with expectant eyes. I looked around the room for a moment before speaking, "Is this where you go and hide when you are sick and tired of everyone, Nathaniel?"

He smirked, confirming that it was indeed that, but after a moment he sighed a little before speaking, **"This office room, along with the two down below are not on the palace's maps. These were ancient safe rooms for when there were sieges. However, since we no longer go Viking, there was a little less need for them. My father, had these three converted to office spaces, however, the only other person who knows that they exist is Tobias, since our father decreed Logan as too unstable to know about these hidden rooms. The only other person who is not entirely royalty is Aurelius, but she can be trustworthy, and quite frankly, she only saw the stairs so she does not know these rooms personally."**

**"You say safe rooms, so does that mean other members of the pack that remember back to those days may remember them too?"**

He looked at Rafeor since Shadow had allowed her to surface, although I knew that Shadow was on the brink of showing back up too. Nathaniel sighed slightly before running his hand across his face and replying slowly, **"I wouldn't say my father was cruel, but he had the staff that had remodeled these office spaces, banished the whole lot. I believe they are in the outlands now."**

"Banished? But why?"

**"To keep this space safe from prying ears. Back then, anyone who was banished did not get a word into anyone who was part of the pack. The pack would not listen to anyone who was banished. Therefore, even if it was said, then they would be taken as fools. That is still somewhat true as of today. Now, before we go further down that rabbit hole. Tell me, who was on that ship that was part of my pack?"**

I swallowed and glanced at Rafeor and knew she wanted to continue with what was said. There was a lot to break down on what was said, that was a lot of hidden information, but I also knew that when Nathaniel was not in the mood to tell anyone the information,  he would allow Basil to surface only enough for the person to drop it afterward. I sighed deeply before speaking, "Sais, Hecktor, Jerad, Summer….. And Arrax."

**"Arrax? What the hell was he thinking?"**

"He chose the wrong friends, my lord, he asked for a trail, but I knew your response well. Since he was there, he got the same fate as everyone else."

Nathaniel bowed before speaking quietly, **"I am disappointed in him. Arrax would have been a great soldier if he continued to do his duties, and not get caught up in the wrongdoings with everyone else."**

"Agreed."

There was a comfortable silence for a moment, before Rafeor asked, "**Why are you acting like Arrax is someone of great importance? What is his significance?**"

Nathaniel glanced up at her and replied, "**His father was one of my top men. Until recently, I thought they were dead, but Morphous let slip at some point that he had some werewolves in his dungeon for over twelve years. The same ones that I mourn ever since they went missing.**"

"**What is his last name?**"

He sighed deeply before looking at me. "**His last name is Damson. His father was Trevoric. A good man.**"

He sighed heavily but shook his head after a moment. Lost in thought. I looked at Rafeor and saw her frown slightly and seemed to want to question it further, but sighed deeply and sank to another couch letting a puff of dust go upward and making her wheeze. I tried hard not to laugh, but completely failed, and chuckled at her. Rafeor's eyes flung upward as she glared daggers at me before she growled, "**Oh shush.**"

I raised my eyebrow before replying, "Make me."

She seemed to be lost for a moment, but Nathaniel cleared his throat, drawing our attention back to him. Rafeor blushed and seemed to have forgotten that we were not alone. Her eyes flickered to me before connecting in the link, "*I will deal with you later, Marius.*"

A shudder rolled through me, knowing full well that she had more than one thing she could deal with that only she could sustain.

Rafeor sighed slightly and drew our attention back to her, she asked, "**So, they are banished, but what now? You had Logan taken down to the dungeons. What will happen to him?**"

Nathaniel looked at her for a full ten seconds, before his eyes flickered to mine. He said, "**I need Rispin here, also Marius. Do you know where he would be currently?**"

"Why don't you just link him?"

"**Because linking would take a while. I would rather know where to find him, and then bring him back here.**"

"Would he know about this area of office space?"

"**No.**"

I sighed deeply and replied, "Do you want me to go get him, or would you rather yourself?"

"**It would be faster if it was myself. I would have the ability to know if anyone was following us.**"

"Why keep these rooms hidden? They were once safe rooms, but…."

"Because there are some that clearly do not see me fit for the leadership. Logan will eventually have to challenge Basil to a fight to the death."

"To the death?"

"Yes, along with yourself, Rafeor. You are Sophoronia's firstborn child. Therefore, royalty. You have as much to lose as I do."

"But it would be to the death? I thought it would be until one submitted."

He looked at me and swallowed hard. We both know why the rule was the way it was, since around a century ago, the last one that was allowed to leave without being killed was deadly and he had caused countless wars and unnecessary deaths. I sighed deeply drawing her attention to myself. I replied slowly, "There is some history behind that. I will tell you while Nathaniel is gone."

"Okay."

I looked at him and he sighed deeply, before standing to his feet before speaking, "**You do that, Marius.**"

He headed towards the entrance, when Rafeor spoke, "**Wait.**"

He turned around and raised his eyebrow at her before replying, "**What?**"

"Why was Sophronia acting differently? You two acted as if you were trying to hide something."

Nathaniel smirked slightly and blushed after a moment. His eyes showed nothing but happiness, and I finally figured out why he was happier. Along with the way Basil was reacting. I smiled slightly before Rafeor seemed to finally click the pieces together too. Her hands flew to her face and she squealed slightly. She squirmed slightly into the chair too, and I swallowed slightly, as Onyx flashed in my eyes at the endearment that she was showing. Nathaniel looked at me for a moment before speaking, "**I think that you two know what I am going to be.**"

"When?"

"**We found out before I left for the channel.**"

I smiled wide before asking, "And you are keeping it quiet because?"

That was where his face fell and he lowered his eyes. "**Because we do not know if the pup will survive. This is the first one since Rafeor, and that was almost nineteen years ago now.**"

For a moment, none of us spoke. We were in silence and finally, Rafeor whispered, "**I'm sorry.**"

**"Don't be, Rafeor, I would not change anything as it is."**

**"But I am not your daughter. Not fully at least."**

**"You are Sophronia's daughter. My mate's daughter. That makes you automatically mine. I would not change anything."**

She looked up at him with tears in her eyes, and he approached her and rested his hand against her cheek before he whispered, **"You are filling in a hole that I didn't know needed to be filled, Rafeor. I would not change anything for anything. Now, as Marius tells you why we would have to kill each other, and the history behind it. Relax and enjoy what we both know."**

She smiled and nodded in acknowledgment. Nathaniel took a step backwards and leveled me with a knowing look. He turned towards the way before connecting to me, *"Do not make me smell your arousal when I get back with Rispin, Marius."*

*"As if I would do it with these circumstances, my liege."*

He gave me a hard look before he descended the staircase.

******

I smirked as I turned my attention to Rafeor before speaking, "Well, what do you want to know about, honey?"

She blushed for a moment before batting her eyelashes at me and replying, **"I want to know how to ease all the tension out of you."**

I swallowed hard and felt my trousers start to have a small bulge in the front. I scowled slightly, closed my eyes, and counted to ten before replying, "That is only in the privacy of our room that we can indulge in said things, Rafeor."

She smirked, and Onyx flared in my eyes for a brief moment, but he soon faded back after a moment. Which brought a brilliant smile to her face, which was way better than when we rescued her only yesterday. I sighed and sat down in the other armchair, as a puff of dust went up into the air. Making her wave her hands in front of her face as the dust danced around. She wheezed, but there was nothing I could do to stop it further. We just had to wait until it came back down and settled.

I sighed deeply as I watched as the dust danced in the little light that streamed through the opposite wall. It may be an old safe room, but every single safe room had a tunnel or a way out in case it was compromised in any way. Along with the wolves needing a way to connect to the earth, otherwise, we become rather rambunctious when kept in a dark room without natural light.

Rafeor cleared her throat, drawing me out of my thought process before asking, "**Alright fine, so I guess my question is why is it to the death?**"

I locked eyes with her and replied slowly, "Are you sure you want to know that history, Rafeor?"

**"I'm sure."**

I nodded and sighed before speaking, "About a century ago, long before mine or Nathaniel's time. There was a challenger for the crown. At the time, the king knew the challenger himself and was a friend of this wolf. So, he allowed his friend to leave…."

I looked down at my clasped hands before continuing, "The wolf that was banished, brought nothing but pain and misery. He attacked the royal pack over and over again. This is before Nathaniel and his father united the surrounding packs, to become under one rule. So, this wolf united several packs that were in the surrounding area and would attack. And attack. And attack, until he was the sole one left. Everyone that had helped him, had perished. Killing hundreds of innocent lives. The king at the time, fought back. However, every single time that they had a face-off, the challenger would run off. The king, under werewolf law, would have to put down everyone who had fought or banished them. Since this is throughout someone else being banished, he had to kill every. Single. Wolf. That had attacked."

A small whine sounded from Rafeor, and I glanced up and saw her eyes swimming in tears, but there was more to this history. I knew that Nathaniel would want me to tell her everything, so I took a deep breath in, knowing full well that the next part would even make my voice crack slightly, "The surrounding packs, stopped supplying the royal pack items, and soon famine happened in the royal pack. However, the surrounding packs did not understand something. They did not know why the royal pack was attacking their friends. At least not until the challenger went towards them for aid at some point. That is when the rest of the surrounding packs understood what was happening, however, it was too late for some. Since they had gone along with the challenger."

I paused and was about to continue when Rafeor cut me off for a moment, "**What was the challenger's name?**"

I swallowed and looked down at the hardwood floor before replying, "Ivanov."

**"How old would it be in history?"**

"About a century ago. Why?"

She swallowed before replying, "**Because Ivanov sounds familiar somehow.**"

I frowned and shook my head in disdain slightly, there was no way that he was alive. However, even Onyx was silent for a moment, which was unusual for him to say the least. He knew something that I did not. I was about to ask him, but Rafeor gestured towards me, and I raised my eyes to her before raising an eyebrow. She smiled slightly, but spoke softly, "**Please continue."**

I swallowed hard and after a moment I continued, "Ivanov, had challenged the pack's alphas. And since it is common practice in the packs, it was to the death. So, none of the alphas had survived his brutal lying ass. That is how he had gained the support of the surrounding packs. Since he had challenged the alpha to a duel, if an alpha did not accept a challenge, then he was deemed unworthy of leading a pack. At least, that is the old way of their logic. Not nowadays."

I paused and looked at her and then looked away when I saw Shadow flicker in her eyes for a moment, "Anyhow, after Ivanov had challenged ninety percent of the surrounding packs, the rest came towards King Lentulas looking for help. At the time, Lentulas was wary of anyone, but after their alphas swore fealty to him, did he do anything. With their united front, they drove Ivanov out of pack lands, and further still. That is roughly when Lentulas was handing the reins to Nathaniel's father when it was made into a pack. The first thing that Nathaniel's father had done after the threat, he had requested that all the alphas that had survived to hand over their leadership to the royal pack, and that we would be merged over. At first, none of the other alphas wanted to, but Nathaniel's father was persistent, and finally woven the rest of the packs into our own."

**"Does the pack acknowledge that the alphas were once leaders?"**

"It is a weird dynamic in that sense, Rafeor. I would tell you how it all works but for now, I think that is all that needs to be immediately addressed."

She frowned after a moment but sighed deeply and her head fell backward, and a yawn escaped her. I blinked once before opening my arms, and without hesitation, she came over sat on my lap, and snuggled in close. Soon after a minute, she fell asleep. Her even breathing was the only thing that kept Onyx quiet. There was one other part of the history that was not told, but both of us did not really want to tell her that.

*****

After a few minutes, Nathaniel and Rispin entered the room. Nathaniel glanced down at me, and blinked once as if he was for sure would smell something that would make us uncomfortable around each other. He sighed deeply, which woke Rafeor, and she jolted hard and whimpered. Which brought Onyx to growl a low warning at Nathaniel, as he tightened his hold around her. Nathaniel held up had hands before speaking softly, "**My apologies, Rafeor.**"

She looked at him with wild eyes for a moment. She seemed to come to terms with where she was and she lowered her eyes in shame. That is when Rispin shook his head before speaking, "Do not even think about doing that. It is understandable on your reaction."

She swallowed hard and nodded once, but did not reply. She was still waking up and I sighed deeply before moving her into a more comfortable position.

Nathaniel looked at me for a brief second before asking in the link, "***Is she okay, Marius?**"*

*"She is suffering from post-trauma, my lord. It is not something that can be cured overnight."*

He nodded slightly and turned his attention to Rispin before heading back to the desk, and sitting down in the chair that he had left. Leaving Rispin to sit next to us, since there were only three armchairs in this office space.

Nathaniel sighed deeply, drawing my attention back to him before he spoke, "**I brought you here too Rispin, because we had recent issues that need my next line of leadership.**"

"Like what could be so dire, that you would bring me to this hidden room?"

I swallowed and Nathaniel motioned towards me, and Rispin's eyes flickered to me before he turned his head sideways slightly and I sighed deeply before speaking, "Before Quinn was told to go home, he was avertedly told to bring me and fly after the human ship. To make sure they were not up to anything bad. However, what I was not expecting was one of our ships following after them."

"How? How is that possible? Nathaniel did not authorize anyone to follow them."

"**That is because they were not on my accord.**"

"Treason?"

"**Treason. Marius, please continue.**"

I took a deep breath, and Rafeor squeezed my hand in support, I raised my eyes to once again meet Rispin's before continuing, "Once Quinn caught up, and landed on the ship, I noticed that it was our pack members. There were a total of six, but I am unsure of the other wolf that was staying with their ship. The five that boarded were: Hecktor, Sais, Jerald, Summer, and…. And Arrax, who got caught up in the wrong friend group. However, while I was being flown over, Basil informed me that anyone who had joined the ones that had committed treason would be banished on sight."

"So, Arrax is now banished?"

**"As unfortunate as it is, we cannot go against our customs for one wolf. We cannot afford to make history repeat."**

Rispin glanced at Rafeor before his eyes flickered over at Nathaniel before speaking, "Does…"

**"While Nathaniel was going after you, Rispin, Marius filled me in on the history. I understand now why it is either banishment or death."**

Rispin looked back at her, and he seemed to glance at me for a split second, and I shook my head slightly. He frowned and squinted his eyes as if wondering what part I did not tell her. However, bringing it up would make it bad on my end too. Nathaniel glanced sharply at me before linking, *"I know that look, Marius. What did you not tell her?"*

*"I didn't tell her about Ivanov taking anyone with him when our forefathers ran him off."*

*"That could have been important information for her to know."*

*"Nathaniel, would you want her to worry? They had left with the threat of attacking once their so-called pack would be strong enough to sustain the war. I would rather not tell her."*

*"You are digging yourself a hole, Marius. You should have told her the whole history."*

*"Nathaniel…."*

Rispin cleared his throat, making us drop the connection, and I blinked once and saw Shadow squinting her eyes at me. Rispin swallowed and looked at anyone else but myself. As if he knew that Nathaniel and I were having a heated conversation about not telling her certain aspects of the history. After a moment, Rispin asked, "So…. if that is the case. Who ordered them to attack? What were they after anyhow?"

Nathaniel glanced at me and raised his eyebrow, that was something I did not have the chance to tell him either. I knew that he was keeping the link up with Sophronia too, since she had requested it. I sighed deeply before speaking, "Logan. Apparently, for whatever reason, Logan was after the blood that Ivenson's mate gave. Don't know why though."

It took a moment before Rispin processed the news, and his wolf, Smoke, growled a low snarl. He may not be of royal blood, but that did not mean he was not powerful. His aura swirled around the room, extended to the other ends of the room, and seemed to sweep down the first staircase. Nathaniel spoke, **"Smoke, reel back in your anger."**

Smoke looked sharply at Nathaniel and seemed to want to challenge. After a moment, his eyes flickered back to Rispin's green eyes. Rispin sighed hard for a moment before whispering, "My apologies, my king."

**"It is alright, Rispin, however, we cannot be leaking out our anger at the moment. We need a plan on what the next steps are."**

"Why don't you kill him?"

Rispin growled. Rafeor took a sharp breath in before whispering, **"Are we talking about killing Logan? The king's brother?"**

Rispin looked at her sharply, which drew out Onyx's protective nature, who let out a sub-vocal warning. Rispin swallowed before speaking, "Logan has done more offensive things than this one. His challenging Nathaniel's rule alone would result in death otherwise. Or banishment, in some cases. However, why are you waiting Nathaniel? He has not once shown any quality reasons to keep him around."

Nathaniel grabbed a feather and had since been twirling it in his hands before he replied, **"Because he is my brother Rispin. Would you kill your sister if she had done this?"**

Rispin swallowed hard before replying, "But this is not the first time he has challenged you personally, Nathaniel. This is the more recent occurrence, but it still does not excuse him for the behavior."

**"So, killing him is the best solution you have come up with?"**

Rispin glanced at her before his eyes landed on mine before replying, "Rafeor, I am sorry to say this frankly. However, you do not know even the tip of the iceberg that Logan has done. There are some things that even the pack doesn't know, but Nathaniel does. Isn't that right, Nathaniel?"

I glanced at Nathaniel and saw him pause in his twirling with the feather before he sighed deeply, **"There are some things that I do keep to myself on his crimes."**

"See? What qualities are you hoping to see out of Logan besides betrayal more than once Nathaniel? Logan is mateless and has no heirs. He drinks his so-called sorrows away, and had not once been…."

**"Logan had a mate and has a stepdaughter. He does not want anyone else to really know."**

"Who?"

**"His mate was killed Rispin. His stepdaughter is Aurelius, who is the last connection to his mate."**

To say Rispin was shocked was an understatement, and he glanced at me before whispering, "How long did you know about this, Marius?"

**"Aurelius and I are friends Rispin. So, at some point, I informed him of it too. But I don't think it was that long ago. Since I had just been here not even six days yet."**

Rispin looked at Rafeor and sighed deeply. He ran his left hand across his face, before looking at Nathaniel and speaking, "When did you find out that Aurelius is his daughter?"

**"I do not need to tell you that entirely. However, I had learned it perhaps a day or so beforehand. When the water was poisoned."**

"Oh. yeah, I kind of forgot about that."

He fell silent and Smoke glinted in his eyes for a split second before Rispin shoved him back down. He sighed deeply before looking at Nathaniel with a pointed look, "I am the only one in the dark in this aspect. Great. Anyhow, back to business. I say we kill Logan. Banishment is too risky, especially since Logan has been in this palace for the entirety of his entire life. We do not want a repeat in history."

**"That may be true, but I am not going to kill him."**

"Why not?"

I asked, earning a sharp elbow in the side, making me wince in slight discomfort. I grumbled, but Nathaniel without missing a beat, **"Because if I kill him, then we lose...."**

Footsteps sounded on the staircase, and we all fell silent. Basil flashed in Nathaniel's eyes, along with Onyx in mine. Rispin stood up, and Smoke took the reins, but he kept his aura down. His hand lingered on the weapon on his hip.

# Chapter 44

Rafeor took a deep breath in before turning to Basil and whispering, "**How does Ghost know of this area?**"

Basil and Smoke looked at each other sharply, before they faded away to let their humans have the reins. Soon, Ghost walked into the room, his eyes flew across the room, landing on me before his eyes flickered to Nathaniel before speaking, "Ah, so this is where you go into hiding."

"How did you find this?"

Ghost looked at Rispin before replying, "Sophronia sent me to be with you guys at this meeting. She said office, and when I went into Nathaniel's public office, no one was inside."

"**So, what did you exactly do to find the entrance?**"

"I connected to Sophronia and asked where the meeting was. She said there was a chance that you were in the chambers behind the red-bound book."

"**Who else knows about it?**"

"Myself, and the rest of my patrol."

"**You told your patrol?**"

"Nathaniel, we do not keep secrets away from each other. Besides, my father mentioned a set of office spaces hidden in the castle somewhere. He never said where mind you, but I think this answers my question on where."

Rispin gripped his sword handle, and Ghost looked at him, raising an eyebrow before speaking again, "Rispin, may I remind you that my father is Tobias, not Logan. As I am aware, Logan does not know where these office spaces are. So, we are safe in that aspect."

"But you told others without asking, Nathaniel."

"I am aware that I had done that Rispin, however, I have only done it because we are becoming part of the royal guard. Shouldn't they know where this area is?"

"**Ghost, none of the current royal guard knows of this place. Rispin didn't find out until a few minutes ago. Same with Marius.**"

"Oh. I thought it would have been known through the royal guard at least."

"Who else did you tell Ghost?"

I asked, drawing his attention to myself slightly. Ghost sighed, shook his head, and replied, "I only informed the rest of my patrol. So Azier, Cyprus, Batis, and Brego. No one else knows. If I said something to them, then they do tend to keep it under wraps."

"How do we know that they won't spill the location of it to anyone else? Especially when they drink,"asked Rispin.

Ghost glanced at him, sniffed slightly, and pulled himself upright slightly before replying, "Have you ever seen them inside the tavern or bar area? According to Azier, the siblings cannot have any drinks that may impair them. So, that would only be Brego that would be the missing link, however, I know Brego has a high no-alcohol rule. He doesn't like the taste, and along with the fact that drinking makes him sick. So, I think we are safe there."

"What if it was compromised? No one is safe from being tortured for information Ghost, "Rispin replied.

Ghost sighed deeply before speaking, "As I had stated before, Rispin, we are training to be royal guards. How many others are being trained to be royal guards? How many get Nathaniel or Basil's attention enough for that?"

Rispin was silent for a moment before he mumbled, "Not a lot."

"Exactly. Not a whole lot. I would never tell something even being tortured. I cannot be bought. Along with the fact that Taryn tells us five stuff that even Nathaniel is not knowledgeable of. I think I am safe to be telling my patrol."

**"I thought it was Azier's patrol?"**

Ghost glanced at Rafeor and sighed deeply and replied, "It is under technical terms her patrol. She is the captain. However, she entrusts each and every one of us to be in command. Besides, not many people are comfortable answering a woman's question. The whole, guy and girl status."

**"What status?"**

Rispin beat me to reply, "The fact that girls and women are typically seen but not heard. They do the household chores and make the food."

**"What does the guy normally do?"**

"He normally works, and…."

Rispin rubbed the back of his head with his right hand and did not continue. Rafeor frowned and wiggled out of my hold slightly, before turning to me with a look across her face. **"You better know here and now Marius, that I will not be like normal women. I want my freedom."**

"As if I could stop you either way," I replied with a small chuckle.

Rafeor rolled her eyes, and Ghost smirked slightly before turning his attention to Nathaniel and speaking, "Are you okay, Nathaniel?"

Nathaniel looked down at his hands and replied, "**If roles were reversed, Ghost, would you be?**"

"Good point. Now, before I joined. What exactly was suggested?"

"We kill him. Either that we banish him, but that has its own problems." Growled Rispin, making Nathaniel sigh deeply and shake his head slowly. Ghost raised his eyebrows and turned slightly to Rispin before replying, "That is not going to work. On either account. There is something else. Nathaniel? Thoughts?"

Nathaniel sighed deeply and shook his head. He seemed to be lost. Ghost looked at me for a moment before speaking, "Isn't there something that Rafeor could do?"

**"Like what?"**

"Like have Shadow strip him of his rank?"

Rafeor's jaw dropped slightly before she whispered, "**But that would…. I am not Logan's alpha. Nathaniel is.**"

******

Ghost looked down at the ground, frowned, and turned slowly around to stare at Nathaniel. He swallowed hard, Basil flickering in his eyes, and he looked away slightly. I put the pieces together quicker than the others before shaking my head, I was shocked. If Nathaniel is ready to hand over the reins that means that something else was told to him alone. I glanced at Rispin and saw him squint his eyes between Ghost and Nathaniel before asking, "What else is being kept in the dark? Ghost is acting like he knows something more than even we do."

Nathaniel sighed and glowered a moment at Ghost before speaking, "**Before Rafeor and Aurelius were kidnapped, Taryn came to me. She said that I needed to hand the pack over to Rafeor.**"

"What?"

Rispin raised his voice. Making Rafeor flinch slightly, and I caged her in my arms for a moment, but knew that Rispin would only get slightly more aggravated if I growled at him. Nathaniel glanced at Rispin. "**She said that I have ruled the kingdom long enough for the next in line to take control. Shadow is more than ready to take command. Along with Rafeor. She**"

**may have only been here for less than a week, but in that time frame she had proven herself to be strong enough to be an alpha."**

"Isn't there someone else to lead the pack? I apologize beforehand Rafeor, however, I must speak my mind."

Rispin paused, and Rafeor nodded once, and he continued, "Rafeor is not a complete werewolf. She is a weapon. The prophecy states that she is the most dangerous creature on the planet and you want…. Her to be in the control of a vast kingdom?"

"Rispin, we have allied with Morphous, therefore we won't get attacked by the shifters…."

"Shut it, Ghost. You don't seem to understand that this would change everything. Rafeor would have two responsibilities. She is not ready to take over a huge pack, along with the fact that the pack would not accept her. I have heard them more than once, Nathaniel. That they would rather die than be led by a monster."

Nathaniel growled a warning, and Rispin raised his hands in surrender before speaking, "I am more of the one saying these things aloud. Do not kill the messenger."

I felt rage, but Shadow replied, **"I have heard what several of them try to keep hidden and away for a long time. However, that is only a small section of the pack. Maybe not even twenty wolves."**

"That may be true, that it is only a couple. However, they tend to spread news like wildfire around here."

**"That may be true Rispin, however, I agree with you on some points you have made. Ghost, is there anything that you know that you can tell us? Why would Taryn suggest the takeover now rather than later? And before you ask, no Rafeor is not hearing anything I say. So, if that is something to be worried about, it is not happening."**

Everyone looked at Ghost and he swallowed hard before replying, "The only thing that Taryn stressed to everyone in the patrol was the fact that if Rafeor, and yourself Shadow did not take command of the werewolves now. That there would be more and more deaths. More than the normal war amount. We could even be wiped out as a whole."

"As a whole? Can you elaborate on that Ghost?" whispered Rispin, he tried to keep his voice down. However, I could see Smoke glinting in his eyes, and Ghost swallowed hard before looking at Nathaniel. Nathaniel nodded once at him, and he sighed deeply, speaking, "Taryn said that if Shadow and Rafeor did not take command of the werewolves. Along with the shifters…."

"Wait. Back up. The shifters? What do they have to do with this exactly?"

Rispin was getting on my nerves, and it seemed that even Nathaniel was starting to wonder if he should have left him out of this meeting. Shadow spoke, "**Rispin?**"

Rispin looked over at her, before Shadow continued, "**Please hold all comments and questions until he is finished. It doesn't do anything if he keeps having to repeat himself more than once.**"

Rispin scowled but his eyes flickered to Nathaniel, who was staring at him. Basil's eyes glinted in his eyes, and Smoke lowered his eyes. After a moment, Rispin lifted his head and nodded to Ghost. He replied, "I apologize, Ghost. Please continue."

Ghost was silent for a moment and looked at Rafeor before continuing, "As I was saying, the shifters would be joined in our pack. We would face the threat that we all face as one."

**"I thought that I was to sign a peace treaty with the leader of the attackers?"**

"That was before certain events happened. Taryn actually informed us a few hours ago, that…. That she was supposed to die when the humans attacked. However, since we have come to a standing agreement, that future snapped out of place. It crumbled to ashes. Therefore, the only way to do this now is to be a united front. And that includes the outlanders."

Ghost paused and swallowed hard before whispering, "The outlanders, the Carpathians, the shifters. They all need to follow under two rulers."

"Two rulers? Who else?" Asked Rispin after a moment, when Ghost did not continue.

Ghost swallowed before speaking, "Logan has a son who survived. I don't know the exact details, Taryn knows more than I do, however, Logan has a son, and he has been raised with the shifters."

Silence. Finally, after a moment, Shadow spoke, "**Wait a moment. I thought that Logan's children were killed.**"

**"I recently found out that Herald may be the missing child. Logan sent his children to learn under the Druids. I am unsure if the children were given to Morphous to keep them alive, but I know Morphous, did not leave any survivors."**

"Then how did Herald get to live with the shifters?"

**"Wait, a moment. Herald? You sure he is the child that is Logan's?"**

"Positive. When he shifted to his wolf form here, he was, as the other prophecy stated. It is in the werewolf community, that a royal-blood werewolf, would one day come in the colorations of his wolf's. Along with the fact, that his wolf spoke differently, whenever someone of royal blood speaks it is different. I could tell that he had rank, I just didn't tie it together until now on why he had a wolf spirit."

"How long did you know that Herald was Logan's son Nathaniel?" Asked Rispin.

We glanced towards Nathaniel who sighed deeply before replying, "**I only just found out that Logan had children. I didn't really tie the connection to Herald until now.**"

Rispin looked like he was lost for a moment, but I asked a question that was now nagging me, "Ghost, you seem like you want Rafeor and Herald to lead our pack and the shifters. Why?" "Because if we are not a united front, we will all die."

"How can you be so sure of that Ghost? We had threats before, and they all fell through."

"Because unlike all the other threats, this one is very real. This one is very dangerous. Remember when the shifters were killed when they attacked the two ships that were coming in on either side?"

We all swallowed. How could anyone forget that? Shadow winced before speaking, "**What about them?**"

"Unfortunately, for us, the humans on this side of the channel have decreed that the shifters were to be hunted to extinction because of Astromic and her children. Therefore, they hired the Sazornoras. Who are supernatural hunters."

"Why does it matter? They are after the shifters, why should we unite together?" Replied Rispin.

Shadow for a moment threw daggers with her eyes at him before she looked at Ghost before speaking, "**Ghost, there is more to this isn't there? You cannot simply say they are solely targeting the shifters.**"

Ghost swallowed for a moment, looked down and took a deep breath in before letting it slowly out. He was worried, and his fingers flickered at his, sides, the only signs that I have noticed that he did when he was nervous. Rispin noticed that too, and he swallowed. As much as he may challenge Ghost, he knew that not many things made Ghost nervous. Rispin's eyes flickered to Nathaniel who was quiet throughout this entire ordeal before speaking, "Nathaniel?"

Nathaniel raised his eyes slightly before speaking, "**While we were coming back across the channel, Ghost and Taryn told me to drop connections to Morphous. They informed me that the four shifters that were going down would be killed. At the moment, I don't think that Morphous is in the greatest of moods to unite us together. He would not let anyone rule his clan without being challenged.**"

He lowered his head and did not speak anymore. Shadow gently pried herself off of my lap, and moved to stand up. She swayed slightly before speaking, "**Nathaniel, you and I both know that something is happening at the shifter palace as of current. However, that is not the time** to discuss that. Ghost, what is making you so nervous? There is something that you are not saying about this group."

"There is some information that I wished I had never known, Shadow, however, now that I know it, I cannot take it back. The Sazornoras are going to be tasked with killing any supernatural being they see since the humans are expanding. They are getting bolder and they are starting to have more thoughts than a few decades ago. The only way that we may survive their attack, and of course, this may change, since nothing is set in stone completely. However, we all, as supernatural beings, need to unite together and become one. The only ones that may have issues with this are the outlanders. Since Taryn saw a vision that someone of the Carpathian family line is with the shifters currently."

"Ummm… how is a Carpathian out of their safety zone? I thought that they couldn't walk in the daylight."

"Normally, you are correct Rispin. However, there are certain artifacts that the Carpathians had created when the druids were still around. I believe they had what is called a daylight ring. They can walk in the sun without being blown away in the sun."

"How certain is Taryn that the shifters have a family member of the Carpathians?"

**"I am pretty sure that it is solid. Since Herald mentioned the need of going to the Carpathians next after us."**

Rispin looked at Nathaniel when he replied. Rispin swallowed hard and looked away before looking at Shadow before speaking again, "So I would need to follow a hybrid?"

He made it seem that he would challenge my mate's authority, and Onyx stirred in my eyes. However, Ghost beat me to speak, "Rispin, it sounds like you are ready to challenge Shadow. Why?"

"Because I would. No offense Shadow, but you are not someone who I would back up."

**"I think that for this to work properly. I would need to challenge Basil to a duel. However, I understand that the customs are to kill the alpha, but that is not going to happen. Nathaniel, can you allow Basil to answer a question?"**

**"What question?"**

**"The question along the lines of him submitting to me."**

For a moment, Nathaniel seemed lost in thought before his eyes flickered to Basil's eyes and he rumbled, **"If I could little one, I would submit to you immediately right now."**

**"However, Rispin makes a point. How would the pack know I can rule them if they have not seen me fight? No one has seen me fight, since you have ordered it to be cleared out for**

my sessions. Therefore, they would need to see it in person. However, we cannot simply move out of this office space and announce the match. No, we can't do that. Basil, you are going to have to make me angry enough to have me surface."

**"Why can't it be immediately out of here?"**

Ghost seemed to be on the same wavelength as he replied, "Because it cannot look staged. If it looks staged then it would be…. Not the greatest thing. The pack would not submit to Shadow. It has to look real."

He looked at Shadow with a look before continuing, "It would make even the wolves that don't seem to be the best of our numbers, to submit to the new ruler. The fact that Shadow is however Sophronia's daughter, makes it slightly better since Nathaniel would only be handing it down to the eldest child. However, when the next two become of age, that may differ if things go the way they should."

It took a moment for everyone to process what Ghost said. Finally, Rispin glanced sharply at Nathaniel before whispering, "Wait, Sophronia is expecting?"

Nathaniel had paled slightly before whispering, "**Ghost. What do you mean by two?**"

Ghost looked perplexed for a moment and then he registered on what was said. He smiled slightly before speaking, "Ummm…. Taryn said that you were going to have triplets….. However…. One will not make it through, but the other two will become strong."

**"How sure are you?"**

"If the events of the current do not do anything horrid, ninety-nine percent, Nathaniel. If things turned worse though…."

He looked down and whispered the next sequence, "None of them would survive."

Basil flickered into Nathaniel's eyes, and he looked like he was struggling with his Lycan for a moment. Finally, Nathaniel won and Basil's eyes faded away. He blinked and looked at Rispin who had his jaw open in shock before whispering, "Is that why you want to hand over to Shadow?"

**"Partially. I want to raise my children. I did not expect it to be that many though. I was only expecting one."**

"Sorry, Nathaniel, but it is two that will survive if things go correctly. However, that is still in shadows on that aspect."

Nathaniel would have smiled if things weren't so grim. He looked at Rispin and then his eyes flickered to mine before speaking, "**Marius, why are you so quiet?**"

Everyone glanced at me, and I sighed deeply before replying, "Because I have not had anything to say on some of these things that are being brought up. I will fully support my mate in the endeavors of the leadership. Along with the fact that the future is looking rather grim for anything nice."

Ghost let out a breath as if he was holding in, and I glanced at him with a raised eyebrow but did not respond. Rispin sighed deeply and drew our attention to him before he spoke, "So, in other words, doom would happen if we did not unite with the shifters and other supernatural beings. However, I see to think of one issue."

**"What issue?"**

"The fact that if the Carpathians are indeed to be somehow brought here, then how would it work in their feeding? How would they even get here?"

I opened my mouth but closed it for a moment. Frowning, he brought up an excellent point. We all have heard rumors about how they feed, and we have heard rumors that they capture and take werewolves simply for the fun of it. Onyx glinted in my eyes at the thought, but I forced him back slightly. He faded in the back and I blinked once and saw everyone staring at me. I swallowed and asked, "What?"

"Onyx started to shake the room in a thunderous growl is what," replied Ghost.

I frowned and replied, "I thought he only flickered in my eyes."

"Nope, it was along with his thunderous growl."

"Sorry."

They all shrugged and finally silence happened once again. We sat in comfortable silence for a few minutes. All thinking about what was said.

*****

Shadow sighed deeply before drawing our attention to her, **"Well... with that said, the question still stands. What are we going to do with Logan?"**

Rispin sighed deeply and replied, "Since you will soon become alpha, I think that is kind of up to your discretion."

**"You would allow me to be your alpha, Rispin?"**

Rispin swallowed before replying, "The laws in our kingdom say that if a challenger is of royal blood, then the former alpha is not to be killed. I will accept you as the alpha if you win against Basil fairly."

Shadow nodded and was about to say something else. However, Ghost spoke, "That means that Basil has to do this the proper way. He cannot hold himself back even slightly, Nathaniel. Everyone knows how strong Basil is here, and they would not want him holding himself back."

**"Believe me, he would not hold back."**

Basil flickered in Nathaniel's eyes for a moment, before fading back into the background. Making everyone shuffle their feet for a moment since Basil let loose the aura of himself. Everyone besides Shadow seemed affected, leading to the fact that she was ready for the role. Even Rispin bared his neck in submission to Basil's little aura he let slip out. Shadow didn't even seem phased by it. I smiled, that proved more than anything that she was ready to take command. If you do not react at all towards an alpha's aura as powerful as Basil's it means you are truly ready to challenge him.

******

It even seems that Rispin understood it. He stood up after a moment, before speaking, "Is that all for now?"

I glanced at Ghost and saw him frown in confusion for a moment. No one would seem to want to get away as much as Rispin is acting, however, after a moment, Nathaniel shrugged and replied, **"I think so. We have covered what we needed with Logan, and…. What will happen soon."**

Rispin nodded and was about to head out when Ghost called out, "Rispin?"

"Hmm?"

"Swear that you will not tell anyone of this to the moon."

Rispin froze. His eyes flickered back to Ghost who did not budge, and he growled, "I am the beta of the pack, Ghost."

"Then you would not mind swearing to it."

Rispin stared hard at him but Nathaniel growled out, **"Why is it suddenly so hard for you to do this, Rispin?"**

Rispin swallowed hard and took a step backward, making Basil surface, and he growled out. His aura swirled around the office room, and even though it was not directed towards us, everyone but Shadow bared their neck. However, I noticed that Rispin seemed to fight his aura. I growled low in my throat, Onyx surfacing slightly before Ghost spoke, "Rispin?"

Rispin looked at him and growled low in his throat, Smoke flickering in his eyes. Shadow seemed to know what was happening though and she sighed deeply before whispering, "**I should have made the connections on why you seemed to challenge everything. Smoke, who is your alpha?**"

Her aura rolled out, and Smoke flinched but replied, "Logan."

**"Not Nathaniel?"**

"He has gone soft. He is making the pack weak."

Nathaniel growled low in his throat, but after a moment, Shadow looked at him, and Basil faded away for a moment in his expression and drew back in his aura. She looked back at Rispin before speaking, "**Is that why you challenged my authority every other time that you could, Smoke?**"

"Yes."

"What did Logan promise you?"

"He promised that I would stay beta when he challenged Nathaniel."

"When was he supposed to challenge Nathaniel?"

"Tomorrow at noon."

"Did you think he would win?"

Smoke swallowed and his eyes dropped slightly before replying, "I knew that he would do something to make it easier."

"Like what?"

"He would poison food or the drink in the morning."

"Did you connect to anyone inside this office space, Smoke?"

Smoke shook his head and replied after a moment, "Couldn't. Nathaniel said we couldn't link anyone out of the room that we were in. I did attempt to, but couldn't get through to anyone."

Marius glanced at Nathaniel and saw something flicker in his eyes before he spoke, "**You were my beta, Rispin.**"

"Were? I am still your beta."

**"Not anymore. You are no longer my beta. You are banished."**

Growled Basil, and we all felt the power and the connection with Rispin snapped. Smoke dropped down to the ground and clutched his chest, banishment is not the easiest thing to manage. It was said it felt like one would be slammed down by a hammer on the chest repeatedly, and without mercy. It would feel the worst for the next few days. Rispin raised his head and swallowed hard before whispering, "I will tell everyone who will listen to me that you are not fit to rule."

"As if they would listen to anyone that is banished, Rispin. Have you thought of why no one took something that is banished seriously? There are laws in place, along with the stereotype that the one banished is nothing but a pile of dung."

Smoke growled in warning before he charged at Ghost. It seemed though, that Ghost knew he would do that, and moved precisely where he would be located. It was almost like he knew that this would happen. Smoke fell hard, and slammed into the desk, and before either of them could do anything, Shadow rolled out so much power, that I glanced at Nathaniel and saw even his flinch, and almost bare his neck in submission. Smoke dropped to the floor and pressed himself to it.

If it affected Ghost, he did not show it. He tilted his head sideways, but he did not submit completely. Showing that the training to be a royal guard was something major, I had thought about it myself but knew that I would not be able to do it. I didn't have the capable hands to do it without…. Without having issues, myself.

Shadow looked down at Smoke before growling, **"On your feet. Hands where I can see them. Ghost, accompany me to escort this filth out of the castle."**

"Yes, my Queen."

Shadow seemed to smirk at the endearment, but she did not pull her aura back in. She raised her eyes to Nathaniel before she walked out without hesitation. With Rispin in the lead, along with Ghost behind him.

******

It was a few minutes later, but we heard the actual office door open and soon shut afterward. Nathaniel sighed deeply and looked at me before speaking, **"You do realize that she will need a new beta because of this right?"**

"I know, but that would be too much work for myself and Onyx. Besides, we have discussed that actually. She wants Ghost or one of the five to become her beta."

Nathaniel frowned slightly and was about to say something, but I continued, "It is either one of the five or yourself Nathaniel."

**"Me? It cannot be me."**

I shrugged and replied, "She said it herself, Nathaniel. I did not even suggest anyone. She said the only ones that she knew would follow her without question were the five, and yourself. Along with the fact that she knew that you would not be killed now that she knows that she is of the royal bloodline."

Nathaniel sighed deeply and rubbed his face with his right hand before speaking, **"Be it as it may, I cannot be the beta of the pack. It would make it seem like favoritism."**

"Along with the fact that others would question why. It would make others think that you simply couldn't handle the duties of the alpha-ship and would go down a peg. However, my question is at this point…. Is what happens when Tobias comes back?"

**"He has stressed to me that he does not want the title. He is comfortable with being alpha."**

"Are you sure of that? After he gets back from being in the Outlanders' territory, he may have different opinions of that."

**"Marius, I am positive that Tobias is not wanting the title. He made it clear to everyone. Besides, if he wanted it then Ghost and Taryn would not have Rafeor take over. Knowing that Ravean would challenge it. I think that Tobias may even welcome her with open arms."**

"I guess that is true. So…. what now?"

**"Now, we leave this dusty office, and we head down to the cellars."**

"And do what exactly?"

**"I want to beat Logan to a BLOODY PULP!"**

Roared Basil, and I flinched backward. Onyx cowered slightly, the raw fury that Basil lashed out in the words would make anyone feel the need or want to drop down to their bellies. However, Nathaniel sighed and pinched the bridge of his nose before he whispered, **"Along with seeing Sophronia, since she did not leave him alone."**

Onyx stirred in my mind, and his eyes flashed for a moment, but he quickly disappeared. I cleared my throat before speaking, "You left your mate with someone dangerous alone?"

Nathaniel lowered his eyes slightly before replying, "**Have you tried to tell your mate no at any point, Marius? It is not an easy thing to do.**"

I shuffled my seating slightly and sighed deeply before replying, "Don't remind me of the punishments that she had dealt out. That is not the best thing to think about."

Nathaniel smirked and stood up, and a cloud of dust swirled around and he sneezed, I smirked slightly before pushing myself out of the seat, and another cloud of dust stirred up. I coughed and he chuckled but we left the office after that.

# Chapter 45

I flew back to the shifter palace and saw a huge groove where something big had been brought down. I sighed deeply, as I landed. Already knowing what had caused such a groove in the earth, the only thing big enough was a dragon, and there were only a few people on site that could. I sighed as I entered the palace, a little shocked that there were no guards posted at the doors. Although, I should not be surprised either. Everyone would be mourning the fallen. Thakur stirred in my mind, he was still angry with how that happened. Mainly because he could have taken out those ships and still be alive. However, I had a feeling that whatever was about to happen shortly was drastic enough for a seer to want death. Thakur settled after a moment, and I knew he felt the air shift around in the palace, ever since I had accepted him as my demon half, and allowed him to take control. He was happier and less vitriol in screaming in the part of the mind he was always chained to. Yes, chained. I had built up mentally a chain to make him be in a small section of my mind without lashing out at people. Just for the fun of it, at least attempted to. There were a few times that Anna had to intervene on some occasions and I would be drugged out of my mind for days until I could control him again.

I paused, sensing we were being watched by someone. I looked around and saw a black beetle, and I smiled slightly before speaking, "Don't you know that it is rude to follow someone?"

Herald shifted to his human self, and I saw how tired he looked. He looked like he could sleep for years, and still needed to sleep. He looked at me with dead eyes before speaking, "Hey."

I frowned before motioning with my head to the side, he hesitated for a moment, before shrugging and following after me.

*****

It was a few turns and twists in the palace before I came across the area that I had found much by accident at one point. I pressed on the brick, and the door opened. To say I was not surprised that it did not squeak means that someone had used this tunnel more than once, and frequently. I frowned slightly but stepped into the darkness, and Herald followed after a moment, grabbing a torch on the way in. Shutting the door and slamming his fist into the wall.

I stared at him in surprise before speaking, "What's wrong, Herald?"

He turned his attention to me before he spat, "I am a fool is what! The man I brought here, Akato, seemed so fucking good and acknowledged my worries and pain. Telling me that some things were not meant to happen, that half of the things father did, did not make ANY sense on why…."

He trailed off for a moment and tightened his fists again before hissing out, "On why he hated my guts. And now…. Now he turns around and acts like I am nothing! Like everyone else!"

I stared at my brother, and swallowed for a moment, before speaking, "Herald…. Do you remember anything from your childhood?"

He froze and turned his eyes towards me. "The little bits and pieces I remember are that people were always wearing the robes or dark blue, with their hoods up, and…. And talking in hushed voices. I remember vaguely of a pair talking about having myself and someone else be moved. However, they were referring to a different name than when I…."

He froze. His eyes sparked in anger, and that is when I knew he had made the connections. I swallowed, if no one had asked him these questions that meant no one else knew. What he had just described though was the druids. They wore robes of dark blue and always talked in hushed tones whenever they were seen. Which was rarely. You had to get an elder to allow one to speak to you, otherwise they did not simply talk to you. They acted as if they were terrified of you.

He stared at me before speaking, "Are we…. Are we even siblings?"

I swallowed and after a moment shook my head, before replying, "No. According to Killian, he went to the druids before Morphous raided them. It was a few years beforehand, which is why we were both led to think that we were."

He stared at me, the fire playing tricks in the limited light that was shown before he sighed deeply, he lowered himself against the wall, and curled his knees towards his chest, before wrapping his arms around them. He looked up at me, and I sighed before edging myself down to the cool ground and speaking, "Although, I will say this here and now. You may not be my blood brother, Herald, but you and I are brothers."

"So, what happens now? What is my next in-line thing that happens?"

I picked up a loose rock, before running my hand over the rough edges and replying, "Honestly? Don't know what is in the future. I know that there is a huge war brewing and…. One that will kill everything we know and love. One that I think the humans will start."

"The humans would be way over their heads if they started anything though."

"That may be true for themselves. However, they hired supernatural hunters."

"What? Since when does anyone do that?"

"Since now, we actually lost four of our people on the way back."

"Who?"

"Feilian, Gillith, Hector, and Conrade."

"Whoa! Three of them were our best trainers. Don't get me wrong, I liked Feilian, but he…. He kept to himself the majority of the time. But none of them deserved to die. So… what now?"

I swallowed and looked at the door before sitting against the door entrance, as if I could prevent anyone from entering the entrance if they found it. Herald squinted his eyes, before he shuffled next to me, and pressed himself against it. He looked over at me and I swallowed for a moment before speaking slowly, "Now we prepare for war. We have been tasked to find the experiment and her family. Along with bringing the werewolves, and probably the Carpathians involved. Along with the outlanders and…."

I trailed off, and he seemed to be on the same wavelength for a moment, "And any and all of the supernatural beings we can find. Then what?"

I did not even hesitate, before I locked eyes with him before speaking, "War."

He swallowed and looked down before whispering, "Where do I fit into all of this, Quinn? What is my destiny?"

I placed my right hand on his shoulder, and gently swayed him to look at me, and when he raised his eyes to meet mine, is when I replied, "By my side."

"How are you so certain?"

"Because we are brothers."

"We aren't though."

"You can make your own family up, Herald. It is not defined by blood all the time. You can make it however which way you want. Do you feel like you belong here?"

He paused as he thought about it, and after a moment he swallowed and replied, "Not sure. I feel a calling to go to the werewolves over than anything else. It does not make sense to me."

I frowned and lowered my hand from his shoulder as I thought about it. I pushed myself to my feet and offered my hand to him. He looked at it for a moment in confusion, but trusted me enough, to take my hand. I pulled him to his feet, and nodded towards the flame, before turning around and going deeper into the darkness of the tunnel.

******

The scrape of our footfalls was the only sound for several minutes, as we went this way and that way. Backtracked a few times, but only when I knew it ended in the wrong entrance. Herald never questioned once where we were going, and seemed quite content on following me around for the time being. I knew he had questions, but he also knew that if I wanted to tell him something I normally did, or if I needed to show him something similar. I would show it or say it. Either way, he would understand in the long term he would find out.

After another moment, I found the entrance I wanted. I pushed a little hard since it had not been used in who knows how long and entered the palace library. For the most part, it was empty, but I knew that there might be more than the ones that were in their human forms at the end of the hall. No one heard a thing, since we were in a part of the library that does not get much foot traffic. Especially since this was a restricted zone, where only the higher of the palace people could attend. So, me being who I was, was allowed into this section.

Herald hesitated on coming into it though, signaling that Killian never took him into this section of the library. I hated that I could spend hours and hours here, but Herald would never be allowed in, according to Killian. I, however, did not really care anymore. I gestured for him to enter, and after a moment, he hesitated before he entered the section.

We didn't say anything, besides me gesturing to place the torch in the hallway of the tunnel, so we can have it when we go back. Since no one saw us enter through the common ways, I did not want to have to make an excuse on how we entered. Herald seemed confused for a moment, but after a moment shrugged and complied. I pushed the door closed when he did. It creaked shut, but other than that, it was almost soundless.

Herald looked at me with a raised eyebrow, and I placed my index finger against my lips, and he nodded. He looked around at the old bounded books before he started to reach for one, I looked at him, before making a small cough. He froze and looked at me. I shook my head, and he swallowed and placed his hands near his pockets. He drummed his fingers against his leg, but that was better than on the tables.

We continued into the library and soon came across the section I was after. I motioned him towards a seat, and he gingerly sat down before whispering, "Quinn, how did you know about this entrance?"

"You learn throughout the years. Especially after a few times that Killian purposely left you down here somewhere. You had to find the hidden entrances and exits. Otherwise, you were as good as dead. I went, I think five days without coming back out. That is when Killian decided to go find me. Even he did not know about this entrance."

Herald looked at me in surprise before speaking, "Is this how you disappear so quickly, and show up after a while?"

"Sometimes, but the majority of the time is because of my job, Herald. Being an advisor has its perks but also more drawbacks that not everyone knows about."

"Like what? Name a few examples."

"Like always being on call, day or night. Always knowing how to run the castle, and know the rotations. The way that it needs to run without it going in the bad places…."

"Is it hard?"

"I almost wanted to tell Morphous to find a different person to be his advisor."

"That…. That's a lot of words from you. You would never say that to anyone else. Why are you just now opening up, Quinn?"

"Because I never know when it is going to be my last, Herald."

He looked at me with a pointed look before replying, "That may be true, but surely there is someone you confided in."

I looked down at the cherry wood desk before drumming my fingers on it more than twice, before replying, "The last person I confided in was not someone that could have trusted."

I was met with silence. I looked at Herald, he looked far away for a moment, and I finally paid attention to the books in front of me, and ran my finger gently over their spines, before I found what I was looking for. I pulled the big black bounded book, and gently placed it down on the table.

Herald glanced at it and read the cover, "Druid and known relationships."

He looked at me with a questioning look, before I looked around for a moment, before speaking, "Before our time, and possibly before Killian came to Morphous, for the advisor duty. I think that you were with the Druids, Herald. This book was recorded and was actually found in the elder's hut at a Druid camp. So maybe there is somewhere that you were also documented."

He stared at the black bounding before he looked at me with his mouth slightly parted, something flashed in his eyes for a moment, but I couldn't be sure since it was so fast. Although I did know that Thakur saw it since he stared a little harder at Herald. He was pretty perplexed about what Herald may be. However, I cleared my throat and turned the pages after a moment. Going to the table of contents, and gently ran my finger across the entries. This was written in a different language, but I was taught by Killian in these different languages since I was to become the advisor. However, it soon became apparent that Herald could not. He looked at me with a weird look before asking, "You can read this?"

I glanced at him and replied, "You can't read it, can you?"

He shook his head and I sighed slightly before replying, "Alright, it's fine. I should have known that Killian is a lousy father."

I chuckled darkly at that comment that I had made. Herald smirked but did not laugh. We both knew that Herald and I were different. We always knew that, but Killian went too far making it seem like Herald was nothing. Meant nothing. Now Herald was struggling with a sense of purpose, and therefore it was solely because of the issue of birthright. I sometimes envied him, since Killian was never hard on him, but now understood why. He was never going to do what was expected as a father figure, and therefore would rather pick favorites. I sighed deeply and drew myself out of my endless what-ifs, and knew that the past I couldn't do anything about. It was the future that I could solely focus on without worry. Well, to be fair, I had to worry about the future, but that is one thing at a time.

Herald cleared his throat, and I looked at him, and he raised his eyebrow at me. I sighed deeply and shook my head to clear my never-ending thoughts. I looked at him with a small smile before speaking, "Sorry, did you say something?"

He smirked a little before replying, "What does it say?"

I had pulled to a page, where it has documented the werewolves since that is where the history is somewhat around the Druids. The shifters were at one point peaceful with them until the prophecies came into play. Then all hell broke loose. I looked down at the elder's handwriting and slowly began to read, "Two young children we brought to our encampment, one boy and one girl. The boy showed gifts, the girl nothing. It was almost as if she didn't belong with the wolves. We did further testing and found that the boy had a wolf. A powerful wolf, which our seer, said that one day he will do great things. He came to us with the name Aurelin, and the girl, Tyrell."

Herald took a deep breath in and I saw something flash in his eyes again and I squinted at him for a moment. But after a moment, nothing happened and I thought I could be wrong, so I went back to reading, "However, after only a few months of having these children, a stranger came towards us. Our seer said that a stranger would come, from a far distant land, wanting someone. When he showed up, we were ready to protect everyone from him. However, Tyrell ran in front of our front, and the stranger promptly slaughtered her where she stood."

I swallowed hard, before continuing, "Seeing his sister dead before him, Aurelin, ran out towards the stranger, and let his other spirit that resides inside him out. The stranger survived, but half of my tribe was dead. The stranger then told me, that he would take the child with him, to spare the rest of the tribe. We obliged. Our seer was wounded, but still aware enough to speak in the prophecy surrounding the child, *he will be great. His wolf will prosper in all that makes him believe. He becomes a great ruler if raised correctly.*"

I paused and stared down at the script. I turned the page, looking for more, but nothing else was written. It was almost as if the elder had to leave in a hurry before he was able to complete it. I looked at Herald and swallowed before speaking, "Wolf."

Herald swallowed before speaking, "Now it all makes sense. Why else does my wolf seem much happier in wolf form than a bird? I am a werewolf. But it doesn't make sense, if I am a werewolf, then who were my parents? Why did they drop me off at a Druid camp?"

I looked down at the book, it was only asking further questions, not answering any. I swallowed before looking at him and replied, "The only one who would possibly know those answers would be Nathaniel. Maybe he knows who your father is."

Herald looked down before shaking his head slowly and whispering, "No, there has to be more to this. There has to be more."

He looked at the pages, and turned his head sideways before speaking, "Wait, Quinn…. Do you see that?"

I looked at him, and for a moment didn't respond, and looked at his eyes. They were different, showing that he indeed was not alone. I swallowed hard before looking at what he was looking at and soon Thakur surfaced enough in my eyes to see the other side of the pen. There were hidden messages within the lines. I swallowed and spoke with my normal voice, but Thakur was still in my eyes, "It appeared the elder Druid knew that eventually someone would erase the Druids from the face of the earth, and wrote in a coded way, only one way that someone else would understand if they had something else in their being alongside themselves."

Herald looked at me with a gulp before speaking, "Your eyes."

I swallowed, a lot has happened since he and I were together last. I sighed and replied, "I have a demon, Herald. I have another being inside my head alongside me. It is scary and intense at the same time."

"Oh. What is its name?"

"His name is Thakur."

"Cool name. I haven't heard the one that resides in me, but I know I have a wolf alongside me. I only know since the Carpathians and the werewolves let me go without injury."

He looked lost in thought for a moment, before speaking, "Do you think that is why they let me go? Because my wolf surfaced and made them listen to him?"

"That is a possibility. Who knows how powerful he is."

Herald smirked before looking at me with a look, before speaking, "So…. if the writing about the boy and the girl is true, does that mean that my true name is Aurelin?"

"I would think it does mean that."

"Hmmm…. I always felt like something was wrong with my current name. Like it wasn't fitting me. Would you think it would make people…? People judge me more if I changed my current name to that?"

"I doubt it, Aurelin, people judge everyone for random crap and it doesn't seem to prevent anyone from being who they are. I think you are safe for most of that. Sure, there will be those that challenge it, but mostly I think people will accept who you are."

"Thank you, Quinn."

"You're welcome, brother."

He smirked but motioned down at the writing before speaking, "Can you read it?"

I glanced down at the writing and swallowed for a moment before speaking, "We had moved camp since our home was compromised. I moved my survivors closer to the werewolf population, where we became friends with the werewolf king and the shifter king. Or soon-to-bes. They were still princes."

I paused, I was slightly confused. Nathaniel and Morphous both however acted as if they were friends way back in the day. I swallowed slightly before reading further, "However, our seer saw something in the shifter prince, that one day he would rain hell on our people. I was tasked with informing the werewolf prince that the shifter prince would one day attack without warning, and bring nothing but misery and pain. At the time, he did not listen, and now weeps for not heeding our warning."

I froze, so it was true, that it was Morphous's fault for the war and the horrible destruction of the druids. Thakur growled low in my connection, but he made sure it was not loud enough for Aurelin to hear.

Aurelin scowled and spoke up after a moment, "Is that all?"

I glanced down at the words and swallowed before something caught my eye. In a very small print, there were coordinates. I frowned before speaking, "There are coordinates."

"What? Why would there be any?"

"Perhaps we are wrong…. That there are still Druids left."

"They had survived for twelve years without anyone knowing?"

"Can't know for sure, until one of us checks it out."

He looked at me with shocked-filled eyes for a moment, before looking down at the words, and speaking, "Are you sure?"

I glanced down at the writing and nodded after a moment. I pulled out a piece of parchment, that I normally carry, so I could write something down when I needed it. Something that I picked up from being an advisor for a king, you never know when something arises that you need to write down. I wrote down the coordinates, 39* 07'03.9" N 106* 26'43.2" W. I handed him the coordinates, and he frowned before speaking, "I've been here before. These are the same coordinates that…. That I had remembered before…."

He trailed off.

******

I would have pushed him for a solid answer, but the door to the restricted section opened, and two sets of footfalls sounded. We exchanged looks, he was not allowed inside, but I was. I swallowed and gestured to him to go around the corner, but he simply shifted to his go-to if he wanted to be hidden from sight, and flew onto me being as a beetle. If I hadn't watched him land, no one would be any wiser. I stuffed the book back onto the shelf and stuck the piece of parchment into my pocket. No way in hell was it getting away from me. I straightened myself out and pulled another book down, it was the history of the Shifters. I turned to a random page and pretended to read it.

I heard the two voices, one I recognized as Takato and the other as Valentin, both of whom were not authorized to come into the restricted section. I frowned, but tuned into what they were saying, "Are you sure that they were banished?"

"Positive. Otherwise, they would have come back and told us."

I frowned and strained a little harder, but they were silent. I turned another page in the book and continued to pretend I was reading. A low growl behind me sounded, and I lifted my head to find Takato standing behind me. I hmph-ed a little before closing the book up and speaking, "Can I assist you with something? Last time I checked, you two did not have clearance to be inside this section."

Takato frowned before growling, "How long have you been inside?"

"Long enough."

"Give me a freaking time frame! How long?"

"Long enough for me to hear you come inside."

He went silent and glanced over at Valentin, before growling, "You heard nothing."

"I heard what I needed."

"What is that supposed to mean?"

"It means that you two are traitors and that something along the lines of someone being banished. So, what were you going to talk about until you found me?"

Takato once again looked at Valentin, before Valentin spoke, his voice rumbled slightly in his throat, "You won't say a word."

He had a blade against my throat, and I swallowed hard, the edge of the blade against my skin, and I caused a few beads of blood to spill. The weapon was recently sharpened to a point. I swallowed for a moment before speaking, "You kill me, there will be a horrible aftermath."

"Then say that you heard nothing."

"I would be lying if I said nothing."

"Your life is in the balance here. You won't get away from my blade."

"This is treason."

"Shut it."

He pressed his blade a little harder, but they both seemed to forget who and what I was. I connected to Morphous within a heartbeat, and…. Well…. I felt him coming, but they were either too dumb to realize this or too naive.

"Whatever you were talking about it sounded as if you were talking about those who were told to leave. Were you talking about Sky and Krool?"

"No."

"Then who?"

"None of your concern. Your life is in the balance here. You seem to think you have the upper hand."

**"Because he does."**

Morphous's voice sounded behind the bookshelf that was connecting to the one before us. He stepped around it, and Takato and Valentin shrunk down before Takato whispered, "M-m-my l-lo-lord!"

He cleared his throat before trying again, "My lord, how did you know?"

Morphous raised his eyebrow before speaking, "**Have you forgotten who is my advisor?**"

That was when Takato and Valentin, seem to connect the dots, and they both paled significantly. Valentin removed his blade from my throat before speaking softly, "My lord…"

Morphous held up his hand and stared at them with a hard look before speaking, "**The only ones that are allowed inside this section of the library are the ones with rank. If I was not mistaken, neither of you have it. So, what is your business inside my restricted section?**"

They glanced at each other and finally, Takato lowered his eyes to the floor before whispering, "We thought no one would be in here. It would have been an easy way to talk in private without interruptions."

**"Talk about what?"**

He seemed to struggle for a moment, but finally, Valentin replied with a heavy sigh, "Talk about the werewolves that were recently banished."

**"The werewolves? And why do they have anything to do with us?"**

"Because a few of the ones that were banished had become our friends across the channel. Sais was…. Was heavily set on getting someone named Logan in leadership, and I…. Being myself, gave him something that no one should."

**"What did you give him?"**

Valentin swallowed hard before whispering, "My blood."

**"Why?"**

"Because he needed it for something. I don't know the entire jest of it, but he said it would help him with something he was working on back home."

**"You willingly gave a werewolf your blood?"**

"Yes, my lord."

I glanced at Morphous and saw the look of shock written across his face. I frowned, it lined up with what had happened, Sais was one of the few that had been on the ship heading back across the channel. Meaning, they had known beforehand that shifter blood was powerful beforehand. I squint my eyes for a moment, before speaking, "What was given in return?"

Valentin swallowed hard and his eyes flickered to Takato and then glanced at Morphous for a moment before he shrunk down. He gulped hard but did not speak. Takato swallowed and refused to look directly at me or Morphous before whispering, "Money."

**"How much?"**

"Enough that we wouldn't have to worry about our futures."

I sighed deeply, this was not the first time that someone had bought it. I glanced at Morphous and knew that if Abacore was able to, he would have surfaced. However, knowing the sedative that was given to him, most likely a day before, would still make him dormant. Morphous however rolled out his aura, and he growled, **"What?"**

Normally, I would have shrunk down, but now that I had embraced Thakur, I no longer bowed down to the kings. I, however, felt Aurelin tremble on my coat, but I connected to him, *"Listen to my heartbeat. Follow it."*

It was a few moments, but he stopped trembling and soon became a black spot. However, I noticed that Morphous glanced down at my coat, and must have seen the movement. My eyes flickered to his and his eyes bore into mine for a moment before he turned his attention back to Takato and Valentin before growling, **"Give me a good reason for not throwing you into the dungeon."**

They blanched for a moment before Valentin replied, "Because you are losing people as you speak."

**"What does that supposed to mean?"**

"Your rule as king is coming to an end. Sais said so himself, and I cannot agree more. You are selfish and arrogant. Someone who I would not see as a ruler."

"You are talking treason."

"It is not us alone that thinks that though. His reign as ruler is coming to an end."

I glanced at Valentin and then at Takato and knew that they highly believed that before Morphous lost his temper. Morphous slammed his hand straight down onto the desk, breaking a corner off, and his eyes flashed orange before he growled out, **"HOW. DARE. YOU!"**

He would have grabbed Takato and Valentin, but I held up my hand, stopping him.

Thakur surfaced in my eyes, and he paused. I looked at Valentin and Takato with a hard look, and they both cowered before me. Thakur turned his attention back to Morphous before speaking, "Enough."

**"Easy for you to say! You are not the one being challenged!"**

"Morphous, I will only say it once more. Enough. Takato, Valentin, explain to me something. If Sais is so smart, then who did he say would lead the shifters?"

Morphous stared daggers at me for a moment, but his eyes flickered to Valentin and Takato who swallowed hard before Takato replied softly, "L-Lo-Logan."

"The same wolf that had committed countless crimes, the one that had tried to kill the current king more than once? The one that had proven more than thrice the amount that he was no king material, Logan?"

They were silent. I looked at them with a raised eyebrow, and they shuffled their feet before Takato replied, "I've never met him. However, other people that were around us seemed scornful that Sais would think he would be a good ruler."

"So, to get this correct, and correct me if I am wrong. You would want to overthrow the shifter crown, and give access to a werewolf, that even his people seem to scorn him?"

"Now, that you put it that way…."

Takato trailed off and looked at Morphous before speaking, "I-I-I'm sorry, my lord."

I glanced at Valentin who was silent and seemed to be deep in thought. I raised my eyebrow again before clearing my throat, and he looked up at me and then his eyes flickered to Morphous before he whispered, "I apologize, Morphous."

I turned slightly to look at Morphous before speaking, "With that being said though, they are up to your discretion on what to do with."

"What? Why?"

"Because I am not a ruler."

"But you are more powerful than he is!"

"That is debatable. Morphous has some qualities that I lack. Therefore, he is superior to me. I would not be one to be stuck in one spot."

"Why?"

"Because it is not my destiny to be stuck in a leadership role."

"How are you so sure about your destiny?"

"Because I trust in the prophecies surrounding myself. The good, the bad, and the ones in between."

"What about your main host? What about him?"

"Did you forget his name already?"

"Would I be in trouble if I said yes?"

I frowned and glanced at Morphous before turning my attention to them before I saw something in their eyes. A flash of wolf light. I growled and grabbed Valentin by the throat and raised him into the air before I growled, "WHO. ARE. YOU?"

"Valentin?"

"The truth."

I squeezed my hand tighter around his throat and he clawed at my hand for a moment, and it seemed like he would just continue to struggle in his human form for a moment, but after a little bit of time passed. Did his eyes flash silver and a low rumble escaped? His fingers elongated and tufts of hair came in on his open arms. Takato backed away, at least attempted to. Someone else had followed Morphous inside and stopped him with a look.

I could not see who it was, but it was clear that whoever it was made anyone in there nervous. It was someone who was not here before. However, I felt Aurelin's displeasure in our connection, meaning he knew who it was. I turned my attention back to the wolf in front of me before growling, "ANSWER!"

Valentin struggled against my hands, but I tightened harder and finally, he stopped fighting and gasped out, "My name is Valentin!"

I dropped him and stared at him as he gasped at the air before he looked up at me. I glanced at Takato before growling, "And you?"

"I was not lying about my name, Takato. Neither of us were."

"How long have you infiltrated the shifter palace for?"

"We never left."

"Then how did you not know who I am?"

They lowered their eyes and their shoulder slumped for a moment before Valentin wheezed out, "Fine, we were positioned here by Logan. He wanted to know intel."

"How much intel did you give your commander?"

I looked at the stranger and raised my eyebrow. He stared hard at me, for a split second before his eyes flickered to Valentin. Valentin swallowed after a moment before replying, "I don't answer to the likes of you."

**"Too bad. Answer, or I kill you where you are."**

Anyone who knew Morphous knew better than to ignore the warning he had given. However, the wolf smirked and replied, "I am connected to my pack still Morphous. Therefore, killing me is an act of war."

"Yet you seem quite happy to be on shifter territory without your king's consent."

"If you are referring to Nathaniel as my king, then you are wrong. My loyalties lie with Logan, and Logan alone."

Morphous exchanged glances with me and then glanced at the stranger before Morphous replied, "**Akato, you know where the dungeons are correct?**"

"Correct."

**"Take them both down there."**

"You can't imprison us!"

**"You are on my terrain. You are on my territory. You challenged Nathaniel's leadership. Therefore, you are mine."**

"I will not go down willingly!"

"Ooh? And you seem like you are itching for a fight there little one. Do you wish to feel my fangs before you head down, or after?"

"Neither."

"You don't get a choice in that aspect."

"That is where you are wrong."

We locked eye contact with each other, not watching them for a split second before they tried to do something incredibly stupid. They tried to kill Morphous, along with the guy named Akato. Which had the outcomes that you would expect. They both lay on the ground, their hearts in the grasp of Akato and Aurelin, who had shifted and killed Valentin before he got to Morphous.

*****

Morphous raised his eyebrows at me before speaking, "**Herald?**"

"I found out that my name is not Herald. My name is Aurelin."

"Ummm. what?"

Aurelin glowered at Akato and rolled his eyes and did not answer him. Thakur had released control when the threat was disposed of and approached Aurelin's shoulder and I gently laid a hand on him before looking at the man before me. He was built I can say that. I sighed for a moment, before speaking, "I don't believe I had the pleasure of meeting you?"

"My name is Akato. Son of Dracula."

"Welcome, my name is Quinn."

"Quinn what?"

"Benik."

The squint in his eyes was the only evidence that he knew something surrounding my last name. However, by the way that Aurelin was behaving, that did not mean anything special. I sighed before looking at Morphous and speaking, "Thank you for coming down here on short notice."

**"I didn't realize that you were back."**

"My apologies. I had something else that had taken my immediate attention."

"Such as?"

"That is none of your business, Carpathian."

Thakur had spoken, and I frowned and raised my eyebrows at him before speaking, "There is normally a reason why he surfaces. Why is he suddenly wanting to make you submit to him?"

Akato shrugged and replied, "Unknown."

I scoffed and knew that he knew something, but was not going to tell me a thing. I shrugged after a moment, and turned my attention to Morphous before speaking, "Come along, Aurelin."

**"Quinn."**

"Yes, my lord?"

**"Why are you being so secretive?"**

"I cannot answer that."

**"Quinn."**

His eyes flashed for a moment, but I went to respond, but Thakur flashed in my eyes, and I fell silent. Something about this was not right. I glanced at Akato, and glanced at Aurelin before gesturing to him towards the main entrance and replying, "Cannot tell you."

"Why not?"

"None of your concern, Carpathian!"

My eyes flickered to Morphous for a moment and connected to him, "*Apparently, I cannot tell you in front of the Carpathian.*"

Morphous frowned but after a moment shrugged and looked down at the werewolves before him before speaking, "**Quinn?**"

"Yes, my lord?"

"**Send a cleaning crew down here.**"

"Of course, my lord."

"Wait."

Aurelin and I paused in the doorway and glanced at each other. Akato approached and eyed me with a knowing look before looking at Aurelin and speaking, "Why did you change your name from Herald to Aurelin?"

"Freedom of speech."

"Why are you lying to me, Herald?"

"My name is not Herald anymore Akato. I choose Aurelin as my name."

"I do not see you as an Aurelin, Herald. Pick another name that suits you better."

"It is not in your right to challenge him on his name."

I butt in then, and Akato turned his attention to me with a sharp look. His eyes flashed for a moment, but Morphous cleared his throat from behind him. Akato glanced back at him before whispering, "I will find you again, Quinn. And you and me will have a nice long chat."

Thakur glimmered in my eyes and fought for control for a moment before I grounded out, "I need to leave."

I turned to go, but Akato seemed to think that he could control me and grabbed me with his hand across my shoulder. Earning a growl from Morphous, whom Akato did not seem affected by either. Aurelin looked between us for a moment, before his eyes flashed again and a new voice boomed out, "**Release him.**"

Akato instantly withdrew his hand and looked at Herald and before he could say a word, the voice spoke, "**My name is Firefoot. Akato, you are not allowed to touch Quinn, or any other shifter for that matter.**"

"You are not my master."

"**Good, then you know your place. I do not want to be your so-called master anyhow. You will, however, obey.**"

"I said…"

**"Shut it."**

Akato looked like he wanted to challenge him, but finally lowered his eyes from Firefoot's before he turned his attention to me for a moment. He looked at Morphous and did not speak. He simply turned hard on his heel and strode across the library, and it took me a moment to follow after him, leaving Akato and Morphous behind with the bodies.

# Chapter 46

I hurried after Firefoot, who was surprisingly faster than he let on. Soon after a few sharp turns, we came across another panel that would let us disappear into the walls, and he pushed the entrance brick without any hesitation and entered. I followed after him after a moment and soon disappeared into darkness.

I followed him into the tunnel for a bit and soon came to a quiet area before he stopped and turned hard and made me trip over my feet as he forced himself the opposite way again. It took me a moment, but it seemed as if he was making sure to make our scent everywhere – as if he had a feeling someone else would come down here. I wasn't even sure if Morphous knew these tunnels. However, I did not question him. There had to be something I did not know.

Soon, he stopped and sat down against the wall before speaking, **"My apologies. I had to make sure that no one would know where we stopped to talk."**

"Why so secretive?"

**"Because there is something that I know about Akato and his father."**

"Which is?"

**"They do not mean anything to the supernatural world. They want to ensure that we as their food banks do not die, therefore Akato was tasked to help Aurelin."**

"Did you know that Aurelin was Herald's true name?"

**"I knew, but I had to wait for him to find his name alone."**

"I guess that is a fair thing to do. Now my question is, what can I do for you?"

**"Let your demon out, and we will have a chat."**

"But I won't remember anything that is said between the two of you."

**"Unfortunately, the information that I have to say, is not quite ready for anyone else to know. Even their hosts are not allowed to know it."**

"What is so important that I cannot find out?"

**"Do you not trust me?"**

"I am wary of you. That is different than not trusting you."

**"I guess that is a fair judgment call. However, I cannot tell you what is waiting for you in the future. So please, let your demon out so we can have a discussion."**

"Tell me one thing, please. Will we make it out of this alive?"

**"I cannot tell you that."**

I sighed deeply and sat down across from him and allowed Thakur to surface. He blocked me completely out since that is what Firefoot had instructed him to do.

****

Thakur surfaced completely and my whole demeanor changed in a heartbeat, Firefoot smiled for a moment before speaking, **"Hello."**

"You got me. Now what is so dire that you couldn't wait to tell me?"

**"I am pretty sure that you know some things that even you don't share with just anyone Thakur."**

"Fair, now what is it that you wanted to talk about?"

**"We need to cross ourselves to our world for a moment."**

"My homeland? Are you sure you want to know that?"

**"Humor me."**

"Fine. According to my father, Falcor, it is a massive grassy land now that the humans think belongs to them. He killed several before he was talked out of it by werewolves that he had brought. Along with talking Severi out of killing his subjects for no good reason."

**"What about the wolves in the outlands?"**

"The outlanders? They haven't approached the camp as of what I know. Although Killian was banished from the shifter palace and territory by Morphous and Abacore so I do not know anything further than what you now know."

**"What werewolves do your father and uncle have now?"**

"Trevoric, Xavier, Averic, Savador, Topaz, Fantar, Arancum and Wilson. Unsure of their last names."

**"I have a feeling that all of them were, at one point, thought loss, otherwise the werewolf population would have fought tooth and nail for them."**

"Morphous had them imprisoned downstairs, doubtful that anyone knew they were still alive."

**"Ah. Well, that explains it."**

We sat in silence for a moment before I asked, "Alright, spill. I heard what you had told Quinn. So, what is so dire that you cannot tell him directly and need to speak to me?"

**"And you promise that he is not able to hear what is about to be discussed?"**

"Firefoot, have I been untrustworthy hence far?"

**"Fair enough."**

He sighed deeply before continuing, **"You know the prophecy surrounding yourself, right?"**

"Of course, I do."

**"Humor me then."**

"I will become someone that has no mate, no love. To get to what I wholeheartedly desire. I will however gain the reputation of being above and beyond whatever it seems fit to be."

**"That is, or is there more?"**

"There's many different forms of my prophecy, Firefoot. Mine isn't set in stone."

**"Ah, I see."**

"Yours, however, seems to be in werewolf, Carpathian, and surprisingly, not in the shifter population."

**"Cause I was never supposed to be in the shifter population. I was supposed to be with the werewolves."**

"Do you know your father and mother?"

**"I do."**

"And?"

**"By the sounds of it, my mother is out of the picture, and my father is not a good one."**

"How are you so sure of that?"

**"Because my father is named Logan Vigolf. And if I heard correctly, then that means that he is not alpha and to be quite blunt, a fucking tool."**

"Oof. I guess I have it slightly better than you on that front then."

**"Shut it. Now, back to business. What do you know of my prophecy?"**

"Personally? Not much about yours. I have solely grown up around mine and Falcor's. I was not allowed to question Killian's methods or interact with Aurelin much during childhood if you so recall."

"Oh, I recall. Although I did not surface until he was at the age of ten. I came early compared to the other werewolves in the werewolf territory. However, back to track. What do you know of mine?"

"I just told you, I have not the slightest ideas."

"Really? Are you just saying that or are you trying to pull my leg?"

I sighed deeply before replying, "Fine…. The little bit that I have read in the werewolf books would be that one day a wolf, with your markings, would come in and become the werewolf king. However, it seems that Rafeor is made to become the ruler and not yourself."

"That is true, Rafeor and Shadow are the first ones who will become the rulers of the current. However, my prophecy is not for our times. I was not really supposed to be here until another few centuries."

"What? Then why are you here?"

"I cannot change what is happening as much as I want to. The moon goddess had placed me onto the earth earlier than planned and knew that one day I would understand why. I have not figured out why. However, it was believed that I was the one to unite everyone."

"Wait, you don't know what you are doing?"

"Far from it. All I know is that the Carpathians will one day become to be named vampires and that the shifters will no longer be purebloods. Therefore, the only ones to survive this are the experiment and her family line, along with anyone else that is in her tree line. Unsure about the werewolves, but I have a feeling that some of them will continue."

"Hmmm… interesting. And why the secrecy on this exactly?"

"Because I am unsure of what is supposed to be shared and not."

"And you are sharing it with me because?"

"Because I have no idea what I am going to become. There is another prophecy surrounding me that even the werewolves do not know about. However, the Druids know it. At one point, it was said that my sister would be the key to preventing it from happening. However, since Killian killed Tyrell, then that prophecy may end up happening."

"Killian killed your sister?"

"Did you not listen to what Quinn was reading?"

"I was, but at the same time I was more of paying attention to the things that he did not read aloud to you."

"What did he not say?"

"What the seer said. She had more to say, but he completely skipped the part, and acted as if he couldn't read anymore."

**"What did it say?"**

*"He will be great. His wolf will prosper in all that makes him believe. He becomes a great ruler if raised correctly. If raised wrong, he will only bring destruction and death upon everything and everyone. Drowning the world in blood and sorrow."*

**"Oh."**

"Yeah. Quinn did not want Aurelin to know that. However, I doubt that it will happen. Considering that you are who you are."

**"How are you so sure of yourself Thakur that something won't come to be in the near future to bring the ugly side out of me, as you say?"**

"Because unlike everyone else, I believe in you. I think that you will become something more. Your destiny and or prophecy does not define who you are. They are more like guidelines anyhow. My keeps changing with the choices I imply with Quinn's actions."

**"I guess that is true."**

We fell into a comfortable silence, and soon a chill ran up my spine.

******

I sat rigid for a moment before I heard a voice further down the tunnels, "WHERE ARE YOU?"

I growled slightly, but Firefoot slapped his hand across my face before shaking his head. I fell silent, and the voice got a little closer, "Come out, come out, wherever you are! I will find you!"

I looked at Firefoot and saw him shake his head before shifting, and I shifted after a moment into a beetle and seemed to be in time too. Since Akato rounded the corner and looked in the hallway we were in before hissing, "I will find you one way or another. Come out and play with me."

We don't respond. I stared into Akato, and saw him look around the darkness but we did not budge from where we were. It was almost as if he was waiting for a heartbeat. However, since we were beetles, he couldn't detect us. It was a few minutes before he turned hard before calling out, "HERALD! COME OUT AND PLAY WITH ME!"

Then he zoomed out and down the hall. I looked over at Aurelin, before I noticed that he had moved and was next to me before speaking in the connection, *"We need to leave, and head to the coordinates. We need to leave the shifter palace."*

*"What about the rest?"*

*"So far Morphous has kept a close eye on Akato since he is an outsider."*

*"But not now though."*

*"He cannot keep a close eye all the damn time on him."*

*"Fair."*

We fell silent as we watched as Akato came back and he looked into the hallway once again before growling, "Come out of your hiding spot! I know you are down here, Herald!"

I swallowed for a split second but did not move. Akato raked his eyes across the bricks and finally, he disappeared once again, but I heard that he was waiting outside of the entrance of the hallway. He did not go far.

*****

I allowed Quinn a little access, and he pointed out the hidden exit, that only a shifter would be able to get out of in a beetle form, and we went that way. We got out into a room, and soon we exited the room, entered the main areas, and disappeared after a moment. It was clear that Firefoot and Aurelin did not know that exit, since they looked at me with curious eyes. I placed a hand on my mouth and shook it side to side. They knew better than to speak though.

We exited the hallways, and carefully left the palace. We ran into two guards, and I informed them to assist Morphous with the bodies in the restricted library. And they hurried to obey. It took a moment, but soon I found Anna's quarters and knew that I would find no one inside, but I quickly took her map down from the wall and scanned the coordinated map, finding the exact spot before turning around and hurrying out. I connect to Morphous, *"I apologize, Morphous, but I need to leave."*

*"Don't blame you. I would. Akato is not someone to mess with."*

*"Truer words never spoken."*

*"Get back safe, Thakur. I need my advisor."*

*"Will try."*

I closed the connection, and Aurelin and I ran out of the building and shifted to birds before flying with the nightly flock that flew past the palace at this hour.

# Chapter 47

We flew with the flock until they veered off to go to their roosters for the evening. We continued, I knew the mountain that the note said and knew that if we hurry, we could reach it within a day. However, it became clear that Firefoot was not accustomed to flying in a bird form, since he was struggling several times to get it in the correct flap sequence. I sighed deeply before heading into the tree line below us. He followed after a moment, and I shifted to a hawk before speaking in the connection, "*Shift into a….*"

I fell silent as I saw something coming at us fast, and realized too late what it was. We got entangled in the net, and before either of us could shift into something else, to get away. We were brought down to the forest floor, where the guy who was waiting down below looked at us in great glee. I struggled in his net and screeched at him, but he grimaced but did not let go of the rope, ensuring that normal birds did not escape.

Firefoot and I exchanged glances, and we both knew that we would have to shift to make him release us, however, by the smell alone, he was not human. At least, not like any I have smelt. I connected to Firefoot, "*We have a few options….*"

**"No."**

*"What do you mean, no?"*

**"Our paths were met to be crossed clearly, Thakur. Let's see where he takes us."**

*"We could easily be food if he doesn't know what we are."*

**"Have a little trust, will you?"**

*"Fine, but if we die because we don't show him what we are now, it's your fault."*

**"Fair enough."**

I scowled in the connection but turned my attention to the boy before us currently. He had approached closer and then I saw a symbol on his arm. It was a circle with a tree in the center, with the markings of wind, fire, earth, and air. I looked at Firefoot, who looked a little smug since he probably knew that this young lad was a druid.

He crouched down and looked at us with unblinking eyes before he sighed deeply before releasing the net. We ruffled our feathers and looked up at him. He looked around for a split second before standing to his feet, coiling the net and rope together, and walking off.

*****

I looked at Firefoot and knew he had questions. Why capture us, and only release us afterward? I knew it caught him equally off guard. He shrugged after a moment, and we followed after him. Although, we stayed in our bird forms, as we did. I limped a little, but not that much.

The Druid boy stopped and turned around, clearly shocked to still see us. However. he was watching me as I limped along. He swallowed but after a moment he crouched down again, before gesturing towards me to come to him. I paused, looked into his green eyes, and swallowed before limping towards him. He picked me up, looked down at my foot, and I knew that he would see nothing since it was an old injury that usually only shows when I am in a bird form. A time when Killian thought the best time to teach me to shift into a bird would be tossing me out of the window and hoping that I would shift before I hit anything on the way down. However, he did it when I wasn't entirely surfaced, and Quinn was still learning. So, one thing led to another and I had a fractured leg. Something that could not be fixed without taking the leg off entirely. Since Anna cleared Quinn, that meant it was okay to be as it was. However, Killian was roasted and reamed for doing it the way he did it.

The Druid boy drew me out of my thoughts when he spoke, "Oh shush… little one. I don't see a new injury on your foot. However, I see a small fracture that must have been here for a few years. Probably when you were learning to fly."

I looked sharply at Firefoot and noticed that he was staring at the boy with a look. I saw something swimming in his expression but did not say a word in the connection. I wondered what he saw in this young boy.

The boy rocked back on his heels before running a hand down his face and whispering, "I shouldn't bring you back to camp, yet something is drawing me to do so. I can't explain it entirely, but I think you are destined to come along with me back."

I looked at Firefoot, who shook his head slightly. I knew that I wouldn't say a word, and neither would he. The boy stood up and swallowed, but I took a limp forward and he seemed to make up his mind and mumbled, "Another verbal lashing here I come."

He picked me up, and got me to sit on his shoulder before he held out his left hand to Firefoot, who hopped on instantly. He turned to look around for a moment, before walking towards the mountain.

*****

It was a little past the high moon when we reached the camp. It was hidden, and would not be able to be seen from the air. It seemed that it had a canopy hiding it from sight. Only someone within it knew where to find it. So, finding the druid boy in the woods was a blessing.

As soon as he walked further into the camp though, did we understand something. The rest of the druids were darker in color and stared at him as he passed them, showing that he was different in stark comparison. Hushed whispers were around and I could not pick up what was said, but Firefoot seemed rather skittish all of a sudden. I looked at him sharply before he connected to me, *"Whatever happens. Do not shift unless we absolutely have to."*

*"What do you know that you aren't telling me?"*

*"Thakur, this is not the same druid camp that I came from. This is a different one."*

*"Meaning what?"*

*"Meaning we cannot trust anyone here."*

*"Firefoot, we came here to find the druids. And here they are. Are we for sure not going to show ourselves?"*

*"Thakur, these are when I was with the druids I remember. We often talked down upon since of their practices."*

*"What sort of practices?"*

*"The sacrifices that they give their goddess, Thakur."*

*"Are you saying that if we shift, then we will be sacrificed to their god?"*

*"Yeah."*

*"This is your idea to bring us to this druid camp, and now you want to back away?"*

*"I didn't say that..."*

*"You are kind of implying it though."*

*"I cannot do anything about it all the same Thakur. I did not know that they were the druids that were here. Neither did you."*

*"As far as anyone else knew, the druids were wiped out."*

*"Hush."*

I would have said more, but looked around and found ourselves inside a huge tent. There was a man there, in the shadows. He sighed deeply before running his hand across his face and speaking, **"Oswald, what is the meaning of this?"**

*"Father, they were injured in the woods."*

**"You know the customs of this group. Anything that is brought into the camp, has to pass the elders."**

"Can't it for once not do that?"

**"You know as well as I do son, that is not possible. Their people have already seen you enter camp with them."**

"But father!"

**"No, Oswald. They were better to be left in the forest than be brought here."**

"But father, I had a dream last night."

His father froze, turned his head sharply, and looked at his son. He stood up and approached and I heard Firefoot take a sharp intake before murmuring in the connection, *"Fergus."*

*"What?"*

*"Thakur, this is Fergus, he was the elder that I remember."*

*"You sure?"*

*"I do not forget a voice as his."*

I let it go at that. I looked at Fergus for a moment before leaping off Oswald's shoulder and landing on a piece of wood that was about shoulder height. I looked into Fergus who was watching me intently, before his eyes flickered to Firefoot. He looked at Oswald before speaking, **"You didn't."**

"I didn't what, father?"

**"You brought outsiders."**

"Father, these are birds though…"

Fergus looked at me for a solid moment before speaking, **"Shift."**

I glanced at Firefoot, and saw him shrug slightly before shifting. I hopped down onto the ground and shifted. We both crouched there for a moment.

I lifted my head after a moment, and spoke, "My name is…."

**"Shush."**

I would have wanted to finish what I was saying when I heard footsteps coming towards their tent. I looked at Firefoot for a moment, before we both shifted to a beetle, disappearing into the dirt floors. If Fergus had not watched us shift, he would not be any wiser on where we were.

Oswald, however, had shock written across his face and his father hissed, "**Wipe your shock off your face, Oswald!**"

It took a moment, but his face became as if it was a normal occurrence.

****

The tent flap opened and three of the dark-skinned druids came inside. Fergus dipped his head to the one in the lead before speaking, "**Dubthach.**"

"**Fergus, I had reports that your son brought something into camp without allowing myself and the rest of the elders to examine them. Show me.**"

"**There is nothing here as you can see Dubthach. My son arrived shortly before yourself.**"

"**Are you calling my people liars, Fergus? After everything we have done for you?**"

"**No, Dubthach.**"

"**Then tell me the truth, did your son bring something into the camp without showing it to the elders and myself?**"

Fergus swallowed hard before speaking, "**I apologize, Dubthach, however, whatever he brought within the camp, has fled. They never arrived inside my tent.**"

"**Are you lying?**"

"**No, Dubthach.**"

Dubthach stared at Fergus before biting out, "**This is not the first time that your boy has tried to bring something to you, without our knowledge. Perhaps, it is time that you are shown what we do at this camp with any outsiders.**"

Fergus stared hard at Dubthach before speaking, "**Please, spare him. He will obey what I have to say to him, Dubthach.**"

"**That is what is happening here though, he is solely obeying your sayings and none of mine or my tribe's customs.**"

"**I apologize, Dubthach, but please. Spare him. He is a bit of a boy.**"

Dubthach looked at Oswald and stared hard into him before shaking his head and barking out, "**Last chance, Fergus. Otherwise, you know our customs.**"

"**Yes, Dubthach.**"

*****

As soon as they left, Fergus stared hard into his son before hissing, "**And that is what exactly happens when you disobey my orders! They want to do it to you now, Oswald!"**

"Do what?"

Firefoot and myself had shifted and were now in the darkest corner of their tent, hidden in the shadows. Fergus did not turn his attention towards us before his shoulders slumped before replying, "**They want to make an example of him. They force their people to live in fear of them. Not the way it should be."**

"What happened to your tribe if I may ask?"

He swallowed before looking to our shadow of a tent spot before looking at Oswald before speaking, "**Anyway, that you can shift and take us somewhere?"**

"Yes."

**"Then take us to the mountain peak."**

I blinked once before replying, "Only a dragon would be able to get to the peak. Nothing else would be able to get past the cloud cover."

**"That is the safest place we can be though. Can you do it?"**

"It would be dangerous if I shifted mid-flight."

**"Not as dangerous as it is here though."**

"I can do it."

I approached them, but the tent flap opened, Dubthach entered and crossed his arms across his chest before speaking, "**You are coming with me."**

The shock written across Fergus's face was somewhat comical, however, I replied after a moment, "No."

**"You are an outsider!"**

"That I am. However, I will not come with you. Our paths were met to cross, until now."

**"How are you so sure that it was supposed to end now?"**

**"Because Fergus is the one that was in my vision to find."**

**"Our seer did not see you coming. Therefore, you are nothing but an outsider!"**

**"If you want to kill us simply because you are not in the right here, Dubthach. I apologize that we had to enter your camp, your home, to get to our person. However, we need to depart."**

**"No."**

**"You do not get a choice in this matter, however."**

**"I am the chief in this camp! You will obey my…."**

**"My name is FIREFOOT! You will let us pass."**

Silence. It was clear by the shadows in the tent that Dubthach knew of Firefoot, and the paleness in his expression was a little funny. However, Fergus glanced sharply at Firefoot and sighed deeply before muttering, "**Aurelin.**"

Firefoot looked at Fergus for a fleeting second, but I did not take my eyes off of Dubthach. He looked at me for a moment before whispering, "**And you? Who are you?**"

"I am nothing of your immediate concern. Unless you are going to continue to block our exit."

*"Tell them."*

*"Ummm… no. What do you know that I don't know, Firefoot?"*

*"Thakur, tell them who you are. Even the druids know of your family name. At least, tell them your last name."*

*"Fine."*

I looked at Dubthach before speaking again, a low rumble from my throat in response, "My last name is Benik."

Everyone in the tent blanched. Their jaws dropped in shock before Dubthach did something that surprised us all. He dropped to his knees and mumbled words to the dirt floor. I glanced at Fergus before noticing that he sighed deeply and rubbed his hand across his face again. It looked like he knew that one day we would come together. He looked at Dubthach before speaking, **"Dubthach, it appears that my destiny has come. I need to leave your camp. Along with Oswald."**

Dubthach looked up at Fergus with a strange look and replied, "**Go, and never come back.**"

**"So be it."**

Fergus went about his way and was shoving things into baskets that looked woven from grass and bark from trees. Oswald stared at us for a moment longer before helping his father.

*****

I turned my attention to Dubthach, and noticed that he had backed out. He left as quickly as he had come in. It was possibly a bad thing that he left without a word, but I was unsure of what happened. I looked at Fergus as he worked to get his items packed. It was not much though, a few dark blue robes, but other than that very little besides.

After a few minutes, they were done packing, except for the cots they had made. I looked at the cots before speaking, "Do you need the cots?"

**"No. They will be left here."**

I nodded in return. Suddenly wondering why, they were being so curtly towards me. Firefoot swallowed slightly but did not say anything. I had a feeling he knew why. However, I could not say a word. I sighed and exited the tent, before shifting to my dragon. My spikes popped out of my hide before I roared into the dawn sky.

I turned my head towards Firefoot before rumbling in the connection, *"You will mount my head, and…."*

***"Thakur, no."***

*"What?"*

***"Fergus will ride your head."***

*"But…"*

***"No."***

*"What do you know that I don't?"*

***"Trust me on this, Thakur."***

I growled at him and snapped my jaws at him. My teeth were razor-sharp. I snarled at him, but Fergus approached me, speaking, **"Hold yourself steady, Benik."**

I turned my attention back to him and shook my head slightly, before leaning my head down close to the ground.

Fergus approached and eyed Firefoot, but threw rope around my shoulders and latched his limited belongings onto my back, fastening them down. Oswald approached carefully before whispering, "Father?"

Fergus looked at him before speaking, **"Get four blankets from the cots, Oswald. They will be our padding on his back."**

"Yes, father."

Oswald disappeared into the tent and came out with four blankets and handed them to his father. He attached one to the items attached to me, before placing one between my shoulder blades, and attached a rope sequence to my spikes and around a few others. He gestured towards his son to come closer to him.

Oswald came towards me cautiously but I did not turn my head at him, but my eyes followed his movement. It caused him to swallow in fear, but he seemed to be rather trusting in his father. Fergus looked at him before speaking, **"You ride here son, mount him. Use his spike here, and here and pull yourself up onto his back. Onto the blanket. When you are settled, lean forward loop your arms through the rope in front of you, and pull backward. It will be a similar feeling to the net you made, son."**

It took Oswald a few times to mount me before he grew frustrated that he couldn't do it. I finally grumbled but lay down on the ground. I brought my left front fore-claw backward and gave him more of an area to get up. It took a few moments to scramble onto my back and soon did. He followed his father's instructions, looped his arm through the rope, and pulled backward, and it sank directly into position. I rocked gently back and forth, getting adjusted to his weight. I felt him tense but did not say a word.

Fergus glanced at Firefoot before speaking, **"Do you need assistance up?"**

**"No."**

**"Then what are you waiting on?"**

**"I wasn't going to mount until you do."**

He smirked slightly and huffed a little as he approached my head before placing his hand on my horn above my eye before speaking, **"I apologize, but I am going to be the one who rides you on your head."**

I rumbled a little but knew that we could not communicate as myself and Firefoot. He took that as an answer enough, however, and he threw a blanket onto my neck before mounting. He did not do the rope sequence that he had done for his son and glanced questioning at Firefoot.

Firefoot swallowed before connecting to me, *"Go."*

*"What? Not without you."*

**"I will catch up with you, Thakur. However, Dubthach would not let you go. Go."**

*"I hope you know what you are doing, Firefoot."*

**"Get out of the camp! GO!"**

I roared into the dawning sunlight and leaped into the air without delay. Oswald instantly shouted, "WAIT! YOU FORGOT...."

The tribe rushed out and held out spears and threw them at me. I growled low in my throat and roared in anger as one pierced into my side. Smoke swirled through my nostrils, but Fergus leaned forward before barking out, **"NO! GET US OUT OF HERE!"**

My eyes flickered to him for a split second, before I roared into the sky and rose into the sky, and flew off. The veil above me broke and shattered the veil in a heartbeat. It rained down upon the ones below us. Another spear stuck onto my belly and I roared into the air and looked down with hatred as I stared down at the one who had thrown it. Dubthach stared at me in fear for a moment but grabbed another spear and would have thrown it, but Firefoot did something that I would have never thought was possible. He shifted to a Lycan, and tore apart the tribe, slaughtering anyone that held a spear.

I felt Fergus look away in what seemed like a shame. I swallowed and flew upwards. I hovered just below the cloud cover for a moment, before a bird flew up, and by the wing beats and uncertainty, I knew it was Firefoot.

I waited until he landed in my claw before I flew upwards. Heading higher and higher until Fergus directed me towards the ledge on the top of the mountain. It was a huge cave inside. I entered, lowered my head down, and he slipped off and assisted Oswald off. Firefoot exited my claw and stood away from us.

# Chapter 48

After everything was off, I shifted into my human form and stared at Firefoot for a moment before speaking, "What the hell? You never told me that you could shift into a freaking Lycan!"

Firefoot looked at me and replied, "**I only channel that side of my anger when I absolutely need to Thakur. Did they give us a choice in the matter? They hit you twice, and would have brought you down if I didn't.**"

"**What anger has boiled in you for these many years?**"

Firefoot looked at me for a moment, before turning his attention to Fergus and replying, "**The man you sent, no gave me away to… he did not want me.**"

Oswald looked at his father sharply before voicing, "What does he mean father?"

Fergus sighed deeply before looking at me and speaking, "**I have a feeling you have another half. Does he know where he is?**"

"He doesn't."

"**Any possible way for him to be fronting, and not yourself?**"

"Why are you wanting him?"

"**Because I personally do not trust a demon.**"

I scowled before replying, "Not all of us are bad."

"**I will not speak again until BOTH of your sides come to play. And that does mean yours too Firefoot.**"

"**My half does not know about my name.**"

"Why not?"

Firefoot looked at Oswald for a moment before sighing, "**Because he doesn't need to know yet.**"

"**Is that his choice or yours?**"

Firefoot was silent for a moment before dropping his eyes from Fergus, muttering, "**Mine.**"

Fergus scoffed before shaking his head and looked at me for a moment before rolling his eyes. He stayed true though, and did not say another word after his little fit with Firefoot.

I sighed deeply before sinking back into my mind and allowing Quinn to surface again.

****

I looked wildly around, gasped, winced, and held my stomach and side. I grimaced before sighing deeply as I took off my shirt. I saw the wounds and grumbled to myself before looking around. I did not realize that we were not alone. I froze when I saw Fergus and Oswald staring at me.  I looked at Aurelin who looked equally confused about where we were, before speaking, "Uhh…. hello?"

**"Hello."**

"I am sorry, but who are you?"

**"My name is Fergus, and my son is Oswald. You?"**

"My name is Quinn. King Morphous's advisor."

**"Morphous Draconis?"**

"Correct."

Fergus seemed lost for a moment before Oswald spoke, "The same guy that wiped out our tribe? That one?"

I opened my mouth to say something but stopped myself and sighed deeply. I ran a hand over my face before I replied after a moment, "Unfortunately, yes. That one."

"Why are you his advisor? Do you agree with what he had done?"

"I do not agree with what he has done, and he doesn't like it either."

"Then why did he attack? We weren't even on his territory."

**"Oswald."**

Fergus barked out in anger. Oswald turned his head to the side., "Why should I be silent, father, he works for the man who killed our family."

**"Enough."**

I sighed deeply, before speaking, "He has a right to his emotions, Fergus. I did not understand the extent of what Morphous had done until quite recently. I apologize for his behavior and actions. However, where are we even?"

**"You don't know anything?"**

"Nothing. The last thing I remember was giving my demon the reins, and that was back at the shifter palace."

Oswald had shock written across his face. "What does it feel like when he does kick you out?"

**"Oswald!"**

"No, it is fine. It feels like I am floating in darkness. Feels disorientated and weird."

"Do you always give him control like that?"

"No, that I do not. I rarely do."

"Do you not trust him to take over more frequently?"

"I only have embraced him in the past three weeks. So, we are still on rocky terms."

Fergus looked confused for a moment before speaking, **"Did you not know before three weeks that you had someone else with you?"**

"My father was not entirely keen on showing me the difference between shifter and demon. I grew up believing I was a shifter. However, that changed after I hit the age of twelve, and that is where the shit hit the fan. I heard a voice in the back of my mind for years but did not let it out. At least, not again."

**"Again?"**

I swallowed and looked around and went to sit on a rock that was nearby. I shivered slightly before I put my shirt back on before sighing. My breaths were coming out in vapor and I knew that we were high up somewhere. Meaning, that Thakur flew us somewhere only his dragon form could reach.

I sighed deeply before shaking my head in frustration as I knew I was daydreaming. I looked up at Fergus before whispering, "I had siblings. More than Herald…. However, once I hit the age that my demon could surface, the shit hit the fan."

**"What happened?"**

"He slaughtered all my siblings except for Herald. And only because my father came into the room then."

Silence. I hung my head in shame before whispering, "My mother had been dead for years before I had gotten my demon completely. However, after my father and she had children, did he tell her what he was. Therefore, she was kept in the dark."

"So…. that means that you are half shifter and half demon. You are the hybrid."

"I am one of the hybrids, yes. The other one that is the cause of the attack on your people would be the one that is currently residing with the werewolves."

"Wait. There was a reason why he attacked without warning?"

I looked up at him before noticing that Fergus had stiffened slightly. He muttered something under his breath and said, **"Was Morphous after an artifact? Was that the reason why he attacked?"**

"Unfortunately, yes. He was after an artifact."

**"The only artifact that could have helped the hybrid would be.... Oh."**

"What?"

**"The artifact that we were guarding. Safekeeping if you want to call it, was one of the artifacts that could harness the hybrid's powers, could make it the most powerful being in the world. However, that was a lie at the same time."**

"What do you mean a lie?"

**"It means that Morphous took an artifact that could harness the hybrid's ability but would also slowly kill it too. The artifact would kill the hybrid if worn for a long amount of time. It was more of a way to kill the hybrid than anything else."**

"So.... in other words, Morphous took something that will kill his daughter?"

**"Daughter?"**

"Yeah."

He stared hard at me for a moment before looking at Aurelin who looked confused and was staring into the cloud cover – as if thinking about jumping. Oswald was also watching him, and without a word, he went over there and stood beside Aurelin without a word.

I looked at Fergus before speaking softly, "Son?"

Fergus looked at Oswald for a moment before slowly shaking his head and replying in an equally hushed whisper, **"Under technical terms, no. Not my son. He was the last survivor of the raid."**

"My condolences on that."

**"We cannot go back in time even though we all wish it. You said that Morphous attacked our camp because he was trying to hide something?"**

"I did not say that, but to be truthful, yes he did attack you to hide someone. He used the attack as an excuse to hide her."

**"He did it to hide his daughter?"**

"Yeah."

**"You seem to know more about her than I do."**

"She is the daughter of Morphous, so shifter king line in her veins. Her mother, I don't know the whole story behind it, but is Sophronia, mate to Nathaniel."

**"So, she's a cross between shifter and wolf. I thought they had lived in separate lives so they do not mix blood."**

"That is the original thing, yes, but it appears that Sophronia and Morphous had an affair or something along the lines…."

**"Not an affair. I know some of the history, Morphous and Nathaniel, the werewolves and shifters overall, were friends until Morphous heard my old seer say that his daughter would be the death of everything that he holds dear."**

"So Morphous acted in fear then? That is why he faked his daughter's death and sold her to the slave trade. Because he was in fear?"

Fergus looked at me with a sharp look and I swallowed before shrugging and speaking, "I may be his advisor, but I only became his advisor after my father stepped down. We came into the shifter palace about a year after the raid. So, I didn't even know about the druid camp until a guard passed down that information to me at a later date."

**"So, you didn't know the unjustness of the raid. Interesting."**

"What is interesting?"

**"The fact that you were only brought into the shifter palace around a year later, where were you before then?"**

"Don't remember that, unfortunately. I was five or six when we came into the shifter palace. My father decided to do the advisor position and ran the palace. I did not understand, however, growing up how he knew the exits and entrances that no one else really knew though. It was as if he was there before."

**"Your father, what is his name?"**

I sighed deeply before looking down at the cave floor and noticed something. The ground was moving. I looked sharply at Fergus before speaking, "His name is Killian. However, may I ask you something really quick before we dive further into the past?"

**"Go ahead."**

"Which mountain are we at currently?"

**"Ummm…. Not entirely sure on the proper name, but the tribe that we have been residing with for the past twelve years call it…."**

He trailed off since I am sure he felt the ground shift under his feet. I stood up slowly before speaking, "Aurelin?"

I looked towards where they were, but they were gone. Fergus and I exchanged frightened looks before I called out again, "AURELIN?"

The ground beneath us shifted again, and I looked at Fergus once before the ground opened up beneath us and we fell downward. I looked up and saw the mountain cave floor close up, on hinges. This meant that this was not an act of a god, meaning it could mean only one thing…. Shit.

******

We woke up after a few minutes of being down there, and it was pitch black. Could not see my hand within mere inches from my face, it was dark. I swallowed and tried to get my bearings before a voice rumbled out, "**What is your business in being in my mountain?**"

I tried to gauge where the voice came from, but I sighed deeply, "I'm sorry, but we did not realize it was your mountain."

**"Are you daft, boy? The locals know of me, they call me their god."**

So, I was right, not a god. Good golly, and by the sounds of his accent, he was a Carpathian. I sighed deeply before speaking, "There was another two with us…"

**"Why are you worried about the others when you are in the same fate?"**

"Because they are my friends and family."

**"I would not worry about their fate, more of my own if I were you."**

"Well, I am unlike anyone else that you have seen."

The voice went silent before he sighed deeply before speaking, "**Annonu, bring me a torch.**"

"Yes, my lord."

A shuffling sounded and soon my eyes squinted in the sudden brightness before I squinted up at the man who held it. He was a pale fellow, with long black hair and brown eyes. However, the one that has spoken more snapped his fingers and drew my attention to him. He was tall, and lean, but still had enough muscles in the correct places. I swallowed and looked at his facial features before it dawned on me who he was. I lowered my eyes before speaking, "Zaros."

**"Oh? You know of me?"**

"It's a little hard not to know of you, Zaros. My father spoke of you for a couple of years."

**"Who is your father?"**

"Killian Benik."

Zaros face fell instantly, and he gripped the sword that was on his hip, turning his knuckles white. However, after a moment, his hands loosened before he growled, **"Father, huh? Interesting that he isn't with you."**

"He would have been with me if he wasn't stupid."

**"Is he dead?"**

"No."

**"Damn, I wish he was."**

"Why?"

"Killian only brought misery to our people. Before he sought the safety he wanted for his little children. Hence the reason why he left us."

**"Annonu!"**

Annonu shrunk down and his shoulder brought inward, and I saw Zaros's eyes flash in rage before he held up his hand to hit. However, what Annonu said caused me to ask a question, "Wait, what do you mean before he left you?"

Zaros looked at me with a confused look before lowering his hand and replying, **"You don't know?"**

"No."

**"Hmmm…. Interesting. Annonu, take him and the other one in this room to the guest chambers."**

"The guest chambers?"

**"Yes."**

"Yes, my lord."

Annonu turned his attention to me before speaking, "Right this way. Follow me, please."

I looked at Zaros who stayed where he was, and turned around to watch something. He seemed deep in thought.

*****

It was not long later that we had entered the rest of the palace hidden from sight, but it was bright. It seems the only room in the entire palace that was that black was the room we dropped into. I looked at Fergus out of the corner of my eye, we locked eye contact for a split second and he shook his head slightly. He was slightly scared, but he hid it rather well too.

Soon after a bit, we had come to a room and Annonu opened the door and gestured towards us to go into it. I paused before entering before speaking, "Annonu?"

"What is it?"

"Where are the others that were brought down here before us?"

For a moment, he looked like he wouldn't answer and finally, he looked down the hallways and then glanced at me before replying, "Dungeons."

"Why are they in the dungeons?"

"Because they tried to fight Zaros."

I frowned and asked another question, "Annonu, what would you do if you were brought down here against your will? Fight or…."

"It is not what I would do. I would know better than to attack Zaros."

I would have said something, but Fergus cleared his throat and I looked at him. He did not seem to want to speak with Annonu there, and I sighed and entered the room. Annonu stared after me for a moment, before shutting the door and leaving.

****

I looked at Fergus before muttering, "You were rather quiet."

**"You seem to not understand something, Quinn. That this is a Carpathian ownership of this mountain."**

"I can tell it is a Carpathian mountain. The Carpathians proved it, didn't they?"

He sighed deeply before replying, **"You don't seem to understand something here, Quinn. Anyone that enters this mountain never comes back out alive."**

"We will get out of here."

Fergus shook his head before snapping, **"You don't seem concerned entirely about us, Quinn. Oswald and Aurelin are in the dungeons for attacking Zaros, and we are inside the**

**main area. We would never get to see them again, since….. The Carpathians are known far and wide that they will slaughter anything that harms them."**

I sighed deeply before replying, "Normal Carpathians yes, that may be the case. However, I noticed on the way in here, that there were no humans and no blood bank people wandering around here behind their so-called masters."

**"Don't you understand though that WE are their blood banks and their food now?"**

I rubbed my right hand across my face when Thakur spoke in the connection, *"We will not become food."*

*"You seem rather confident in that, Thakur. Mind telling me why?"*

*"Because you said it yourself, that no blood banks is walking around. Meaning these Carpathians practice something else. Find out what they practice, Quinn."*

*"We should leave here though."*

*"Quinn… there is only a handful of people that have made it into Zaros mountain and be his guest. Are you really going to toss that opportunity away?"*

I sighed deeply and looked at Fergus who looked rather stunned for a moment before speaking, **"Did you mean to have your demon speak as if he was talking to me?"**

"What do you mean?"

**"I heard your demon in my mind, Quinn. How is that possible? We did not share any blood or anything on that matter."**

I frowned and Thakur spoke to both of us at the same time, "It is because the Carpathians in this mountain don't really allow anyone to mind speak alone to each other. Which is why there are more people talking."

**"How are you okay with them bringing us inside a room and locking the door behind us? Along with Oswald and Aurelin being inside their dungeons?"**

Thakur sighed deeply before speaking, "We are not locked inside this room. We could leave if we wanted to."

I frowned and turned to look at the door, wondering if he was correct, that we could leave any time we wanted. I sighed and looked back at Fergus before speaking, "Do we want to try to leave?"

"Leaving would end in your death. Stay in the room, or I will kill you."

Boomed a voice further inside the room, making us jump. I looked at Fergus and knew he was scared now. I sighed deeply before raising my head, rounding the corner of the cave, and finding a Carpathian reading a book on the couch. He looked up at me and then his eyes landed on Fergus's before speaking again, "Welcome to my humble home. This is my room, and I am unsure of why Zaros wanted you two in here with me."

I frowned and Thakur spoke out loud, "Cornelius?"

The Carpathian stiffened for a moment as he looked up and seemed to judge me hardcore for a moment before he whispered, "Not possible. Are you… are you, the son of Killian?"

"Yes, should I know you?"

Cornelius put his book down and sighed deeply before replying, "I guess not. If you don't know who I am, then that means that your father failed to mention me growing up for his reasons. It does sadden me though that my nephew does not know me though."

**"Nephew? In what way?"**

"Killian has a stepbrother, myself, and learning about each other was quite by accident may I add."

"How is that possible? My father is a demon."

"True, he is. However, at some point in time, his mother had met my father who was a traveling Carpathian at that time era and…. One thing led to another, and I became what I am. So, in a way, I am a hybrid, but my Carpathian is more prominent than the demon. The demon gene skipped me."

I stared at him with a hard look before speaking, "How is it possible that I have a Carpathian uncle?"

Cornelius gave me a look before looking at Fergus who had a confused look written across his face. However, he was rather quiet about the matter too. Cornelius sighed and replied, "Well… you see…. When two different…"

"No! No, no, no. I understand that aspect of how the creation works. However, my mind is still processing the gist of it. Why didn't my father talk about you?"

Cornelius sighed deeply before replying, "Because we had a fight, and Zaros who was a young ruler at the time had different views on how to deal with it than Killian did. So…. one thing led to another, and Killian fled leaving me here to deal with Zaros."

"Why are you sounding so defeated as if you don't like your ruler?"

"Because Zaros may be the ruler of this strand of Carpathians, but he is not my ruler. Dracula is my king."

**"Then how did you become to be here of all places?"**

"Dracula did not want anyone that was inbred. Also known as me. Therefore, he had banished me from his court, and I fled and stumbled onto Zaros place of residency. And here is where I haven't left."

It was clear that Fergus and myself was not familiar with any of this history and Cornelius sighed deeply before speaking, "Before we go deeper into this history, what are your names, please?"

"My name is Quinn, and my demon is Thakur."

"Nice to meet you two, I barely remember you two, you left when you were very young. And yourself?"

He turned his attention to Fergus and Fergus swallowed and looked down before replying, **"Fergus."**

"Nice to meet you, Fergus. Now what was that about two others being down in the dungeons?"

"It appears that…. That my idiot brother, who is no by blood, may or may not have attacked Zaros on the way down here."

"Attacked Zaros, and he is still alive?"

He seemed rather perplexed by that, and I felt that Fergus wanted to know a question, Cornelius sighed after a moment before speaking, "Normally anyone who attacks Zaros is dead before they even know it. However, since Annonu said they were in the dungeons, it means that whatever happened was not serious. Either that Zaros, wanted to know something."

"Like what?"

"Where exactly did you come into this mountain? Did you come in the way that the druid tribe gives us their sacrifices or a different way?"

**"Different."**

"Different, how?"

"We came down from the cave."

"The cave, that is above the cloud cover. The cave that only a dragon can reach the cave. That cave?"

"Yeah… why?"

Cornelius sighed deeply and ran his hand across his face before replying, "Because only one other person came down from that way, and that is the same one that is your father, Quinn. In the times of the old, when dragons were more prominent in the way of the earth, that cave belonged to a dragon. One that ruled this entire section of the mountains as far as his eyes could see. However, after some time had passed the humans worked together and brought the mighty beast down. However, that is only part of the history. The other part of it is that the dragon had built these chambers and rooms with its own talons."

**"Why would a dragon build something not for itself?"**

"Not sure on that part, but I do know that it was a mighty feat. I personally do not remember that day, but I know that Zaros's father may know of the dragon that built their home. Unsure, of course, but it would make sense."

"Wait a moment. You said that my father was the only other person who had come down from the entrance that we had come from. If the legends are true, about the dragon, why did the cave seem…. Alive?"

Cornelius looked at me with a weird look before looking at Fergus before speaking, "What does he mean? Alive?"

Fergus looked at me for a moment before sighing deeply and replied, "**Before the ground came underfoot, the cave floor seemed to breathe in and out as if it was breathing.**"

Cornelius frowned and scratched his head for a moment before muttering, "Not possible."

"What's not possible?"

He frowned as he looked up at us for a moment before speaking, "Anyway that you can take me to the cavern?"

"Wouldn't Zaros need to be informed of that?"

"He doesn't keep a leash on anyone here, Quinn. We can even leave if we desire to."

**"Then why stay here of all places?"**

"Honestly because I don't want to socialize with anyone else. It was a way that I could be who I am without anyone saying that I was different or…. A burden. This is where it would have been the ideal place to grow up since there are next to no rules here."

"Surely, there are some rules. Otherwise, this place would be in chaos."

"Okay, there are some stricter rules, yes, but none of them would result in banishment."

I looked over at Fergus before replying, "Any way we can get the two idiots from the dungeons before we depart?"

Cornelius stared at us with a weird look for a moment before he sighed and replied, "Unfortunately, I do not have clearance to go down there myself. Even though I have lived here for the past few centuries, I do not have the authority to go down there. At least, not without Zaros's approval."

"So, flying up to the main cavern is different because?"

"Because he doesn't mind where we go as long as it is not outside of the mountain for the most part."

**"But that doesn't make sense, you said you could leave the mountain if you desired to do so."**

"I did say that, yes. However, it highly involves around you two. I can go as much as I please, you two though, unsure on that aspect."

I glanced at Fergus and saw the look written across his face. He wanted to depart and head home, or most likely wherever we went. Since our fates are intertwined apparently. Cornelius sighed after a moment before speaking again, "How did you four even get up there anyhow?"

"Thakur flew us up there."

"How often have you flown?"

"Killian had me train the moment I could. It gave me something to do, other than slaughter every fool that made their…"

"Thakur, enough."

I sighed deeply and rubbed the bridge of my nose before looking at Cornelius and Fregus who looked mildly perturbed by what Thakur was saying. I shrugged once before I spoke, "One of the reasons why I don't let him full access. I cannot trust what he would do."

"Probably the best that you would do the flying then, Quinn. We cannot kill anyone here."

"Why not?"

"Because that would result in your death. And I am pretty sure that your fate is already messy and adding an angry clan of Carpathians at your back is not something that you would want to add to the reputation. Now would it?"

Thakur scowled in my mind, and I smirked in response. I held out my hand to Cornelius before speaking, "Wow, you made him fall silent for once in his anger."

**"What happens normally?"**

"He tends to take control of me and would hunt the victim. Unless, I, of course, was working and disagreed with someone. Then he allowed me to deal with whatever it was. Although there were a few incidents along the way, being in the shifter palace helped a whole lot more than you would think."

"In what way?"

"They would heal, and rarely need the medical's attention. Unless, of course, Thakur went too far. But after our massacre with the rest of our siblings, that has not happened since."

It took a moment for Cornelius to process what was said. His eyes flew into a rage before he thundered, "You killed your own blood?"

"Do not make me remember that."

"Why?"

"Because they were getting on my nerves. They pushed me too far, and I lost my temper."

"What ended up stopping you?"

"My father."

"I assume that would be Killian's demon correct?"

"Yes."

Cornelius shook his head in disgust before turning his attention to Fergus and speaking, "I apologize, but where do you exactly fit into this mixture? I do not believe my brother would allow someone like yourself to be with his son."

"I fit into this because I am the second to last druid that Morphous had raided the camp. I was residing with the tribe before Thakur and Firefoot showed."

"Wait… back up. Firefoot is here?"

"You know of Firefoot?"

"Ummm…. Firefoot is the one that would bring nothing but prosperity in the supernatural world. He should be recruiting the supernatural species, to unite them, and then we face off the ones that were commissioned to kill us as one species."

It took us a moment before my eyes flashed with Thakur's for a split second before, I reined him back in before whispering, "How do you know that we are being hunted?"

Cornelius sighed deeply before replying, "You are a druid, aren't you?"

Fergus shuffled his feet slightly before replying, "**Yes.**"

"Do you want to tell him how this came to be?"

Fergus swallowed and looked around for a moment before moving towards a recliner, lowering himself into the seat and looking down at the cavern floor. He sighed deeply before looking up at me with a look, speaking, "**There is a prophecy that my people knew. I don't know if it is solely mine that knew this, but Dubthach acted as if he never heard of it when I**

**mentioned it to him a few years back. However, the prophecy stated that the supernatural world would have to unite as one to defeat a species that was hired in. My seer, at the time, did not believe that any of the werewolves, shifters, or Carpathians would be able to work together as one to defeat the same enemy. However, it seems that the prophecy is coming to be."**

"How do you know it is coming to be?"

Fergus looked at Cornelius before Cornelius sighed deeply before running his hand across his face. He looked at me for a solid ten seconds, and I shuffled my feet in waiting, he sighed deeply again before murmuring, "There is a reason why Zaros has it so we can come and go as we please. We are not locked underneath his rule, not entirely at least. However, the last time I went out, there was talk about the supernatural hunters that were hired and sent out. After some more listening to the humans, I found out that their church has funded this project of theirs, and are now hunting the shifters. I am unsure if the shifters they were tasked to hunt were the experiment and her offspring, or if it included the purebloods. However, after some of the humans were talking, I asked them if they had met these hunters personally. Since I have been friends with various hunters in the past."

He paused and scowled for a moment before muttering, "Stop giving me that look. It helped keep me safe from harm."

I scowled after a moment when he gave me a pointed look, and I sighed after a moment and sat down in the other recliner. After a moment, he continued, "Anyhow, after I got to talking with them, one of them said they have personally never met these hunters, but they never miss their targets. They hunt and hunt to their last dying breath, but never have failed in a mission. The name that most of the people know them by is Zhukov. That is all I know. However, I did some digging on my own, here in the massive library, and came across the name Zhukov, and realized something. That these are supernatural hunters. Not the common human hunters either, these were…. Born to be what they are. They are faster and stronger than any supernatural, even alphas in the werewolf territory. Along with the shifters. So, after I came up on that little tidbit of information, I did not go out and about again in the human world."

It took us a moment to process what he had said, and after a moment Fergus spoke, "**So if that is true, that they are hired to hunt the shifters, then why was the prophecy targeting the entire supernaturals?**"

"**It is because Zhukov is not the common one who listens to his client entirely. He will hunt every single wolf, shifter, and Carpathian until we are wiped out entirely.**"

We all jumped and glanced at the entrance and saw Zaros standing there. His arms crossed and I stood up and replied, "Can we please have the two in the dungeon?"

"Why? So, you can leave? I am sorry to bust your bubble, but you are not going anywhere for a while."

"Why not?"

"Because you are something else. I do not want you to disappear and never come back, since that is how it would happen."

"How about this? You give us the two that are down in the dungeon, and we won't leave immediately?"

"What are you doing, Quinn?" Muttered Fergus, but Zaros did not let his eyes flicker to him before he sighed deeply and looked at Cornelius. Cornelius swallowed slightly, but Zaros sighed deeply. "Fine, as long as you do not leave immediately. However, it is more to keep you safe than anything."

"Keep us safe?"

He had since turned around and now had his back to us. He froze for a moment before turning his attention back to us and sighing deeply. He looked at the door, and motioned towards it, before speaking, "Cornelius, please find Vernius, and tell him to bring the two new accounts from my dungeon."

"Of course, Zaros."

*****

Cornelius departed, and after a moment, Zaros turned to face us for a moment before speaking, "So, I take it that you have found out why I had you placed into this chamber?"

"Yes, but why did you set us in here?"

"Because no one should not know they have family. Along with the fact that Cornelius needed a reminder that he was worth something. He has kind of fallen off the horse slightly, and his depression was eating him away."

"How would you know that?"

"Has it not occurred to you, that my entire palace has no way that anyone can connect? Along with their other halves being able to speak freely and be heard by all? That is something I have here. However, that has a cost actually."

"Cost?"

He had a grim smile on for a split second before his smile faded and his shoulder slouched inward for a moment before he replied, "**There is something else in the mountain, I would have thought that since you were on its doorstep it would have claimed you as its own. Not send you down to me.**"

It took a moment to match what he said, and we both were silent. Our heartbeats rose and seemed to thunder in my ears. I swallowed nervously before whispering, "Cornelius made it sound as if the dragon was dead though."

"**He is, but his offspring is not dead. Another young dragon is living up there.**"

"What is his name?"

Zaros shrugged and replied, "**Not entirely sure, have never met the dragon myself. However, I do know that he doesn't typically let anyone leave once he does have them in his cavern. Especially after what happened to his father before him. He doesn't trust anyone, but since his father allowed my father to be down here, he has not really bothered us.**"

"Do you feed him?"

"**Honest answer, okay. No, he is a wild animal, and we have not fed him once.**"

"**Then what happens to every single offering that the tribe gave you? Once they entered, no one came back out.**"

"**They live here. The tribe thinks that we are monsters, and pay tribute. However, that is not how I run things. I never approved of the ways that Dracula had his people act in fear of being around him. However, that does not mean that I do not follow some of his customs. We all have to feed at some point. I keep a strict rule here, that the tributes, are to be used only enough until we can go to a human village to get our proper fill.**"

"So, the humans here and the other offerings are living here peacefully?"

"**As peaceful as they can I should say. However, they cannot leave. That doesn't include you by the way, same with the two that Cornelius will have shortly. You four are different.**"

"Different how?"

"**The dragon let you down here. You were up in his home, in his sanctuary and I am surprised that he did not kill you where you stood. However, since he did not kill you, it would not suit me in any way, in doing so. He spared you all because he saw something that no one else had. Unsure on what it is entirely, but I am sure he knows more than we do in this aspect.**"

"**Any way that we can talk to the dragon? Maybe he knows more than we know here. As you said.**"

"I am unsure if he would talk to anyone. Regardless of what the topic they want to talk about. He is known to slaughter anything that comes back up from this chamber section."

"If that is true, then why didn't he kill us when he had a clear chance to since we did not know he was up there."

Zaros shrugged and replied, "As I said before, I do not understand why he let you out of his cavern without meeting his flames. Normally, he would have slaughtered everything in his cavern."

"Hmmm….. Interesting. I wonder what his name is."

Zaros shrugged again and motioned us to follow him. After a brief hesitation, we followed after him and disappeared down into the lit areas.

****

It was a few minutes later when we reached an office space and that is when I asked the question that was starting to bother me, "So, out of curiosity. Why is the place where we came into was very dark?"

"Because that is where the offerings come into. We did not expect to find a werewolf, a druid boy in the darkness. And later a hybrid, and a druid elder. It is because the tribe outside believes we live in darkness. They have never seen us personally, but have heard my voice more than once when someone strays too close to my entrance."

"Ah, so…. You don't want offerings?"

"The offerings are nothing more than blood banks, but they are treated fairly as possible. Yes, they can never leave and that is the unfortunate thing, but we cannot allow them out now that they have seen what we are. It is the same with the human villages. We don't tend to feed on people all at the same time, we bring one back or we have more than five join the person, and they all…. Well… you know, suck the person dry for the most part, and put them into an unmarked grave. It doesn't happen often mind you, but it does happen at least every other three months. At a random interval."

That brought us to a standstill, I stared at him before speaking, "You say that so calmly, you are murdering people."

"I am very selective in the people that my people do it to. My strand of Carpathians can read people's minds. So, we use that on the humans as much as we can, so we do target the ones that are typically cruel to anything."

"You are weeding out the bad ones?"

**"You can say that. Yes, but in another way, no. It is a bit of bad fortune since the majority of them were led down the wrong pathway by their forefathers. However, we must feed at the same time, so.... Unfortunate as it is, yes, we weed out the ones that target weaker individuals for their own gain."**

I looked at Fergus and saw his conflicted look for a moment before he replied, **"I normally don't like anyone feeding off someone else, however, I have heard stories that all the problematic people in the human territories are disappearing slowly. No one looks for them, even their children and spouse. So... I guess that is a fair assumption that you are doing the proper thing in this world."**

I blinked a few times and looked around the office, I agreed with what had happened. The way he has his people target the ones that only do the most harm, however, there had to be a point where someone disobeyed his orders, and I looked at him before speaking, "What happens when someone disobeys your direct orders?"

Zaros froze, and his hands lingered on his sword handle before his fingers gripped it slightly before his voice went dark, **"I read everyone's minds when they arrive back. If one of them has feasted on someone that is not to my standard, they are dead."**

"You kill them?"

Zaros looked directly at Fergus without missing a beat and replied, **"I do not tolerate anyone disobeying my direct orders. That is the one rule that everyone here knows better than to question me. That is one of my top rules here."**

Fergus swallowed and took a step backward, it was almost instinctual for Thakur to take a step forward. Zaros's eyes flickered to mine before he released his hold on his sword handle and said, **"I do not mean either of you any harm."**

Thakur faded in the background, and I sighed deeply before rubbing my face before the door was opened with Cornelius, along with Oswald and Aurelin.

*****

Cornelius looked between us and glanced at Zaros before speaking, "Do you wish for me to stay, Zaros?"

**"If you want to stay, you may. Otherwise, it is up to you if you want to or not."**

Cornelius looked at us for a fleeting moment before replying, "I would request that I stay, Zaros."

**"Alright."**

I glanced at Cornelius before noticing something. He had a red welt on his chin that he was trying hard to hide from Zaros, but I caught it. My thoughts must have leaked slightly, since Zaros froze and looked sharply at Cornelius before speaking, **"Cornelius, why does your chin have a red welt on it?"**

Cornelius lowered his eyes from Zaros before replying, "I…. it took a while to convince Vernius that I had been under your command. Until I said something that you alone would have said."

**"Did he hit you?"**

"Yes, Zaros. He hit me."

Zaros's eyes turned murderous suddenly, and he touched his sword before growling out, **"Guards."**

Two guards instantly entered the office and seemed ready to take us, but Zaros stopped them in their tracks, **"Bring me, Vernius."**

They looked a little shocked, but quickly left to go find him.

Zaros looked at Cornelius before speaking quietly, **"I do not want you to hide what happened next time. I do not want to read someone else's thoughts, to get to the answers I seek. Talk to me, Cornelius."**

"Yes, my lord."

Zaros for a moment smirked, before turning his attention to us and speaking again, **"I request that you enter the top of my study, go up the ladders and there is a small seating area on top. Stay there, stay silent. But I do not want you to leave the office space. Understood?"**

We all nodded, and we went to the ladders, suddenly wondering why he wanted us to stay when it clearly would have been better for us to leave the office and come back later after he dealt with his punishment.

*****

It was a few minutes later when the guards returned with Vernius. He was a tall, dark-skinned Carpathian, with thick wavy black hair. His chin jutted out slightly, and he seemed rather arrogant. At least, that is what I got off of him upon entrance. He walked with authority with every step, however, I noticed that he was slightly nervous, his fingers lingered at his side for a moment before he spoke, "You requested me, my lord?"

Zaros did not hide his emotions, and he looked up from his desk before locking eye contact with Vernius and speaking, **"Did you strike Cornelius?"**

Vernius Adam's Apple bobbed before he replied, "That I did."

**"Why?"**

"Because I thought he was solely trying to get the prisoners out for a feast. That is what others have attempted to do when they noticed two newbies heading down there."

**"How often does Cornelius request to go on our hunting trips? Or actually feed, Vernius?"**

Vernius swallowed hard before whispering, "Not often, my lord. What is this about, if I may ask?"

**"It is because you struck Cornelius, Vernius. He was on my direct order. What did he tell you?"**

"He told me that you had requested their release, and to be brought up to your office."

**"And what did you do to him after he said that?"**

"I jabbed him in the jaw before he said to bring the two new accounts from the dungeons. I know that you solely are the one that say accounts, then people."

**"That is correct, that is my go-to phrase when I say that, Vernius. Which is why I am perturbed that you hit someone who was doing my bidding."**

"I apologize, Zaros."

Zaros drummed his fingers onto the desk, before leaning into it and replying, **"You owe Cornelius ten darics, for the hit, and you owe me twelve darics. For the inconvenience."**

Vernius let out a nearly soundless whine at the total, and it seemed that the guards themselves were shocked by the amount that was said.

Vernius fished into his pouch on his hip, pulled out the amount that was told, and placed the stacks onto the desk. He stepped backward and swallowed hard. Zaros approached the stacks, when Vernius quickly whipped out his sword, and tried to slash Zaros's stomach. A collective gasp went up in the audacity that he had done. However, he was no longer standing. Faster than he could move, Zaros had whipped his blade out and killed him within mere seconds of being slashed. Vernius's body dropped to the ground, and his head tumbled a few times and stopped at Cornelius's feet.

Zaros placed his weapon onto his desk before staring at the bloody mess his eyes stared murderously at the guards before barking, "**GET. EVERYONE. IN. THE. DARKNESS.**"

"YES, MY LORD!"

They chorused and quickly disappeared. Zaros's eyes rose to us, before he spoke with venom venom-laced voice, "**Stay here, please. I do not want any of you to leave my office.**"

"Okay. We will stay."

"**Cornelius, stay with them. You did nothing wrong, but the people have some questioning actions. I need to figure out who disobeyed my orders.**"

"Yes, my lord."

Zaros grabbed his bloody sword and was about to walk out when Cornelius stopped him. Zaros froze and turned his murderous eyes towards him, but Cornelius did not even swallow hard before speaking, "May I wipe your sword off, my lord?"

Zaros looked down at his bloody weapon before replying, "**Fine, but do it fast, Cornelius.**"

"Of course."

Cornelius quickly got a piece of fabric and wiped the blade off quickly, before handing it back to Zaros, who thanked him and looked up at us. Zaros's eyes were glinting in rage, but he spoke with calmness, "**Do not leave.**"

"**We won't,**" replied Fergus. Zaros nodded once, before disappearing into the main area.

# Chapter 49

We watched as Zaros left the room, before I spoke to Cornelius, "The darkness?"

Cornelius swallowed before whispering, "The place that you came out from. That is called the darkness. It is the place where Zaros has people meet their end, without everyone knowing that they are being hunted."

"How often is this carried out?"

"Very rarely. No one wants to cross Zaros. He may be better than Dracula in several things, but he is still a good ruler. He has some things that he does not tolerate, and this is one of them."

"What does he not tolerate?" asked Oswald.

Cornelius sighed before going to the ladder and climbed up. We were all sitting at the table there, there was one more seat that was not in use. Cornelius sat down with a grumble before speaking, "He does not tolerate his people ignoring his direct rules. He is very firm on the feeding habits, which I am sure you were talking about before Oswald and Aurelin were brought up. I will allow you to fill them in on that if you wish them to know. Along with, anyone going down to the dungeons, no one is allowed down there except for a certain few Carpathians, and now that Vernius has said that others have requested Oswald and Aurelin's blood, that makes him furious. Since no one is really allowed down there. So, he will weed out the ones that had requested the new additions, and…. Well… he is very firm on the belief that they do not deserve to live longer than that."

There was silence for a few moments, before I asked, "So what happens to the ones that are not guilty?"

"They live as they are. After everyone who has committed the crime has met their end, he dismisses everyone."

"What happens if they are the fathers or mothers of your children?"

"Not possible here."

**"Why not?"**

"Because the majority of the Carpathians here are barren. They cannot have children, so in more than one way, they were sent here from their communities, since they knew Zaros would take anyone who doesn't have a home. At least, with other Carpathians. Unless you challenge his rules, you don't really have to worry about him too often."

"So, to clarify, these mass massacres are of the Carpathians who cannot have children at all?" Aurelin asked.

Cornelius cut his eyes to him before his eyes looked at me for a fleeting second, he replied, "Correct. But at the same time, they are not massacring."

"They are massacres if you round up people only to kill them all over again."

"Zaros is very strict on who gets killed and who doesn't. Zaros will know who committed the crimes, and who hasn't. Zaros knows how to weed them out."

"How does he know the difference?"

"Because he has the ability to read people's thoughts, and minds overall. He is not some Carpathian who does not understand how to not do this. He is part of the strand that knows how to do this easily. I don't know if Dracula can, but I assume he does know how to."

"Regardless, how does he know the difference between those who have thoughts of doing it and the ones who had done it?"

Cornelius sighed deeply before muttering, "I am starting to question why I am even here."

"Because Zaros told you to stay with us," replied Aurelin helpfully.

Cornelius looked at me with a pleading look in his eyes, and I sighed deeply again before speaking, "Alright everyone. Yes, Zaros is going to do something that no one really wants to hear. However, he has his people to take care of. My now question is, now what? What are we going to do?"

"What do you mean?"

"Do we stay here for a few days, or try to leave as soon as Zaros gets back?"

**"I would suggest that we head up to the cavern that we came down from."**

"And do what exactly?"

**"You said it yourself in your chambers, Cornelius, that you wanted to go up there and look around."**

"That was until after Zaros told me of what was up there."

**"He told you?"**

"Yes, he told me. He only came into my chambers because of what he overheard. Otherwise, he would have left us alone."

"What are we missing here?" asked Aurelin, who looked equally confused as Oswald.

I sighed deeply before running my right hand across my face and summing up, "While the two of you were taken down to the dungeons, might I add was a very dangerous thing you managed to do without getting killed. However, myself and Fergus were brought up here after I told Zaros of who I was. Along with being brought to Cornelius. We talked for a while and soon Zaros himself entered the room, and informed us why we cannot go up to the cavern we came down from."

It took a moment before Oswald asked, "Wait, why not?"

**"Because it is being guarded by a dragon."**

"A dragon, dragon. Or one of them?"

He pointed straight at me, as he said the last part. Thakur purred under the attention, and I rolled my eyes in response. The needy beast. However, after a few seconds, Cornelius replied, "Dragon, dragon. The ones that do not shift back into any other form."

"I thought they were all slaughtered in the great purge centuries ago."

"That is what was believed. I thought that myself, until after Zaros informed me."

Silence met his words for a moment, and finally, Aurelin looked like he was going to ask another question when Fergus spoke, **"Regardless of what we do next, we have not slept for the last twenty or so hours. Cornelius, are we safe here to fall asleep?"**

"No one would dare enter into Zaros's office without his direct permission. Otherwise… well, you all saw what his temper is like."

We all nodded and Fergus looked at me before speaking, **"Any way that you two can shift into a wolf, and we sleep next to you?"**

"I mean we can, but why?"

**"More comfortable than sleeping on hardwood floors."**

"I guess that is fair."

I stood up and hesitated for a moment before looking at Cornelius with a look before I shifted into my wolf. I shook myself out, stretched out before trotting to the corner, and laid down. I blinked my blue eyes up at them, before placing my head onto my paws.

Aurelin looked at me for a moment, sighing as he yawned, stood up, and shifted to his wolf. He trotted to the opposite corner and lay down. We were bigger than common wolves, and it looked like it, for a moment, that Oswald and Fergus were not going to use us as planned. However, Cornelius spoke softly, "Their wolves are rather large."

**"In the werewolf population, the larger the wolf, the more power he or she has. So, these ones look like they are betas or almost alpha ranking. This is what I would take for Aurelin's wolf since he is the son of a werewolf. However, what caught me off guard is how big Quinn's wolf is."**

I lifted my head before replying, since they could all hear my thoughts, "Keep in mind that I am a demon. Thakur is rather large for who he is. Everything of mine is larger than the common ones that are seen."

"Interesting."

**"What is interesting?"**

"Perhaps the dragon knew that you four were important in something, and did not kill you because of your destinies."

**"That is a possibility. The only way to know for sure though, is by asking him."**

"Why are you four set on trying to fry yourselves alive?"

**"Because we need answers. And so far, he may be the only one to answer some of the harder and older questions. It was believed that all the dragons were killed off centuries ago. How often do you actually meet a dragon, that is not a shifter?"**

Cornelius went to answer, but I huffed at Fergus before speaking in my thoughts, "We do not know how long the darkness will take, Fergus. Come on, come sleep on us as you said. We can touch base on this later after we wake up."

**"Fine, I cannot argue with your logic at this current time frame."**

Fergus stood up, moved towards me, and sat down before scooting himself backward until he was up against my side. I turned my head slightly and looked at him before looking at Oswald as he curled up beside Aurelin. I looked at Cornelius before speaking, "Are you going to stand watch?"

"You will be safe, regardless. But yes, I will remain awake."

"Thank you."

I lowered my head back down, closed my eyes, and drifted into a slumber.

*****

I headed into the entrance of the darkness. I felt everyone's fear in the room, but since no one could see anything, they did not know why they were called down there. I went to the area

615

that I had become used to knowing in the darkness before I addressed everyone, "**It has come to my attention that some of you have requested to feast off of the two new additions to my dungeons, and have tried to go get them WITHOUT my permission.**"

Silence met me, and I looked into the darkness. No one could see me, but I had a fair idea of where everyone else was. Since I had been taught how to train inside this very hall with my father. It was somewhere that even I knew that no one else could know the ins and outs without knowing where the secrets. I opened my connection to hear everyone's thoughts and found the five that were the ones that have approached Vernius. My eyes flashed dangerous, but no one knew that, since no one could see me.

I silently walked through the people and soon found one of them. I removed my blade before killing the man before me. He crumbled to the ground. I moved to the next, and the next, and the next. Finally, everyone who had tried to get into the dungeons had perished. I stayed where I was for a moment before calling out, "**DISMISSED.**"

The survivors scrambled out of the darkness, and after a few minutes, I exited the hall. I was met with a few startled guards before one bowed to me and whispered, "My lord?"

"**What is it, Erabius?**"

"Are the rumors true? That you allowed outsiders inside the mountain without being used for nourishment?"

I paused before surveying the crowd before replying, "**They had come down from the mountain shaft.**"

A collective gasp sounded since no one was able to go up there and live. So, the fact that they had come from his cavern, meant that it was something special. Erabius swallowed before whispering, "I apologize, my lord. Forgive me."

I looked at him before replying, "**As long as you know your place, we are fine. Those who went against my ruling have already met their end.**"

"Should I try to find…"

"**No.**"

"Yes, my lord."

The rest of the people scattered after a moment, and soon I was left alone. I sighed deeply before sighing deeply. My sword hung limply in my hand, blood dripping onto the cavern floors before a timid guard came forward. I looked at him with a hard look for a moment. He bowed to me and held out his hand towards my blade. I handed him my sword, and he quickly wiped off the blood from those who had gone against me, without a word. He bowed, as he backed away, and disappeared through a tunnel entrance. I sighed deeply as I walked back towards my office. I paused before entering it, before closing my eyes and turning around slightly. With my back to the wall, I said, "**I hear your thoughts, come on out.**"

A timid guard stepped out of a room and approached me. I knew everyone by name and I sighed deeply as I spoke, "**What can I do for you, Felius?**"

"My lord, is it true that you have people that were not brought to the nutrition area?"

"**That is correct, Felius.**"

"Why are you hiding them from the public? You never hide the sacrifices."

"**They aren't sacrifices.**"

"They aren't?"

"**No, they came from the cave shaft.**"

"But that means the dragon did not harm them. How is that possible?"

"**I do not know his motives, Felius.**"

"Understood."

He twirled his fingers together, and I had a feeling he had something else to ask but was wary of asking. I sighed before turning completely to him, and gave him my complete attention before asking, "**What is it, Felius?**"

"It's nothing, my lord."

"**Do not lie to me. I know it is not nothing. Do not make me look into your thoughts.**"

He swallowed before dropping his eyes, he swallowed hard before speaking slowly, "I wish to leave your mountain, my lord."

I was not expecting that request, and after a moment I replied, "**Why?**"

"Because I want to travel the world. See the differences that are sure to be out there. And possibly even see if I have a mate somewhere."

I sighed deeply, I knew Felius was told to come to my mountain since he had not found his mate back a century ago. Therefore, she could be alive now, and would not even know he existed. I sighed deeply again before replying, "**Do you have a ring?**"

"No, my lord."

"**Go see Helius for your ring.**"

"Thank you, my lord!"

He turned to leave, before I spoke again, "**You do know the customs of my mountain at this point, Felius. If you come back with your mate, then you both get moved up a few chambers.**"

He paused and looked back at me with a small smile, before leaving. I offered that to any of my people who are under my care. If they desire to go out into the world and find their mates, they can leave as they want. Along with taking a daylight ring. They get the couple's rooms, and they are higher up in the mountain. My chambers are higher, but my office is down here, so I am available for the people who need my ruling. I turn back to my office before hearing the gentle breathing already. A small smile came across my face, and I turned around and went back to the main section of my mountain, leaving the guests to their slumber in peace.

*****

I woke up after a few hours it seemed, I would have stretched but Fergus was against me, and by the sound of his breathing, he was still passed out. I sighed and looked up at Cornelius who was staring at a wall. I looked at the others and found that they were still passed out. I sighed deeply, drawing Cornelius's attention before speaking, "How long has it been?"

"Five hours."

"And Zaros has not come back yet?"

"He was outside the door about an hour ago. I believe he heard you all sleeping, and left you to it."

"Is that a normal thing for him to do?"

"Unsure since not many people are allowed to be inside his office. Unless they request his audience."

"Ah. Well… Should I wake them up?"

"No, let them sleep. I have a feeling that you are going to do something that Zaros is not going to approve of entirely."

"You know we kind of have to ask the questions though."

"I know that personally. However, he is different. He may not allow you to go back up there."

"When we exit the mountain, then Thakur will fly us up to the mountain entrance."

Cornelius shook his head and sighed deeply. However, it did not wake anyone else up. I looked at Fergus and then at Aurelin and Oswald before I looked back at Cornelius. I sighed a bit before speaking again, "It is not like we want to go against him, you know. However, the dragon may have answers to something that we need."

**"Like what exactly?"**

Cornelius jumped slightly, and Zaros came up the ladder and stared at us. He looked at everyone else, who was passed out asleep. His eyes landed once again on mine, I sighed slightly before replying, "Like what does he know of the past? There has to be other things that he knows more about overall."

Zaros looked like he wanted to challenge that, but he leaned against the guard rail before replying, "**And you think you will get the answers you seek if you go back up there and irritate the dragon?**"

"I wouldn't call it irritating the dragon. I have a feeling he let us go because of Thakur since he flew up there in a dragon form. So, I have a feeling he will at least talk to me."

**"And if he wants to roast you alive for disturbing his peace?"**

"Then I will gladly take the heat from him. But I have a feeling we were met to meet him."

Zaros would have said something more, but Oswald started to talk in his sleep, "*Corimid. Will answer questions. He knows all. Sees all.*"

Zaros and I looked at him sharply. Fergus jolted awake and stared at Oswald before whispering, "**What did he just say in his sleep?**"

**"Corimid. Will answer questions. He knows all. Sees all. Do you know someone named Corimid?"**

Zaros looked directly at Fergus who looked a little confused. He replied, "**Oswald is different than anyone else. His mother was my seer in my old tribe. He, of course, does not know that, so no one says anything. However, I have a feeling that Corimid is the dragon you have in the cavern up there.**"

**"How are you so sure of that?"**

**"Who else knows all, and sees all?"**

Zaros grumbled slightly before replying, "**I guess that is fair, even I don't know all. Cornelius, are you going to join them?**"

I looked at Cornelius and saw him hesitate, before I replied, "I am unsure if that is wise though. Cornelius is at home in your mountain, not with the outside world. Along with the fact, that your mountain is rather secluded and probably won't be on the radar of the hunters."

Zaros stared at me before replying, **"I've heard about these hunters. If the rumors are true, then they will find any hidden communities, regardless of how secluded they are."**

"What you have up there though, may stop them from entering your mountain. I doubt that they would try to tackle a dragon to get to you."

Zaros sighed deeply and replied, **"As I said before, he does what he wants. I cannot control his motives. We don't even go up there to see him. I have never once seen him personally. So, I have not the slightest idea of what color he is either."**

**"Interesting."**

Zaros sighed deeply and shrugged before looking at us all, and I noticed that Aurelin did not wake up yet before I spoke, "Do you have any supplies that we can have? Since I am pretty sure that you had taken what was up with us."

**"Nothing came down, so Corimid may have your things. But I will still supply you with what you need."**

"Thank you."

Cornelius swallowed hard, and looked at Zaros before speaking, "Would I be allowed back if I decided to come back here, Zaros?"

**"Yes. You know my customs here as is, Cornelius. You did nothing wrong. Just head down to Helius for your ring."**

"Ring?"

**"Carpathians cannot walk in sunlight, otherwise, we burn up and die. We have daylight rings."**

**"How in the world did you manage to get daylight rings?"**

**"I cannot answer that."**

I could tell that Fergus wanted to challenge that, but I sighed deeply, waking Oswald and Aurelin, who were still sleeping until then. They jolted awake and looked wildly around for a moment, but finally, they sighed deeply and Oswald rubbed his eyes and yawned. He did not appear like he knew what had happened. Fergus looked at us all sharply and shook his head. Zaros sighed deeply after a moment, **"What supplies do you need?"**

I looked at Fergus and cocked my head to the side, and he sighed deeply before listing, **"Baskets if you have them, dried beef, a cooking pot, flint...."**

**"Why dried beef?"**

**"It lasts longer than fresh."**

"That is true. Zaros, would you want me to stop by the kitchen to get some of their supplies?"

**"That works for me, Cornelius, since they have to wait for you to get back."**

"Why do we have to wait for him to get back?" Aurelin asked.

Zaros looked at him and sighed deeply before replying, "**Because that is my order.**"

Aurelin looked like he was going to challenge, it but I huffed at him and he gave me a look, but kept quiet. I looked back at Zaros and replied, "Understood."

Zaros straightened himself back up before angling himself to go back down his ladder. Fergus spoke, "**You seem rather calm in us going.**"

Zaros paused and looked at Fergus before replying, "**Because it is not in my discretion to stop you from what you are going to do. I may highly suggest, otherwise, but I don't believe that you would follow my directions. At least, not entirely. Especially, after all that I have overheard. It is clear that two of you are not accustomed to hiding your thoughts, and the other two can.**"

Fergus frowned before he glanced at me and Aurelin. I shrugged before replying, "That may be true, that we had no training in that field. However, there are not many people that can read minds where we come from either."

**"That may be true, but you also have to know that the dragon will know the old ways. I am pretty sure we had traded blood with his father at one point since not many other Carpathians can mind speak."**

**"That doesn't make sense if all of your people can do the same thing though. It would make more sense if the walls of the cavern and chambers were enhanced with something,"** replied Fergus.

Zaros looked like he would say something else, but seemed to think better of it before he went backward, disappearing.

*****

I went down to the ring bearer room, where countless rings were in small crescents of the wall. Felius was also down there, already engaged in conversation with Helius, who looked like he wanted to strangle him. It was very rare, that someone asked for a ring, and the fact that both of us were allowed to go into the day, meant that we wouldn't be needed for much. Helius glanced up from his conversation with Felius and spoke, "What do you want, Cornelius?"

"I need a daylight ring. Zaros sent me down here to get one."

"How do I know that this isn't a trick? First Felius, and now you? Didn't you say at one point that you did not want to go back out in the real world?"

"That I did, Helius. However, my nephew is here and I am going to join him in his adventure."

"Nephew? I thought that you were not allowed to see him again."

"He came on his own accord, Helius."

"Ah, go ahead and pick any one of them that you want. Preferably that they fit you. So, test them out."

"Thank you, Helius."

He grunted in response and looked down at Felius who was about a head or two shorter than him. Felius looked perturbed for a moment before speaking, "You know as well as I do, Helius, that Zaros let us out in the day too! Come on, give me a ring."

"I was not informed that you were allowed a ring, Felius."

"Were you informed that Cornelius was in need of a ring, Helius?"

Helius scowled before replying, "Cornelius has been under this mountain longer than yourself, Felius, I trust him more."

Felius sighed hard before muttering, "I was sent down here by Zaros himself, and now you won't give me a ring because you do not trust my word. How is that possible anyhow? I have been down here for a century and a half, and you now don't trust me. What made you stop trusting people, Helius?"

"When people come for rings and do not do what Zaros had told them to do."

That caught my attention, I turned around before asking, "Like what exactly do they not do, Helius?"

I had a ring on my left-hand ring finger, and he looked down at the ring before looking back at my face and replying, "Feed on humans that Zaros has deemed for. There have been countless Carpathians that have come through here, and go against what Zaros's orders are."

"Have you informed Zaros of this?"

"I didn't want to trouble him with such affairs, Cornelius."

"But you are actually helping the ones that are getting away with this behavior. When Zaros finds out, then it would look bad on you not saying anything to him on this topic."

Helius looked conflicted for a moment. He turned his attention to Felius before asking him, "What do you plan on doing with the ring, Felius?"

"I plan on traveling the world, and looking for my mate."

"I thought you had been kicked out of your community solely based on the fact that you couldn't find your mate back a century ago."

"That is true, but a century is a hundred years, Helius. I believe that my mate is out there somewhere, without the knowledge I exist since of how remote this mountain is."

Helius sighed deeply,  gesturing to the rings before muttering, "Fine, find a ring, and get out of my hair."

"Thank you, Helius."

Helius grunted in acknowledgment, and I looked at him before speaking, "You know I speak the truth, though right? If you don't tell Zaros about the ones that take rings without Zaros permission, then you are their accomplice in this."

"Alright, alright. I'll tell him."

He looked conflicted again, and I was suddenly wondering who they were for his hesitation, but I knew better than to ask that question. I had no business in asking that question. I looked down at the ring, and looked at the little rubies embedded in the black band before I looked at Helius and said, "I picked this ring."

He approached and looked at it with a hmph before replying, "**That is a good ring. Whatever adventure you are on, I hope it is filled with adventure.**"

"Oh, believe me, it will be filled with that."

He chuckled slightly, before turning his attention to Felius who had a ring on his right ring finger, and was looking down at it with a small frown. He sighed, and clapped his right hand onto my shoulder, speaking, "Be safe out there, Cornelius."

"I will try. You try not to get in trouble more, Helius."

He barked out a laugh but turned around and went towards Felius. I turned out of the ring bearer area and went to the kitchens.

*****

It was a few minutes, but soon I made it to the kitchens, and I walked in as a big puff of steam came up from the hot cauldron that was being stirred with some sort of stew. Yes, Carpathians survived off of actual food too, it is not always blood. Although we do tend to eat raw foods more than anything else. The cook, Cervix, was behind the steam and she waved the steam away before barking out, "What do you want?"

I swallowed hard before replying, "Zaros ordered me to ask for a few baskets of dried goods."

She stepped away from the cauldron before snapping, "Dried goods? You know that we do not really carry said items. However, I will send you along with some of our freshly made canned goods."

"Thank you, Cervix."

She hmphed before she turned to a kitchen aid, barking at him, "Stay here and stir this. Do not let it burn again!"

"Yes, Cervix!" He mumbled.

I swallowed and glanced at Cervix as she went beyond the cauldron and went to get a few bags of something. I stayed where I was, since the last time that anyone that was not kitchen staff entered further into the kitchen, was hit with a scalding metal spoon, that was near the coals of the fires.

After a few minutes, she appeared again, and dropped three baskets at my feet, before looking at me with a hard expression across her face and shaking her head. She turned away and came back after a moment with fire starters and a few knives. She placed them into a basket, straightening out before she eyed me thoughtfully. "And where are you going that you need these supplies? It appears that you got approved to leave since you have a ring on your finger."

I looked down at the daylight ring, then looked back at her and replied, "My nephew came back on his own accord, and now I am joining him in his endeavors."

She looked at me with a raised eyebrow before shrugging and replying, "Have with that. You better come back here at some point and tell me about it."

My jaw dropped slightly Cervix never said anything like this to anyone else, to my knowledge. Even her kitchen aid looked sharply at her from the steam that was coming off of the pot. I swallowed and bowed to her as I gathered up the three baskets, and noticed that two were significantly heavier than the third. I swallowed and wondered how I was going to get it up to Zaros's office without dropping it. She seemed to come to the same conclusion since she went back to the cauldron before snapping at the kitchen aid, "Help him take his baskets wherever he is going. Then come back immediately."

"Yes, Cervix!"

He stepped back, and walked briskly to me, picking up the two heavier baskets, and looked at me with expectant eyes. I cast my eyes onto the steam cloud before speaking, "Thank you."

"Get going."

But in her voice, she sounded rather pleased that I personally thanked her for the goods.

****

I looked at her kitchen aid and turned around after I had picked up the basket. I walked through the halls and soon came back to Zaros's office, where the kitchen aid hesitated before entering his office.

The kitchen aid followed after a moment, and placed the baskets onto the ground before bowing to me, turning around, and pausing at the door before speaking, "Something is different about Cervix when she talked to you."

I looked at him and replied, "I thought that myself too."

He nodded and departed quickly since Cervix was not one to have the patience for chit-chats.

******

I looked up the ladders and sighed before climbing up, and finding that they were still up there, but they had blades against their throats. Four Carpathians were holding their blades nestled against their throats. They did not see me, and I crept back down and immediately went to find Zaros.

# Chapter 50

I went to the known areas where Zaros tends to hang around when he was not in his chambers or office. But did not find him in any of them. I swallowed hard before going up to the level where his chambers were, since no one went to his chambers, everyone knew better than to go to them. I, however, was in no condition to go against four Carpathians who were going to harm my nephew. I hesitated at his door, and finally worked up my courage and knocked twice. For a moment, there was no sign of movement, and I started to second-guess myself when Zaros opened his door.

He looked at me with a hard look before speaking, **"What do you possibly want now, Cornelius?"**

"Ummm… there are four Carpathians inside your office."

He squinted his eyes before growling, **"Of course, someone is in there."**

He turned around and grabbed his sword, and departed. His trench coat that he wore flared behind the brisk pace that he set. We soon made it down to his office, and Zaros placed his fingers across his lips. I nodded at him in understanding, knowing better than to speak.

*****

Zaros entered his office before climbing the ladder, and speaking, **"What are you doing?"**

The Carpathians, who I thought would have surely departed before now, froze. Two of them had Oswald in their grasp and were drinking his blood, while the other two held their weapons against the throats of Aurelin and Quinn. While, Fergus, lay on the ground in a bloody heap. They swallowed before removing their fangs from Oswald, one of them replied, "Drinking from those that you are hiding apparently."

**"They were not food."**

"Anyone that is brought here, is food."

**"Are you challenging my authority?"**

"Yes and no."

They swallowed and all of them looked like they had recently fed since their faces were more colored than anyone else. Meaning they had fed from Fergus before moving to Oswald, sparking Zaros's anger. He pulled himself upright and looked at the four before him before growling, "**Since when does anyone enter my office without my consent?**"

"Are you saying that these had your consent to be in here?"

"**Yes.**"

They were silent, and two of them eyed Zaros's grip on his sword before their eyes flickered to mine and they sneered before speaking, "Even Cornelius is allowed?"

"**Cornelius has my consent. You four do not.**"

They were silent for a moment before I spoke, "Did you kill them?"

"What makes it your issue?"

"Answer my question, did you kill them?"

"We do not answer to you."

"**But you do answer to me. Did you kill them?**"

They swallowed before they looked at Fergus before one muttered, "I wanted to, but the others reminded me of your rule inside of this mountain."

Zaros looked at the Carpathian sharply before his eyes sparked in rage. He hissed, "**Wolves, shift back.**"

For a moment, I looked at the back of Zaros as if he was nuts in asking Quinn and Aurelin to shift back. After a moment, they both did, surprising all four of the Carpathians. They swallowed hard before they eyed both of them, who actually were carrying their weapons. Quinn had the most, and Aurelin looked like he had a few.

Zaros looked at them before speaking in a quiet deadly voice, "**What are some of my top rules in my mountain?**"

The Carpathians shuffled their feet and one mumbled, "No one enters your office without consent. No one is to suck the ones that cannot leave the mountain dry, they are to be treated fairly. No stealing from others. Knock before entering…."

"**And how many rules have you broken already? And what tends to happen to those who ignore them?**"

They all swallowed before one whispered, "It was my idea, not theirs."

"**Regardless of whose idea it was, all of you are guilty in this action since NONE OF THE OTHERS sought me.**"

Zaros's voice rose in rage, and after a moment he stopped talking. The Carpathians before him shrunk down in fear. I looked at them before speaking, "Quinn, you okay?"

The Carpathians glanced at Aurelin and Quinn. Quinn replied, "Would you be if roles were reversed?"

I sighed deeply and knew that he was right. I would not be at the greatest point of this. I looked at Zaros's back before he spoke again, "**Throw down your weapons.**"

"I would rather not," replied one of the Carpathians. It was clear to me though, that they all knew their end fate, and the fact that they refused to throw their weapons down, sealed it further. Zaros gripped his sword before growling, "**It was not a suggestion.**"

"I would rather fight for my life than be slaughtered where I stand. I will not go down the way that it appeared that Vernius did."

"Vernius tried to attack Zaros, he had it coming."

Zaros turned his head slightly in my direction but did not look at me directly, but I could almost hear his tongue lashing if I continued to speak. I fell silent and mumbled, "My apologies, Zaros."

He turned his head back to the four in front before speaking, "**Throw your weapons down.**"

"No."

"**Do it.**"

"No, like I had said. I would rather go down fighting than being slaughtered where I stand."

Zaros gripped his blade before replying, "**Then let my guests leave your positions.**"

"No."

"**No?**"

"Yes, no. I am not in the mood to let your so-called guests out of our area since you would simply try to kill us afterward."

"**It wouldn't be trying. I would instantly kill you.**"

"See? My point exactly."

I saw the look written across Aurelin's and Quinn's faces as they looked at the four Carpathians before them. Quinn threw out his thought towards me and Zaros, and somehow managed to block it from the Carpathians before him, "Are they good as dead?"

Zaros stared at Quinn, nodding his head slightly. Quinn replied, "Then I will take care of them."

"They are harder to kill than you think."

"Doubtful."

Surprising me and Zaros when his voice changed. He blinked once and his eyes showed a different color all of a sudden. Aurelin glanced at him and backed a step away, but did not draw attention to them.

Zaros glanced at me with a side eye, but it seemed that he understood what was about to happen. He did not remove his hand from his sword handle though before he addressed the Carpathians before him, **"One last chance. Throw your weapons down."**

"No."

Zaros locked eye contact with Quinn's demon and nodded once. He took a step backward, and the Carpathians in front of him scoffed before one of them yelped.

 His comrades looked at Quinn sharply, but he had the Carpathian's heart in his hand that he had ripped from his chest in one fluid movement. His eyes showed glee in the death, as the body tumbled to the ground next to Fergus. I swallowed hard as the other three Carpathians tried to kill him, but they quickly learned that they had no chance before him. Quinn did not remove his sword, at all. Not once did he grab the handle of it, and ripped another Carpathian's arm off, and blood poured out of the wound, making the Carpathian scream in pain. He instinctively grabbed his stump of an arm and tried to stop the bleeding, but Quinn's demon did not hesitate as he moved to the other two. After a few minutes, none of them were alive. They were a bloody mess on the ground and wall.

Quinn was caked in their blood, along with Aurelin, who looked like he was used to this. He did not even wipe his face from the blood splatter from his face. Showing both Zaros and myself, that this was not the first time. I felt the unease flow from Zaros, but he was quickly able to hide it before Quinn's demon blinked once and faded from Quinn's eyes.

Quinn swayed for a moment, before looking at the bloody mess before mumbling, "I am sorry about how...."

**"It is fine."**

"Do you need help in cleaning up this mess?"

**"I'll have someone else do it."**

"Okay."

Quinn glanced down at Fergus before dropping to his knees and checking his pulse, sighing in relief. Aurelin checked Oswald's before nodding his head at Quinn. Quinn sighed in relief before looking up at Zaros before speaking, "We need to stay a day or so. Until they can be functional. Is that okay with you, Zaros?"

**"Stay as long as you need."**

"Thank you."

Quinn rocked back onto his heels, before standing up and looking at the bodies that his demon had dropped before sighing deeply. He picked up Fergus, who looked heavier than Quinn himself, but he picked him up as if he was not a burden. Aurelin picked up Oswald, before Quinn spoke to me, "Cornelius, would it be okay if we stay in your chambers?"

"Of course."

"Thank you."

Zaros looked at me and we locked eye contact for a brief second before Quinn looked down into the office. He had Fergus in a fireman carry. His eyes flashed once before he shifted with Fergus in tow. He flew down in a bird, landed, and shifted back. Fergus was still in the same position as the last time he was up here. Making Zaros stare at him in shock, he placed Fergus down, before climbing up and grabbing Oswald from Aurelin before doing it again.

Aurelin got down the normal way, picked up Oswald on the ground, then looked at Quinn for a moment and nodded once. Quinn looked up at me before speaking, "Are you going to escort us to your chambers, Cornelius?"

I looked at Zaros bowed slightly, and he connected to me, *"Come back after they have entered your chambers. I think we need to talk."*

*"Okay."*

I turned around, went back down the ladder, and lifted the heavier basket before I walked towards the office door. I looked back after a moment and saw that Quinn and Aurelin had also picked up the baskets, and were carrying them in one hand - showing that they were rather strong. I looked up at Zaros and knew that he did not miss anything. I dipped my head towards him, before leading them to my chambers.

*****

I was thankful when I had the first choice of the chambers that were opened since they had two bedrooms. I directed them into the spare room, where Quinn placed Fergus and Aurelin placed Oswald side by side. Quinn looked at me before speaking, "You can go to your meeting with Zaros, Cornelius. We will be safe here."

"How did you know that we have a meeting?"

"By the way that the two of you looked at each other. I had filled in the pieces of the needed information. Go."

"You sure?"

"Cornelius, you witnessed what I can do without a weapon. Do you really think that I cannot defend ourselves?"

I swallowed backed away from him and bowed slightly in his general direction before I turned around, to head out. When a thought occurred to me, I turned around to look at Quinn before speaking, "Did Killian teach you how to fight without the use of weapons?"

"It is also a shifter practice. We are trained to be good with anything that is available. And even if we have weapons, we do tend to not use them. However, Thakur more of wanted to kill them since they were going to die anyhow."

I nodded in understanding before I turned to leave. Aurelin spoke, "Who were those Carpathians anyhow?"

"Personally, I don't know. And by the sounds of it, Zaros did not address them by name. So, they must have been the most recent members."

"Ah."

Aurelin and Quinn exchanged looks, and Quinn shook his head slightly. I suddenly wondered what they were doing, but nothing was coming into the thought process – that meant they were connecting to each other. I swallowed in the knowledge that I would not know what they were saying. I headed back to Zaros's office after a few hesitated moments.

# Chapter 51

We headed down to the cellars, where Sophronia was watching the cell door where she had placed Logan. Onyx flared in rage for a split second, but I quietly hushed him. I glanced over at Nathaniel and noticed that his eyes changed from Nathaniel's eyes and Basil's a constant switch. His hand clasping and unclasping, as if he was trying to stop himself from hitting something, or someone. I glanced at Sophronia before bowing my head slightly before speaking, "Sophronia."

**"Marius."**

She glanced at Nathaniel before approaching him, and rested her hand on his bicep before whispering, **"Shush honey, it will be alright in the end."**

Nathaniel looked down at her and swallowed before Basil disappeared from his eyes. Nathaniel dropped his eyes to the ground, and Sophronia gently placed her fingers on his chin, and raised his head again, speaking, **"Nuh-uh. Keep your head up, my love."**

I looked away and knew that Nathaniel wished that they were alone, but now that we were down here, I knew that Logan could probably feel Basil through the door and feel the rage rolling off of him in response. I sighed deeply before clearing my throat, drawing Sophronia's gaze towards me, I spoke softly, "Has he said anything, Sophronia?"

**"Not a word."**

**"I think he knows that he is in the wrong at this point. And that his life hangs in the balance of what your mate decides to do."**

Sophronia glanced sharply at Nathaniel and her eyes sparked for a moment before looking at me. I smiled slightly and looked down at the ground. I kept my word and kept the link open with her since I had better control than Nathaniel did with Basil. She sighed before speaking, **"Are you sure she is ready?"**

"Without a doubt. She took everything rather well, along with not bowing or baring her neck to Basil when he does flare up. Along with the fact that she orders Basil around as if he is not the alpha."

Sophronia looked at her mate, whispering, **"She has gone through so much as it is. First being with us for not even a week and being abducted. Along with the fact of whatever they had done to her across the channel. Are you sure you want her in this position, Nathaniel? Have someone that is not even experienced in this?"**

I looked at Sophronia sharply before speaking, "Why are you acting like this is the worst idea? You sounded like Rispin."

Sophronia gave me a sharp look before snapping, "**As much as I had liked Rispin, I am nothing like him. He was a good beta, but nothing more. I can be a protective mother, even though I never got the privilege to raise her as my daughter.**"

"Okay, okay. Sheesh. I was more of bringing it up based on your reaction."

She scowled at me and would have said something else, but Nathaniel chuckled a little before placing his fingers under her chin and drawing her attention to him, speaking, "**She is ready for the role, Sophronia. Most of the pack already respects her.**"

"**You are correct in that honey, most of the pack. But not all.**"

"**There will always be those who do not see the king as their true alpha. It is the same as it is now. Although, I have no idea how long Logan has been working on getting people on his team. According to Rispin, before he got banished, he was ready to challenge Basil tomorrow at noon.**"

Sophronia scoffed before speaking, "**Logan may be powerful, but he is nowhere near Basil's level.**"

"Which is why Rispin also mentioned that he would sabotage Nathaniel in some way."

Sophronia's eyes sparked Evenor's for a fleeting second before she glanced at the cell door. She squinted her eyes before looking further down the dungeon hallway before speaking, "**Gray, open the door.**"

I looked behind me and Gray stepped out of the shadows. He blinked once and stared at me and Nathaniel. I glanced at Nathaniel and saw him stare hard at Gray before Sophronia cleared her throat. Drawing our attention off of Gray, she gave us a pointed look.

Gray comes closer to the door before placing the key into the keyhole and turning it. It shrieked on the hinges as it was opened. Evidence that we should get the doors oiled soon, so they glide open without issues. The door swung inward, revealing the dark cold cell. The only light was from our side now as it crept into the creases of the obsidian blocks.

*****

Logan was huddled against the corner, looking up at me before his eyes flickered to Gray's. He swallowed hard before speaking, "**Marius, Gray.**"

"Logan."

It was clear he did not see Sophronia or Nathaniel, and I glanced behind Gray and saw that Nathaniel's eyes were between Basil's and his. It was clear that Nathaniel may not be ready to interrogate his brother. I sighed slightly before looking at Logan and speaking, "Logan, are you ready to answer questions?"

His eyes showed he was scared, but he spat at me, snapping, "**Oh? Is Nathaniel too scared to do it himself? Sends his gamma down to do his dirty work is he now?**"

I was about to reply, when Basil's aura rolled out, and Logan instantly cowered more. Basil stepped slightly around Gray, who at this point was cowering and keeping his head low. Logan swallowed hard before Basil spoke, "**Gray, thank you. You are dismissed.**"

Gray scrambled to his feet and promptly departed. His footfall was the only sound in the hallway since Sophronia was keeping silent behind the wall. She was leaning against it as if this was an everyday occurrence. I partially wondered if she stayed down because she was keeping Basil to a minimum power.

Logan glanced at Nathaniel before speaking, "**Brother.**"

Basil snarled in response and Logan dropped his eye contact, speaking, "**I am sorry that it had to come to this, brother. It was not entirely planned.**"

"You act like you did not corrupt Arrax, Rispin, and who knows who else. You are the one to blame for some of our best pack members to fall."

Logan frowned before replying, "**I didn't corrupt Arrax, he did that to himself.**"

"But the others?"

"**I had a hand in that.**"

"What did you promise the others that Nathaniel would not have been able to do?"

Logan glanced at Nathaniel and swallowed before replying, "**I'm not going to tell you that.**"

"**It is either tell us on your own, or we force it from you.**"

Logan's Adam's apple bobbed in his throat. He gulped hard before whispering, "**You are going to go low to torture your brother, Nathaniel?**"

"**You caused me more grief than anyone else, Logan. More than one pack. More than one wolf is being corrupted by your beliefs. When you sent my pack members after the humans, that was the last straw. What business do you have with shifter blood?**"

Logan swallowed, Basil was one hundred percent in Nathaniel's voice. Logan seemed to struggle before he hung his head down and spoke, "**I was going to give it to the highest bidder at the human town closest.**"

"What would you gain from doing that?"

"**I doubt you would understand anything, Marius. You do not seem like you are down to what I have found out.**"

"What have you found out?"

"**Huh? As if I would tell you.**"

"**Tell me.**"

Basil rolled out the command, and Logan struggled before finally submitting, "**I found out that the humans want the shifter blood to heal their injuries. Along with giving them a longer life than their normal puny lives. I also found out that the humans created the shifter project to eliminate the werewolves and the vampires. Therefore, we should be working on getting rid of the current shifters.**"

"Not all of them are bred to be what you claim they are."

"**True, but that is what the humans believe anyhow. They believe that the world would be better with only humans and nothing else.**"

"**Is that why they had hired the Sazornoras to hunt the shifters?**"

"**Partially. However, the humans had asked to get a few live specimens of the shifters for the blood bank. However, I doubt that the leader is going to allow that sort of thing. Since they are supernatural hunters. And have been for their entire generations.**"

"How are you so confident in talking about the Sazornoras and the human population? It is almost as if you are friends with the people who will kill everything and everyone you know."

"**It is because I am confident in talking with them. I have actually spoken with Zhukov before, we met at one of the human meetings.**"

"Didn't he comment on you being a supernatural?"

"**He didn't know that I was one.**"

"I think he lied about it then. The Sazonroras seem to know when someone is supernatural and not."

"**As if you know what you are talking about, Marius.**"

I opened my mouth to reply, but Basil side-eyed me and I swallowed and dropped my gaze for a moment. Basil looked at Logan before speaking, "**Enough. Answer my question, Logan, what are the Sazornoras going to do?**"

"**Isn't obvious, Basil? They are going to kill everyone.**"

"Then why are you talking to them?"

Logan swallowed, and that made it suddenly click why he got friendly with the humans and had met Zhukov personally. He was making it harder for them to kill him and possibly whoever was going to follow after him. I glanced at Basil and knew he must have been on the same wavelength as he spoke, "**So, to get this right, you are getting friendly with the enemy because you think they will spare you?**"

"**Partially correct, brother. It also means that I can live with anyone who is with me. So. any pack members that I have already corrupted would be safe.**"

"You do know that the Sazornoras are not ones to really think that would work. They will go back on their promises solely because you are a werewolf."

"**As if they can kill all the werewolves and vampires.**"

"You left the shifters out of that equation."

"**Because Zhukov told me himself that they were hired to go after the shifters. Therefore, I doubt that any of them survive their onslaught.**"

"Hmmm… surely, there is something that can prevent them from killing the shifters."

"**Have you not been listening, Marius? They will be hired to kill the shifters, but they will also kill anyone who stands beside the shifters. This is why I should be king, I would not be beside the shifters. It would become the world it should be.**"

"**The world you are describing, Logan. will never happen.**"

"**Really? Or is that what you solely want to believe, Basil? If we do not gain the shifters, along with placing Rafeor into the leadership role, we won't have a target on our back.**"

"Yes and no on that aspect, Logan. We will still have a target on our backs because we are supernatural beings. And since we are taking prime areas to live, that means the humans will eventually get restless and try to expand. Once they do that, they will try to run us out of our homeland. Who do you think they would want there?"

"**They would want a werewolf pack to protect them, Marius. I wouldn't care if they moved next to the pack lands.**"

"**You are forgetting something here, Logan. If they do, in fact, move this far down, then we would be going after the same resources.**"

**"We can manage without some of our resources if we can live in peaceful neighbors. Not everything is about violence with me, Basil. I agree I have the tendencies of causing issues, but I would seek no harm to the humans and I would be alpha, to make sure none of my pack members starts things with the humans."**

"You are making it seem like you have talked this with the humans. Have you?"

**"I have been keeping in contact with the humans, yes. However, I have been doing it to survive. The Sazornoras will come after the whole supernatural besides the few that the humans have befriended."**

**"How are you so sure that they will be your friend in a few weeks or months after the downgrade of the rest of us?"**

**"I will get a document signed, giving us the section of the land. Along with a peace treaty in a sense. It is the best way I can keep our people safe, Basil. Surely, you thought about doing a peace treaty."**

I glanced at Basil and saw him frown. I glanced at Sophronia and saw her frown before she tapped her forefinger onto her chin before speaking, making Logan jump slightly, **"We were informed by Taryn to not do the peace treaty."**

**"Taryn is a fool that she did not advise you to do it."**

"She is no fool though, I have spoken with her on this topic even. She said that…."

**"No."**

I looked at Basil and saw him staring at me hard. I looked down and fell silent. I knew better than to say anything to Basil. Basil looked at Logan before snapping, **"Are you ready to answer some other questions? Or should I get something to force it out?"**

I heard the rasp of want in Basil's voice, and by the look written across Logan's face, he knew he was in deep shit as is. He swallowed before replying, **"I'll talk as I am currently, Basil."**

Basil slouched slightly as if he was hoping that Logan would say that he would refuse. However, I looked at Logan and saw him swallow hard before asking, **"What is your first question, Basil?"**

**"How many of my pack members do you have under your paw?"**

**"About a third of the pack."**

**"Is that why you thought you had enough pack members behind you to challenge me tomorrow at noon?"**

**"How did you find out?"**

**"Answer my question, Logan."**

Logan swallowed before lowering his head down and mumbled, "**Yes.**"

"**What? A little louder, Logan.**"

Logan lifted his head, looked at Basil, and swallowed before replying, "**Yes.**"

"**Is this what the Sazornoras and humans wanted you to do for them?**"

Logan stared at him, and his jaw dropped slightly before he whispered, "**How did you know to ask that question?**"

Basil growled low in his throat, and Logan swallowed before replying, "**But to answer your question, yes. That is one of the conditions that the humans have come to request. They want a pack that is more open to their needs than anything else.**"

"And you think that they will allow a werewolf pack to live in peace?"

"**Yes, I have their word that if I can get the pack under my authority, they will leave the werewolves alone. Which is why I have insisted to be king.**"

"**Why do you think I would not be open to a peace treaty with the humans?**"

"**Have you seen yourself, Basil? They would not want something so…. Dangerous to be their neighbor.**"

"And you are not considered dangerous, Logan? Have they not witnessed you and your drinking?"

"**Their booze is weaker than the things I have at home.**"

"Did you tell them that you would be able to take the throne?"

Logan clenched his jaw down and did not reply. Proving that he did insist that he was powerful enough to take Basil down without issues. Basil growled, "Well?"

"**I did inform them that you had gone soft over the years, Basil. I thought that you would be easier to take down than a couple of years prior.**"

"**So, how long have you gotten the other wolves underneath you?**"

"**This is coming up on the second- or third-year, Basil.**"

"**Second or third year?**"

"**Yes.**"

"**So, you have thought about becoming alpha for that long?**"

"**Yes, Basil. I have thought about it. Along with most of the pack. You have gone soft, and the older generations are getting restless. Along with the newer generation too.**"

"I don't believe that lots of the generations think that Nathaniel and Basil have gone soft."

**"Belive what you want, Marius, but it is the truth. The majority of the pack thinks that the next in line should be me, and not anyone else. I am after all our father's son too. Therefore. I have a right even before Rafeor."**

**"That's not true. It belongs to the firstborn and the children of theirs. Not the second born and their children."**

**"It is time for things to change, Basil. I have a third of the pack behind me currently."**

**"Are you talking about the ones who are already banished in that number?"**

**"I had considered that, Basil. I knew that you would banish my members slowly but surely. However, they do their jobs without grief and follow it through to the end."**

**"Collateral damage?"**

**"In a way yes, but the ones that you had banished as is knowing that I will allow them back into the pack afterward."**

**"After you challenged me?"**

**"Yes, after I challenged you."**

"How would you challenge, Basil though? He is stronger and makes you cower under his aura as is. How would that work entirely?"

Logan swallowed hard and appeared that he did not want to answer my question. However, Basil growled softly, and Logan finally replied, "**Okay! Okay, fine! I would poison his food or drink in the morning. Then after that, it would be a breeze.**"

**"You would have committed treason in that."**

**"Only if I was caught."**

**"Well, you were caught."**

**"The fact that I am in the cell must give you great pleasure, Basil. What are you going to do with me now though?"**

**"I'm going to let fate decide that."**

Basil turned around and walked down the hallway. I watched him in shock for a moment before moving to follow him, when Logan spoke, "**You do know that the third I have under my paw will not allow anyone besides myself to be king right? Even if a different challenge would happen.**"

I glanced at him before stepping backward, grabbing the door handle on my way out, and slamming it into place.

****

I turned to look at Sophronia who looked confused, she murmured, "**Things are getting worse and worse.**"

Her eyes lifted and I saw tears in her eyes, she whispered, "**And this is the world my child gets to grow up in.**"

I swallowed and gently placed a hand on her shoulder and squeezed it gently in support. She looked at me with a small smile before turning and walking away. I looked at the cell door before calling after her, "Who should I post on the door, Sophronia?"

She paused and turned slightly before replying, "**Only someone you trust.**"

I nodded and would have linked someone when Brego came from the hallway and bowed to Sophronia as she departed. He strolled over to me before speaking, "Get going, Marius. I have the door."

"How did you know?"

"Basil got in contact with Ghost, and he directed me down here."

"Ah."

"The patrol will be on rotation, Marius. I have the first eight hours, and then everyone else will decide on the times that they want to do it. Everyone except for Azier."

"Why not Azier?"

"Because Taryn does not want her down here. Along with the fact, that only males are going to be down here in case."

"Does Azier agree with this rotation?"

"She doesn't get a choice in this. Basil agrees too, so there is that factor also."

"Ah. Yeah, I would assume so."

"Anyhow, get going to your mate. She has her hands full with those three oddball children that she talked in keeping."

I sighed deeply before replying, "So, that is where she went after she took care of Rispin."

"Yeah."

"Okay, thank you."

He nodded once, and I turned to leave. I paused before looking at Brego and asking, "Who is your alpha?"

"King Nathaniel."

"Good."

I turned to leave, when Brego growled, "Why did you ask that question, Marius?"

"You can never be too careful. Heads up, he has about a third of the pack in his claws. So, do not be surprised if someone tries to get him out."

"I will ask the same question that you had asked then."

I nodded in agreement before I turned around and was finally able to go away from him.

# Chapter 52

I went into our bedroom chambers, since Shadow and Rafeor both insisted that the children be in our chambers, Nathaniel had allowed us to move to the bigger chambers. I walked in as Johnathan screamed, "YOU ARE NOT MY MOTHER!"

I instantly growled, "Anyone else would have taken you elsewhere."

Johnathan jumped and looked at me with a hard look before dropping his eyes to the ground. I looked at Rafeor and saw the hurt in her eyes, she whispered, "**I may not be your mother, but I am here now that she has left you.**"

"And whose fault is it that she left us? You killed our father, along with countless others."

"You didn't seem to have an issue with coming with us over the channel, Johnathan. Why the sudden change?"

"There is talk about war as it is. Along with the fact that we do not get along with the other children here. Their eyes change and…."

"Their eyes change because we are werewolves, Johnathan."

**"Not helping Marius."**

I looked at Rafeor before sighing deeply and speaking, "Would you rather not be here, Johnathan?"

"I would rather be home."

"And where is home for you?"

"Across the channel."

I looked at Rafeor and saw her shoulders slump. She replied, "**You don't mean that, do you?**"

"You cannot be serious. There is talk about war, and we would be safe on the other side."

**"Even Espi?"**

"Espi wants to stay here. However, myself and Annie must go back over there."

"Why do you must have to?"

"Because it is not safe over here when you are preparing for war. I have seen the weapons. It is not the place where we should be."

I glanced up at Rafeor and saw the sorrow in her eyes. As much as I want to disagree with him, it may be safer for them across the channel. However, after a moment I replied, "And what? You know as well as anyone. Once you get back over there, there is no one in the mansion where we had raided. Therefore, you would be at the mercy of others."

A whimper escaped Rafeor, and she wrapped her hands across her chest as she thought back to her past. I swallowed and felt the fear in the bond, however, I needed to pass this test. I looked at Johnathan before speaking, "Would you want to place Annie and yourself at the mercy of others?"

"You may be correct, that it may be worse over there, Marius, however, it is not safe over here either. I pride myself on being protective of my siblings, and Espi wants to stay here, but I know it is not where Annie should be. She needs to grow up with other humans."

**"We have a few humans here."**

"They are slaves working for your pack though. This is not the best place for a young girl to grow up. I want to go back across the channel."

Rafeor looked over his head and looked at me with a pleading look. However, I slightly agreed with Johnathan. We were not ready for children, and after what Rafeor has gone through, it means that she will be more likely to be injured. Words hurt a lot when they are spoken in a way of harm. I sighed deeply before replying, "And how do you think you are going to get across? There is no shifter here."

"That's not true. There is a shifter here. Her name is Anna. She can take us across the channel."

I looked at Rafeor and saw her lower her eyes in anguish.  I asked Johnathan, "You may want to go back across the channel, but have you thought about where you would go? Anyone across the channel can, and will abuse you. Just like your father did."

Johnathan sighed deeply. "We need to go back across the channel. Either you help us, or I will find a way to do it alone."

**"Absolutely not."**

"You do not get a fucking say in what I do! You are not my mother!"

Onyx surfaced slightly, and stayed in my eyes as I growled at him, "She may not be your birth mother, but you need to show her some respect, Johnathan! She took you under her wing, and now you want to go back less than five days later."

"I want to go back home!"

**"This is your home!"**

"NO IT IS NOT! I WANT TO GO BACK ACROSS THE CHANNEL!"

We were about to go back and forth on this further when a knock on the door sounded. I glared at Johnathan for a moment before I opened the door. Taryn stared at me and then glanced back at Rafeor before speaking, "Rafeor, Marius. A word?"

I looked at Rafeor and saw her hesitate beside Johnathan before she walked past him, and into the hallway. I glanced at Johnathan and closed the door behind me with a click.

*****

Taryn looked at us both before speaking, "I am sorry Rafeor, however, he is right. He needs to go back across the channel, along with Annie."

"What about Espi?"

"Someone would kill him since he is an albino. They are believed to be bad luck which is false, but anything different is looked down upon. However, I stress that they need to go back over there."

**"Who would take them?"**

"I do not know that answer Rafeor, however, things on this side of the channel are too dangerous. They have to go back over there in the next few days."

"What happens in a few days, Taryn?"

"I cannot tell you what is about to happen. However, I can tell you that it is safer for those children across the channel."

**"What about the other children that we had brought over here?"**

"They stay as they are, Rafeor. Nathaniel has already begun to move them somewhere that should not be affected as much as the…. the event, which is to come up."

Rafeor's shoulders slumped before she whispered, "**Am I being a bad parent?**"

"I wouldn't go that far, Rafeor. You are doing the best you can with what trauma you have endured. However, it is time for them to depart. I know not what you want to hear, Rafeor, however, it has to happen. Otherwise…."

She looked around cautiously before dropping her voice, "Otherwise, they will die, Rafeor. They are not safe here. It is somewhat safer on the other side of the channel since they do not have the werewolf, vampire, or shifter population as this side does."

"So, we have to prepare for war in other words?"

Taryn looked at me with a look before her eyes flickered around before she nodded slightly. I swallowed hard and whispered, "How long do we have?"

"I am sorry, but I cannot answer that question. Nothing is set in stone yet, Marius. And I would rather not say how many I think it could be."

Rafeor sighed deeply and drew Taryn's attention, who approached Rafeor and hugged her. Onyx got a little grumpy that his mate didn't do this together, but Taryn was a woman and it seemed that Taryn knew that Rafeor would need a hug. A hug that only a mother would be able to provide. After a moment, Rafeor pulled herself back a step and Taryn let her go. She looked at me with a small smile before speaking, "I know not the news you want to hear Marius, Rafeor. However, it needs to be done."

**"How do you suggest we do this?"**

Taryn swallowed before looking directly at Rafeor and replying, "You fly them across the channel."

"Wait! Back up. You want my mate to fly them across the channel?"

"Yes."

"Why not the shifter, Anna?"

"Because she is not powerful enough to fly two young children across the channel."

"You sound so sure of that."

**"Because I also know that she is not that powerful. She may be a medical in the shifter community, but that does not mean she is dangerous. Or that she has the stamina to keep flying for two ways."**

I groaned and closed my eyes as I knew that there was nothing more than that I could do. I looked at Taryn before asking, "When?"

**"The earlier the better I think. Right, Taryn?"**

"Yes, that is correct."

**"I will depart immediately then."**

Rafeor turned around to go back through the door, when I asked Taryn a question, "Is there any danger in the water at this time?"

Rafeor looked over at Taryn and her eyes swirled with different emotions before she finally shook her head and replied, "She should be fine for the time being. If she waited a couple more days…. That would change everything."

"How would it change?"

"I cannot tell you."

"Stop talking in riddles, Taryn. How would it change?"

"As I said, Marius, I cannot answer that."

"Why not?"

"It would change the order of events. I have seen all the outcomes. It would be better that Rafeor leaves immediately and not later."

"We are talking about the safety of my mate here."

**"Marius."**

I winced slightly as I looked over at Shadow's eyes, she continued, "**You will be coming with me.**"

"He cannot go."

Shadow's eyes cut to Taryn as she said that. I growled and tried hard to keep Onyx back but was failing entirely. Taryn swallowed before speaking, "You are needed here, Marius. There are not many wolves that Nathaniel trusts now. Therefore, he needs his gamma in charge for the time being."

I would have argued, but I knew the logic behind what she said too. I sighed deeply and looked at Shadow with a look and sighed deeply again. Shadow looked perplexed for a moment before sighing deeply herself. She seemed to understand that aspect.

****

Taryn looked conflicted before she started to walk away. I watched after her before I turned around to look at Shadow, who looked perplexed and spoke, "**Alert Nathaniel of this for me, Marius. I will be back in a day.**"

Onyx growled in my mind at her leaving without us, but at the same time, we understood why Nathaniel would want us to be at his side. Since we did not know who was friend and who was foe. Before Taryn got to the end of the hallway though, she froze and must have thought of something. She turned around and came back towards us. Shadow looked at her with expectant eyes, and she spoke, "There is someone you can take, Shadow, Aurelius, and Azier won't have anything to be doing in this time frame. If you want company."

Shadow frowned slightly before replying, "**You sure you want your daughter on my trip?**"

"Positive."

**"Sounds good to me then."**

"I will tell them to meet you in the back gardens."

Shadow simply nodded in response. She turned to go back into our chambers before she paused and looked at Taryn with a look, but did not speak. It was almost as if Shadow and Taryn knew something that they were not going to tell me it. I scowled slightly before Shadow disappeared into the room, leaving me and Taryn to stand outside the door.

****

I headed to the room when Taryn spoke, "Like it or not, Marius, you cannot join them on this mission."

"Why not?"

"Nathaniel doesn't trust many of our guards or anyone currently. Especially with what has happened with Logan. Therefore, you are now his current beta until a certain someone appoints someone else. You will have the same duties as Rispin had."

"Damn it."

"You knew it was going to happen though, Marius. That if one person of leadership falls, then it goes to the next one in line. However, since Nathaniel cannot trust everyone that means he skips the current customs and goes to his gamma. Ghost will assist you when he can, along with the patrol. Since they are for sure not corrupted."

"Alright. Do you know where Nathaniel is currently?"

"Last time I checked, he was in his chambers. So, you are not immediately needed. Although be warned though, the rest of the beta blooded-of-age ones will seek him out to find out why he has not appointed them as his new beta."

"Isn't Ghost beta blood?"

"He is, but he is waiting for the next one in line to take the throne."

"Why not do it now?"

"Because there are only so many guards that Nathaniel trusts, and since we have a certain someone down in the dungeons currently. He doesn't want anyone else but the patrol to take care of them."

"Alright, that is also understandable."

A yell sounded on the other side of the door and I sighed deeply before I headed towards the door again. Taryn sighed deeply and I looked at her with a look before asking, "What?"

"Unfortunately, the two children that are leaving, Marius, will not be in a good situation when they get back unless you can manage to find Blackwell. The advisor to their king so to speak."

"What is the advisor going to do to them?"

"He would raise them correctly, however, everyone else will treat them like trash. Inform Shadow of this, Marius. She must find Blackwell to give them a good chance in this life."

"You are really morbid sometimes, Taryn."

"I know, but it is the thing that comes with the bells and whistles of being a seer."

"I do not envy your duties."

"No one does. Azier is the same as myself, along with Cyprus. It skipped Batis, but I was expecting at least one of my children to not have the ability."

"Ah, well…. I'm going to help my mate, and then I will go find Nathaniel and whatever else that needs to be addressed."

"That is a good plan. Have a good evening, Marius."

"Same to you, Taryn."

"Thank you."

"You're welcome."

She smiled slightly before she turned around once again, and this time she did not come back.

*****

I looked at the door and sighed deeply. I entered the room and found Johnathan scrambling around looking for something. Shadow stared at him, panting since something happened in the time frame that had happened while I was talking with Taryn. I locked eye contact with Shadow for a moment, but she simply just shook her head for a moment, before cutting her eyes to look at Johnathan scramble on the ground. Finally, he found what he was looking for, and I frowned as I noticed the photograph and saw four people on it, with a baby in the woman's arms.

Showing that it was what the family looked like before the shit hit the fan. I sighed, rubbed the back of my neck, and watched as Johnathan scrambled around again. He stuffed his belongings and Annie's belongings into a bag.

Espi came out of the room that was closer to ours, and watched as his brother scrambled around before speaking, "Are you sure that this is what you want brother? Even after mother said to stay together?"

Johnathan paused, looked at Espi, and saw his blank face. I noticed that Espi kept himself completely voided of emotions, showing that he had gone through some trauma while he was across the channel. Johnathan sighed deeply before replying, "I am sorry, Espi, but it is how it needs to happen. You know what others across the channel will think of you."

"Then why don't you stay here? This is not a bad place, and sure we all get weird looks, but that is common now. Come on, brother, are you for sure saying that you would rather break up the family? Solely because something is coming?"

"It will be better on the other side of the channel Espi."

"How are you so sure of that, Johnathan? How can you say it will be better than what we have here? We have all of our needs met here, without issues. Why change?"

"I am done talking about this, Espi, this is going to happen. Without you since you wanted to stay here."

"I think you are making a mistake in this decision of yours, Johnathan. I think you will one day come to the knowledge that I was in the right mindset."

"Shut up."

Espi closed his mouth in a grim line before looking at me with a look and disappeared back into the room. He closed the door with a gentle slam, and Johnathan winced slightly, but he did not attempt to speak to his brother.

I looked at Shadow and saw her frown. We were both under the impression that Espi wanted to stay, but now that we have witnessed this conversation, it appeared that Espi wanted to go with his siblings. To be a family, and not be separated from them. I sighed as I linked Shadow, *"Taryn highly suggests you find Blackwell. The king's advisor."*

**"The same advisor that had the sword stuck out of him?"**

*"Yeah, that one."*

**"What is his business in this?"**

*"Taryn says he will be the only one willing to take care of them."*

Shadow's eyes sparked in anger before she nodded once in acknowledgment. I knew that once she had come to terms with something, she would follow through with it to the end. I sighed deeply before rubbing the bridge of my nose and sighed deeply. After a few minutes, Johnathan had Annie ready to go. Espi has not exited the room, and I linked Shadow, *"Are you taking Espi with you?"*

*"No, I think he wants to stay here. Even if his siblings are leaving."*

*"Okay."*

Shadow dropped the connection and looked at me with love in her eyes. She sighed before speaking, "**Ready to leave?**"

"Yes."

"**Then out the door.**"

Annie walked up to me and hugged my legs. I cleared my throat and knew that I was going to cry. They may have not been here for long, but they have definitely been a part of my life now. It would feel weird after they are gone. I could feel the pain of the mate bond with Shadow and Rafeor and knew that they were feeling the same, but they also respected Taryn and her wisdom. If she said something would happen, and it would happen, it usually meant that it was going to get bad. I sighed as Johnathan glanced up at me and swallowed hard. He held out his hand, and I grasped it. He was never one for hugs, since I believe his father beat it into him that he was nothing. However, I pulled him into a hug, and he stiffened for a moment before relaxing himself. He clasped his hands across my back and squeezed gently before stepping backwards. It was only after a moment that I released him.

I looked at Shadow and saw the tears glittering in her eyes, but she nodded and we embraced after they went into the hallway.

*****

After she left, directing the children in front of her, Espi came out of his room. He looked at me with a sniff, and tears began to stream down his face. I opened my arms and he walked into my open arms and wrapped his hands across my chest, whispering, "Am I to blame for them leaving?"

"No, you are not to blame."

"How are you so sure? Even my own father didn't want me."

"Your father was a cruel man, you will be loved here."

"Promise?"

"I promise."

"What is going to happen now?"

"We will know later on how things will end up."

"So, nothing is set in stone?"

"Not that I know of."

"Can I go outside in the gardens? It's peaceful there."

"Sure, as long as you know how to get back here."

He chuckled slightly before whispering, "Thank you, dad."

My breath caught in my throat, and he tensed underneath me. I looked down at him as he looked up at me with startled eyes. He swallowed nervously before whispering, "Is that okay? To call you dad?"

"Yes."

I tightened my hold and he nestled into my arms before whispering, "I never had a good dad hug. Is this what it feels like?"

A lump was in my throat, but I cleared it before replying, "Yes, this is what it feels like."

"I like it."

"Me too."

"When you have children, would I become a thing of the past? A burden?"

"No, you will be our eldest."

"Promise?"

"Promise."

He stepped backward and whipped his nose on his tunic before smiling at me with a lazy smile. He headed to the bedroom before he paused and looked over at me, over his shoulder, speaking, "Thank you."

"You're welcome."

The smile that radiated off of him, was intense. He finally entered the room and closed the door with a small click.

If I had known that I would be a father to someone else's child, then I would have called you nuts. However, after finding my mate, and dealing with everything, with the trauma and things with her, I knew that I had room and time for taking care of someone else. I would not change anything.

# Chapter 53

We headed down to the gardens, and Azier and Aurelius were waiting. I headed towards Aurelius before embracing her. She smiled slightly but was a shell of what she was before the kidnapping. I sighed slightly before stepping backwards and nodding at Azier. She dipped her head but did not speak. I directed the children closer to them before I stepped backward and got about twenty feet from them before I allowed Remmu to take control. She quickly took control and roared into the sky. Shaking the trees, a few branches fell with a thud somewhere in the forest.

****

I looked over at them before rolling my shoulders and leaning downward. I was crouching, making good room for them to climb onto me, before I straightened back to my full height. For a moment, Johnathan looked like he was going to refuse, but after a moment Annie ran forward and giggled as she placed her tiny hand against my scales. I watched her out of the side of my eye and smiled slightly. Not enough to show my fangs, but enough that they saw some little whiteness.

After a moment, Johnathan swallowed and came forward and rested his hand against my scales before he looked up. He was still very far down to the ground, there was no way that I could get lower than what I was though, he and his sister were going to have to climb onto me.

Azier came up and stood beside my left foreclaw, whispering to Johnathan, "Have you ever ridden a dragon before?"

"No."

"Okay, think of her as a giant horse. You have ridden a horse, right?"

"Yeah."

"Okay, it is similar to riding a horse."

"How is it similar to riding a horse?"

"Well, for one thing, the head controls where we go, which is where I will be to direct the direction of her. Her back, between her horns on her spine, is quite comfortable to ride. I will place Annie up first, then I'll help you up. You two will sit together so Annie doesn't fall off."

"Is it easy to fall off?"

"If you are not careful, yes. Otherwise, as long as you hold onto the spike in front of you, you will be fine. It is almost like a horn on a saddle."

I looked at Azier with my left eye, and she patted my face gently before she turned her attention to Johnathan who looked as white as snow. He swallowed before speaking, "Why can't we take a ship across?"

"A ship is more dangerous than riding a dragon. You never know what is in the water."

"And that is how the air is too? Is it safe to be so high up?"

"It will be safe enough."

"That doesn't sound exactly strong in the sense. Is it safe?"

"Let's put it this way. Have you ever fallen off a horse?"

"Yes."

"What do you do when you fall off a horse?"

"You get back on."

"Yeah, same deal here."

"If we were to fall, how would we get back onto her?"

"I will be watching you from behind you. I will make sure you are on her soundly."

Johnathan looked at Aurelius before looking back at Azier. He swallowed before whispering, "I don't know."

"This is the only way you would get across the channel safely. This is your one chance. Do you want to or not?"

He looked back at me with a look of terror in his eye, he swallowed hard and whispered, "Go."

"Okay, give me a few moments to get Annie up there. Aurelius, are you comfortable getting onto her without assistance of would you want me to help you?"

"Help would be nice, but I can manage without."

"Okay, you go up first, and if you need further help. I will assist you."

"Okay."

She started to climb onto my leg, boasting herself up, using my horns along the back. I turned my head sideways as I watched Johnathan. He seemed rather nervous, but he swallowed hard and pulled himself together. He looked down at his little sister and swallowed hard. He suddenly wondered if he was doing the right thing, but now that Aurelius was in position, it took a few moments. She was ready for the handoff. Azier approached Annie slowly before picking her up. Aurelius leaned over and helped raise her to the spot in front. Azier looked at Johnathan now with an expectant look. He swallowed hard before he tried to scramble up my leg. However, he was unsure of his movements and did not get that far up. Azier approached him and boosted him up and soon he scrambled across my back and sat behind Annie.

Azier looked at me with a gentle smile before speaking, "Are you ready to go?"

I rumbled in response. She smiled before she gripped my horn on the side of my head before she pulled herself up. She sat at the curve of my skull. I swayed back and forth, adjusted to the added weight before I stood up completely.

I heard a little shriek and turned my head to look at Johnathan as he looked straight down, which was high in the air. I easily stood even with the palace, which had three stories, just shy away from being taller than it. I turned my head back to see the darkness in the sky. The sun was setting now. My element was during the night, I partially wondered if flying in the dark was part of the requirement to get them home safely.

I moved gingerly away from the palace, before opening my wings. The black webbing stretched out and I flapped my wings once, twice, three times, before I got enough air in my wings to get airborne. I could not do what I normally did when I got airborne, which was to leap into the sky and then flap my wings. That was not the most comfortable aspect of flying with riders. After I got airborne, I beat my wings against my body four times, to get the altitude where it would be the safest with wind currents. I glided across the wind and soon evened out.

******

I watched out my window as Rafeor's dragon left, I knew that it was only a matter of time before something else happened. I, for now, have to figure out a way to get Logan out of the cells. He has business to deal with. I had been on the hunt to find Rispin, but for the past several hours I have not located him. Then I felt the line break, alerting another member being banished. My wolf growled low in his throat. There was only one person that may have been banished and that is Rispin. I tried to find him, when I ran into Ghost who was walking away from the front door woods. He looked pissed. I swallowed and smiled at him before speaking, "Ghost! What news?"

Ghost paused and looked up at me with a squint before speaking, "Not much, Ehsan."

"Whose line broke from the pack?"

"A traitor."

"Who?"

He looked at me with a look before replying, "Rispin."

I tried hard to control my facial features, especially since Ghost was one of the top warriors. He would have skinned me alive if I tried anything. However, he was preceptive. He looked at the steps and me, before speaking, "What are you trying to hide from me, Ehsan?"

"Nothing."

"Liar."

I swallowed slightly before replying, "You wouldn't understand."

"Understand what?"

"Why I have to do what I have to do."

"And what would that entitle entirely, Ehsan?"

"None of your concern, Ghost."

"I am making it my concern. Answer me."

"I would rather not."

"Swear on the moon. Who is your alpha?"

I froze. Swearing on the moon for a werewolf would be bound to the moon goddess, and breaking her vow would result in death. My wolf whined in the back of my mind before I whispered, "Logan."

"Logan? You know that Nathaniel is king right?"

"Currently."

"That is treason, Ehsan."

"As if you have the authority to do anything to me."

**"He does though."**

I jumped in the air as I whirled around and came face to face with Nathaniel, who looked like he would kill me, Basil glinted in his eyes. I swallowed hard. "What are you going to do to me?"

**"Ehsan, you are banished."**

I felt the pack link break and I swallowed hard before taking a step backward and speaking, "You will regret this."

**"Leave."**

I turned around and saw Ghost stare at me with hard eyes suddenly. They had switched to his business face quickly. His hand gripped his weapon at his side. I was seen as a threat to Nathaniel. I swallowed as I quickly edged my way around him and ran for my life. Knowing that if I had done what I was going to do before I was dinking around, I would be hunted. Someone else had to get Logan out of the cells.

*****

I watched as Ehsan ran away from us, I would have given chase but knew that Nathaniel came out here to find me. I looked up at him before speaking, "My king?"

He looked down at me before speaking, "**Meet me at my office. And if you can, bring Marius, and whoever is not watching Logan's cell.**"

"Yes, my lord."

I passed him on the stairs, paused, and came equally upon him before speaking, "You are a fair king, Nathaniel. I would not follow anyone else."

**"Not even your father?"**

"My father has some good qualities, but he told you and me himself, that he would not want that title. He is comfortable being alpha of a pack."

**"Are you sure after all these events that have happened, that he will see it the same way as before?"**

"I can assure you on that aspect, Nathaniel. My father is happy with doing what he is doing. We cannot force him to do something that he doesn't want to do."

**"That is true."**

A small smile broke across Nathaniel's face, and I grinned slightly. It was an accomplishment, since after everything that has happened. He is faced with death, and pain.

****

I instantly connected to everyone but Brego and Azier, since Brego was watching the cell, and Azier was flying across the channel with Rafeor and Aurelius, alerting them to meet in Nathaniel's main office.

I would have normally connected to Marius, but I had time now, and would rather find him than anything else. I went towards his chambers and found Espi coming out of the door. I paused, I thought that the children would all go. It appears not though. Espi looked at me with a look, before speaking, "Hello."

"I thought you would have gone with your siblings."

"I am a freak, and no one across the channel would allow me to be in their homes."

I growled slightly, and Ghost lit in my eyes before he faded away. Espi swallowed and looked down before asking, "What is your wolf's name?"

"Ghost."

"I thought your name is Ghost though?"

"We prefer to be called the same name."

"If you don't mind me asking, what is your name then?"

"My personal name is Asaro, but please call me by Ghost."

"Okay, I wasn't going to call you by your name. I was more curious about what it was."

I smiled slightly. Espi was kind, and even if he was an albino, it did not mean he was anything but a good kid. He looked down before speaking, "You came up here to talk to me? Or did you come for my dad?"

That took me by surprise, and replied after a moment, "Your dad."

"Ah, I assumed so, since you are one of the top warriors here."

I smiled slightly. This kid was so perceptive of the ways that this castle ran as is. I wondered if I should try to train him since he could benefit the pack. However, after a moment, Espi ducked back into the room and all I heard was murmuring for a moment before Marius came out. He looked at me and looked at Espi and spoke, "You still okay with going alone?"

"Yeah, I'm good."

"Have fun then."

"I will. Goodbye, Ghost."

He walked by me and continued down the hallway before he turned towards the entrance to the gardens.

****

I looked at Marius before speaking, "Uh…. dad?"

"He called me dad as his siblings left."

"And you are okay with that?"

"Yes, he may not share any blood with me or Rafeor, but we are his parents."

"Ah, ok. Nathaniel has requested you in his office."

"You too?"

"Always perceptive you are, Marius, but yes. He wants the patrol, besides Azier and Brego."

"Makes sense. Let's go then."

We walked down the hallway, and I noticed that two of the doors were cracked open and I knew that instantly that whatever was said was not private. Whatever Nathaniel had to talk about would remain hidden since no one else knew about the hidden ones.

****

I glided across the cloud cover, listening to Johnathan and Annie's wonder sounds. I knew that the others felt the same, but kept their sounds closed off since they were enjoying the moment. I passed over a dark cloud, and a flash of lightning flashed on our left, making a boom. I winced slightly but knew that we weren't in any sort of danger besides being in the storm itself. The rain started to dribble onto my body, and I felt Azier shift herself around, to look at the children, and I knew that I needed to get higher. I pumped my wings hand against my body, as I rose into the sky. Soon, we glided across the darkness of the cloud, and I saw an area a few leagues away that was not dark. I headed that way before I went back below the cloud cover.

It was another forty minutes to an hour later when I saw the other side. I felt Azier tense underneath me, as we flew past the barge that I had come across on. I felt Rafeor tense in my mind, but there was nothing I could do about it. Yes, it had some horrid memories on that barge and the events afterward were equally harsh and cruel. However, it did not make a difference for me. I might be her dragon form, but we did not share to same pain. As much as others thought that we were the same, we weren't. She had to ask me if I wanted to surface, if I didn't, then I didn't. However, that was only sometimes, there had been a few times that I had not allowed her access, like the time that we first shifted. She was in a rage, and whenever we were in a rage, we tended to shift into anything that we wanted to. I was just more prominent that fateful day. I sighed deeply before angling myself down, it was still stark black outside, so the humans would not really see me unless they had torches. I saw a mansion in the background, and I flew towards it, gut instinct telling me this was where Blackwell would be located.

I landed in their garden and heard dogs barking up a storm. I crouched there for a moment before Azier slid off my head. She looked at me and whispered, "Wait here."

A plume of smoke came from my nose in response, and she smiled at me before looking up at my back and placing her fingers to her lip – signaling to the children to keep quiet. They must have nodded since Azier went on ahead to scoop the place out.

A dog ran around the corner, barking up a storm before it saw me, it tucked its tail in between its legs, cried out, and scampered back the way it had come. I huffed in amusement. After a few minutes, Azier came back before whispering, "I believe this is it."

I looked at her and blinked once, and after she helped the children and Aurelius down off my back, I allowed Rafeor to shift back.

****

I stumbled around and breathed heavily for a moment. Azier steadied me before she looked at everyone else. She placed her fingers across her lips and we all hunched over and moved towards the building.

A few dogs ran around the corner, barking at us. They stopped within a few feet and were causing a ruckus, Shadow surfaced only enough to huff at them in warning. That got their attention and they backed away, whining.

We soon came across a door, and it was clear that whoever was living here thought that no one dared enter their living quarters in the dead of night since there were no signs of guards anywhere. We entered the side door and came across three guards. They looked startled as they took in three women and two children. I straightened myself out slightly. **We came to speak to Blackwell."**

"Blackwell? What is your business with him?"

**"It is none of your concern. Where is he?"**

"Uh… does he know you are here?"

"Why does it matter if he knows or not? We are here, and we need to speak to Blackwell. Please take us to him."

The guards swallowed before one looked at the others before speaking, "Right this way."

He turned hard on his heel and headed into the mansion. We passed the other guards, and I saw the shock written across their faces. It was clear that they were not expecting anyone to show up on their doorstep.

****

It took a few minutes, but finally, the guard paused outside the chamber door. He swallowed before he rapped three times and spoke through the door, "Blackwell? You have visitors."

It was a few minutes later, that the door opened and a groggy Blackwell stuck his head out and stared at us in confusion. The guard shifted his footing before speaking, "Your orders?"

**"Uhhh…. You are dismissed. Come on inside. please."**

He ducked inside his chambers, leaving a startled guard for a moment before we passed the guard into his chambers. It took us a moment to adjust to the darkness but after a moment, Blackwell moved around with a pair of flint stones and lit the surrounding candles, illuminating the space. His bed was half-made, showing that he was alone.  After a moment, he cleared his throat, drawing my attention to him. He rested his hands on the corner of his table before speaking, **"Who are you?"**

**"My name is Rafeor."**

**"Rafeor? The same one that was captured and brought over here? What are you doing here?"**

**"I was hoping you would be able to take care of them."**

I motion Johnathan and Annie forward. Blackwell's eyes fell to them, and his Adam's apple bobbed before his eyes flickered to Azier and Aurelius before speaking, **"Why? Why leave someone here?"**

"Because our side of the channel is getting ready for war. My mother said that you would be the safest and the most noble one to take care of them."

**"I don't know about that. There are countless others that can take children in."**

"But any as fair as you?"

It took him a moment before he sighed deeply and shook his head in response. He looked at me before speaking, **"Does your…. Do leaders know you are over here? I do not want any issues."**

**"The one that it matters to, does know. The other has not attempted to contact me."**

**"Okay."**

He drummed his fingers onto the table before he spoke, **"You do realize that I am a King's advisor right though? I have countless duties to do. How would I make time to raise two children?"**

"Teach me, " whispered Johnathan. Blackwell looked at him before speaking, **"Teach you?"**

"Yes, teach me. Teach me the layout of the mansion, and what duties you have to perform. I can help you. Please."

**"Hmmm…. I don't know."**

His eyes flickered to mine before speaking, **"Where did they even come from?"**

"We came from the mansion that Rafeor and Aurelius were held captive at."

He looked at Johnathan, and his eyes flickered back to Azier before whispering, **"They are human?"**

"Yes."

**"That makes it somewhat easier. I thought they were your kind. No offense."**

"None taken."

**"I can take them in. How long do you think it will be?"**

"The rest of their lives."

**"So, you are giving up the right to be their guardian?"**

**"Yes."**

**"Okay, I will have to ask Drake then."**

"Drake?"

**"He is the owner of the mansion. My king."**

"Why does he get a say in this?"

**"Because to train anyone in the ways of being an advisor, I would need his permission. Along with Lucius since he is next in line."**

**"Are they nice?"**

**"They may be more inclined to do what you ask since you are the ones who assisted us with Lucius's injury."**

Azier frowned slightly but did not reply. I glanced at her out of the corner of my eye. She knew something. I wondered what she knew and what she was keeping to herself. It was a few moments later that she sighed. "We unfortunately cannot wait around for morning. And waking either prince or king up before dawn is no ideal business. This is not entirely dire either."

I frowned slightly, wondering why we couldn't wait. However, I was getting restless, the guards looked at Aurelius and me with hunger in their eyes. They did not know what we were, except walking sex toys to them. I swallowed hard, it was taking a lot for me not to tremble in front of Blackwell as was. Azier glanced at me out of the corner of her eye but did nothing. Blackwell sighed deeply before speaking, **"Okay, then you can leave them here. I cannot say for certain that they will be welcomed with open arms though."**

"Understandable. Thank you, either way, you will be a good father figure to both of them."

Blackwell froze and looked at Azier with a partially open mouth. He whispered, **"How do you know that?"**

"I am the daughter of our seer."

**"Oh… that suddenly makes sense. Is that why you sought me alone out?"**

"Yes."

**"Okay. I will do all that is in my power to make sure these children are taken care of. What is your name? So, I can inform my king and prince."**

Azier hesitated before she replied, "Azier, I cannot tell you my last."

Blackwell sighed deeply but he nodded in response. **"And you?"**

He looked at Aurelius, who swallowed nervously before whispering, "Aurelius Fiore."

He paused and stared at Aurelius before his eyes flickered to us before speaking, **"Okay, you may leave. Although, how did you get here?"**

**"I flew here."**

**"You flew here? Carrying all of them?"**

**"I was in my dragon form."**

**"Dragon form?"**

**"Yeah."**

He opened his mouth, then closed it, clearly puzzled. Azier chuckled slightly before speaking, "If you get some shoes on, you can escort us to the gardens again. That is where we landed."

"**You landed in the garden?**"

"Yeah."

"**Damn it. That means the flowers are torn up.**"

"**No, I landed in the clearing. The big grassy field.**"

"**Did you kill anything as you landed?**"

"**No.**"

"**Thank goodness for that then.**"

"What's in the field?"

"**Horses. And overall cattle.**"

"Ah, yeah. We did not land on anything. If we did, we would have paid handsomely for it."

"**And what is handsomely to you?**"

"Three golden pieces."

His jaw dropped before he whispered, "**And how in the world have you earned that coinage?**"

"I am the seer's daughter, along with being a top warrior."

"**Ah, that makes sense. Anyhow, if you say you cannot stay, it is best that you depart now.**"

"Agreed."

Annie turned to look at me and made grabby hands. I leaned down and picked her up, she yawned huge and snuggled into me. I swallowed hard but did not do anything. Blackwell watched our interaction before commenting, "**It almost seems that you two don't want to separate.**"

"It was my idea to come back over here. Not theirs."

"**And why do you want to be over here?**"

"Because it is not safe over there."

He looked at us all before it dawned on him what was said earlier. He swallowed hard before speaking, "**War? Why are you bringing them over here then?**"

"Because it will not reach this side of the channel."

"**Oh.**"

He looked down at Johnathan and then glanced up at Annie before sighing deeply and replying, "**I will take care of them as best as I can.**"


****


We turned to go out the way we had come, however, a rapid knock pounded on his door. He froze and eyed the door with a frown before speaking, "**Along the wall, behind the door. Quick, all of you.**"

Azier squinted her eyes but grabbed Johnathan's hand, walked to the left door, and went up against the wall, along with Aurelius and me on the right. Blackwell took his time and yawned as he approached the door, and opened it a crack. His behavior changed slightly before he opened the door further, "**My king?**"

Drake entered his chambers and did not look around before he heard the door shut behind him. Blackwell glanced at us and shrugged slightly before he spoke, "**What brought you to my chambers?**"

"**We both know why Blackwell.**"

He turned around and was slightly surprised to see us. However, it appeared that he knew we were here too. He sighed and pinched the bridge of his nose before speaking, "**And... they are still here.**"

"**Yes.**"

"**Welcome, but why did you come at the night hours?**"

"We came at night since it is safer for us to fly here."

"**Oh? Fly? How so?**"

I went to speak, but Azier spoke above me slightly, "None of your concern. However, we need to leave before day breaks."

"**Why so dire in getting out before day?**"

Azier bit her lip before she replied, "We flew here on a dragon, Your Majesty. Not many people are accustomed to seeing a flying beast. Which is why the cover of darkness is more needed than anything else."

"**A dragon? A flying beast?**"

He scoffed it as if he did not believe us. He looked at Blackwell before speaking, "**And you believed this nonsense?**"

"How else did they get here from the other side of the channel? It makes sense."

"Other side of the channel?"

He looked at us sharply, sighing deeply, "Oh. This suddenly makes more sense. What brings you across?"

"These children. We respectfully asked Blackwell to take care of them."

Drake froze and looked at Blackwell before speaking, "And you have time to take care of two children?"

"I'll be taking the boy under my wing, to train him as my trainee."

"And the little girl?"

"I'll do my best to support both of them."

"Sheesh. You have yourself a handful, Blackwell. You have your own duties to perform, don't let them take away from your duties. Otherwise, I will have to get one to be taken care of elsewhere."

"I don't want Annie to be separated from me!"

Drake froze, and Blackwell swallowed hard. Drake turned his eyes to Johnathan before asking, "What was that?"

"I-I… I don't want my sister to be separated from me, Your Majesty. Please."

Drake sighed hard before looking at us and speaking, "Alright, it is time for you to leave then. Daybreak is two hours out."

"Thank you, Your Majesty."

Azier curtseyed and Aurelius followed suit. I, however, stayed as I was, since I was royal blood, along with holding Annie in my arms. Drake looked at me for a moment before his eyes flickered over to Aurelius before he made the connections. His face fell slightly and whispered, "You two…. You made it known what shifters are to me."

"Don't do anything stupid."

Azier hand gripped her blade at her hip, and her eyes were trained on him. Drake scoffed before speaking, "You are out of your bounds."

"Not really. I am protecting my next Queen, along with the niece of the current king."

Drake cut his eyes towards us suddenly and his jaw dropped slightly before speaking, "Queen?"

"Yes."

**"But you are so young."**

**"So are you."**

**"I am older than you."**

**"That may be the case, but I am the age to take leadership either way."**

**"Most likely across the channel."**

**"Yeah, across the channel."**

He rolled his eyes but motioned us to leave. We turned around to go out the door when a knock sounded on the door. Drake and Blackwell looked at each other. Finally, Drake motioned for us to stay where we were, before he barked out, "**Enter.**"

*****

We headed to the office, and soon entered, finding the remaining of my patrol and Nathaniel. He looked sour for a moment before we entered into the office space. I could tell that none of them had spoken about being asked into the office, and soon two more people entered the office, Sophronia and Taryn. Sophronia looked at us all before motioning towards the red-bounded book. Nathaniel looked at the five of us: Marius, Taryn, myself, Batis, and Cyprus. He nodded slightly before nodding to his mate, to go to the hidden entrance.

The shock in the bond between my patrol was clear as day since they did not know it was there. I swallowed, I only knew about it because Sophronia had informed me of where to find it. Even though I had told them before about it, it still shocked them that I was not lying. Although we had a pact that we would not lie about something like this. So, finding out that it was not a stretch was a shocker to them most likely.

We headed into the office space, pausing on the stairs before Nathaniel joined us. He looked at us all before closing the entrance and pointing downward. We went down three spirals downward before we came up to a large conference room. We entered and I sat down, and a puff of dust went instantly into the air. I coughed slightly, waving my hand across my face. However, I knew that requesting someone to dust down here was not going to happen, because of how dire things were.

Nathaniel placed himself at the head of the table and looked at every one of us before speaking, "**Our home is threatened. You lot are the only ones that I immediately trust now. You will be on rotation with Brego, but only within this patrol.**"

"Except for Azier."

**"Why leave her out of this, Taryn?"**

"Because she is a woman, and women tend to get the most brutally injured when someone wants something. In this case, someone. I do not mean any offense to my daughter, however, she will not be one of the few who watches Logan."

"How long will he be in our cells?" Batis asked.

I looked at Nathaniel and saw him swallow before he sighed and spoke, **"Unsure on time. He is too valuable to be let go."**

"How is he valuable if you don't mind me asking?" I asked.

He looked at me and was about to reply when Sophronia replied, **"As much as we don't like Logan, there is a reason why we have not killed him all this time. When even one event that he has committed would have killed another wolf. The reason behind it is because he is…."**

She trailed off and swallowed hard before Basil spoke, **"Before we continue. Swear on the moon that this is not going to get out to anyone else. Swear it."**

"I swear on the moon."

"I swear on the moon."

"I swear on the moon."

"I swear on the moon."

"I swear on the moon."

After we were all sworn in, Basil dropped away from Nathaniel's eyes. We all breathed a little easier once he disappeared from his eyes. Sophronia sighed deeply before speaking, **"It is because he is the true alpha of this pack."**

Silence. After a moment I asked, "What do you mean?"

**"My father had Logan first. Logan is the firstborn under technical terms. I was the second born, and Tobias was the third born. However…."**

"However, I had a vision the night before they would have announced the eldest. That the firstborn would break the pack apart, and bring it down to the ground. That the second-born would be the strongest," replied Taryn.

We all froze. Marius looked equally shocked. We all swallowed if that piece of information went out, then we would be in trouble. Nathaniel grimaces before speaking, **"That is why we cannot kill him. As much as we want to, we cannot. Otherwise, there could be issues. If someone did any tests, then it would be found out what happened."**

"Okay, so Logan is the true alpha, but that doesn't make sense on why this is hidden. The ones that should know about this should have been alerted of this," replied Cyprus.

He looked perturbed that he was not informed. Nathaniel looked like he was going to reply, but Marius beat him to it, "I understand why we were not informed. Look at it this way, Rispin was the freaking beta and he still went about it the wrong way. He was the second in command and therefore he was on the higher end of things. What would you think he would do if he had that tidbit of information?"

"That may be true, but not all of us are corrupted."

**"Regardless if you are corrupted or not, we kept it hidden since we had been sworn to."**

"Then why are you telling us this now? If you have been sworn to keep this a secret then why tell us?"

**"Because, if Logan were to poison or attempt to kill me, that makes it easier for him. Along with the fact that we didn't swear on the moon. We were sworn to say nothing except to the ones we trusted. Since I was unsure of when to bring this up, it did not make sense to tell anyone beforehand. When would have been the best time to bring this up?"**

"Ah, that makes sense. There was never a good time to say this."

I frowned and looked at Sophronia and Nathaniel before asking, "What now? Since we cannot kill Logan, what are we going to do with him then? He cannot stay down in the cells for the rest of his life."

Nathaniel sighed deeply and pushed himself into a standing position before he paced back and forth for a moment before his back was facing us. He was staring at the fire pit that was in this certain office space, before he spoke, **"I am going to be leaving that up to the next in line."**

"Next in line? Who is next in line?" asked Cyprus.

I looked over at him for a moment and raised my eyebrow. Did he really not know? Nathaniel turned to face us after his shoulders slumped slightly before he turned around and spoke, **"Rafeor."**

"Rafeor? I apologize before I say this. However, she is new to the pack Nathaniel. You are already having issues with the pack now, think about what will happen when you announce that you will be handing the pack to her."

"She won't be handed the pack. Shadow will challenge Basil to a fight for the title," replied Taryn. Cyprus looked at her for a moment before speaking, "But wouldn't it look staged?"

**"There will always be someone who will challenge the alpha for their title. However, unlike other wolves, Rafeor will not kill Nathaniel. She is of royal blood. She is the eldest."**

"But you…. You do realize that that rule only rolls to the one with royal blood. Pure royal blood, when it falls onto that aspect," replied Cyprus. He looked conflicted but finally, Taryn spoke, "Not necessarily. Rafeor is half werewolf and half shifter royal. She is pureblood in both aspects. And if anyone dares to challenge her for the title…. Shadow will put them down."

For a moment, it was silent in the room, as everyone thought of what was said. Finally. Marius spoke, "I see one flaw in this plan though Nathaniel. Wouldn't the normal thing to do for a duel be the other one to be banished?"

Our eyes flew to Marius for a moment until they trained on Nathaniel. He swallowed hard before he opened his mouth to say something, but Taryn spoke before he could utter a word, "Under normal circumstances yes, but since Rafeor is the eldest. That does not happen in this case."

"And you are for sure of that?"

"Fine, I am ninety-eight percent sure of that. However, the pack would accept Rafeor. Some have seen her train recently, and they have seen Shadow in action. Nathaniel, does Basil ever hold back during training?"

Nathaniel sighed before speaking, "**Not really. Shadow gives him a fight. Sure, we monitor it, but when Shadow challenges him, it will solely be him in his element.**"

"Are you saying that there will be no way to make him not injure my mate severely?"

"It unfortunately has to be a real fight. Basil has to go all out to keep his title, and it has to be real. I am sorry, Marius, but if anyone witnesses that Basil holds himself back at all, they would think this is staged. Which is why this has to happen soon."

"How soon are you thinking, mother?"

"A day after Rafeor and them get back."

"What do you know that we don't?"

Taryn swallowed and looked at Cyprus and me for a moment. Both of them sighed deeply before I spoke, "The war will happen in a few days. We have to unite with the shifters, along with the outlanders in the next few days."

"What about the Carpathians?"

I locked eye contact with Taryn and she seemed like she didn't want to answer. Finally, she sighed deeply before speaking, "Unfortunately, they are siding with the enemy."

"How sure are you on that?"

"I have seen several outcomes of this Marius. None of them have the Carpathians on our side."

"Shit."

"Agreed."

Sophronia rubbed her stomach for a moment before she sighed deeply and spoke, "**Taryn, can you tell me that my child will be okay during this?**"

Taryn has purposely avoided looking at Sophronia up until now. She lowered her eyes and swallowed hard. She did not reply. That was an answer in itself. Sophronia gasped and covered her mouth with her hand, and one hand clutched her stomach and she backed away for a moment. She swallowed hard before she asked, "**How does it happen?**"

"Nothing is set in stone yet, Sophronia." I replied.

I knew the ways that Sophronia would perish, but there was a way that she could survive, and live to her end of days, being the mother that she would be amazing at. However, that would result in her and Nathaniel leaving completely. Off the face of the earth, and head across the channel to start, before they ran for the rest of their lives. Same with Tobias and anyone else who wanted to live. There was going to be the majority of us dead, and there was no way to change it. I even knew that there were people in this very room to die a horrid death.

Taryn looked at me with a knowing look after a moment. She must have thought the same since she did not speak a word though. She lowered her eyes but did not say a word.

Nathaniel had come over to his mate, wrapped her into his arms, and caged her to his core for a moment. He was silent and he rested his head on her head for a moment before taking in a deep whiff of his mate's scent. I swallowed as I watched their interaction. I have not found my mate yet, and I know that the chance of surviving would be slim now. I sighed deeply before looking at Marius, who had a perturbed look on his face. However, he did not say a word.

*****

After a few minutes, I finally asked, "Well…. What is the next phase of action?"

Nathaniel sighed deeply before taking in a deep whiff of his mate before speaking, "**Now we prepare for war. I thought we had more time than what we do. Batis, get the blacksmiths going. Ghost, Cyprus, I want you to help Marius with training the pack. Keep your ears open. Batis, when Brego needs to be relieved, you will be first to take his position. So, after you alert the blacksmiths, go catch a few hours of sleep.**"

"So more intense training. What do we tell the pack of this?"

"Nothing. Tell them that this is the new protocol."

Replied Taryn. However, she glanced at Nathaniel as if seeing if he was going to reject that idea. Nathaniel looked at her with a squint in his eyes before he asked, **"Taryn, what do you know that we don't about this aspect? Why can't we be upfront on this?"**

"It is because we do not know who to trust. It is better that we only tell them that this is the new protocol and I think that the pack actually wants more of a challenge. Don't you agree Marius?"

"That is true, a few of the pack members actually want to fight more and more. They are all getting restless. A few actually asked if they can train to be elites."

**"Hmmm…. Only the best of the best become elites. Do you think that those said wolves are ready to become elites, Marius?"**

"A few of them are more than ready. However, Rispin had ignored my recommendations of those who would become other elites. It now makes sense why he refused though. Any elites would be the pack's strongest members, and harder to win over if things get hairy."

**"Hmmm…. Then if that is the case, get those wolves training to be elites. Ghost, you will be training them hard-core on this. That means that you Cyprus will be Batis, and Brego's replacement. Since Ghost will be dealing with the new elite training, along with Azier when she gets back."**

"Azier is exempt from watching the cell. Fine, but why can't Ghost be babysitting the cell?"

I looked at Cyprus, it seemed as if he wanted to keep pushing for a solid answer each and every time. However, after a moment, I shook my head and was going to reply when Sophronia replied, **"Because Ghost is Tobias's son. You are Taryn's son, Cyprus. The other pack members look up to Ghost, they…. More of tolerate you since you are part of the elite and soon-to-be royal guard."**

Cyprus scowled in response. I smirked. It was known that he was a royal guard, but here was the thing though, I was beta blood. He is delta. So even though he had respect from the pack, they did not exactly look up to him for leadership. Cyprus looked at my smug look and scowled deeper than what he already was, and I chuckled at his facial look. He growled softly, as his wolf surfaced. I shrugged and looked away from him. There was no reason for Ghost to get involved in something so trivial. He actually snorted in our connection, before he turned around and fell asleep again.

Nathaniel sighed and released Sophronia before speaking, **"That was harsh, Sophronia. However, it is true in a way, Cyprus. The pack looks up to Ghost since he is Tobias's son."**

Cyprus sighed deeply, turned his back to me, and kept Nathaniel in his peripheral vision. He was silent for the next few moments, not acknowledging anything or anyone. I went to speak when Ghost sat up in my mind with a growl. I froze and my eyes sparked his eyes for a moment before his eyes dimmed. However, I looked at Taryn and saw her swallow hard. Getting Ghost to react to anything was hard, and something in our gut told us that something was wrong, seriously wrong.

****

Nathaniel froze as he looked at me, and a moment later, ran up the stairs, and carefully exited the safe room without a word. I followed up the stairs but stayed in the hidden entrance when two royal guards slammed his door open. He looked up from his desk, he had a piece of parchment in his hand. As if he was doing paperwork. He frowned at them before speaking, **"What is the meaning of this?"**

"My lord! Someone broke into the dungeons, and one person escaped."

**"Who escaped?"**

"Logan."

**"Dismissed."**

"But…."

**"Guard my door, but shut it. Leave me, "** growled Basil.

It was a few moments later that the guards complied with his orders. I pushed the bookcase forward before looking at Nathaniel before speaking, "Shit."

**"How did it happen? How did Ghost know that something was wrong first?"**

"I don't know why or how he knew first. It sometimes does not make any sort of sense."

Nathaniel sighed deeply before muttering, **"Shit, shit, shit."**

"What are your orders?"

He swallowed and looked up at me before shaking his head in response. He was at a loss for words. I sighed and was about to say something else when Taryn spoke, "Brego, what happened to him?"

I swallowed hard and replied, "He's alive I can tell you that much, I still feel his life force."

Taryn looked at me sharply but knew better than to challenge me. She may be a seer, but I was someone more brutal than anyone here. I kept Ghost on a short leash and rarely let him out for full control, and everyone knew that too. She sighed after a moment before speaking, "Okay, I guess that will be okay for now in knowledge."

Cyprus entered the office room, and glanced at us for a moment before speaking, "I'm heading down to the dungeons."

**"To do what?"**

"To see who would do this."

**"Alright, take Batis with you."**

"I can handle myself alone," he snapped.

I looked at him, speaking, "Cyprus, how many times has Brego tossed you around like a rag doll?"

He glowered at me in response, but shuffled his feet before muttering, "A few times."

"What do you think happened to Brego? He would not have gone down easily."

He fell silent and finally sighed deeply before muttering, "Fair."

Nathaniel looked at me with somewhat of an amused look but Taryn looked at Cyprus with a frown before she snapped, "Cyprus, stay here. Ghost, take Batis down with you."

"Ummm…. Okay?"

I looked at her with a look, but she had her eyes hard on Cyprus, as he shuffled his footing. He swallowed hard. He did not want to be stuck in a room with his mother. And I, frankly, do not blame him either. Taryn may be a seer, but that does not make it easier for her to be a mother to three children. Azier may be her sole daughter, but they were never taught differently growing up, as much as I knew about them at least. A mother will always be a mother, and you better hope you stay on her good side, otherwise, you will always see the angry side that you never want to witness on Taryn. I had caught it earlier in past years since I always hung out with them as kids, and we all got in trouble. I shuddered thinking about some of the punishments that we had to endure. Like scraping the chicken coops with a spoon for several hours. That was brutal and took us two whole days to clean up. It was disgusting and I thought that I would get out of it since I was not her child, but my father wholeheartedly agreed with the punishment.

Taryn cleared her throat, and I blinked a few times when I noticed that Batis was standing by the door. I bowed to Nathaniel before I left.

*****

The door opened and a guard closed it quickly as a young man walked through the door. He was still white, and pale, but was walking soundly. He was about my height, at five-eleven, and looked at Drake and Blackwell with a hard look before he spoke, "**Father, Blackwell. What is the meaning of this meeting?**"

"**Uhhh….**"

He looked at Blackwell with a hard look, and Blackwell shut his mouth instantly. He looked at Drake before snapping, "**Well?**"

"**It is because someone from across the channel came to deliver two young children.**"

"**Stop lying to me! There is no way that someone traveled across the channel without you being alerted of it first. What is the meaning of this meeting?**"

"He is correct, it is because we were delivering two young children."

The lad froze, turned sharply on his heel, and stared at us in shock. It was clear he wasn't expecting anyone to be here besides Blackwell and his father. He stared at us in shock before he looked at his father and Blackwell for a moment. He sighed before speaking, "**Who is going to raise them?**"

"**I am.**"

"**You? Have you dealt with children before, Blackwell? Along with your duties as the advisor?**"

"**I will be training the boy in my duties.**"

"**And the little girl?**"

"**I will do the best I can in supplying what she needs.**"

"**Father, are you going to be helping Blackwell in this?**"

"**It seems like I will son.**"

"**They aren't replacing me, right?**"

"**They aren't.**"

"**Good, then I have no qualms with the children.**"

He looked at us before speaking, "**How did you get here though without being seen on the harbor?**"

"We flew."

"**Flew? On what?**"

"A dragon."

"**A dragon? What the fuck is a dragon?**"

I grinned for a moment before setting Annie down on the ground, and speaking, "**A powerful beast.**"

He looked at me now and sighed after a moment before speaking, "**If it is a powerful beast, where is it?**"

I glanced at Azier and she bit her lip. Blackwell looked between us for a moment but kept himself silent, and finally, the lad turned around before raising his eyebrow and speaking, "**Well? Where?**"

"**I am it.**" I replied after a moment when Azier nodded at me.

He scoffed for a moment before he read the room and frowned before looking at his father and back at me. He swallowed before speaking, "**It was your blood that they forced down my throat?**"

"**No, that was a pure-blooded shifter's blood. I am a half-blood.**"

"**Half-blood? Between what entirely?**"

"**Shifter and werewolf.**"

"**You are from across the channel then. Those are where those species are located. Although, I guess not much longer. Considering the hunters are already out.**"

"**Hunters?**"

"**You don't know? There are twenty supernatural hunters, they are called Sazornoras. I only know because I have met one once, and he informed me of what he was.**"

"When?"

He looked at Azier before replying, "**About a week ago. I was on death's bed still, and visitors were allowed into my chambers to give me good wishes.**"

I glanced at Drake and saw the stark fear in him for a moment. He did not seem like he knew of this interaction. I looked at his son before asking, "**What did he want?**"

"**That is the weird thing, he wanted nothing. He gave me a vial of blood, and left.**"

"Do you still have this blood?"

"**Yeah, I still have it.**"

"Can I see it?"

**"Why?"**

"Please."

**"Fine, but I would have to go to my chambers to get it."**

"We'll wait."

He glanced at Blackwell for a moment before speaking, "**Blackwell, accompany me, please. I do not want a filthy guard directing me.**"

**"Why are you calling your people filthy?"**

**"Because the guard that took me was drunk out of his mind. He was staggering everywhere. I was helping him more than him helping me."**

**"Oh."**

**"Yeah."**

Drake looked like he would storm the castle to find the guard, but I cleared my throat. They looked at me before I looked at Azier before speaking, "**I will be in the field, Azier.**"

"Sounds good, Rafeor. I'll see you there."

I nodded once and looked at Drake for a moment, and he sighed before offering me his arm, and I snaked it into him before Blackwell opened the door and we stepped out. Aurelius put Annie and Johnathan to bed and walked out since Annie was turning into a pumpkin and was falling asleep in my arms.

****

We exited the chambers and seemed to shock all the guards before they stood taller and one tried hard not to look at Drake or his son directly in the eye. Drake instantly tensed but said nothing to the guard. He glowered at him, as we passed but nothing else. I knew that Drake would not punish his men in front of us. After a few minutes, we got to the field.

I slipped out of his hold and kept walking into the field. I stopped about halfway before I looked around to make sure that nothing would be killed in my shift. I allowed my dragon, Remmu to take control.

****

I shifted fast, raised my head into the sky, and roared. It shook the few trees, and the dogs began to bark in fear. Drake's jaw dropped as he looked at me. I turned my turquoise eye towards him and blinked once. Aurelius walked past Drake and instantly scrambled up my leg and sat in the spot where Johnathan and Annie had vacated a couple of hours before.

Drake scrambled backward after a moment and lowered his eyes to me. I smirked a little but did not really care in the slightest either. I turned my head slightly before I saw Azier coming towards us, along with the boy and Blackwell. Azier expertly got onto my head and I lifted my head after a moment. Drake, his son, and Blackwell stared at me in shock. Before I leaped into the sky without a word.

I angled myself slightly and flew over the mansion, and flew homeward. I made sure that I had one of my scales fall off in the flight since no one would believe them if they said a dragon. It also would make an excellent sword if done right.

****

We got back home without many issues, there was one spot where we had to go higher than normal, and that was to avoid detection of the humans below. Since we do not want any hunters after me. We continued after a while longer and finally we reached home. Where I saw evidence of something being off. I hovered in the air and looked down upon the mansion and beach and realized why it seemed off. There were a lot of werewolves hidden in the bushes, I felt Shadow stir in my mind for a moment before she asked me to land.

I landed with a boom, but Azier looked at Aurelius and whispered, "Don't leave her side."

"I won't."

Azier slid off of me, checked the nearest wolf, and frowned before looking over at me and whispering, "Knocked out. Not dead."

I blinked at her to acknowledge her. Azier stood up and finally approached a few more, and seemed to come to the same conclusion. However, since none of the other pack members were everywhere, meant that this was more than one wolf behavior. My eyes sparked orange for a moment since I was somewhat outraged. A low rumble came out of me, and Azier looked at me and placed her forefinger on her lips and I instantly fell silent. She looked around for a moment and found about twenty wolves knocked out in total. The ones posted on the outdoor posts. All of them.

I frowned but did not know what to think of it. Azier finally found one that was waking up slightly. She came towards him before whispering, "What happened?"

The guard coughed a little before wheezing out, "Logan escaped. He and the pack that supported him did this."

I had heard every single word. Azier stepped backward before speaking, "Anyone dead?"

The guard shook his head and wheezed out, "No."

"Thank the goddess."

Azier looked at me and saw that I was having somewhat trouble before she looked at Aurelius before speaking, "Aurelius, you can get off of her."

Aurelius slid down instantly and allowed me to shift into Shadow.

****

Shadow crouched down on the sand before growling out, "**Who did this to you?**"

"I don't know. They attacked us from the mansion side."

"**Okay. Rest. We will get to the bottom of this.**"

She stood up and towered over everyone and I had to crane my head up to look at her before she spoke, "**Azier, protect Aurelius. I can protect myself.**"

I would have said something, but knew better than to challenge her in front of others. I nodded once, and I went towards Aurelius as we entered the mansion.

# Chapter 54

Shadow entered the mansion first before she called out, "**Hello?**"

I cringed as her voice echoed. It was proof enough that the mansion was compromised, but now I was not entirely sure if it was. Nothing happened. We crept forward, and soon found more and more guards down, proving that the mansion was compromised. As we went further, we finally found Nathaniel's office. It was empty, but by smell alone, it was clear that he was in there not twenty minutes before. His scent was still fresh.

Shadow looked around the room and finally went towards a bounded book before she pulled it down. My jaw dropped slightly as the bookcase went up, revealing a secret staircase. We entered and Shadow grabbed the bookcase and pulled it back down. We headed down and soon found Nathaniel with Sophronia. Their eyes flickered to us before Nathaniel spoke, "**When did the three of you get back?**"

"**Not until after we saw everyone knocked out.**"

"**Everyone?**"

"To our knowledge, yes. The guards outside and the ones inside too. All knocked out, but alive."

"**I guess that is one good thing about this situation then.**"

"**What happened?**"

"**Logan's followers broke him out.**"

"**Any casualties in that aspect?**"

"**Thankfully none.**"

I glanced at Sophronia and noticed the small bulge in her stomach, and I looked up slightly before I noticed that my mother was there with Cyprus in the corner. Cyprus looked like he might bow down before her, and I suddenly wondered what he had done to get her attention on him. Normally, Cyprus was the most respectful member of my patrol, but he had a mouth, and I wondered if that was what happened in this case currently. I sighed before speaking, "What is the next order of business?"

Nathaniel sighed deeply before shaking his head and speaking, "**We can do nothing. We will let them go for now.**"

"What? And do nothing?"

"Yes."

"Why?"

**"Because that is what needs to happen. We have to prepare for war."**

I glanced at Shadow and saw her squint slightly before she replied, **"I do not tolerate being kept in the dark, Nathaniel. Tell me, what was being discussed in this office?"**

**"Swear on the moon that it will not get out."**

**"As if I would tell anyone. I swear on the moon."**

"I swear on the moon."

"I swear on the moon."

He looked at us and sighed deeply before replying, **"Logan was firstborn, but Taryn had a vision before the announcement ceremony that he would bring only destruction and devastation. That I, being second-born, would be the best leader. So that is what happened. That is why we cannot kill Logan."**

"We can't kill him, but can't we bring him close to death?"

**"You would want to bring your step-father to that sort of pain Aurelius?"**

"He was the one that made it possible for Finn, myself, and Shadow to get over the channel. He had his hand in all these backstabbing aspects. What do you think?"

Basil flared in his eyes for a moment before Nathaniel chuckled slightly before replying, **"Fair point in all of that."**

"What else was discussed?"

"The Carpathians are not going to fight on our side."

I looked at my mother and smiled slightly, but she did not return it. Her eyes were far away, and I saw her eyes scan the area and swallow hard. She knew something that she was not informing anyone in this room. She gets more intense seeing compared to myself and Cyprus, but we keep Ghost in the loop since he asked. Along with the fact that Taryn had said at one point that Ghost was to be told everything. He would help keep us safe along the way.

I sighed deeply and looked at Nathaniel and saw him with a frown across his face, as he too was watching Taryn. He knew that she was hiding something else. I sighed slightly and plopped myself into a seat, and instantly regretted it since a plume of dust went up, making me sneeze. Nathaniel chuckled slightly but stopped after a moment as the bookcase entrance dinged. Yes, there was a bell down here apparently. We all went silent.

****

Ghost, Batis, and Brego came down. Well more of, Ghost carrying Brego in a fireman carry. Ghost placed Brego down on the ground before straightening himself before speaking, "He is alive thankfully. However, he is in high need of medical services."

**"Has he said anything?"**

"No, he is in no condition to speak, Nathaniel. By the looks alone, he has taken on five traitors."

Basil surfaced and he gripped the table corner and was about to snap it off, when Sophronia placed her hand onto his. He stopped instantly before inhaling her scent. It was a few moments later that Basil disappeared from his eyes, and his aura fell again. Nathaniel sighed deeply before speaking, **"Sorry."**

"Don't be sorry, Nathaniel, you are being extremely cautious and able to control Basil somewhat. It makes me wonder what had happened too."

"It seems that this was a well-thought-out plan."

"That it was, they knew that we were missing. The best time to strike was when Nathaniel was in his office. When Shadow was on her mission. Same with you Azier, it makes it much easier when the next in line people are out of sight. And somewhat unreachable."

**"Where's Marius?"**

**"He went to find Espi."**

**"Find Espi?"**

**"Espi went out on his own a bit after you took off Shadow. I'm sure he is fine."**

**"Are you for sure of that?"**

**"Marius knows where we are if he needs assistance in finding him Shadow. He is going to be okay."**

It looked for a moment that Shadow was going to challenge it but stopped herself when she cocked her head to the side. **"If you are so sure, then why is my mate sending fine tremors of worry through the bond?"**

Nathaniel looked like he was going to say something, but Shadow turned around slightly and headed towards the staircase before she looked over her shoulder, growling, **"I'll be back."**

She went out, and without a word I went to follow her when Taryn spoke, "Azier you stay, Ghost go with Shadow."

I looked at my mother with a look, but her face was set. I knew better than to challenge her though, and fell silent. Ghost seemed perplexed before he followed Shadow, who had already entered the normal office space and headed further towards the exit.

*****

After they left, I looked at my mother before asking, "Why?"

"Because one of the visions is that Logan's men took him."

**"Ummm…. Are you sure about that, Taryn?"**

"I unfortunately believe it. If Marius hasn't been able to hide his anxiety from Shadow in the bond, means that he has not found him."

"You do know that Shadow will go hunting for him, right?"

"She cannot take on the third of the pack."

**"She considers that child as her own through, Taryn. She will go through hell and back for her family."**

Taryn looked at Sophronia before she swallowed, turning her gaze towards Nathaniel and speaking, "She cannot leave Nathaniel."

**"I cannot stop her when she has a rage, Taryn. She beats Basil in a fight, and I don't have the slightest idea if that is the best idea either."**

"Best idea for what? To try to stop her? I know Shadow and Rafeor quite well. Once she has a mission, it takes a tranquilizer to make her stop."

"Been talking to Marius have you, brother?"

"Yeah, I asked him what it is like to have a mate that is both shifter and wolf. He says that it is rare that her shifter comes into play as often as Shadow. However, when both her dragon and Shadow agree….. It is damn scary."

He shuddered in response, making Nathaniel smirk. Sophronia frowned before speaking, **"Have you thought about her dragon at all, Nathaniel? What is going to happen when we bring both the shifters and the rest of the pack together?"**

I sighed and knew that this was on everyone's minds, that if Shadow in deed took the leadership, like how Batis informed me on the way in. It was common knowledge in the patrol that Basil and Nathaniel were stepping down to Shadow when the time came. Nathaniel sighed heavily, drawing myself out of my thoughts, as I looked at him. He swallowed hard before replying, "**Her dragon will help lead the shifters to battle.**"

"**But that doesn't do anything for the pack.**"

"Yes and no."

I looked at Cyprus as he rubbed the back of his neck as if he was nervous. Nathaniel glanced at him with a look before speaking, "**Explain.**"

Cyprus glanced at our mother, and she shrugged in response. Cyprus sighed deeply before replying, "It will do both in helping in uniting the shifters and the pack. However, Shadow and Logan's son will both lead."

"**LOGAN'S SON IS NOT LEADING THE PACK!**" roared Basil.

Everyone flinched backwards, including Sophronia. Basil had his hair growing in before Aurelius spoke, "B-ba-Basil."

Basil looked at Aurelius with a murderous glower, and his talons elongated and his face started to turn into a snout. Nathaniel was losing this battle between being in control. I would have said something, but aura strong swept through the room, and Shadow showed back up.

****

I glanced at her out of the corner of my eye before she bellowed, "**BASIL! DOWN. NOW.**"

Basil stared at her and pulled back his lips in response, Nathaniel was not going to win this one. Shadow stared him down before growling, "**Don't.**"

He snarled in response and leaped at her, and Shadow met him in the air and slammed him to the ground. Batis had barely enough time to move Brego out of the way, as they landed where he was a moment before. Basil had his face to the ground, and Shadow stood over him. She was breathing heavily. She snarled, "**BASIL! RELEASE CONTROL! NOW.**"

She pushed her aura out completely, and I flinched back at the intensity. If it was directed at me, then I would have my nose to the ground and as low as I could be. Basil whimpered after a few minutes of this and finally submitted to Nathaniel. Shadow moved back as Nathaniel surfaced and panted.

Nathaniel glanced at Shadow's eyes and they were sparked with rage. Everyone could feel the anger flow through the pack bond. So, Taryn was correct, that Espi was taken. Shadow straightened herself out before she growled, "**He's gone. He is no longer in the palace. Meaning he has been taken.**"

She stated it as a growl, and everyone winced and backed away. Cyprus moved quietly in front of Sophronia. Shadow's eyes flickered around the room before she sneered slightly at the sight before speaking, "**As if I was to hurt my mother.**"

"Better be safe than sorry," Cyprus replied. His eyes still trained on Shadow. Shadow sneered in response but turned her attention to Taryn before speaking, "**You knew.**"

"That I did."

"**What am I supposed to do in your eyes?**"

Taryn swallowed hard before whispering, "You let him be, where he is."

"**Are they going to treat him horribly?**"

"I don't know the details, Shadow."

"**Is my son going to make it? Yes or no.**"

Taryn swallowed for a moment and cowered slightly. Answering the question for everyone. Espi would not make it. Shadow's eyes flared in response, they were orange before she growled, "**If I leave him where he is, what are his odds, Taryn? Will he be better off than if I go after him?**"

"It's fifty-fifty."

I glanced at my mother and knew that she wasn't telling Shadow anything wrong either. It looked like this was true, that it was a fifty-fifty chance. I swallowed before glancing at Ghost who had come back, along with Marius who looked deflated.

Ghost and I locked eye contact, and even though that we could not connect to each other, we knew each other well. Ghost glanced at Cyprus, and then at Batis, and it seemed that Batis was on the same wavelength because he was watching us. However, Cyprus was shaking his head no, but the majority of the patrol would go in a heartbeat.

Shadow glanced around the room before speaking, "**I am going after him.**"

"**No.**"

"**Nathaniel, he is my son.**"

"**And you are my daughter.**"

"**I am going, Nathaniel.**"

"**No.**"

**"Nathaniel, you don't have any say in this. I am going to get my son."**

**"You heard it yourself though, it is fifty-fifty."**

**"Nathaniel, even though Taryn said no a few minutes ago. She just admitted that it was a fifty-fifty chance."**

**"It is dangerous though. We have a war to plan for."**

"That may be the case, but this is the one time that Shadow will be able to go," replied Ghost. I glanced at him and saw Taryn frown before she glanced around at the patrol and swallowed. She knew the moment that I looked at Cyprus, and Ghost. She took a breath in sharply before shaking her head and speaking, "No, absolutely not, Azier!"

"Mother."

"No."

"As if you could stop us from doing our duties. Shadow is the next in line for the throne, and that is clear as day. What do you know about this that we do not know?" Ghost asked. We all turned our attention to Taryn as she fidgeted a bit before she finally sighed hard. "Nothing."

"That is a big fat lie and you know it. What do you know?" growled Batis, who looked ready to leave at a moment's notice. Taryn looked at him and replied, "Everyone there knows your scent. No one is going to let you get him out of the camp safely."

**"Who says that I will be myself?"**

"What are you talking about?"

**"They are going to be expecting a seven-foot-tall white Lycan, right?"**

"Yes."

**"Then I'll go as my shifter half."**

"How sure are you on this rescue mission?"

**"I am going to go after him, Taryn. I am not going to let them kill my son."**

Taryn looked deflated for a moment before she glanced at Marius and spoke, "Marius? What are you going to do?"

Everyone glanced at Marius and I saw his throat bob for a moment before he replied, "I am going to support my mate."

**"No, you are not."**

Everyone froze. Marius looked at Shadow for a moment and replied, "Why not?"

**"Because they all know your scent. No, actually no one from the pack goes."**

"If you go alone they will slaughter you!" Ghost growled in response.

Shadow shook her head and replied, "**I won't be alone.**"

"Then who are you going with?"

**"None of your concern."**

"Shadow."

**"No."**

Marius looked like he wanted to challenge it, but fell silent after a moment. He frowned, but looked at Nathaniel with a look across his face, speaking, "What now?"

Nathaniel sighed deeply before glancing at Shadow and speaking, "**Nothing. We prepare for war.**"

"Okay."

Marius looked at his mate for a moment and sighed deeply and seemed to think that this was his fault, I would have moved to speak to him when Shadow moved and rested her taloned hand onto him. She leaned down and whispered, "**It is not your fault, Marius. This is fate.**"

He looked up at her with a look, before he sighed deeply before whispering, "I will feel more comfortable when you tell me who you are going with."

**"It is better that you do not know whom I am going to go with."**

Marius looked about to challenge it, but Shadow removed herself from the room and left promptly, startling us all by the abruptness.

****

I started to follow when Taryn spoke, "No, let her."

"Mother."

"No, she is right. This is something that she has to do alone."

"Taryn, what do you possibly know? My mate is hell-bent on going on a mission alone."

"I know that she will get what she is after."

"Mother."

"No, that is all that I can say."

Everyone grumbled slightly. Marius sighed the deepest before speaking, "I'm going to check on the guards. See if any need further medical services."

**"I'll go with you,"** replied Nathaniel.

He looked at Sophronia before speaking, **"Do you want to join us, Sophronia?"**

**"I am safer down here, Nathaniel."**

**"Fair enough."**

Nathaniel and Marius left after a moment leaving: Sophronia, Taryn, myself, Ghost, Batis, Cyprus, and beat up Brego in the office space.

# Chapter 55

I looked at my mother and glanced at Sophronia, but she seemed to be in her little world momentarily. Finally, after a few moments of silence, Sophronia stood up and walked down the other flight of stairs without a word, leaving my patrol and Taryn in this office space.

Taryn looked at us all before swallowing. It was clear to her that Sophronia had left us to discuss whatever we needed to without someone hearing it. Finally, Ghost sighed deeply before speaking, "Alright spill. What do you know?"

"I know we have a slim chance at winning this war."

"Slim chance? Or a high chance of winning?"

"It is unfortunately slim."

"Why?"

"Because a certain someone will cause a whole ruckus that may damage what needs to happen."

"Who?"

"You know that I cannot tell you, Ghost."

"Are you going to tell Azier, Cyprus and Batis though?"

"No."

"But they are your children."

"They may be my children, but they still have much to learn."

"Then teach them. Who is going to cause a whole ruckus and cause our fight damage?"

"I cannot say, since it will alter the course it needs to stay on."

"Taryn, how can we help if you do not tell us?"

"I am not going to tell you who it is."

"Taryn."

"No."

"Mother?"

"Yes, Azier?"

"If there is a slim chance that we win the war, does that mean that the shifters, werewolves and Carpathians as a whole get destroyed?"

"No."

"So, that means that some of us survive this thing?"

Taryn fell silent. She sighed. "Yes, some of us will survive. However, at a terrible cost. The survivors may wish that they had been killed alongside."

"If that is the case, Taryn, why didn't you say anything?"

"Because that means there is hope. I don't want you to get your hopes up."

"Is it really that bad to hope?"

"In this case, yes. Yes, it is. Which is why I said nothing about it to everyone else."

"If that is true, then why are you telling us this, mother?"

"Because you will eventually get these visions yourself, Azier."

"That may be true, but why does it have to happen now?"

"Why does what need to happen now?"

"This course of events. Isn't there always another path? A new one that forms?"

"That is a small possible train of events, Azier, and you know it."

"It may be slim, but it is a chance."

Taryn scowled, folded her arms across her chest, and stared at me with a frown. Ghost sighed deeply before looking at Cyprus, speaking, "You are awfully quiet, Cyprus."

"Cause I don't have anything to add to this."

"Why not?"

"Because I agree with my mother. That some things are meant to happen. That this train of events is going to happen one way or another."

"So, you are not even slightly curious about other aspects in the next train of events?"

"Okay, you got me there, Ghost. I am slightly curious, but I also know the more questions we pester my mother with, she will make us do something to resolve it."

"That is an understatement, boys," replied Taryn with a smirk.

Ghost scowled before Cyprus chuckled a little before Batis spoke, "Mother, surely there is something else that you can tell us?"

"Fine, someone in this very room area is not going to make it."

Silence. We all stared at her before we glanced around at each other. My throat constricted. I did not want any of them to be dead. However, Taryn whispered, "But it is not yet set in stone on that aspect either. But be warned, it is in more than three trains of events that one of you is not going to make it."

"Who?"

"Cannot tell you."

"Please?"

"Sorry, Ghost. I cannot tell you anything else."

"But…"

"No, that is the end of it."

Ghost looked like he would continue to challenge it, but Cyprus hung his head, speaking, "Okay, we know that someone in this chamber is not going to make it. Here is my question though. What is going to happen when the shifters join us?"

"That is a good question."

"What do you mean, a good question? You act like you don't know, Taryn."

"Because I don't know. That is not entirely in the vision."

"So, there is a chance that this could all be avoided?"

"Possibly, but I am unsure of the shifter king. What would Morphous do if he had to bow down to someone powerful?"

"He will do the right thing for his people."

"How sure of that are you, Ghost?"

"Every great leader has to have sacrifices, surely, Taryn."

"Yeah, keyword great." Chuckled Cyprus. This caused Taryn to look at him for a moment with a look. Cyprus shrugged his shoulders and crossed his arms. He did not seem indifferent to what was being discussed. It seemed he was okay with the thought that one of us would not make it. I looked at Ghost and saw him frown before looking at Taryn and speaking, "Taryn, what else do you know?"

"Nothing that is good. Ghost."

"Please, Taryn."

"Fine, I can tell you a little. Swear on the moon. All of you."

"I swear on the moon."

"I swear on the moon."

"I swear on the moon."

"I swear on the moon."

Taryn glanced at Brego and spoke, "Batis, check on him."

Batis dropped to the ground and pressed his fingers onto his throat. He looked up after a moment before replying, "Alive, but does not have an awake heartbeat. He is still out cold."

"Okay, good enough."

Taryn continued, "It is still unclear what will happen with the shifters and the outlanders. Mainly because their leaders are unhinged. It may take Tobias more than the time that we have to win them over at all. Along with the fact that Tobias has to fight the demons."

"Demons?"

"Yeah, apparently, Killian is there along with someone else. Unsure of who they both are, but since Quinn is a demon, I would assume his father is one too. Therefore, I have a feeling that the challenge of the alphas over there isn't going smoothly. Since he has to challenge someone dangerous."

"Is my father going to make it out of that situation alive, Taryn?"

"Your father gets back here, but he is changed compared to what he left as."

"In what way?"

"I cannot say for certain, Ghost."

"Taryn."

"I am sorry, it is hazy in that field of things, Ghost."

Ghost sighed deeply before shaking his head in defeat. Now that they knew that Quinn was not the only demon, it meant a couple of things. If we could win them over, then we could win the war. However, that was a maybe. It is still clouded in shadows and hazy as Taryn said. I looked at my mother before speaking, "So there is a chance that the demons would be on our side?"

"That is clouded in shadow, Azier."

"But there is a chance?"

"Yes, there is a chance. However, I am unsure of how likely that is."

"What do you mean?"

"The other person may be in charge and I have not the slightest idea how it would work."

"It would work better if we know who the other person is," replied Cyprus.

Who looked at our mother with a pointed look. She sighed deeply before replying, "Mind you, I don't know if this is true or not. However, the visions say that Killian is with someone named Calio."

"Calio?"

"Yeah."

"Huh, interesting."

"What is?" asked Ghost, looking at me with raised eyebrows.

I sighed. "I had a vision that they would come back over here. Someone had that name in my dreams."

"When was this dream?"

"Three nights ago."

"And why are you only saying this now?"

"Because it didn't make sense."

"Do dreams ever make sense?"

"Fair point. They don't always make sense."

"Then why did you think it would change now?"

I would have replied to Ghost, but after a moment, Taryn growled, "Shush."

The bell dinged and we all fell silent. Someone was coming down here.

*****

Aurelius arrived back down, with a platter of baked goods and drinks. I had not realized that she had gone out at some point. She looked around wildly before she set down the platter, stepped backwards, and locked eye contact with me. She could tell that we were discussing something that she had interrupted. I glanced at mother and saw that her lips were in a grim line. She did not even look at what Aurelius had brought down and turned around to face the wall.

Ghost sighed after a moment. "Thank you, Aurelius."

"Uh, you're welcome."

"When did you leave to get all of this?"

"Right when Ghost and Shadow went out to see if they could find Espi, I think."

"Ah, well Sophronia is down the stairs if you want to keep her company."

"No, leave," growled Taryn, her eyes daggers in Aurelius's direction suddenly. Aurelius gasped slightly and took a step backwards before bursting into tears as she fled up the stairs and out of the hidden entrance.

*****

I turn slowly around to face my mother, snapping, "Why such venom for someone who did no wrong?"

"It is because she will be the reason why someone in this room dies."

"So, you are taking it out on her now?"

"Yes."

"Mother, that is not fair to Aurelius as of current. You should apologize to her when you see her next time."

"If I had my way, Cyprus, there would not be a next time."

"Mother, that is treason talk."

Cyprus glowered at his mother, his wolf flickered in his eyes in response. Like Ghost, his wolf was somewhat harder to trigger a response out of, and you never know he was done until something happened. Taryn glowered at Cyprus and was about to say something, but Ghost beat her to it, "Taryn, Aurelius does not mean any of us harm. I doubt that she will purposely make us die. There has to be some sort of trap that we walk into."

"That is where you are wrong, Ghost. She will willingly put one of you in that danger."

"I doubt that she will. Not unless they have something or someone that she wants," replied Batis. He glowered at our mother for a solid moment before growling out, "Correct?"

Our mother kind of squirmed a little before muttering, "Correct."

"See? You are harming a young girl as is, mother. You are so quick to judge others. Even before certain events happen. I am glad that this gene skipped me."

"You don't mean that!"

Taryn sounded outraged at the thought that Batis thought that. He shrugged and crossed his arms across his chest before replying, "I can think what I want, mother, it is what I believe. I am glad that I did not get the seer gene. I am glad that one of us children came out like dad."

"DO. NOT. BRING. UP. YOUR. DEAD. BEAT. FATHER!" bellowed Taryn. Her wolf surfaced enough to make me frown. Dove usually never sparked in mother's eyes, even growing up, she never really surfaced. She never really ran with the pack either on our nightly runs. Even though everyone knew that Dove would love to, Taryn refused to let her out. I wondered why she never let Dove out to play and be with her pack members. I suddenly wondered if it was because she considered Dove to be beneath her, and that was why Dove never got to surface and have fun.

Ghost stared at Taryn before he spoke quietly. It was rare, extremely rare for Ghost, the actual Ghost to speak and when he did it was with precision, "Taryn, it seems that you are trying extremely hard to not let Dove out. Why?"

Taryn froze, Ghost blinked his golden eyes at her. She swallowed hard before speaking, "It matters not, Ghost."

"It matters to me. Why are you suppressing Dove? She deserves to come out in the open."

"She is weaker than I am."

"And yet, you say that our wolves are superior to you. Why are you suppressing Dove?"

"I don't have to tell you that, Ghost."

"I am of higher rank than you. Do not make me Alpha command you."

I gasped. Cyprus glanced at Ghost and for a moment no one spoke. Finally, Cyprus whispered, "What do you mean, Ghost?"

"I am an alpha wolf. Asaro and I both didn't want to be alpha, he was fine being a beta, and therefore Tobias had allowed us to have everyone believe we were. Now answer me, Taryn. Why can't Dove come out to be who she is?"

I glanced at my mother with a sudden thought, she never let Dove out, not once during childhood. Not once did Dove come out, now I slightly wondered if Dove was the wolf that my mother always claimed that she was, which was a vicious beast that she had to keep a very tight, short leash on. I wonder if it was the completely opposite.

Ghost did not back down, he stared hard at Taryn and finally, Taryn muttered, "I suppress her because she is not what I want to be."

"Explain."

"I don't want to, Ghost."

"EXPLAIN."

He growled in warning, making us all flinch as he rolled out his alpha aura, something that must take a lot of mental strength to keep back. Since everyone believed that he was beta-born. Taryn gasped in response and Dove's green eyes flickered to light before her voice whispered out, "Help me."

My wolf likes being called, pretty much each and everyone in my patrol, our wolves' names were the ones that handle everything. At least, they had their names, and Taryn had accepted that our wolves' names were the names we would go by. She growled and flickered in my eyes. Brego who had been out for most of what had been happening, growled low in his throat. His eyes flashed. Every single one of our wolves had surfaced. Not a good sign for anyone to be on the receiving end. Taryn swallowed.

****

She would have said something but Sophronia came upstairs, blasting Taryn with her aura, and was pulling from the pack. Taryn sat down with a whimper and I glanced at Sophronia and wondered what she had heard – what if she was eavesdropping in on this conversation? However, Sophronia seemed to know what I was thinking but she shook her head and replied after a moment, "**It is extremely rare for Ghost to let go of his alpha aura. When he does, it goes everywhere.**"

"Oh."

Sophronia spared me a small smile before turning her smile back into a frown. "**Dove, what do you mean, help you?**"

"She makes it so I cannot come out freely, my lady. She is keeping me under lock and key so to speak."

"**Why? Taryn?**"

"Because she is weak."

"**How is she weak?**"

"She would tell everyone what we see. She cannot be trusted."

**"Dove, why does she think that?"**

"Because some of it is the truth, I would tell some of it. However, I would be selective in what I would say. I understand somewhat why Taryn doesn't allow me to come out, but all the time? I did not even get to play with my mate before Taryn rejected him after he gave us children."

"You…. rejected dad?"

"This is why I don't allow her out! She is giving away too much in…"

"ENOUGH! Taryn, you had caused a hard rip in your children, they believed that their father rejected you. That is why they have helped you hence far since they BELIEVED IT WAS THE OTHER WAY AROUND!"

Ghost flared in rage, and I noticed that he was drooling more, along with sweat on his brow. It showed that Asaro was trying to keep him down, but was being ignored in command. Uh oh, I looked at Cyprus, Batis and Brego before linking them, since for whatever reason we could link each other in the office space, *"Slowly edge away from Ghost and Taryn. Do not do it fast though. Protect Sophronia."*

Cyprus and Brego glanced at Ghost and seemed to notice the difference too. Brego sighed, picked himself off the ground, walked slightly, and caught Taryn's gaze in this act. Brego stared at her for a moment before speaking, "Hey, I'm still stiff, okay?"

Taryn snorted in response but her eyes flickered to Batis and Cyprus, suddenly wondering what could have happened in the past few moments.

I glanced at Sophronia and she seemed to realize that Taryn was goading Ghost. She glanced at Ghost out of the corner of her eye and seemed to know that she was in no condition to move away from him. It would trigger a train of events that should be avoided.

I felt something in the pack link and knew that Taryn may or may not feel it too. Ghost stepped towards Taryn for a moment with a hard look. Before anything could happen, the bell jingled, announcing someone was coming down here.

*****

A triad of power swept through the stairs and room. Taryn bared her neck instantly, Ghost, however, was unaffected, but everyone else besides Sophronia bared their necks. Sophronia glanced in the doorway and I spared a look and saw Basil highly in Nathaniel's eyes before he boomed out, **"What. is. Going. On. here?"**

His voice was rather calm, and I noticed that Taryn wanted nothing to do with how calm he was. Whenever a wolf went dead calm before a fight or asked a question, meant that you were in the dog house. Not even a little bit, a lot. Basil glanced around the room, at all the wolf-lit eyes before speaking, **"Ghost, answer me."**

"Taryn has been suppressing Dove, her wolf, for years. Along with the fact that she released the information that she rejected her goddess-given mate after they had their children together."

**"Taryn, is that true?"**

"Yes, Basil."

**"Explain."**

"She is a weak wolf, Basil, she would tell everyone of the dreams and visions. She had to be kept on a short leash."

**"Explain to me why your mate had to suffer your choice though."**

"It was either reject him or find a way to kill him."

Ghost stared at Taryn as she said it so easily, however, I could tell that my mother did not want to say that. However, she was under bound by the alpha command, that Basil was giving out every word.

Basil hung his head slightly before speaking, **"Ghost, Brego. Escort Taryn down to the dungeons."**

"Yes, my king."

"But wouldn't that be punishing Dove at the same time though?" Brego asked, making Basil look at him.

Brego flinched but held himself steady as he looked at Basil who looked conflicted for a moment. He looked at me, Cyprus and Batis before replying, **"It is a discussion that needs to happen without her in it. Take her down to the dungeons. I apologize now, Dove."**

"I understand, my king, "Dove replied.

Taryn tried to struggle slightly when Brego approached and tried to get her to come with him, but Ghost had no qualms though. He went up to her, threw Taryn over his shoulder, and carried her away. She swayed back and forth and pounded on his back, but everyone knew that she would be stuck, and Brego was left following after Ghost after a moment.

****

I glanced at Basil and saw him bring in Sophronia so her scent would calm him. Soon, Nathaniel blinked after a moment and he sighed and rubbed the bridge of his nose before he whispered, "**Well, it is now up to the three of you on what you want to happen.**"

I glanced at Cyprus and saw Batis hanging his head down. Batis replied after a hesitated moment, "We cannot do anything to her. She is the seer."

"That is not entirely true, once she goes, then it will pass to the next one in line."

**"You want to kill your mother?"**

Nathaniel seemed shocked at the response that Cyprus gave. Cyprus swallowed hard before replying, "She has made it hard for anything to be fun. She has dictated our lives and has made it a living hell in some form or another. Although, there has to be a way that Dove gets left alone in this process. I have no qualms with Dove, but I have qualms with Taryn herself."

Nathaniel glanced at us, Batis and me. He saw the conflict in our eyes for a moment. Batis sighed deeply before speaking, "As much as I agree with that, are you two prepared for that? Has she trained you entirely in knowing when to tell someone something?"

I glanced at Cyprus and we both slowly nodded before replying, "Yeah, she had trained us the moment we had dreams that were becoming real. We were about four in age when we could speak freely."

Nathaniel looked conflicted. "**So, you would rather see your mother dead, and keep her wolf alive?**"

"In sums, yes. That is what we would want to happen."

He glanced at Batis and me as he was speaking. We both nodded after a hesitated moment. As much as Taryn taught us how to be who we were, she had no excuse for what she had done. Nathaniel seemed shocked and would have said something when Sophronia replied, "**How long has Dove not been able to come out?**"

"As far as we know, she has not let her out once. Not even to meet her mate when our father was in the picture."

Sophronia lowered her eyes for a moment and sighed heavily before looking at Nathaniel. There was only one person who could separate a wolf and a human from each other, and that was a druid. However, since Morphous's raid, they were gone. Nathaniel looked at me for a moment before speaking, "**Azier, is this truly what you want?**"

"She has wronged too many people otherwise, Nathaniel. She has to face her punishments."

**"That may be true, but the only way to separate a wolf and a human would be by a Druid."**

I swallowed after a moment and glanced at Cyprus, who looked conflicted for a moment. He finally sighed heavily before speaking, "The Druids are still alive."

**"What?"**

"There is a tribe at the base of a mountain, and they were harboring a member of our tribe that we had protected. However, I am unsure of when they would come back."

**"They?"**

"In my part of the dream, they were with Quinn. I am unsure about the other's face, but I do know that they were traveling together."

**"How sure of this are you two?"**

"Positive that this is going to happen. Whenever something like both of us dreams the same thing, it usually always means that it is going to happen."

**"Does Taryn know?"**

"With all that has been happening, we haven't had the chance to inform her of this."

**"But if you two had the same dream..."**

"It is weird, but it doesn't entirely work like that. Taryn explained that if we both had a dream that was the same base, we needed to inform her immediately. However, since we have been on duty, there have been other more pressing things than talk about a dream."

**"How can you be sure that Taryn did not have the dream though?"**

"If it remotely mattered to her, it would have. However, I believe that the goddess gives us different dreams. Taryn may have the ability to know when some sort of catastrophic event may happen now, but when she moves onto the next world, that means that she will be no longer in the thick of things. It would go to the next one, which in our case would be myself and Azier."

**"Hmmm. Interesting logic in that aspect, Cyprus. Azier, is that true?"**

"It is true, Taryn always sat us down the next morning and we used to inform her of the weird dreams that we had during the night while they were still fresh in our minds. However, this may have a small issue, since we have moved on with our lives, Taryn has been more and more aloof than normal."

**"Meaning?"**

"Meaning that she may know something that she has not informed us of. There has to be a reason why she has not communicated anything for the past week and a half with us."

"That is a good point in that, Azier. Taryn always sought us out every other day, but it has been a while since she has tried to get in contact with us."

**"Hmmm. That would mean that she knows something."**

"The question is what does she know? Since our dreams and stuff are different. It is like a puzzle somewhat. We each get a piece of the puzzle and we don't know the whole story until we discuss it."

**"So, it is best to keep her alive then?"**

"If we can separate Dove and Taryn from each other, that is the best plan at this point. Taryn will still get the dreams, but Dove will be able to play and be as she pleases. Since Taryn has suppressed her for so long," Batis replied.

I looked at him and thought through what he had suggested. I knew that Cyprus would rather see her dead, but also understood that it would benefit us that she would be that. I glanced at Cyprus and saw him frown as he thought through what Batis had suggested when the bell dinged a few times.

****

Ghost and Brego entered the room, and glanced at us all before Ghost spoke, "Is all safe?"

"Yes, Ghost," replied Cyprus. Ghost nodded and looked at Nathaniel before his eyes fell to Asaro's eyes. Asaro blinked a few times before he panted and gasped out, "Damn."

"I agree."

Asaro looked at him and smirked slightly before turning his attention to me and speaking, "You good, Azier?"

"Yeah, Ghost."

Asaro smirked before his face fell slightly. He sighed deeply before speaking, "For the time being, call me by my name. Ghost is on edge."

**"What does he sense?"**

"Something is coming our way, that we won't be ready for since most of our pack is a traitor."

Silence. I looked at Nathaniel and saw him tighten his hold on Sophronia. I glanced at Cyprus and saw him frown slightly before he began to speak, "There may be a way that your children grow up, Nathaniel, since this does not look like it is going in our favor."

**"What suggestion are you thinking, Cyprus?"**

"Send Sophronia across the channel."

Nathaniel stared at Cyprus as if he lost his marbles. I swallowed but did not drop my eye contact with him. Nathaniel stared at us all before whispering, **"Will I be in their lives?"**

"If current events happen, not likely," replied Cyprus in a hushed whisper.

Asaro looked down and spoke after a moment, "Taryn told us all that we had to keep it a secret, Nathaniel. That if Sophronia stays over here, she and your offspring will not survive. However, the war will not cross the channel. That we know for sure."

Nathaniel removed himself slightly from Sophronia before looking at her for a moment, with tears in his eyes. However, Sophronia shut us all down, **"I may not survive over here, but the one and most important thing in my life is Nathaniel. I am not disappearing from my mate."**

**"It sounds like you would die though, Sophronia…."**

**"Nathaniel, we have been through hell and back. This is war, honey, and I will stand by your side to my bitter end. How the goddess sees fit. I will not tolerate anything else."**

**"Are you sure?"**

**"Nathaniel, we have made our vows. Do you not remember the last one?"**

**"Until death do us part."**

**"Until death do us part, yes."**

She glanced at us and whispered, **"I would rather die with my mate near me, rather than flee."**

"Honorable," replied Asaro.

I glanced at him and knew that he wanted his mate for years, but she or he, unsure of which he would choose. Has not come to the pack in search of their goddess-given mate. I swallowed, even I wondered if I was blessed with one. My patrol was all over eighteen, old enough to find their mates, and Asaro was the oldest by two years compared to Cyprus, he was twenty-five. Asaro was twenty-three, and everyone else, Brego, Batis, and myself were twenty-one.

I sighed heavily as I got out of my immediate thoughts bringing the attention to myself before I spoke, "What is the plan now?"

**"The plan is to get ready for what is to come."**

"Okay."

I pushed myself towards the stairs and paused before looking over my shoulder at my family and I smiled slightly before I turned and headed out. I would oversee the training, at least some of it since I knew that was where it was needed the most. War was coming, and we had to prepare.

# Chapter 56

I have searched the hidden tunnels in this bloody shifter palace, but they were no longer there. Their scent was dimming, and fading from the walls themselves. I scowled and backed out of the entrance, heading towards the dungeon entrance. I have found this area much by accident, there were a few tunnels in the dungeon that I had stumbled on since I was now allowed to move freely down here. Morphous only had a handful of prisoners, and two that were further down the tunnel, those two he forbade me to touch. However, I had entered the woman's cell once and found out that she was his so-called wife. However, she was not entirely joyful. She had dull eyes and only a skeleton of what she must have been when she was above ground. I didn't know anything about the shifter lines entirely, so I did not take blood from her. The other one though, Sammuel, I one hundred percent did take his blood. He was rather tasty, and I knew I would be coming back down there for his again soon. I may not be like my father and older brother, but I did have my share of drinking blood from those unwilling.

Soon, I made it back to the dungeons and found that I was not alone down there. I looked around and spotted a figure in the darkness. He stood up and walked into the flame before I could make out that it was Morphous. I scowled slightly before speaking, "Come down here to gloat, did you?"

**"Far from it, Akato."**

"What do you want?"

**"I want the truth."**

"As if I would give that to you."

He stared at me for a moment before replying, **"You traveled back here with Aurelin, for months. And you never once let it slip on what you are doing here with him."**

"He didn't need to know the details."

**"Are you so self-centered that you do not see the benefits of confining in someone?"**

"I am not self-centered. If I was, then there would be an issue. My father sent me here to do exactly what I am currently doing. Also, you are one to speak. You have your wife down here in the stinking dungeons. What crime has she committed that deserves that treatment?"

**"Treason."**

"What does treason look to you exactly?"

**"She tried to have several of my members killed."**

"Yet, you make it so I cannot feed on her? Why?"

**"Because that is not what she will do. Along, with the fact that she is a shifter."**

"That doesn't entirely concern me, Morphous."

**"It should though, has your father informed you of what happened to someone like yourself that had tasted shifter blood? And what happened to them?"**

I stared at him for a moment before replying, "No, he has not said anything on that aspect. Do you know what happened?"

**"Vaguely, it was before my time."**

"Do tell then."

**"The Carpathian in question went nuts. I think this was when your father was pretty young himself, however, he was the ruler of your realm. Anyhow, the Carpathian in question had changed. He had begun to show signs of being a mutt."**

"A mutt?"

**"Yes, he started showing that he was not a pure-blood Carpathian."**

"Not possible."

**"It is too possible. Have you wondered how your species came to be?"**

"We came to bring nothing but pain and misery to the humans, and the gods at the time thought we had done our duties well, and granted us immortal life. Therefore, created the superior species."

**"Really?"**

"Yes really. Why? What have you heard?"

**"I heard that you were placed on this earth because you had trifled with the wrong god, and had angered it so much that it banished you to live your life sucking the life out of others."**

I scowled in response before growling out, "What do you possibly want, Morphous?"

**"As I told you, I want the truth."**

"What truth do you seek then?"

**"Why are you here?"**

"I already told you that the day I arrived."

**"Humor me, and tell me again."**

"Why should I humor you?"

**"Because I will hurt you if you don't."**

I raised my eyebrow at him before speaking, "Ah, I was wondering when you were going to show yourself, Abacore. What was in that concoction that your medic gave you?"

His eyes narrowed in response, but did not reply. I smirked before shaking my head, crossing my arms, and raising my eyebrow slightly before speaking, "You know full well where I stand. Where my father stands too. We are done Morphous, Abacore."

**"Has it occurred to you that if you helped us, and did not fight against us, then you would have more chance people willingly give you their blood?"**

I paused, "I had the same thoughts at one point too, however, going there with Herald, showed me that the shifters were the one species that was not supposed to be here. They were supposed to disappear and die. My father had sent me a message at one point, informing me that I was not banished as I had been. That I could come home, but yet again, I had more sights to see. More to see overall. It was eye-opening to see how the shifters worked along with the other limited species I had met so far. It showed me that I had more to see, however, that did not mean that the shifters were in the clear to be here. The Sazornoras were going to rain down on the shifters, and eventually the werewolves, but to make it work in our favor according to my father, I had to make sure to work alongside the leader of the Sazornoras to make sure that they leave the humans, along with the werewolves alone. So, we have our food bank."

He cleared his throat and raised his eyebrow at me, I scowled and suddenly remembered that we were discussing, but I had dismissed him. I raised my eyebrow before replying in a snapping tone, "What do you want more of, Morphous? I already answered your questions. Leave me."

**"Answer mine."**

"No, we are done."

**"Akato, this is where the communications are stopping at. Come on, tell me what the reason why you are here. Along with the fact that you are fighting against us, has it occurred to you that we have been protecting the nature of things? You would be tossing that away."**

I turned around and had my back to him before I growled out, "I am done talking, Morphous. Leave me."

**"Akato…"**

I turned sharply on my foot and spun around, if I had my weapons, I would have killed him. However, I knew that I could not kill him. I would get the wrath of all the shifters. Morphous squinted his eyes at me and growled a low warning. However, I hissed, eyes are red at this point, "OUT!"

**"Last time I checked, I am in my home, Akato. This is MY DUNGEONS!"**

I squinted my eyes at him. He rarely raised his voice, and when he did, it usually was not the best place to be. I noticed that his eyes turned orange, but they did not turn red. I rocked back on my heels and turned to go back down the hallway, to disappear into the walls, when he spoke again, **"You are not allowed down in the dungeons any longer, Akato. Find your own food."**

I froze, and a flash of rage flared through me. However, I turned my head slightly before snapping, "So be it."

I disappeared into the hallway and left him standing where he was. If I had the authority, I would fucking take this excuse of a leader out. However, I knew that I was not destined to take out Morphous Draconis. Even though he was a prick, he was a good leader for his people.

*****

I had turned more than once, to make sure that he did not follow me. However, since I did not need a torch, meant that I could see him way before he saw me if he decided to come after me. Finally, after a bunch of this way and that way and backups, I had finally made it to the area I wanted. I shoved the door open, letting the air of the crisp night air into the entrance, which has been long since forgotten, and walked out. I knew that the shifters did not know this entrance, and kept myself extremely quiet about the hidden entrance, and exited. I was going to use it to assist the Sazornoras into the palace.

After a few minutes, I stopped walking and headed towards the stables. One of the hands stared at me with bleary eyes, since I had made my presents known. He was a young lad, not yet old enough to know better. However, he looked at me with a frown before speaking, "Can I help you with something?"

"I need a horse."

"You would need Morphous's permission to get a horse."

"Do you know who I am?"

His throat bobbed, but he raised his head slightly higher before speaking, "It doesn't matter. No one gets a horse without Morphous's permission. Regardless of whom they are."

I scowled. I was about to argue, when the boy spoke up, "My lord…."

**"It is alright, Will, he can take a horse. Pick one for him."**

"Right away, my Lord!"

He stood up and scrambled to his feet. I noticed that the horse in the stall was a big black stallion, I walked towards him and would have touched him, when the boy spoke up, "Not him."

"Why not?"

"He has strangles."

"What is that?"

"Fever, nasal discharge along with swollen lymph nodes. In other words, won't get you anywhere."

I stopped and looked at the stallion, he wheezed in response, but other than that he did not do anything else. He looked like he was suffering, so I did the thing that my father would do, and quickly put the horse down.

His body dropped after his neck snapped, and Will stared at the animal before whispering, "Y-yo-you…. You killed him."

"That is what happens with animals when they are sick. You put them down."

"That…. That doesn't happen here! You killed a horse that was getting better!"

I shrugged and replied, "And how often were you taking care of it?"

"For a few days, he was getting better."

"A few days too long."

Will looked at Morphous. I turned slightly and saw Morphous staring at the black stallion before speaking, "**Will, stop. He has made it clear that he cannot be trusted with anything that we have.**"

"Thank you, my lord."

Will stepped away, still staring at the stallion I had killed, before walking away with his head hung low. I raised my eyebrow at Morphous before speaking, "You should have seen that coming, surely."

Morphous looked up at me with a hard stare before whispering, "**You just killed a shifter.**"

"What?"

I was not ready for that, I knew that they could shift into other animals, and had seen a few trained ones even. However, none as a horse. Morphous stared at me with a hard look before finally speaking, **"Part of our training here, Akato, is to be one of the animals. It is our core training, and you just killed a shifter."**

I looked at the dead stallion and swallowed. I knew the laws that the shifters here follow and knew the moment that Morphous continued did I understand, **"Get out of here, Akato. Get out before the family of their loved ones comes. Although, they would know it is you since no one else would be so cruel. You are not allowed to come back here."**

"Morphous...."

**"Out."**

"How was I supposed to know it was a shifter?"

**"You weren't! Part of the training we have here is that you wouldn't know if it is or not until they shift back."**

I swallowed and growled out, "That is your fault for not alerting me that there are shifters as animals!"

**"Get out of here, Akato! You are BANISHED!"**

His eyes flared Abacore's for a solid ten seconds, as he tried to force himself out. However, after a few moments, Morphous got him under control again. Morphous shook his head and hissed, **"Go."**

I backed away, and looked at the other horses, wondering which was which. However, none of the others had shifted back, and they nickered in response at my attention. However, Morphous looked at them all, and seemed to talk to them and they all turned their heads down and fell asleep again. Except for one, who was a buckskin stallion. His eyes stared hard at me before he looked at Morphous, but did not go to sleep. Morphous glanced at the buckskin before glowering at me before moving away.

I sighed, I knew that moment that I had fucked up. Although now, I understood something. Shifters could be animals, and part of their training would be as animals, therefore they were harder to detect. I needed to inform Zhukov of this finding.

# Chapter 57

I got back to Zaros's office without a hitch, no one stopped me in the halls. He was still leaning against the railing, looking at the gore that was on his floor and walls. I cleared my throat and Zaros looked down at me before motioning me to join him. I hesitated for a brief second, before complying. After I got up beside him, he turned to speak softly, "**Cornelius, I can assume you did not know that your nephew could kill without the need for weapons?**"

"I did not realize that until today, Zaros. Before now, I thought I would never see Killian's son."

**"Do you hold any resentment for what he did?"**

I was silent for a moment before replying, "Do you hold resentment for what Killian had done, Zaros?"

**"I do believe I asked you first."**

"No, not really. I am sure that Killian knew that his son would eventually make his way back here."

**"So, you are aware that when you do go out, there is a chance that you come across Killian?"**

"Aware, but unsure on the cost of it."

Zaros looked perplexed for a moment before he nodded slightly and looked at the bodies before us. I tried hard not to look at it, but couldn't help it after a moment. I looked at the gore that was scattered and swallowed hard. Zaros sighed deeply before gesturing me to the lower level of his office. I instantly complied with his wishes and scrambled down the ladder. There was still one body here, but Zaros did not heed it any. It was less gruesome than the ones on his platform.

Zaros looked at me as he sat in his chair rocking slightly before looking at me with his calculated look and speaking, "**I am sure that you know that I want you to keep your nephew away from the dragon, however, I am aware at this point that there is no stopping him when he is set. Do you think there is any way to keep him from going up there?**"

I sighed deeply before shaking my head in response. I looked down at the blood splatter and swallowed slightly before replying, "As much as we both want to keep them inside the mountain, we both know that we cannot keep them down here."

**"I know that I cannot keep them down here as much as I want to. It still doesn't mean I want them to go up to Corimid."**

"I agree, I don't want to either."

**"Then talk them out of it."**

"Have you tried to talk them out of something? You have heard everything one way or another, Zaros, you know I have tried to prevent them from going up."

**"That is not entirely true either. You at first wanted to go up there. It was only after I informed you of what is up there that you backpedaled."**

"Alright, that is true. However, I am not in the mood to get roasted alive at the same time though."

**"Don't blame you."**

We both fell silent for a moment before I looked up at him, he was watching me intently. I asked him a question, "Why are you allowing me to leave, Zaros? You could have said no."

**"Because you had done nothing wrong. You are free to come and go as you want."**

"That may be true in some forms, Zaros, but you must have an alternative motive."

Zaros sighed deeply and leaned back into his chair which creaked under the movement. He replied, **"Alright, there is one alternative motive. I wanted someone I can trust to be on the outside."**

"What do you mean?"

**"There was something that my father has passed down, it is from generation to generation. However, we cannot speak freely here as much as I wish it so. Come along, Cornelius."**

He stood up, and without waiting for me to reply, he was already out of the door. I was left to follow in his wake.

*****

We went up, and up, and up. Finally reaching the caverns even above his. I swallowed and knew that this area entirely was restricted. I hesitated before entering after him when he paused to enter another room. He entered and I was surprised to find another office space set up. A little dusty, but it seemed well cared for either way. I could tell that he knew what I was thinking but also did not inform me of the why's. He sat on the chair, and a small cloud of dust went up, but he did not seem to be disturbed by it either. I sat down across from him, and another small dust cloud went up. I waved it across my face, coughing slightly. I looked around the room for a moment and finally looked back at Zaros who gave me a look. I swallowed and dipped my head towards him in acknowledgment.

He sighed before speaking, **"Not a word to anyone else about this place, Cornelius. There was a time when this was my father's study before he passed away."**

"Wait, your father died? When?"

**"You didn't know?"**

"No."

**"Hmmm. Well, he passed away three winters ago, Cornelius. I was surprised that you did not know."**

"Oh."

**"Anyhow, that is not what I brought you up here for. I was going to tell you some history. Ready to take some more?"**

"You know that I like reading history."

**"That I do know since you are allowed in the semi-restricted area to get the books you seek."**

I frowned, I did not realize that there was a difference between a restricted area and a semi-restricted area. Especially when it came up on the knowledge point. It should be open to everyone. However, I could tell that Zaros was not in any mood to change what had been working for him for centuries. I sighed and rubbed my hand across my face before speaking, "I didn't realize that they were in the semi-restricted area, Zaros."

**"No heed to it, Cornelius."**

He fell silent for a moment before asking, **"Answer me truthfully, where do your loyalties lie?"**

"You know that I still consider Dracula as my king, however, you have shown me what a true leader does with his people. I will follow you to my death, Zaros."

For a moment, Zaros did not speak but finally nodded once before speaking, **"Good, since I need you to swear on something."**

"On what though?"

**"Something that means a lot to you, Cornelius."**

"I swear on my father's grave that I will not tell anyone."

"Not even your nephew?"

"He does not need to know everything, Zaros."

"Good."

He leaned forward in his seat before speaking, "**As I was going to say a couple of minutes ago, what I am about to inform you has been passed down several lines. My father told me when I was of age to challenge him. He informed me that one day Firefoot would make an appearance, that he would rule the entire supernatural world in peace and harmony. However, there was something that my father did tell me before he passed. There were rumors that this prophecy that should happen was succumbed in the shadows. There is something out there hunting us. We both know what it is, and I am sure that I had let you check one a book that my grandfather had written, do you know which one I am referring to?**"

I swallowed hard before whispering, "I thought that was more out of common spot for that book. I thought you would have it locked so that no one else could gain access to it. However, I know why you allowed me to now."

"**And why would that be exactly, Cornelius?**"

"Be-bec-because…. Your grandfather ran into Zhukov himself, along with his entire family tree."

"**Exactly, and I can assume you have read the entirety of the book?**"

"I have."

"**And you know what they will do to the shifters when they get their hands on them?**"

A lump formed in my throat as I whispered, "I do."

"**Then you also understand why I am against them leaving. Since it seems to me that Quinn and Aurelin are hell-bent on heading back home.**"

I swallowed hard and looked down before whispering, "What do you want me to do exactly, Zaros?"

He leaned forward, regardless of the puff of dust that flickered up before he whispered, "**I want you to reach out to me for help. I know that Dracula will only see this as his food source disappearing and will side with the threat. However, he will be the main cause for the Carpathians to go down. You know I have enough rings for my entire army here, Cornelius.**"

"Why help the shifters and the rest if they have done nothing to help us in the past though?"

"**Because without a world with the shifters will be the biggest mistake that humans can possibly make. The human race will burn, kill, slaughter, and above all, destroy the earth** that we know it now. They will become smart and will move into the areas that we deem home. Along with the fact, that the shifters can shift into anything at will. They can help populate the natural animals' wildlife when humans get too greedy."

"So, you want me to go with them, and send word to you, so you can prepare for war?"

"Precisely."

"But I thought that you wanted to stay out of this as much as possible. You would have to cancel or change your blood-bounds since everyone needs to be at their full strength."

"That may be true but think of it this way though. You will have someone answer your call of help, regardless of what the other Carpathians of the Dracula strand do."

"But I am…. I am not a full Carpathian."

"I knew that already, Cornelius."

"Therefore, Dracula's army is going to be deadlier than me."

"One thing that I do know that Dracula does not have a ready supply of though, Cornelius, is daylight rings. They cannot meet the sun."

I frowned before replying, "Out of curiosity, how did you manage to get that many?"

Zaros leaned back into the chair, making it creak under him before he replied, "We are not alone in this mountain, Cornelius. This is the last floor before the other one starts."

"What do you mean? Besides Corimid?"

"Corimid's father, unsure of his name, had made daylight rings for my father. Many, many, many of them. Knowing that there will be one day of war and bloodshed."

"Wait, if that is true then, why are there more floors above us?"

"Because we harbor more than one thing above us. Corimid is protecting it from the top, and I am protecting it from the bottom. Hence why my chamber is where it is."

"What are you two guarding?"

"Dragon eggs."

"Dragon eggs? Really?"

"Positive."

"But all the dragons died out centuries ago. How did some of their eggs make it?"

"Because for a dragon to come into the world it has to meet their handlers. My father was gifted Corimid's egg when he was but a baby, so he does not know the ceremony that goes with it. However, that was many, many seasons ago."

"So, you are saying, that we are guarding dragon eggs and no one else knows of it?"

**"Correct."**

"Why are you telling me this though?"

**"Because I have a feeling you will need to go through those chambers to get to Corimid's."**

"But Thakur can fly us up there."

**"No, I have a feeling that there is another reason why they were brought here. Besides showing us that Firefoot is indeed here in power. It means that we need to have them come through this way."**

"How are you so sure that they are allowed through the eggs?"

**"Cornelius?"**

"Yes, my lord?"

**"When have I ever really been wrong about something?"**

"Rarely."

**"So why are you questioning it now?"**

"Because I thought that the dragons had died out centuries ago."

**"Ah, yeah. That is what a lot of people believe. However, you cannot tell them why you are going through the tunnels. Whoever the dragon eggs call to though, do not direct them any other way. The dragon and the one who opens the egg will be perfectly alright."**

"If that is true, then why hide the dragons from everyone else here?"

**"Has the five bodies in my office not been enough evidence?"**

"Fair point."

We fell silent for a moment before I replied hesitatingly, "If that is the truth, and if someone is drawn to the hatchlings, then what will happen?"

**"The eggs will hatch."**

"Then what?"

**"You will take the hatchling to Corimid."**

"But I thought that dragons were extremely dangerous towards someone else's hatchlings."

**"I am unsure of what the direct line between Corimid and them is, however, I think that they are related somehow. My father was very vague on them since no one else is supposed to know about them."**

"If your father knew of them then why didn't he allow anyone up there? Perhaps, he had missed someone worthy of finding the eggs."

**"Believe me, Cornelius, at the time. No one was worthy of those dragon eggs. The only person I have ever considered bringing up there is you after you had made it clear where you stand with everything."**

"Me?"

**"Yes, you."**

"Why me?"

**"Because you have shown me that you are trustworthy throughout all the centuries you have come here, Cornelius. I am unsure of what it will feel like. But if you feel something weird upon entering the cavern where they are, do not second guess it."**

"Okay."

I frowned and stood up after a moment, making his eyes follow my movements. I popped my back and looked down at him before speaking, "Although, why take them that way? Other people will know that they are moving and we may be followed."

**"No one will follow you."**

"How are you for sure?"

**"Because I will be having a meeting in the darkness."**

"That doesn't mean that everyone will attend."

**"Cornelius?"**

"Yes, my lord?"

**"Has anyone disobeyed my direct orders from meeting in the darkness?"**

"No."

**"Then why would someone start now?"**

"Because I am unsure if someone will try again with the same feat as the ones in the office."

He sighed deeply before muttering, **"Fair point in that. However, I will need you to go along with the plan all the same. We cannot have anyone follow you."**

"You want me to enforce that no one follows?"

**"Do whatever is necessary."**

"But that would include death."

"**Cornelius, no one is supposed to be away from the darkness meeting. Therefore, they are being traitorous and you are simply doing me a favor.**"

"But everyone knows the rule about not killing one another in the mountain."

"**Cornelius, you would not be the one to kill them. I will allow you to tell Thakur and Firefoot about this. But other than that, no one else.**"

"Why Thakur and Firefoot? Why not Quinn and Aurelin?"

"**Because their other halves will know what is at stake.**"

"Why have this meeting alone if you want to include them?"

"**Because they do not need to know everything that we have yet to discuss. Cornelius.**"

"There is more than the given rings and the dragon eggs?"

"**I am going to make you my next in heir.**"

My jaw dropped and I shook my head in response. "Me? You are surely kidding."

"**I am not kidding, Cornelius.**"

"Why me? Of all the people to choose from, Zaros, I am not the leader that you would want to rule your people."

"**Times are changing, Cornelius, and whether we live through the battle or not, we need to set up something. Since I know that my destiny is to not rule forever like my forefathers before me. I know that something else is coming.**"

"How are you so sure that you want me to be the one in command though?"

"**I knew the first minute I saw you all those centuries back, Cornelius. My father would have approved of the choice, too. He had seen how you treat others and would approve.**"

"But what about you? What do you know of your destiny?"

"**I cannot alter my destiny more than I can say, Cornelius. As much as I know you wish to find out, I cannot tell you that.**"

"If the battle is won, and we are in victory and you and I are both alive, you want to step down and away from what you know?"

He fell silent and finally replied, "**My father had warned me against telling someone my destiny, however, I should tell someone. My destiny is to be the next person who raises the next line of Carpathians. In the next few centuries, we will be known as vampires, the shifters will be still shifters as well as the werewolves as werewolves.**"

"Wait, vampires? But we are the Carpathians."

**"The Carpathians are pure-blooded for the most part, Cornelius."**

"Wait, aren't you full blood though?"

**"Not entirely full blood. Although I have the behavior of my father through his teachings, that is about it. I will be the one who will hopefully assist you in the coming of leadership, but unsure."**

"Why are you unsure?"

**"The battle, Cornelius. I am unsure of the outcome to be. I know Zhukov, and I know that he will attack any that stands in his way."**

"But I thought that if we stayed out of it, then we would be safe though."

**"That is what the humans wish, however, Zhukov would go against them slightly, and go after any supernatural beings."**

"Not all of us are threats though."

**"I agree, but his family is supernatural hunters. You cannot call someone away from their tendencies."**

"That may be true in some cases. However, can't we simply ask him to not go after us?"

**"Did you not read what my grandfather had mentioned in his book about the same person we are talking about?"**

I fell silent. Already knowing that I should have not gone down this rabbit hole. Knowing that Zhukov would kill any supernatural being without cause. I sighed and rubbed my hand through my hair before speaking, "So no chance that the future is in shadows? That you would want to step down?"

**"I am positive, Cornelius."**

"Okay, I will back you up on that. As long as I survive this battle."

**"That would be amazing that you do."**

"I am sure it will be for your sake."

**"Enough."**

He frowned as he stood up abruptly and I froze. He went towards the entrance of the cavern and soon dragged two Carpathians into the room. I instantly recognized them, they were the newer additions.

# Chapter 58

Zaros stared down at them and fury lit his eyes before he whispered dangerously, "**And just what the hell are you doing up here?**"

"We…."

"**We what?**"

They glanced at each other before they swallowed and whispered, "Please don't kill us."

"**And why should I allow you to live?**"

"Because killing them would result in others finding out that you have other hidden chambers up here, Zaros."

Zaros stiffened and turned his attention towards the door before speaking, "**Kruse.**"

"Zaros."

A stiff silence involved around us and after a moment Kruse's eyes flickered to mine and he raised his eyebrows at me before looking at Zaros and speaking, "Apparently not alone. I would have thought for sure you would have been in your chambers."

"**You went to my chambers?**"

"I want answers, Zaros. Why do you have outsiders inside the mountain?"

"They are my family members."

Kruse looked at me with a hard look before rumbling, "Uh, last time I checked, Cornelius, I did not address you. I addressed Zaros. If it was up to me though, you and your likes would be out of this mountain."

"**But it is not up to you, Kruse.**"

Kruse looked back at Zaros and did not flinch before he replied, "Currently not. I, however, want to challenge you, Zaros, for the leadership role. You are allowing others to get ahead of you."

"I take it that you are the one that is making Helius nervous?"

Kruse froze, and his eyes landed on the ring on my finger before he turned his attention to Zaros and swallowed slightly. Zaros stiffened and glowered at me, but I did not mean to let that slip out of my mouth. However, Kruse's stiffness confirmed it was his doing though. The way he moved back a step too was also a considering factor.

The two lower-ranking Carpathians tried to move away right then, but Zaros without a single hesitation, killed them both where they were. Their heads rolled towards Kruse who had to step out of the way as the cavern floors made them head towards the door, stopping at the entrance. Kruse's eyes and head followed their direction, but he did not once let his guard down. He looked back at Zaros before speaking, "Unless, of course, you are too afraid to accept my challenge?"

**"We do it in the darkness."**

That was the moment of fear in the fool. Kruse knew the layout of the training room since it was lit, but he had never gone into the darkness willingly. He knew the laws though and had expertly made his thoughts and everything that would inform Zaros of his treachery a secret. His Adam's apple bobbed before he replied, "I thought it would have been the challenger that chose the area."

**"Not in this case. This is my mountain. Anyone else can concur that this is the way it has been for centuries."**

He swallowed and held his head down before replying arrogantly, "When I become ruler, those that you deem safe in your home are the first to go."

"You will kick out any that don't see you fit to rule?"

As soon as that was out of my mouth, I knew I should have kept silent. He turned his attention to me and snarled. His eyes turned red in anger. However, I felt something stir in my mind, but something about it was calling to me. I glanced up at the cavern ceiling above me, and suddenly realized what it would be. I glanced at Zaros, before backing up before Kruse's advance. Zaros moved forward for a moment, but Kruse snapped his fingers and more than thirty other Carpathians swarmed the area – blocking Zaros from getting to me. I swallowed and stepped backward. Fear was sweeping from me since I carry no weapons.

*****

A thunderous growl sounded from the entrance. For a moment, no one moved and soon Quinn stepped into the tunnel entrance without hesitation. He surveyed the area before speaking, "Any of those who would attack Cornelius or Zaros will be brutally killed. Except for you."

He pointed straight at Kruse before continuing, "Since you are the only one who wants to challenge him for the right to lead. Everyone else will be killed."

"You have no right up here!" snarled Kruse.

He was within striking distance from me now, and I swallowed as I noticed that he did not come empty-handed. Quinn, however, did not budge before replying, "Nor do you."

A few of the Carpathians in the group stepped slightly away from Zaros in response. Quinn looked at Kruse before speaking, "Do not challenge me here, Kruse, I doubt that you would be able to take on me."

I stared over Kruse's shoulder, suddenly wondering what the hell he was going to do. He was challenging a full-blood Carpathian. They are faster than they make it seem. However, I also knew that Kruse did not know the extent of his strength either. Kruse eyed him up and down before his eyes flickered to Zaros. "I will fight you for leadership, Zaros, but after I deal with this kid."

For a moment, Zaros looked conflicted, but when we locked eye contact, there was no possible way that Kruse knew that he would die before this so-called kid. I glanced at Kruse when he turned his attention back to me, before hissing, "And AFTER I kill him, you will be next."

My Adam's apple bobbed in response, but I did not shy away from him before replying, "If you kill him."

He scoffed before replying, "He is nothing but a child, Cornelius."

I looked over at Zaros and saw a smirk in his eyes before Kruse could look back over at him, did it fade away However, I could tell that the surrounding Carpathians knew something was wrong. However, they had no rank and probably knew that Kruse would shut them down the moment that they spoke out.

*****

Quinn stared at the group of Carpathians before Zaros spoke again, "Any of those who wish a quick death, come forward."

"NO! They are not to be harmed until I deal with you."

Quinn glanced at Kruse before replying, "They will die one way or another."

"As if."

"You are challenging two powerful people. Cornelius may look weak, but he is far from it. You had the galls to bring weapons up here. You were looking for trouble."

Kruse swallowed hard, and he stepped slightly away from me. I glanced at Zaros and knew that he was thinking the same thing. Kruse had not challenged two powerful beings, he challenged three. Quinn would make Kruse a fool, although I wonder if Thakur will be the one to put him down. However, after a moment, Kruse growled out, "Training room."

"So be it."

Quinn backed out slightly before eyeing the Carpathians and Zaros said, "After you."

Kruse sneered at me before turning his eyes to the Carpathians. Zaros snapped, "Go."

They instantly filed out of the chamber, and Kruse hesitated to follow after them. Eyeing Zaros's sword before he passed us.

****

Leaving Quinn, myself, and Zaros in the chamber. Quinn looked at me for a moment before speaking, "Can the two of you show me to the training room?"

**"How did you know to come up here?"**

"I followed the giant group of Carpathians."

**"But how did you know they were not supposed to come up here?"**

"Based on the areas that I have seen. Along with their hushed whispers that they are not supposed to go up the floors."

**"What have you heard?"**

"Nothing that you need to worry yourself over, Zaros. I am no threat."

Zaros fell silent and eyed me for a moment before gesturing me to depart. I swallowed as I passed Quinn before heading down the levels.

****

I stared hard at Quinn before speaking, **"What did you find out?"**

"I will tell you after I put Kruse down."

**"You have to know he will not do it fairly once he realizes that he is no match for you."**

"I am aware of it."

**"Then afterwards-"**

"I will tell you everything that I have overheard from the group. I followed them up here, but was too far away from the chamber to hear anything that you were speaking about."

**"Are you lying?"**

"You can check my thoughts, Zaros."

I fell silent and did indeed do it, and found that he was one hundred percent telling the truth. I sighed and sighed after a moment and finally gestured for him to follow me. We both departed after a moment and soon went down to the training room.

*****

I got to the training room before everyone else and looked at the fools before me. They claimed to want a new leader, a better leader than Zaros, but the moment that the fucker showed himself, they all froze. If it was up to me they would have both been killed in that chamber, not being in the training room to figure out how to win against this outsider. Whom, I had never once laid eyes on, just knew that the rumors and data from others had made it seem like Zaros was making an exception to his rules. Choosing favorites.

I looked at the one I would have as second in command and walked up to him. He looked up at me before speaking, "Kruse."

"What was that behavior back there, Manu? You chickened out at the last second?"

"Quite the opposite actually, Kruse. Has it occurred to you, that Zaros's family line has been allowed to live here? You forcefully taking this sanctuary will not be the best for you."

"That is a different tune compared to what you said the other night."

"That may be true, Kruse, but have you seen the peace that Zaros has in this mountain? He is not strict on his rules."

"Except for feeding."

"Except for feeding, but that is an understanding one if I say so myself."

"Are you running scared now, Manu?"

His Adam's apple bobbed once as he swallowed hard before whispering, "No."

"Then why are you suddenly questioning what Zaros is doing with the said mountain?"

"Because there are a few things that Zaros is doing that should stay."

"Like what?"

"This is a sanctuary for those who have no home. That should stay…."

"You want weaklings being in your home?"

"Kruse, we all are misfits. We all have no mates, and therefore our communities did not want us. Zaros opened his home for us…."

I wrapped my hand around his throat, and he stuttered in shock before his eyes flared red. His fingernails elongated before he hissed, "Kruse."

"I say you are smitten by Zaros, Manu. Why should I let you live?"

"Because that is the least you should do for someone who has stood behind you, Kruse."

I stiffened released Manu, and turned around slowly to stare at Cornelius before growling, "Where is the outsider and Zaros?"

"I do not answer to someone like you, Kruse."

"Answer me, and I will put you down quickly."

"No."

I took a step forward when the outsider and Zaros entered the training room, along with the rest of the residents of the mountain. I swallowed as I watched as my father entered the cavern. His eyes flickered around before his eyes landed on mine and he squinted his eyes. He sat down in the front row before scooting over for Zaros to sit beside him. I had no love for my father, but seeing him sitting there made a small amount of rage surface, sure he supported me, but I was currently unsure whom he would support. Me or the outsider. I turned my back on him before the rest of the residents trickled into the area, and got themselves sitting – leaving the outsider and myself on the floor alone.

I turned around after a few moments and stared at the outsider before snarling, "Last chance."

He did not seem fazed and dared to yawn, speaking, "How will this work? Weapons or by hand-to-hand combat?"

"Both."

He raised his eyebrows in response before shrugging and speaking, "So be it."

He removed his coat and that is when I saw for the first time how well-toned he is. I swallowed and eyed him thoughtfully before hissing, "What are you?"

"Something that you will learn quickly enough."

He had a sword on his hip, and one strapped across his back. Neither of which he touched and looked rather calm. I withdrew my sword and stared at him. However, he stared at me before speaking, "Why are you hesitating?"

"Because that is the least I could do before I slaughter you where you stand."

"How about this, when I take you down, you forfeit your challenge to Zaros. Along with your leadership with these Carpathians and have to serve Zaros for his troubles?"

"You act like you will survive."

"Cause one way or another, I will be walking out of here alive. You on the other hand? Will not."

I glanced back at the stadium, he had said it loud enough for the rest of the population to hear, but it was Zaros who frowned at the statement. However, he did not say anything. His eyes never left the outsider. I looked at the outsider before asking, "Your name?"

"Why? So, you know who killed you?"

"No, so I know who I defeated."

"Quinn."

"Quinn what?"

"Quinn Benik."

I froze and stared at him before whispering, "Benik?"

"Yes."

I swallowed hard before seeing my father's eyes staring down at me. It was as if he knew I was about to back out, and he turned his head in shame. I burrowed my eyebrows and gripped my sword before growling out, "Prepare to die then."

I lunge forward, full of my Carpathian full blood speed. However, at the last second, he stepped away and I ran right past him. I whirled around staring at him before charging again, but this time anticipating his moving out of the way. I swung my sword and would have caught him if his blade had not met mine with a solid thaw. We backed off for a moment and we met again. I was using two hands on my sword, which seemed stupid now watching him move with his with his left hand. He looked relaxed and soon I found out that he did not seem to need to wait for another attack, he advanced and kept coming. It was all I could do but to block and deflect him. Not one drop of sweat dripped into his eyes, and he acted as if he could continue long into the night and day. I, however, had a small coating of sweat already and I blocked his advancements, which leveled more than anyone else I had fought back before.

Soon, after he had slashed my clothing, and nicked my skin he paused before speaking, "Do you submit?"

"No."

I panted out. He shrugged and replied, "I can go on for longer than you, apparently. Full-blood or not, you are no match for me."

I scowled at his easiness and growled, "Switch to your dominant hand."

He raised his eyebrow and replied, "Dominate hand, eh? That would cause you a whole line of hurt."

"Regardless, switch."

"So be it."

Without warning, he tossed his sword into the air, twirled around, caught it, and stared at me with a dangerous glint in his eyes. It was almost as if he knew the moment had changed. I swallowed and suddenly wondered what was in his eyes, they seemed to change for a brief moment, but then went away.

I stared at him and backed away. A collective gasp went up and soon a roar of laughter. I snarled at them, but they did not stop. I glanced at my father and noticed that he did not move his eyes from Quinn. His eyes flickered to mine for a moment before he slowly shook his head. I swallowed and threw my weapon down after a hesitated moment. It clanged to the ground without a wince.

I looked up at Quinn, swallowed, and whispered, "I submit."

"Good."

He quickly put his sword into the sheath and turned his back to me, I lunged forward, grabbed my sword, and threw it at him. A collective gasp came from the crowd. A few standing in the stands, before a voice echoed, "NO!"

However, Quinn did something that no one else could have done, not even Zaros would have been able to do it. He turned around fast and caught the blade in the air, mere centimeters from his chest. He sighed deeply before dropping my sword to the ground, with a clatter. His eyes were coal black and he breathed heavily before growling, "You attacked someone with their back turned. This is the action of a coward."

I froze and stared back at him before whispering, "What are you?"

"Did the last name Benik do nothing to alert you of what I am?"

I swallowed hard, so the rumor was true, that the Benik's were indeed still around. He turned his head slightly before speaking, "Zaros? Any use for this filth?"

My eyes flickered to where Zaros was standing, his hand on his sword hilt before he replied, **"None."**

"Good."

"WAIT!"

Quinn froze for a moment, and looked over his shoulder at someone in the stadium before speaking, "What?"

"Wait, please."

Quinn backed up slightly and looked at Zaros for a moment. I could tell that Zaros would have said finish me, but the man coming forward was Manu. Manu bowed his head in Zaros's direction before speaking, "Surely, there is another way, so, there is no more bloodshed?"

"Manu-"

I said warningly, but Zaros spoke cutting me off, **"Manu, last time I checked, you were in the group that had challenged me in my chambers."**

A collective gasp went up, everyone knew better than to go to Zaros's chambers without just cause. I swallowed and glanced at my father, and saw the shame in his eyes. He looked away after a moment. I bowed my head and swallowed hard. I should have been killed here and now. Not standing here for the pity of Manu.

Manu swallowed before he addressed Zaros, "I apologize, Zaros, but yes that is true. However, without Kruse in command, I would have left you alone. Not all of those who were with us were traitorous to you."

**"And I am to believe that you are stopping Kruse's execution because he is the sole one in his action?"**

"Negative, my lord. There are a few in our numbers that were bribed by Kruse."

"How does this fit into what is happening at this current time frame exactly?"

Manu swallowed as he looked at Quinn before replying, "Because before you kill him, I wanted to make sure that you two know that not everyone who participated wanted to. Before Kruse is killed."

"You act like I have been killed already, Manu!"

**"Because you have been, Kruse. You will not be alive in a few minutes."**

"I challenge you, Zaros!"

Zaros looked like he was going to scoff, but my father spoke, "No."

"What?"

"You do not get the right to challenge him, Kruse. You failed to kill an outsider. What makes you think that you will win against our ruler?"

"Father-"

"You are no son of mine, Kruse. You changed after we came to seek refuge with Zaros three weeks ago. You find him weak, but I see the power behind him at the same time. No."

"Father…."

"YOU ARE NO SON OF MINE!"

I stared at him before hissing, "What would mother say?"

"She would be disappointed in what her son became. Quinn, you may kill him now."

I glanced at Quinn and saw him picking at his nails before he looked at me with a look written across his face, shrugging before pulling a sword from his sheath. He took a step forward but Manu stepped in front of him before speaking, "Don't. Zaros, banish him from your mountain."

**"Why? So, he can come back and injure the rest of us?"**

"Please."

**"No."**

"Surely, death is not the only answer!"

I looked at Manu, why was he so set on trying to prevent my death, but soon a woman stood up and walked down the stairs. One I know full well since I bed with her some evenings. However, her scent was different. No, it can't be true. Manu glanced at the woman who was approaching and swallowed hard before he turned to Zaros and speaking, "He is the father of the child, Zaros. Surely, you won't kill the father of someone."

Zaros strode over to us then, and looked at the woman beside Manu at this point. **"Felisa?"**

"It's true…. He is the baby's father."

Zaros turned to Quinn before speaking, **"What do you suggest to be done to him, Quinn?"**

I scoffed for a moment before growling, "You got to be kidding me! He gets to choose?"

**"If it was up to me, Kruse, you would be dead already."**

"You are letting an outsider decide."

**"Do you want your head to roll, Kruse?"**

I did not reply, and he looked at me, lifting his right eyebrow at me. Waiting for an answer. I looked away, and he scoffed before looking at Quinn. Quinn looked perplexed for a moment but finally, he replied, "If he finds his way out of the darkness in twelve hours he is safe. Otherwise, kill him."

Felisa blanched and looked over at me for a moment before whispering, "The darkness?"

"It is the one spot where someone has a chance to escape."

"But it is not a high chance though!"

"I am sorry, but that is my decree."

She stared at Quinn before whispering, "No one has escaped from the darkness."

"But he has a chance."

She looked at me for a moment, speaking, "I am going with him."

**"No."**

"Zaros, you cannot stop her from going, " replied Manu, who looked slightly shocked by Quinn's decree. However, Zaros turned his attention to Manu before speaking, **"Every single person from the chamber goes. You have twelve hours to find an exit. Or I will come kill you."**

"What about me though?"

**"Alaister, escort Felisa to the dungeons."**

"Of course, my lord."

I looked sharply at my old man before stepping forward and blocking his way. "That child is your grandchild!"

"As I said before, Kruse, you are no son of mine."

I scowled and backed off slightly. Zaros snapped his fingers and guards instantly stood up and approached me, along with the other group that I had talked to in switching. A few looked like they wanted to vomit, but a few held their heads high before one growled at Zaros, "You are not fit to rule!"

Zaros glowered at the Carpathian who spoke but did not reply. He watched as the rest of us were shoved into the darkness, and the entrances back into the mountain were closed off. Sealing before we were in complete darkness.

# Chapter 59

I looked around the stadium before speaking, "**Anyone else?**"

No one moved. I looked at Quinn before speaking, "**You will be departing soon correct?**"

"Correct."

**"How soon?"**

"As soon as Fergus and Oswald are well enough to move."

**"Cervix."**

"Yes, my lord?"

**"Go with Quinn and Cornelius to see if they need any of your healing broth."**

"Of course, my lord!"

She rose from the stands and moved towards us, before stopping and looking at Quinn with expectant eyes. I stared at him before jerking my head towards the exit. Quinn bowed to me before he turned around and left.

*****

I looked at the remaining Carpathians before speaking, "**Prepare for war. Our home is under attack. We must prepare. Helius, allow every loyal member a ring.**"

"Yes, my lord!"

I turn around to leave when a voice calls out, "War?"

I paused, looked at the one who had spoken, and replied, "**The Sazornoras are on the move.**"

Hushed whispers sounded, and finally, someone else replied, "Rumors are that they are after the shifters."

**"That is partially correct. They were tasked to go after the shifters. However, when has a supernatural hunter ever solely go after those whom they are paid to go after?"**

Silence answered. Since everyone knew that I was right. We all know the Sazornoras one way or another. Finally, a few of the older Carpathians, who remember my father in their youth, nodded in thoughtfulness before one spoke, "Your father would be proud of you, Zaros."

A lump formed in my throat at this certain Carpathian's thoughtfulness, and I bowed my head in his direction, since he was my father's advisor before he stepped down when my father had passed. I had learned a lot from him. He stood up, and soon the other elders did the same, and looked beyond the others before calling out, "To the king!"

**"TO THE KING!"**

The room echoed, and the elders looked down at the center of the room before they vaporized and came down before strolling away, leaving the last of the followers where they were in the stands. I turned around and left, since no one else called out.

****

A few minutes later, we got back to Cornelius's chambers and soon found out that Fergus and Oswald were awake, but they were still weak. Cervix looked at them once before speaking, "They are weak, I will go get my aid to bring up some of my broth."

"Thank you."

She looked at me for a moment, but she did not reply as she left. I looked at Cornelius before asking, "What?"

"You could have gotten yourself killed, Quinn."

"But I didn't."

"What would your father say to you now if he knew what you have been doing?"

"It doesn't matter what he thinks."

Cornelius looked like he would continue, but after a moment, the aide came back, and he panted before shoving two large glasses at us before disappearing without a word. I looked down at the broth and wondered what was in it. However, I was not about to go ask the cook or her aide. It was clear that they were going to be busy.

I walked towards Fergus and Oswald, offering them the broth. Fergus looked down at it and sniffed it and frowned before speaking, **"I'll pass."**

"It will help you, though."

**"I said I'm good."**

"Father-"

**"Hush, Oswald."**

I glanced around the room and noticed that Aurelin was not near them. He was not in the room at all. I looked at Cornelius before exiting and found him in the living room, with his head bowed. I rested my hand on his shoulder, he jerked away for a moment before looking up, and sighed deeply. "Oh, it's you."

"What happened?"

"Nothing much. When Fergus woke up, he said we planned for this to happen, and I said a few choice words that I wish I could take back now."

"What did you say to him?"

"I told him that without us, he would not be safe."

"And what did he say to that?"

"He said he was safe enough at the base of the mountain with the other druids."

I would have said something else, but when Fergus came into the room, he was staggering, but he was still walking when he stopped and looked at me with a hard look. I raised an eyebrow before speaking, "Fergus?"

**"After the dragon, we will part ways."**

"I thought that you would be joining us."

**"Not after everything that has happened."**

"I cannot alter what has happened. Nor can I alter what is to come."

**"I understand that you cannot alter what will become, but leaving me and Aurelin alone? That was not so great for you to do."**

"Why?"

**"Because you are part of the cause for most of my people's deaths."**

Aurelin fell silent and hung his head, and I replied after a moment, "Surely you knew that something was to happen to your people one way or another, Fergus."

**"I am not going with you besides the dragon, Quinn. That is final."**

"Then how are you going back down the mountain?"

He opened his mouth to retort, but fell silent. He did not think that far ahead in his plan, apparently, and finally shook his head, scowling before accepting Cornelius's help with the glass of broth. He downed it in five gulps and grimaced after a moment before speaking again, **"Fly us down to the base, and we will part from there."**

"Are you sure?"

**"Positive."**

I sighed after a moment, rubbing the back of my neck before replying, "Fine."

Cornelius looked like he was going to reject that idea, but I shot him a look, and we all fell into silence. It was after a few minutes that Oswald came into the other room, and by his behavior alone, he was good to travel. I glanced at Fergus and noticed that he was getting better, too. I saw him frown for a moment before speaking, **"What was in that?"**

"Something that Cervix brews up every other week."

**"But what is in it?"**

"Don't know. She won't allow anyone else besides her kitchen aid inside."

Fergus looked at Cornelius with a scowl, but did not reply. He seemed to know better than to ask again since he would get the same response. He looked at Oswald and glared at him, but Oswald spoke, "I'm not going with you, Father."

**"You are but a boy."**

"Father-"

**"You are staying with me."**

"No."

**"Oswald-"**

"Father, the only time that no one scorns me for being in the same area as they are. These are the same people."

**"One of them killed your family."**

Oswald swallowed hard before whispering, "Then it must have been fate."

Fergus stared at Oswald as if he had slapped him across the face, and we all fell silent. Finally, after a few minutes, Fergus looked at me with a hard look before speaking, **"Chances of our survival?"**

"You know that is not fair to them."

**"Hush."**

"Father-"

**"Oswald."**

Oswald scowled but fell silent after a moment. Fergus looked at me, and finally, I sighed deeply before speaking, "I cannot promise anything."

**"Fine."**

He looked at Oswald for a solid thirty seconds before sighing deeply and speaking, **"We will stay with you. However, the moment that it becomes evident that you will abandon us since we are the druids, then we will depart."**

"I won't abandon you."

Fergus glowered at me for a moment but did not respond. He went into the next room and picked up one of the baskets and sighed deeply before throwing it over his shoulder. He winced, but I went forward for a moment before looking at Aurelin before speaking, "Aurelin?"

"Hmm?"

"Shift into your wolf, and we will strap the baskets onto you."

"Okay."

For a moment, Fergus looked like he would refuse, but after a moment, he sighed as he watched Aurelin shift into his wolf form. He stared at me for a moment, but said nothing. I picked up the other two baskets and got them onto his back, and looked at Fergus for a moment. Fergus sighed deeply and handed over the other basket after a moment of hesitation.

I took his basket and loaded it onto Aurelin, who grunted under the weight. However, we had been trained hard on how to do it. He sighed after a moment, but did not complain more than a huff. I looked over at Cornelius before speaking, "Where is the exit?"

**"You are not to fly up there. You are walking up the cavern."**

I blinked and looked over at Zaros, who stood in the doorway before bowing to him slightly before speaking, "Forgive me, but you made it seem that going up your caverns is the worst idea that we would do."

**"Unless someone has the explicit permission to go up further, that does stand. However, you are different."**

"Thank you."

**"Are you all well enough to go?"**

I looked at Fergus and Oswald, and Fergus sighed deeply before replying, **"Yes."**

**"Then you will depart immediately."**

"What's the rush?"

"You are causing too many issues being down here."

"I apologize."

"It is not your fault, though. It is equally mine."

"In what way is it your fault?"

"All the new people I accept are the ones currently in the darkness."

"I thought that area was reserved for your sacrifices and meetings."

"Currently, it is housing around forty new Carpathians that I had allowed in my home, who had wanted to overthrow me. Quinn challenged their ring leader."

"Is that where you're going off to?"

"Yes, you were safe enough with Aurelin, and I knew that no one would try again…. At least partially thought after what has happened."

"Ah."

"Yeah."

"So, what happened to lead to that discussion?"

"The ring leader slept with an unmated female, and now they are going to have a child. Therefore, for the father to have a fighting chance, it was decreed that he and his followers would get twelve hours to find an exit."

"Did they get daylight rings?"

"No."

"Good."

Silence wrapped around us before I looked at Zaros before speaking, "Thank you."

Zaros eyes rose to meet mine before he cocked his head slightly before replying, "**For what?**"

"For allowing us to be alive down here in your mountain. Along with protecting us."

"**I can tell why Morphous keeps you as his advisor.**"

A grim look settled onto Fergus as he looked at me before speaking quietly, "**I agree.**"

I swallowed and bowed my head to Fergus and Zaros before Zaros spoke again, "**Got everything?**"

I glanced at Fergus, and he nodded once. Zaros frowned before speaking, "**So be it. You will leave now. Cornelius, you know the way you are to go.**"

"Thank you, Zaros."

**"Remember what I told you earlier, Cornelius."**

"I will."

Without further discussion, Zaros departed.

*****

I looked at Cornelius before speaking, "What?"

"Not your immediate concern at the moment, Quinn."

I scowled but followed after Cornelius without further questions. Knowing that Aurelin will carry the baskets and that Fergus and Oswald will follow.

# Chapter 60

We headed past the few Carpathians who were lingering in the halls, but none of them moved towards us. None of them even addressed us. As if knowing will cause further conflict. We moved silently, and soon we came to another level, and another and another. Soon, going further and further up the mountain. Not once did Cornelius backtrack; it was as if he knew where he was going. Soon we reached the tunnel where I had found them before, Kruse could attack them, but Cornelius continued to rise. It was after a few minutes that Fergus spoke, **"Where does this lead?"**

"To Corimid."

**"It would have been easier to fly up."**

"Easier, yes, but not the most entertaining nonetheless."

I glanced back at Fergus and saw him scowl, but did not reply. It was after a while that Thakur stirred. So far, he had not really surfaced, except when Kruse challenged him. Well, more of them took my turned back to attack me when my back was turned. That would not fly in his books, and quite frankly, neither does it for anyone sane. He showed his true colors when he attacked someone from behind.

Fergus stopped walking, and it took me a moment to realize it. I stopped and looked back at him before speaking, "You good, Fergus?"

**"Something is calling me. Something is luring me to it."**

I frowned, since I did not sense anything ahead. However, Cornelius paused and turned to look back at Fergus before speaking, "Are you positive you feel a draw?"

**"Being a druid elder has its perks sometimes, Cornelius. I am positive that something is calling to me. I have not yet discovered what it is, though, so no clue what it is."**

Cornelius looked for a moment, perplexed, and looked back up the trail before looking the way we had come. Finally, he sighed deeply before looking at me and Aurelin before speaking, "Quinn, Aurelin. Please let your other beings surface."

"Why?"

"Because there is something that needs to come to light, but I have been warned not to tell the two of you."

"Why does it matter so much that Thakur and…. Aurelin's half finds out before us?"

"I am sorry, Quinn, but I cannot go against my promise. Please."

I grumbled, but looked at Aurelin, and saw him sigh in defeat. He seemed to relax, and after a moment, his eyes turned the color of Firefoot's. It was eerie in the darkness of the tunnel, especially when he blinked. I looked at Fergus before speaking, "If it is not serious business, please keep me informed."

**"It highly depends on what Cornelius will inform us, Quinn."**

I glanced at my uncle, sighed deeply, and finally, allowed Thakur to take control.

****

I blinked my eyes and glanced around for a moment before sighing deeply before pinching the bridge of my nose, and speaking slowly, "What is so dire that Quinn cannot get the information, Cornelius?"

"I apologize, Thakur, but I had to swear on my father's grave to be told something. One of which is what is drawing me and Fergus. It appears that not all the natural dragons are dead."

He paused, and I stared at him with my jaw dropped open. Did he just say what I thought he said? That there were still dragons besides Corimid? A scoff sounded behind me, and I glanced back and saw Oswald scowl before speaking, "Do you really want us to believe that there is more than one giant flying beast alive?"

"I am sorry, but yes. There is more than one, apparently."

**"It makes sense now."**

Fergus muttered. I glanced at him before cocking an eyebrow before snapping, "What makes sense?"

Fergus turned his eyes to me and replied, **"Why did the dragon do what he did. He allowed us down into the lower chambers since he knew that at least one of us was destined to have one. However, it does not make sense to me why he allowed us all down here."**

I glanced at Cornelius before speaking, "So, back up, you think that there is more than one dragon, and they are so-called calling whomever they want?"

**"Have you paid any attention to the history of the dragons, Thakur? Or has Quinn?"**

"Not to my knowledge, why?"

**"Because the dragons have to come out of eggs first. For the dragon to hatch, it has to have a handler. The dragon will call the handler when it sees someone fit to lead it comfortably.**

**Although it doesn't see who it is, quite the opposite, actually, it senses who is worthy. No matter the distance."**

I glanced at Firefoot and knew that everyone else had heard him since Fergus was nodding and Cornelius seemed rather shocked for a moment. Oswald looked like he did not know what to believe. I was in the same boat, though. However, after everything that has happened, though, it should not be a surprise that it has happened. I sighed and ran my hand through my hair before sighing deeply before speaking slowly, "So to get this straight, there are dragon eggs that are calling Fergus and you, Cornelius…. Then why hasn't all of us been drawn to a dragon egg?"

**"The dragon chooses who is worthy to have them. Not the other way around."**

"Great, just what we need. Two fire flaming dragons to add to the mix."

**"Last time I checked, Thakur, you are another fire-flaming dragon."**

"Only when I bloody want to be one. This is different from what I can shift into."

**"In what way? Is it the fact that you don't know what you are doing because you have never experienced something like this before, and you simply do not like the fact that someone hasn't called you? You should be grateful that someone in your group has even been called to such a beautiful creature of the sky and earth."**

I scowled in response, but knew that Fergus was correct. That this is a huge blessing, not a burden. My words and actions are making it seem like I don't want another dragon in this world. I sighed deeply before speaking, "What are we waiting for? Then go find your critters."

"You okay with not being the center of attention, Thakur?"

"It may not be my destiny to be a dragon handler, but I will do my best to protect those who are. There are only two known ones at this point."

"Two?"

I looked at Oswald for a moment, and ran my hand down my face before looking at Fergus with a look. He shook his head in annoyance, but did not reply to Oswald. Firefoot sighed and spoke again, "**Cornelius and Fergus are getting the dragon hatchling. However, my question is, though, who is going to raise them? It cannot be a shifter, or a demon, sorry Thakur, but that does include you too.**"

I grumbled, but did not reply. I glanced at Cornelius, who swallowed before whispering, "You are correct Firefoot, it is no shifter or demon. It will be Corimid himself."

**"But aren't dragons rather brutal to those who are not their kin?"**

"Unsure of the relationship to Corimid they have, but I have been informed that they are somehow related to Corimid. Along with the fact that he is guarding the eggs. As well as Zaros from the bottom."

Fergus glanced sharply at Cornelius before speaking, **"It suddenly makes sense. Why does he have the strict rules he has? Along with the fact that he and his people have been allowed access to this haven. It is because they are guarding something. It makes sense now."**

I sighed deeply and looked down at the cavern floors, and saw the scrap marks, ancient but still there. Showing the dragon that has scraped the cavern floors to be what it is now. Finally, after a moment, I looked at Cornelius and gestured with my hand to move forward. For a moment, Cornelius hesitated. However, after his eyes flickered to Fergus and the others did he started back up.

*****

It was another two levels up that Cornelius stopped dead in his tracks. He looked to the darkness of the left corner, disappearing. He swallowed hard, but I came beside him before speaking, "Just go."

He looked at me for a moment and swallowed hard again, but nodded without a word. He disappeared into the darkness and soon disappeared entirely. I waited, and soon after a minute, I heard him coming back. He was not alone, I felt myself stir in anticipation, knowing that he had a dragon with him.

He soon came back and looked down at the dragon in his hands, his hand covered in slime and goo. I scowled as I noticed that it was all over his trousers and shirt, but he did not seem bothered by the reddish goop in spots. He was staring down at the golden dragon, who looked at him with dark red eyes. His little wings, tipped with black and ran down his spines. I looked at Cornelius before speaking, "What did you name him Cornelius?"

Cornelius acted as if he hadn't heard me for a moment, and I was about to repeat myself. However, after a moment, he raised his eyes to me and swallowed before speaking, "Salvadorious."

The dragon mewed like a kitten at the name, but brushed its head against his wrist, leaving small indents where its scales indented. Once or twice, drawing blood from him. However, Cornelius looked like he had preferred it. He looked down at Salvadorious with a small smile. I looked over my shoulder at Fergus, who was watching the interaction for a moment in silence, but finally looked at me. He shrugged and finally, after a hesitated moment, spoke, "**I don't feel anything calling on this floor.**"

"Okay, then let's keep going."

I looked at Cornelius before speaking again, "Do you want to lead, Cornelius?"

He looked up at me in a daze for a moment, blinking his eyes as if he was waking up from a dream, before he whispered, "No, Fergus needs to lead. So, when he finds his, we are there to support him."

I looked over my shoulder at Fergus and saw him swallow, but he moved ahead of us and started to lead the way again.

*****

It was another two levels before Fergus stopped dead in his tracks. He was staring to the right of the cavern and frowned. He glanced back at us, but said nothing and didn't need any prompts to move. He swallowed hard, but moved into the darkness. My curiosity got to me, and I was about to approach the cavern where the eggs were, but Salvadorious growled a warning. I looked back at him, and saw his shoulders were hunched up and he was baring his small razor-sharp teeth at me in warning. I looked up at Cornelius, who looked equally shocked, but looked at me before whispering, "No one besides the ones that are called into the dragon chambers can go into them."

"How do you know that?"

"Salvadorious told me."

"How does he know that, though? He just hatched."

"**Thakur?**"

I turned my attention to Firefoot and cocked an eyebrow, "**It is better to not question these things when we are outside of our elements. Even dragons that just hatched know things that we don't.**"

"Fine."

I turn my attention back to the cavern, and hear a shriek and a small sob, and a scream of pain. Soon, though, Fergus stumbled into the chamber. His eyes were wide in shock, and his eyes blurred, and he went forward. I lunged forward and caught him in my arms, easing him down to the cavern floor. I glanced up at Cornelius, who took a step backwards and swallowed hard. I looked down at Fergus and saw the flame marks and the blood. Lots and lots of blood. I looked over at Cornelius, but before I could say anything, Fergus whimpered, drawing my attention to him again. His eyes were swollen shut, and his breathing was harsh. I looked at Firefoot, who instantly came over and sniffed him everywhere before speaking, "**He's not going to make it."**

"WHAT? NO! FATHER!"

I winced and looked at the druid boy, and felt his pain radiate off of him. I swallowed and looked back at Cornelius before speaking, "Cornelius."

My voice held the questioning tone, along with venom in it too. He swallowed hard before whispering, "I don't know what to say…."

I looked down at Fergus before I leaned down to his ear, "Fergus, your injuries are making you suffer more than you should. Do you want me… Me to put you out of your misery?"

Oswald stared at me with scared, frightened eyes before he started shaking his head rapidly before speaking, "No…. there has to be a way to save him. Please, he is my only family I have left."

I looked at Firefoot, but he looked at me knowingly, and I looked back at Cornelius before I placed my hand on the back of Fergus's neck, and was about to snap his neck when a mewing of a kitten sounded in the chamber that Fergus came out of. We all tensed as a dark red dragon, with golden spikes and black wings, crawled out of the cavern. His eyes were a milky white color, showing his blindness. Oswald took a sharp breath when he saw the baby dragon and looked at Fergus for a moment, and swallowed before he approached the creature.

I was about to stop him, but Cornelius spoke softly, "Don't."

I looked at him in anger, my eyes flashing dangerously. Cornelius has not seen all my strength as of yet, but if he doesn't explain himself, he will soon find out how much I know. However, I turned my attention to Oswald when he let out a whimper. I noticed that the dragon hatchling had scratched him, along with burning his hands. Although now we know it was not knowing. It did not know that Fergus did not mean it any harm. Oswald looked up after a moment before whispering, "I-it…. He didn't mean to harm his handler…."

He looked up at me for a moment before whispering, "Please though Thakur, there has to be another way. Please…. I can't lose my only family that I have left. Please."

I looked at Firefoot and sighed before speaking, "I cannot promise anything, Oswald. His injuries are making him suffer."

"Please."

I sighed deeply before standing up and looking down at Fergus, before looking at Cornelius, and speaking, "Is your dragon telling you anything, Cornelius?"

"No."

"Are you lying?"

"I would not lie in a time like this, Thakur."

I sighed deeply before glancing down at Fergus's face, which was showing excruciating pain. I sighed for a moment and spoke, "We are taking him with us then."

**"Uhhh…. I wouldn't if I were you."**

"Why not?"

**"We have no idea if Corimid is going to… You know…. Eat him."**

I glanced at Oswald and saw his Adam's apple bob in response and I looked back at Firefoot before smirking before speaking, "Really?"

He looked at Oswald and smiled sheepishly before muttering, "**Sorry.**"

For a moment, Oswald stared at us before shaking his head in disbelief and looking down at Fergus and whispering, "I'm not strong enough to carry him."

"You won't be the one carrying him, Oswald. I will."

I looked back down at Fergus and picked him up after a moment. Fergus let out a whine of pain and grimaced in pain as I adjusted myself. I looked at Cornelius before speaking, "Lead away, Cornelius."

He hesitated for a moment, but soon nodded and kept his eyes low as he got ahead of us and kept going.

****

After another ten levels, we soon reached two large entrances. He paused and swallowed before speaking, "We are here."

"Which one?"

"Uhhh…. Not entirely sure. Salvadorious won't tell me either."

I scowled and was about to say something when a deep voice spoke in all of our minds at once, "*Enter the right chamber.*"

I swallowed and looked at Cornelius who shrunk himself down before swallowing. He took a small step forward and soon stopped dead in his tracks and looked at me with terrified eyes. I rolled my eyes and took the lead, and strolled straight into the right chamber without hesitation.

# Chapter 61

Unlike the other sections of the tunnels and chambers, it had great big torch spots hanging on chains from the high ceilings that disappeared into the darkness. They were gently swinging in the area they were, showing that something was making them swing, or they were in the breezeway. Which seemed to be the latter, since nothing caught my immediate attention in the chamber. I looked around, and only four of the eight torches were lit; every other one. Two on our side of the giant chamber and another two at the end. There were two other chamber entrances, one bigger than the other, and I took a deep inhale, knowing that the larger exit was the way to the outside. Possibly even the entrance where we had landed when we first arrived three days ago. I looked at the other chamber and saw the most recent scale shedding that Corimid had; his old scales looked blue, but I was unsure if it was indeed blue or if they had lost their color once they were shed.

I glanced at Cornelius and saw him shrink down and swallow hard. I looked back at Firefoot and saw him cock his head to the side, but he did not say a word. As if knowing that by speaking, it will break the spell of uncertainty. Oswald was looking around the chambers before he whispered, "Wow, this is amazing."

As if a spell was lifted, all the torches became lit, and soon a hot breath seemed to breathe deeply further into the chamber. I shrank down and quickly handed the controls back to Quinn.

****

I gasped at the sudden change and looked wildly around, and swallowed hard before looking at the chamber before us. I looked down at Fergus and frowned at his injuries, but could not question it since I knew that speaking would only draw Corimid out. I swallowed and looked back at Aurelin, and only stared at Firefoot's eyes and sighed deeply before I turned my attention back to the main chamber, down about one hundred yards, and started to walk forward. For a moment, none of the others took a step forward, but finally they followed after a moment.

Soon we stood in front of another chamber, it was wide and tall. Reaching beyond what the torch lights can reach, disappearing into the darkness. I swallow hard but spoke out, "He-hel-hello?"

*"Enter."*

I looked at the others and knew that they felt the same, and I saw that Cornelius cowered slightly, but I was unsure of why. I entered first, and soon after a moment the rest followed suit. The interior of the cavern was filled with tall, towering statues of Egyptian gods, and Greek gods. Well, more of the Greek, but of the Egyptian gods there are: Horus, Anubis, Osiris, Ra, and Set. The Greek gods that I recognized from my various readings:  Gaia, Artemis, Uranus, Nyx, Erebus. There were five others that I could not name, though.

I swallowed and slowly put down Fergus before placing my head down to the cavern floor. The others hesitated before following suit. After a dead silence for a minute, there was a rumbly huff of hot air, before the voice sounded, *"Stand up."*

I swallowed before I got to my knees, and looked up, there was nothing but darkness in the room besides the torches where the statues were, but that was a small fraction of the chamber. I swallowed as I picked myself back to my feet and winced as I stepped onto a sharp stone that jabbed into my foot, since my shoes were losing their soles. I took a steadying breath before speaking, "Where are you?"

*"Here."*

A huge, vibrant, dark blue, almost shimmery in color, tail swept out of the shadows, and a purple iris opened. I swallowed the lump in my throat before speaking, "Why did you allow us to go down to the other chambers below?"

*"Because your destiny is not to die at my flames."*

"Sounds so reassuring."

I would have turned sharply to stare at Oswald, but Corimid chuckled before speaking, *"It is quite all right, Quinn Benik. I take no offense at Oswald's thoughts."*

"How do you know my name?"

*"You should know better than to ask that question. I am older than you. I know much."*

"Can you answer our questions?"

*"The answers you may seek may show the horrors of what is to become. Are you for sure you want to go down into that dark place for answers?"*

"Yes."

*"I am giving you a fair warning, Quinn, once it is said. Nothing can erase time."*

"I understand, Corimid."

The giant eye blinked once and withdrew, making the wind increase as he moved backwards. His tail whipping around, although careful of the statutes in the room, and giant, shimmery, dark blue forepaws showed in the gathering torchlight. For a moment, I could not see anything but the talons, which were longer than me and I looked up and up, and up before I saw the shadow of his head. I swallowed hard before I swallowed hard again. He flexed his talons three times before rumbling, *"It has been a long time since anyone has called me by name, Quinn. Not since my handler has met his end three winters ago."*

"Your handler?"

*"Zaros's father was my handler. We spoke constantly, even on his deathbed. He passed to old age."*

"I thought that Carpathians were immortal…"

*"Some claim to be, but they are not. They are the same to kill. Although for some, sunlight will kill them instantly, others a staked to the heart, or simply beheading. The myth of garlic would only cause them a sneezing fit, but wouldn't cause them death. They are mortal, but live long lives."*

"So, Dracula…. Will eventually die?"

*"Dracula will meet his end in this war."*

Corimid snarled in reply, making us cower before him. His talons scraped the floors of his cavern, making them screech under the sharpness. He huffed low and soon bent his head down to lay his head on his foreclaws, looking at us. I swallowed as I looked at him before speaking, "Who will kill him?"

*"I cannot say for certain what his end will be. However, you must kill the entire Dracula followers and kin."*

**"Why all of them?"**

*"Because if one is left alive, he or she will continue to use the survivors as their food source. The time of Dracula and his ways is over."*

**"How would we kill him? He may not be immortal, but he would be heavily guarded, especially since he will be guarded by the Sazornoras."**

*"I did not say it would be easy. However, it is a must to kill their line in this fight. Otherwise, the future generations would forever be bound to a Carpathian."*

We fell into silence for a moment, no one speaking. Absorbing what he said. I looked at him before speaking, "Would you be able to heal someone?"

*"It depends, if you are talking about healing yourself from your demon, no. That cannot be done. Along with not bringing others back from the dead. That cannot be completed. If you are referring to Fergus below you, then yes. I can heal him. However, there is a cost."*

"What cost?"

*"I want your firstborn child, Quinn."*

"Why would you want my firstborn? And who said anything about a child?"

*"That is my price, Quinn, I have countless years before me. Do not make haste."*

**"Why claim someone who has not been on the timeline?"**

*"That is my business, Firefoot, not yours. Do we have a deal?"*

I swallowed before looking down at Fergus and gulped in a deep breath, what Corimid wants…. Would I be able to do what he asks? Be able to hand him my firstborn child for Fergus? I swallowed as I looked back at Oswald, who was staring at me in shock, and swallowed hard in response when his eyes met mine. He knew it was ultimately my choice to refuse, but he would lose his only family member. I close my eyes before slowly speaking, "I accept your condition Corimid."

Corimid blinked once, but he moved his right foreclaw forward, making me move backwards, as he moved Fergus in his direction. His talons curled under Fergus without a second hesitation, and soon rotated his closed claw to the right, to look at Fergus in his paw. His thumb claw went down, straight into Fergus.

I leapt backwards in shock and stared in horror as Fergus's blood ran through Corimid's scales and onto the cavern floor below. I shouted, "WE HAD A DEAL! YOU KILLED HIM!"

Corimid ignored us and removed his talon from Fergus before licking him. His tongue was forked at the end, like a snake. He sighed in bliss for a moment before he repeated the process of licking him. I swallowed hard, and Oswald ran forward, but I caught him before he could reach Corimid.

After a tense minute, we all heard a gasp. Corimid placed his foreclaw down and gently moved his claws backwards before speaking, *"It is done."*

I released Oswald and approached Corimid cautiously, and soon saw that Fergus's eyes flickered open before he gasped once again. I swallowed as I looked up at Corimid before climbing onto his clawed hand, and reached Fergus. I slung his arm over my shoulder and stood up after a moment. Soon I got him to the edge of the hand, and swallowed as I looked down at the several feet down before slinging him into a fireman's carry and shifted to a bird before landing at the bottom, before shifting again.

I looked up at Corimid timidly, and swallowed as his purple eye looked at me for a moment before he looked at Cornelius before speaking, *"Cornelius."*

"Y-ye-yes?"

*"Do not fear me. Whom have you brought forth?"*

"Salvadorious."

*"Fitting name. And yours?"*

Corimid looked directly at Oswald in question. Oswald swallowed before speaking, "He's not mine."

Corimid's eyes flashed in rage before he bellowed, *"ONLY THOSE WHO WERE CALLED IN THE CAVERN CAN UNLEASH MY BRETHREN! PREPARE…."*

**"WAIT!"**

Corimid's head whipped towards Firefoot before he snarled, *"Wait? Are you telling me to wait?"*

**"I apologize Corimid, however, there is an explanation. Oswald did not enter the chamber for the egg. Fergus was the one who was called. None of us entered the cavern even though we heard him scream in pain. It was only after he stumbled into the main hallway that we saw his injuries."**

*"Are you lying?"*

*"He is not lying. Fergus was the one who was called to the egg. Only his dragon was born blind and was defending itself. Hence the injuries."*

I turned my head towards Salvadorious, who was now perched on top of Cornelius's shoulder, as he looked at Corimid. Corimid looked at him for a moment, and looked at Oswald before speaking, *"Swear that you did not enter the cavern."*

"I swear on my mother's grave that I did not enter the cavern."

Corimid blinked once and withdrew his head and breathed out deeply before speaking, *"Good."*

Corimid relaxed after a moment and breathed out deeply. I have since brought Fergus back, and had laid him down next to Firefoot before looking up at Corimid before speaking, "Would you be able to answer questions now?"

*"Only after Fergus tells me his dragon's name."*

"Why after?"

*"Are you challenging my decision?"*

I swallowed before replying, "Partially."

*"You and humans have one thing in common."*

**"Which is what?"**

Corimid looked over at Firefoot before snorting in response. I swallowed before Oswald mumbled, "Your impatience."

Corimid turned his head towards Oswald before speaking, *"Correct, you are."*

I scowled slightly as I looked down at Fergus before speaking, "Out of curiosity, how did you heal him?"

Corimid looked down at me and blinked before looking down at Fergus before responding, *"Dragon saliva has many properties in it. If someone is not dead, it can heal any wounds."*

**"So, a fraction like shifter blood then?"**

*"You don't know the history of the shifters?"*

No one spoke, and I looked at Firefoot with a questioning look, but even I didn't really know the history of the shifter species entirely. All I know is that the shifters have healing abilities and can shift into dragons if they are purebloods.

Corimid sighed deeply before speaking, *"I guess you don't know the history of the shifters. Probably know more history on the demons, but they are involved in this now, too. So, I will tell you while we wait for Fergus to awaken."*

"Thank you."

*"Might as well sit down. It will be a long history lesson."*

I hesitated for a moment, but finally sighed and sat down, and looked behind me to see Oswald, who carefully sat down while holding the blind dragon. Cornelius swallowed hard before he sat down and dropped his gaze from Corimid's. Which kind of made me question, what did he have to hide before the dragon? However, Corimid did not seem surprised by his behavior and did not say a word. Firefoot huffed at me, and I looked at him with a raised eyebrow before I realized that he was still carrying the baskets. I sheepishly got back to my feet and took off the baskets from him. He looked up at Corimid before he spoke, **"May I shift back into my human form?"**

Corimid blinked his eyes once in response, and Firefoot took that as a yes, and quickly shifted to his human form. Crouching down, he rolled his shoulders slightly and sat down, and stretched slightly. He shuddered when he felt the cool breeze from our level, but Corimid blinked in surprise before he rumbled, *"What is the name of your human form, Firefoot?"*

**"His true name is Aurelin, but for the majority of his life, he has been called by the name of Herald."**

*"Hmmm…. Interesting."*

I frowned up at Corimid before I could ask him what was so interesting, Fergus stirred and mumbled something incoherent. Our attention immediately went to him and we all held our breath slightly as he cracked open his eyes and after a moment he scrambled to his feet and looked wildly around. Soon his eyes fell onto Oswald with the blind dragon, and his face instantly softened and approached Oswald.

Oswald swallowed as he looked up at Fergus, who instantly gestured to take the hatchling. Oswald swallowed hard, but he gently handed him the baby dragon, who mewed like a kitten in his handler's hold. Fergus looked down at the little dragon before whispering, **"Shush, I know you did not mean to harm me, Alethraziel."**

The hatchling purred like a kitten, and Corimid froze. He brought his head down to our level before rumbling, *"What did you just call it?"*

**"Alethraziel."**

I looked at Corimid sharply, and saw his eyes widen for a split second before he flexed his talons against the cavern floor. For a moment, he did not reply before he looked at Cornelius, who was staring at Fergus as if he had spilled burning oil onto him. I suddenly wondered what the issue was, but I was unsure why. I was about to ask when Corimid rumbled, *"Leave."*

"Wait, what?"

*"Leave."*

"But I thought…."

*"DO NOT TRIFLE WITH ME, QUINN! LEAVE! And take your hatchlings."*

"I-i-i…."

I glanced at Cornelius sharply, but Corimid looked at him for a moment before rolling his eyes in response. He lifted his head up, and it disappeared into the darkness, before he pushed himself to his feet. His talons scraping the cavern floor.

Firefoot scrambled to his feet and grabbed Oswald before hightailing it to the cavern entrance, shouting, **"MOVE QUINN!"**

I glanced up and saw Corimid lift his clawed hand, and it coming straight down where I stood. I scrambled instantly and shifted into a wolf. I sprinted past Oswald and Firefoot, heading to the entrance that was bringing in the cool air. I got there first and forced Thakur to surface, and soon he begrudgingly surfaced to shift into his dragon form. Firefoot and Oswald rounded the corner, with Cornelius on their backs. Fergus was nowhere in sight, though.

Oswald skidded to a halt and looked back over his shoulder as he watched Fergus running slightly towards us, but was being careful with his hatchling. Cornelius grabbed his shoulder and forced him ahead of him before Corimid rounded the corner. His eyes sparked in something I could not describe as I looked back at him. However, he simply rumbled, *"Fly back home."*

For a moment, I stared at him in shock, wondering what had angered him so much between now and Alethzariel's name? Although he was allowing us to leave with the hatchlings, I thought that they would stay with him to learn the dragon ways.

Firefoot climbed onto my head and reached down and grabbed Oswald, and pulled him in front of him. Cornelius and Fergus mounted between my wings and gripped my spikes in response. Only one was scared, and that was Cornelius, since he had not ridden a dragon before. However, I stood up and looked up at Corimid before speaking, "Can I come back to ask questions?"

*"Go."*

"What changed?"

**"QUINN! GO!"**

I rotated my eyes slightly to look at Firefoot, but saw his ashen face, and I sighed before looking down the mountain and bunching my shoulders, before leaping off the mountain. Falling before I opened my wings to catch the wind. Cornelius screamed on the way down. I glanced once up and saw Corimid staring down at us from his mountain home, watching us disappear into the cloud cover.